Rivers Run Deep

Tim Holden

2022

1st Edition – Published by Monkey Time Books in 2022
22 Heigham St
Norwich, NR2 4TF, UK

ISBN no: 978-1-9162448-1-8

For more information on this book, and others
by the same author, visit:
www.timholden.com

To my beloved boys, George & James,
may you always discover the gifts
concealed in every misfortune.

Prelude

Anyone who met George Croghan gave him the benefit of the doubt. Whether it was due to his smooth Irish lilt, the constant crooked smile, or the clash of piercing blue eyes and ebony hair, not even he knew; yet something about this man in the prime of life made him easy to like – and easy to forgive.

Croghan jumped from the bow of his canoe, his boots splashing in the shallows of the landing area, then took a moment to survey the rolling wooded hills that surrounded the river running through this virgin land. How it differed from the dank Irish peat bog that had surrounded his family homestead. God had punished his community with failed crops, famine and sickness. Deprived of the charity of the absent Protestant landlords, Croghan and his family had boarded a transit to the New World. In Pennsylvania, they had found a toleration of their Catholicism. After four short years, he now found himself here; at the edge of the known world, a very long way from home. *The Lord truly does work in mysterious ways,* he thought.

This particular canoe journey from his base on Lake Erie had taken ten days. The only challenge had been the thirty-mile portage, where they'd had to change rivers, carrying the canoes and cargo. The journey had otherwise been straightforward: paddling in the mild spring weather had been comfortable, and the nights camped on the riverbanks had been cool, but bearable for the seasoned frontier men that made up his trading party.

The Iroquois village, which the Europeans called Logstown, was by

1

some measure the largest in the territory. A gathering of Iroquois children surrounded the landing area, excitedly awaiting the arrival of the white men. At the margins behind them stood the occasional brave: the young Iroquois warriors, their stony faces and folded arms affording only the most suspicious of welcomes.

Croghan turned to his crew and ordered them to drag the canoes clear of the river. He stepped up on the bank, parting the assembled children. There, waiting to greet him was Thayonih, Chief Tanacharison's eldest son. Croghan knew a smattering of the Seneca language; they exchanged traditional greetings, swapping wampum, strings of tubular-shaped shells, arranged in coloured sequences to denote one's credentials. With Croghan's provenance confirmed, Thayonih offered to show him the village before taking him to his accommodation. The meeting with his father would take place tomorrow. For now, Croghan was eager to get on with the business of trading furs, but knew better than to rush matters, given his hosts' preference for ritual.

He ordered his crew to stow the canoes and prepare their tributes. They were a rag-tag bunch of illiterate men from all corners of the British Isles. No sooner had their boats docked in the New World, had they succumbed to Croghan's temptations: promises of riches and adventure on the lawless frontier.

As he walked up the slope, Croghan noticed a parade of ten canoes already jettisoned on the ground in front of the village maize plantation. Behind them, a white man stood guard, resting his hands on the muzzle of his musket. Bearded and unkempt, he winked at Croghan and spat his tobacco towards Croghan's feet. The canoes were laden with goods, covered with blankets and secured to the gunwales with cord.

The French are here too. Their presence would make negotiations interesting; he'd assumed – wrongly – that he would have the benefit of a private audience with the village elders.

In small numbers, the French had been actively trading in the Ohio Valley for years. They'd only ever settled the land to the north, New France, but had since developed trade networks to the south with the native tribes. Croghan had intended to secure a slice of this trade for himself, under the flag of the peoples of Great Britain. The presence of the French didn't mean his profit would be any slimmer, for the canny Indians were as well-practised as any European merchant when it came to achieving the thinnest bargains any man could stomach. Croghan would have to be careful not to provoke further hostilities between the rival nations, for they were once again – technically – at war, but the conflict hadn't yet reached far beyond the coastlines of Nova Scotia and Massachusetts. This far inland, it was in the interests of all parties to conduct their business without the disruption – or cost – of bloodshed.

Croghan left the boats under the capable supervision of his crew and followed Thayonih into the camp. It was dominated by a great wooden longhouse, outside which a posse of women sat cross-legged pounding cornflour. They all smiled at the dashing Irishman, admiring his beaver skin hat and deerskin waistcoat. He winked at them, prompting giggles as he passed. Behind the longhouse was a flat grassy plain, strewn with tepees, housing fifteen hundred Indians. Between them came the occasional drift of a smoking campfire. The maize plantation extended to his right, while to his left was a corral of fine-looking horses, another European import to the New World that, together with guns and alcohol, the Indians had taken to quickly. The camp fell quiet as people stopped to inspect the new arrivals.

'It's big, yes?' said Thayonih.

Croghan nodded. 'Very impressive.' The Iroquois who resided in this pleasant riverside village were a collection of independent tribes that had gradually banded together in response to the arrival of the white men on their shores. United, their scattered tribes now dominated the land to the west of the mountains which bordered the British colonies. The growth in the Iroquois trade with the French meant it was convenient for the tribes, who feared the illnesses of the white man, to have a more permanent settlement in the Ohio Valley. Croghan supposed it was a ploy to pass the cost and effort of transporting skins onto the white man. The Iroquois could now make deals on their own turf, rather than having to venture into white settlements. For intrepid men like Croghan, this gave him the chance to corner the fur market. Given the French were here too, somebody would be walking away empty-handed.

3

***

The first night passed without incident. Croghan and his companions kept to themselves and were treated to a simple evening meal of corn and bread round the campfire. The French did likewise on the far side of the settlement.

The next morning, Thayonih arrived and explained it was time to present gifts to their great Chief, Tanacharison. Once received, he and the council of elders would listen to any exchange that Croghan wished to propose, but Thayonih warned that he should be mindful that the village had all the provisions it required. Croghan kissed the small wooden Celtic cross that hung on his leather necklace. 'Father, Son and Holy Ghost, I'll be needing all three of you today,' he whispered to himself.

Back at the canoes, he found his man, who was supposed to be guarding the vessels and their cargo, playing chase with the Iroquois children, under the watchful eyes of some young Iroquois women. Fortunately, everything was as he'd left it, so he didn't trouble to mention it.

Croghan collected his gift, carefully concealed in a rolled-up blanket. Indians would only trade if first you greased their palms with gratuities. It was a practice that didn't sit well with his European notions, but as the proverb went: *When in Rome...* Carrying his gift, Croghan walked toward the longhouse, feeling butterflies in his stomach. He'd staked everything he had on securing a trade of furs. All his backers' money had been spent on this gift; he hoped the Chief would like it, for if he didn't, all was lost. Putting his fears aside, he rejoined Thayonih by the entrance to the longhouse and was invited inside. As his eyes adjusted to the dark, he could make out a dais at the far end on which sat the Chief. His tanned face was beginning to show the first creases of age around his eyes and across his forehead, while his chestnut hair had streaks of grey, placing him, Croghan assumed, in his mid-forties. Dozens of wampum necklaces hung around his neck and over his sleeveless chamois waistcoat. At the foot of the dais, the Frenchman stood waiting and introduced himself as Croghan took his place alongside him.

'Pierre De La Frontesse.' They exchanged a handshake. His head

4

tilted back, giving him a haughty air. 'I've not seen you about these parts, m'sieur?'

'I dare say you'll be seeing a great deal more of me, my friend,' replied Croghan easily.

'I was born in New France. I've trapped and traded furs my whole life.'

Ignoring the boast, Croghan assumed Pierre must be a similar age to himself, in his late twenties.

Croghan bowed to show his respect to Tanacharison, and in his best Seneca said, 'Greetings, Great Chief. I am honoured to meet you and receive your audience. Please accept this string of wampum as a token of my appreciation.'

The Chief said nothing, but gently nodded, his piercing dark eyes boring into Croghan, while his face remained stony still.

Croghan briefly looked round to acknowledge the other Iroquois gathered at the edges of the room, their faces lit only by the smoke hole in the crudely thatched roof. No women or children, only a selection of men of all ages and decorations. All silent.

Thayonih invited the Frenchman to present his gift. Pierre walked forward and laid a bottle at the feet of the Chief, who inspected it, removed the cork and sniffed its contents.

'The very finest French brandy,' said Pierre in his fluent Seneca. 'I have fifty bottles just like it outside. I would be honoured if you would accept my humble offering.'

The Chief smiled.

'But I must object to the presence of Monsieur Croghan here,' Pierre continued. 'Your people are allied to France; you have an exclusive agreement to trade with us. This man's presence brings shame to our alliance.'

Croghan couldn't follow all that was said, but the Chief didn't appear to rise to the Frenchman's remarks. He waved him away and invited Croghan forward. He laid the roll of blankets at the Chief's feet, glancing up to catch the Chief's expression, which only betrayed the briefest twinge of disappointment, just as Croghan had hoped for. The longhouse was silent as he slowly began to unroll the blanket, explaining it was of the finest English lambs' wool. He unfurled the final layer, exposing the flintlock musket that he'd hidden inside and

held it aloft for the Chief to inspect. Mahogany stock, solid steel barrel, cast in Birmingham and decorated with silver plate.

The Chief's mouth turned upwards, unable to hide his smile once he saw the silver plate was engraved with the image of a noble Indian chief in traditional headdress. He took the gun and looked down the barrel, checking it thoroughly, then nodded his appreciation. Croghan felt a brief moment of hope as the gifts were cleared away by two aides and the Chief was passed a lit pipe. After inhaling some tobacco and exhaling a silver cloud, he offered it to Pierre, who did likewise. Next, Croghan took a heavy draw on the pipe. He'd become accustomed to tobacco here in America, and sighed as he enjoyed an instant relief to his craving.

After a few more rounds of smoke, the Chief broke the silence. 'You will trade with my son.'

Thayonih invited both men to take a seat on the earthen floor, while he remained standing. He opened his palms and looked directly at Croghan. 'Please. Make your offer.' The young Indian was firm, but courteous.

Croghan would have preferred to have gone second so he could hear the terms offered by the Frenchman, but as he was the new face in these parts, he assumed this was out of respect for the longevity of the Indian tribe's relationship with Pierre. He threw caution to the wind.

'I'll take as many skins, deer or beaver, as you can supply,' he said. 'I'll pay you three musket balls for each hide.'

Thayonih turned his hawk-eyed gaze to Pierre, who shifted nervously.

'The Englishman...'

The inaccuracy provoked immediate offence in Croghan, who was about to bite back, when he realised Pierre was deliberately riling him. Despite having an English name, there was no quicker way to loosen an Irish temper than to call it English.

'...is bold. These people are rarely to be taken at their word. Anyone can make grand promises.'

'You yourself promised us gunpowder, Pierre. Yet we have not seen it,' Thayonih pointed out.

'My supplies have yet to arrive. I can only assume they have been held up on the great ocean. But on my honour, they will come.'

'I seem to remember you saying the same thing last time.'

'You must be patient.'

'You test our patience, brother.'

Pierre held his palms open to accept the accusation. 'I should warn you, our wise father, the King of France, would be very disappointed to learn of his allies, the Iroquois, entertaining English traders here.'

'We too are disappointed, for he sends us no weapons with which to protect ourselves. What sort of friend leaves his allies defenceless?'

Croghan did his best to follow with his limited Seneca as the two men went back and forth. Finally, the Frenchman made his offer:

'One thousand beaver pelts for one thousand musket balls and enough gunpowder to fire them, by the winter.'

Thayonih's face was a mask. Croghan thought he had a fair chance and contemplated upping his offer as Thayonih turned his back and received another gentle nod from his father.

Thayonih turned to the Frenchman, reached for the tomahawk tucked into his belt and with a swift swing of his arm, buried its blade in Pierre's forehead. It struck with a sickening thump. Pierre's eyes rolled up in his head as he fell backwards onto the floor. Dead.

Every hair on Croghan's body stood to attention. The Iroquois sat motionless as blood began to seep from the Frenchman's forehead.

'Will you also include gunpowder?' Thayonih said to Croghan, his voice even.

'Yes,' said Croghan, nodding furiously. He felt his face drain of colour. He'd have agreed to run round Philadelphia in woman's undergarments, or anything else for that matter.

Thayonih held out his hand and they shook. 'Our trade is good, brother. Please accept this string of wampum as a token of the friendship between our peoples.'

'To be sure, it's been a pleasure!' said Croghan, letting out a deep sigh as his shoulders slumped. Fearing the vomit that swilled at the back of his throat may spill out of his mouth, he requested permission to take some air outside.

PART 1

—

1747

1

George felt the first pang of nerves in his stomach as he looked out at the miles of lush, ankle-length grass that stretched out under a cloudless sky. The green blades shimmered under the golden sunshine of another fine spring day in Virginia, as if in anticipation of the races. Beyond the field, through the thicket of trees were the well-spaced red-brick buildings of Williamsburg. George caught a glimpse of the charred remains of the Capitol building, razed in an arson attack that January. The arsonists were still at large and remained the talk of the town. For now, this sad sight served as a stark reminder of the tensions simmering beneath the genteel surface of this, England's wealthiest American colony. It should have been the jewel in the burgeoning crown of Great Britain's Empire. Yet, the multitude of different peoples that poured in would never get on, as his mother always said, bemoaning the arrival of yet more Africans, Irish, Scots, Germans, Dutch and English with their foreign ways.

But today was about racing. Not only had fifteen-year-old George already far outgrown the boyish physique advantageous for jockeying, but his ever-dependable mare was no racer. He'd brushed her coat, trimmed her mane and blacked her hooves, so she would at least look presentable as she crossed the finish line – most likely in last place.

It had been his own idea to enter today's race. Lawrence, his elder half-brother, had been against it. Now that he was in the saddle though, George regretted being so foolhardy. Everyone who was

11

anyone in Virginia would be watching and he dreaded them seeing him fall off, or finish last, or his horse refuse. *Just don't embarrass yourself.* He nudged Lisbeth into a trot to join the other riders and crowd of gentle folk who congregated at the finish line, eagerly awaiting the first race of the day.

The end of the racetrack was denoted by two lone white posts. No bigger than broom handles, they stood upright in the ground. In the distance, away from the town, another two posts marked the start line.

The various heats and races for the largest prizes had already been settled in the preceding days, so today's schedule was an opportunity for young horses or nags, riders old and new alike who couldn't compete for the bigger prizes, to try out the turf.

The bravado that had deserted George when he'd first seen the field began to return as his body settled into the rhythm of the horse's trot. Amongst the crowd at the finish line, men sported brightly coloured tailcoats, an array of hats, white shirts and breeches, mingling with women in silk and cotton frocks, shaded under bonnets and parasols. The seven other riders of the first race held their horses by the reins and chatted with spectators. Off to the side, a large circular pen made from crudely sawn posts and rails corralled the horses for the later races. Saddles and bridles hung over the rails, ready to be tacked up by the attending negroes when the time came.

The day's spectacle had drawn a modest crowd of working folk, tradespeople and indentured servants from the immediate surroundings. Barred from competing, they stood on the far side of the course, placing bets and catching up with – and most likely embellishing – the gossip doing the rounds in the colony.

George heard his name called out. Amongst the sea of faces, he spotted Lawrence waving to him. He rode over to join his brother.

It was three years since Lawrence had been elected into the House of Burgesses, to represent the county of Fairfax, named after his in-laws whose interests he was placed to guard. Sitting in the Lower House of colonial government, which dealt with all affairs local to the colony, he now came to Williamsburg every two months and rubbed shoulders with the great and good. With business for the sitting concluded, no more trials to hear or bills to vote on, the town hosted a week of dinners, dances and horse races so the men of influence and their families could relax, socialise and gamble.

'Ladies and Gentlemen,' said Lawrence, his booming voice full of his characteristic swagger, drawing the admiring attention of all those around him, 'I present to you Virginia's best-kept secret, about to make his name as a horse racing prodigy, Master George Washington!' Lawrence smirked. George raised his cocked hat and bowed his head to receive his half-brother, his wife Anne, and the assembled company who swooned in Lawrence's orbit. Whatever dignity George tried to convey felt brittle thanks to Lawrence's taunt.

Anne looked beautiful as usual, her lustrous dark-brown hair pinned into curls under a straw hat trimmed in pink silk, as she wished him good luck for his first race. The gentle features of her face were whitened with blanc, her slender cheeks accentuated by rouge. She was always kind and accommodating towards her husband's young sibling and George frequently stayed with them, as Lawrence, fourteen years his senior, did his best to influence his upbringing. Such proximity to Anne, who was only nineteen, forced George to suppress the certainty that he too, could easily let himself develop a romantic attachment to her, had his brother – once again – not got there first.

George's lingering gaze was interrupted by the imposing tone of Colonel Lee.

'A fine morning for your first race.' The sight of Thomas Lee, wearing a top hat over a wig of long silver curls, set the butterflies in George's stomach aflutter. Colonel Lee stood with his wife Hannah on his arm, her coat matching the bright blue sky overhead. Lee was a member of the King's Council, the Upper House of Virginia's Government, the conduit between the colony's elected body and its absent Governor in London. Not the sort of people to whom George wanted to be remembered by humiliating himself on the racecourse.

'Jolly good luck to you boy,' said Lee. 'I never met a man standing over six feet who could make a fine jockey.'

Uncertain if Lee was teasing him, George gritted his teeth and said nothing.

'Lawrence invited George to join us on the trip to Williamsburg,' Anne remarked to Hannah. 'It's George's first time here. Lawrence thought it time to introduce his younger brother to Virginia society.'

Hannah Lee forced a smile.

George removed his cocked hat, made of black beaver pelt and decorated with a now shabby silver brocade round the rim, and handed it to Lawrence. Like most of George's clothing, it had belonged to someone else first: in this case, his late father, who had died four years ago this week. George still felt the loss keenly, having not known his father in adulthood. Thus, the hat, one of the few possessions he'd inherited from his father's estate, all of which had been dispersed amongst various other siblings, held sentimental value greater than its worth.

'Just hold on tight and kick her flanks until she hasn't an ounce of puff left,' said Lawrence, tucking George's hat under his arm. Lawrence wore the red tunic of the British army's American regiment. It was five years since he had seen active service in the Caribbean, but he still wore his officer's uniform to all civic occasions. George hoped that now he was coming of age, it wouldn't be long before he too could parade alongside his brother, dressed as a gentleman soldier.

Mr Drummond, the race organiser, joined their party. A short fat man with cheeks reddened more by drinking than the sun, he held out an upturned top hat. George waved his palm in Lawrence's direction.

'He says you're covering his entry? Two pistoles, please,' prompted Drummond.

Lawrence nodded, and fished into his waistcoat pocket. The coins chinked as they fell against the others in Drummond's hat. George nodded his head in thanks to Lawrence, who winked in reply. Racing was an expensive pastime, and it was Lawrence who'd inherited the lion's share of their late father's legacy. Currency was still scarce in the colonies, even amongst the landed classes, so they frequently used the locally available Spanish dollars and pistoles in the absence of sterling. George, much to his chagrin, didn't yet have two coins of any denomination to rub together, so relied on Lawrence's charity.

'Ladies and Gentlemen,' boomed Drummond, 'we are about to start our first race of the day. A one-mile point-to-point of eight riders. First prize is a fine leather saddle from Button & Co in England, with a value of forty shillings. Second prize is a bridle, value of twenty shillings. Third prize is a leather riding crop with a silver pummel. Riders, please make your way to the start and await the sound of the trumpet.'

George's stomach somersaulted. It was time. *Come, Lisbeth,* he pricked her flanks and they began their canter towards the start. He repeated his mantra to himself: *Just don't embarrass yourself.*

***

'Good luck, George,' chuckled Lawrence. His younger brother was of a serious temperament and cut a determined-looking figure astride his horse. George would be well advised to be less competitive and just enjoy himself. He had nothing to prove, after all. He'd never even raced before.

Colonel Lee placed his arm around Lawrence's shoulder and leant his head in conspiratorially. He tapped George's hat under Lawrence's arm. 'Major Lawrence, I have something I need to discuss with you. An opportunity.' He ushered the younger man away from their wives. Satisfied there was sufficient distance from prying ears, he continued, 'It concerns a race of an altogether different kind. You're the first person I have told of this, Major Lawrence, so I wish you to keep this to yourself.'

Lee's face was ruddy and drawn, interrupted by a long, thin nose, well suited to looking down at others. His eyes were sallow and drooped from yesterday's boozing, giving him a docile impression, quite at odds with the razor-sharp intellect concealed within.

'I've petitioned His Majesty, King George II, for a land grant,' said Lee. 'For a million acres of the Ohio Valley.'

Lawrence's eyes bulged. Lee's glinted.

'Bloody hell, Thomas, that's bold. Why would the King give you all that land?'

'He won't. But he might give it to *us*.' Lee tapped his finger on the cream lapel of Lawrence's red tunic.

'What do you mean? He's got no idea who I am.'

'Don't let that trouble you. That land is beyond the western frontier of British territory. It's ripe for settling. Teeming with trees, rivers…'

'And Indians,' Lawrence put in.

'Yes, them too, but that's where you come in. You're in charge of the Virginia militia, we'll need you to defend our interests.'

15

'Ha! That's absurd, Colonel, there's forty militiamen. Farmers and blacksmiths, mostly. All of them need to be prised free of their own parish. The idea that they could clear that land of Indians...'

'Ah, but we don't need to clear the land of Indians, Lawrence. The land will be the cheapest in the Kingdom, the settlers can take their own chances. We, on the other hand, need the Indians. For these,' he tapped George's hat again, still tucked under Lawrence's arm. 'Beaver pelts. I have it on good authority that the French in the area can no longer compete with us. Pennsylvania has the fur trade all to itself, which doesn't strike me as very sporting. Our tobacco fields are growing spent. If the land is granted to Virginia, we can monopolise the beaver trade rather than leave it to those northern Quakers. The Indians will be dependent on trade with us. We'll ply them with worthless trinkets and rum to yoke their obedience.'

Lawrence shook his head. This foolhardy notion was typical of a man accustomed to scheming when he'd never done a day's work in his life.

'You, Lawrence, will need to secure the trading posts from French harassment.'

'Harassment? That's a thousand-mile frontier, Thomas.'

'Yes, and if there's more than two hundred Frenchmen between the Great Lakes and Louisiana then you can call me a fairy and bugger me yourself. You'll have them chased off in no time, especially with help from the Indians.'

Lawrence shook his head. 'The Indians are contrary creatures, Colonel. They fight by your side one day and scalp you while you sleep the next.'

'Come, young man, as the French themselves say, one can't make an omelette without breaking eggs. Now, once we've populated the land, we'll clear them off, like we did here.'

The trumpet sounded. There was a ripple of excitement and cheers from the crowds on either side of the finish line. A mile away, eight horses and their riders broke into a gallop.

Neither man took any notice. Despite his light-hearted quips, Lawrence could see Lee was serious.

'There aren't enough people in the British Isles to fill that land,' said Lawrence, keeping his tone even. 'We'd have to empty Britain...'

'Lawrence, you think too small, that's your trouble! Europe's always ablaze. I couldn't care less what nationality they are. Their money's as good as the next man's. As long as they're Protestant, they're welcome.'

'You'd be talking millions of people.'

'Yes. All landing here, coming through our land. Buying our goods,' said Lee. 'There's a bloody fortune to be made. I nearly wet my britches every time I think of it.'

'Even if this mad scheme of yours were possible, we could never cope,' said Lawrence. 'There's no harbour here; they'd head for New York instead. Or Philadelphia even; that's closer still.'

'You're right – that's why we'll need to build a harbour. Start a town of our own. One to rival the towns of the northern colonies.'

Lawrence laughed. 'You're mad!'

'No, I am deadly serious. You're married to the daughter of that old windbag Fairfax. You'll persuade him to hand over the land for a town.'

'Jesus, you *are* serious…'

'Oh yes, I've thought of everything,' said Lee, looking even more smug than usual. 'Old man Fairfax will make a fortune auctioning off lots for the town. Would be worth us buying some too.'

The ground below their feet began to rumble from the pounding of horses' hooves. The crowd cheered, calling out in support of their respective riders.

'What we do here, Lawrence, will make history,' Lee hissed in his ear. 'We'll change these lands forever. And Virginia – better still, you and I – will be at the centre of the new world we shall create.'

'I'm not sure I want anything to do with it—'

'Too late, dear boy. I have already put your name down on the petition. As far as King George is concerned, you're a co-founder of the Ohio Company.' Lee pulled Lawrence to his breast, sour wine still on his breath. 'We're going to have such fun, Lawrence.'

Their backs still turned, neither man saw the line of horses gallop past. For Lawrence, the loud cries of the spectators faded in the background as his mind grappled with what Lee had planned. He didn't see his younger brother cross the finish line.

***

The moment George crossed the finish line, the connection he had felt between horse and rider vanished. He grinned like a madman as he became aware of his heart pounding in his chest; he'd finished third. Lisbeth was blowing like an easterly wind, bless the old girl, she'd given it everything. He tugged the reins to slow her to a canter. Without congratulating the victors, he turned her round and cantered back towards his brother, who was deep in discussion with Colonel Lee. *Why wasn't he smiling too?*

'Bravo, George,' said Anne. Hannah Lee feigned a smile.

'Lawrence, did you see me?' George called, breathless.

Roused from whatever had occupied his thoughts, Lawrence looked up and seemed surprised to see George. 'Sorry, you're back, yes, well done, how did you do?'

George's heart sank. He'd done brilliantly and Lawrence had missed it. Today was supposed to be about George. Anne, even Hannah Lee, had managed to watch him, yet Lawrence apparently had better things to do than watch his brother finish in the prizes in his first-ever race. Spectators gathered round, offering their congratulations on a valiant effort, but their words fell on deaf ears, for there was only one person's praise George sought. Whatever kind words Lawrence now summoned, they would be empty.

As his elation reduced to disappointment, George wondered what had been so important that it had demanded his brother's attention during those brief moments when it had finally been George treading the boards of the stage.

2

Life was all about timing, and George Croghan's couldn't have been any better. He was in the right place, at the right time.

Thank God for the Royal Navy! It was a curious time for such a thought to cross his mind, as he ejaculated into the loins of the Indian woman beneath him. Had it not been for the navy's blockade off the coast of Nova Scotia, things might have been very different. He dismounted and collapsed beside her on the bearskin that covered their bed. She smiled, watching him as he let out a deep sigh. He'd fallen into the fur trade by chance. Unlike most colonists, who weren't willing to venture out into Indian territory, Croghan made friends easily, and hadn't given a second thought to leaving the safety of Pennsylvania's boundaries. It was two years since he'd cemented an alliance with the Iroquois at Logstown, and now he was courting the Twightee, a smaller independent tribe still allied to France. Staying at their camp as their guest, it was thanks to the ongoing war between Britain and France that he was finding their hospitality more forthcoming. Unlike their French allies, he had access to what the Twightee wanted above all else: muskets and ammunition.

Is there anywhere more dangerous on Earth? Croghan wondered as he lit a cigar and puffed out a plume of smoke. Yet he never felt uneasy; if anything, the ever-present danger amongst the Indians only added to life's colour: each sunset was richer when it wasn't assured. During his time on the continent, he'd learned that just like Europe, the American interior was a tinderbox of tribal alliances and blood vendettas, with each tribe seeking to keep the strength of its neighbours in check. Justice was biblical, an eye for an eye. Yet it was the conflict between the age-old rivalries of Britain and France, now in full swing, that threatened to disrupt the uneasy balance of power in these fertile Indian hunting grounds. With French ships unable to dock in the New World, their merchants were unable to restock and, with so little to sell, the French cowered in their villages, leaving the Indians who were allied to them in a state of restless vulnerability.

France's loss was Croghan's gain, for he now found himself one of the very few British people west of the mountains, not only with goods to trade but Indians eager to buy them. Croghan's promise of English cartridges had ensured him a warm welcome in the Twightee Indian village on the shores of the great lake, for they feared an Iroquois attack as a result of their differing European allegiances. Sensing the French powerlessness, the Twightee had deserted the French camp at Detroit.

When Croghan had appeared over the horizon, hauling a wagon loaded with powder and shot, the Twightee chief had invited Croghan to build a permanent storehouse in his village. Since then, Croghan had wanted for very little. Every day, trapping parties would return to the village with skins of all manner of beasts they caught along the Cuyahoga River. The pile of furs ready to ship east grew bigger over the winter. His men had built him a strong house, and he now enjoyed its comforts, while practising the native tongue, drinking with the Chief, and sampling the unmarried women.

The best part, thought Croghan as he exhaled a plume of smoke, was that it was all paid for with other people's money. The lure of fur trade profits was too tempting for the wealthy Philadelphia merchants. Even Thomas Penn, the colony's owner, wanted a slice of the pie. They threw hitherto unimaginable sums of money at the Irishman, who, having arrived penniless, couldn't spend it fast enough. He'd hired a retinue of workers, bought property on the frontier, and bestowed lavish gifts to the Indians, whatever their persuasion. Feeling in a celebratory mood, he took a swig of last night's half-full whiskey cup on the bedside table, savouring the instant tingle of the alcohol.

Somewhere, many miles to the south, his herd would be waking, his slaves would be pouring the corn to fatten his cattle, his horses would be brushed and worked, his fields planted, people engaged in his service – it was a thought he would never tire of. He didn't have to lift a finger; as long as the skins travelled east, all was good.

He drained the whiskey, rogered his courtesan again, and went outside to take a restorative swim in the lake. It was a fine spring morning and the sun shone bright. Winter had passed and the brilliant blue sky, like Croghan's life, was cloudless. He controlled his breath as his body battled against the freezing water, then dunked his head and took a mouthful of fresh water. Just a few moments' discomfort before he would feel revitalised for the day. He surfaced, water running down his face, and roared, his voice lost in the vast expanse of the fabulous land, rife with opportunity. As he listened to the echo of his roar, Croghan knew with total certainty, this was his time. The reward for all the hardships he'd suffered, and the courage he'd shown in overcoming them. God would continue to reward his pluck.

Energised by his swim, he took a bowl of cornmeal for breakfast and went to find the Chief. Croghan took the track affording him a view over the lake, the grassland in the foreground, dotted with a forest of tepees. Beyond the accommodation, Croghan found the Chief in the woods, playing a game with his granddaughters. He stood behind the young girl and covered her eyes so she could not see her cousins run to hide amongst the trees.

'Top of the morning, Chief,' said Croghan, announcing his arrival to the short, powerfully built Indian, whom he'd nicknamed Old Briton. Despite the Chief's passing years, he'd lost none of his strength and still looked capable of besting any young upstart tempted to challenge his hold on the Twightee. He removed his hands from the girl's smiling face.

'Butterfly, butterfly, show me the way!' she ran forwards in search of the hiding children.

'Wait!' called Old Briton, holding her back. 'Look. Listen. Then search.'

She keenly searched the trees and undergrowth. Old Briton pointed to the wet, loamy soil.

'Here, this leaf is crushed. There's another, notice the signs, then you will find your prey.' The girl nodded before charging off into the trees.

Old Briton shook his head in mock exasperation. With his proud nose and greying hair, he had the bearing of a man enjoying the sight of his legacy: his offspring. A yelp came from the trees as she found the first of the hiding children.

'They have good luck to be young,' said Old Briton, practising his pidgin English.

'Aye, spared the decisions facing their elders.' Croghan turned to look at the Chief. 'Have you decided if you'll make firm our alliance and formally join the British?'

The Chief's eyes narrowed. 'We make a good trade. You welcome here.'

'Aye, but people are asking questions. They don't want the cartridges I'm selling you to be fired back in our direction.'

'I left the French, didn't I?'

Croghan nodded. More yelps emanated from the trees as the girl found another hider.

'Old Briton...'

'Why you call me this silly name?'

'Because, Chief, I know you're for Britain, even if you don't yet.' Croghan winked, provoking a frown on the Chief's face, exaggerating the lines weathered on his dark skin. He waved a hand, swatting away Croghan's comment as a horse's tail might dismiss an irritating fly.

'Chief, I'll talk plain. I don't give a horse's shit who you fight for, or against. If you sell me skins, what you do with my goods is your decision.' Croghan paused to let the Chief's understanding catch up. 'But my people – they ask me questions. I can't just walk into a store and buy a wagonload of ammunition. It's controlled. They let me have it only if they think it's in their best interest.'

'You did before.'

'Aye, to show what is possible, to lure them in, like a mistress opening her legs for you. Now, though, the mistress wants to be your wife. My Governor wants to know you're on his side for life, before you grow too strong.'

'If you want skins...'

Croghan threw up his hands. 'I do, but you're not talking to the right man; I'd sell you my grandmother, but my Governor takes a different view. You want to come meet him?'

Old Briton squinted, then shook his head and turned his attention back to the girls creeping through the trees. Croghan wasn't sure the Chief fully understood.

Croghan continued, 'France is finished.' He drew his fingers across his throat. 'Quebec has been captured. The sooner you join us, the better it will be for you.'

Old Briton's eyes widened in alarm. 'Quebec is English now?'

Croghan nodded. It wasn't. But how would the Chief find out he was peddling bullshit? 'The longer you make me wait...'

'I decide when I ready. Now go.'

Stubborn bastard makes an Irishman look flexible, thought Croghan as he walked back along the shore of the lake. He knew better than to force his point; Indians did nothing in a hurry. He'd try again tomorrow. He grabbed his cane pole and spent the afternoon fishing.

That evening, he walked back to the cabin, his fingers hooked under a fish's gills. Outside the wooden strong house, he found two of his men dispensing whiskey to three Twightee braves.

'What are you two doing?' he demanded.

'Jesus, boss, it's just a drink.'

'Enough, be gone.' He shooed away the braves. 'You can't be giving this lot drink. There's no telling what they'll do. They aren't used to it. Don't ever give them booze, you understand me?'

'But they offered us women.'

'Boys, don't be so daft. You want a woman? Have mine, but don't be giving the braves grog. You'll be blamed for creating a bloody havoc.'

With their telling-off concluded, one of them noticed something in the distance. 'Look, boss,' he said, pointing behind Croghan's back. On the bluff overlooking the lake, a horse-drawn wagon, piled high with what looked to be animal skins, wound its way towards the Twightee village. Five white men dressed in animal skins accompanied the wagon on foot. Croghan watched as the wagon rolled down the slope toward the tepees. These were the first white men he'd seen since the fall.

'Lads, fetch the guns,' he called over his shoulder. While he waited, he helped himself to a slurp of whiskey from his flask. Once armed, they ventured out to meet the arriving visitors.

The wagon was already surrounded by the Twightee. Old Briton arrived at the same time as Croghan and his men.

'*Bonsoir, mes amis,*' said their leader, a tall man whose long dark hair was receding from his temples. He bowed his head and presented Old Briton a string of wampum.

'Gentlemen, welcome to Sandusky,' said Croghan, conspicuously resting his musket against his shoulder.

'*Anglais?*' Their leader's surprise evident from his wide-eyed expression.

Croghan, who knew a spattering of French, only nodded.

The Frenchman smiled. '*Enchanté. Je suis Jacques De Silva.*' He stretched out the open palm of his hand.

Croghan hesitated.

'We come in peace,' said Jacques, reverting to English.

Croghan glanced at Old Briton who was watching him intently. He refused Jacques' handshake. 'That's a lot of fur you got yourself. Where did you get that?'

'The Cuyahoga River. May we rest here with you tonight?'

'Don't ask me, it's not my village.'

The Frenchman turned to the Chief and spoke in French: 'Chief, we travel to Detroit, to visit our mutual friend Lieutenant Céloron. If it is convenient to rest here tonight, we'd be very grateful, although I see you have company already?'

The Chief nodded his agreement. The Frenchman put his arm around the Chief. *Treacherous bastard,* thought Croghan. *That's a month's worth of furs going straight into French pockets, right under my nose.*

'You could buy a lot of powder with that,' he called out. One of the Frenchmen tapped the horse's rump and the wagon lurched forward. Croghan grimaced at the sight of Old Briton walking side by side with Jacques. He noticed the Chief's hand reach for his hip. Old Briton drew out a knife and as he turned, slashed the Frenchman's belly. Jacques groaned and doubled over, collapsing to the ground, a pool of blood spilling from his guts. The horse stopped. The four remaining Frenchmen froze. The Chief nodded to one of his braves, a lean and well-built man in his twenties, who carried the serious face of a warrior. The young man hollered a war cry as he drew his tomahawk and brought it crashing down into the skull of the nearest Frenchman. Other braves followed his lead, hacking the Frenchmen to the ground. The camp fell silent as the soil turned red with French blood.

Holy shit was the only thought that passed through Croghan's mind as he watched the Frenchmen being butchered and relieved of their scalps. He turned to see the Chief methodically wiping the blood from his knife with a leather patch.

'There's a wagon of skins there for you, if you bring us powder.' The Chief smiled. 'We on your side now.'

Jesus, thought Croghan, stunned by another merciless dispatching of his trading rivals. *Don't ever let me get on the wrong side of these people.* He held out his hand with contrasting feelings of horror and relief to secure his next allegiance.

The Chief put his blood-spattered hand on Croghan's shoulder. 'I want your English rum too. I never taste it.'

Jesus, you lot on rum, you'd kill everyone within a hundred miles of here. 'Sure, Old Briton, I told you. But if we're to be allies now, you'd better come to Philadelphia with me.'

'No! I not go. Too many white man's illnesses.'

'Fine, tell you what, let's enjoy a drink, then we talk more, eh?'

Croghan sighed as the Chief nodded his agreement. He needed a drink. A strong one. He had his men take the French skins to the storehouse and joined the Chief in his tepee, a draft of rum in hand, sensing for all the risks, a strong prospect of impending riches.

3

October 10ᵗʰ, 1747
Fairfax County, Virginia

Viktor should have been happy – or at the very least, satisfied. He was neither. He picked up the head of the cask and laid it atop the tightly packed bundles of tobacco leaves, then proceeded to fit the hoops around the barrel so it was secure. He took the iron from the fire and branded his father's initials 'HN' and their pattern onto the cask, scenting the open-sided barn with the smell of charred oak. A year's work, a full crop of Oronoco leaves compressed into two hogsheads, ready for shipping to England.

His father, Hans, limped into the barn and inspected his cargo. His skin was still brown from the summer sun and weathered by a lifetime outside. His beard and hair were long, grey and unkempt. He drew a small flask of rum from his jacket pocket.

'Good work, Viktor, let us celebrate our labours.' Even after fifteen years in the colony, Hans' English was still heavily accented with his native German, unlike Viktor who could remember nothing of his life in Hanover, save for being perpetually hungry; he had only been three when the family had made the crossing. Now he passed for a native Virginian.

Viktor didn't feel the urge to celebrate, but the cool October evening held a chill that the rum would keep at bay. He upended the small tot and held it out for a refill. His brother Daniel should have been with them, but he remained confined to his bed with a fever.

'You're quiet, son,' his father prompted.

26

That was rich, thought Viktor, whose father was renowned for keeping his thoughts to himself. He'd always assumed it stemmed from wanting to hide his Germanic origins, or lack of confidence in his English.

He let the second tot of rum burn his throat, but it didn't loosen his tongue. Two measly hogsheads of tobacco didn't offer much promise for betterment. He watched as other planters grew their enterprises and produced evermore of the bountiful weed.

'It's time we got some negroes, Father.'

Hans returned the flask to his linen jacket pocket and shook his head. It was an argument they'd had many a time.

'Our neighbours grow fat and rich,' continued Viktor, 'yet they barely lift a finger. You, though, you make us live like hogs!' Viktor held up his hands, revealing the brown stains left from handling the tobacco leaves.

'So long as I live, Viktor, a negro will never be forced to work our lands. I raised you a Lutheran. We don't believe in the bondage of one man to another...'

Tired of his father's sermonising, Viktor interrupted. 'That's the whole point, Father. Masters have a duty to teach their slaves Christianity, for their salvation.'

'Listen to yourself, Viktor, it's absurd—'

'Yet everybody else does it! They can't all be absurd.'

'Just because everybody does it, doesn't make it right, Viktor.'

Viktor shook his head. 'So why does Pastor Reynolds stand up in church and preach that negroes will be spared the curse of Ham by their enslavement?'

'Has it not occurred to you that even if the Pastor had a different interpretation, he is surrounded by slave owners?'

Viktor threw his arms in the air. 'Listen to yourself. Everyone holds negroes, the Pastor endorses it, yet you, the only person who thinks differently, are the one in the right? Do you think we shouldn't also keep cattle, hogs, sheep? Should they be emancipated too?'

Viktor felt himself flush with victory as his father turned to walk away. Yet too stubborn to concede, Hans stopped and turned back to his eldest son. 'If you ever want to inherit this land, then you will abide by my wishes, even after I am gone.'

27

Viktor snorted. 'There won't be anything left to inherit. Twenty acres is barely a hobby farm. There's scarcely any good land left this close to the coast, certainly not that we can afford. We can't hope to keep up with the big planters off two measly hogsheads.'

Hans squared up to his son, finger extended. 'When we landed here, we had nothing.'

Viktor rolled his eyes. *Here we go again.*

'I served a master for seven years so we could be free,' Hans continued in a strident voice. 'Look at us now: already we have land of our own, our tobacco is the finest in the county – not because we use negroes to toil against their will and neglect our craft, but because we tend to it ourselves. When you take these for inspection tomorrow, people will see that "HN" branded on the barrel, and know that it's the finest Virginia can produce.'

Viktor ground his teeth; his father just couldn't see sense. 'Father, everyone takes credit – they buy land and negroes and grow richer by the season from hundreds of hogsheads. Even if they aren't as good as yours.'

'They grow deeper and deeper in debt, son. And you mark my words, it will be the undoing of this colony.'

'Well, I don't see them wearing homespun cotton!' said Viktor, tugging at his shirt.

Hans hobbled away, grimacing in pain from his arthritic feet. The conversation had ended as it always did: Father and son unable to understand one another.

***

The next morning, the low sun poured through the small window of the room Viktor shared with his younger brother. Daniel was sleeping still; his face, a younger version of their father's, was pale and his breathing shallow as he battled the illness.

The family cabin was a simple construction of interconnecting rough-hewn logs. Two bedrooms, separated by another larger room, in which all their homely functions were conducted.

Viktor washed his face in the water bowl under the window, its shutters ajar, to let the light in, and combed his blond hair, checking himself as best he could in the reflection of the bowl. A trip out, if only to the tobacco warehouse at Hunting Creek, was an infrequent and rare opportunity to meet people. The fairer sex had little cause to visit a tobacco warehouse, but still, Viktor hoped today, perhaps, he could meet somebody on whom he could make a good impression. Not that he held much hope; dressed in a simple cotton shirt and old woollen trousers, doing the work of a negro, he was hardly the catch of the Tidewater, despite his broad shoulders and muscular frame. His father's stubborn ways kept him not only poor, but unromanced.

Hans was already outside the barn, tacking up the horse, a chestnut mare, barely bigger than a pony. After enduring Viktor's persuasiveness, he'd reluctantly agreed to stay home and care for Daniel, entrusting the crop to his son for the first time.

'You're to take these hogsheads by road. You're not to use Fitzbarton's wharf.'

The neighbouring plantation had a wharf, where for a fee you could transport goods by boat out of the creek that led to the Occoquan River, and then onto the Potomac River, where the nearest tobacco warehouse was situated. Viktor had never managed to pry out of his father why he was so averse to Fitzbarton.

Instead, the cumbersome hogsheads would be dragged, one behind the other, in between a simple metal harness attached to the horse. Everyone complained about London's insistence on receiving tobacco in hogsheads, the largest type of barrel. The unwieldy loads made a small planter's task of transporting them awkward, but their use was mandated to deter smuggling and the subsequent evasion of Parliament's duty.

'Sell it to a factor, don't consign it to a merchant,' Hans ordered. 'We need the money now and can't chance crossing the ocean at our risk. Get a new bracket for the hoe and a knife-grinding wheel from the store, but nothing else. The rest goes to our account.'

Viktor nodded and mounted the horse. Without a goodbye, he set off on his journey, their year's work trundling haphazardly behind him. There was an art to rolling barrels like this. Slow and steady, so as not to damage the tightly packed tobacco within, and always stopping on an incline so the loose barrels didn't crash into the horse's legs. All of which was far easier said than done on Virginia's rolling hills and potted roads, which were mere rough tracks cleared between the trees.

The morning was sunny and crisp, with a thin dew on the ground, the leaves, ready to fall, were warm browns and copper. He was soon clear of his father's land as the track led him back through the neighbouring Fitzbarton land, which surrounded their plantation on three sides. It was thickly wooded, with the occasional clearing where six weeks ago would have stood a crop of tobacco plants, yet now was nothing but bare soil, furrowed and exposed to the elements.

Viktor was glad to keep his own company for the day. By the time the tobacco was inspected, assuming it could be done today, it would be nightfall when he returned home. He fantasised about engaging with a loose woman, susceptible to his charms and looks... Perhaps he might spend the night in the throes of illicit passion. However much he entertained such arousing thoughts, he knew there was as much chance of seeing snow in July. But hope was hope, and in a man just turned seventeen, it was a commodity well-guarded.

In previous years, he'd accompanied his father, who'd taken the lead, but this year he'd entrusted Viktor to negotiate the sale on his own. Hans put it down to the pain he suffered when he walked, and the need to nurse his youngest son, Daniel, but Viktor knew it was his father's way of engaging his impenitent son in their small plantation. It didn't change Viktor's frustrations, but he did feel the burden of responsibility. While they kept a few loose leaves at home to use as local currency, this sale would be their sustenance for the year, reluctant as his father was to indulge in the easy credit from London, on which the colony operated. Viktor would take his time; his father had schooled him repeatedly in the art of negotiation. All the talk was of how the indifferent weather had led to lower yields, so tobacco was fetching a high price. The war with France was over, so no disruption to trade was expected, the transfer to Britain should be safe, and all the European markets were open to Virginian leaf.

After three miles through the woods, the road was joined by a side track that led back to the Fitzbarton wharf on the Occoquan River. Viktor had barely travelled fifty yards beyond the junction when he found a tree felled, blocking the road. Two negroes, in their homespun clothing, stood on top of the fallen oak, stripping off the bark with their knives. On the ground laid two axes and a buck saw. Seeing

Viktor, the younger one gave a sharp whistle. Moments later, another whistle pierced the air, a delayed echo of the first. Then another.

Viktor gently drew his horse to a halt, and the tobacco barrels jolted back and forth to a standstill. On the right, under the red leaves and bent branches of the treetop, was a large moss-covered knoll. The trunk end was thick with brambles. Both sides were densely packed with sappers and trees.

These two buffoons couldn't have picked a worse place to fell a tree, thought Viktor, seeing the road was entirely impassable.

'You bloody idiots have blocked the road!' he barked.

'Master said he want this tree cut into staves,' said one man.

'We should be done in a week. Maybe two,' said the other.

'No. I'm passing through now.' Viktor leapt from his horse and strode over to the tree. He pushed the trunk. It wouldn't budge.

'Come on, you two. Help me clear the road.'

'Master says…'

'I don't give a damn what your master says, I have to get this to market!'

Sluggishly, the negroes slid from their perches and took up positions either side of Viktor. He met the eyes of the older one. Could he see a drop of menace in his dark-brown pupils? *Am I in danger?* The thought flashed through his mind. Was this a trap? Blocking the road at a convenient choke point. Outnumbered, unarmed and unable to flee with his cargo? He put his fears to the back of his mind.

'Heave,' he commanded.

They pushed and shoved, but it was futile. The tree would not move.

Viktor cursed. He picked up their discarded axe from the road. Feeling safer, he ordered, 'Help me clear a path round the tree. Here.' He pointed to the trunk end.

'Master say…'

'Bah. You've no right to block a road. You'll help me pass or I'll report you to the authorities and your master will have all sorts of questions to answer.'

The negroes picked up their broad-bladed machetes and hacked at the undergrowth. Viktor felt a wave of relief. This was just a frustrating setback, nothing more sinister. It would cost him a few hours though. He'd have to find lodging for the night. Maybe he would end up in the arms of a woman after all. He took the axe and attacked the suckers blocking the verge.

Nigh on fifteen minutes had passed when the rhythm of slashing and chopping of wood was interrupted.

'My niggers working for you now?'

Viktor turned around. Astride a white stallion, clothed in white – stockings, breeches, shirt, silk waistcoat and neckerchief – was Mason Fitzbarton. He cut a large figure in his mid-forties, his brown hair, now peppered with grey, was pulled back tightly in a queue. His face was pale, with a short pointed nose that drew the lines of his forehead toward it, giving the man a stern demeanour.

Viktor suppressed his irritation and summoned suitable respect.

'They blocked the road.'

'I can see that. They respond well to your command, Master Neumann.'

Fitzbarton twitched his ankles and the stallion strode forward to the edge of where the undergrowth had been cleared.

'You've grown up to be a fine specimen of a man, Viktor.'

Viktor nodded.

'How's your father?'

'Well, thank you.'

Fitzbarton turned to study Viktor's horse and cargo.

'How many more do you have? Hogsheads.'

'That's it.'

'You won't live well off of that,' Fitzbarton purred.

He was right but Viktor wasn't going to give him the satisfaction of agreeing with him. Instead, Viktor turned his back and swung his axe into the tree he'd been clearing.

'That tree you're hacking at belongs to me,' drawled Fitzbarton.

'Well, this road you've blocked belongs to Virginia.'

Fitzbarton smirked. 'Sell your crop to me, I'll have these two take it off your hands now.'

Viktor returned the smirk. 'No, sir, my father would not condone it.'

'That's the trouble with fathers, always telling you what to do and what's for the best. It must get very frustrating.' Fitzbarton paused. 'How is Hans? I never could understand why his opinion of me is so sour.'

Viktor shrugged. 'He's fine, thank you for asking.'

'Come now, this won't do, Viktor, you'll be all day clearing this path,' said Fitzbarton. 'You're quite right, this tree shouldn't be blocking the road. Unfortunately, when one owns so many negroes, you can't supervise their each and every move. You two are damned fools,' he said, turning his attention to his slaves, with an unconvincing reprimand. 'I'm too soft on them, Viktor, that's my trouble. They need a strong, young man like you to drive them hard. Come, let us take your cargo to the wharf, where we'll see it loaded onto a boat alongside my own.'

Viktor was surprised at Fitzbarton's sudden change in tone. 'Thank you, er, no, Mr Fitzbarton, we won't be paying you any fees for using your wharf…'

'Pah! No, of course not. You're quite right. My men have blocked your passage, the transit will be my gift, to compensate you for your troubles.'

His father's words rang in his ears. He must go by road, and not use the wharf. But his father was too miserly to pay the fare – if it was being offered for free, then…

'The Lord approves of a man who can use his initiative,' Fitzbarton cut into his thoughts.

Viktor hesitated. Fitzbarton smiled and beckoned him to follow. He seemed sincere enough.

'Mr Fitzbarton…'

'Please, Viktor, call me Mason, we are neighbours after all.'

'Very well, sir, that would be most gracious of you.'

'Excellent!' Fitzbarton clapped his hands together twice, 'Charlie, Chalky,' referring to his slaves, 'turn this horse around and we'll save the beast the burden, roll these barrels by hand.'

Wow, thought Viktor, this wasn't the treatment he expected from the man his father was so wary of.

'It's better for the tobacco, Viktor. Don't want it spoiling by bashing those hogsheads together. Come, ride with me, I'll escort you to the wharf so we're certain you won't be impeded again.'

Together, they trundled back down the road, past the junction and further on into the Fitzbarton estate. Riding side by side, Mason Fitzbarton showed polite and sincere interest in the Neumann farm.

'What does your father wish to achieve, in the fullness of time?' asked Fitzbarton as they crossed a plank bridge over a small stream. Beyond them, the trees opened up and an enormous tobacco field lay empty.

Viktor thought that this one field was nearly as much as his father's entire smallholding. 'I'm not sure what he wants, other than for me to take over one day.'

'Naturally. Is that what you want, Viktor?'

Viktor felt coy about sharing his true feelings.

'Do you want his way of life for yourself, Viktor?'

'Well, there are things I believe he should do differently.'

'For example?'

'Negroes. He refuses to slave them, preferring to do the work by his own hand – and mine.'

'I always wondered how long he would maintain that stance. My father ran this plantation before me, Viktor. It's quite natural for the son to see the errors of his father's ways. It's what allows one generation to build on the efforts of the one before. Alas, that is not a tradition I am able to perpetuate, childless as I am.'

After a short pass through more woods, a large clearing opened up before them. In the centre, resplendent in the morning sun, stood the house. Viktor had stolen glances at it through the trees before, but never by invitation. A large red-brick façade sported a portico, supported by four pillars on a balcony, on top of four more pillars astride the entrance doors. A tiled roof, neatly interrupted by a series of dormer windows and two substantial chimneys topped it off. The main house was flanked by annexes, forming two one-storey wings with oversized windows.

'My new orangery is to the left and a gallery lies on the right. It has been a pleasure to make alterations since my father died.'

'It's very impressive, Mr Fitzbarton.'

'Please, Viktor, call me Mason, I insist. When I took over, we produced a hundred hogsheads of tobacco in a good year. This year, we'll ship close to four hundred. I'm at the point where I want my own vessel, so I don't have to haggle with greedy sea captains for space. My ship can return from Britain with a hull full of the most fashionable furniture, clothes, art, as well as the usual tools and materials, all to sell here in the colonies. In between, I can run flour, pork and rum to the Indies, and return laden with sugar.'

Viktor envied Mason's future. What a life this was, so very different to his own, and yet they dealt in the same crop.

'Of course, like everyone else, I always need good men to ensure things run right, with more land, so I can diversify.'

Viktor was distracted by the sight of two young slave women husking corn by the barn. One was mulatto, lighter in colour than her companion. She wore a simple linen dress, while the darker had a cloth shawl shrouding her upper body, concealing the curves that Viktor's eyes instinctively searched for. Neither looked a day over twenty. Behind them, a negro baby crawled on the grass, mute, a vacant expression in its eyes. Viktor noted Mason's grin to himself.

Beyond the farm buildings, the track ran past the simple wooden slave huts. The slope had been cleared ahead of the white cedar and chestnut trees that covered the land to the creek. The two men were silent as they rode through the trees, until they finally arrived at the water's edge. A large wharf of newly sawn wood abutted the land, laden with dozens upon dozens of hogsheads. Negroes were loading them onto flat-bottomed boats, ready to be taken for official inspection.

'Have these two loaded on right away,' Mason called out. 'Mr Neumann here will be accompanying you today.'

Viktor imagined the journey that would have lain before him, across the rolling roads, concentrating hard to avoid damaging or losing his barrels, navigating bumps and holes... *Thank heavens for that fallen tree,* he thought. Now he could sit back and relax as the water did the work.

'Thank you kindly, Mason, I am very grateful...'

'It's nothing, Viktor. I have matters to attend to here first, but I'll follow on shortly, and make sure you get a fair price for your crop. What are neighbours for, if not for helping one another?'

Mason turned his horse and trotted back towards his home.

His father couldn't have been more wrong about Mason

Fitzbarton, Viktor decided. He'd been every inch the gentleman.

After waiting for the last of the tobacco to be loaded, Viktor climbed aboard and sat on top of a barrel, watching as the lines were loosed and the boat pushed off. As it gently drifted downriver, Viktor daydreamed of a life where he was Mason Fitzbarton. Buying whatever he wanted, never lifting a finger, having the pick of the few available women in the colony – and some unavailable ones too, no doubt.

It was a far cry from his own existence. Something Viktor intended to change.

1748

4

For twenty-eight days of each month, much of Virginia's rural expanse was quiet. Unless travelling on specific business, folk tended to their plantations, their vegetable patches and livestock, and other such domestic pursuits, in solitude. The exceptions were court days. For those two days, while court was in session, residents descended on the county courthouses.

Hans, Viktor and Daniel always made the twenty-mile journey to Fairfax on foot, stopping for the night at a friend of Hans', who lived halfway between.

They arrived in Fairfax mid-morning. On any other day, one could pass through Fairfax unaware that the simple one-story clapboard building at the crossroad was a courthouse. There was nothing to distinguish this building as the seat of the county's administration from a private dwelling. During the six brief years which it had stood, the toll of Virginia's punishing climate was evident in the rotting bargeboards and peeling paint. In a far better state of repair was the tavern, a large wooden barn with a veranda around the ground floor and glazed windows for the rooms above. In the morning sun, it cast a long, cool shadow over the courthouse. Over the road, a red-brick church lay dormant until Sunday. Reverend Green, like everyone else, was keen to partake in the opportunities that court days provided: gossip, intrigue and scandal. By the church was a small jail, also made of brick, bar the wooden door which enclosed offenders in its cramped single room as they awaited trial. Not that any criminal cases were being advertised this sitting. The stocks, too, were empty. The clerk's house sat behind the church. He, the taverner and the storekeeper were the only people to reside in Fairfax all year.

Completing the hamlet of Fairfax was the store itself, which sold the essentials: everything from flour to iron nails. It was a long building, with bay windows displaying wares to those travelling past. The large yard on its far side held lumber, hogsheads, and other large items, though today, instead of being patrolled by the owner's dog, it was thronging with chatter. Hawkers mingled amongst the crowd, peddling their goods. Straw bales were being arranged for cock fights. Drinks, be they from the tavern or the illegal distillers, were already in full circulation. Two Gloucester hogs and a negro woman were chained to the wall, and a merchant waited for bids on either, hoping, in time, the drink would loosen people's grip on whatever they used for barter. Most working folk lacked the means to hold accounts in London, so were denied its endless credit. Instead, they used tobacco as currency or swapped goods, agreeing between them the value of the items in trade. A gang of mucky-faced children played fives against the rear wall of the yard. Caught up in their game, they knocked into a woman, spilling her drink and receiving a clip round the ear from her husband for their troubles.

For Viktor, each time he came to court, he felt his stomach flutter as he swapped the slow monotony of farm life for the vibrant – though brief – bloom of Virginian humanity. Each month he hoped for the arrival of an eligible woman making her way inland, eager for company. Each month he returned home, his dreams dashed. Those ladies present were either too young or their families had already overseen their introduction to a man with land to his name. Viktor watched a young couple, standing hand in hand, dressed in their Sunday best, their lives ahead of them, full of promise. The thought had occurred to Viktor that perhaps it was time he saved to buy land of his own. Land was cheap and even he could get some if he ventured west toward the frontier – assuming he persuaded someone to extend him their own credit. Yet, as appealing as a homestead and farm would be to a potential mate, he would be unable to make a sufficient living on his own without children to help, and he couldn't afford slaves. One failed crop, and he'd be thrown onto the charity of others.

The bell rang, interrupting his thoughts, signalling that court was now in session.

'Come on boys, let's go inside,' said Hans.

Viktor dutifully followed his father and brother, looking longingly over his shoulder at those folk who didn't bother themselves with court proceedings, instead remaining outside to drink and chatter in the shade. That was how the seeds of romance took root.

The small courtroom was full, with standing room only. The Neumanns took their place at the back, huddled amongst the audience.

***

George loved court. Strutting about in his new clothes, he made his way through the courtroom where the machinations of the colony would play out like theatre, grinding its people, slowly, clumsily toward a better future, progress of some kind. He was fascinated by the nods exchanged across the courtroom, the winks, the bargains struck in the bar. He had a front-row seat as he coat-tailed his elder half-brother, Lawrence, who shook hands with the good and the great of the county, listening to the woes of those with enough land to vote; it all contributed to an understanding of the issues of the day. Lawrence was a natural; he mingled with anybody who could vote, knew their names, where they farmed, and what they were up to. It was this God-given ability to listen, show interest and broker solutions, together with the wealth of his wife's family, that put him in government. These were the people he represented; he needed their vote, and court time was when Lawrence earned it – or bought it. They were lucky to have him, thought George, as he looked about the assembled crowd, his own emotions mixed: pride in his half-brother, envy of his talents, and wonder at the trail he so effortlessly cut. All the gifts bestowed by an education in England. A cachet which, unlike Lawrence, George had been denied by his mother as she'd assumed responsibility for him, following his father's death. He knew his second-rate education would forever be his cross to bear in polite society. Despite the practicalities of Virginian schooling, the absence of parity still irked George, that his brother's bread had, as usual, been buttered on both sides.

Time with Lawrence always left George feeling uncertain about his own path. He was making a respectable living as a surveyor, he had cash to his name, but no woman on his arm. As respectable a profession as surveying was, he questioned if it would ever be enough for him. He knew the answer was no. George enjoyed the precision of his work, but he was capable of more. He *needed* more, but of what he wasn't sure; and why…well, he'd never considered it.

Lawrence nudged him with his elbow. 'Look, that's Fry, the new justice of the peace.' He pointed to a short, wiry man in a scarlet robe. His wig and narrow pointed face and spectacles gave him an officious manner. 'Come, George, let us make ourselves known to him.'

George followed Lawrence to the front of court, stepping over the bar that held the people back so they could see the magistrate and clerk, who were seated to face them.

'Justice Fry?' said Lawrence.

'Yes?'

'Delighted to make your acquaintance at last! Lawrence Washington.' They shook hands and Lawrence introduced George. 'How are you adjusting to life in the colony?'

Though Lawrence attempted to engage him in some trivialities, Fry remained tight-lipped. His answers were clipped, factual, with no niceties returned.

'Well, I am delighted we can meet and I look forward to working with you, Justice Fry,' Lawrence went on. 'I am sure you know, I am the representative in the House of Burgesses for this county.'

Fry didn't look impressed.

'I see that the first case on the docket is Christopher Gist against Mason Fitzbarton.'

Fry nodded.

'Gist is a good man. Very reliable with an unblemished character.' Lawrence leaned toward Fry and lowered his voice, 'From what I know of this dispute, the court ought to be finding in Gist's favour.'

Fry's eyes narrowed. 'Mr Washington, you are welcome to your opinion, but it is I who will decide the merits of the plaintiff's case. If you think you can curry influence with me, sir, then let me disabuse you of that notion straight away.' Fry straightened his waistcoat and lifted his head. 'This is the trouble with the colonies, Mr Washington: doing your business on a nod and wink, with little regard for the rule of law. Well, let me make it clear that the days of you and your friends doing as you please are over. Parliament is dismayed that His Majesty's law is being so poorly applied in his colonies. Myself and my fellow upstanding men have been sent here to ensure things are smartened up. In Britain, Mr Washington, the law is paramount, and so it shall be in her dominions.'

George bristled, yet Lawrence smiled. 'I couldn't agree more, Mr Fry. We're lucky to have your expertise here, to strengthen the colony.'

Fry's expression softened.

'You must come to Mount Vernon,' said Lawrence. 'It is my humble abode. Won't you join us for dinner?'

The man warranted a slap and yet Lawrence would have him to stay! George watched in fascination as Fry nodded and excused himself.

'Be seated,' he commanded the courtroom, which began to quieten.

'*Dinner?*' whispered George as they took their seats.

'The man needs educating on how we do things here,' replied Lawrence in a hushed tone.

George chuckled. 'You have your work cut out with him, brother.'

'Keep your enemies close, George. Besides, if he won't toe the line, I'll see him moved to some tumbledown shit-hole out west.'

George laughed, attracting Fry's attention, who shot him an irritated glance from his seat at the front of the court.

***

'Court is in session,' announced the clerk seated to Fry's right.

Fry introduced himself and thanked the gallery for their attendance. 'I look forward to ensuring the law is a fit and proper instrument for the good of this county. I shall endeavour to be fair in all my undertakings.'

There was some minor heckling from the rear of the room. Viktor, standing between his father and brother in the crowd, laughed as Fry's face turned the same colour as his robe. He banged his gavel and called for silence.

'First on the docket is the matter of an unpaid debt brought by Mr Christopher Gist of…' Fry consulted the papers on the small desk in front of him, 'of no fixed address. Hmm.' He double-checked, a look of disapproval on his face. '…Brought against a Mr Mason Fitzbarton. Gentlemen, will you approach the bar, please.'

Mr Gist walked from the back of the room through the narrow aisle between the cheap wooden chairs. Fitzbarton was already standing at the bar. He turned and offered a nod of reassurance to his wife, who was sitting in the front row behind him.

To Viktor's eyes, Fitzbarton cut a dashing figure, his head held high, his broad chest puffed out, filling his silk waistcoat. He cradled his beaver skin hat under one arm, revealing hair tied tight in a queue. His cream breeches were impeccable. Viktor wondered what his outfit cost. It was immaculate and appropriately understated for summer court.

'Nice to see Fitzbarton finally come a cropper,' whispered Hans. Viktor rolled his eyes.

'Mr Gist, would you care to explain the complaint you bring here today,' prompted Fry.

'Thank you, sir,' said Gist. His back to the gallery, he too cut an impressive physique, but with an altogether less impressive wardrobe. The creases in his shirt and the dirt marks on his breeches gave him the look of a man who'd just completed a lengthy journey. 'In the summer of last year, I sold two negroes to Fitzbarton here. We agreed to thirty days credit, but both the bill for fifty pounds remains unpaid and interest on the debt would now be due. I'd like the court to see the bill settled.'

'Do you have a receipt for the goods?' asked Fry.

'With the passing of time, I have mislaid it.'

Fry frowned. He turned to address Fitzbarton. 'What of Mr Gist's account do you take issue with, Mr Fitzbarton?'

'Well, it is true as he tells it, Your Honour, but what Mr Gist neglects to mention are the details of our contract. Mr Gist was selling his house slaves: two negroes, one male, one female, both nearing their mid-twentieth year. I was desiring of an additional negro to work my fields and a trained house slave, so we agreed a price and, acting in good faith, executed our contract.'

Hans tutted at the mention of good faith. Viktor looked at his father, perplexed. He was a man who espoused the virtue of English law, and yet he'd clearly made his mind up already. In Hans' head, Fitzbarton had already been denied a fair trial. Was it out of jealousy at his success? Viktor shook his head and continued watching the trial.

'Having taken receipt of the goods, it was no more than a week before the male negro turned sick. Despite the best attention of his people and their medicines, he died a mere week later in a terrible fever. Being as this all occurred before the bill was due, and whatever the condition that afflicted the sickly beast, it would have been contracted under the ownership of Mr Gist. Therefore, I trust the court will find he sold me defective goods.'

'What say you in reply, Mr Gist?'

He shrugged. 'I'm no doctor. Fitzbarton inspected the goods before buying them. Mighty unlucky, I grant you, but the buyer takes on the risk.'

Fry's eyes narrowed as he considered this.

'There is the matter of the female slave, Your Honour,' Fitzbarton continued. 'She transpired to be with child. An act which occurred under the ownership of Mr Gist. I didn't buy a slave to lose her attention for six years while she raised a child.'

'You got a free negro,' Gist retorted.

'Thank you, Mr Gist,' said Fry, in a warning tone.

'I wrote to Mr Gist, informing him of the events and offering to return the negro child to him, for his benefit, while I kept the mother. I received no reply.'

'Mr Gist, why did you not reply?' asked Fry.

'I never received any such letter.'

Fry frowned. 'To where did you send your letter, Mr Fitzbarton? My papers indicate Mr Gist is of no fixed abode.'

There was a subtle intake of breath as the audience watched to see if there was a hole in Fitzbarton's account. Without breaking stride, he stated, 'Mr Gist left no forwarding address, so I sent letters to the taverns that he was reputed to attend.'

'Mr Gist?' prompted Fry.

Gist shrugged. 'My surveying work detains me for long periods in the western frontier. I have no need for a home, being as I never spend any time there. With no need for it, I sold my property and my excess slaves and invested the money in the Ohio Company venture. My earnings from surveying are sufficient to house me at taverns in the meantime. I have indeed been to the taverns that Mr Fitzbarton claims to have written to, but I never received anything.'

Fry sighed. 'What became of the negro woman and child?' he asked Fitzbarton.

'I released them, to return to Mr Gist.'

'I take issue with that,' said Gist, raising his gruff voice. 'They've never been seen. Any man of Mr Fitzbarton's commercial understanding would have kept them and sold the child when he came of useful age.'

'That is conjecture, Mr Gist,' said Fry. 'We are concerned with what *actually* happened, not what you would have done had you been in Mr Fitzbarton's position. If you choose to sell goods, and be of no fixed address, such that you cannot easily be contacted, or the goods easily returned, then I find in favour of Mr Fitzbarton. If it should transpire that he retains possession of the goods, having relinquished his title to them, then he may look forward to a suitable punishment in future, but for now, I consider the debt invalid.' Fry banged his gavel and the audience began to chatter about the verdict.

'Lying bastard,' muttered Hans.

Viktor rolled his eyes. *Innocent until proven guilty.* He watched as Fitzbarton thanked Magistrate Fry, then turned and nodded towards his wife, satisfied yet magnanimous in his victory. *What Father doesn't realise*, thought Viktor, *whether Fitzbarton is liable for the debt or not, that's how you get ahead in life.* Standing your ground, guarding your money, taking issue with those who crossed you, bending the truth if need be – winning. As Fitzbarton walked down the aisle, some people stood and congratulated him on his victory.

'Where are you going?' asked Hans.

Viktor ignored his father. Like a moth to a flame, he was drawn into Fitzbarton's orbit.

'Mr Fitzbarton, may I congratulate you,' he said. 'I am glad to see that you achieved justice today.'

'Viktor! Thank you. Good to see you again. How are you keeping?'

He is a good man. He recognised me straight away. Viktor glowed with pride. 'I am well, sir, thank you.'

'And this year's crop, how is it looking for you?'

'Good, thank you,' said Viktor, forcing a smile which felt unconvincing. The crop in the fields was fine, but it was pathetic compared to what Fitzbarton produced, and Viktor knew it.

'Come now, son,' said Hans arriving behind him with Daniel in tow, 'that's enough. Leave the man to his business.'

'Hans, good to see you,' said Fitzbarton. 'You have a fine son here.'

Hans remained stony-faced. 'Come on, Viktor.'

Viktor didn't move, captivated by Fitzbarton, hoping the exchange would continue.

'Well, if I can ever help again, you need only ask,' said Fitzbarton, smoothing over the awkward pause.

'Thank you, sir, that's most kind of you.' Viktor nodded and doffed his hat at Mr Fitzbarton's wife. Her reaction was cool, but Viktor paid her no mind. He could feel his father's fury emanating from him. *Here we go.*

As soon as they were outside, Hans rounded on him. 'What did he mean, help *again*? What's he done for you?'

Viktor frowned. 'For me? No, Father, for *us*.'

Daniel looked worried. He knew.

'He helped ship our tobacco to the warehouse last fall.'

'What?' Hans grabbed his son's shirt and twisted it in his gnarled hand, pulling Viktor towards him. 'Have you been dealing with that man behind my back?' he growled, his voice hushed to avoid a scene.

'No! The road was blocked, so he offered to load our hogsheads on his boat. He didn't even charge me, Father. He did it out of charity.'

Hans frowned. 'Nonsense. Tell me, Viktor, what blocked the road?'

'A tree.'

'You see. This was his doing.'

Viktor shook his head. 'You're paranoid, Father. A man like that has better things to do than trouble himself with us.'

'Oh no, Viktor, you're wrong. We've just seen that man lie in a courtroom, so he doesn't have to pay his debt to a man of lesser means. He grows rich by trampling those around him.'

47

Viktor pushed his father's hand away. 'We've just watched the magistrate clear him and find in his favour.'

'That doesn't mean anything.'

'It means everything! Father, this is absurd. This is about slaves, isn't it? You can't bear anyone to prosper by using slaves.'

Hans' face turned crimson. 'You're bloody naïve, boy.'

'*I'm* naïve? You have no idea how *naïve* you sound!'

'I'll be in heaven with a clear conscience, resting for eternity, while Fitzbarton and all the slavers burn in hell.'

'Good for you, Father.' Viktor turned to walk away.

'Come back here! We're going back inside.'

Viktor shook his head. '*We're* not going anywhere!'

Hang what he wants, Viktor thought, crossing the road, leaving his father and brother to attend the next hearing.

A cock fight was about to get underway in the store yard; a ring of straw bales had been set up, around which were gathered a crowd of rowdy spectators, mostly young men. A curly-haired man of a similar age to Viktor, with a broad nose and a recent scar from a nasty slice to his cheek, paraded the cock for inspection. Its feathers were red, the same colour as its owner's hair, and it too had a menacing manner as its head jerked left and right, spoiling to get in the ring. The bird knew what was coming.

'You placing a bet?' asked a tall man Viktor had seen previously but didn't know.

To hell with it. Viktor nodded. His father had forbidden it, so he would do it. 'That one, the red bird.'

Overhearing the exchange, the bird's owner commented, in a thick Scots accent, 'Aye, good choice, laddie, he be a nasty wee bugger.'

The cocks were placed in the ring. The opponent, a black-feathered creature, began to circle the red one. Both birds crouched as they paced, eyeing each other. As one, they suddenly leapt, clawing at each other in the air, their spurs scything back and forth, sending a shower of feathers floating to the ground. A ripple of cheers ran round the ring. Up and down the birds jumped, furiously slashing at each other. The red bird mounted its opponent and pinned it to the ground, pecking at its head. Viktor yelled, 'Go on, finish it!' along with the rest of the spectators, all in a state of frenzied excitement or anxious desperation, depending on which bird they'd backed. The black bird wriggled free and leapt again, but the Scotsman's bird sensed victory, its legs flailing wildly. The black bird fell. A beat passed. It didn't stand. Its owner stepped over the bales and picked it up, eager to save it for another day. Cheers rang out from those who'd bet on red. Viktor clapped, delighted by the distraction. He collected his winnings, a small roll of tobacco, and congratulated the Scotsman, who was returning the victorious cock to its wooden cage. The man lifted a demijohn.

'Any of yous wanna dram o' cider?' he offered. 'Half a shilling's worth of baccy – that's half what that robbin' bastard at the tavern next door 'ul charge yous.'

Viktor took a long draft, savouring its dry flavour, then wiped his lips on his sleeve. He took another. 'It's good. Thank you.'

'Aye, that it is, pal. Barney's my name. You?'

'Viktor.'

They stood chatting, passing the cider to and fro, while Barney waited for someone to challenge his bird.

'I've not seen you here before,' said Viktor.

'Aye, I tend to travel where my nose takes me. Suits me nicely.'

Viktor felt envious of the man's freedom. He was trapped under his father's wing, yet Barney, no older than he, could come and go as he pleased. Scraping a living, by the look of his attire, but not bound by anyone's rules. Viktor passed him another chaw of tobacco from his winnings and upended the cider bottle.

'Oi! I saw that!' called out an irate voice.

Viktor finished his swig and turned to see Paul, the tavern keeper, striding over, waving a stick in the air. 'Begone and take your grog with you!'

Barney took the demijohn from Viktor. 'What's your problem?'

'You are. Selling drink. Where's your licence?'

'I was nae selling it, pal. Just what I had left from my journey.'

'I saw him pay you!' the taverner protested, pointing at Viktor.

'Nae, pal, yous wrong there.'

'Nonsense.'

'It's true,' said Viktor, standing beside Barney.

'Bollocks, Neumann,' said Paul. He prodded Barney in the chest

49

with his stick. 'Be gone or I'll have you clapped in irons.' He pointed to the stocks with his stick. 'Shoo! Be gone. I'm the only one selling drink here. If you're thirsty, you come to my tavern and buy it from me. Like the law demands.'

Barney squinted. A quiet menace exuded from his glare. 'Come on, Viktor. We best be off before I fix this man a new nose.'

Viktor followed Barney, his heart racing from the confrontation. In the woods behind the tavern kitchen garden, Barney fished out another demijohn from amongst the undergrowth.

'You've more?' said Viktor.

'Aye. Fell off a boat somewhere. Yous wanna help me drink it? I don't want tae be carrying it all with me when I leave.' Barney popped out the cork and took a swig. Viktor took another mouthful and followed Barney, who found a comfortable tree against which to rest his back. He placed his cockerel, recovering in his cage, by his side. Viktor sat at the base of the next tree and relaxed as the cider began to take effect.

'Where you headed?' Viktor asked.

'Eh?'

'You said you didn't want to carry the cider. Where are you going?'

'Oh, I dunno.'

'I'm guessing you aren't native Virginian. How long you been here?'

'Nae long. Eighteen months or so.'

'How are you finding it?'

'Aye, suits me well. Warmer than the Highlands.'

'You came here for the weather?'

Barney offered an ironic smile and took another draft of cider. 'I'm here because the British government sold me.'

Viktor frowned. There was clearly more to this story. Without further prompting, Barney seemed at ease to continue:

'Me and a hundred of my fellow clansmen. By rights, we should have hanged, but you know about this new British state – if they can make an easy quid, they will. Judge said he didn't want to provoke our people by hanging us – real Christian-like, but I know for a fact he took a backhander when he sold us all to a merchant. There's money to be made here in America; I guess the judge wanted his share. Just as well, else I'ze be in the ground, cuddling daisy roots.'

Viktor took another mouthful of cider. He wasn't accustomed to criminal company. They were a common and unwelcome presence in the colony and his father would have forbidden him from mixing with such unsavoury persons, but he didn't feel threatened by the Scotsman.

'What did you do?'

Barney's stare settled into the middle distance as he searched for the memories that had brought him here...

Sleet blew across the treeless moorland of Culloden in the Scottish Highlands, stinging the cheeks of the two opposing lines of Scotsmen facing each other, muskets raised, ready to fight. The grass fluttered in the wind under a troublesome grey sky. The armies waited. One, blocking the route to Inverness, were wearing the blue bonnets of the rebel Jacobites; four and half thousand clansmen, all determined to put a Stuart back on the Scottish throne. Their Monarch-in-waiting, Bonnie Prince Charlie, stood to their rear, pulling his cloak tight about him to keep out the icy chill. Their opponents were fellow Scotsmen, cousins, neighbours, rival clans, decked in British army red coats, cutting a thin bloody line across the moor. Their union flags quivered in the wind.

Having been born twenty-three years after its inception, Barney had never known a time before Great Britain. In his sixteen short years, he'd been fed a steady diet of his father's and grandfathers' vitriolic tirades against the British project. What England had failed to achieve militarily, it had since succeeded in, subjugating the people of Scotland by the hammer of finance and politics. A Tory scheme, under the cover of the then Queen Anne, a descendant of the Scottish House of Stuart. The Clan MacGregor, to which Barney belonged, had been against it from the beginning, seeing it for what it had been: conquest by stealth. English acts of Parliament took precedence, preventing the Scottish people from choosing their own monarch. What they couldn't settle in government would now be determined on the battlefield.

Barney didn't claim to understand it all, but he'd been raised to hate the English, so any Scotsman who sided shoulder to shoulder with them was his enemy. Like every boy, glory on the battlefield was a noble notion, yet now the time had come, he tried hard not to show the fear that danced wildly in his belly, his cold hands gripping his broadsword tightly. There hadn't been enough targes to go round, so without a shield, Barney would have to trust his fate into God's care. He believed.

Teeth clenched, eyes narrowed, he stared at the distant line of red soldiers, too far to make out their faces. Today he would prove himself, and by evening, he could swagger into the tavern in Inverness, boasting of the soldiers he'd slain. He would have done his part in bringing down the regime that had subsumed Scotland. A government that so feared losing its Protestant stranglehold on the country, it would put a German, King George, rather than a Catholic on the throne.

The Jacobite cannon fired, its blast echoing across the bleak moorland. It missed. But that didn't deter the stomach-churning roar of the Highland men as they readied themselves to inflict on their enemy their infamous Highland charge.

Puffs of white smoke ran in perfectly ordered sequence, like falling dominoes, up the course of the British line. The boy standing beside Barney, his cousin Jamie, vanished soundlessly as he was swept off his feet. Barney glanced over his shoulder; Jamie, also sixteen, lay ten feet behind him, dead. A cavity punched into his chest. The boom thundered across the sky like a hundred storms in union. Barney's hunger faded as he felt panic course through his veins. All along the rebel lines, men howled in agony, having absorbed the first enemy blow. Thunder came from the middle of their line. The Mackintoshes were charging. Other clans followed. Barney roared as his group broke into a sprint. It was disorganised, chaotic, and unsightly, but it must have put the fear of God into their opponents as they leapt across the rough ground.

More puffs of white smoke came from the British lines. More screams as men were cut down by canon fire. Barney didn't stop to look. He heard the crack of gunfire as they unloaded their muskets into the oncoming chargers. Strangely devoid of the fear that had dogged him all day, Barney's body moved with the power of a racehorse, propelling him towards his fate.

His ginger curls were tied at the nape of his neck, hidden under his bonnet, and together with his broad nose and manly jaw, he appeared tough, strong, and terrifying. He raised his sword and yelled as he covered the last few yards, ready to barge into the man unlucky enough to face him. A tall, pale man in the same red coat and cocked hat as every other government soldier, his musket, bayonet fixed, pointed inexplicably towards the ground, leaving his torso undefended. Barney dropped his left shoulder, turned his head and tucked his sword handle tight to his right hip. Like a bull, he braced for impact. The enemy raised his musket. Barney never saw the bayonet that stabbed into his left cheek before glancing across his mouth. He felt the slice, but not the pain. Knocked off balance, he cannoned into the man's legs. Dazed, he got to his feet and parried a bayonet lunge before headbutting his opponent, hearing the crunch of the man's nose. He kicked at his knee and felled the redcoat, driving his sword into the man's belly.

The first skirmish over, he wiped his free hand across his cheek. The skin was loose, split from the corner of his mouth to his ear. Blood poured from the wound, soaking his chin and neck. So, he had his first battle scar, one to tell his grandchildren about. The sneaky lowland bastards were striking the men to their side, not to their front, catching the clansmen off guard. Without hesitation, he lunged at the redcoat to his left, his blow deflected but he managed to slash his sword across the soldier's gullet. Blood spattered across Barney's already blood-soaked face. To the right, more Highland chargers arrived, and barged into the thin red line. Barney swung his sword, thrashing wildly at anything red. Behind the British line, he saw more smoke. Hundreds of puffs in unison. There was a second British line. A musket ball glanced off the tartan covering his shoulder. He stopped, unsure what to do, the momentum of his battle rage interrupted. Every other man in the distant line of soldiers dropped to their knees and began to reload their muskets. The alternate men remained standing, muskets prone to their shoulders as they waited for the command which Barney realised was imminent.

'FIRE!'

As one, they loosed their musket balls, decimating the Highlanders. The redcoats who had survived the initial charge fought with renewed vigour. Barney stood motionless and watched as the firing ranks mechanically performed their reloading and firing. Supplied, practised and out of range, Barney knew the day belonged to the enemy. It must have occurred to his fellow men too, for they began to fall back. Without any order, the Highlanders charged again, but this time off the battlefield, past their fallen brethren, gunfire ringing in their ears, under pursuit from the King's dragoons. The cause was lost.

Viktor sat in awe, listening to Barney's tale, and quietly imbibing the cider. It was so far removed from his own world of pulling up weeds, tending to seedlings, and packing hogsheads. Indians and thieves were the only menace he'd ever had to contend with. To take up arms against your own people was unthinkable.

'Fighting your kin? I just can't…why?'

Barney smiled grimly and took back the cider. 'Our hatred of the English goes back a long way and we've long memories.'

Viktor shook his head. Everyone in the colony was loyal to the King. They were proud of their English origins. It made them stronger against their common enemies, or so he'd been led to believe. His father said that Britain was a beacon of tolerance and liberty. He'd uprooted their family from Hanover and chosen for them to become British subjects. That somebody from within would take up arms against this system was an idea he couldn't comprehend. Yet it wouldn't surprise him if this misplaced loyalty was another thing his father had got wrong.

'Take my word, Viktor, the Britain I know is a different beast to the one you've been fed. It kills, deports, and beats its own people without mercy. Parliament would sell their own mothers for a fair price.'

'So, what happened to you?'

'We hid up in Inverness overnight, but redcoats found us the next morning. With this,' pointing to the scar on his cheek, 'I cannae be denying fighting. They put us in gaol but there were too many of us. Couldnae lock us all up, so theys made us draw lots for hanging. I drew the short straw. Honestly, lad, dunnae mind saying, my knees was trembling like a sapling in a storm. Was no pleas in court. Judge banged his gavel and that was it. We was guilty o' treason. Hanging be the punishment, but judge says we's not beyond redemption, him sat there, his pockets full a gold.'

'And that was it, you were free?'

'Nae. Merchant bought me. Shipped me here. I was sold to a rice farmer in Carolina. Seven years slavery. Nae thanks, pal, I was gone.'

'You ran away?'

'Too right I did. Not slavin' for no man.'

'And they didn't pursue you?'

Barney shrugged. 'They must a' done, but easy for a Scotsman to move about. Nobody asked me any questions and if they did, I'd shoot them a look to make their blood turn cold. Different story if you've the black skin, mind. Then yous is definitely running from someone.'

Viktor's mind sifted through all he'd learned. He couldn't help but feel foolish. There was so much he didn't know, his life being small and sheltered. Barney's had adventure. But the thought of ever facing the noose made him shudder.

***

Court finished at five and, with justice served for the day, people reconvened in the tavern or spilled outside. They debated the day's rulings, petty criminal matters, and gossiped about the fate of the prosecuted. The tavern's side room was reserved for the county's betters. There was no definitive rule for who could or couldn't enter, but if you had to ask, then you weren't suitable. The wealthy were assured enough to know. For those who tried before their time, found their attempts at conversation unreturned. It was here that the Washingtons mingled. As usual, Lawrence bought the drinks, the price of their votes.

George looked across the crowded room. Its décor was simple, with well-worn wooden floorboards, the few chairs moved to the edge of the room so women and the elderly could rest themselves. The diminutive pepper-pot figure of Mason Fitzbarton's wife sat alone, by the window, her glass empty.

George signalled to the waiting negro to fill her drink, then mustered the courage to approach.

'Congratulations on your husband's victory today,' he said, emulating Lawrence's habit of parleying with those with whom he'd differed. Gist was Lawrence's acquaintance, so they had naturally taken his side.

Her head tilted upwards to take in George. Her podgy cheeks and the curl of her dark hair gave her a cherub-like appearance, at odds with the creases across her forehead, the signature of a burdened mind. Her dark eyes drooped, with a vacant glaze. She forced a half-smile.

'We've not been introduced; George Washington,' he said.

She held out her hand and he bowed to kiss it.

'Enchanted.'

She said nothing. George began to regret coming over as he watched her polish off half the drink. 'Tell me, how does today find you?' he continued, not wanting to appear rude by leaving.

'Mmm. Fine. Thank you,' she replied, her slurred voice thick.

'A victory for your husband; I imagine he must be satisfied?'

She snorted. 'Satisfied? My husband? Not likely.'

Sensing she was now loose with her tongue, George continued, 'Really? Is he a difficult man to please?'

She glared at George. He wondered what drink-riddled thoughts danced across her mind. She drained her glass and swayed in her chair. 'He's a cunt.'

George's eyes bulged. Never in his life had he heard such a word from the mouth of a lady.

Finally, he recovered his thoughts. 'I am sure he's…'

She glared at him and he changed tack.

'Yes, well, I, er, none of us are born perfect. I dare say he has some redeeming qualities.'

'Money.' Tears welled in her eyes.

This was all going rather badly. She was three sheets to the wind.

'Can I get you any food?' he suggested.

Mrs Fitzbarton rose to her feet, swaying. George wondered if he should offer his arm, but didn't want to appear too familiar. He moved out of her way as she stumbled and fell to the floor with a crash. Her empty glass smashed, sending shards of glass across the floor.

The room fell silent as heads craned to see what had occurred.

George felt eyes resting on him, and uncertain what else to do, he held up his palms. Mason Fitzbarton, his face crimson, left the men he was talking to and swooped across to gather his wife. Shooting a suspicious glance at George, he lifted his wife and held her limp body up by her armpits as he attempted to obscure her with his bulk. The manoeuvre was executed with an ease that suggested to George it had been performed before. He began to offer a denial to Fitzbarton, but the man was in no mood to hear it. In one smooth gesture, he removed his debilitated wife from the room and the negro serving girl appeared with a dustpan and brush to sweep up the glass. The chatter gradually returned to the room. George sidled back to Lawrence.

'Pleased to see you haven't lost your touch with the ladies, brother,' Lawrence quipped. 'You always could make women weak at the knees.'

***

As dusk turned to night, Viktor, now drunk from a day's intake of cider, watched the tavern from behind a tree at the rear of the building. Behind the next tree, Barney drained the last of his cider. The tavern's windows glowed in the darkness. Viktor wasn't sure what they were doing. He'd spent the day chatting with Barney and had decided he wasn't an easy fellow to like, but he'd lived and that was something Viktor felt resolved to do more of from now on. He'd be eighteen in October; it was time to step clear of his father's shadow. Hans and Daniel would have left to stay at his friend's cabin for the night. They'd be back tomorrow, but for tonight, Viktor was unsupervised.

'Rite, yous ready?'

Viktor nodded, though for what he wasn't sure.

'Roll down ya sleeves.'

Viktor did as instructed.

'We's gonna teach that tavern keeper the price of his licence, eh? Rite, that window on the left is open. See 'at?'

Viktor nodded, sobered by the excitement of the misdemeanour that lay ahead. Between them was open ground, then a large vegetable garden, fenced with wire to keep out the rabbits.

'Let's go.'

Crouching low, he followed Barney along the treeline. They stopped thirty yards in, when they came to a collection of beehives. Barney lifted the wooden lid off one and carefully laid it on the ground. The bees were sleeping.

'You take one of these too,' said Barney, lifting the frame out of the hive. Bees began to stir as the night air disturbed their honeycomb. The surface of the frame was thick with bees. 'Quick, go!'

Viktor lifted a frame and ran after Barney. The drink numbed the first sting to his finger as he raced across the open ground. He had three more stings by the time he reached the vegetable garden. He cleared the fence and cut through the neat lines of greens. Barney tossed his frame through the open window. Viktor did likewise and brushed the bees clear off his hands. Panting, they peeked through the window as the bees began to swarm. A woman screamed and expletives filled the air as people flapped their arms to deter the angry bees circling them.

Viktor hesitated to join Barney's laughter. The tavern keeper ushered everyone into the safety of the gentlefolk's room.

'You won't be selling too much grog tonight, you prick,' chortled Barney. 'Quick, let's get out of here.'

Viktor, his footing unsteady from drink, chased after him into the dark of the night.

5

There must be some honest folk living in London, but Sylvia Coppell had never encountered them. As she woke in the mid-afternoon, sharing a bed with her younger sister and brother, she remembered today was special: it was her eighteenth birthday. The age the posh girls performed their coming out ceremony. This evening, Sylvia was going to the theatre to celebrate her own version of this custom. Her head was fuzzy from this morning's gin, the air heavy with the snoring bodies crammed into the small one-room tenement her family shared with another; she thought about how her life had turned out. When she was little, her mother would tell her stories of princesses, adorned in jewels, living in castles and dancing with dashing princes. Fairy tale weddings and families. Life in London couldn't be more different. Her father had vanished when she was ten, never to be seen again. Her mother had worked every waking hour: servant work, tavern work, stable work, night work; whatever she could do to put meagre food on the table, she had done. Sylvia had been left to raise her four siblings, of which only the two she shared a bed with now remained.

Once Mother had died, their lives hadn't changed much, for they had barely seen her before. Life, trapped in the pit of London's humanity, didn't afford you long to grieve. Each day was a battle to be fought, against hunger, disease, violence and misadventure. Each night they retired, knowing any of these could take them tomorrow. By begging, stealing and turning tricks, Sylvia had kept her family from becoming parish children. At the expense of the law, she had protected them from a life of beatings, slavery and becoming the carnal fodder of their masters. Rarely though, did Sylvia think of her future, more concerned as she was with the challenges of the present. But today she was turning eighteen. She lay daydreaming amongst the chorus of snoring bodies: To have a house of her own, a husband to love, money in her pocket, children in her arms, servants to wait on her, a jewel around her neck… Was it too much to ask? Far too much.

Her daydreams were interrupted by a loud fart from her brother Jacob. Eager to escape the Dutch oven, she climbed over her sister Caroline and out of the bed. She tiptoed across the floor, choosing a path between the sleeping bodies of the rest of the Whitechapel gang, whose turn it was to sleep on the floor. Seven of them shared the cramped space: Two years ago, her family had joined with the Nicholsons, who'd suffered similar hardships. Between them, they eked out an existence.

Sylvia went outside and found the slop bucket brimming with foul-smelling waste from the stomach malady that had worked its way through the building. The stench was unbearable. She emptied the bucket onto the straw in the courtyard outside and then relieved herself in the same straw. The night-soil boys hadn't been paid yet so wouldn't collect it until their palms were greased. Putting practicalities out of her mind, Sylvia was excited at the prospect of donning rich people's finery for tonight's visit to the theatre in Covent Garden. It would be the closest she had come to the princess of her childhood imagination.

Once the light of the evening sun turned amber, a gentle breeze blew through the open shutters of the tenement. The youngest Nicholson girl, Mags, brewed tea for all. The tobacco smoke from Jacob's pipe masked their collective perfume. They never wanted for luxuries, for Simon and Billy, the eldest Nicholsons, worked on the river trade, opening hogsheads. By day, as coopers, they'd mend the broken casks, prising them open and smuggling their content out in Mags' pockets, posing as their apprentice. By night, the boys were lumpers and mudlarks: they'd return to the ships in the early hours once the watch had finished, lump cargoes overboard to accomplices waiting in the mud of low tide. Brought ashore and sold, the rest they kept for the household: tea from the Orient, sugar from the Caribbean and tobacco from Virginia. They emulated their betters, consuming all they could from the new worlds. Such luxuries made the rest bearable.

Sylvia was excited as she finally put on the dress for the first time, acquired just for this occasion. On her tall, slender body, the green satin dress flared out on hoops, giving her the silhouette of a town crier's bell. The train draped on the ground, hiding her tell-tale leather sandals. A matching waistcoat drew in tight across her waist to accentuate the curve of her slim hips. To look totally convincing, it needed a stay to accentuate her bosom, but her sepia blouse would have to suffice for tonight.

'Sis, you look just like one of them,' said Jacob.

Sylvia fluttered her eyelids, mimicking the gentry class. She stroked the fabric; it fitted perfectly. 'Made to measure, don't you think?'

'I'd have ya!' Simon Nicholson, the eldest of the Nicholson boys, teased. He always flirted with her, but while he might grope her after too much drink, both knew there was nothing in it. Abe, their youngest brother, clapped his hands together.

Sylvia smiled at him. He was easy to excite, being a simpleton. By day, Abe was a beggar, deploying his ragged clothes, squint eyes and flat face; he was perfectly placed to elicit donations from the wealthy. Beyond his small contributions to the gang's coffers, he was their eyes and ears. Watching everything, all day. What boats came and went, who was saying what to whom, what cargo was stashed where... All the intricate details of London street life were noticed by Abe. Underestimating him, people's tongues loosened in his vicinity. He rushed past Mags and up to Sylvia, only two-thirds her height, and offered his arm to chaperone her.

'I always wanted a pretty lady on my arm!'

'Bless you, Abe.' She leaned down and planted an affectionate kiss on his cheek. He went red as his brothers teased him.

'Rat!' shouted Jacob. He threw his knife at the large rodent that scurried across the far side of the skirting board. He missed.

'You're not bringing that knife with you tonight, are you, Jacob?' asked Sylvia. 'If you're found with it...'

'Nah.'

'Right, sis,' said Caroline, 'let's do your hair.'

Sylvia sat on the edge of the bed struggling to accommodate the skirt beneath her. 'I don't know how rich folk manage with all this stuff, none of it's for comfort.'

'They've no sense,' said Caroline, tugging a whalebone comb through Sylvia's auburn hair. Its teeth slid through her fine strands with ease. 'I love your hair,' Caroline sighed. 'Mine is so frizzy compared to yours.' She pulled it tight and fastened it up with some clips. 'Time for your wig.'

Mags brought it over and placed it on Sylvia's hair. She started laughing. 'You look so funny.'

'I hope not! I need to look like I belong.'

'You'd fetch a good price tonight, gal,' said Simon.

She stood and they all offered a round of applause.

'You look the part,' said Jacob. 'Here, have a tot of brandy, for luck.'

Once the silver flask had been shared around, Mags and Caroline said goodbye and wished them luck. Sylvia took a handful of ash from the cooking fire and followed the boys as they filed down the rickety staircase at the end of the dank corridor and out into the yard. Once on the street, the sight of Sylvia dressed up to the nines elicited wolf whistles from the barrow boys and street vendors as they packed up their wares for the day. Sylvia mocked them, swinging her hips from side to side in an exaggerated manner. She could afford to be light-hearted when she was chaperoned by Jacob, Simon, Billy and Abe.

They were silent as they walked down Whitechapel, Leadenhall, Cheapside and past St Paul's Cathedral, a beacon of white stone shining bright and large amongst the grime of brown cobbles, horseshit, beggars and slang of London. As they passed it, they left behind the squalor of East London and made their way up the Strand towards the gold of the setting sun, and the City of Westminster. Tonight's theatre trip had been in the making for some time; procuring Sylvia's outfit had been the hardest task. It was exciting to think that tonight, finally, it was all happening. A beautiful performance awaited.

As the light faded, they approached Covent Garden where the streets were wide enough for three carriages to pass. The stone buildings were new, all tall and symmetrical, displaying the wealth of the merchant class, earned in the East End and spent in the West. The streets were quieter. Pedestrians wore bright finery and wigs as they paraded themselves in front of their peers. Despite the contrast in wealth, Sylvia wasn't intimidated by the prospect of rubbing shoulders with the good and the great. The pairs of prostitutes waiting at each street corner were a reminder that the folk in these parts were no better than Sylvia's lot: all on the make, indulging in sin, feeding off the efforts of others. Here, they just did it in fancier surroundings.

'Time we left you to it, before we attract any attention,' said Simon. 'Happy birthday gal, have a great time tonight.' He winked and without further ceremony, the Nicholson boys drifted away. Jacob, who'd brushed his coat and wiped clean his trousers for the occasion, offered his arm and they made their way to the theatre, past the street vendors and gilded carriages that rattled into the square. They approached the nightwatchman, who was just starting his shift. Sylvia said hello to the hulk of a man whose curved shoulders mirrored the curve of his bald head. Jacob winked at him and discreetly passed a large coin as they shook hands.

'Enjoy the show,' the man grunted as he swung his wooden cudgel over his shoulder. Outside, the theatre carriages unloaded their well-to-do cargoes, both sexes bedecked in tall wigs, painted faces, elaborate clothing that used enough fabric for two people. Sylvia began to feel nervous, fearing her blouse gave her away. In the street, people greeted each other with exaggerated kisses and waving arms as they drifted between the pillars and up the steps under the theatre's portico. The coachmen whipped their horses, moving their carriages away so the next ones could arrive to unload. As a coach drew alongside them, Sylvia shuddered when she noticed that the coachman carried two pistols in his belt. So preciously guarded were the English sensibilities of liberty that they preferred to go out into the night armed to the teeth rather than endure a French-style police presence in their cities. Authority was to be mistrusted; it was expected of every man and woman to come to the aid of those in distress.

Sylvia and Jacob walked past the front of the theatre and waited in the side alley as the city fell into darkness. Tonight, as every night, the gas lanterns were unlit. Unwilling to pay the tax to subsidise their street lighting, Londoners preferred to take their chances in the dark. For Sylvia, her journey back would be dangerous whether light or dark; at least in the dark they could go home unnoticed.

Inside, the performance ran its course with the faintest hum of applause and cheers discernible from the outside. When the theatregoers began to stream out onto the street, merry from drink, it was time. Sylvia and Jacob made their way to the roadside, taking position just on the edge of the light cast from the burning lanterns of the theatre building. On the street, carriages jostled and crammed towards the doors, to collect their passengers. Sylvia watched the huddled crowd exchanging goodbyes and comments on the play. Simon's head could be seen bobbing through the crowd as he ran past the theatre entrance. Sylvia felt the nerves in her stomach flutter as he approached her. As he passed her, glancing his shoulder against hers, she screamed, 'Thief!'

Heads turned toward the noise from the edge of the shadows.

'Stop that man!' shouted Jacob, giving chase after Simon.

'Don't leave me,' screamed Sylvia. 'Help! Somebody, please, help!' She took a step back into the shadows. A man from the crowd gave chase after Jacob and Simon. Another couple came to Sylvia's aid. She cried as the elegant woman comforted her to her breast. The man, wearing a velvet coat drew a pistol and held it in the direction of her assailant in case they should return. Sylvia pulled away. Her eyes now well-adjusted to the dark, she could see the man was in his late twenties and finely dressed. From her clenched fist, she threw the handful of the ash she'd held all evening into his eyes. He yelped as it stung. Sylvia snatched the pistol from his unsuspecting hand. His lady companion shouted in horror, but Sylvia swung the pistol across the woman's blanc-covered face, felling her to the ground. From the shadows, Abe ran and cannoned into the gentleman, sending him flying. People outside the theatre began to realise something was amiss, craning their heads towards the commotion in the murk of the night. They moved tentatively towards the scuffle. Sylvia raised the pistol, firing a shot over the heads of the theatregoers. The night sky filled with their screams. Billy arrived, swinging the nightwatchman's cudgel, felling a man whose curiosity had brought him dangerously close.

'Quick boys,' shouted Sylvia. She pushed the pistol into her coat, pressed against her breast, then leant over to yank the wig from the fallen woman's head, and ripped the necklace from around her neck. The woman screamed as Sylvia tore the ear-studs from the woman's lobes, stuffing them down her blouse. Jacob and Simon returned from their imitated chase and helped Abe relieve the fallen man of his possessions, until he was left lying naked on the ground. Sylvia struggled to wrench the woman out of her jacket.

'It's a robbery!' shouted someone from the crowd, approaching en masse. Billy swung the club wildly as they advanced.

'Time to go,' he yelled as they threatened to overwhelm him by force of numbers. He gave flight, closely followed by Sylvia and Simon. A gunshot rang out. Its loud crack sent a shiver down Sylvia's spine. Stolen wig in hand, she turned to see young Abe stumble and fall to the ground, clutching his chest. His fingers turned dark as blood gushed from the wound.

'They got Abe!' she yelled.

Simon and Billy turned and dragged their younger brother across the cobbles, causing the injured lad to scream in pain.

'Stop there or I'll shoot,' shouted Sylvia, despite having already discharged her pistol. There was another crack of gunfire. More screams from theatregoers. The shot whistled past Sylvia and disappeared into the darkness.

The Whitechapel gang, clutching their loot and dragging their fallen member, gave flight into the darkness. Once clear of Covent Garden, they slipped into a side alley, breathing frantically. They glanced back into the pitch gloom to see if anyone had given chase. The theatregoers would be summoning the hue and cry, but the gang had already greased the palm of the night watch. Provided the watchman was good to his word, he would bungle his efforts.

'How is he?' asked Sylvia, kneeling to comfort Abe.

Blood trickled from Abe's lips as he spoke, 'I'm scared. I'm dying. Please no.'

'Abe, ssshh,' said Sylvia, recovering her breath. 'We'll get you home.'

They hadn't reckoned on making their return journey with an invalid. Two and a half miles home. Every few streets, there would be a new watchman. To bribe them all was as unaffordable as it was impossible. Someone would turn them in, in hope of a reward. If they happened upon other criminals, they would be relieved of their loot. Perhaps it had been too ambitious to come this far west, thought Sylvia.

'We're buggered!' exclaimed Jacob.

Sylvia shushed him. Wallowing in their predicament wouldn't get them home.

'Don't leave me,' pleaded Abe, blood spluttering from his trembling lips.

'We won't,' she assured him, clenching his hand in hers.

'Simon, you take his legs,' said Billy.

'Where are we gonna take him?'

'We can't stay here!' Billy slid his arms under Abe's, causing him to shriek in pain.

Sylvia clasped her palm over Abe's mouth, stifling his screams.

'We can't move him, Billy,' said Simon, unable to hide the panic in his voice.

'I'm dying!' said Abe, his words muffled by Sylvia's bloodstained palm.

'You two,' Sylvia hissed at Billy and Simon. 'Just wait. Hold your brother.'

They knelt round him, while Jacob kept watch at the end of the alley. Abe cried and trembled. Precious blood drained from his chest and mouth. His breathing became frantic. Tears rolled down Sylvia's cheeks. *Poor Abe.* He was beyond help. Moments later, his body turned limp, and his breathing stopped. He was dead.

An hour later the Whitechapel gang silently trudged up the stairs of their tenement. An anxious Mags and Caroline took fright at the sight of their bloodstained hands.

'Where's Abe?' quizzed Mags.

'He's dead,' said Jacob, matter-of-factly.

'No!' Mags become hysterical and had to be restrained by her brothers. 'Where is he? You can't just have left him?'

'We had no choice, Mags,' said Sylvia. Tears rolling freely down her cheeks, she reached out to comfort Mags, who swiped out at her.

'He needs a burial!'

'We couldn't carry a dead body back through London, Mags,' said Billy.

Mags cried. Caroline too, as she comforted her young friend.

'He's at peace now,' said Sylvia. Abe, the simpleton, hadn't had an easy life. He'd been bullied, teased and tormented, but had remained cheerful despite it all. He'd had a good heart. Loyal to his family, and their gang. He'd deserved better than the watery grave the River Thames afforded him. They'd offered a brief prayer as they committed his body to the river's edge. Fortunately, the tide was in and would take his corpse out to sea. The thought of the fish or rats feeding on him drew more tears from Sylvia. They'd yet to examine their haul, but even if they'd taken the crown jewels, it wasn't worth Abe's life. She regretted the whole scheme.

As she grieved, her jaw grew firm. It was her birthday, so she was granted a wish, which she hadn't yet used. She closed her eyes, picturing Abe's terrified face as he had died, and made a promise to herself. She would mend her ways. Henceforth, Sylvia Coppell would endeavour to make an honest living.

1749

6

April 30ᵗʰ, 1749
The Washington Farm, Fredericksburg

Lawrence stepped out of the carriage and approached the farmhouse. Like his own house, this one had also been built by his late father – both were made from clapboard, bookended by brick chimneys, the roof interrupted by four dormer windows on the first floor. They were simple, comfortable dwellings, both overlooking rivers. Though unlike his, which stood overlooking the Potomac towards the shore of the Maryland coast, this one had a prospect of the town of Fredericksburg, its church spires and smouldering chimneys piercing the sky over the far bank. Once Lawrence's mother had died, his father had married Mary, George's mother, and built the property after she had refused to live in his father's former marital home. Lawrence hadn't complained, for he'd been the beneficiary of her obstinacy, inheriting his family home, which he'd since renamed Mount Vernon.

It was scarce that he had occasion – or rarer still, an invitation – to visit George at home. He knocked on the door, which was promptly answered by the negro house servant. Lawrence, dressed in his cream and red army uniform, stepped inside the central hall. He called for George.

'Who's that?' barked Mary, leaning forward from her seat in the adjoining parlour. 'Oh, it's you,' she said as Lawrence strode past.

'George, get your things, you're coming with me.'

'And where do you think you're going?' said the diminutive widow.

'Hello Mary,' said Lawrence, filling her doorway. 'To a party at the

Lees'. Anne was too poorly to make it so I thought George might enjoy it.'

George's footsteps came pounding down the stairs. 'Lawrence?'

'Put on your Sunday best, George, we're going to a party.'

George ran back upstairs, the floorboards above creaking as he readied himself.

'Don't you be putting any more of your ideas in that boy's head,' said Mary, her frosty glare hanging over her downturned mouth. 'You in your fancy uniform, leading my boy astray.'

'He's not a boy, Mary, not anymore.'

'Well, I don't want him coming back, his imagination filled with more fantasies about fighting in your navy.'

'Come, Mary…'

'No. I won't hear it. Whatever possessed you to do such a thing, I just don't know. He hasn't stopped sulking since.'

Lawrence had arranged for George a position of midshipman in the navy, but Mary had prevented him from enrolling.

George reappeared, short of breath, in his blue velvet longcoat. 'Where are we going?'

'Bye, Mary,' said Lawrence.

'Goodbye, Mother,' said George, as he followed his brother out of the house.

***

Fifty miles later, George was relieved to hear the hooves and carriage wheels finally crunching over shingle. With all six feet of him hunched over in the small wooden box of their carriage, his back had protested as they had bounced along the dirt tracks that passed for roads, to their destination for the weekend: Stratford Hall. Home to Colonel Lee, who, as Lawrence had briefly explained en route, was hosting a gathering to discuss a venture he'd founded called the Ohio Company.

Lawrence coughed into his hanky.

'You're coughing rather a lot, Lawrence,' said George.

'It's like being with Anne, you fuss nearly as much as her! I'm fine.'

The carriage drew to a halt and the footman opened the door. George stepped out of the carriage and groaned with relief. Before him stood the robust red-brick façade of Stratford Hall. He admired the simple and solid geometry of its structure. The south-facing frontage was dominated by eight large windows positioned above smaller ground-floor windows. Two protruding wings sat astride a recessed centre. It was a grand building, but simple enough to have been designed without the benefit of an architect, a profession which proved scarce in the colony.

George rearranged his chestnut hair, pulling it tight and fastening it at the nape of his neck with a black ribbon.

A negro butler, dressed in a silver tailcoat over white stockings and sporting a periwig, came down the steps and across the lawn to greet them. He welcomed them to the Hall and invited them to take tea indoors.

Lawrence issued instructions for the unloading of their luggage, and they made their way across the front lawn, George admiring this thriving tobacco plantation. It was a hive of self-contained industry with its own wharf, grist mill, workshops for carpentry, blacksmiths, coopering, and weaving, as well as outbuildings for tobacco drying and slave accommodation.

At the top of the stone-cut steps leading to the front door stood their hosts for the weekend, a smiling Colonel Thomas Lee and his wife Hannah.

'Apologies that we should be late, Colonel,' said Lawrence.

'Nonsense, my dear fellow, we're delighted you could join us at our humble abode, Major Lawrence,' Lee welcomed them with no small degree of false modesty.

Lawrence bent and kissed Mrs Lee's hand. 'I'm sorry my wife Anne is too unwell to join us. I brought my brother George in her stead, I trust that's all right?' said Lawrence as he shook Colonel Lee's hand.

'We're sorry to miss her,' said Mrs Lee.

George bowed. 'Enchanted, Mrs Lee. Thank you for having me.'

Hannah Lee flashed a brief smile. 'We're delighted to make your acquaintance again, Master Washington.' She turned to her husband. 'I'll change the table plan.'

'What's this I hear about you turning down a position in the navy?' Lee asked George.

'Well, it's...'

73

'A long story – differing opinions in the family,' interrupted Lawrence, much to George's relief, as he didn't like to give voice to his opinions of his mother.

'Pah!' sniffed Lee.

'We'll have him serving his country soon, Colonel, mark my words,' said Lawrence.

George doubted Lawrence spoke the truth. His mother would never permit him to endanger himself. Instead, he'd opted to train as a surveyor. Using some old tools of his father's, he'd practised the trade around the farm to complement his studies. What the profession lacked in excitement and glory, it made up for in providing stability and a respectable income. It wasn't without its adventures though. He'd just completed his first expedition west to the Shenandoah valley, where he'd lived wild, surveying the land, dividing it into plots, ready for sale to settlers arriving from Europe.

Inside the house, cooled from the spring warmth, George surveyed the large reception room: brightly decorated walls adorned with oil portraits, contrasting with the dark varnished floorboards, off which echoed the chatter of Colonel Lee's assembled guests. Servants moved among them imperceptibly, serving tea and collecting cups and saucers.

'Best we say hello to Lordy,' said Lawrence, tipping his head at the sight of his father-in-law, William Fairfax. George followed Lawrence as he picked a path through the guests, who, since his election to the House, now ranked as Lawrence's peers.

'The Washingtons!' Fairfax effused when he saw them. In his mid-fifties, Fairfax had the tell-tale signs of good living: a portly belly, ruddy cheeks and soft hands. He was an energetic man, who waved his hands around in a manner George found overly feminine. 'Fabulous to see you, young George, it's been so long!' He leant in and tapped the side of his nose with his dainty index finger and whispered, 'Culpeper county needs a new surveyor. I put in a good word for you, George. Come, I want you to meet someone.' Fairfax propelled him to the far corner of the room, seeking a middle-aged man in clothing that, to George's eye, would look more at home in a tavern than at a colonel's party. 'Gentlemen, it is so fortuitous that you should meet: Christopher Gist, George Washington,' Fairfax introduced them.

'We've met, actually,' said George and was soon abandoned by Fairfax, who returned to talk with Lawrence.

Gist was as tall as George. His lank, shoulder-length hair was chocolate brown, his tanned skin was partially hidden by a beard, but he wore no powder or colour. His penetrating dark-brown eyes suggested he wouldn't flinch if he witnessed a man scalped.

'I never did offer you my commiserations on the court case,' said George. 'Rotten luck against that scoundrel Fitzbarton.'

Gist shrugged. 'I was surprised to see Fry here, that judge who found in Fitzbarton's favour.' He nodded to the far side of the room, where the shrew-like Fry stood alone with his wife.

'Perhaps Lawrence is trying to bring him round to see things his way,' George commented. 'Keep your enemies close and all that.'

George and Gist, relegated to the fringes of the room, discussed their shared profession in truncated fashion until they were both relieved to hear Colonel Lee announce, 'Ladies and Gentlemen, if you would care to please follow me, we shall dine.' He smiled and retreated from the hallway towards the dining room.

The modest-sized room was plain and functional, and the polished wood dining table had been extended with a series of cloth-covered trestle tables to accommodate all the diners. This arrangement meant there was scant room to negotiate round the table to find one's place.

George found his seat on the corner nearest the door. The square formed by the tables left the arrangement with a hollow centre so servants could pass in and serve the plates.

George introduced himself to his neighbours; to his left, a Virginian widow by the name of Sophie Montague. He estimated her age at thirty. She was inoffensive in appearance and wouldn't remain a widow for long in the colonies. Men still outnumbered the fairer sex, affording available women the pick of the litter. At seventeen, George had little to offer, bar dreams and unrealised ambitions.

George had drawn the short straw, for to his right were Fry and his wife Mary. After grace, George tried to engage them in conversation as the devilled eggs were being served, but finding them to be most reserved, he turned his attention back to Ms Montague.

'So, who are you related to – did you say it was Major Washington?' she asked, eager to understand his lineage.

George pointed out Lawrence and then spent the rest of the first course regaling her of the exploits of his recent surveying trip; meeting Indians, sleeping in his clothes like a simple negro, fording rivers, and foraging for food. Ms Montague nodded politely throughout. Thereafter, George expanded on his hopes: he would continue with his surveying and indeed hoped to speculate with land of his own, but when he reached his majority, he still yearned to become a commissioned officer in the Royal Navy to serve his country, whatever demands and sacrifices it may require.

'My, what a precocious young man you are.'

George failed to construe her meaning and continued to indulge himself. People often remarked on his aspirations. He'd seen his father, like so many others, die before their time in Virginia's swampy climate. Time was precious, and not to be frittered away.

Mr Fry then joined the conversation, much to Ms Montague's apparent relief.

'You wish to serve in the military, Master Washington?'

'As an officer, yes,' said George.

When Mr Fry didn't remark further, George puffed out his chest. 'Did you ever serve in your youth?'

Fry placed his knife and fork down on his plate. 'I have and I may offer you one piece of advice, Master Washington. An officer of the army, like any other gentleman, should be primarily acquainted with the notion of what he may do for those in his charge, and be firmly disabused of the thought of what the army may do for him.'

'Yes, of course,' stuttered George, his cheeks reddening at Fry's rebuke. 'I very much agree.'

'Empty vessels make the most noise, Master Washington.'

George took a sip of his wine. 'Do you work, Mr Fry, beyond your responsibilities as a justice of the peace?'

'I teach mathematics at the College of William and Mary. I do a little surveying. And since I found myself unceremoniously bumped out of Fairfax and relegated west to Albemarle, I have since been elected to represent the county in the House of Burgesses. Tell me, George, was it your brother who had me moved?'

'Goodness, I can't imagine he would do anything like that,' said George, unaware of Lawrence's machinations. He suspected Fry spoke the truth. 'I am sure Lawrence will look forward to working with you in the House.'

'We'll see,' said Fry, dabbing his pursed lips with a napkin.

George could imagine Fry as a teacher. His self-satisfied manner lent itself well to reciting answers. Despite his instinctive dislike of Fry, they both mellowed a little over the course of the afternoon's meal: roast pork with sweet potato, followed by syllabub.

As the servants cleared away the desserts, the host, Colonel Lee, took to his feet. 'Ladies, we thank you for your gracious company and now invite you to take refreshments in the drawing room.'

Once the ladies had filed out, Lee continued, his tone more mischievous, 'Gentlemen, I am honoured to entertain you this weekend, and trust that you will find our simple home comfortable enough.' As he spoke, the negro servant, a thin girl in her twenties, offered each guest a cigar from a walnut box. George declined.

'There is an ulterior motive for your invitations. I have it on very good authority that His Majesty, King George II, has approved a land grant beyond the mountains of our western frontier: half a million acres of the Ohio Valley.'

Lawrence coughed as the room began to fill with tobacco smoke. Lee took a swig of his wine and invited John Mercer, a prominent lawyer, to continue.

'Thankin' ye kindly, Colonel,' said Mercer in his distinctive Irish accent. 'We await the formal confirmation. The Board of Trade are drawing up the contract and it is expected to arrive this summer. However, my son has been handling the Ohio Company's affairs in London, and has just returned to Virginia. In exchange for an annual rent, payable after seven years, the King has granted the Company the valleys surrounding the Ohio river basin.'

I wasn't aware it was the King's land to sell, thought George.

'His Majesty makes some stipulations, as is his prerogative: The first two hundred thousand acres are to be divided between no less than one hundred families. That's two thousand acres per family, enough for a sizeable farm. However, his subjects residing in the valley must be safe from harassment, so the grant is dependent on the Company financing a fort and its garrison, so they may live in peace. If all that is done in seven years, then His Majesty will kindly offer us a further three hundred thousand acres.'

The stony-faced guests listened intently, and even the cigar smoke seemed to hang in the air.

'But,' interrupted Lee, rising to his feet, 'I have seen too many noble ventures fail because of unwieldy governance. As the founder of the Ohio Company, which consists of myself, Major Washington, Mr Mercer and his son, I am restricting the shareholding of the company to sixteen people, all of whom will invest two hundred pounds of their own money, at risk. You, gentlemen, are the lucky ones.'

Mercer cautioned Colonel Lee's haste. 'Alas, gentlemen, we are not the only people in the bidding. The Pennsylvania Quakers are mounting a bid too.'

A groan rippled round the room. Once a Swedish settlement, the land that now formed the Pennsylvania colony had later been taken by King Charles II and given to the Penn family to use for their private benefit, in relief of the King's debts. The Penns had intended it as a refuge for Quakers, and had since succeeded in turning it into a dumping ground for every wayward religious minority in Europe. To call Pennsylvania a British colony was a gross exaggeration in the minds of the assembled Virginians, whose own colony, although started as a private company, was now the property of the Crown.

Lee continued, his passion now inflamed. 'This is the biggest westward expansion since the founding of Virginia. We were here long before the other colonies, and I'll be damned if I'm going to let any of them beat us to this prize. There's a fortune to be made and I want all the Ohio Valley connected to roads that lead its wealth and trade home to Virginia. It should be us to prosper from it, not only in the initial land investment – which, once developed with roads, churches, and farms will double in value – but the subsequent trade: the beaver pelts and buckskins travelling east from Ohio, down our roads, through our harbours, to Britain and beyond to her territories. To the west, we shall sell our own goods that settlers require: saws, nails, clothes, tea, sugar, flour and iron from our mines. The inns to house the new arrivals and the sailors, the breweries supplying their beer... We shall be in the middle of all this trade. Virginia: fat, happy, and rich!'

'I'm in!' quipped Lord Fairfax. 'Where do I sign?'

'Our harbours?' asked Fry, quick to pick up on the discrepancy. 'Norfolk is our only harbour. Philadelphia or New York are just as close to the Ohio Valley. Why wouldn't settlers go there—?'

'Which is why we must build one,' cut in Colonel Lee.

Lawrence cleared his throat, 'We've found some land, at the navigable limit on the upper Potomac River, by the Hunting Creek tobacco warehouse.'

Fry grunted as Lawrence and Fairfax exchanged a nod.

'I shall put a bill before the House next month to establish the town of Alexandria, for the purpose of helping us develop the interior of the continent.'

George couldn't believe that Lawrence hadn't disclosed any of this to him the whole time he'd been plotting such an ambitious scheme. He'd even asked him to survey the site. George hadn't thought to ask why a new town should be needed. He'd done as asked and collected his fee.

'Tell me,' Fry continued, 'what exactly is His Majesty contributing here, in exchange for the rent?' His tone was assertive, bordering on impolite.

A frown descended on Colonel Lee's face. 'Have you ever sold land, Mr Fry?'

Fry shook his head.

'I assumed as much. Well, let me tell you, when somebody has spent three months huddled in the bottom of a boat, lying in their own filth, clutching his life's savings, he tends to be careful in how he spends it. Likewise, an indentured servant, having toiled for another for seven years, likes to know when he can finally acquire his own land, and achieve the independence which is the envy of all Englishmen. They tend to feel a damned sight more confident when the deeds to the land bear the crest of the lion and the unicorn. People believe they are spending their money on something real, something that won't disappear before them like a playing card in the hands of a trickster. And should a foreign entity later try to deprive them of it, then they can be comforted that the King may send his armies to recover it.' Lee's cheeks were red from his impassioned speech.

Fry simply shrugged; George could see he wasn't convinced.

Lee took a large swig of wine. 'It is my contention, gentlemen, that one day this fine colony of ours will be an independent nation. The Virginian people are too enterprising and too far from home, in a continent that is too large for any one country to rule over.' He stopped to allow a moment's silence, letting his words sink in. This was close to treason.

What utter nonsense, thought George. The colonies were the jewel in the British crown. That Virginia should ever want to depart the safety of Britain's blanket and the reach of her naval fleet was absurd.

Satisfied he'd provoked sufficient thought amongst his audience, Lee continued. 'Any westward expansion *must* be Virginian, so we remain the dominant power on this continent.'

That, George could agree with.

'Other than greasing the King's palms, what is the £4000 raised from shareholders to be spent on?' asked Fry, unmoved by Lee's emotion.

Mercer intervened before Lee could take further exception to Fry. ''Tis used as capital to fund the company's expenses. For example,' he paused, 'recruiting the settlers alone would require advertisements to be placed in newspapers across Protestant Europe. We'd need agents in the ports of London and Rotterdam to register the settlers and organise their transportation. Most likely, Bristol and Liverpool, too. Then, trade goods for the Iroquois; strings of wampum won't be enough to persuade them to relinquish this much land. Guns, ammunition, powder, rum...'

'You'd sell the savages guns to use against us, if they so chose?' Fry said in disbelief.

Gist's deep voice cut through the exchange. Heads turned to see what had necessitated a quiet man to speak.

'As the only man here to have been to the Ohio Valley, I can say that the settlers will only survive with Iroquois consent. Indians are not one united body, but a series of ever-sparring tribes, with their own territorial disputes and vendettas. They depend on guns and ammunition to protect themselves from each other. Only guns preserve the balance of power. You will need to yoke their loyalty and their protection. But be warned, I've traded with them, they'll drive as hard a bargain as any Jew and are twice as slippery.'

'I would have thought once matters were agreed in a treaty, they would be dependable,' said Fry.

Gist grunted. 'I doubt it would be worth the paper it was written on.'

'The law is paramount, Mr Gist. It is what separates us from animals,' said Fry, adopting his magistrate's tone.

Gist smirked and looked away.

Fry, emboldened by taking his share in the debate, spoke as if addressing a class, 'So, let me make sure I understand: the land would be sold to the settlers?'

'Sold or rented,' Mercer replied. 'In either case, rent will form part of the Ohio Company's revenues, of which each investor is eligible for his share. Furthermore, you would be free to sell your shareholding, with committee approval, to other investors at any point.'

'So, it would be mine to buy, but not mine to sell?'

Lee sighed. 'If I allow you to invest, yes.'

Fry's face betrayed he'd been rankled.

'Because, Mr Fry,' continued Lee, leaning forward, 'I don't want my venture spoilt by in-fighting.' He rapped his knuckles on the dining table. 'By controlling the ownership, we limit the potential for dispute. None of us wants to be tied up in expensive litigation.'

'Except perhaps me!' said Mercer to lighten the mood, and the guests laughed at the lawyer's quip.

Fry, chastened by the Colonel's hostility, sat quietly while the Colonel took questions and basked in the enthusiasm of the other guests.

'Gentleman, I propose a toast of rum,' said Lee, raising his empty glass. The servant girl distributed some measures of rum, and all assembled raised their glasses. 'To the Ohio Company!'

'Now, if you wish to invest,' said Lee, 'place your funds with Mr Mercer here and he'll issue the relevant certificates. There will be plenty of time to discuss business, but for now, I trust that you will enjoy your stay here and join us for some cricket on the lawn in the morning. We'll be short some players, but I'll have the niggers field!'

Amongst the laughter, and the cigar smoke, George Washington felt very privileged to have a seat at the table. Whatever his usual jealousies of Lawrence, he had his brother to thank for affording him the opportunity to invest in the Ohio Company, the biggest land speculation of the age, and make his fortune. He was a little short of money, but a few more lucrative surveying jobs and he'd have enough. Any way he could, he wanted in.

***

On Sunday morning, the Washington brothers were readying themselves to leave when Colonel Lee appeared at their bedroom door.

'Don't mind me,' he said as he sauntered in.

'Thank you for a lovely weekend, Colonel,' said Lawrence, as he folded a shirt into the open trunk on his bed.

'Indeed. Most importantly, I think we've got most of our guests.'

George frowned as he tucked his shirt into his breeches.

'Excellent,' Lawrence beamed.

'Did Fry speak with you?'

Lawrence shook his head. 'No. I think it was a mistake to invite him.'

'Yes, I fear you are right. I'd thought, given his election to the House, it might be better to have him in the boat throwing his rocks out, rather than the other way round.'

'Well, it's done now. It will be his loss, not ours.'

Lee sighed. 'He left early this morning. I suspect he was avoiding me.'

'I don't like the man. Bit Whiggish for my tastes.'

'Me neither,' nodded Lee. 'Let's knobble him.'

The two men embraced heartily, and George watched with a pang.

'By golly, we're going to be the richest men in the Americas!' crowed Lee.

The brothers travelled home by sloop. Rather than returning to his mother's house in Fredericksburg, George had decided to accompany Lawrence back to Mount Vernon. A good wind filled the sand-coloured jib sail that whisked them through the cold waters of the Potomac. The cotton wool clouds that adorned the bright blue sky cast shadows across the glistening river surface. As they rounded a wide bend, the land was little more than a green slither of trees that demarcated the water from the sky. Standing next to Lawrence at the starboard gunwales, George spotted a porpoise cresting the water. It swam alongside them and glanced up occasionally as it broke the surface.

'A wonderful spectacle to mark the end of a wonderful weekend,' said George. 'I must thank you for inviting me, Lawrence.'

The two brothers had barely had a moment alone to talk, despite sharing a bed for the weekend. When they had returned to their room to slumber, they were so bloated from Colonel Lee's hospitality, it was all they could do to perform their ablutions and retire to sleep. George had been granted a tour of the estate and he found himself full of zeal to create such a plantation for himself. To be self-sufficient, with a parcel of land to call his own, in its centre a place of comfort, but also of industry, to supply all he and his future family should need… Yes, it was a worthy goal. He could barely contain his enthusiasm to accrue such wealth and escape the confines of his mother's roof and her stifling influence. Freedom and contentment beckoned. *Has there ever been a better time in history to be alive than now?* he'd wondered. He had never been to Britain and sampled her sophistications: theatres, bustling cities, ports crammed with the swaying masts of ships, coffee houses awash with more capital than the rest of the world could muster. But despite these luxuries, many of his fellow Virginians regarded their slice of the Empire to be the envy of every Englishman. As he daydreamed about a wife and children running around his brick mansion, slaves attending to his every whim, he began to understand why, for he was living in the right time, in the right place, on the cusp of history as the English peoples pushed west into the rumoured expanse of the American continent. *It is my destiny to be involved,* he thought.

Perhaps one day I can be Governor, he dreamed, the King's man in Virginia, trips to London, liaising with the Crown. He was giddy at the very prospect of it – he just needed the money.

'I must say, Lawrence, what an exciting venture the Ohio Company is. How long have you known?'

The boat began to change tack and leaned to port. George turned and sat on the bench rail that ran the length of the boat's side. The boom swung towards them, and at the stern, the captain busied himself tightening ropes.

Lawrence continued to rest on the gunwale, looking out across the large expanse of river. A dozen similar craft plied their own courses between the tide and the breeze. As he waited for Lawrence, still deep in thought, George studied the three other passengers opposite him on the port benches. A married couple sat hand in hand, quietly enjoying the warmth of the sun's rays on their faces. The other man in a cocked hat and wig carried a leather case, which gave him an official appearance.

'Eighteen months, I suppose,' Lawrence finally replied, 'I wasn't convinced it was feasible at the outset, but Lee has a persuasive manner, as you have seen.'

'Hasn't he just – I wanted in, there and then. I'd have given him my life savings, if I had any!'

Lawrence chortled.

'Brother,' said George, 'I'd love to be a shareholder of the Ohio venture. I just don't have the money yet, but if I get the appointment to be surveyor of Culpeper County, I will have a regular income. Could you cover my shortfall in the meantime?'

Lawrence's smile vanished. 'George, it's a very risky venture. Its chances of success are at best limited. You are in no position to be gambling money you don't even have.'

'But I will have it, soon.' George felt himself getting frustrated. 'I would pay you back, even if it went wrong.'

'I wouldn't want to put you in that situation, brother. Two hundred pounds is a significant sum of money. Think what you could do with that. Buy a house of your own, get out from under your mother's feet.'

'But I could earn as much in as little as two years.'

'You could, if you ate nothing, bought nothing, went nowhere. You'd basically have to hibernate.'

George clenched his jaw.

'The time isn't right for you, George,' Lawrence went on.

'I've just turned seventeen, Lawrence. I am not a child, damn it! I could be halfway through my life already.'

'You haven't reached your majority, George. It would be irresponsible to have you sign up for such debts at your age. I would be accountable to your mother…'

'She wouldn't have to know.'

'Look, George, I didn't invite you to Colonel Lee's so you could become a degenerate gambler. I thought I should offer you some exposure to the affairs of the colony's elite, as part of your education.'

'Because I wasn't lucky enough to be schooled in England like you?' snapped George.

'Hold your tongue, brother. I am trying to do my best by you and don't take kindly to your tone. Besides,' said Lawrence, flattening the creases in his breeches with the palms of his hand before taking a calming deep breath, 'I am not made of money. I am no pauper, but my wealth is through marriage, tied up in land and tightly controlled. I don't have a spare two hundred pounds I can lend for you to gamble away.'

'When I do it, it's gambling, but when you do it, it's investing?' George could feel his cheeks reddening.

Lawrence started coughing, his body shaking as his lungs hacked up the impurities that troubled them. George was too irritated to feel much sympathy.

Struggling to recover, Lawrence continued, 'I am fourteen years your senior, George. I have waited a long time,' he coughed again, 'for such opportunities. You too must learn the virtues of patience. Similar opportunities will come to you, brother – in time.'

Bloody nonsense, thought George, too irritated to notice Lawrence's coughing fit. There was a gaping opportunity facing him right now and he didn't want to miss out.

'Fetch me a drink, would you?' wheezed Lawrence.

Indignant, George got to his feet and walked along the side towards the hold, muttering to himself, 'It's all right for him, he's got to do everything he ever wanted... School, army, fight, marry, own property.'

As George fetched a mug of water for his brother, he continued to seethe with frustration at his lack of advancement. *I am damned by my family,* he decided. The only one who had believed in him was his father, and the Lord had seen fit to take him into his care before he could witness any noteworthy achievement attained by George: his teaching himself to survey, his performance at the Williamsburg horserace – all had been missed. Worse still, George knew that with this opportunity of the Ohio Company threatening to pass him by, he was sentenced to a life where every occasion – from landmark birthdays, marriage, the birth of his children...in fact, every accomplishment he would go on to attain – would all go unnoticed and unremarked by the one person to matter most in George's life: his father.

7

To Joshua Fry's mind, the imposing brick college, the oldest in the colonies, stood for man's most noble pursuit: the quest for knowledge. Yet the wood-clad walls of the great hall now gave way to man's baser instincts: the attainment of power. An animal urge, which must be kept in check by human measures. Bright sun poured in through the arch windows under the hall's high ceiling. The portrait that usually hung above the empty fireplace at the far end had been replaced by the royal crest of English lion and Scottish unicorn. *We'll see what that's worth today,* thought Fry as he took his seat on the long bench that ran the entire length of both sides of the room. Today he estimated there must be close to seventy members present, not quite the full complement of the colony. Each county elected two members to represent their interests in the colony's government. Under the royal crest, the Speaker was seated behind a table covered with green felt, on which sat the mace, the symbol of the colonist's right to self-determination.

After prayers, the Speaker got the morning's business underway.

It was mid-morning by the time the vote to establish the town of Alexandria was held. The Speaker stood. 'The votes being now cast, forty-two yeas to twenty-nine noes. The yeas have it: the House votes in favour of the founding of the town of Alexandria at the site of the Hunting Creek tobacco warehouse.'

First blood to them, thought Fry, as he watched a self-satisfied

Lawrence Washington congratulating his fellow committee members, all a part of Virginia's old guard. Descendants of the first settlers to arrive at these distant shores, they occupied the coastal plain. Through length of tenure and weight of finance, these men still liked to think of Virginia as their personal possession. A tool for their perpetual enrichment, of which Alexandria was just another attempt.

Fry grimaced at the sight of them backslapping each other. For now, they could have their town, though he was sure it would falter. Like many towns before, it would likely amount to nothing more than an unfulfilled dream. The people fleeing the squalor of British cities travelled far in search of their own land to farm, rather than to swap one urban stench for another.

The chamber settled down as the Speaker rose to announce the next bill. 'A public bill, raised by the Ohio Fort Committee, for the erection of a fort to protect settlers dwelling in the Ohio Valley.'

Fry sneered as Washington once again readied himself to take the floor. Emboldened by the passage of his first bill, Washington's colour had returned to his grinning face. He stood, and after a brief cough, began to describe the design of a fort and the size of garrison needed to secure the surrounding land.

Washington was little more than a farm boy, thought Fry. An oversized body, clad in military garb, an accent turned English with practice. He'd married well, and now masqueraded as one of the tidewater set. Their tobacco lands now spent from over-farming, they needed new ventures to sustain their opulent lifestyles as they sought to imitate their aristocratic counterparts in Europe, sponsoring the likes of Washington to do their bidding in the House.

In the short time since Fry's arrival in Virginia, he recognised in those vulgar Virginians across the aisle the same forces that had prevented his advancement in England. No sooner had he stood up to Washington and his cronies, he had found himself reposted out on the colony's frontier. What they hadn't bargained for was how much easier it was to get elected in those remote backwaters. Now Fry intended to show this nouveau nobility he wasn't going to sit quietly in relative exile while the King's men did as they damned well pleased. There was a new roundhead in the house. He remembered stories of his grandfather's struggle to overturn the Crown during the English civil war. Power must be checked.

Washington continued in his attempt to persuade the House that they should fund a military outpost, neglecting to mention that he and Colonel Lee needed it for their Ohio Company venture. Fry had been tempted to join the Ohio Company when he'd been given the opportunity but his instincts had led him to a plan of his own. The whole reason for seeking a fresh start in the New World was to be free to command his own destiny. His stance wasn't without its risks. While he could give Washington and his cronies a run for their money in the House, Colonel Lee sat on the Governor's council, the colony's Upper Chamber. Its role, much like the House of Lords in London, was to revise the bills of the Lower House. Yet, unlike its London counterpart, the Governor's council held a power of veto over the Burgesses, and could call elections to refresh the membership of the Lower House. Lee could make his life difficult, but that was a chance Fry was willing to take.

When the Speaker of the House invited the debate, Fry wasted no time in rising to his feet. He turned to address his fellow members. 'That this should be a public bill, defies conscience! This fort, which Major Washington intends to fund from our taxes, is for his personal benefit. The land which it is intended to guard is to be considered the private property of the Ohio Company, of which Major Washington is a founder shareholder, is it not, Major?'

If looks could kill, Fry would have been struck dead by Washington's glare. Far from being intimidated, Fry continued, 'If he and his friends want this distant land to themselves, then it is they who shall benefit from it, *exclusively*. So, why should the good folk of Virginia stomach the cost?'

'The member Mr Fry is correct,' Washington cut in smoothly, 'but I should point out that the wider benefits of opening the interior of the continent will be of immeasurable value to the colony of Virginia. The processing and housing of people, the goods on which they depend and produce, will all flow through Virginia ports—'

'Like Alexandria, the port you've just established in your father-in-law's district?' said Fry.

Washington coughed.

'So,' Fry continued, 'I put it to this house that the fruits of this venture will not be shared equally by the colony, but instead the lion's share will go to those first-generation Virginians. I thought when I'd left England that I'd seen the last of hereditary privilege and primogeniture, but it seems they're alive and well here in Virginia. While there's breath in my body, I shall not vote for this scheme. Let those who benefit most be burdened by the costs.'

'Hear hear!' rang out across the chamber in support of Fry's rhetoric.

'Furthermore,' continued Fry, sensing the momentum of the House was with him, 'The land earmarked by His Majesty, in his limited wisdom, encroaches the hunting grounds of French trappers and traders, and their native allies. Should his plan bring us into conflict with our perpetual enemy, does Major Washington intend to indemnify the colony for the costs incurred should his scheme throw us into a dispute with France?'

Washington struggled to reply as he coughed into his hanky.

Fry held up a document for the House to see. 'I have here a petition to the Speaker, signed by over forty of my peers.' Holding it aloft, Fry walked up to the front table and passed the document to the Speaker of the House. 'For the formation of the Loyal Company of Virginia...'

'Sit down!' barked one of Washington's committee members, waving his own papers at Fry.

'Mr Fry, I remind you that this colony was founded in the very same manner as I am proposing here,' said Washington, fighting for breath.

'Nearly one hundred and fifty years ago, Major. Would you also have us return to the literacy rates of that time too? Or the living conditions?'

Fry waited. Washington said nothing.

'You native Virginians are forever asserting your claims to this land. I ask you, why do you wait for the King? Why should we be required to pay rent to him when he isn't here to collect it? Let me remind the members, in England it is Parliament that is sovereign, yet here, an ocean away, we still sit at permission of the King? Gentlemen, the New World needs to catch up with the old. It is us that will clear the land. I say we shouldn't wait for the King's blessing; let us survey this land and sell it ourselves, free from His Majesty's stipulations. The war with France is over, let us not tempt another by the costly erection of forts that will serve only to antagonise our French neighbours. Nor, in a time of peace, should we encourage the formation of a standing army to man this unnecessary fortification. For an idle army is the thin end of the wedge that leads to tyranny. My company, The Loyal Company of Virginia, proposes our expansion be aimed further south, to the land the natives call *Ken-tuc-ee,* thereby providing us with a suitable buffer from the French in the Ohio.'

More cheers of support ran around the room.

'The Loyal Company of Virginia,' announced Fry, 'will be open to all investors, not just the privileged few, and I commend it to the House,' concluded Fry, his voice raised to be heard over the din of the member cries, leaving his petition on the table in front of the Speaker.

'Treason!'

'Hear, hear!'

'Order, order! That's enough, Mr Fry,' said the Speaker, trying to quiet the House.

While cries of the competing factions rang out, Fry remained indifferent to their charges, for members were free from the threat of arrest for expressing their opinions. He looked directly at the representative from the Virginia Gazette newspaper. His nod provoked a smile on Fry's face.

He returned to his seat, aglow with inner satisfaction. He would rather be damned than line the grubby pockets of Lee's cronies with a two-hundred-pound investment, so they could pick and choose who benefited from the virgin land west of the mountains. Virginia was changing and the old guard would need to accept this was no longer their private reserve.

Fry sat down and, from all sides, hands came to pat his shoulders in congratulation.

One commotion was interrupted by another; there was a collective gasp as Major Washington collapsed to the ground. A coughing fit, his face puce, as he fought for air.

8

Viktor was in purgatory, reading about heaven and all the things he mustn't do to get there. The family Bible was the only book they owned. Summer evenings, when the work was done and the light still good, they would sit outside and take turns to read passages to each other. It was one of the various impositions Hans had made since Viktor's transgression with the honeybees. It had been the first and only time Viktor had misbehaved, but he'd learned just how fast bad news travelled. The next day, knowing himself to have crossed a line, he'd travelled home alone. Hans and Daniel had returned later that night, and Hans had beaten him as he lay in bed. Not only had Viktor absconded, but his actions had also been the talk of the county, and his father had taken great exception to the family name being sullied by such accusations. Nobody could say for sure it had been Viktor, but his absence had been enough to confirm their suspicions, though it was insufficient evidence to bring about a charge of disturbing the peace. In addition to the beating that had left him bruised and battered, Viktor had since been denied attending monthly court visits and was confined to their smallholding. He was a prisoner, isolated from the outside world so he could do no more harm to himself – or the family reputation.

'Do not judge,' continued Viktor, reading from the book of Luke, 'and you will not be judged. Do not condemn, and you will not be condemned. Forgive, and you will be forgiven.' He closed the tatty cover of the good book. His reading had at least improved as a consequence. Hans bid them goodnight and turned in for the night. Viktor, who was nursing the last of a summer cold, and Daniel did likewise, retiring to their shared room. Viktor climbed onto his straw mattress, releasing a plume of dust up into the warm air. The shutters were closed, dampening the song of crickets outside. He lay prone while Daniel climbed into his bed on the other side of the small room.

'It's two years since the court day. When do you think Father will forgive me?' Viktor said into the darkness.

'He may never.'

'Not very Christian, is it?'

'I forgot to tell you,' said Daniel, changing the subject as he always did when Viktor tried to point out their father's hypocrisies. 'While you were in your sick bed yesterday, Father and I were in the fields. He told me what happened between him and Mason Fitzbarton.'

Viktor propped himself up on his elbows, his annoyance at Daniel being taken into his father's confidence ahead of himself playing second fiddle to his curiosity.

'It went back to before Father bought this place,' said Daniel in a hushed whisper, mindful of the thin wooden walls. 'He'd got wind of a stretch of land coming up for sale upriver, west of here. Forty acres with river frontage. Was ideal. We could have got the crops straight onto the river. No land crossings. Our own jetty. Anyhow, Father needed to borrow the money – it wasn't cheap, being only a day's journey to the inspection warehouse. Somebody tells him Mason Fitzbarton is always in credit, so Father approaches him and they speak about a loan. Fitzbarton agrees it with him, and they shake hands. All proper. Father leaves thinking all is good as Fitzbarton says his lawyer will draw up a contract. Father doesn't hear nothing. After a month, he gets anxious. He goes to Fitzbarton's place, but the man won't see him. Father makes enquiries of his own. Turns out, Fitzbarton bought the land for himself. Same price Father had agreed. He only knew about it because of Father, yet he pinched it from under his nose.'

Viktor thought about it while Daniel continued.

'Father didn't want to go way out west. Wasn't safe. Long transport. So, we ended up here instead.'

'Hmm, doesn't it strike you as odd, that after all that, Father bought a plot right next door to Fitzbarton's?'

There was silence while Daniel thought. 'Maybe.'

'I know what Father's like, he wants to get one up on him. Fitzbarton prevented him from getting what he wanted, so he's done likewise. Virginia's plenty big enough, but Father, stubborn mule he is, can't let it go.'

'Anyway, that's what happened,' said Daniel flatly.

Viktor laid his head back down. 'How come he tells you these things and not me?'

'Because he knows you'll point out his faults. Whatever he tells you becomes an argument. You two are like oil and vinegar.'

Viktor couldn't disagree. What Fitzbarton had done was wrong, but Viktor had to admit it was also clever – that was how people got ahead. Father was too honest for his own good. Too petty as well. Hans Neumann would always be poor. And so would Viktor. For the millionth time, he considered running away. Life was passing him by. But his father kept watch of the money; he'd be leaving empty-handed. A runaway. Would people still remember what he'd done with the bees? All he knew was tobacco farming. What did he have to offer the world? *Not much.* The little he knew of the outside world came from his younger brother, which was humiliating in itself. He sighed at his predicament. The words of the Bible came to mind: *Forgive and you will be forgiven.* But his father wasn't the forgiving type.

***

The next day, they were de-flowering the tobacco plants, encouraging their leaves to grow bigger. While Daniel was up the other end of the field, Viktor approached his father.

'Daniel told me about what happened between you and Fitzbarton.'

Hans grunted as he stooped to pull up a weed.

'He's our neighbour now. He could be useful to us,' Viktor pressed on. 'How long are you going to hold it against him?'

'We've no use for him.'

'He has a jetty. We could ship our produce by water. If you let me speak to him…'

'Let me tell you something,' Hans rounded on his son. 'If someone betrays your trust, you can never rely on them. Ever. Psalms: *It is better to take refuge in the Lord than to trust in man.*'

'And does that apply to me too?'

'Mason's a snake. You're not like him. You're just a fool.' Hans went back to pinching off the buds.

'Do not judge and you will not be judged,' Viktor recited. 'Do not condemn, and you will not be condemned. Forgive, and you will be forgiven.' said Viktor, repeating last night's verse.

Hans stopped and appraised him. Viktor couldn't determine what his face betrayed.

Father and son stood, face to face, silent under the beating midday sun.

Hans nodded then embraced his son briefly, before carrying on with his labours.

Viktor was left stunned.

'Now, we'll be having no more talk of Fitzbarton, and that be the last of it,' Hans called out over his shoulder.

Viktor got back to work.

9

Croghan had been enjoying a lively drink in the King's Tavern when he'd overheard two men talking about the Ohio Company. His drunkenness interrupted by a sudden sobriety, he'd grabbed the man by his lapels, and extracted from him the details of a land grant made to a consortium of Virginians – by the King, no less. He'd left immediately and travelled west on horseback.

This development was certain to upset matters. He'd got things in the Ohio going just nicely. Old Briton had relocated the Twightee from Sandusky and taken a spot even further west on the Miami River. His camp blocked the French from venturing south from Detroit, from where he could harry French traders. Relations with the Iroquois were also good; they acquiesced to Croghan's trading with the Twightee, as the neighbouring tribe acted as a buffer to French reprisals. From both tribes, a steady stream of furs travelled east, meaning Croghan raised more money as merchants were eager to cash in on the boom in furs. While Croghan skimmed some for himself, he spent the rest on goods to trade with the Indians. Occasionally, London merchants credited his account, and rather than settle his debts, Croghan bought more goods, more land, hired more people. If these rumours about the Virginians were true, he would need to slam the door to the Ohio before they arrived.

He rode day and night, stopping off at his farmstead to collect the last of the ammunition stored there for just such an emergency. Since the war with the French had finished, the supply of lead and powder had been prohibited. The barrels tightly strapped to the wagon trundling behind his farmhands were now an even more valuable cargo.

Ten days after leaving Philadelphia, an exhausted Croghan arrived at Logstown. The welcome of the Iroquois people was subdued.

'Where's Tanacharison?' he asked the sombre-looking son of the Chief.

'The council of elders are meeting in the longhouse,' said Thayonih. Croghan followed him in. The doors were open, allowing a gentle breeze from the river to calm the stifling summer heat. Twelve Iroquois sat cross-legged in a circle. Tanacharison invited him to take a seat amongst them.

'Buck,' said Tanacharison, using his native Seneca tongue, 'tell us what is happening?'

'With the Virginians?'

Tanacharison frowned. 'No, the French. They come here and tell us not to trade with you.'

'Just me?'

Tanacharison nodded. 'They offered us a bounty for your scalp.'

Oh Jesus, thought Croghan. 'When?'

'Yesterday. They left this morning.'

Another Iroquois interrupted, 'There were over two hundred French men. And fifty-five Huron.'

Holy shit, you prodded the hornet's nest this time, Georgy boy.

'We've never seen so many white men before.'

'We must surrender our alliance with the British,' announced one of the Iroquois seated on the far side of the circle.

Be calm. 'What do they want?' Croghan asked.

'They say this land is theirs. We can stay here in peace, but no British people must come into the Ohio Valley. We must only trade with the French.'

'We should accept their lesser trade terms,' said one council member. 'Poor terms are better than French anger.'

'I agree,' said another Iroquois.

'But this land is yours,' said Croghan. 'They can't just take it! I wouldn't dare piss you lot off,' he added in English.

'There were too many for us to fight.'

Tanacharison stood and fetched an oval-shaped metal plate. 'We found this, fastened to a tree, at the fork in the river.' He passed it to Croghan. French words were engraved onto it.

'What does it say?'

The Iroquois next to him took the plaque and translated it:

> *In the year 1749, of the reign of Louis the 15th, King of*
> *France, I Céloron, commander of a detachment sent by*
> *Governor General of New France,*
> *to re-establish tranquillity in some Indian villages of*
> *these cantons, have buried this Plate of Lead,*
> *this 29th day of July, near the*
> *river Ohio, as a monument of the renewal*
> *of the possession we have taken of the said river Ohio*
> *and of all those which empty into it, and of all the lands on*
> *both sides as far as the sources of the said rivers.*

'You can't let them get away with that,' protested Croghan in English. His debts, which he'd abandoned at the back of his mind, now came surging forward. If he lost his trade with the Indians, he was done for. He owed thousands of pounds; his name would be mud in the New World.

'What did you say about Virginia?' asked Tanacharison.

Croghan cursed himself for opening his big mouth. He frowned, pretending confusion.

'When you came in, you said the Virginians,' pressed Tanacharison.

'Well, could be nothing, but I hear rumour that men from Virginia show interest in these lands.'

Uproar spread across the assembled Iroquois.

'See, the British are no better than the French!'

'We should kill them all.'

'You can't trust the white men!'

'Hold your horses, it's just a rumour,' said Croghan.

'What do they want with us?' boomed Tanacharison.

Croghan stood. 'I don't know, but look, we make good trade together. To me, the trade we share matters more than anything. If you need protection from the French or Virginians, I will lead it for you. I know these people, they fear you. If you stand strong, it's bloody fool who crosses the mountains against your wishes. Trust me.' He looked round at the silent faces. 'I'm on your side. We want the same things. To trade and to leave you in peace.'

'Buck, you must leave us now,' said Tanacharison.

'I leave you to your debate.' Croghan thanked them for their courtesy, knowing they had paid him a great honour by letting him join their council. He left the longhouse, a sinking feeling in his gut. Cursing himself for encouraging the Indians to clear the valleys of French traders, it was obvious now that there'd be a reaction. But the frontier had been within his grasp. You'd need the self-restraint of a priest not to reach for something so close and so valuable.

I need a drink.

***

In the early dawn, two days after their council meeting, Tanacharison stood in the horse corral. He ran the palm of his hand over the hair on his skewbald horse's back. Smooth and dusty. He brought it to a rest on its rump and felt the strength of the muscles. He admired its nobility and power, qualities that he strived to bring out in himself. He breathed in, absorbing the animal's potency. He would need it, for the winter ahead was certain to be a perilous one. The peace between the French and English had brought to his camp a great many problems. If word spread that his tribe was low on ammunition, they would be a sitting duck for anyone able to challenge their hold on the valleys of the Ohio. The peace had unrestrained the white men. The French were arriving in numbers never seen before. Talk of men from Virginia too. Tanacharison's people were caught in the middle. While the council fretted and fussed, he was reassured that both sides were courting his loyalty. He could exploit this, so long as they viewed him and his people as powerful.

But they would have to choose, and that would bring its own problems. The council had been unable to agree on whom they should favour. They feared the French, but trade was better with the British, who at least hadn't yet claimed their land with plaques or treaties, or any other devices white men used.

Tanacharison searched his soul for an answer. The white men who had arrived at the shores of his ancestors' lands had brought many problems. Their diseases had killed more Indians than all the tribal wars combined. They had settled the coastline, killing or pushing back the native peoples, sparking tribal disputes as one tribe trod on the foot of another. Yet, they had brought with them a great many other things on which his people now depended. He'd heard Croghan saying, 'You can't unring that bell.' He finally understood what he'd meant by that. The white men – once a distant convenience, a tool to use as required – were here to stay. Their earlier ambitions were being superseded by new ones. Tanacharison feared that unless he took action, his descendants would be condemned to live under the threat of the white man forever, be that sickness, the trickery of their words, disguised as law, or their capacity for violence.

A bald eagle soared high in the morning sky above him. A bad omen to see one flying at dawn, circling high to spy its prey.

'Sadögweta, Chief,' said Croghan, appearing from between the tepees.

'Hello, Buck.' He'd given Croghan the nickname on account of his energy and his seemingly limitless desire for deer skins. This early, he wore the bleary eyes of a man dragged from his slumber. 'You will ride with me.'

Tanacharison leapt up onto the horse's bare back with a sprightliness that belied a man in his fiftieth summer.

Croghan let himself into the corral, replaced the fence rail behind him, then spent several moments persuading one of the horses to let him mount it.

'You are trapped, Buck,' laughed Tanacharison, as Croghan saw he had corralled himself with the horses. 'You must jump the fence!'

'Jesus, it's a little early for this.' Croghan took a tight hold of the horse's chestnut-coloured mane, gripped with his thighs, and kicked his feet into the animal's ribs. The horse leapt, clearing the fence, and dumped Croghan on the ground with a grunt.

Tanacharison let out a belly laugh.

Dusting himself off, Buck said something in his own language and remounted.

'Follow me, Buck.' Tanacharison kicked his mare and broke into a canter. He heard the white man curse behind him.

He thundered past the tepees of his sleeping people and headed east into the forest. Finding his rhythm, he gripped hard with his legs and gave himself over to the animal's stride, its hooves almost silent in the soft loamy soil of the forest. Giant trees dashed past the fringes of his view; their canopy too towering to trouble him with branches at this height. He let the horse choose its own path as it weaved between the trees, scattering the birds and animals of the forest as it went. He glanced behind and saw the white man hanging on for his life, terror fixed on his face.

Riding a horse was one of the great joys of Tanacharison's life. Beast and man connected in a harmony of movement, one responding instinctively to the other, with man nominally in control. Nothing healed the ailments of a man's innermost thoughts more than being out with a horse. Whenever fate determined Tanacharison to die, the spirit horse would take him from this life to the next – but until then, he would trot, canter and gallop to his heart's content.

The white man managed to keep up with him all morning as they headed along the hunting trails, through the clearings, over the hills and round the valleys, stopping only to water the animals.

It was midday when Tanacharison brought his horse to a halt on the bluff overlooking the confluence of the river, where the waters of the Ohio split into the Allegheny and the Monongahela.

It was a very tired-looking Irishman who slid from his horse, relieved that his aching body would not have to travel any further.

'Down there, at the fork of the river, is where my scouts found the plaque we showed you. The French, they travelled down from here,' Tanacharison indicated the Allegheny River, which ran left from the fork of the confluence. 'They came all the way from their station on Lake Erie in the North. They have built a portage road to connect the lake to this river. From here, the French can travel to the Mississippi and the warm seas in the south, where I hear they have a settlement called Louisiana.' He turned to face Buck. 'I need your help to stop them.'

'Sure. How exactly?'

'I need ammunition.' He pointed his finger at Buck's chest, 'You must get it for me.'

The trader laughed. Not the response Tanacharison had hoped for. The white man raised his palms. 'Chief, I told you, I can't. Britain makes peace with France. They have an agreement not to supply arms to Indians. No British person would dare sell me muskets, bullets – anything. We'd be blamed for starting another war.'

'No. You have to.'

'Why? So you can attack the French? Or the British maybe?'

'No. So I can protect my people.'

'That's not how the Governor of Pennsylvania would see it. I'd be hanged for breaking a treaty. As much as I love a deal, I value my neck.'

Tanacharison continued to stare into Buck's eyes.

'Trust me, if I could make money selling you guns, bullets – bows and arrows even – I would, Jesus, I'd sell you my own mother if you gave me a good price.'

Tanacharison smiled, his temper waning. Buck always had amusing comments at the ready. Satisfied that Buck was telling the truth, he turned his gaze out across at the river, its dark waters shimmering in the midday sun. His people depended on this river for water, fish, travel and trade. It brought them life – but with it, the white man.

He dismounted and stroked his horse's brown and white patterned neck, then let it go to graze. He patted Buck's horse too and the animals began to sniff the ground.

'I must protect my people, Buck.'

'Look, it may not be in my best interests to say this, but would it not just be easier to trade with the French?'

Tanacharison found a comfortable patch of ground. 'Come, sit with me.' He untied his leather pouch to share some dried deer meat. They sat side by side watching the distant river's current. Tanacharison felt his mood ease once the food found his belly.

'Why did you come to these lands, Buck?' he spoke into the easy silence.

'My family's land failed. We were starving.' Croghan paused as he wrestled with the memories of his past. 'I left Ireland to survive and because I didn't trust myself not to do something that might cost me my life.'

It was a rare moment of solemnity. In all their dealings, Tanacharison couldn't recall seeing Buck so sad.

'Besides, if I must be British, I may as well enjoy some of the benefits that come with it – and profit from their Empire.'

Tanacharison frowned. 'You don't love your own people?'

'It's complicated. I suppose I don't see myself as British.' Croghan paused and considered his words. 'Your Iroquois confederacy is six nations united under one Chief. Britain is four nations ruled by one King. Only, in Britain, the King is German – a different tribe altogether – and his council rules the isles by force. The English are the dominant tribe, and for centuries they have sent armies and settlers to conquer my homeland. So, their King may rule the land, but I don't belong to their tribe.'

These people are mad, thought Tanacharison, unable to grasp the reasoning behind such an arrangement. 'Now you come to my land and do to me as they did to you?'

Croghan sighed. 'I fancy that makes me a hypocrite, yes, but I am just trying to survive in the best way I can. Hobson's choice.'

'What does that mean?'

'Something my father used to say, God rest his soul. When you don't have a choice, there is only one answer.'

Tanacharison grunted. His father would have disagreed. *You always have a choice.* 'I don't remember my father. The French captured me when I was young. Their allies, the Huron, ate my father.'

Croghan winced.

'I swear it on my life and on his spirit, the French will never have these lands,' said Tanacharison.

'Chief,' Buck turned to him with a sincere look, 'if the French don't take these lands, then the British will.'

Tanacharison knew that Buck was right. 'You are not like the other British. Why do you tell the truth?'

Buck shrugged. 'I like you. My livelihood depends on our trust. It is better to be honest with you.'

Tanacharison nodded; it was a rare quality to find in a white man. 'What do you think the Virginians want?'

'Land, I'd imagine. They're farming people. Furs too, I'm sure.'

'That is bad for you?'

'Yes. *If* you make terms with them, instead of me.' Buck looked gloomy. 'But they won't have ammunition.'

It was as Tanacharison feared. He was safer when the white men were at war with one another.

'Wait!' Buck jumped to his feet. 'I have an idea! You want to keep the French out, and the Virginians too?'

Tanacharison nodded and took another bite of deer meat.

'So do I. I want to trade with you. So...what if you sold this land,' Buck turned and cast his arm across the view beyond the fork in the river, 'to me.'

Tanacharison sat still and said nothing as his mind mulled over the consequences.

'It would mean the land was protected, so you could hunt,' Buck went on. 'If we had a proper contract drawn up in a Pennsylvanian court, the Virginians would have to recognise my deeds. They'd be prevented from taking it if I had already bought it from you.'

'And the French? They will offer a bounty for your head.'

'Well, I haven't got that far yet...'

While Buck paced up and down, grappling with the holes of his plan, Tanacharison considered how he felt. Buck was a white man. He spoke plain and was more honest than all the others he'd dealt with. But the white man valued land so highly... If Buck betrayed his promises, they could kill him. One white man owning land was easier to control than thousands of white men with their notions of property and law.

'I think if I could persuade Pennsylvania to fund a fort,' Buck was saying, 'it would peg the French back and guarantee the furs for their merchants, rather than Virginians. It might just work.' He waved his hands as if that might shake the remaining answers from the depths of his mind. 'But it will need to be a lot of land, to form a bulwark against the white men. At least half a million acres.' Buck stood waiting for a reaction.

Tanacharison stared back at the white man; the gleam had returned to Buck's eyes. *He will betray us in time,* thought Tanacharison. *He is given to temptation. It will be too great for him to resist.*

'What you thinking?' said Croghan in Seneca.

'If I can trust you,' Tanacharison said slowly.

'I'm a fur trader, pure and simple. The only way I can continue is if you're safe and willing to trade with me.'

'If I agree, what would you do with this land?'

'Well, I'd build a house and a small farm for myself. But that's it. If you promise to trade only with me, I will prevent any white men from settling on that land.' The corners of his lips hinted at a smile.

Tanacharison shook his head. 'That land has great value to you. What could you give me for it?'

'Remember that I have great value to you too. I am the only white man who will honour your wishes. I will act in the interests of your people.' Buck knelt down in front of him. Their eyes met. 'Chief, what if I told you I had a small supply of ammunition?'

'You said you had none!' barked Tanacharison.

'No. I said I had none to trade, and that I couldn't buy any more. This is my own supply, which I was keeping for my use. One hogshead, full to the brim.'

It wasn't much, but if they were careful with it, they could make it last a year. 'What else can you give me?'

They haggled back and forth. Buck was unable to hide his excitement at the prospect of owning so much land. Tanacharison extracted from him a very great price along with the ammunition, but he still wasn't convinced Buck's scheme could work.

***

Croghan was close to pissing himself with excitement. Obviously, he didn't have the money to complete the trade, but that much land was unthinkable for the Irishman, whose family had barely survived on five waterlogged acres of Irish turf. This wasn't even landing a fish – he was about to catch a whale. He'd do and say whatever he needed to get his hands on the trade goods the Chief demanded. He'd divert funds intended to pay for furs. His creditors would have to wait. He could pay them off in land if he had to. Once it was his, Tanacharison wouldn't be able to stop him. They'd just have to be patient.

'Virginia can't take the land from you?' Tanacharison asked.

'No. British law will prevail. They'll have to respect my rights.'

'You will build a fort?'

'Yes, definitely.'

'I will need to discuss it with the council,' said the Chief.

Shit. 'Of course. You honour me by considering it.'

***

Tanacharison stood, looking down at Buck kneeling at his feet. 'Swear your loyalty to my people, Buck.'

Buck did so without protest. Still, Tanacharison didn't trust him entirely, but he was the lesser of evils and should be kept close. 'You must join us. Sit on our council, be as one with our people.'

'Whatever you need, Chief,' he winked. 'I'm your man.'

Tanacharison went to find his horse, and briefly smiled to himself, for only he knew his real plan, and it was now in motion.

10

Today, Sylvia turned nineteen. One year had passed since little Abe had died in her arms. Since then, some things in her life had changed – but most hadn't. The Whitechapel gang still shared the same small tenement. Abe's space had been filled by Rebecca, whom Jacob had married shortly after meeting, on discovering they had conceived a child together. Their baby was expected any day. In the meantime, Rebecca's swollen body filled the chair in the corner of the tenement as she cradled her belly, endlessly complaining of discomfort. If she didn't end her moaning, Sylvia was minded to give her sister-in-law something to really complain about. Such violent thoughts were wishful thinking, for she could never harm her brother's wife.

The artefacts they'd stolen outside the theatre – jewellery, a silver cigarillo case, a walking cane, the pistol, some coins – had long since been traded and spent, keeping them in rent and new clothes for a few months. Sylvia had wanted to keep the lady's necklace, but she couldn't wear it, knowing that it had been traded for Abe's life. Her promise to leave behind her life of crime had proved hard to fulfil. In the absence of good references, and with more people than there were jobs, it was nigh on impossible for a known member of a London gang to find respectable employment, no matter how hard they wanted to reform themselves. She'd secretly attended Sunday church, and found the congregation shunned her. So much for their Christian charity.

'Come on, sis,' said Jacob. 'There's no good us moping about here all evening. What say I take you and Caroline out for a drink?'

'What about me?' asked Rebecca.

'You can't come, not in your condition,' said Jacob, much to Sylvia's relief. 'We'll go early, before it gets rowdy. Just one gin, for your birthday.'

Sylvia was keen to escape the confines of the room, but she had misgivings about being seen celebrating on the anniversary of Abe's death. Reading her mind as siblings could, Jacob said, 'You'll hopefully have a great many birthdays to come. You can't stay home wishing Abe hadn't died.' He was right, and a break from Rebecca's whining would be welcome.

'The boys won't mind,' said Mags, referring to her brothers, the other half of the Whitechapel gang. 'There's a load of boats arrived, so they've work.'

'Very well, come on Caroline, let's go,' said Sylvia, leading the way out of the door.

The air was so thick with coal smoke, it obscured the late afternoon sun. They walked together, sandwiching Jacob, who chaperoned a sister on each arm, carrying his stolen pewter flagon in one hand and a knife tucked up the sleeve of his other arm. They passed the Tower of London and stopped by the riverbank of bustling Lower Thames Street. They bought a pint of illicit gin from a street peddler and took a seat on the riverbank.

'To Abe, God rest his soul,' toasted Jacob. He took a swig and passed it to Sylvia, who did likewise. The acrid-tasting gin was little better than poison, and the after-effects were little different, but she didn't care, it was her birthday. They shared the flagon and watched the tall ships struggle to manoeuvre in and out of the river's extremity, blocked by the bridge. Sylvia remembered the same scene from her childhood. Even in her short life, the ships had grown bigger and the river busier. Tall masts bobbed in the current, amongst which little row boats picked paths across the brown water and between the great wooden hulls congesting the river. The watermen of the empty boats shouted up to the gunwales of the ocean-going ships, bargaining to unload their cargo for less than the next man. Those successful would return to shore so fully laden, they were perilously close to sinking below their waterline. Their pilots shouted for others to get out of their way, attempting to avoid collision with ships that further piled into the pool of London. The street was chaos too. Carters lugged hogsheads to and from the customs house and warehouses. Horses and carts ferried in merchant men, keen to secure space in the warehouses. The street urchins and pickpockets, who would have once counted Abe among their number, slunk through the crowds in search of opportunity and unguarded belongings. The air was filled with shouting, cursing, bargaining and waving arms, as London did its business, absorbing all the goods of the world through one small, congested stretch of river.

'Made a wish for your birthday, sis?' asked Caroline.

'The same one I make every year,' said Sylvia, aware the gin had loosened her tongue. 'Not to die a poverty-stricken spinster.' It wasn't for a lack of male interest that she remained stubbornly unattached at her advancing age. She attracted plenty of interest, but they were all ne'er-do-wells, quick to make promises and quicker still to break them. None offered her betterment, and she'd seen too many girls trapped in squalor, caring for the screaming brats they spawned while absent husbands drank their earnings, and beat their wives as soon as they complained. She may be stuck in the sludge of the London gutter, but she wasn't going to fasten an anchor to her feet in the process. But on days like today, without a man of her own to share her birthday with, she felt her loneliness all the keener.

'Enough of this, let's go for a proper drink,' she pointed to the Copper Kettle tavern on the far side of the street. 'We've enough for a round, and we can always persuade a man to buy us one, can't we, Caroline?' she said, feeling defiant. It was her birthday, and she could do as she pleased.

The Copper Kettle was frequented by newly paid sailors and dock workers. She noticed *him* the moment she stepped inside. It was as if the crowd of drinkers parted to lead her to him, the tall, dark-haired serious man standing at the bar. Unshaven, weathered skin and gnarled hands were at odds with the smart purple velvet coat and white stockings. She knew at that moment she would be intimate with this man. She offered a coy smile as she took her place next to him at the bar. He forced a smile too, but his expression remained serious.

Caroline nudged her sister with her elbow.

'What's your name?' asked Caroline. Jacob pushed himself forward, his presence indicating his sisters were accompanied and not to be taken advantage of.

'Captain John Reid.' He never asked for their names.

'Not very friendly, is he?' remarked Caroline to Sylvia, who was indulging her imagination as to this man's nature.

Captain Reid grunted. His jaw was wide and determined. Sylvia noticed a small brooch on his coat, studded with a small gemstone.

'What is that?' asked Sylvia.

''Tis a sapphire, from India,' he replied.

Feeling mildly irritated at his manner, she persisted, 'Is it being at sea that makes you a man of few words?'

A thin smile broke across his face. 'Aye, maybe.'

'Let us buy you a drink and loosen your tongue,' suggested Sylvia, waving away Jacob's protestations.

When four ales were placed on the bar, the Captain paid, which silenced Jacob and restored Sylvia's belief in her course.

They supped their drinks. Reid was impervious to Caroline's flirting as he eyed Jacob with suspicion and Sylvia with an infuriating indifference. Having finished his drink, Reid excused himself to empty his bladder.

'Will you be returning?'

'Aye, if you're buying.'

'Four ales, please, barkeep,' announced Sylvia, determined to win this man's attention.

With Reid gone, Caroline whispered, 'He's very handsome. Should we pickpocket him?'

'You take him in the alleyway, once he's aroused…'

'No,' said Sylvia, interrupting Jacob. 'I've a feeling about him.'

'Ooowww,' teased Caroline.

'You two make yourselves scarce, once he's had his next drink.'

Reid returned. He took a sip of his ale and looked over his shoulders to see who was in earshot. 'You folk look like good honest thieves. I need to arrange for my cargo to be stolen tonight. Can you help an honest sailor save some duty?'

'That depends,' said Sylvia not in the least surprised to hear such a request. 'What's in it for us?'

He looked her directly in the eyes. 'What do you want?'

She was undone by the simplicity of the question. An image of Abe appeared in her mind. Her instinct told her to take this chance. 'Let me speak with Captain Reid alone for a moment.'

Jacob acquiesced to his elder sibling; he trusted her but didn't like being left out of negotiations. He spoke directly to Reid, 'We'll be just over here, so don't be getting any ideas with my sister.'

Reid nodded. 'So, you're the master of your house, eh?' he asked Sylvia once they were alone.

'Mother and master, for ten years.'

Reid nodded, looking vaguely impressed. 'So then, what are your terms?'

'You asked me what I want. Well, I will speak truthfully to you, but I warn you it will not be what you are expecting.'

The indifference of Reid's gesture suggested he'd heard all sorts in his time.

'I don't want to steal anymore.'

At that, his face did register some surprise.

'I'm not a bad person, truly I'm not. I've made a living from peccadilloes because I had to. For years, we've been lucky, for the most part.' Again, she thought of poor Abe. 'But it is time to quit while I'm ahead. To live an honest life. To raise a child of my own, rather than the children of my parents.'

Reid ordered two more ales. 'You should go to the colonies. Leave your past behind. Your past doesn't matter in the Americas. Far easier to make an honest living, they're always short of labour. Regardless, though, a pretty woman like you – you'd find a man easy enough.'

She felt herself blush a little. He *was* attracted to her.

'Help me tonight and I'll give you free passage,' he said.

She glanced at Jacob and Caroline. *What would become of them?* Caroline would be forced to turn to prostitution. The Nicholsons would get the better of Jacob. She shook her head. 'I can't.'

Reid saw her predicament for himself. 'I know a man. A Methodist. Jeremiah Benson, from Cheapside. He's keen on returning lost sheep to the flock. I could request an introduction.'

'What would he want with me?'

Reid shrugged.

'Can't promise you anything'll come of it. But if you get my tobacco stolen for me tonight, I'll take you to meet him.'

'But,' she felt her temper straining, 'it would cost you nothing to ask him first. Then I'd know if there was anything in it for me before putting my family at risk to steal your own cargo, just so you can save a few quid.'

'Well, if you've a better deal elsewhere…'

You bastard. His face was stern; she felt her attraction to him wane.

'You don't have to do it yourself. Send your brother, you'd have me as an alibi.'

She scowled at him. Was he suggesting intimacy?

'How's about another deal, you have *me*. For your pleasure. In return, I—'

Reid shook his head. 'No, you're very pretty for sure, but with your sort there's always a risk of waking up naked, to discover all my clothes and worldly possessions have taken flight in the night.'

'I'm no whore!' protested Sylvia, offended.

'Those are my terms, girl. Your salvation for another night's work.'

He was a hard man, for which he deserved a begrudging respect. 'Very well, but you take me to Cheapside first. Then, if all's well, we'll help.'

'No. If nothing comes of it, you won't honour your side of the bargain, and if Mr Benson smells the booze on your breath, you won't get past the front door.'

She squinted at him. 'How can I be sure I can trust you?'

Reid shrugged. His indifference was infuriating, not least because she was willing to accept his terms. They shook on it.

***

The watch finished at midnight. Sylvia spent the rest of her birthday keeping lookout while the boys of the Whitechapel gang climbed aboard Captain Reid's ship, the *Relief*. They worked all night, ferrying hogsheads to an empty storehouse in Southwark. They kept one for themselves to cover expenses. It was a bleary-eyed Sylvia who waited outside the Copper Kettle for Reid to arrive.

He ambled up the busy street despite being an hour late, for which he didn't apologise, beyond explaining that the revenue men had been grilling him over his missing cargo.

'Well then, let's go,' said Sylvia. Without further ado, they walked to Cheapside and knocked on the black-painted door of a three-story townhouse made from yellow London stock bricks. The door was finally answered by a man whose advancing age manifested itself in grey hair, heavy features and a withering frame. He wore a large pair of ivory-framed spectacles, whose round lenses made his eyes look unnaturally large.

'Who have we here? Mmm, Captain Reid, and a lady I don't believe I've met before?' His voice was clipped and mildly effeminate.

'Pleased to make your acquaintance, Mr Benson, Sylvia Coppell.' She curtsied and offered a broad smile, which he briefly returned.

'And what brings you both to my door on this fine day?'

Sylvia glanced at Reid, not sure if she should speak.

'I've not got all day,' prompted Mr Benson.

Both Sylvia and Reid spoke at the same time, then stopped to let the other continue. Reid broke the awkwardness, explaining he'd offered to make an introduction on Miss Coppell's behalf.

'What is it you want, young lady? Out with it, it will be getting dark at this rate.'

'Employment. Sir.'

Benson, despite his advancing years, was still blessed with a sharp mind, for his head sprung in Reid's direction. 'You can vouch for her?'

'No, not really.'

Sylvia ground her teeth in frustration at Reid's obstinacy. He only gave the very minimum of himself. She was minded to set his hogsheads ablaze.

'I met her last night. She wants to make an honest living.'

Damn him! He'd as good as told him she was a criminal. Benson appraised her with fresh interest. She felt pathetic and offered a pleading smile.

'You better come inside, young lady. Captain Reid, I shall speak with the lady alone. You may wait in the hallway if you wish.' Benson turned around and disappeared into his hallway. Sylvia was confused. Reid had as good as sabotaged her chances, yet the old man invited her in anyway. Reid gestured for her to follow Benson inside. He was holding a door to his parlour open, waiting for Sylvia.

Closing the door behind her, he invited her to take a seat on a wooden chair by the fireplace. The room was tasteful, and a world away from her own lodgings. A Persian rug covered the floorboards. A painting of the Virgin Mary hung above the wooden mantle over the fireplace. Opposite was a settee with bright cushions, on which slept a ginger cat. The scent of cut roses in the vase on the side table gave it a very homely feel. Mr Benson took a seat in a plush-looking armchair adjacent to the unlit fireplace.

'I can see you're a pauper, Miss Coppell, for which I don't judge you, but if there's one thing above all else I prize it is honesty, so if you please, tell me of your circumstances and don't be tempted to sugar-coat it.'

There was a brief silence while Sylvia considered how to tackle his invitation. She explained how she had raised her siblings and that she shared a tenement.

'How do you make your living?'

'Well, I…'

His eyebrows raised as she hesitated. His manner was disarming, and she threw caution to the wind.

'I steal, mostly. Pickpocketing. Robbery. We trade smuggled goods, tobacco, tea, calico…' she checked for his reaction, which appeared impartial. She felt ashamed as she confessed to the life she led. She didn't hold back, giving voice to her worst offences. It was agonising listening to herself but there was a peaceful silence once she'd run out of sins.

'Now, how do you feel for that?'

She let out a deep sigh and wiped away the tears that formed in her eyes. Outside her gang, she'd never shared the grim reality of her life with anyone. Years of ducking and diving, thinking on her feet seemed to leave her conscience in the presence of this old man's parlour.

'Well, Miss Coppell…'

She sobbed, knowing this was the moment he would dismiss her for being the vile scum she was.

'I think you've done very well, looking after your family. God has given you a great many challenges to overcome.' Seeing her surprise, he remarked, 'Yes, you have sinned greatly, for which you must atone, but you are alive, by your own merits and guile. You have resisted the temptation to prostitute your body. You are a brave girl.'

She tried to stop the tears from escaping her eyes, but they relentlessly trickled down her cheeks. She was utterly disarmed by his generosity. She wiped her nose on her sleeve and dried her tears. This was proving to be the most extraordinary day.

'Tell me, what is it you wish for?'

Her shoulders lightened. She described her dreams of marrying a man and raising a family.

'Are you willing to forsake your deviant ways, Miss Coppell?'

She nodded.

'Truly?'

'Yes. Truly, I want to be a good person.'

'Do you worship God?'

They exchanged a knowing look. 'Not as much as I should.'

Mr Benson nodded. 'I am a Methodist. Have you heard of Methodism, Miss Coppell?'

She shook her head.

'We believe that those who stray from the flock should be welcomed back. That any Christian can be reborn, to live in God's care and by His laws. Are you willing, Miss Coppell, to live by the commandments in the Bible, to forsake your habits, to take the second chance if you are offered it?'

She nodded. 'Yes, sir, truly I am.'

The door to the parlour opened. A tall man, of similar age to Mr Benson, leaned into the room.

'Who are you talking to, Jerry?'

'Come in, let me introduce you to Miss Sylvia Coppell, she's our new parlour maid.'

'Oh, I see.' The man looked shocked at the news.

Sylvia got to her feet to curtsey, which put the newcomer at ease.

'I'm Hugo Somerton. Delighted to make your acquaintance.' He smiled and then took a seat on the settee.

Mr Benson continued. 'You'll receive board and lodgings. There's space for you in the attic, it's draughty but you'll be comfortable enough. Are you literate?'

'No.'

'Very well. You won't be paid, and this is a temperate house, so no drink will pass your lips, nor will you swear, and if you steal or commit any wrongdoing you'll return to your current life.'

Sylvia nodded her understanding, unable to hide the smile that broke across her lips.

'There's more: You will be required to learn letters and numbers. Every evening you'll be schooled and once educated, you will be required to perform this service for others like yourself. It will be a life of service, not just to Hugo and me...'

She glanced at Hugo, wondering what their arrangement was.

'But you will assist me with my preaching, serving God, as together we educate the folk of London in the true ways of God, so they become good Methodists, just like you will become.' He cleared his throat, 'Are you willing to accept our terms and become a Methodist, Miss Coppell?'

She sniffed. 'Yes, sir, I'd be delighted.'

'Then we'd be delighted to welcome you into our home.'

Again, she glanced at Hugo, then back to Mr Benson.

He leaned forward in his chair, 'I haven't judged you for how you have lived in the past, Miss Coppell; I ask you to extend us the same courtesy and refrain from judging Hugo and I for how we choose to live?'

She nodded eagerly. 'Thank you, I won't disappoint you.'

He finally shared a big, warm smile. She couldn't believe the events that had brought her here. The Lord truly did work in mysterious ways.

1750

11

Anne carried baby Sarah up the stairs to bed, while Lawrence took a sip of warm milk, relieved by the removal of the baby to another room, where the walls at least might dampen the incessant crying.

'Can I pass you anything, brother?' asked George, closing his journal, and placing it at the base of the candle that had illuminated his prose. He'd come to stay as soon as he'd heard the news of young Sarah's birth, hoping he might be of use in some way. There was little he could do that the house slaves weren't capable of, but it had served as a good excuse to get out from under his mother's roof. Despite reaching his majority, she insisted on keeping him around for his company and her convenience.

'Maybe, I'll have a look through the newspaper, see what I've been missing.' said Lawrence.

George passed the paper and a candelabra for Lawrence to read by, then resumed his seat by the fire. 'Do you miss it, being in government?'

Following Lawrence's collapse in front of his peers, he'd returned home to rest. No sooner had he returned home than he and Anne were confronted by the death of their third child, Mildred. Having lost two children already, Lawrence stepped down from the House of Burgesses. Anne needed the comfort, and he was determined to rest and finally conquer the affliction which plagued his lungs.

'I miss being in the know,' Lawrence admitted. 'As for the

procedures and the politics…no. In the army, one becomes accustomed to using orders to execute a mission. The House is less precise – too many opinions and competing factors. I found it unwieldy and tiresome, to be honest.'

Lawrence opened the paper and began skimming through the stories. The cries from the baby subsided and a weary Anne returned to the parlour. She poured herself a large rum and slumped onto the settee next to Lawrence. George contemplated doing a sketch of the two of them, but dismissed the idea. In a few short years, Anne had gone from a radiant beauty to an exhausted and bereaved mother, with creases around eyes that no longer sparkled. In that same time, Lawrence had lost weight, his clothes hanging limp on his once masculine physique. Despite a trip to a specialist in London that summer, his cough hadn't improved. They both feared his condition was consumption, but never gave voice to it – not in front of George at least.

'Good heavens!' said Lawrence. 'The Lees have died.'

'The Colonel, or his wife, Hannah?'

'Both! It says here she passed away first. Grief-stricken, he went a few days later. They were buried in the family cemetery.'

'Poor things,' Anne commented and crossed herself.

'What about the Ohio Company?' asked George, with a small sense of relief he hadn't tied his own money up in the venture. Since then, he had managed to scrape together enough money to buy his own plot of land. As Lawrence and the now late Colonel Lee hadn't let him in on their venture, he'd taken a leaf out of Fry's book and taken matters into his own hands. It was only a few acres eighty miles inland, though nestled amidst German and Scots settlements, at least he could call it his own. He intended to turn it into a plantation that would one day rival the Lees' home, Stratford Hall.

'Well, the company has just lost its president, and the colony its governor.' Lawrence put the paper down. 'That's about the worst thing that could happen.'

'To the Lees, yes, I should think so!' said George, with a wry smile as he tried to comfort his brother.

Ignoring his joke, Lawrence continued, 'We've lost our man on the council. Whilst he was acting governor, Lee managed to tie up Fry's company in legal proceedings. If these don't continue, we're back in a straight race with Fry, with no one leading on our side.'

'You could put yourself forward,' Anne suggested.

The two began to debate the merits of Lawrence nominating himself, balanced against the risks to his health and what his absence at home would mean for Anne.

I've heard enough, thought George as he got to his feet. 'Goodnight, everybody.'

It would be just like Lawrence to turn a man's death into an opportunity for personal advancement. Every time he falls in muck, he gets up smelling of roses, lamented George as he climbed the stairs.

12

December 26th, 1750
Belvoir Mansion, Virginia

'Tally ho!' cried George as his horse overtook Fairfax's. He held his breath as his steed leapt the creek, landing on the far bank with a jolt. George gripped the reins tight and felt the wind rush through his hair as he closed on the hounds ahead. The terrified fox scarpered across the wet grassy slope into the woods. Behind him, George heard the blast of the huntsman's horn. He couldn't conceal the smile that stretched across his large, pale face. His skin tingled as he tore across the tidewater in pursuit of their quarry. Others may regard it as poor form to lead the chase on a neighbour's hunt, but the thrill was too alluring to ignore. He shot through, letting his horse choose its path, trusting entirely in its judgement. Ahead, the lead hound knocked the fox over. The pack descended. Seconds later, the fox had vanished, pulled to pieces. A quick and noble death for a creature that had been the most fantastic sport. George pulled up and admired the gleeful hounds, their mouths coated red.

Afterwards, with the hounds returned to the kennels and the horses to their stables, the riders gathered on Belvoir's lawn, in the shadow of Fairfax's grand house. A new brick mansion, it would have looked equally at home in the green and pleasant land of the mother country. Neighbouring Lawrence's land, it too overlooked the Potomac River.

Lawrence, wrapped in a large bearskin coat, his wife Anne by his

122

side, greeted the hunting party. A negro held a tray of sloe gins.

'To the fox!' toasted Fairfax, raising his glass.

'How was it, George?' Lawrence asked.

'Marvellous! Plucky little fellow, gave us a great chase.'

Lawrence's smile couldn't hide his disappointment at missing the Boxing Day hunt, as his ill health prevented him from riding in the cold weather.

'We should get you indoors, Lawrence,' said Anne.

'Nonsense, woman, quit your fussing.'

She raised her eyebrows at George, an oft-repeated gesture.

'Major Lawrence, 'tis a fine sight to see ya up and about,' said the lawyer John Mercer, who approached from behind George. 'We've missed you in the House this season. Are you feeling better?'

Lawrence squared his shoulders. 'I am sure to be myself again in time for the next elections.'

'To be sure,' said Mercer. 'Since Colonel Lee died, I'll admit we've rather lost our way.'

'Well, we should find out who's going to replace him soon,' put in Fairfax, referring to the Ohio Company. 'You, Lawrence, need to get the new man invested in our little venture. A task you shall have little difficulty in accomplishing...'

George glanced at his brother. Lawrence appeared confused.

Fairfax continued in his mildly effeminate manner, 'Since Colonel Lee died, I am pleased to confirm that the shareholders have unanimously agreed that you, Major Washington, will take over the presidency of the Ohio Company.'

'Good heavens, Lordy, that's marvellous news,' said Lawrence, a delighted smile spreading across his face. 'What an honour!'

'To Major Lawrence,' said Fairfax, raising his glass.

George raised his glass. His own smile was forced. He was pleased for Lawrence – proud even – of course he was. But Lawrence's star seemed ever in the ascendancy, leaving George melancholy that his own destiny should remain ever in the shadows. Though Lawrence was his best friend, George envied him all the things he wanted for himself: the primogeniture that had led to an English education, the commission in the army, the family estate, the beautiful wife and daughter... The fruit from the tree always fell into Lawrence's outstretched palm. George took a sip of his sloe gin, its sweet taste soured by the notion that his was but a supporting act in the great play of Lawrence's life.

'Come, let us go indoors and warm ourselves by the fire,' announced Fairfax.

George stood, the low winter sun in his eyes. The assembled crowd all offered his brother their congratulations as they made their way inside. George upended the last of his gin and looked about the genteel surroundings of the Belvoir mansion: its ornamental gardens, cream shingle pathways, lush lawns, Georgian brick geometry, and colonnaded porch. He was, he supposed, lucky to be here. But it wasn't enough to simply be here, he wanted to be a part of it. He was tired of being the poor relation, the man who couldn't return an invitation, the man who lived under the roof of his mother and in the shadow of his brother. This was the New World, where anyone could make of themselves whatever they wanted – not by birthright, but by endeavour. All around he saw men advancing their cause, and yet his progress seemed glacial by comparison. He still needed to work for a living, while these were men of leisure, living off the fat of their assets.

No rank. No woman. *No longer,* he said to himself, as he turned to join the hunting party, his riding boots crunching the shingle underfoot. George would be twenty in two months' time. He made a promise to himself.

'I'll show them what I am capable of.'

***

That evening, with the children in bed and after a fine dinner of cold cuts and hot soup, the stragglers from the hunting party, all shareholders in the Ohio Company, dismissed their women and gathered on the settees around the fireplace in Belvoir's drawing room. Flames licked the logs in the grate, casting a warm, orange light across the assembled faces. In the armchair nearest the hearth was Lawrence, coughing again; his condition always seemed to worsen before he retired to bed. He held his handkerchief over his mouth and stared into the fire's hot coals, deep in thought. Next to him, on the two-seater settee, George's bulk seemed even more oversized beside the slight frame of the middle-aged John Mercer. Mercer swirled the brandy around the bowl of the snifter cupped in his petite hand. George abstained. Never given to suffer the temptations of drink, he was especially cautious when his mood was black, for drink only exacerbated the darkness. Directly opposite the fire, in a wingback leather chair was Fairfax, also with brandy in hand and cigar in mouth. His hairline receding and his cheeks red from fresh air and good living. On a matching settee was the introverted surveyor, Christopher Gist. Nathaniel Chapman, the company's treasurer, returned from relieving his bladder. He helped himself to a brandy from the side table and took the empty armchair on the opposite flank of the fireplace to Lawrence. He belched as he sat down. 'A fine meal, Lordy,' he said, nodding at Fairfax. 'A fine day. Thank you for your hospitality. Never wanting, as always.'

'Gentlemen, following my appointment as president today, for which I remain honoured,' said Lawrence, turning his attention away from the fire to face the men, 'I'll be candid in that I have found our progress to date wanting. Our priority must be to select a suitable location for a fortress. Somewhere with command over the rivers. Given the trouble we've had in clearing the Shenandoah valley of Indians – which is much closer to home – we can't hope to appeal to settlers if they cannot feel the safety of the King's protective blanket.'

In unison, heads nodded at Lawrence's pragmatism.

Lawrence continued, 'We only have one chance to gain a foothold. No sooner have we erected a fort, the French will seek to repel us. So, we must choose our move wisely. Without a working map of the territory, I propose we commission a survey of the Ohio Valley and its rivers.'

George's ears pricked up. Lawrence was about to hand him a meal ticket. The Ohio Valley was an enormous territory. He sat upright, keen for his brother's next words.

'I propose you, Mr Gist, to survey the valley.'

Gist's eyes widened and a smile spread across his face, exposing the missing teeth in his lower gum.

'You can start tomorrow,' said Lawrence. 'One hundred and fifty pounds should be sufficient to cover your expenses and compensate you for your time.'

George couldn't believe his ears. *What is he playing at?* Lawrence had just handed a slug of company revenue to a man outside the family. George was a more-than-capable surveyor. He made no attempt to hide the disappointment that fell heavy on his face.

'Gist, I want you to map the rivers and the topography,' Lawrence went on. 'Then separate these into smaller maps, so we can divide the land into plots. Make notes. List the advantages pertaining to each plot, such as access to wood, soil condition, rock, defence, wildlife. Be specific. The more detail we have, the more we can charge. People will need to be given certainties so they may be confident to move out so far west.'

George closed his eyes and tilted his head back. He could have done this. Done it very well, excellently even. It was too much. He stood up and left the room.

An hour later, he stormed in unannounced to Lawrence's room.

'Forgive me, Anne,' he said, silencing her gasp.

Lawrence, undressed, sat on the edge of the bed.

'Brother, what in damnation? Gist? You favour him over me?' exclaimed George. His voice may have been hushed to prevent others from hearing, but his frown and outstretched arm suggested he wished to shout his remonstrations. Lawrence shook his head and began to cough.

Anne protested, 'George, please, it's late...'

'No, Anne. Tell me, Lawrence, why Gist? Do you think him more capable than me? The man's a brute.'

Lawrence met his brother's fierce eyes. 'George, it's too dangerous – the Indians will trade your scalp for wampum, the French...'

'I've dealt with Indians before.'

'Not like the ones in Ohio...'

'Pah! I may be your baby brother, but I'm not a bloody child. I am more than capable-'

'George, you had malaria this year, you're in no state to...'

'Poppycock, Lawrence!' replied George. His voice grew louder.

'George. No – Gist is going, and that's the last I'll say on the matter.'

'Enough,' interrupted Anne. 'George, your brother is tired and ill. Leave us.'

George left, slamming the door, sending a loud bang through the quiet, dark corridors of the Fairfax house.

Damn family! Cursing them, he stomped back to his room.

1751

13

May 2nd, 1751
Neumann Plantation

Viktor had no desire to get out of bed. Today, they were felling another oak tree to make staves for this year's hogsheads. Another day's labour, swinging axe blow after axe blow, until the tree succumbed to his blade, at which point his arms would feel like hog fat. For Viktor, the days, weeks, months and years were all merging into one long wasted life. He was twenty now and had all but given up, resigned to a life ruled by his father, who was determined to see him suffer a livelihood he didn't want. Daniel didn't seem troubled by the grinding wheel of their existence, but the more Viktor's thoughts were drawn to an outside world he didn't know or understand, the more he suffered, and the longer and more interminable the day ahead would be.

Daniel began to stir in his bed. Viktor could hear his father pottering about in the room next door. He nudged the shutters open, letting the sunlight seep in. By the orange tint to the daylight and the slant of the shadow cast from the tobacco barn, he reckoned it must be close to seven. He left the shutter ajar and swung his heavy legs out of bed. His ankle itched from a mosquito bite, the first of many this year. They always seemed to prefer the taste of him, leaving his brother untouched.

He pulled on his trousers and linen shirt, both overdue a wash, then tugged the bedsheet covering Daniel and left the room before he could witness his brother's protestations.

His father was kneeling at the fireplace, stirring a cast iron pot of porridge. Neither bid the other good morning.

Viktor took a seat at the table and his father passed him a wooden bowl of steaming porridge oats. Hans joined him and, once he'd yelled for Daniel to come and get his breakfast, they ate in silence. Hans told Viktor to check on the seedlings before joining them by the oak tree he'd already chosen to be felled.

'We've had plenty of rain, they'll be fine,' said Viktor, feeling argumentative.

'Just do as I ask.'

His father insisted he check the seedlings every day. Every morning, he was supposed to trudge into the woods where, in March, they had carefully planted the thousands of tiny tobacco seeds in the sheltered, loamy soil beneath the trees. There they would stay until June, when they would be large enough to transplant into the open fields. These would need to be burned and cleared of weeds since last year's harvest. The weather had been kind, so Viktor was sure the seedlings would be fine. Fed up with the monotony of this daily routine, it had actually been three days since Viktor had last checked them – instead, he would disappear into the woods to check his snares, spy on the female slaves on the neighbouring Fitzbarton plantation or swim in the creek.

With breakfast finished, it was Viktor's turn to wash the bowls. Hans stood and took the saw and axe from beside the door. He and Daniel headed for the oak tree. Once Viktor had finished, he put on his wide-brimmed hat and headed out of the door.

It would have been much easier to have the seedbeds close to the house, he thought, but the ground beyond the ridge overlooking the farmstead was better suited. The air blew clear through, whereas round the house it tended to hang in the depression, liable to cause rot or mould on young seedlings. He climbed the path, past their vegetable garden, over the ridge and into the trees, as he had done a thousand times, daydreaming of a life that lay beyond the confines of their canopy: of men fighting for the country, of young women brimming with unfulfilled desires, of ships that crossed the oceans, of money passing hands. It was a world in which Mason Fitzbarton moved freely, and in which Viktor was denied passage.

Within half a mile, he arrived at the first of the seedbeds. Viktor stopped with a jolt. Something was wrong. The seedlings, still only measuring a few inches tall, were dull, their leaves had lost their vibrant green sheen. Viktor frowned and hurried his approach. Crouching down, he inspected a seedling. Its leaf was pitted with small pox-like scars. The next seedling was the same. And the next. His eyes were drawn to a small movement. He nudged a seedling in front of him. Climbing the stem of the plant was a tiny flea beetle. No bigger than a ladybird, its menacing black shell shimmered green as it climbed the stalk, on its way to devour more leaves. Viktor's heart thumped in his chest. He looked about the seedlings and his skin began to tingle with fear. Everywhere he looked, he saw flea beetles. An army of them devouring the crop. He skirted round the seedbeds. They were riddled with the critters. Though it had only been three days, in that time a plague had taken hold. The bed was too far gone to be salvaged. He broke into a run to check the next bed, a hundred yards to the east, hoping beyond hope that the beetles hadn't made it that far. Otherwise, they were ruined.

***

An anxious-looking Hans knelt down to inspect his tobacco seedlings. A flea beetle landed on his hand. He crushed it between his forefinger and thumb. Panic set in as he scanned the scarred leaves of the seedlings, tightly packed together in their seedbeds.

I don't understand... He and Daniel had burned the ground before the planting, destroying the larvae in the soil. And yet they were infested – not just one bed, but three out of four. It didn't make any sense.

He turned to face Viktor, whose head was stooped in shame. 'Tell me you checked these yesterday?'

Viktor's lips twisted.

As Viktor struggled for words, Hans closed his eyes and took a deep breath to control the rage that swelled in his belly. He wanted to thrash the boy, but the reprimands would have to wait.

'You boys go back to the house. Fetch some buckets of soapy water and come straight back.'

The boys ran through the trees back to the house, leaving Hans alone. He wiped his eyes on his sleeve as tears began to well. It had been a long and unforgiving journey to this point. His wife, Agatha, had died shortly after giving birth to Daniel, their third child. The eldest, also called Hans, had died at only three months old, an experience so painful, Hans senior had never been the same since. When he'd lost Agatha as well, he couldn't face life as he knew it without her. Ignoring his neighbours' warnings, he'd sold everything he'd ever owned – which wasn't much – to pay his part-fare to the New World, in the hopes of creating a new life. His young boys had survived the crossing. On landing in Norfolk, Virginia, he'd indentured himself, then endured seven long years before finally earning his freedom. That so prized state, in which one hoped for so much, but he soon learned that freedom brought problems entirely of its own. He'd worked night and day making hogsheads and had raised enough capital to buy his own smallholding of twenty acres. The land's former owner, an elderly planter, had also shared a dislike of Fitzbarton and hadn't wanted his land to end up as part of Fitzbarton's plantation. On his death, the small estate had been divided between his three sons, one of whom was wayward and soon fell into debt. Hans had swooped in and bought his share. For the first time in his life, Hans owned a tract of dirt from which he was determined to craft a living.

But now it all hung in the balance. If this crop failed, without money he'd be at the mercy of their own subsistence. He could borrow money to support the family, but he'd seen many a smallholder fall deeper into debt as crops failed. He'd spent seven years at the whim of another man and had no desire to return to such an uncertain existence. As he knelt in the dirt, he realised for the first time that to lose what he'd travelled the ocean and worked so hard for would be worse than never having attained it.

Resigned, he began plucking out seedlings that were too far gone. The boys returned with pails of soapy water. Hans tested it with his fingers. Satisfied, he removed his shirt, then dipped the sleeve in the water and began carefully wiping the seedlings. If they were gentle enough not to damage the plants, thorough enough not to miss a spot, and if the mixture of soap and water was sufficiently balanced, they stood a chance. The boys followed suit, slowly drowning the flea beetles in suds. In a few days, they would know if they had a crop, and a means to make it through the year.

That evening, all three of them slumped into their chairs, too tired to light a cooking fire. They had cleaned two of their four seedbeds by hand. Conscious of losing the light, and with time being of the essence, they'd simply doused the third bed, tipping the suds straight from the bucket.

'Viktor, tomorrow at sunrise you ride to the store to pick up some more soap as soon as they open.'

Viktor grunted his agreement.

'If you can be trusted,' continued Hans, 'to actually do as I ask?' It was the first time he'd referred to Viktor's neglect of his duties since the discovery of the flea beetles.

Viktor said nothing, knowing the scolding was now due.

'That's why we check things. Every day. Whether we think we need to or not. If you had found those bugs three days earlier, then we…'

Viktor was tired. His mistake was obvious, the lesson was self-evident. 'Yes, Father, you are right,' he snapped.

'You've put our survival at risk, because of your idleness,' he shouted. 'One day you'll have a family of your own and maybe then you'll understand that a man has duties to perform, or his family suffer.'

'How am I supposed to have a family?' Viktor protested. 'All I do is toil in your fields. When am I ever going to meet a woman and have children?'

Hans grew fearful of what he might do to Viktor if his juvenile provocation continued. 'You're still too much of a child to attract the attention of any sensible woman.'

'I could be the most handsome man in the colonies and no woman is ever going to notice me here!'

'Did either of you notice the dead tobacco leaf amongst our seedlings?' Daniel asked suddenly.

Hans frowned; his attention had been entirely focused on saving the crop. The forest could have been on fire and he would not have noticed.

Daniel continued, 'I remember thinking at the time that it was odd to see a mature leaf amongst the seedlings.'

Hans sat upright. 'Somebody could have smuggled a leaf covered in beetles into the seedbed, knowing they would soon migrate to the young seedlings.'

'Why would anyone do that?' said Viktor dismissively.

'It's possible.' Daniel shrugged.

Hans clicked his fingers as the idea took shape. 'It was Fitzbarton. He's the only one with a grudge against us.'

'Or maybe,' said Viktor, his tone sarcastic, 'here's a novel idea; perhaps the leaf was blown in by the wind!'

'No. This has the hallmarks of Fitzbarton's doing.'

'That's absurd,' Viktor laughed. 'He's got better things to do than to go prowling around in the night with beetles in his pockets! Father, you are an idiot.'

'Why would our seedbeds succumb at once?' Hans demanded. 'We burned the soil. They must have been introduced! It's Fitzbarton. I know it.'

'Let's say you're right – instead of just paranoid and obsessed. Why would he have cause? Is it because you went out of your way and brought land next to his, just to prove that you could?'

Hans leapt to his feet and punched Viktor square on the nose. The cartilage crunched under the weight of his fist. Viktor, knocked out of his chair, jumped to his feet, blood streaming from his nose. Daniel leapt up to restrain him as he made towards their father.

Hans avoided his son's glare and returned to his seat, shame flooding through him.

Fists clenched, Viktor calmed himself. It was time to be the bigger man. He took a deep breath. His body was trembling, but his words were steady. 'Your theory says more about you than it does Fitzbarton, Father.'

The words stung. Their eyes met.

'He's devious as a snake,' said Hans. 'You're too blinded by his wealth to see it.'

'Listen to yourself, Father.' Viktor's expression was one of pity. 'You're pathetic.'

Hans sprung back up to his feet. Years of toil had got him his independence, the freedom to do as he chose – now it was all risked by his son's negligence. The boy should be thrashed within an inch of his life. He pointed a shaking finger at Viktor. 'If you'd done as I told you,' he shouted, 'none of this would have happened! Wouldn't surprise me to learn you're in cahoots with him! Did he put you up to this?'

Viktor pushed past Daniel, squaring up to his father. 'It's my fault for not checking the seedlings, but to accuse me of conspiring to starve us off our own land is – is – it's bloody madness, Father! If that's what you think of me...' Viktor's face contorted in confusion and hurt. All his life, he'd slaved on his father's farm, and now *this*? He spat at his father's feet, then turned and left the room, slamming the bedroom door. He gathered his scant belongings: clothes, knife, razor and hairbrush, stuffing them into a hessian sack.

The door opened behind him and Daniel entered the room.

'What are you doing, Vik?'

'I'm leaving. I'm not suffering this for another minute. If you've got any sense, you should too.'

Daniel shook his head. 'Father wouldn't manage here on his own.'

'That's up to you, Dan.' Viktor swung the sack over his shoulder and walked out of the bedroom, past his father, and out of the door.

He stepped out into the warm Virginia evening. He was free of it all. With nowhere to go.

14

The first that Mason Fitzbarton knew of the dawning of a new day was the ache across his forehead, his parched mouth, and an erection that pressed against his Egyptian cotton bedsheets. Last night had been the same as so many others; it had started out civil. He and Mary had taken a small supper of biscuits, cheese and bacon, and washed it down with four bottles of wine. Now, he rolled over onto his back and cursed himself for his latest overindulgence. His body was weary of this familiar morning routine, his soul heavy with regret for the succession of seemingly minor, but poor choices that each day conspired for him to start the next in a state so utterly physically and mentally disadvantaged.

His head cushioned on the plump goose-feather pillows, he glanced around the bedroom. The light of a fine spring morning poured through the large window; the heavy velvet curtains were still ajar. The cherubs, grapes and wheat sheaves carved into the uprights of his four-poster bed towered over him, supporting a luxurious tapestry. The lace curtains that should have enclosed the bed to keep the mosquitos at bay had been left invitingly open. Yesterday's clothes were strewn across the floor, discarded in a hurry before his drunken body had lurched the final few yards to slumber, relying on the most primary of instincts. At least he'd managed to undress, he consoled himself as he stared unseeingly at the fine fabrics, imported from Europe, that he'd taken such pride in. They were now cast aside like rags. Grace would put them in their proper place in the mahogany wardrobe.

The thought of Grace, the negro housemaid, put evil urges in his body. The trouble with negroes was that they were always available to him; a daily temptation that he was forced to battle and overcome.

Mason closed his eyes and took a deep breath. He faced another choice. He couldn't go through the day with this craving unpurged. He could end his suffering within two minutes, or he could do the right thing. His hand begged for permission to reach for his manhood. He refused to be reduced to the humiliation of masturbating like an adolescent. Today, he would break the self-inflicted cycle of disappointment. He swung the bedsheets clear and prized himself out of bed, took a sip of water from the glass on his bedside table, and followed his jockum's lead to his wife's room.

Bright light crept around the edges of the curtains, affording Mason's bleary eyes some relief as he entered her dim chamber. It was light enough to see by, but dark enough to cover the embarrassment of making his carnal visit. Unlike him, she'd managed to pull her curtains to. Mason was continually perplexed by her capacity to function when he'd matched her drink for drink: she'd folded her clothes, emptied her bladder, washed her face. She, the architect of his daily downfall, set the pace, and yet slept soundly like a babe in a crib. At one time, he had loved her devoutly.

Though Mason crept across the room, she was woken by the creaking floorboards.

'What do you want?' she asked, her eyes still closed.

'My wife.'

She grunted.

Mason lifted the sheets and mounted the bed.

'Go away, Mason.' Mary rolled over to turn her back to him.

Mason cuddled up to his wife's soft body. Once a well-proportioned thing of beauty, life's kindnesses had been cruel; the overindulgences of good living had left her thrumpy. It was not a condition that aroused Mason's taste.

But today, he couldn't afford to be so choosy. His clammy skin pressed against her warmth. The stale smell of wine hung in the air. The tip of his prick prodded against her backside.

'Get that thing away from me, Mason.' She swung her arm behind her and pushed against him.

'I'll be quick.'

'No!' she snapped. 'I'm sleeping.'

'No, you're not.'

'Because you just woke me up!'

Mason's embarrassment turned to anger, rummaging between the sheets.

'Get off me!' she shrieked, elbowing him in the ribs.

Mason grunted in pain and his temper flared. He grabbed her as she tried to squirm away.

'Why not? We always—'

'Leave me alone. How dare you come in here—'

Mason ignored her protestations. This was his house and he'd do as he pleased. And after all, it was her drinking that so often caused him to wake in such an unsettled state. He wasn't prepared to live like this anymore. He would take his satisfaction. He gripped her forearms behind her back and used his legs to pin hers down. As she thrashed to escape his clutches, he pressed her head into the pillow, muffling her complaints. He hated that she brought this out in him, so she ought to face the consequences of her behaviour.

He prodded himself between her buttocks but she wriggled defiantly as he tried to thread the needle. Releasing her head, he raised his hand and brought it down in a stinging slap across her cheek. Her cries were muffled against the pillow.

'Lie still, or there's more where that came from!' he ordered.

Her resistance ended abruptly. His relief began. She lay prone while he thrust his hips. Speeding up, it wasn't long before he groaned, spilling himself inside her. Finished, he climbed off and left her to cry alone.

The comfort of his release was tempered by the shame he now felt for what he'd done. It had been six months since they'd last taken a turn among the cabbages, that time consensually. Mary could not fall pregnant. For all the times they'd tried, God had never blessed them with children. His subsequent impregnation of a negro slave had determined that the issue didn't lie with Mason.

He sat at the breakfast table reading the Virginia Gazette, hair brushed and tied back, clothes immaculate, his puffy eyes the only trace of his excesses. The newspaper carried the usual array of stories: runaway slaves and sailors, a ferry crossing out of commission, a sighting of pirates on the edge of the Chesapeake.

Grace brought him a china plate with two fried eggs and cornbread for dipping. He asked for another cup of tea, and as she left the dining room, Mary appeared, stiffly walking past Mason and taking a seat at the far end of the polished walnut table. He glanced up and saw beyond the candelabra that her head was turned deliberately away from him. Arms folded, chin held high, she stared out of the window. Mason had seen this routine before. *Suit yourself, woman.*

Grace returned and placed his tea down in front of him. She scuttled up to the far end of the table in her simple grey dress and white apron. 'Good morning, ma'am. What is you wanting to eat, Mrs Fitzbarton?'

'Nothing!'

Grace scurried out of the room.

'I've lost my appetite.' Mary picked up her silverware and slammed it down on the table.

Unwilling to indulge her, Mason's eyes shifted to the oil portrait of his father, Mason Fitzbarton I, hanging behind Mary at the far end of the dining room. His father's ever-judgemental gaze rested on his son. Pictured with his leg raised on a fallen tree trunk, his hands pressed into his hips, the eye was drawn to his loins. Painted in the classical style and surrounded by hunting dogs he'd never owned, he was depicted as the archetypal English gentleman: refined and powerful. He may be in heaven, but Mason still felt his father's presence in the house. *'You've made your bed, son, now you'll lie in it,'* he would say of his current predicament. And lie in it, Mason would. For all Mary's less savoury traits, they had made a vow before God.

Mason finished his breakfast. Not a further word was spoken.

***

After breakfasting, he donned his wide-brimmed hat, checked his appearance in the hallway mirror, and went outside to supervise his plantation. Tobacco too was a demanding mistress: every few years she required fresh ground, so woods had to be cleared. What Mason didn't know about tobacco wasn't worth knowing and he'd learned it all from his late father. Once established, it was a hardy enough plant, but in germination, it was a delicate seedling, whose success depended on attending to the finest details. You could never leave it to the negroes. Their neglectful manner would see your season abandoned.

Mason knew he needed to diversify, especially as most of the family land had now been cleared and was close to exhaustion. The plantation's best days were behind it, unless Mason changed things. He had reserves; he could stomach a bad harvest – even two – but he felt drawn to new commodities. His land could sustain wheat and pork, both of which were in frequent demand in the local market, unlike tobacco which had to make the dangerous voyage to England. Sugar was the most lucrative of the New World commodities, but it required the Caribbean climate. It was now in such sufficient demand from the New England distilleries that money could be made shipping it up the Atlantic coastline to Boston, rather than venturing capital on the riskier ocean voyage to England. He yearned for his own ship. He'd be able to move cargo at reduced cost, and insulate himself from the vagaries of the tobacco harvest.

But practicalities aside, he was a third-generation planter. Other families who'd arrived in Virginia alongside his grandfather had amassed enough wealth to finance ships. His father would have expected him to be keeping pace with their rivals. If he didn't get into shipping, Mason feared he would be left behind – permanently. One day, his portrait would adorn the dining room wall, but precluded from having children, what would people say of him after he was gone? *That's Mason Fitzbarton, he married badly, squandered his inheritance and his estate was subsumed by other, more enterprising, planters.'* He may be stuck with barren Mary, but he would not countenance being the black sheep to end the family line. This fear ate away at him during his rare periods of indolence.

His ambitions would take cash. Lots of it. And connections. Which meant time away. What he needed first was white men, willing and capable of attending to matters here. Yet any white man worth his salt worked for himself. There was no shortage of convicts and vagrants, dumped out of England, who – although capable of whipping the negroes snatched from Africa – were unreliable, untrustworthy and didn't have the first clue about the crop on which his livelihood depended.

Mason walked past the workers' accommodation. The sunny Virginia morning was interrupted by the metallic thud of the blacksmith's hammer pounding away in the foundry. He caught a whiff of smoke from the furnace. In this simple brick building were the only two white men he employed: a carpenter and a smith, but their talents were wasted overseeing negroes. Left unsupervised, the slaves were so slow as to be overtaken by snails. To say nothing of the fact they dangerously outnumbered the whites on the plantation. Mason wondered if Mary drank to quiet the fear that lay dormant, lurking in their backyard. Any unfamiliar noise in the dark of night plagued him with nightmares of a slave uprising. It wouldn't have happened in his grandfather's day, but over time, as plantations had grown more powerful and their competing owners more ambitious, it was the Africans who'd borne the brunt of their masters' ambitions. In the passing decades, matters had grown ever worse. One was well advised to sleep with one eye open.

Skilled workers were much sought-after, and their lack was the greatest impediment to the prosperity of the colonies. Mason would have to go to great lengths to find someone who knew his Oronoco from his sweet-scented. For the more he dirtied his own fingers, the more he neglected to rub shoulders with the right people. Entry to opportunities like the Ohio Company kept passing him by.

As he made his way towards the woods where his delicate seedlings germinated, a formation of ducks flew overhead towards the coast.

'Boss, boss!'

Mason turned to see Charlie, one of his better negroes, running across the lawn towards him.

'What is it?'

Charlie fought to recover his breath. His bare feet were dusty. 'Mr Mason, sir, I seen the older Neumann boy on the road. I found him sleeping by Dunn's wood. He tell me he headed for upriver, looking for work.'

'Fetch my horse.'

Mason ran back to the house to don his riding boots.

Moments later, he was cantering towards the road. It may have been an ungentlemanly sight, but to ride one's beast in haste through the trees was a treat not to be missed. In a place where life's pace was governed by the passing of the seasons, the ebb and flow of the tide and the punishing heat of the sun, cause to act in a hurry was the surest way to get one's blood flowing. Mason's worries lifted as the road ahead took his attention, leaning into corners, ducking under low branches, avoiding potholes.

He caught up with Viktor Neumann by the duck pond before the turning to Colchester. Easing to a trot until he'd drawn level, he saw that Viktor was unshaven. His blonde hair was dishevelled, and his homespun clothes were creased and dusty.

'Viktor, you look like you've crawled out of a ditch,' said Mason, regaining his breath.

Viktor glanced up but carried on walking.

'You look troubled, Viktor.'

Viktor stopped in his tracks and faced Mason. 'Did you tamper with our seedbeds?'

Mason frowned. 'How dare you accuse me of impropriety! I resent the accusation. You forget yourself, young man.'

Viktor's shoulders slumped. 'I apologise, Mr Fitzbarton, sir, only my father put the thought in my head.'

'What thought?'

'A plague of beetles appeared on our seedbeds.'

Mason nodded but said nothing, leaving Viktor to continue.

'We found them yesterday…'

'And now you are travelling with all your worldly belongings on your back?'

'My father and I have trouble seeing eye to eye nowadays. He's convinced you did it.'

'And you disagreed with him?'

'I reckon you had more pressing matters.'

'Indeed. Viktor, your father is a good man, but he's suspicious by nature. Quite why he thinks I should wish him ill, I don't know. But you vouched for my character, and for that I am grateful.'

Viktor shrugged and walked on.

'That I should be the cause of this dispute pains me, Viktor. How can I make this right?'

Viktor stopped, his face contorted with dejection.

'Where are you headed?' Mason asked.

'In search of work…'

'What manner of work?'

'Anything,' Viktor sighed.

'Well, there's no need to travel. I'll find you work. There are a hundred matters on my plantation competing for the attention and intelligence of a young ambitious man like you.'

'My father would never…'

'Viktor, you've left home. Unless I'm mistaken, the only person with a stake in your destiny is you. Poppycock to your father's wishes. Come and oversee my negroes, I'll pay you handsomely. I'll teach you how to run an estate.'

Mason could see the lad wavering under the force of his persuasion. *I know just the blow to strike this nail home.* 'I make you no promises, Viktor, but my wife and I are not blessed with children. As I age, more and more my thoughts turn to the legacy of my enterprises. Nothing would give me greater satisfaction than grooming the heir that I have never been blessed with, to take over the running of my affairs once I'm gone.'

Viktor's eyes bulged. Mason could see him thinking about it, but the lad shook his head.

'Have you a better offer?'

'No.'

'Come then. Join me. We'll live well. We'll prosper and grow rich together.'

A smile spread across Viktor's face. 'Very well, Mr Fitzbarton, I accept your generous offer.'

'Excellent. Better the devil you know,' he winked. 'Let us return and get you some clothes befitting of your role.'

Together, they headed back to the Fitzbarton plantation.

Nothing in this life happens by accident. Every providence is the result of prior conception. Splendid work, Mason, he said to himself.

15

Sylvia sneezed as she swirled Mr Benson's and Mr Somerton's laundry around the warm water in the copper kettle. Even after two years, the smell of the stale urine added to the laundry water still made her eyes stream. Every morning, come rain or shine, she could be found in the backyard to the house, warming the clothes that had soaked overnight above burning coals. Today it was the turn of the bedsheets. She fished out the sheets on her wooden pole and transferred them to the larger wooden bucket full of soapy water. She applied extra soap to the stains then kneaded the sheets on her board, forcing out the soapy water, taking with it the sweat, semen and blood left by her two masters. Her fingers were red raw from performing this routine each day.

She took her wooden battledore and pounded the laundry, beating the last of the water from it. Today, as so often, she hit it far harder than was necessary. Not in resentment to her employers, who despite their buggery, were decent people. More in frustration with her own existence for she was bored beyond words. The monotony of her daily routines left her weary and worn down. Once the evening meal was cleared away, under the candlelight, Mr Benson forced her to learn numbers and letters. In her time, she had learned to write sentences and perform simple addition and subtraction. It hadn't proved a useful skill. She took no pleasure from reading. She had written two letters to her family, not that they were able to read them. Even then Mr

146

Benson had delivered them on her behalf so she couldn't fraternise with her former gang. 'You've been delivered from temptation,' he'd explained. She missed them all and worried for their welfare. Mags would be of childbearing age by now. Jacob's baby would be a toddler. No doubt Rebecca would still be whining; Sylvia even missed being angry at her sister-in-law. But Mr Benson had made it very clear: she was not to abscond.

Despite his preaching the freedom of God's religion, he practised a servitude that wouldn't have looked out of place in a workhouse or prison. For she was not allowed to leave, other than to collect water, buy groceries or to attend church, in the company of Mr Benson and Mr Somerton. She was never hungry, or especially cold, and she slept well but, increasingly, she longed for a pint of gin, if only to numb the boredom to which she had succumbed. She hadn't cheered at a hanging or a flogging, or pilfered so much as a flower since living under this roof. Occasionally, she daydreamed about Captain Reid, whom she'd never seen again since he'd delivered her into Mr Benson's care. She didn't miss him, as he'd proved a difficult man to like, but when she'd first seen him, she'd been certain she would give herself to him, for reasons she couldn't quite understand. Something about his self-absorbed manner attracted her. Alas, Captain Reid proved to be a mere fleeting fancy, she thought as she doused the coals and hung the laundry to dry.

The ginger cat scurried past her as she entered the house from the rear door; she heard the knocker on the front door. It was unusual for the mollies, as she privately referred to Mr Benson and Mr Somerton, to get visitors. They were out, so whoever was calling would be disappointed. Sylvia gasped as she opened the door and saw her brother Jacob and sister Caroline standing there. She leapt forward and hugged them tightly.

'Hey, sis!'

'How did you find me?'

'I saw him delivering your letter, so I followed him back here. Kept watch on the place until they were out,' explained Jacob.

She was overjoyed to see them. Jacob looked just like himself. Caroline had pox scars on her cheeks.

'You going to invite us in?' asked Caroline.

Sylvia hesitated until she noticed Caroline's brow furrowing.

'Be quick.'

'They won't be back until afternoon. They're at court, they go every month,' said Jacob who had clearly performed inquiries on her masters.

She showed them round the ground-floor rooms. The house took on an air of excitement as she saw it through the eyes of her family. It was harmless, but it was the first illicit thing she'd done in a long time. Her heart quickened from the thrill of it. They stopped in the parlour, where Jacob picked up a clay figurine from the mantelpiece.

'Put that down,' said Sylvia.

Caroline made herself comfortable on the settee, putting her feet up in a manner that would have made the mollies seethe.

'How's your child?' Sylvia asked Jacob, taking a seat in Mr Benson's chair.

Jacob shook his head. 'Pox.'

'Sorry.'

'Why don't you come and visit us?' asked Caroline, whose previous excitement at seeing her sister seemed to cool.

Sylvia explained the terms under which she lived as a prisoner in this house.

'There's a fortune to be made, we could clear this place out.'

'No,' Sylvia said firmly. The mollies weren't perfect but they had placed their trust in her. She wasn't willing to betray them.

'You've changed,' remarked Caroline.

It had been so long since she'd seen her family that only now did Sylvia appreciate the effect that nightly Bible readings and being in the company of devout Methodists had had on her.

'You should come and see us,' said Jacob.

'I can't.'

'We'll come and see you then.'

A shadow passed the window, and she heard the voices of Mr Benson arguing with Mr Somerton.

'Quick, they're back early!'

Caroline leapt up off the settee and Sylvia shooed them down the corridor and into the kitchen. The front door shut; the mollies continued their heated conversation in the hallway.

Sylvia silently opened the door to the rear yard.

'What's that smell?' she heard Mr Benson asking.

'Quick, out,' she whispered, following them and pulling the door to behind her. 'Over the wall.'

Jacob snatched the damp sheet from the line and folded it up, placing it over the shards of broken glass and bottles that had been set into the top of the wall surrounding the backyard. He leapt up.

'You coming with us?'

Sylvia was tempted, but not ready to make a snap decision. 'Go. Quick. I go to the market on Saturdays and Wednesdays,' she added.

He nodded and heaved himself over the wall. Sylvia gave Caroline a leg up and she too cleared the wall. Sylvia yanked at the bedsheet, which snagged on a shard of glass, tearing the cotton. Mr Benson appeared at the back door as Sylvia unfurled the folded sheet. Her heart was beating like a racehorse.

'Oh, hello,' she said, trying to look calm.

'Is everything all right?'

'Yes. Well, no. I mustn't have pegged this sheet properly. The wind seems to have caught it. I'm afraid it got snagged on the wall. I'll mend it, sir.'

Mr Benson hobbled over and examined the tears in the sheet. He looked her in the eyes. She held his gaze, holding her breath and praying her cheeks wouldn't colour.

'No use crying over spilt milk,' he said eventually.

Sylvia nodded. 'I'm very sorry. I will mend it.'

'Good girl. Here, I bought you an orange.' He walked back inside, leaving her to regain her composure, a damp bedsheet in one hand and an orange in the other. She smiled to herself. She hadn't felt this alive in a long time.

16

George studied his face in the mirror. Such a cruel disease that it should leave a permanent reminder of its presence on the most visible part of the body. He wondered if he would ever be rid of the heavy funk that accompanied his disfigurement. Since recovering from the pox, each time he looked in the mirror, hopeful of some further progress, he was crestfallen at the scabs marring his once pristine face. Would that he were already married; perhaps he'd have been spared the full pain of the humiliation. His mood darkening, he discarded the hand mirror and left the room. It was teatime.

He was relieved to find Lawrence alone, seated in the tropical garden. In the six weeks they'd spent at the house, a succession of guests had passed through. Some also suffered with consumption, hoping that the mild sea air would ease their condition.

'You look better,' said Lawrence, who himself looked gaunt in the afternoon sun. He held a better colour for their stay, but his cheeks were hollow, and his once thick brown hair had turned grey and brittle.

George shrugged as he took a seat at the ornately forged metal table, its paint peeling. 'We came here to get you better, yet it is I who falls ill!'

'Have some tea.'

George poured himself a cup from the pot on the table and refilled Lawrence's. He added three sugars to his brew in the hopes it would lift his spirits.

A gentle breeze softened the sun's heat and freshened the humid air. George enjoyed the smell of salt that blew from the sea. Would he have tired of it, had he been allowed to join the navy, he wondered.

The trip to the Caribbean had done nothing to quieten his anxieties about his future. The people he'd met hadn't been impressed on learning of his career as a surveyor. He'd boasted of the land he'd purchased, but he knew the plantation of which he talked was nothing more than scrub waiting to be cleared. He wondered if his heart was really in it. The sour reality of building a farm from nothing lacked the sweetness of the dream. Last night, he'd dreamed he was a small boy, tall enough to see the feast on the table, but too short to reach for it. He was on the periphery of the wealthy, yet he was a bystander, watching and listening to the grand machinations of others, but too poor to play the game with his own hand. Part of him envied a simple farmhand who knew his station in life and displayed no desire to reach for more, for his life must surely be more contented than George's.

'George, this may seem a strange thing to say, but look upon your smallpox as a gift. What doesn't kill you, makes you stronger.'

'If you have any more gifts, you can keep them!'

Lawrence coughed into his hanky. 'Better to have survived than died from it. When I served out here, we lost six thousand men – not to fighting, but to disease. It was the scourge of our army.' Lawrence's face hung heavy at the memory. 'Six thousand, George, all brave British lads, gone before their time. It sickens me when I think of their suffering, just so a few men in London could continue to enrich themselves by selling slaves to the Spanish. The world's a rotten place.'

George frowned. Lawrence always seemed so proud of his service; he'd never heard him talk with such melancholy about the events in which he'd partaken.

'Trust me, brother,' Lawrence continued, his lungs protesting as he spoke, 'the more illnesses you can survive, the better your chances of a long life.'

Usually, George relished his brother's pearls of wisdom, but he found them unwelcome today.

'Brother, I have made no improvement during our time here,' said Lawrence. 'I think it best we prepare ourselves for the fact I will not accompany you home.'

The birdsong in the garden seemed to quieten.

'We'll stay until you do recover,' George said staunchly.

'Alas, I have responsibilities I am neglecting.' Lawrence held a piece of paper aloft. 'A letter from Anne. She and the baby are doing well. But she writes that we have our new Governor. Robert Dinwiddie. Do you remember him?'

George shook his head.

'Lived in Virginia for a while. Scotsman. Total bastard.'

George smirked.

'He arrived shortly after we departed,' said Lawrence, sipping his tea. 'We need his support for the Ohio Company. All the shareholder funds have been spent, and with Fry still blocking further funds being raised in the House, we need Governor Dinwiddie to veto Fry's plans and secure us treasury funds. Then we can finally build the fort the King stipulated.'

'Couldn't you get money from London? It was the King who issued a land grant, after all.'

'No. The policy is not to spend British taxpayers' money in the colonies. The British public wouldn't wear it; the Tories would make a great play of it, and use it as an opportunity to get back in.'

'That's a bit short-sighted – think of the trade London would gain.' During their time here, George had heard a great many frustrations from the island's gentry. He'd been surprised by the derogatory manner in which the sugar planters referred to London, berating Parliament for not enforcing the laws they created. They lamented the money they wasted greasing the palms of Britain's politicians, only to see colonists from New England sail past their ports to do business with the French, Dutch and Spanish, in direct contravention of the Navigation Acts.

At dinner last night, their host had become very animated, condemning the 'free traders' and haranguing the navy for not enforcing the will of Parliament. George had gone to bed thinking that if the colonists attended Parliament in London, many of their complaints could be addressed.

Bringing George's thoughts back to the Ohio question, Lawrence continued, 'To get this venture off the ground, we've got to do it ourselves, locally. That's the price we pay for not sending taxes to Britain.' Lawrence shrugged. 'So, I need you to go back to Williamsburg – now – and speak to Dinwiddie. Offer him a chance to invest in the Ohio, so he has an incentive to get the funds organised. Then we can build our fort and start selling some land.'

George took a sip of his tea and returned the cup to the saucer. He tried to suppress the indignation he felt as he looked back towards the sand-coloured house that had served as their home.

'What is it?' asked Lawrence.

'Dinwiddie is allowed to invest. Yet you deny me the same opportunity.'

'George, there's a good chance I won't recover from this consumption.'

'Don't say that—'

'Listen, I've made my last Will. Should the worst happen, I've left my shares in the company to you.'

The bright colours of the garden seemed to pale as George looked at his brother, who, having spoken of his own death, suddenly took on a new frailty. *Lawrence is so strong. Nothing has beaten him, ever. No,* George thought, *he'll recover.*

'George, get yourself on the next boat home, but whatever you do, don't tell Dinwiddie or anyone else of my condition. We don't want to spook the horses.'

1752

17

January 25th, 1752
Governor's Mansion, Williamsburg

Two months had passed since Robert Dinwiddie had been obliged to return to Virginia and he was still feeling bitter. His wife Rebecca lay in bed, still asleep, but no less bitter herself. Dinwiddie, dressed only in his nightshirt, stood by the window looking outside at the dawn frost that covered the palace green of the Governor's Mansion. The tree-lined lawn was deserted at this early hour. Like his wife, most of Williamsburg was still sleeping. He sighed at the thought of all the time he'd spent away from home; after a career spent in the colonies, it was seven years since the Scotsman had finally secured himself a post in London and had been able to return to Britain's green and pleasant land. Unfortunately, the death of Colonel Thomas Lee had left Virginia's affairs in the less-than-capable hands of Lewis Burwell. A series of complaints had been dispatched to London, forcing the Earl of Albemarle, the colony's Governor in absentia (who'd never stepped foot on American soil) to make a new appointment. Wanting the affair done with swiftly, the Earl had sought a man experienced in Virginian affairs – thus, a few months later, Dinwiddie and his family were aboard a ship destined for Norfolk with an order signed by the King, instructing him to act as the Governor's Lieutenant.

Now, here he was, aged fifty-nine, many thousands of miles from home, and even further from his long-awaited retirement.

He'd previously spent four years in Virginia, serving on the Governor's council, before returning to London in 1745, so he knew the ropes. It hadn't compared favourably to the seventeen years he'd spent in Bermuda. Island life had been relatively stable. There was something about the sheer quantity of land available on the continent and the boat-loads of people pouring into it that brought out the basest instincts in its inhabitants, as they squabbled over the spoils like starving dogs around a carcass. It was with this notion in mind that he'd decided to compensate himself for the inconvenience of the posting. He'd arrived with one solitary aim: to amass not land, but as much money as he could. If his greed should be the cause of his early return, then so much the better. He intended to hold the Virginians to ransom. Once the General Assembly met in the spring, he'd demand a fee of a pistole for each time he had to use his patent seal. A career spent collecting taxes had accustomed him to being unpopular. The colonists would pay, they'd have no choice. No seal, no standing in court. No title. All it would take was the impatience of one person to relent, and the rest would follow. Satisfied, he scratched an itch on his arse.

The rest of Dinwiddie's morning passed without incident. He composed letters: to the Board of Trade in London, confirming the dire state of the colony's coffers; to his counterpart in Pennsylvania, agreeing to the request for cooperation on dealing with the Indian menace; and to his tailor in London. After lunch, he took a brisk stroll around the town, stopping opposite the Capitol building to see how its rebuilding was progressing. The slaves huddled around a fire. He barked at them that they might feel a good deal warmer if they did some work. Reluctantly, they dragged themselves back to the wooden scaffolding. The brickwork was now above the first-floor windows, and soon the roof could be rebuilt. Dinwiddie hoped it would be completed this year so he could at least carry out his duties in fit and proper surroundings.

During his absence, the House of Burgesses had held a vote to move the Capitol. The colonists had narrowly voted in favour of remaining in Williamsburg, much to the relief of the inhabitants, whose businesses depended on being near the centre of government. Many bribes were said to have been paid to the delegates by the tavern keepers, shopkeepers, and tradespeople of Williamsburg. Following the burning of the Capitol building (whose perpetrators still remained at large), the other towns' landowners had smelled an opportunity to lure away the elected representatives. For lack of a coordinated effort, Williamsburg remained the seat of colonial government. It rather summed up the colonists in Dinwiddie's mind; they couldn't agree on anything. He blamed the absence of a ruling class, with each subject being free to express his will without fear of contradicting his betters. When their interest collided, rather than having a Lord to arbitrate, they were quick to settle their difference using the law. How they might benefit from a spell in the mother country to quell the independence of their spirits, he lamented, as he turned his back on the building site.

Walking back, he was approached by a tall young man carrying a letter.

'Lieutenant Governor, good afternoon. George Washington, how do you do?' he said, his palm outstretched.

'Good day to you, sir,' replied Dinwiddie. Washington did not move, indicating he wanted to talk. He was a thick-set lad with a serious demeanour. Heavy powder couldn't quite conceal the smallpox scars on his face.

'I have here a letter of introduction from my brother, Major Washington.' He offered the letter. 'May I walk with you?'

'Very well,' said Dinwiddie, stuffing the unopened letter in his pocket and fearing his time was about to be wasted.

They engaged in small talk as they passed the neat clapboard properties that ran either side of the cobbled street. George apologised that he and Lawrence had not been here to welcome the Governor on his return to the colony, having set sail for the Caribbean a few days beforehand.

A gust of icy wind swept by as they passed the tavern and walked across the green towards the small brick courthouse. George pulled his longcoat tight across his chest. 'I must have grown soft in the Caribbean sun,' he remarked.

'You didn't come find me to complain about the weather, Washington. Speak your mind. What is it you want?'

'Indeed. Thank you. It concerns the affairs of the Ohio Company. Are you aware of my brother's venture?'

'Tell me,' said Dinwiddie, concealing what he'd already heard.

Washington explained about the King's land grant, the opportunities for enrichment, land speculation, control of the beaver trade, the importation of European settlers. When Dinwiddie paused to turn right towards the Governor's Mansion, he glanced at the young man who, sensing his time was nearly up, looked awkward.

'There are rival schemes,' Washington said quickly, 'mere imitations that don't have the King's blessing. Joshua Fry's Loyal Company of Virginia, for instance – well, my brother believes the colony's effort would be best served by concentrating our expansion through one effort.'

'His, presumably?'

'Naturally.'

'You're probably right,' said Dinwiddie as they arrived at the mansion gates. He carried on walking, leaving Washington behind.

'May I come in?'

'No.' Dinwiddie smiled to himself, the gravel crunching under his feet like the ticking of a clock.

'But, sir, the colony depends on it!' Washington called after him.

Dinwiddie turned and regarded the young man. 'I expect it does.' He walked up the steps and reached for the door handle.

'But you too, sir, could prosper!' pleaded Washington.

Dinwiddie grinned and turned back to face the young man, who looked forlornly desperate at the risk of losing his audience. Young men were so easy to tease.

'There's a tidy fortune to be made,' Washington went on.

'Tell your brother to come to supper tonight and tell me what his Ohio Company can do for me.'

'But, sir – he can't.'

'Too bad.'

'He's ill. Well, recovering, actually, in the Caribbean. But I'd be delighted to attend in his place.' Lawrence had forbidden him from disclosing his infirm condition, but George sensed opportunity, for once, for himself.

'Very well. Six o'clock. Bring your wife, if you wish.'

A relieved smile broke across the young man's face, creasing the blanc. 'I'll be unaccompanied. Thank you.'

***

George arrived at six o'clock on the dot. He'd donned his finest silk waistcoat and linen shirt. Powdered his hair and tied it back, then reapplied the blanc to his face. His excitement at dining with the Lieutenant Governor was tempered by the fact he still had no stake in the Ohio venture and had already betrayed Lawrence's wishes. But he resolved it was for the good of the scheme, for he couldn't have risked being passed over. Nor, he later consoled himself, could he begin an important relationship on a lie, not even for Lawrence.

A footman led him indoors, beneath the union flags that adorned the candlelit hallway. George was grateful for the dim lighting as Mrs Dinwiddie greeted him and he followed her through to the dining room. She was a short, grey-haired woman, at least ten years her husband's junior, who'd gone to some trouble to hide her accent. George suspected she was of Germanic descent but thought better than to ask. The Lieutenant Governor stood by the marble fireplace, cradling a brandy as he stared into the flames flickering in the grate.

'Washington, good evening!'

A negro butler brought George a glass of wine, at which point he was peppered with questions from Mrs Dinwiddie, who obviously didn't share her husband's disdain for pleasantries:

'Where were you born? To whom? Have you travelled? Are you betrothed? Why not? What do you think of the Gin Act?' Then it turned to politics. 'Who holds your sympathies, the Tories or Whigs?'

George did his best to deflect her questions, lest he made plain his ignorance on the subjects she mentioned. He suddenly felt out of his depth in such esteemed company. He slurped his wine, before offering a bland reply, 'I simply wish to serve the colony in whatever way I can.'

'Since Parliament runs the country, not the King, do you not think colonists should have the vote?' asked Dinwiddie, sensing his unease and finally joining the conversation, as they were seated for dinner at the small mahogany table under the chandelier.

George considered what might constitute an appropriate answer to the question, as a negro appeared and took the napkin from the table and placed it over his lap. 'I suppose, until now, I've been interested in affairs closer to home. For the challenges facing us in Virginia are different to those in London, are they not?'

Dinwiddie took a large swig of wine and held the glass aloft for a refill. 'Spoken like a true colonist: colloquial in outlook, unwilling to contend with the politics of the globe.'

George suppressed a wave of irritation and instead tilted his head. 'Please, if it isn't too tiresome, educate me.'

A servant girl served a slice of turkey breast to Mrs Dinwiddie, and her husband leant back to allow her easy access to his plate. 'Ships, Washington, be they Spanish, French, Dutch, Portuguese – English even – can travel to the farthest reaches of the globe. A globe, which we know to be spherical, and as European trade, technology and influence spread, the affairs of any given nation are not contained by their own borders, or even those of their neighbours. It's a scramble for who controls the whole world. In this age in which we find ourselves, it is he who controls the sea, who then controls the land. And it will remain as such until our scientific pursuits afford us the gift of flight. For now, mastery of the seas dictates who prospers, and in that at least, England has the better of France.'

George smiled and Dinwiddie continued, 'I predict a war that will engulf the globe, such that no corner of the world remains unaffected, as the European powers attempt to assert their dominance over one another.'

'Oh, do be quiet about your war, Robert,' said Mrs Dinwiddie.

'Are we not perpetually at war with our rivals?' asked George.

'Yes, although these are mere skirmishes. What I foresee will be an all-consuming global contest, with a nation's full energies mobilised to defeat the enemy.'

'So pessimistic a view for our enlightened times?' tested George, beginning to find his feet.

'Man is always a base creature, Washington, no matter how many smart clothes he may wear. His instincts are to covet and take from his enemy. The winner's spoils will be unlimited – an empire that will make Rome look like a village fair.'

'Rule Britannia!' George raised his glass, 'May I presume to make a toast? May we forever rule the seas.'

Mrs Dinwiddie remained still. Her husband raised his glass and clinked it with George's.

'Which is why you'll never get a vote in Britain's parliament.'

George's confusion must have been self-evident as Dinwiddie continued.

'Fifty years from now, there will be as many of the King's subjects living in his colonies as there will be Britons in the homeland. No parliament would entrust its matters to a population that's dispersed across the world. To say nothing of the practicalities of counting a vote. It would completely derail Parliament's political agenda, especially when many of them are increasingly of alien heritage. Besides, the British people are at heart as parochial as you colonists. On the rare occasions that they have work, warm food in their bellies, beer in their tankard, tea in their cup, perhaps a pouch of tobacco too, they want for little else. All of life's small comforts, for small-minded people.'

'So, why go to the trouble of ruling the seas?' It had dawned on George that asking questions of his host, kept him from having to contribute his opinions. Instead, he could play the keen student.

'To stop anyone else from ruling the seas. And to make certain that our sugar, tea and tobacco are brought home safely.'

George took a sip of his wine and considered Dinwiddie's words. He'd never really thought about events on such a large scale, or rationalised by higher powers. He wasn't sure if he agreed with the old man's point of view. Virginia without Britain was unthinkable, yet he recalled the late Colonel Lee had made a similar prediction during his party.

'So, the war and the world you've described... I don't understand, how does it end?'

'Same way everything ends, George: badly. I've spent a lifetime in government. Trust me, none of it works, and if it does, then not for long, and never for everyone. This world, this land, our country, our government – it's all flawed. All one can truly do is enrich oneself on the way up, such that you might enjoy some proper comfort from the spoils, when others are choking on the stink.'

'Mmm.' George found such cynicism as unsettling as it was fascinating. He thought it about time he attended to the reason for his visit. 'Well, the subject of enriching brings me nicely to the matter of the Ohio Company. To comply with the King's grant, we need funds for materials and manpower to build a fort.'

'Then raise them. It's your company.'

George was taken aback. 'But, you see, it is the colony that will prosper, so surely she should bear the burden...'

'Are you claiming that you and your fellow shareholders are doing this as a charitable act for Virginia? Pull my other leg, Washington. It's your venture. You want the reward, you pay.'

'Alas, we also need to ensure the Indians are voluntarily bound to our will,' George pressed on. 'We fear they will not honour any agreement unless it is backed by the colony's government. Plus, they'll be expecting gifts.'

'Mr Washington, I dare say you and I could sit here for the rest of the night while you regale me with the difficulties facing your company. You want my assistance. Yes?'

George nodded.

'Right, what have you to offer me?'

George hesitated.

Dinwiddie leaned in and met George's uncertain gaze with his hard brown eyes. 'You want my help – give me a stake, make me a shareholder.'

'Oh, I see,' said George. Why should Dinwiddie get a share, when he didn't have one himself? Finally, 'I will speak to my brother. Currently, the articles restrict shareholders to sixteen people, perhaps...'

'Perhaps I'm wasting my time dining with you, if you can't act with autonomy?'

'No, no, we'll – I mean – *I* will make an exception. The stake is two hundred pounds...'

Dinwiddie shook his head. George fell silent. The shares weren't his to sell.

'The stake for me, son, is my cooperation. I want a share equal to yours. And I won't pay a penny for it. Only then will you have my ear and the full weight of my assistance.'

'Well, that won't cost you anything.'

'That's the spirit! Now we're getting somewhere.'

'No – I mean, I don't have a shareholding yet!'

'Ha!' Dinwiddie leaned back in his chair. 'Some brother you have! Gets you doing his bidding, but doesn't give you a piece of the pie! You poor bastard!'

George felt his cheeks colour.

'Older brothers!' quipped Dinwiddie, shaking his head. 'I had one too. He got the titles, the estates, and I got sent to the far side of the world. To serve in stinking heat, surrounded by mosquitos, niggers and their diseases. You need to sort that.'

'He's bequeathed his shares to me.'

'Dying, is he?'

'No! Goodness, no. Not at all,' said George, backtracking.

'Take it from me, George, if you want something, take it. Don't let your elders or your betters determine your fate.'

George nodded. Dinwiddie seemed sincere; he too must have suffered similar frustrations.

Dinwiddie smirked. 'Anyway, enough about you. If your brother wants my help, I want shares. Can you arrange that, George?'

George scratched his chin.

'If not, you can leave before dessert,' said Dinwiddie.

'Robert! Don't be so cruel,' said his wife.

'Well, if the boy's been entrusted to do the company's dirty work, then he can be entrusted to make some decisions. Otherwise, there's no point us entertaining him, is there?'

Don't dither any more – act, George urged himself. 'May I propose another toast?'

Dinwiddie shrugged.

'To welcome you, Lieutenant Governor, to the board of the Ohio Company.'

They raised their glasses and upended the contents down their gullets.

'Have your lawyer send the paperwork here, at your expense, along with a list of your queries. Splendid work. Now, that's done, let's get drunk.'

'In which case, I will excuse myself,' said Mrs Dinwiddie. 'It's been lovely to meet you, Master Washington.'

George, relieved to have somehow navigated his way through his faux pas, stood to acknowledge Mrs Dinwiddie's departure. 'Enchanted.'

Dinwiddie stayed seated.

George spent the rest of the evening carefully nipping at his wine, listening to Dinwiddie's many theories and opinions, so freely offered. Later, as he walked back through the icy night air towards the room he'd rented in the tavern, he reflected on his experience. He was surprised to find he'd enjoyed himself. He'd spent so much time in Lawrence's company – in his shadow even – that it was nice to tread the boards on his own. He felt he'd handled himself well; he hadn't caused or taken any offence. He'd been pressured into making certain promises on behalf of his brother's company, but as he stared up at the full moon that lit his journey, George honestly thought that had Lawrence been placed in the same position, what could he have said different? Even after being practically extorted, George had remained polite as any Englishman should, and hadn't drunk too much – which perhaps wasn't in keeping with most Englishmen, but seemed prudent on account of his youth. Dinwiddie talked to anyone who was willing to listen, yet for all these failings, he was a clever man, educated, and experienced. George wasn't sure how to feel about Dinwiddie's suggestions of a war across the whole world, or how each nation was doomed to fail. It seemed melancholy, yet Dinwiddie wasn't a dour man. These weren't the ramblings of the tavern drunk. He'd travelled, he understood far more about the world than George did, and so, whilst he didn't agree with Dinwiddie, he was drawn to the old man's ideas, if only for their novelty.

George would write to him tomorrow to thank him for his hospitality and support. The Lieutenant Governor was an acquaintance who, if fostered, might one day prove auspicious.

***

Weeks later, a weary Robert Dinwiddie followed his wife and daughters into the box pew for the Sunday service. The church's congregation, enlarged by the sitting of the General Assembly, fizzed with the week's gossip, filling the high ceiling with the reverberations of their chatter of who had said what and to whom, who had too much to drink, who had made a pass at whom. Politics, too, was carried out; wives proposed bargains between their respective husbands, greasing the wheels of progress, and men ignored their foes and whispered conspiratorially to their allies. Younger ladies hung from the arms of their beaux, or shepherded their young children, all the while eyeing others in their Sunday finest: brooches, necklaces, shoes, hats, fabric – the trimmings of society that subtly distinguished those on the rise from those whose fortunes ran against them.

Dinwiddie nodded acknowledgements to various people as the congregation began to settle. The box pews were full, standing room only. The Pastor mounted his pulpit and invited them to sing the new Easter hymn, *Christ has risen today*. It was an untimely and unwieldy effort that would have benefited from musical accompaniment. An organ was one of the many things that the parish wanted. But, as with so many things in the colonies, the skills required were in short supply. Adverts went unanswered. Britain was the only source of so many of the desirable accoutrements of modern life. The colonists would make do without, as they had done for generations. Dinwiddie reflected on the noise of the previous week, letting his mind choose which issues rose to the fore and which fell away. In the background, the church service passed without great consequence.

As they filed out of the building into the pleasant spring sun, he felt an arm on his shoulder. He turned to see the unmistakeably shrew-like face of Joshua Fry, the mathematics teacher whose pale, grey skin left Dinwiddie wondering if the man was even capable of sunburn. 'Mr Fry. Good day to you.'

'And to you, Governor. May I speak with you?'

Dinwiddie nodded to his wife, who continued mingling with the dispersing crowd.

'Rumour has it you've sided with the Ohio Company?' said Fry, once they had some relative privacy from prying ears.

Dinwiddie looked down at Fry, four inches his inferior. An image flashed through his mind of Fry naked. He blinked away the picture of the wiry sinew of the man's feeble frame. 'What of it?'

'I'll come to the point. Your interests would be better served in the Loyal Virginia Company.'

'Give me some shares then.'

Collecting himself, Fry replied, 'No, Governor. You'll need to put your money alongside your mouth.'

Dinwiddie scoffed. 'Why should I?'

'Because the Ohio venture is going nowhere. It's leaderless. Rumour has it, its president Washington is languishing overseas, too sick to work. The House will never agree to pay for the obstacles the King has erected in its path. And most of all it's too close to the French. Nobody wants to provoke them unnecessarily. It would threaten war, again.'

'It would have a better chance if you didn't insist on blocking it in the house, Mr Fry.'

'Why should we bear the cost of the King's stipulations? Did the King pay for the forts of the first settlers to arrive here? No, they did it themselves. This is the New World, where a man is free from monarchy's interference, relying instead on his own endeavours.'

'It's a little different nowadays.'

'Well, one thing won't change – I have the majority of the burgesses in my pocket. We won't vote for your funds. You'll not be getting a penny from Virginia's coffers.'

'Very well, you have made your point, Mr Fry. But for either scheme to work, they both need the Indians on side.' Dinwiddie rested his hand on Fry's shoulder. 'You can help me to help you. Get yourself out to the Ohio, parley with the Indians. If you come back holding a treaty with the savages, then I'll give you my money for your Loyal Company.'

Fry's mouth fluttered as he searched for words. Dinwiddie enjoyed watching the man struggle. Finally, Fry said, 'Will it be worth the paper it's written on?'

'To me, yes. I have masters in London who expect due process to be followed, otherwise I'll be stripped of office and my pension with it. So, if only for my own protection, you get yourself out to the Ohio and bring me a watertight agreement with those savages. If not, I'll veto anything and everything your company petitions for. I am adept at building obstacles of my own, Mr Fry, and I have the full weight of the colonial treasury behind me. We'll see how quickly your investors turn turkey, as they say in these parts.'

Fry frowned, his skin rippling across his jaws as they gnashed together. 'I won't…'

'Oh, you will, you shit, and let me tell you why: the King would take great exception to hear of your rival scheme. I'll write to him this very afternoon.'

'My company was approved by the Governor's council, therefore—'

'Not on my watch, Mr Fry. Imagine my dismay when I discovered the previous Governor's errors. The King will be very pleased when he learns of the mess I've cleared up…'

'Very well,' sniffed Fry. 'If I come back with a treaty, we'll have your full support – and in return, you will agree to see that the Ohio Company is left null and void?'

Dinwiddie nodded. 'It's a lovely day for a trip out west, Mr Fry.' With that, he walked away, hands un-shook.

Always better to back two horses, thought Dinwiddie. As he walked back to his mansion, he felt a surge of warmth from his impending wealth.

18

February 6th, 1752
Fitzbarton Plantation

If a man is to truly appreciate another man's lifeline, then best wait till he's drowning. Only then, with his mouth full of water, will he concede to the terms of another. The tobacco harvest had been pulled up, dried, packed, sold and, God willing, unloaded in London's warehouses. By now, the proceeds – or in Hans Neumann's case, lack thereof – would be fully apparent. For Mason, it had been a good harvest. The weather had been kind and Viktor had harvested a bumper haul of leaf. Spared the cost of war, Europe bought all the tobacco London could import. Prices were good. For those who had managed their estate well, commerce was good. For those that had lost their seedlings to flea beetles, not so. With snow covering the ground and winter supplies looking thin in the larder, the time had come for Mason to act.

He rubbed his hands together as he walked out of the back door of the house toward the stables. Dressed in his Sunday best, white breeches, cotton shirt under an indigo silk waistcoat and lambswool tailcoat, he donned his top hat as the snow covering the rear lawn crunched beneath his leather riding boots.

Behind their accommodation, the negroes were huddled together, trying to stay warm while practising their obscure religion. Mason was expected to teach them Christianity, but he resolved it was kinder to deny them the hope God offered.

In the stable, Viktor had already tacked up his horse and it was ready and waiting for him. Mason checked the buckles himself. He didn't yet trust the Neumann boy. He probably never would, for he knew it wasn't in his nature to trust others. 'Jolly good,' he said to himself, seeing that the tack was in order. Running a plantation was a continual practice of checking other people's labour. He'd learned that the hard way; you could never rely on others to attend to matters with the same degree of diligence that he himself exhibited – but that was why he lived in the big house, and not them.

'Mr Fitzbarton, sir, I wonder if I could trouble you for my pay?' said Viktor timidly.

Mason climbed into the saddle and looked down at his farmhand. 'How long have you worked here now, Viktor?'

'Nine months this week.'

'And how many slaves have you lost in that time?'

His expression looked pained. 'Just one…'

'*Just* one! How much does a slave cost, Viktor?'

Viktor looked away.

'An adult male, like the one you let escape, costs thirty pounds. That's thirty pounds for the slave. Six pounds for the clothes you are wearing. Two pounds for the dogs I've had to buy, so the next time you lose a slave, we'll be able to hunt him down. You've cost me thirty-eight pounds. Which is eleven and a half months' pay. You'll be paid in May – provided, of course, you don't lose anyone else.'

Viktor looked dejected.

'Quit your sulking, lad. I've run this place for years and never lost a slave. You take your punishment, and you'll be a better slaver for it.'

Before Viktor could plead further, Mason cut him off. 'I never said it would be easy, Viktor, but if you want to rise, you must learn the hard way. Now come, you've only two more months to wait.' Mason twitched his heels into Fortune's ribs and rode away.

***

Viktor was left in the stable, the musty smell of disturbed straw filling his nostrils. His mouth hung open. Tears began to well in his eyes. He wiped them dry on his sleeves and shook his head, determined to stop

171

the leak of emotion before it poured freely. It had been his decision to leave his father. He had come here a free man and whatever setbacks he suffered, he was determined to make the best of it. He walked out of the stable, his eyes adjusting to the glare of the snow. In the yard, the negro toddler, Benji, was building a snowman. Viktor stopped and watched the boy pack the snow tightly. Benji's father had died shortly after he was born, and his mother had passed in the summer. Everyone knew that negroes didn't have the same feelings as white men, but Viktor wondered what the boy's life would be like. Was it better to have lost a father he had never known, or be in Viktor's position and have an estranged father who you no longer loved? He crouched down and made a snowball, then hurled it at Benji, hitting his torso. The boy laughed and bent to make a snowball of his own. They lobbed snowballs at each other, ducking and feinting. As Viktor crouched to make a snowball, Benji caught him in the face with one of his. He jumped up in triumph, laughing. Viktor laughed too and they traded shots at each other.

A shrill whistle interrupted their fun. Viktor turned around to see Billy, Mason's carpenter, calling from an open window, 'You didn't ought to be doing that,' he drawled at Viktor. 'Ain't your job to play with the slaves.'

Viktor sent Benji on his way, sad that their brief moment of fun had come to an end. As he walked back to his accommodation, he supposed Billy was right. The slaves ought to fear him, not that he thought that was how to get the best out of them. But he couldn't afford to lose the respect of the plantation's white folk. As he lay back on his bed, his gloom briefly lifted by the warmth of the child's smile, he thought about the last year. It had started well enough. On his first day, the stern faces of the negros had struck terror into him. To talk of owning slaves was easy, but to command them was a different matter. Mason had taken him under his wing, the tobacco harvest had gone well, and if negroes had sensed his fear, they hadn't exploited it. He was respectful to them, and they, in return, had proved compliant. Time passed slower when supervising the work of others than when he'd been doing the work himself. But all had changed when the negro had escaped. It had been Mason who'd spotted the absence. In that moment, his manner had changed completely towards Viktor.

Viktor reflected on what he'd achieved in his first year: he may be better dressed, but his pockets were still empty. He consoled himself with the fact that he was learning from the best. He would, in time, prove himself worthy of Mason's favour. The rewards would come. He was certain of it.

***

Mason trotted along the snow-covered road, leaving wisps of warm breath dispersing in the chilly air. He arrived at the Neumann farm half an hour later. The crudely sawn cabin was a poor excuse for a home. The three inches of snow on the roof couldn't hide its humble squalor. The shutters were left ajar and smoke drifted peacefully from the stone chimney. Yesterday's footprints to and from the door were still visible under the fresh dusting of snow.

'Good morning,' Mason shouted.

The door opened; Hans leant against the door frame, blocking the dingy view of the interior. 'What do you want?'

'That's not very neighbourly.'

'Neither are you.'

Mason grinned. 'Aren't you going to invite me in?'

'No.'

The younger son's face appeared at the window.

'How was your harvest?' Mason asked.

'Poor. Beetles got my crop.'

'Oh dear, my sympathies, Hans. The tobacco trade is a fickle business.'

'What do you want, Mason?'

'Well, I confess I'd heard you'd had a poor year. My negroes travelled past and saw some of your fields unplanted. You know how they like to gossip.'

Hans stood silent, his arms folded across his chest.

'Do you need money?'

His head tilted back, but Hans' mouth stayed firmly closed.

'I can help, if you've fallen on hard times?'

'I'd rather drink my own piss.'

How dare he, thought Mason, *that jumped-up little German.* His horse shifted on the hard ground. 'I'd like to make you an offer for your property.'

Hans spat on the snow.

'I'll clear any of your debts,' said Mason, undeterred. 'You can keep your crop and equipment.'

'I must be getting on. Don't come back.'

'You could live here – for a small rent – or work the field in lieu of payment.'

'For you, Mason? Never. I'll take my chances.'

'Without tobacco, what have you to trade?'

'I'll find a way,' said Hans, 'but it won't involve making a pact with the devil.'

'How dare you!' shouted Mason, 'You'll show me some respect.'

'That's what you want, isn't it, Fitzbarton? To be respected, part of the aristocracy. Your family was nothing in the old country, so they came out here and emulated what they could never truly be. There's more nobility in that horse than there is in your common blood.'

'You're a fine one to talk – look at you in your hovel.'

'I know what I am, Mason, and I don't try to be anything else. You can keep your money. I wouldn't sell to you for all the tea in China.' Hans turned to go back indoors.

'How's your son, Viktor?' Mason sneered.

Hans stopped and looked back at him.

'He works for me now, Hans, whipping my negroes. You're welcome to pay him a visit.'

'You're welcome to him. He's dead to me.' Hans went inside and shut the door.

'He's brighter than you, Hans! I'm filling his head with my poison,' he shouted. The younger son was still at the window. 'Why don't you come and join your brother? Make some real money on a real plantation?'

Hans moved his son aside and closed the shutters.

'You know where I am, Neumann. I'll have your farm one way or another.'

Mason turned and rode home. He had the money and the means. The stubborn Hun couldn't hold back the tide forever. Mason would have his land, one way or another. It was inevitable.

19

May 28th, 1752
Logstown, Ohio River

The red British ensign fluttered from the stern of the lead canoe. All morning they'd battled against a headwind buffeting their canoes from one side of the river to the other. Yesterday, they'd suffered rain of biblical proportions. The day before, the sun had been equally relentless. Since their departure, the Virginia party, under the command of Joshua Fry, had faced three of the four seasons. Fry couldn't help but wonder if the Almighty had designs on frustrating their mission. If this was a divine test to prove that they, the English, were truly deserving of the land to the west of the Appalachian Mountains, then Fry was satisfied.

Gunfire! Fry ducked to shelter behind the gunwales of his canoe. Birds fled the trees that lined the river. More shots filled the air. Fry looked about; nobody seemed hurt. Christopher Gist, the frontiersman Dinwiddie had recommended as a guide, sat in the stern of the next canoe and began to laugh. He held his musket aloft and discharged a round into the sky.

'What are you doing?' hissed Fry.

'They're saluting us with their gunfire. We're here. The journey's over!'

Fry sat upright and straightened his jacket, his embarrassment soon replaced with relief to be finished paddling as his feet splashed into the shallows by the Iroquois village. Thirsty, hungry, tired, and with damp clothes, he'd had to row his own canoe after two of their negroes had absconded and his elbows now protested with shooting nerve pain. He'd cursed Dinwiddie repeatedly for making him lead this detachment from Virginia. The only advantage of attending in person was he could be certain he wouldn't be betrayed. He was charged with conducting the negotiations with the Iroquois. Word had it that Lawrence Washington had been furious on learning that the Loyal Company of Virginia would be taking the lead role, leaving his Ohio Company as good as dead. Dinwiddie, too, seemed to be on board, for he had proposed Gist to attend as Fry's deputy, to ensure he returned from the east with his scalp still attached to his head. Gist had proved a quiet travelling companion, keeping his thoughts to himself, a simpleton, who seemed more at home in the woods eating whatever he'd foraged than brokering treaties. Fry thought there was something familiar about Gist's shabby appearance, he wondered if they'd met before, but he couldn't place him. One met so many strangers in America as people moved freely inland and up and down the seaboard. New arrivals settled in new towns, moving with the work; Fry observed they lacked the long-held communities of home that would have felt so familiar to an Englishman.

Gist helped Fry step ashore. Their canoes were dragged from the river by the five other white men and two remaining negroes in their party. Fry looked around the village. By the standards of the savages, it was large and well-developed, yet a lone stone building and some extra tepees didn't make up for the Indian shortcomings. They were uneducated, ignorant of civility, science and law – all the things the mathematics teacher and magistrate prized as the triumphs of their race.

They were greeted by a red-skinned savage. Fry didn't offer his hand.

***

George Croghan had problems of his own. That evening, in his tepee at Logstown, his Iroquois concubine sleeping soundly on the bearskin beside him, he reread the letter from his lawyer by the light of a candle:

Dear Mr Croghan,

It is with great regret, sir, that I write to confirm that the colony of Pennsylvania is unwilling to finance, or in any such way assist in the construction of a fortification at said place where the Allegheny and Monongahela rivers merge with the Ohio River, or in any such similar place that may be recommended, beyond the territory which is inhabited by its subjects. The colony does not recognise Mr Croghan's claim to any land east of the aforementioned fork in the rivers, as such, no deeds will be forthcoming.

Yours Sincerely,

William Wainwright

Attorney at Law

Damned Quakers! The colony's religious tolerance had been what had attracted his family here, but now the Pennsylvanian government, founded on such peace-loving Quaker beliefs, was too lily-livered to fund anything that might promote the use of violence. No matter what Tanacharison had promised him, if it wasn't recognised in law by the colony, it was worthless. Having parted with his ammunition and a whopping £1,000 of trade goods, he had little hope of getting his goods back from the Chief if it fell through.

The Irishman folded his letter and held it to the candle flame. Watching the paper burn until it singed his calloused fingers, he blew out the last ember and lay on his back in the darkness, contemplating how he could keep all parties happy. Tanacharison needed a fort built at the confluence of the rivers to keep the French at bay. Pennsylvania wasn't willing to finance the construction and manning of a fort, yet he and his backers from the state needed to retain their hold in the Ohio fur trade. If Croghan could square this circle, then he stood to profit from the land Tanacharison had promised him, provided Pennsylvania would honour the deeds.

On top of all that, the Virginians had arrived, eager to grab some land for themselves. Somebody was going home empty-handed. To ensure it wasn't his backers, they had sent an agent, Andrew Montour, to 'assist' Croghan. Some time had passed since he'd sent furs east, and Croghan took Montour's arrival as a sign that his backers were questioning their faith in him.

All that mattered to Croghan was that he got the land Tanacharison had promised. He rolled over and kissed his woman, who was in the deep slumber of one who had engaged in the pleasures of the flesh.

***

The next day, figuring he might as well get to know the measure of his opponents, Croghan went to introduce himself to the Virginians. He found them bathing in the river. He stripped off his clothes and joined them in the shallows, recognising Gist straight away. He'd appeared in the Ohio the previous winter, to survey the land for the Ohio Company. Croghan had given him a tour along the river, stopping at Logstown before continuing west to his other base with the Twightee on the Miami River. He'd been keen to impress upon Gist his influence in the area.

'Mr Croghan. Nice to see you again,' said Gist, shaking his hand. 'Let me introduce Mr Fry, who commands our delegation.'

To Croghan, the short, wiry man scrubbing his body in the water looked like he wouldn't last a day alone in the backwoods.

'Much obliged to make your acquaintance, sir,' said Croghan.

'My man, I can barely see you without my glasses,' said Fry as he outstretched his soapy hand.

'What do you want here?'

'Well, that's between me and the Iroquois chief, wherever he may be,' said Fry.

'He'll appear when he wants to. He's probably watching us right now. Be wary of him. I watched him split a Frenchman's head open once.'

Fry shuddered.

'What is your business here, Mr Croghan?'

'I've been trading furs here for years. Today, my job is to stop Virginia getting any land, or furs.'

'Hmm,' grunted Fry.

'Well, you gentlemen have yourselves a nice day,' said Croghan, plunging his head underwater to hide his smile.

***

Tanacharison returned to Logstown, as the white men called it, his permanent base on the Ohio River, two days after the delegation from Virginia had arrived. He'd watched them arrive from the top of the hill on the far side of the river, but instead of returning, he'd opted to hunt in the forests to the south. *Make them wait.* This conference had been organised at their behest, but it suited his plans too. Croghan and another man from Pennsylvania were in attendance. To Tanacharison, they were all white men bent on taking his land, be they French, Virginian or Pennsylvanian. He arranged his belt to display with prominence the scalps he'd just collected. They'd happened across a Huron raiding party who had either been spying for their French masters or planning to ambush the Iroquois. The English would pay him a bounty for each circular shrivelled patch of skin. He'd sell them to Buck, who would sell them to the authorities on his return to Philadelphia. But today, as he walked back into camp, they served as a reminder to the white men that they could never travel in confidence through the woods and rivers of this continent, without fear of being relieved of their scalps. They were guests of the Iroquois people. Welcome or otherwise.

***

From the Virginians' arrival, it took three days before they were all granted an audience with Chief Tanacharison in the longhouse. They sat in a circle on the earthen floor, with Tanacharison looking relaxed on the dais, one knee raised to the thatch above. Behind him, the double doors were open, casting bright sunlight into the shadows. His fellow elders, and his eldest son Thayonih, sat to either side of him, all wearing the usual deerskin apparel, their dark eyes serious, their expressions obscured by the daylight behind them. Exposed to the glare of the sunlight was Fry, dressed in a wool suit, his round glasses perched on the end of his pointy nose. Gist, looking shabby with greasy hair and an untrimmed beard, sat next to him, wearing buckskin trousers and waistcoat, a reminder that he was accustomed to dealing with Indians. His tatty cocked hat lay in his lap. Croghan sat to one side, so he could watch both the Virginians and Tanacharison. On his right was Montour, the man he suspected had been sent to spy on him. He was a short, stocky fellow, balding, with a crooked nose that suggested it had encountered a few punches.

The gathering followed the usual protocol: the parties swapped wampum and paid each other compliments, reaffirming their friendship. Tanacharison thanked them for making the long and perilous journey. Croghan volunteered Montour as translator. It would afford himself some thinking time and distract Montour from whatever brief he'd really been given. 'The Great Chief says had he known you were coming he would have met you halfway,' said Montour. 'Please open your hearts to us and speak freely.'

Croghan smiled inwardly. *Tanacharison knew they were coming the moment they crossed the mountain top.*

'Mr Fry, on behalf of Pennsylvania, may I welcome you to the meeting, and invite you to speak first,' said Croghan, eager to see what the Virginian had to say.

Fry's voice was clipped and officious, his accent still wholly English. 'At the Treaty of Lancaster, in the Year 1744, between the Governments of Virginia, Maryland, and Pennsylvania, you made a deed recognising our great King's right to all the lands as far as it was then peopled.'

He paused to let Montour translate.

'It is the design of the King of Great Britain, our Father, to make a settlement of British subjects on the southeast side of the Ohio Valley, so that we may be united as one people, by the strongest ties of neighbourhood and friendship.'

The Iroquois sat stony-faced while they listened to the translation, then shared knowing looks on hearing the Virginian intentions.

Montour nodded to Fry, who rearranged his glasses before continuing.

'From such a settlement, greater advantages will arise for you. Our people will be able to supply valuable trade goods, even cheaper than now. They will offer you support, should you be attacked by our common enemies. Rest assured, the King's laws will prevail, and good men will be appointed to punish and restrain any disorderly white people.'

There was another pause for translation. Again, the Iroquois said nothing, beyond nodding to confirm their understanding.

'Brethren, our King never had any intention of taking your lands from you, but that we might live together as one people, and keep the land from the French, who would be bad neighbours. The British King, unlike the French King, who calls himself your father but endeavours with an armed force to take possession of your land, by depositing inscriptions on trees, and along the rivers.'

'You wish us to live as one people, yet under your laws and customs?' asked a sceptical-looking Tanacharison.

Once translated, Fry nodded his confirmation of the Chief's understanding.

The Iroquois conferred in hushed tones, then Tanacharison spoke.

Montour translated, 'The Chief says your white people cross the mountains and settle these lands, although they are not supposed to. They commit many injuries to our people.'

He was right. Only last year, Croghan had set fire to an illegal settlement of English folk, torching their wooden houses. With each boatload that had docked, homeless people poured west to claim the land beyond the limits of the colonial governments, rubbing up against the Indians. No sooner was a settlement destroyed, did they relocate, fell more trees and begin again.

'They tempt our people,' continued the Chief, 'with their liquor, trading a barrel for five buckskins.'

Croghan liked a drink as much as anyone but, with great sadness, had seen for himself how Indian families had been laid to waste by the liquor the white men brought. For a measly five bucks, crops would go neglected, the hunt would be forsaken, men would beat the women, and children would go hungry. It was a scourge on a people who weren't accustomed to the instant gratification of alcohol.

Fry interrupted, much to the annoyance of the Chief. 'Your people stray from the roads on which they are required to travel into our territory. They cause great alarm to our people when they appear in our settlements without warning. Indeed, in my county, one of your people is wanted for the murder of an innocent woman and child.'

Croghan saw his own reaction mirrored in Gist's frown. Fry was antagonising them over misdemeanours.

'It is true that the chain of our friendship may have picked up some rust,' interrupted Croghan, 'but here we seek to burnish the rust so we might forge a strong union together, against the French who would do us a great harm.'

Scolded, Fry puffed out his chest in defiance. Fortunately, he didn't continue speaking.

'This man will be dealt with by our people,' said Tanacharison. 'We are sorry for his crimes. He will be suitably punished.'

Croghan looked at Fry, who was about to speak, and gave him an imperceptible shake of the head.

'The French are a cruel folk,' said the Chief. 'They have committed great crimes against me and my people. It is my wish that you build a fort in the forks of the river, a day's journey upstream from here, so you can prevent them from coming further into our lands. This is my condition.'

'A fort would only provoke the French further,' Fry protested. 'It is too risky and expensive to man.'

'I have spoken,' said Tanacharison with steely eyes.

'We are willing to accept this condition,' said Gist quickly.

'No, we are not!' rebutted Fry.

Croghan's ears pricked up. *The two Virginian men disagree?* His mind quickly added up the pieces. *Croghan, you fool, the answer's been staring at you all along...* 'Thank you, Chief,' he said in Seneca. 'I need to relieve myself; I suggest we break and resume this afternoon.'

They took a lunch of venison and maize under an arbour to shield them from the midday sun. Croghan kept his eye on Gist's movements. When he stood to take a walk, Croghan did likewise. He followed the man past the tepee field and caught up with him at the horse corral.

'Hey, friend. Your man Fry fumbled over the fort, didn't he?'

Gist smirked. 'It's a long story. Suffice to say, although we're here on behalf of Virginia, we ain't on the same side. I represent the Ohio Company. Fry has his own company, the Loyal Company of Virginia.'

'But you can pay for a fort?'

'What are you thinking?'

'Look, Tanacharison will only deal with me,' said Croghan. 'He trusts me, I'm on their council. You boys never stood a chance. He'll listen to what you say, but only *I* can get him to agree to what you want. And you'll need to build that fort.'

'What if we can't?'

'Well, that's your problem. But if you can, I think I can swing it your way.'

'You're from Pennsylvania – what's in it for you?' Gist squinted at Croghan.

'I get the two hundred thousand acres east of the forks in the river, recognised in law by a Virginian court. Or you leave here with nothing.'

'Has he promised you that land already?'

Croghan nodded. 'You can take the land to the southeast that leads back to Virginia, then we don't clash. The Chief won't like it, but it's the best he's going to get.'

'What about Pennsylvania?'

Croghan snorted. 'Who cares, it's all America isn't it? You don't need me to tell you it's every man for himself out here. You put a fort at the fork in the river and recognise the deeds to my land. I'll get you the Chief's blessing.'

Gist smiled. 'You've got yourself a deal, Croghan.' They shook hands and Gist started laughing.

Croghan, unable to hide his beaming smile, danced a jig in the dust. He was a big step closer to becoming a very rich man. The two men embraced. Gist couldn't stop laughing.

'What's so funny?'

'I don't know what I am happier about,' said Gist. 'Getting the Ohio Valley secured for my employers, or Fry missing out on the biggest land deal in history!'

***

That evening, Croghan asked to accompany Tanacharison on a walk along the river.

'Chief, I need to be honest with you,' said Croghan as they walked side by side under the pink hues of the setting sun, reflected off the relentless flow of the Ohio River. 'Pennsylvania won't build a fort. Virginia is your only hope.'

'Then I have to concede land. I don't like it.'

'It's not ideal. You'll still have my land as a buffer.'

'You will sell it to white men, Buck,' snarled Tanacharison.

'Aye, then you'll kill me, most likely.'

Tanacharison snorted.

Croghan stopped and turned to face the Chief. 'Look, if you don't take this chance, you're left with the French. They've already shown their hand by claiming your land. At least the British will give you something in exchange for it. And they make better trading terms than the French. I know it's not what you wanted, but I fear it's time to choose your poison: Virginian or French.'

'Very well. Thank you for your advice, Buck.'

***

The next day, they took their places on the floor of the longhouse and the conference resumed. A relaxed-looking Tanacharison spoke first, addressing Fry and Gist. 'Our council has spoken and we have made the following decision: You men from Virginia, you will build me a fort at the fork in the Ohio River, to protect my peoples from the French, and in return, we shall grant Virginia access to our lands so we may trade together, via Buck,' he pointed at Croghan, 'through whom you shall conduct all your negotiations.'

Fry sitting on the ground, shuffled awkwardly. As he translated, Montour glared at Croghan, who hid the smile that concealed his glee. The ranks of onlooking Iroquois were silent.

'I object!' declared Fry.

Tanacharison glared at him, then turned his gaze to Gist. 'I understand your King also wants a fort to keep the French from travelling south.'

Gist nodded. 'He does, Chief. There are men in Virginia ready and willing to honour your request.'

'Hold on one moment, this man is not entitled to negotiate on behalf of Virginia,' protested Fry.

'I think you'll find, Mr Fry, Mr Gist represents the Ohio Company,' said Croghan.

Fry scowled at Gist 'You're Washington's man?'

Gist winked.

'Be damned! You cursed snake.' Fry's face glowed red as the treachery came clear to him. It was Dinwiddie who'd recommended Gist. He would have known, he must have bent to pressure from Washington. Then he remembered where he'd seen Gist – the courtroom in Fairfax, some trial about missing negroes. Major Washington had attempted to persuade him towards Gist's cause. *The double-dealing conspirators!* 'How dare you undermine me!'

Fry got to his feet. Tanacharison signalled to his son, Thayonih. The brave leapt to his feet and drew his tomahawk from his belt, raising it aloft, light from the smoke hole glinting across its blade.

'I'd sit down if I were you,' insisted Croghan.

Fry froze as indignation gave way to terror.

'Sit down, Mr Fry,' repeated Croghan.

Thayonih remained standing, calmly lowering his tomahawk as Fry returned to the ground.

'Chief, we have a deal,' said Gist, 'I am happy to accept your terms on behalf of Virginia's Ohio Company.'

A furious-looking Montour translated.

The Chief nodded his agreement and crossed his forearms, indicating a trade had been made.

After discussing points of detail, they broke at mid-morning. Croghan was glad to stretch his legs. He'd said nothing, for the outcome was one he was delighted with. As his eye adjusted to the light outside, Montour tugged his sleeve.

'What are you playing at? You're supposed to represent Pennsylvania, not Virginia!'

'Calm down. You could see for yourself: Pennsylvania won't guard the river. Their interests are finished here.'

'But—'

'It wasn't my decision, I had no choice. Be sure to tell your people that. They lost the Ohio Valley.'

'You owe them money!' exclaimed Montour.

'Sure, look, it'll be fine, I can still send furs their way, you heard the Chief, I'll control all the Iroquois trade.'

'Croghan, there's a long list of people you owe money to and you haven't sent nearly enough furs back to settle your accounts.'

'All the more reason we need a fort on the river, to keep the French out. If the good folk of Pennsylvania didn't think all men were as pious as them, then my life and theirs would be a lot easier, and we'd both be richer. In Philadelphia, you might all sit in a circle, holding hands, forgiving each other's sins, but out here, it's bloody wild, man. You don't go anywhere without a loaded gun. Ever. Or you're dead.'

Montour stayed silent and Croghan could see his argument was carrying the man's opinion.

'You need to make them understand that. Tell them that I'll send them furs. I'm good for the money. Remember, I have the Twightee now. Your people's money has been invested in a trading post west of here. As soon as we're done here, I'm headed to the Twightee to fetch the winter's haul of furs. Tell my backers, by the summer, they'll be up to their eyeballs in pelts.'

Seeing Gist approach, Croghan thanked Montour and excused him. 'Congratulations, Mr Gist, a good morning's work, eh?'

'Aye. Major Washington will be delighted. I thank you for your assistance.'

'How's your man Fry?'

'Spitting feathers!'

Croghan laughed.

That afternoon, the treaty between the Iroquois and the Virginians was committed to paper. It was a very solemn Joshua Fry who signed his name to the papers requiring his colony to erect a fort at the fork in the Ohio River.

The Iroquois elders were equally disappointed; all except for Tanacharison. He'd expected such an outcome. But he knew the nature of the white men and was satisfied they hadn't realised he'd played them at their own game; overjoyed with their accomplishment, they were totally unsuspecting of his intentions.

20

At first glance, the Twightee village of Pickawillany, nestled against the bank of the Miami River, was a picture of serenity. Deep within the continent, two hundred and fifty miles further west than Logstown, the river's green water sparkled in the evening sun as it flowed gently past the camp. Tepees encircled a large dome-shaped council house covered in reed matting. Behind the Twightee camp, incongruous with the native setting, was a stockade of log posts driven into the earth to encircle and fortify the storehouse and cabins of George Croghan's newest trading post. Four years had passed since he'd converted Old Briton's Twightee tribe from the French persuasion. Since switching sides, they'd ruthlessly pursued the French from the territory, proving their allegiance to Croghan beyond any measure of doubt.

For Croghan, it had all gone swimmingly. So far west, their animal skins were cheaper and beyond the range of the other British traders who now regularly appeared in the Ohio Valley. Old Briton benefited too, as Croghan came every season and collected his haul. The Twightee no longer had to paddle their wares through the lands of Tanacharison's Iroquois confederacy, who, much to the Twightee's displeasure, had blocked the river. Perched in the middle between the Twightee and the British colonies, Tanacharison had levied a mark-up on the Twightee skins that passed through his territory. If he caught the Twightee moving skins under his nose, he would execute them – a fate he couldn't very well impose on Croghan, or any of the British, for killing his buyers was to his own detriment.

When Old Briton had murdered the French traders at Sandusky on the banks of Lake Erie, Croghan could never have envisaged that things would have developed so smoothly. Together, they now stood side by side in the newly finished storehouse. Two Twightee children rolled a hogshead past them. Tilting it up on its end, they removed the lid and fished out a pelt, then shook off the sawdust and passed it to Croghan to inspect. He smelled the pelt, inhaling the scent of vegetable oil and sawdust from the barrel. Now that it had been rolled, the skin was shiny and pliable. He deemed it good. Helped by men Croghan had hired in Philadelphia, the Twightee children added them to a heap on the floor.

'That's all?' said Croghan.

Old Briton nodded.

It was less than Croghan had hoped for, compared to previous years. 'You holding some back?'

Old Briton, bare-chested, wearing only buckskin trousers and a goose feather in his hair, frowned. He explained in his pidgin English that Croghan bought them faster than the beavers could breed. Each season, it was becoming more difficult to supply the demand of the white men.

'That's all we catch,' he finished.

Jesus, that's not enough to cover the cost of my lads, thought Croghan.

'Very few. Price is higher now. I want ammunition,' said Old Briton.

'Sorry, Chief, I can't get it.'

'My people defenceless.'

'Aye, but look, I did get you these, I have a hundred of them.' Croghan signalled to his companion, who brought forth a large blanket. They were stolen from the Hudson Bay Company, a British venture that monopolised the rivers in the very far north, above the French lands. Croghan had won them from a Boston-based trader in a card game.

'I cannot keep my people safe with blankets,' protested Old Briton.

'Well, you can keep them warm, and they'll look great.' Croghan held one up and draped it across the Chief's bare shoulders. 'See, you'll be the best-dressed Indians in the valley. Quite the picture.' He winked at the Chief.

Old Briton said nothing.

'English wool. The best in the world. It's warm. Keeps the rain off. It looks great, don't you think?' He draped a blanket over his own shoulder, modelling it.

Old Briton protested. Croghan shrugged. They went back and forth, round and round. Croghan chucked in some copper pots and pans, some knives, belts and two axes. Old Briton got agitated, waving his arms about. Croghan had seen it all before. He was at his limit, but he knew the Chief had no option. The Iroquois would give him even less, and the Indians allied with the French would kill him to protect their own trade. Croghan signalled to his men that it was time to pack up and go.

Old Briton grimaced as Croghan extended his hand and they shook on the deal. 'Pleasure doing business with you, Squire.' Croghan tried to hide his smile. In a few weeks, he'd have these paddled, hauled back to Philadelphia and consigned to London, to receive a credit note on his account. Owing to the shortage, prices were high. This little stash would see him through the winter and cover what he'd given Tanacharison to secure his promise of land east of the forks. *Please God, don't let beaver go out of fashion,* he thought as he followed Old Briton back out of the stockade. The Chief shouted something Croghan didn't understand and a brave broke into a run. The two men shared a brandy in the council house, toasting their trade.

Old Briton indicated for Croghan to join him on the floor.

'Brother,' he said, 'my men see many Ottawa people moving here. They are a bad people. Very treacherous. Not good trade for you.'

Through the tent entrance came four young women clad in deer skin. The eldest was probably twenty, her face was square and scowling, but she had ample curves and bosom. The youngest couldn't have been a day over twelve. The middle two looked like sisters, with jet-black hair over blue eyes and pleasantly flat noses. There was probably only a year between them, fifteen, sixteen for the elder.

'We capture these women from the Ottawa, to replace our people they killed. None have found husband yet. Which one you like?'

Croghan finished his brandy and pointed to the younger of the sisters. Chief nodded at her. She removed her clothes and lay naked on the floor. The others filed out while the girl on the floor beckoned Croghan over, faking a desperation to lie with him.

'You may have her, if you swear you not trade with the Ottawa?'

'You got yourself another deal, Chief.'

'Help yourself. She yours while you stay here.'

Croghan led her back to his cabin in the stockade, where he would enjoy her tonight.

***

He woke in the early dawn to find her still sleeping at his side. Sliding out from under the blanket, he crept across the small cabin. The door creaked as he stepped outside. His naked body shivered in the cool air of the early morning. He walked round the side of his cabin and began to relieve his bladder. As his discomfort passed, his senses began to stir. *Something's not right.*

There was no dawn chorus. In the grey half-light, he saw a flash of red pass the loophole in the stockade wall. The hairs on his neck and arms stood proud. Another movement passed the loophole. The silence was shattered by a hollering war cry.

A painted Indian body appeared at the top of the stockade wall. Croghan ran for his door as the Indian raised his musket towards him. Splinters burst from the cabin wall as the musket ball narrowly missed him. The crack of gunfire ricocheted around the wooden fence that surrounded them. Croghan leapt back through the cabin door, scrambling for the clothes left abandoned on the earthen floor. His girl, roused from her slumber, held the blanket over her breasts as her terrified face searched Croghan's for reassurance. He donned his shirt and trousers, still belted with his hunting knife, and stepped into his untied boots. He grabbed his musket, his hands trembling as he bit the tip off the cartridge, pouring the acrid gunpowder down the muzzle, followed by the shot. A quick plunge, he cocked the hammer, then poured the last of the powder into the pan. More gunfire outside. He glanced round the door. The Indian was now striding across the ground towards his cabin. Croghan pressed himself against the wall by the door. He looked back to his concubine, lifted his finger to his lips, lest she gave him away. The Indian filled the doorway. The muscles of his bare body rippling as he walked into the gloom, his tomahawk raised ready to strike, he surveyed the room in search of his quarry. Croghan lowered his musket muzzle towards the Indian, who flinched as he sensed the movement to his rear. Croghan pulled the trigger. A flash of fire and a deafening blast trapped in the confines of the cabin drowned out the scream of the girl. The Indian lurched forward, a musket ball embedded in his spine. He stumbled and slumped onto the floor. Croghan leapt forward and drove the stock of his musket against the skull of the fallen savage. Still, he wriggled. Croghan wrenched the tomahawk from his grip and with a swift chop, buried the blade in the Indian's skull.

The girl continued to scream as he glanced back outside. His fellow white men were now raised from their beds and firing at the Indians who were jumping over the wall in droves. Croghan reloaded his musket and glanced back to see an Indian, bedecked in war paint, rush his youngest crew member at the door to the neighbouring cabin. The boy screamed as the savage gripped his hair and sliced off his scalp. Croghan aimed and fired. It was too late to save the boy, but he felled the Indian. He reloaded then ran across the open ground to the far end of the stockade. Through the loophole he saw Indians swarming the tepees of the Twightee village. There were hundreds of them, hollering their ear-piercing cries as the Twightee roused themselves only to be cut down. Smoke drifted up from the council house. The flames soon took hold, reaching into the morning sky. Tepees were torched. Women screamed as their children's throats were slit, only to suffer a similar fate.

Croghan saw a white man amongst the carnage. Then another. They must be French. Behind him, gunfire and screams of agony filled the stockade. Indians had forced open the gate and were streaming in, puffs of gun smoke obscuring their approach. Two of Croghan's men were felled. Spotting him alone, two Indians ran towards him. Croghan slung the musket strap over his shoulder and scrambled up the face of the stockade. A tomahawk thwacked into the wood inches beside his head. He heaved himself up to the top, feeling their hands clutching at his feet. He lost a boot. Without looking back, he launched himself over the top and crashed to the ground on the far side. A musket ball glanced past his shoulder. More Indians charged towards him. Pain shot through his arm from the fall. Croghan fired his musket, bringing down the first Indian, then swung the musket, clubbing the other around the jaw. He ducked the tomahawk blow of the third Indian and surged forward, knocking the man off his feet and slamming him into the ground. Pulling out his knife, he drove it deep into the man's heart.

Without a beat, he pulled the knife free and ran. His legs had never moved so fast, his remaining boot was untied and slid off. Gunfire, shouts and cries all followed him as he dashed towards the river. A wisp of a shot overtook him. He crouched as he ran the final yards to the riverbank, took a large breath then launched himself forward, diving as far out as his legs could propel him. The cool water silenced the death and carnage behind him. He swam blindly underwater, streaks of musket balls cutting through above and below him. He forced his way down deeper into the river and let the current pull him away from the danger. Just as he feared he might drown, he surfaced, gasped for air, before submerging again.

When he finally dragged himself out of the water, several miles downstream, the sky behind him was streaked with grey from the burning of his stockade, furs, canoes, men, the Twightee and their village. There would be nothing left.

French cunts. This land would never be safe until they were wiped clear of it.

It was a long walk home, barefoot. Croghan had plenty of time to think about how he might contribute to the removal of the French from America, and how he might explain his losses to his creditors.

21

Viktor bit a chaw of tobacco from the twist he kept in his pocket. The midday sun beat down hard. Sweat beaded between his forehead and the lining of his hat, trickling down his face. The sour taste of the leaf filled his mouth as he mulched it between his molars, before using his tongue to push it into the pocket of his cheek, from where its benefits could seep out. He cleared his throat and savoured the relief, his breathing softening.

He patrolled the margins of the tobacco field while the negro gang walked in lines between the crops, pulling up the weeds that competed for the rainwater. His whip curled over his shoulder; he'd never yet had to use it. He'd practised with it on many an evening, swirling it over his head then bringing his arm back, which, when done in the right motion, produced a crack not dissimilar to a small pistol shot. It was his father who'd said that the purpose of a weapon was to deter, not to be used. Viktor knew the day would come when it was required, but so far, he'd treated the negroes with respect, and they had responded in kind.

Last week, one evening when his negroes had finished for the day, he'd walked back to his father's farm and looked at this season's crop. The fields were full, and he'd been surprised to find himself moved to tears. He didn't know how his father and brother had survived last year's failure but was relieved to see them carrying on. He didn't miss his father, but he was glad to know that he and Daniel were all right. Though he missed Daniel, he reassured himself that it was better for his brother if he didn't reach out. Viktor was one less mouth to feed and Daniel could inherit the farm and their father's ways. Viktor's path would lead to prosperity. *One day, I will go and visit them, and prove to Father that I was right.* As he scanned the field of pale green tobacco plants, he gripped the coins in his fist. For after badgering Mason, he'd finally been paid – and in currency, not with tobacco for barter as Mason had originally tried. Tobacco would spoil, and trade goods could be damaged or stolen. Viktor had no account in London, so credit was of no use to him, whereas coins of whatever denomination could be saved, their value trusted. He wished he could show them to his father, for they justified his joining Mason. He would hide them, saving them for his future. Maybe clothes to impress a woman, or to buy her gifts... Not that he'd met any available women, for the slave women were the only females he regularly saw. He found himself fantasising about them with increasing regularity.

His daydream was interrupted by Charlie, who had cut down the tree blocking his route. Of all the negroes, Charlie was possessed of the most gumption and, as such, acted as the foreman. His linen shirt was wet and bore the accompanying smell of a slave at labour. He smiled, exposing his large white teeth.

'We's finished, Master Vik.'

Viktor hadn't noticed that the slave gang had arrived at the far end of the field, where they now waited for his command.

'Good. Let's move to the next field.'

'I suggest the nun-tip field is ready for weeding now, Master Vik.'

'You lead the way, Charlie,' said Viktor, unsure where the nun-tip field was. Viktor didn't see any need to impose his own ideas on those who were so far proving capable of employing the initiative that white folk frequently deemed them incapable of.

After an age, it was done, and the afternoon had turned to evening. Viktor marched them back to their huts, counting them in. Every night since the runaway, he'd returned a full complement of slaves.

He lay on his bed and smoked a handmade cigar to pass the evening, listening to the tune of the field crickets outside. His accommodation was simple. Bare walls – clean, at least – a bed, chair, and table served their purpose with tolerable comfort. Unlike his father's cabin, the floor was boarded and the window overlooking the tobacco barns was glazed. Across the corridor was Billy the carpenter, and further down was Granville, who operated the forge, and whose snoring shook the very foundations of the building.

Viktor exhaled a plume of smoke and watched it twirl and twist towards the rafters. He'd thought he might have had more interaction with Mason, who oversaw his work but rarely commented. Nor had he been invited to any social engagements. Mason's promise of one day leaving him the plantation had sparked fantasies of sitting at the dining table with the family, talking over a glass of wine about how to develop the enterprise. So far, his meals were prepared by Grace, the negro cook who worked in the main house, and delivered to his room by the footman Zebedee.

On a few occasions, he'd shared a bottle of rum and played brag with Billy and Granville, but not only had they beaten him, leaving him in their debt, but he found their company boorish. They encouraged him to flog the slaves and teased him when he showed hesitation. They joked about his father losing his farm and teased him about his virginity. Every time he was with them, he was reminded of why he preferred his own company.

The following morning, he was woken by his door crashing open. Mason stormed in, cursing, his voice slurred. Viktor's eyes struggled to adjust to the faint dawn light.

'Wake up the niggers!' barked Mason, brandishing a pistol in each hand.

Viktor heaved himself from his bed as his tired mind grappled with Mason's unexpected arrival.

'Drag those thieving beasts from their bunks,' he ordered, kicking Viktor's bed frame.

Viktor donned the shirt that was hanging on the back of the chair.

'I'll thrash the treacherous shits,' cried Mason, spittle flying across the room. His shirt was untucked, with a stain down its front and on his breeches. His hair was ruffled and his eyes vacant. He swayed as he walked back to the door.

He's drunk! A bad feeling swelled in Viktor's gut. His father's words reverberated in his mind: *'He's a bad man'.*

He fumbled with the buttons on the front of his cotton trousers as he followed Mason out of the door. Billy and Granville were roused, and they all made their way to the slave huts behind the workers' accommodation.

Moments later, Viktor watched as Mason forced the slaves to parade out of their huts. Their bleary eyes couldn't conceal the fear and uncertainty with which they observed their master.

'Which one of you filthy wretches stole my rum?' slurred Mason, pointing his pistols at them.

Viktor glanced across their faces as fear turned to surprise. They stood as still as statues in the hazy morning dew, waiting. He felt bad seeing the terror in young Benji's eyes.

'Which one of you was it?'

'Loosen your tongues you vermin,' Granville added.

'Was it you?' Mason staggered forward and waved his gun at a young man.

'No, boss.' His eyes wide open, his palms raised, he shook his head in denial. His relief was clear when Mason's attention turned to another.

Something struck Viktor as out of place.

He quickly counted them while Mason spilled forth threats and accusations. *Thirty-eight.* 'One's missing!' he blurted out.

'Find it!' shouted Mason. 'Bring me back my nigger.' Viktor, Billy and Granville spread out to search the property. Granville set off to fetch a horse and scour the roadway. Billy went to search the plantation buildings. *They won't hide there*, thought Viktor, fearing the loss of another ten months' pay if the missing slave couldn't be found. He mulled over the remaining places. Something in his gut urged him to check down by the water's edge.

He stopped running once he was behind the barn, out of Mason's sight. He'd spent enough time skulking in the woods to know that speed was what got you seen or heard. Better to move slowly and sneak up on your quarry. His heart began to calm, and his thoughts turned to why a negro would steal rum. Never had he seen them drink. Poor souls were so dog-tired by sunset, they had little fortitude to tackle rum in any quantity. Unless one of them was suffering a painful ailment... The track to the wharf led through the maple trees, whose canopies were filled with the dawn chorus. He studied the trees; a young rabbit nibbled at some wildflowers, but otherwise the scene was as still as could be.

He checked his footsteps as he neared the brow that overlooked the wharf. Moving to the verge, he hid behind a tree. Amid the morning's tranquillity, he could hear the faint sound of voices. Poking up his head over the crest of the road, he inched higher to see the dusty slope that led to the wharf. Crouched there was Charlie, conversing with a white man in a rowing boat at the water's edge.

Found him. Viktor crept forward and stepped out by the edge to walk casually up to the wharf. Charlie had his back to him and was deep in conversation.

'Morning pal,' said the white man when he noticed Viktor approach. Viktor gulped in surprise: it was Barney.

Charlie's head snapped to the side, eyes wide.

'Barney, long time no see, what are you doing here?' said Viktor, keeping his voice low.

Barney and Charlie exchanged a look. 'I'm just talking to your man here.' His Scots accent was as thick as ever and his ginger beard was interrupted by the scar on his cheek; he was exactly as Viktor remembered him the day they'd thrown the bees through the tavern window. Resting between his legs were three large bottles of what looked like rum.

'What's going on?' asked Viktor, turning his attention to Charlie. 'Is that Mason's rum?'

Charlie's expression fell, betraying his guilt. Barney nudged his boat away from the wharf, drifting it slowly out into the clear water.

'Nope. That's three bottles of my rum between my legs,' Barney grinned.

Viktor noticed Charlie was clutching an instrument between his bent knees; it looked like a banza.

'Charlie, what are you doing?' Viktor asked again.

'Nothing, boss. I just talking.'

Viktor looked back at Barney. Behind him, the bow of the boat was covered by a grey wool blanket, concealing some sort of cargo.

'I come through these parts each July,' said Barney, 'when the river is full with the worm and the big boats are confined to the brackish water far out in the bay. If there's anything you need – tools, meat, grain, clothes – I can get it for you.'

'A wife?' quipped Viktor.

Barney laughed. 'Aye, I ain't got one on here. For now, I got three bottles of stolen rum I can trade yous?' Barney winked.

'Boss, if I swap this music back for the rum, nobody need know,' said Charlie.

Viktor shook his head. 'Too late, Charlie. He knows it's missing, and I sure as hell ain't getting tangled in your crimes.'

'Mr Barney, we swap back?'

Barney, now floating several feet clear from the wharf, tilted his head and his expression hardened. 'I'll give you one bottle for it, but it ain't worth three, pal.'

'Hey, you is not playing fair…'

'Fair int nowt to do with it, and I ain't playing. I don't want a nigger banjo, but I'll give you a bottle of grog for it, to help you out of a jam.'

Charlie leapt up and pointed at Barney, shouting abuse in a language Viktor didn't understand. Barney grinned and dropped his oars in the water, then began his stroke out of the inlet. 'Enjoy your music, Charlie. Nice to see ya again, Vik. I'll be back in a fortnight at sunrise if you want anything. Cannae promise a woman though.'

The boat rounded the corner of the creek and its bow waves lapped at the wharf, the only noise in the morning's silence. The orange glow of daylight replaced the grey tinges of dawn.

Charlie's forehead bore a heavy frown. 'We gotta make this right.'

'*We* haven't got to make anything right. *I* have to take you back to Mason. The rest is yours to answer for. Come let's go.'

'I can get you a woman, boss? Betsy let you ride her.'

Viktor paused. Charlie was desperate. He'd offer the moon if he thought it would save his skin. But he was Viktor's foreman. He owed him a little help.

'Leave your banza here, then we go. We've been too long as it is.'

Viktor waited while Charlie stashed his instrument in the trees. They made their way back up the track to the plantation buildings.

The scene remained unchanged. The slaves stood still under Mason's armed supervision. Billy and Granville had both returned.

'Where was he?' asked Mason, whose anger hadn't subsided during the delay.

'At the wharf,' said Viktor.

'My rum?'

Viktor shook his head.

Mason grunted. Billy and Granville smirked.

'Send these lot out to work, now,' said Mason to Billy and Granville, pointing at the rest of the slaves.

Billy cracked his whip and they hurried together like a flock of sheep into the field, on empty stomachs.

'Viktor and I are going to find out what happened to my rum.' Mason aimed a pistol at Charlie's forehead.

Charlie raised his shaking palms and garbled his denials.

Viktor's stomach churned. Charlie had been good to him. He'd hoped he could protect him a little and lessen his punishment.

'Tie him up, Viktor.' Mason nodded towards the whipping post that stood in front of the slave accommodation.

'Please no, please, don't…' said Charlie as Viktor tried to grab him by the arm. Charlie fought him off.

'Don't just tickle him, Viktor!' Mason commanded.

'Charlie, please,' Viktor whispered.

'Tell him, it wasn't me, I didn't take his rum…'

No way was Viktor getting enmeshed in Charlie's misdeeds. His leniency had already implicated him. If Charlie said anything to Mason, Viktor feared he would be punished as well.

Mason stepped forward and swung the butt of his pistol down on the back of Charlie's head, dropping him to the dirt. 'Strip, nigger.'

Charlie staggered to his feet, tears welling in his eyes. 'Please, don't…'

'Strip!' barked Mason. 'One more word and I'll shoot you.'

Charlie's trembling hands pulled his shirt over his head. He undid the string that held his trousers up and they dropped around his feet. Without further protestations, he stepped out from his trousers and offered himself against the whipping post.

Viktor shuddered as he saw the scars on Charlie's back and legs. He picked up the rope that hung ready on the hook on the rear of the post. It was nothing more than a tree trunk, stripped of its bark, and sunk into the ground, standing six feet tall, stained with blood.

'Grip that post good and tight,' said Mason, in a hushed tone every bit as vicious as the anger it replaced.

Viktor bound Charlie's hands together on the rear side of the post.

'Please, go easy, don't kill me,' whispered Charlie.

Viktor said nothing. He pulled the knot tight and stepped away to join Mason.

'One hundred lashes,' said Mason, passing Viktor the whip.

'No, please, no,' Charlie pleaded.

'You can stop when he tells you the truth.'

Viktor looked at the whip, unable to take it from Mason's hand.

Mason frowned. 'Whip him!' he growled.

Viktor took the whip, his hand trembling. He'd never beaten anything or anyone. His body refused to move.

Mason squinted at him. 'You religious, boy?'

Confused, Viktor nodded.

'You recall the ten commandments, given to Moses?'

Viktor nodded.

'Thou shalt not steal. That's one of them. There isn't one that says thou shalt not whip a thieving nigger.' Mason leaned into Viktor's face, the smell of rum on his breath. 'Are you willing to pay the price?'

Viktor frowned.

'Are you willing to pay the price, Viktor? You think all this,' Mason spread his arms indicating his plantation, 'just magically accumulates? You think that tobacco picks itself? You think I just harvest money straight from the ground? With no risk of crop failure? Thieving? Ships sinking? The cost must be borne, order must be kept. You want paying, you pester me for money, to have the things you want, to be the man you want to be – sure, of course you do! But are *you* willing to pay the price?'

Viktor gritted his teeth and took the whip. He stepped forward and unfurled the coil of leather on the dirt. His arm froze.

'Are you willing to pay the price, Viktor? If not...'

Viktor pulled back his arm and flicked it forward, lashing the leather against Charlie's back.

Charlie screamed.

'Whip him hard, Viktor! Ninety-nine to go,' Mason ordered.

Viktor brought the whip down again, slicing the skin on Charlie's back. The crack pierced the morning air. The third lash on the open wound sent Charlie howling, fighting against the rope that restrained him.

'That's it, Viktor. Now faster, we haven't got all day. This bird will soon start to sing.'

With every lash, Viktor felt increasingly sick. Charlie was defenceless. As soon as Mason sensed him hesitate, he reprimanded him. After twenty lashes, Charlie's back was cut to ribbons. Blood ran down his buttocks and legs, staining the dirt red. Charlie cried. Tears trickled down Viktor's cheeks, He slowed his pace and began to use less force.

'Gimme that!' Mason snatched the whip from his hand and pushed him out of the way. He brought the whip down hard on Charlie's buttocks, spraying blood in the air. Again and again and again.

Viktor wiped his eyes. Unable to look, he turned around and looked towards the house on the far side of the lawn. In the downstairs windows, he saw the house slaves watching.

'Did you steal my rum, nigger?' snarled Mason, bringing the whip down hard on the back of Charlie's head, knocking it against the post.

'YES!' he cried.

'See, Viktor! I told you. *Never* trust a negro.'

Viktor's eyes widened and his stomach churned. If Charlie confessed what Viktor already knew, he might be joining him on the post.

Mason let fly another lash. 'Where is it?'

'It's gone, master.'

'Who drank it with you?'

'No one!'

Another lash.

'I swear. I traded it.'

Another lash.

'For a banza,' howled Charlie.

Satisfied Mason, nodded. 'Viktor, did he have a banza?'

'Not when I found him,' said Viktor, trying hard to sound convincing.

'You thought I wouldn't notice?' said Mason. 'You think I'm

stupid, do you, Darky?'

'No,' sobbed Charlie.

'Not even you'd be stupid enough to come into my house and steal it. Who got it for you?'

Charlie's body shook as he sobbed.

Mason took one of his pistols from his belt and passed it to Viktor. 'Put this in his mouth.'

Viktor's hesitation was met by the muzzle of the other pistol. He walked to the post, shuddering at the sight of the blood trickling from Charlie's back. He raised the pistol at arms-length, unable to look Charlie in the eye, he felt the muzzle clank against Charlie's teeth as he forced it into his mouth.

'Pull the trigger,' said Mason with all the nonchalance of offering a guest a seat.

The sight of Charlie's contorted face, bloodshot eyes, and sodden face was too much to bear. Viktor turned his head away and braced himself. Tears streamed down his cheeks.

'Grace. It was Grace,' shouted Charlie, his voice muffled by the pistol.

'That wasn't so hard, was it?' said Mason.

Viktor let his arm fall limp and walked back to Mason, returning his pistol.

Mason put his hand on the back of Viktor's neck and pulled him in. 'You did well, son.'

Viktor sighed with exhaustion and relief.

'Now let's fetch Grace.'

No! thought Viktor. *I can't do that to Grace.*

'Sir,' said Viktor, pulling out of his master's embrace, 'perhaps I should go and look for the banza? It must be hidden down by the wharf.'

He caught another whiff of the booze on Mason's breath; his eyes were bloodshot.

'Let me find it, Grace isn't going anywhere, she can wait,' Viktor reasoned, willing to say anything for this all to be over.

'Very well. Go and find it. I need a piss.'

Viktor turned his back on the scene, leaving Mason urinating on Charlie's limp body. He broke into a run as he passed the house, unable to look at the faces of the house slaves watching from the windows. He passed the lawn and safely ducked into the obscurity of the trees, where he wiped his tears away and dry retched onto the ground. Fighting to control his breathing, he began to walk towards the wharf, head down, thinking about the path he'd chosen: he recalled how his father had always resisted his suggestion to buy negroes.

He retrieved the offending banza from where Charlie had hidden it. It reminded him of an oversized wooden soup ladle, an animal skin stretched over the spoon end. He plucked the four strings, producing a series of unrelated twangs. *He must love music to risk all that.* He doubted Charlie would ever get to hear it played. It occurred to Viktor to pretend he couldn't find it; perhaps it would bring some meaning to Charlie's suffering. He dismissed the brief temptation. After what he'd just experienced, he was not willing to fall foul of his master. He worked for Mason, not Charlie.

Viktor rested in the woods for an hour before walking back to the house, hopeful that the punishments would all be dispensed by the time he returned.

The front door was answered by Grace. Her normally radiant skin was pallid with fear. Her dark eyes were darting about and, although frightened, she had no bruises. Of all the slaves, she was the healthiest, sustained by kitchen scraps, one of the many benefits of her posting in the house.

Viktor was relieved to see her unharmed. His labours kept him outside, so their paths rarely crossed – aside from his night-time fantasies, in which the young and attractive Grace made regular appearances. Viktor would imagine them walking in the woods together, holding hands. One forbidden pleasure led to another... He was certain such dreams would never be reality.

'Is the master in?' he asked.

She nodded. 'He sleeping.'

'Can you give him this?' Viktor passed over the banza.

Her lip curled as she took it, fear briefly replaced by anger. 'Is Charlie alive?'

Viktor detected a note of steel in her voice. He nodded, unable to meet her eye. He wanted to offer her some comfort, to protect her from the reprisal that must still be coming, but no words were sufficient to ease whatever Mason had in store for her. He bid her goodbye and the door shut sharply.

Viktor walked around the house across the lawn, in between the tobacco barn and workshops, toward his accommodation. He glanced left over his shoulder; Charlie lay slumped as he'd last seen him. Checking there was nobody about, Viktor darted across the grass and checked on Charlie, relieved to see the small movement of breath from his ribs. He waved away the flies, the gashes beginning to dry at the edges. 'I'm sorry, Charlie,' he whispered.

Viktor went to his room where Zebedee had left him a breakfast of buttered bread and ham on his table. He sat, unable to eat and in no hurry to return to the fields, where Billy or Granville would be supervising in his absence. Thoughts of his father kept popping into his mind, and feelings of guilt and regret swelled in his gut. Tormented by his thoughts, he could stand a delay no further, he reached for his whip, only to realise he'd left it outside. His stomach turned as he realised he'd have to face Charlie, for he couldn't go into the field without his whip – not after what had happened this morning. With a heavy heart, he went to the whipping post, where Charlie lay slumped on the ground, his hands still fastened around the post – the knot that Viktor had tied held firm. Lying on the ground, caked in blood and dust, was his whip. His hand trembled as he reached for it, his stomach turning at the flecks of flesh that clung to the leather plaits. He wanted to apologise to Charlie, but he could find no words to do it justice. He walked off, trailing the unfurled whip behind him as he went in search of the slaves.

Fearing repercussions, both Billy and Granville stayed in the fields with him as a precaution. The rest of the day was mercifully uneventful. The slaves were quiet, refraining from their usual songs. By sunset, they had finished topping all of Mason's plants.

Charlie was still tied to the post when they returned, his head up and alert. Viktor avoided his eye and, after declining Billy and Granville's offer of a game of cards, retired to his room. He undressed, washed the dust from his skin in the bowl, keeping his face submerged while he held his breath, the cool touch of the water a balm. Slumped into his wooden chair, he closed his eyes, glad the day was over. In the quiet privacy of his room, he felt a confusing mix of emotions. He'd imagined that owning negroes, as men of any substance did, was a path to enrichment. He'd never considered that such a path was strewn with brutality. For the first time since arriving on Mason's plantation, Viktor questioned whether he could do what was required of him. Mason's words of *'paying the price'* rang in his ears. Perhaps he would harden to the demands in time, but did he truly want that?

A knock at the door interrupted his thoughts. The door opened before he could invite the visitor in. It was Mason, freshly shaven and washed, in a clean white shirt and breeches, with a small book in his hand – a stark contrast to how he'd appeared in Viktor's room in the early hours of that morning.

Viktor sprung to his feet.

'Please, stay seated,' said Mason, leaving the door ajar.

Viktor resumed his seat.

'You did well today, Viktor. I am pleased with you. You returned my negro to me along with the instrument he traded for my rum.'

'Thank you, master…' said Viktor, uneasy at the compliment.

'Discipline must be maintained, otherwise anarchy reigns.'

Uncertain of what to say, Viktor nodded.

'This is the King James Bible.' Mason held up the book in his hand. 'It's my wife's and occasionally I am prone to read it. It is, after all, the scripture of our kings, God's chosen representatives on Earth. Let me read you this section.' Mason opened the book and began to read: 'Paul's Epistle to the Ephesians, VI, 5-7. Servants, be obedient to them that are your masters according to the flesh, with fear and trembling, in singleness of your heart, as unto Christ; not with eye-service, as men-pleasers; but as the servants of Christ, doing the will of God from the heart; with good will doing service, as to the Lord, and not to men: knowing that whatsoever good thing any man doeth, the same shall he receive of the Lord, whether he be bound or free.'

Mason closed the Bible. There was a silence as Viktor considered the word of God.

'It is natural that one man should command another,' said Mason. 'We have a King, who commands us. I have negroes, a wife and you to command. Nature's law binds us to one another. If we don't observe this law of nature, our efforts won't amount to a hill of beans.'

Viktor sighed and nodded. Who was he to argue with the Bible?

'I want better for you, Viktor.'

Viktor felt emotion swell in him as their eyes met.

'You did well today, Viktor. Enjoy your reward.'

Viktor frowned. He hadn't expected a reward.

'Come in,' commanded Mason, raising his voice.

The floorboards creaked and Grace appeared in the doorway. She was in her grey dress and white lace coif, but without her apron. Her eyes were damp with tears.

Viktor froze.

'She smuggled the rum from my cellar. So, since she has seen fit to do as she pleases with my goods, tonight, you may do as you please with my goods. See if you can father me a little mulatto slave child.'

Mason winked at Viktor, then left, closing the door behind him. Grace continued to sob. Viktor stood to comfort her. She turned her head as he tried to wipe her tears away with his thumb.

'Come, sit here,' he indicated the bed. Viktor was uncertain what to say or do, as the long-awaited prospect of forsaking his virginity finally presented itself.

She sat as commanded and turned her body away from Viktor.

With her gaze averted, Viktor grew nervous as he indulged himself in the unrestricted sight of her curves. He imagined breasts baying to be set free from the confines of her tight dress. Hips so rounded they would have to be prized out. He studied her dress, unsure how to remove it. His thoughts were interrupted by her sobs.

'Can I offer you some water?' he asked.

She shook her head, wiped her nose on her sleeve and made no attempt to dry her eyes. Viktor grappled with how to put her at ease, so he might finally enjoy the fruits of a woman.

'I'm frightened too,' he offered. It was met with more sobs. Grace's head fell into her hands.

'Mason expects me to...'

Grace groaned, unable to control herself. 'Just get it over with, fool!'

Viktor was speechless. No words would draw forth her consent. He fumbled at the buttons of her dress that ran down her spine, revealing her dark skin beneath. He pulled the dress clear from her shoulders and tugged it from her arms. Grace didn't resist, nor did she assist. Nude from the waist up, Viktor was afforded his first view of her breasts. They hugged her body, flatter than he'd imagined. She met his eyes with a scowl.

Viktor felt uneasy; she may protest, but he was only doing as Mason had ordered. It hadn't been his design. *Perhaps it will be better for her if I'm naked too.* He removed his trousers and underwear. The sight of his naked body set her sobbing again. He knelt down in front of her on the floor. Her head twisted away from him. He leant forward and kissed her tenderly on the cheek. She remained frozen. Putting his hands on her waist, he felt the soft warmth of her skin and ran his fingers up her flanks, cupping her breasts in his palms. Grace began to howl.

'Ssshh,' Viktor tried to silence her. Snot streamed from her nose and her body trembled.

'This is ridiculous.' He pulled back, grabbing his trousers. Hands trembling, frustrated, humiliated, he dressed himself.

Mason would have beaten her into silence. Viktor didn't want the memory of his first time to be the crying of an unwilling victim.

'Look, if Mason asks, tell him I...'

She nodded, then wiped her eyes and put her arms back into her sleeves, recovering her modesty.

'Would you like some water?'

She shook her head again.

Viktor returned to his wooden chair and for half an hour they sat in awkward silence, while the sky outside turned from dusk to night. Grace finally got to her feet, holding her unbuttoned dress against her bosom.

'I should go now.'

After she had left, Viktor undressed and lay on his bed. Time passed slowly; he shifted and turned, but he couldn't find comfort. His thoughts skipped between Charlie's lacerated back, Grace's howl, the booze on Mason's breath, the cold judging looks on the faces of the other slaves. From the outside, the plantation had looked like the essence of civility. But within, it was as violent and primitive as anything Viktor could have imagined.

From outside came a cry of pain. He climbed out of bed and dashed to the window.

Charlie was still tied to the whipping post. In front of him, the dark of night was interrupted by the orange glow of flames. The banza was burning.

22

Sylvia was alone in the kitchen, washing up the plates from her masters' lunch of chicken stew. Flies hovered over the bucket by the backdoor, filled with the bird's entrails that she still had to dispose of. The house bore a heavy atmosphere; the mollies were having another one of their tiffs. Such fallings out had become increasingly frequent over the last year. Sylvia would crook her ear to the doors as she passed. Hugo Somerton, who was woman in all but body, was upset with Mr Benson for something, which Sylvia could not yet discern. Mr Somerton seemed to find it hard to practise the forgiveness that their religion preached, but all the while, Mr Benson patiently endured his lover's outbursts. They had retired upstairs, presumably to sort out their differences.

Sylvia dried the plates and stacked them up on the shelf, marking the end of another lunch during her time in their employ. She cut herself a slice of bread and took an apple from the bowl and sat at the table. The boredom was crushing. She couldn't even summon the energy to rebel against it. She was halfway through her apple when the door burst open. A red-faced Hugo bounded in.

'Where is my ring?' he demanded.

'Which one?'

'You know,' he hissed, 'my gold ring! It was on the dresser. It's gone.'

She shook her head. 'I haven't seen it.'

'You must have, it was there this morning.'

'I haven't been in your room yet today.'

'Jeremiah, she says she hasn't seen it!' he yelled up the stairs, his face turning more puce by the minute.

'I'll clean your room next, see if I can find it for you.'

'Oh, I see, because I'm too silly to find my own ring!' He noticed the expression on her face change. 'Go on, what were you going to say?'

Sylvia was tempted to make a joke about Mr Benson having a good idea of how to find Hugo's ring but thought better of it. 'Nothing. Once I've finished my apple, I'll look for you.'

'Well, I'm going out, but it seems I better wait until our maid has finished her lunch, can't be interrupting you eating your precious apple, just because I've lost my gold ring. Jeremiah gave me that ring. I've had it for years. Now it's gone!'

'Fine, stay calm…'

'Don't be telling me how to behave, young lady!'

'…I'll go and look for you.' Sylvia got to her feet and walked round the table towards the door.

'Oh, I see, so you can show me up. Well, there's somewhere we ought to check first, isn't there?' Hugo moved to block the door. 'Empty your pockets.'

'Me? You think I've taken it?' Sylvia could have punched him. She'd never been so honest in all her life. For nearly two years, she'd bowed and scraped to her masters, living like a bloody saint, only to be accused of the ways she'd left behind in her past.

'Once a thief, always a thief,' he huffed.

'How dare you!'

'What have you to hide?'

'You want to see my pockets? Fine.' Sylvia pulled out the inners of her pockets, turning out the fluff and dust that gathered there. 'Here, one handkerchief. Satisfied?'

Mr Somerton huffed again.

'You want me to strip?' she said, incited by his disappointment.

'That won't be necessary,' said a sombre-looking Mr Benson, arriving in the doorway behind Mr Somerton. 'Sylvia has been a good servant, Hugo.'

'Oh, that's so like *you*, Jeremiah, take her side.' Mr Somerton stomped up the hallway.

An apologetic look creased Mr Benson's face further. 'Hugo's not quite himself today, we must be patient with him.'

The stare they shared said everything that needed to be said. 'Come, it will pass. God will shepherd us through these times.'

God this, God that. Sylvia had had enough of their deferring all responsibility to God. She stepped past Mr Benson and ran up the stairs into their bedroom. She checked the top of the dresser, where two dishes were left for their jewellery. Neither contained a ring. She got down on her knees and pressed her cheek to the floor, scanning the floorboards. There was a thick layer of dust under the dresser, which she'd need to clean. Nothing. She turned and checked under the bed, moving the unmade covers that draped over the edge onto the floor. There was a small ting, as Mr Somerton's gold ring dropped onto the floor. It sat in plain sight. She'd found it in less than a minute. If he wasn't so quick to blow his top, he would have found it too. She stared at it, the light from the window shining against the lustre of the metal.

'Sod them,' she whispered to herself as she picked it up. She glanced over her shoulder and slipped it past her breast, tucking it into the fold of her undergarment. She made a play of checking the rest of the room.

'He's right,' she announced to Mr Benson as she came downstairs, 'it's nowhere to be found.'

'Thank you for looking. It'll turn up somewhere.'

Sylvia smiled. 'I expect so.'

An hour later, Sylvia stepped out into the street, a wicker shopping basket over her forearm. The afternoon sun had turned London into a smoky furnace, noxious with the smell of coal, dung, entrails and humanity. She rounded the corner and bumped into a man.

'Hello, sis.' It was her brother, Jacob.

Composing herself she hugged him extra tight. 'Am I glad to see you.' She explained the events around Mr Somerton's ring. Jacob laughed as she produced it from her breast. First checking over her shoulders, he examined it. 'What will you do with it?' he asked, as they walked down the street.

'I think I'll keep it, in lieu of payment.'

'Good idea. They owe you that much.'

It was true. They'd been kind. She could read and write. But she'd be twenty-one in a month's time. She may have forsaken crime and drink, yet her life remained stubbornly unfulfilled. Many would say a woman of her station had no right to expect a husband, family, or home of her own. But the more she wished for them, the further away they seemed.

'We should melt this down, turn it into something else. I know a bloke on Chancery Lane who'll do it for us.'

Sylvia felt a rush of excitement. If she was to be accused of the crime, she might as well have the benefit of the proceeds. Once it was fashioned into a pendant, she could claim it was a gift from an admirer. Satisfied they had sufficient time, Jacob slipped the ring in his pocket, and while they walked, she caught up on the gossip from the East End. Past St Paul's and up to the Strand, the street was wide, the main thoroughfare between the cities of London and Westminster. The mansions of previous centuries had been demolished and replaced by chop houses, coffee houses, taverns and shops, filling the space left vacant as the well-to-do continued their march west, upwind in search of the fresh prevailing winds.

Outside the Star tavern, a well-known brothel, a rotund middle-aged man was sweeping up broken glass on the ground. All the building's windows were smashed. Two rosy-cheeked whores looked down from the second-floor window.

'What happened here?' asked Jacob.

The man's temper flared. 'Bunch of sailors came into port last night. Once they'd finished with my girls, they accused them of stealing all their wares!' Spittle flew from the man's mouth as his vitriol poured forth against the sailors. 'Scoundrels tore up my place. I'm trying to make an honest living!' he barked as Jacob and Sylvia said nothing and continued walking.

They heard the shouting as they turned right into Chancery Lane and were confronted by a mob standing outside another brothel, shouting abuse up at the open windows. Sylvia's senses came to life. The men were clearly drunk, brandishing brickbats and clubs. One of them urinated against the door to the brothel. Another launched a brick, smashing a first-floor window. A scream came from within. Cheers ran through the crowd of men. Street urchins slunk between the sailors, looking for any opportunity. One of them was struck down by a sailor for trying to pick his pocket. He was spat at as he lay on the street.

Riotous protest was not an uncommon sight in London, regarded either as bringing attention to a legitimate cause, or – more likely in the case of these marauding sailors – good sport.

The brick that had crashed through the window was returned with interest, striking a man full in the face. A night-soil bucket was upended from the top floor, sending the mob surging away from the filth that splattered on the street. Curses turned to violence as bricks were thrown in retaliation, more glass was smashed, and the front door charged. The wood creaked under the weight of their press.

'I think we'd better find another way,' said Jacob.

Sylvia gasped as she turned to see a line of red-coated soldiers forming up at the entrance to Chancery Lane, blocking off their escape.

'Shit,' said Jacob.

An officer on horseback, wearing a black hat with oversize plumage, was mounted high over his ranks of men who were lined up three-deep, their muskets drawn.

'Company!' shouted the officer, gaining the attention of the mob. 'Go get 'em, boys,' he commanded, a wide grin across his face.

Jacob grabbed Sylvia's hand and ran towards the mob. Filled with drink, they showed no desire to run, squaring up to the advancing soldiers. Jacob tried to barge through the ruffians, dragging Sylvia in his wake. Her wicker basket slipped from her grasp. She felt a sailor grope her, uttering profanities as he pulled her towards him. She smelled the brandy on his rancid breath and screamed as she lost Jacob's hand. The soldiers charged, roaring as they clashed with the front lines of the sailors. Sylvia wriggled free, falling to the ground. A man trampled her ankle as he dashed forward. The man who'd held her, gripped her hair and pulled her away. The pain through her scalp was like nothing she'd ever felt. Jacob returned and punched the man in the jaw, felling him. Seeing this, the sailor's mate swung his club catching Jacob across the jaw, knocking him off his feet. Sylvia scrambled to her feet and with all her strength kicked Jacob's assailant in the groin. He yelped and rolled on the floor, fighting for breath. Jacob staggered over to Sylvia. Gunshots sounded, the bangs echoing against the buildings astride the street. Screams came from somewhere amongst the mob as men stopped the shot with their bodies. Those able to run fled the scene. Dazed, Sylvia and Jacob were knocked over as the sailors rushed away.

'That'll do, lads,' shouted the officer nonchalantly, as his horse ambled up the street. Ignoring him, the soldiers, in pairs and threes, kicked and beat the fallen men. Injured sailors struggled to their feet.

'Shoot anyone that moves,' the officer shouted.

'Scum!' came the cry from the damaged brothel. Sylvia wasn't sure if this was directed at the sailors responsible for inciting the trouble, or at the soldiers. Despite their actions to control the riot, people still resented the soldiers – after all, these men were of their own kind, society's poorest, who were now being turned against them. Used without mercy or consequence, and yet still paid by their taxes.

As fallen sailors groaned on the ground, a sergeant brandished his musket at Jacob, ready to fire. 'On your feet, against the wall.'

'My sister and I were just passing,' protested Jacob, only to receive another blow to his jaw from a musket butt.

'Oi, it's true! We were just passing,' said Sylvia, struggling to get to her feet.

'Shut your trap, you little tart!' said the sergeant.

The dishevelled figures took their place against the silversmith's shop, opposite the brothel. Sylvia attended to Jacob, examining his swollen jaw. Soldiers stood guard, the musket poised, ready to fire at anyone who ran. Faces began to appear at the broken windows of the brothel. 'Burn in hell, you scum!' came the shout from the damaged brothel window.

The officer steadied his horse and studied his captives as his men went down the line, frisking them down, searching for weapons. As a soldier began to shake down Jacob, he protested to the officer, 'We were just passing, honest to God we were, we had nothing to do with...'

'I saw you in the middle of the riot,' said the officer, his voice low and steady.

'That's my basket,' shouted Sylvia, pointing to the mangled heap of wicker on the shit-covered street.

The officer didn't turn his head to look where she was pointing.

''Ere,' said the soldier frisking Jacob. He held up a gold ring, 'He had this stuffed in his pocket.'

Jacob looked terrified. Sylvia shouted, 'That's mine!'

The officer glanced at their clothes, then laughed.

'Company, march these reprobates to Newgate. They're going to prison, where they'll face trial for disturbing the peace,' he paused and looked directly at Jacob and Sylvia, 'and for thievery.'

23

July 25ᵗʰ, 1752
Quebec, New France

The Marquis Du Quesne had barely been in Quebec long enough to settle his sea legs. He'd sent orders ahead of his arrival, recalling all French military officers to be in Quebec, ready to receive him as soon as he disembarked. Regarding himself in the mirror, he straightened the long silver wig that curled over his shoulders. His ruddy cheeks and yellow eyes betrayed his penchant for fine living. He smoothed his thick moustache and plumped his cravat. He was ready. The colonials had made a pig's ear of matters in the Americas. The King had ordered him to take personal responsibility for securing the rivers of the Ohio Valley for France, lest the dithering British be afforded sufficient time to organise themselves, driving a wedge between New France and Louisiana. He picked up his cane and left his private chamber.

Trotting down the stairs, he ignored the acknowledgements of the house staff and strode through the double doors leading to the banqueting suite.

'I am your new commander,' he announced to the rag-tag assembly of personnel who were the basis of his military command. 'From this point on, the Americas will no longer be a source of embarrassment for France. We will purge the southern valleys of the English. This land belongs to the King and he would very much like to realise a profit from it.'

Lieutenant Céloron, his most senior officer, bristled at the criticism. It had been his foolish escapade to plant lead plaques along the rivers. The man's mouth was open, as he waited for an opportunity to justify his failures. Du Quesne had no interest.

'There is only one thing the English understand,' he continued. 'Strength. Tomorrow, you will ready the largest detachment of the French population from these provinces. Every male of fighting age will be seconded to assist in building the mightiest chain of fortifications outside France. Is that clear?'

There were some nodding heads.

'How are we to treat the Indians?' came a voice.

'They are not to be harmed. We will welcome trade with them, but if they wish to trade with the English, they will have to do so beyond French borders. From now on, not one Englishman will set foot on French soil. Everything west of the Appalachian Mountains is France, and your King orders you to defend it with your lives. Céloron, attend to the details and report to me by Friday with your plan.'

Du Quesne waved an arm and turned to leave the room, a renewed sense of zeal in his stride. *Woe betide these English for underestimating France.*

24

The grey light of dusk was settling over Lawrence Washington's house as his brother arrived. George left his horse in the barn and then stopped outside the front door to compose himself. Upon reading Anne's letter, he'd abandoned his plans, and raced the forty miles from Fredericksburg. His heart was still thumping like a drum. This home, which housed so many fond childhood memories, was cast in a pall. He knocked on the door and waited.

Anne opened the door, her face pale and weary. 'George, thank heavens you made it in time. Come in.'

The small hallway was lit with candles, and an invisible fog of sadness hung in the air.

'He's upstairs.'

George strode up the steps two at a time, then took a deep breath outside the bedroom door before going in.

The small room was dim, a lone candle on the bedside table. The open dormer window let in a cool evening breeze, but it wasn't enough to clear the musty scent of decay. In the bed lay what little was left of Lawrence, emaciated from consumption. George knelt beside him and watched him gently dozing, his breath shallow and feeble. He'd deteriorated more than George thought possible: his brother was unrecognisable. He laid his hand on Lawrence's forehead. The skin was cold to the touch. His eyes were sunken, his cheek and jaw bones, once concealed by ruddy cheeks, now stood proud and the skin draped over them like wet washing hung out to dry.

Tears welled in George's eyes and trickled down his cheeks. They'd tried everything to help Lawrence recover. Their trip to Barbados, Lawrence's trip to London, they'd made repeated journeys to the warm springs at Bath, in the west of Virginia. All of it, to no avail.

George took Lawrence's hand in his, closed his eyes and offered a small prayer. He wiped the tears from his cheeks on the back of his coat sleeve. Lawrence's eyelids opened a crack and George saw the smallest of upward twinges in his brother's lips.

'I love you, brother.' George wiped his nose and sniffed. 'I will miss you more than you will ever understand.' Tears streamed freely down his cheeks, unable to restrain the emotions that wanted to escape his body. 'I will make you and Father proud, and when one day we meet again in heaven…' Words failed George as he broke into a fit of sobbing. He felt a tiny squeeze of his fingers and then Lawrence's body fell still. His breath ran out and peace descended on the room as he departed this life.

George held his brother's limp hand in his own and cried out. The shock of the inevitable having now, finally, occurred hit him like a hammer to his heart. He slumped to the floor. He was vaguely aware of Anne comforting him as he sobbed, unable to restrain his grief.

The most important person in his life was gone. What comfort he might have hoped for in no longer seeing Lawrence suffer had yet to make its presence felt.

***

The next morning, as was customary, Lawrence's body was laid to rest in the family tomb with his kin. Once the formalities had been attended to, George spent much of the next two days sleeping in the guest room.

He finally surfaced in the early evening and found Anne sitting outside at the back of the house in her rocking chair, a closed book resting on her lap.

'May I join you?' It was the first time he had spoken in days.

Anne nodded and forced a smile. George kissed the top of her head, savouring the smell of her hair, and took the seat left vacant by Lawrence.

The trees on the riverbank had been cleared, opening up the view to the Potomac River and Maryland's wooded shore beyond. The water rested at slack tide and a half-moon hovered low in the sky.

George wondered if Lawrence was looking down on them. Like everything else his eyes settled upon, the thought reminded him of his loss. Every inanimate object, the shoes by the door, the coat on the peg, the hairbrush on the sideboard, all these surpluses of daily life reflected a constant reminder of the one being who was no longer present. Lawrence's absence was inescapable.

'What are you reading?' George nodded to the book.

'*The Discourses of Epictetus*. It was Lawrence's favourite. I'm losing the light for reading but holding it makes me feel close to him.'

'How are you?' asked George after a pause.

'I have moments when I am glad it's over... His suffering, being forced to watch his deterioration. Then there are moments when I can't believe he's gone, and I wonder what on earth I'm going to do without him.' Anne blotted her eyes with a handkerchief. 'What about you?'

'I'm not sure. I...can't bring myself to believe that he's gone...' Saying it aloud made him crumble with grief. Tears poured, his nose ran. A pain deep in his heart robbed him of breath. 'It's so unfair, it makes you wonder if there really is a God. Why would he take him? I have nobody now. What am I going to do without him?' George broke down again, curling over in his chair. 'My life has been turned upside down...'

'Pull yourself together, George,' snapped Anne. 'Do you grieve for Lawrence or yourself?'

George sat upright and wiped his eyes.

'I'm left a widow,' Anne continued. 'Sarah is two years old and will never remember her father. I've lost everyone bar her, and yet you sit here and cry for yourself.'

'Anne, I'm so sorry, I didn't think—'

'It's time you stopped pitying yourself and grew up, George. You always complained about Lawrence sheltering you. Well, now he's gone.'

The two sat in silence and watched the sky slowly fade to darkness. George's thoughts were finally interrupted by Anne.

'I'm sorry, George, I shouldn't have snapped at you.'

'No, Anne, you're right,' George sighed. 'I was being foolish.' He was no stranger to death and had known that Lawrence would not recover. 'I feel numb. Like I've fallen in freezing water, but I'm not cold.'

Anne placed her hand on his. 'Grief is the price we pay for those we love. You should read this.' Anne passed him the well-worn book. 'It's the wisdom of the Stoics. They teach us not to desire the world as you would have it, but want it as you find it, for every event is part of a greater whole.'

'Well, right now there's a lot I might change about this world.'

'They would say that you'll spend the rest of your life embittered. The only choice we –any of us – have is how we respond to events beyond our design. No matter how terrible the event, we must all search for the gift within it.'

'Maybe.' No matter how sage the advice, it felt impossible to take when the wound was still so raw.

'What was it Shakespeare said?' Anne continued. "Tis nothing good, nor bad, but thinking makes it so?' She cleared her throat. 'Or something like that.'

'You're a wise woman, Anne. Lawrence was lucky to have you at his side.'

She snorted. 'Lawrence was the wise one in this household. Whatever I know is by virtue of being with him.'

'I always envied Lawrence his education in England. The people he met, the teachers he had. Alas, another dream that my mother poured cold water on.'

The door opened and Clarence, the house slave, brought them a plate of buttered bread and biscuits. Anne declined; George tucked in, suddenly aware of how famished he was.

'Life rarely goes to plan, George. But your fate will be decided by your character. So the Stoics say,' she said, tapping the book that rested in his lap. 'If you want to realise your ambitions, then it is not enough to dream them, George – you must act.'

'What do you mean?'

'You've always wanted to serve in the military. Well, Lawrence's position as adjutant to the Virginia militia is vacant.'

'He wouldn't want me to have it.'

'Well, he's not here to deny you any more, is he?'

George shook his head and sighed. 'Mother would never allow it.'

'You're twenty now, George, in the prime of your life. It's time you stepped clear of your mother's shadow. She, like Lawrence, only wanted to protect you, but you can't spend the rest of your life cosseted in cotton wool. In my opinion, they do you a great disservice. You should experience the world. We're lucky to live in an age where you can sail the Atlantic on a whim and be in Europe before the season changes. It's not natural for young men to be cooped up.'

George thought back to his conversation with Dinwiddie. The importance of the sea, his premonition about a world war. It seemed so farfetched, especially here on the fringes of the globe. He'd always dreamed of serving with the army, fighting for his country, but it was a notion he'd since dismissed.

'I don't know, Anne, I'm making a respectable living surveying, I have ample work.'

'George, no man who measures land his whole life will ever amount to anything. That classless mother of yours has filled your head with petty ambitions and peasant attitudes. I'm a Washington now, and I'd like to say in future I'm proud to still be one – but not while I'm related to a man of trade. It's common, it's beneath you.'

'I didn't get given the chances Lawrence did,' George protested.

'Poppycock, George,' she turned to look at him directly. 'For years I've listened to you whingeing about the chances you've been denied. You say you want to serve your country, but when the moment presents itself, are you going to blink?'

'That's not fair—'

'Men of honour don't complain. They do something. You should speak to Governor Dinwiddie. Have Daddy put in a good word for you, if you must.'

What was it about death, wondered George, that liberated the normally restrained tongues of those around you? There was an honesty to death. Pretences were discarded and opinions offered freely, to be received without judgement or insult. Perhaps words did less harm when you were already in such pain.

'When are you finally going to demand the best of yourself, George?'

George snorted.

'These aren't my words, George, but the Stoics'.'

George ate the last biscuit and thanked Anne for the book, taking it with him as he retired. Grief had been replaced by restlessness. Aware it was a temporary wave, he decided to seize it. He sat at the small writing table in the spare room and wrote in his journal by candlelight. Rather than document his grief, he wrote about the life he imagined for himself. However fanciful, he committed in ink his ambitions. A Royal Commission in the army. Heroic deeds celebrated by a grateful nation. A wife and children. A plantation like that of the late Colonel Lee. By the time the ink well had run dry, he was in a state of quiet excitement.

After performing his ablutions, he poured himself a glass of wine and retired to bed. He opened *The Discourses of Epictetus* and began to read.

***

It was two days later that George walked under the ornate ironwork of the entrance gates to the Governor's Palace in Williamsburg. Topped by a golden crown, it was sandwiched between two brick columns that supported the English lion on one side and the Scottish unicorn on the other. He stopped and flattened the creases in his cream waistcoat, adjusted his neck scarf, removed his hat and gathered his breath. His legs were jelly from the hundred-forty-mile journey. He'd left Mount Vernon early, not wanting to burden Anne further, and had ridden hard the length of the colony. He should have been tired but what lay ahead was of too much importance. He approached the compact brick mansion, admiring the tall windows neatly spaced over two floors with dormers in the tiled roof above, crowned by a glazed cupola. Any sense of foreboding was eroded by the experience of dining here as the private guest of the Lieutenant Governor just six months ago.

The imposing door was opened by a footman in a green coat.

'George Washington. Seeking an audience with Governor Dinwiddie.'

The footman retreated indoors. Moments later, he reappeared and held the door open. George passed through the dark wood hallway, beneath the union flags that led to the ballroom.

'The Governor is about to take tea in the garden if you'd care to join him?' said the footman.

They passed through the long, carpeted ballroom with garish blue wallpaper and into the adjoining supper room, where the open doors led to a classical-style garden of neatly arranged shrubs and flowerbeds divided by symmetrical pathways.

Sitting at a small table in the middle of the pea-shingle path was Governor Dinwiddie, opposite another man with dark hair, whom George didn't recognise. Appraising the stranger, George concluded the creases at the corners of his eyes placed him in his thirties. His dark hair was greasy, his clothes were well-worn and his tatty shoes were not appropriate for the Governor's Mansion. George felt himself irritated that he would have to share his audience with Governor Dinwiddie, who had dispensed with his wig, leaving it on the tablecloth. Both men were in shirt sleeves, which George didn't consider proper.

'Hello Washington,' said Dinwiddie in his Scots accent. 'Care for some tea?' George joined them, reluctantly offering the stranger his hand. Dinwiddie remained seated and ordered a negro servant positioned out of sight by the door to fetch another chair.

'So, this is the Major Washington I've been hearing about?'

The man was Irish, George realised. That explained the shoes.

'Him? No.' said Dinwiddie, shaking his head. Before George could explain his brother's fate, Dinwiddie continued, 'It's opportune that you should arrive, Washington, I'd like you to meet another George, George Croghan. An Irishman, who became a Pennsylvanian – but don't hold that against him, now he's chosen to be Virginian,' Dinwiddie chuckled. 'You know one is not at liberty to choose one's religion down here, don't you, Mr Croghan?'

George grinned politely, Croghan's first impressions didn't make him an obvious entrant into refined Virginian society.

Before the Irishman could reply, Dinwiddie continued pontificating. 'This all started when we put that Dutchman William of Orange on the throne.'

George noticed Croghan frown, but Dinwiddie was holding court, just as he had done over dinner.

'If people choose their own king, their religion, their homeland,' he continued, 'where will it all end, I ask you?' Dinwiddie drew breath and took a sip of tea. 'Now we've got those hopeless Hanoverians on the throne. Will we discard them when it suits us? The whole thing makes a mockery of the hereditary monarchy! Gentlemen, what enlightened times we are living in – supposedly!'

'What brings you to Williamsburg, Mr Croghan?' asked George as his seat arrived. He noticed Croghan glance at the Governor.

'Washington's brother, Major Lawrence, is the president of the Ohio venture.' Dinwiddie waved his hand.

A lump came to George's throat at the mention of Lawrence. He hadn't yet heard himself say the words out loud to anyone that his brother was dead. He hadn't even gone home enroute to Williamsburg. Mother had never been Lawrence's greatest admirer and he hadn't wanted to risk saying something he'd regret when she inevitably upset him. George clenched his teeth as he battled to control his emotions.

'I was just telling your man here,' said Croghan in a manner too informal for the surroundings, 'that if you Virginians want any chance at land in the Ohio you need to act through me – and fast.'

George looked to the Governor and was surprised that he didn't seem to register the same offence to this man's manner.

'It's thanks to me that the Chief of the Iroquois struck a treaty with Virginia, not Pennsylvania,' said Croghan.

George bristled at the suggestion that this Irishman was to credit for Virginia's land grant from the King. Authority came from the top of society, not the bottom.

'But,' continued Croghan, 'you need to be aware of how bad things have got in the Ohio. Since the peace, the Iroquois have limited supplies and won't hold out long against a French advance.'

'A French advance?' George repeated.

'Aye. Be under no illusions – they ain't going away.' Croghan recounted events since the discovery of the lead plates claiming the land for France, up to the sacking of his trading post on the Miami River. 'If you want any chance of securing that land, you need to get out there and lay some markers of our own down,' he finished.

Who the devil is this man? thought George as the tea arrived. How dare he tell the Governor what he should be doing. It was contemptible. As the drinks were served, Croghan pulled a hip flask from his breeches and poured a nip of rum into his tea. George declined when offered. The Governor did likewise.

Dinwiddie turned to George. 'We'll ask Lawrence to raise the militia—'

It caught George off guard. He interrupted, 'He died. A few days ago.'

Dinwiddie put his tea down. 'My condolences, George. He was taken before his time.'

'Yes. Quite.' George was relieved as his emotions remained in check. The Irishman said nothing. A long pause ensued as they sipped their tea.

Eager to break the silence, George said what he'd come to say: 'Perhaps it is appropriate, given Mr Croghan's news, for me to volunteer my services?'

The Governor looked quizzical.

'Lawrence's passing leaves his post of adjutant vacant. I believe you will find me to be a most capable replacement.'

The Governor took a sip of his tea. Another awkward silence settled on the table.

'How old are you, Washington?' asked Croghan, his frown making obvious his opinion.

'Twenty, Sir,' said George, resenting the insinuation.

'Have you military experience?' probed Croghan.

George bridled at the implication. Lawrence had taught him a great deal of military matters.

'Fucking Jesus, you colonists; you can't be serious? The Ohio is no place for amateurs.'

George's temper stirred, yet he controlled his response, 'You forget yourself, Mr Croghan, such language...'

'Now, now, you two,' interrupted Dinwiddie, before turning his gaze toward George, 'I like you, Washington, but that notwithstanding, you know nothing of commanding men...'

'I'm a fast learner, Governor, I know I would be gifted at it. Let me prove it to you.'

'Young Washington, I dare say you're an honourable lad,' said Croghan patronisingly, even though it wasn't his place to reply on the Governor's behalf. 'When the French and their allies, the Huron, raided my trading post, they slaughtered everyone.'

There was a pause. Finally, George rebutted, 'Except you, it seems.'

Croghan leaned forward. 'Let me tell you what they did to my partner, Old Briton, the Chief of the Twightee. I watched with my own eyes as they captured him alive.' He jabbed his finger into the table. 'They put him in a pot and boiled him. Then, they ate him.'

'Quite the pot that must have been. A pity you couldn't save him,' said George. *What nonsense.*

Croghan scowled. 'It's not all balls and dances out there.'

'How long have you lived in America, Mr Croghan?'

'Long enough to know the frontier is no place for inexperience.'

The temerity of this man, thought George, who'd lived here his whole life. *This fellow's ill-clad shoes are barely dry from stepping off the boat and he's lecturing me on the dangers of my homeland!* He returned his attention to Dinwiddie, 'Governor, I must impress upon you my desire to serve my country as adjutant to the militia.'

Dinwiddie corrected him, 'We're a colony, Washington, not a country.'

'I meant Britain, sir.'

'Ha!' scoffed Croghan.

'Sir, I must say I find your manner most objectionable,' George fought to keep his voice calm. 'I cannot imagine what transgression I have performed to agitate you against me.'

'You've done nothing wrong, son,' said Croghan. 'I stand to gain hundreds of thousands of acres of the Ohio myself – provided we can keep the French at arm's length. That's a lot of land by anyone's standards – especially for a poor boy from Ireland who, unlike you, grew up without a pot to piss in; so don't be offended if I find it repulsive that my future might be resting in the hands of a boy not yet wise to the ways of the world. That's all, George, it's nothing personal.' Croghan winked.

'He has a point, George,' said Dinwiddie.

'Well, let me tell you both, I am not a boy, and since my brother's unfortunate passing, I too stand to gain land in the Ohio. He has bequeathed his shares in the Ohio to me. So, you can both be assured I have plenty of my own to lose.'

The servant appeared and refilled the teacups. This time, the Governor took a tot of rum in his.

'If what Mr Croghan says about the Iroquois is true, they'll welcome me with open arms, won't they?' George tried another tack.

'I'll say this for you, Washington, you're not short of confidence.'

'Then, sir, I implore you, let me…'

'No,' said Dinwiddie. 'One wrong move could provoke the French.'

George took a sip of his tea. He was no stranger to being told no. All his life he'd been too young or too inexperienced. Well, as Anne had said, until he acted differently, how could he expect different results? Determined, he returned his empty cup to its saucer.

'Governor, I too have friends in high places.' He referred to Anne's father who sat on Dinwiddie's council. 'All are capable of making your life in this colony very much harder than it already is. These people also know those in London who might have a say on your next posting. I hear the mosquitos in Georgia are very big.'

Dinwiddie laughed. 'You'll go far, Washington, of that I'm sure. Tell me, with everything Mr Croghan has said, why are you so keen to join the affray?'

'Because, Sir, I believe with every fibre of my body that I am destined to be a soldier and lead men in battle, for King and Country.'

'God help us,' muttered Croghan.

'Very well, Washington, I hereby appoint you to command the militia—'

'What? Are you mad?' Croghan protested.

'No, but my job might be easier if I were. Do you think, Mr Croghan, I have a queue of people daft enough to risk their necks for these posts?' snapped Dinwiddie. 'Washington, with immediate effect you will take charge of the militia…'

A smile beamed across George's face.

'…of our southern district.'

'Southern district?' George's smile vanished as quickly as it had formed.

'Yes. Civilising those southerners will serve as a great proving ground for someone without any military experience and such high ideals. Although, I hear the mosquitos are bigger down there.'

'Sir, I must protest! I want to be involved in the Ohio – I am not from the south...'

'No, Washington,' Dinwiddie leaned forward, pointing his finger at George's chin. 'Let me remind you who's in charge here; you join me at my table as my guest and then threaten me. I give you a post in the militia and then you complain that it's not the right district. By damn, I've never experienced such temerity.'

George wiped off a speck of the Governor's spittle that had landed on his chin. Rebuked, embarrassed, irritated, upset, George was lost for words. The southern part of Virginia was a wild and uncivilised place. All sailors and criminals, no balls or dances.

'But, Governor, what of the Ohio, I have shares in the venture?'

'That's for me to worry about.'

'But...'

'I do you a great honour, Washington. I'd be grateful if I were you. Now, if you'd care to excuse Mr Croghan and me?'

Croghan winked at him as George stood to make his departure.

'What rank will I hold?'

'Major. For being a major thorn in my side!' barked Dinwiddie.

As George left the mansion and walked towards the tavern, feelings of bitterness toward Croghan and Dinwiddie gave way. He consoled himself, he had won a partial victory. Anne's advice to take action had been right; it had been a bruising encounter, but George was taking the mantle from Lawrence. Losing his older brother had been devastating, but following in his footsteps, George would do his brother's memory proud.

He would write to thank the Governor and apologise for his presumptuousness. Perhaps Anne's father could insist Dinwiddie transfer his responsibilities to the northern district.

He'd order a uniform from London. For, irrespective of the dingy posting, the boy who had spent so much of his childhood playing with carved wooden toy soldiers, was now one himself.

Ready to tread the stage and fulfil his destiny as an officer.

25

August 2ⁿᵈ, 1752
Fitzbarton Plantation

Time was a blur for Viktor. The days were a monotony of watching others labour. He hadn't seen Grace in person since she'd left his room. Nor had she visited his imaginations. Whatever dreams of their coupling he may have once had, his thoughts of her were now tarnished with sorrow.

Charlie had recovered sufficiently that he'd rejoined the slaves in the field. He had not spoken to Viktor since, instead relying on curt head nods and cold stares.

Mason had gone away on business, leaving his wife, Mary, nominally in charge. It was two weeks until the tobacco would be ready to pull up, and Mason would be back by then, but in the meantime, Mary had decided she wanted to extend the lawn in front of the house and had ordered Viktor to have the trees felled. When Viktor asked if Mr Fitzbarton was in accordance with her instructions, he'd witnessed her temper for the first time.

'You'll do as I damn well say, or I'll have my husband throw you off this plantation,' she had hissed. Her delivery had been more distressing than the threat itself; since the banza episode, Viktor had found himself flirting with what lay beyond the plantation. Virginia, America, Britain and all her territories. An entire world and the means with which to explore it lay beyond, yet his whole life was confined to a few small acres of Virginia countryside. But even Viktor knew that the reality of such daydreams was filled with innumerable practical difficulties. Although he had some coins hidden, they wouldn't last long. He had no trade, no reference, no means of supporting himself. Here, at least, he had a roof, a bed, clothes and good food in his belly. He would do as Mary required.

He gathered ten of the youngest and fittest slaves, including the still-silent Charlie. Billy accompanied him, bringing axes and saws from his wood shop. By mid-morning, the crack and fall of timber echoed through the plantation.

'You got any tobacco, Viktor?' asked Billy as they supervised the work.

Viktor checked his pockets. 'No. Not on me.'

Billy groaned. 'I'll nip back to quarters and get mine. You all right here for a minute, Vik?'

Viktor nodded. Everybody was busy with chopping, sawing or moving wood.

Billy ran back across the lawn. Viktor's thoughts returned to Betsy, the slave girl Charlie had suggested he could have all those weeks ago, when he'd bargained to avoid his punishments. She wasn't nearly as pretty as Grace, but as time passed, Viktor's mind had become more open to the prospect. Out of the corner of his eye, he noticed two slaves down their tools and begin chatting. Irritated, Viktor cracked his whip in their direction. The saws fell quiet and the axes ceased to chop. The slaves turned and stared at Viktor.

'Back to work,' he shouted.

He cracked his whip again, but the warning was ignored. As one, the slaves moved towards him. Viktor took a step back as Charlie approached, his axe in the air. Viktor went to crack the whip again, but Charlie shook his head, his eyes narrowed in determination.

Viktor's mouth went dry. He tried to shout, but Charlie raised his finger to his lips, silencing him. Viktor began to shake as he was encircled. From behind, hands grabbed his arms to restrain him.

'Please, don't…'

'Ssssshh, white boy,' said Charlie, his eyes dark and menacing.

Viktor tried to move but was held firm. Charlie reached out and grabbed Viktor's balls in his hand. His grip tightened. With his other arm, he raised the axe blade to Viktor's throat; the blade brushed against stubble.

'We can come for you anytime we want, Viktor,' Charlie whispered. 'When you sleep. When your back is turned. You are not safe here. We can kill you whenever we choose. You remember that, white boy. You touch my Grace again, I'll cut your balls with this axe. You hear me, little white boy?'

Viktor nodded.

Charlie squeezed his balls, then released his grip. He winked, just as Mason had done.

Viktor staggered as he was released. As one, the slaves returned to their duties, and the morning was once again filled with the sound of sawing and chopping wood. Viktor's heart slowed, and he released the breath he'd been holding. Bending over, he thought he might be sick.

Moments later, Billy returned. 'Here you are, you want a bit of this, Vik?'

Viktor snatched the twist of tobacco from Billy's hand. He took a bite and crushed it between his teeth.

'Jesus, Vik, you look like you seen a ghost. You all right?'

'Yes. Thank you.'

Billy began talking about something he'd seen as he'd passed the house, but his words washed over Viktor. His mind knew he had to escape this awful place. Whatever comforts it afforded, it wasn't worth his life.

'You all right, Vik?' Billy repeated.

'Yeah, yeah, fine. Must be the heat.'

Billy continued to chatter while Viktor began to plot his escape. Pride prevented him from returning to his father's farm. There were only two ways out: on foot, or by boat.

26

Never had the phrase 'out of the frying pan and into the fire' held as much meaning as it did today for Sylvia. For the past fortnight, she'd resided at His Majesty's pleasure, in the abjectly filthy conditions of Newgate prison, while she and Jacob awaited trial for their alleged involvement in the Strand riots.

Her brief prison sojourn had undoubtedly been the worst experience of Sylvia's life. With no foreign wars to occupy the country's poor, the gaol was overcrowded. The inmates, having been charged for their entry, were then left to their own devices. Drunkenness and disease were rife, and the most canny of them exploited the internal hierarchy, of which the gaolers were naturally at the top.

Having escaped its violent confines for the day, Sylvia and Jacob found themselves under the full intensity of the public glare at the Old Bailey courtroom. The earlier fizz of gossip in the gallery had given way to attentive silence as the audience looked down upon the performance. A stage filled with the props of justice. A plaster portico clung to the wall in front of Sylvia and Jacob. On its top, His Majesty's lion and unicorn pranced astride the royal arms, and underneath, the sword of justice was fixed above the judge, who, in his silver wig and red robe, was listening to the prosecutor as he delivered his closing remarks to the jury box. There sat twelve silver-haired men, good and true. Arranged in three rows and surrounded by carpentry, they

233

resembled chess pieces in a box, and represented a selection of London's middling sort, tradespeople, artisans and shopkeepers. They enjoyed enough of life's advantages to make an honest living, but not so much to be sufficiently insulated from suffering the crimes committed by those less fortunate than themselves. Sylvia felt their stares resting on her as she tried to suppress her short and rapid breaths. By her side, surrounded by the wood panelling of the dock, was her brother Jacob. His face still black and blue from the beatings he'd endured in gaol. His mouth was missing teeth and his fingers were broken. The injuries had been blamed on his fellow inmates, but she knew they'd been delivered by the clenched fists of the Thief Takers, who'd mercilessly beat confessions out of him.

Following Jacob and Sylvia's arrest, the soldiers, in exchange for gratuities, had passed custody of their captives over to the Thief Takers, ever sharp-eyed for opportunity. With their connections in the criminal underworld, Jacob had soon been identified as a member of the Whitechapel gang, responsible for numerous acts of petty theft, muggings and other peccadilloes. Their attack on theatregoers some four years ago was still on record, and their victims now sat in the gallery, having offered a reward for their apprehension. All these years later, they were still willing to honour it, despite their possessions having long since been traded. Sylvia avoided their adjudging stares.

The lawyer prosecutor concluded his summary, 'So, here we have two notorious criminals whose crimes have been a blight on society. Arrested at the scene of the disturbance, and found in possession of a gold ring, for which no credible explanation has been offered. Two footpads, schemers and now rioters, I urge the members of the jury to condemn them.'

A tear appeared in the corner of Jacob's bruised eye.

'Hear, hear,' shouted a man from the gallery, whom Sylvia recognised from the night of the theatre robbery.

'Order!' called the judge. 'Do the accused wish to offer a defence?'

Her hands trembling, Sylvia said meekly, 'We do.'

'Speak up, woman,' said the judge, who looked surprised that it should be her and not her brother who spoke. 'And you will remember to address me as Your Honour.'

'Yes, Your Honour. Sorry.' Not a great start. 'The jury have been told lies. I am employed in the service of Mr Jeremiah Benson of Cheapside. My brother and I was running an errand for Mr Benson, and my brother agreed to chaperone me.'

'Can you prove this?' interrupted the judge.

'Yes. Mr Benson will confirm what I say is true.'

'Then you may wish to call him to testify as your witness,' said the judge, looking impatient as he made notes with his ink quill.

'Very well.' Sylvia caught Mr Benson's eye, looking solemn as he sat next to Mr Somerton in the gallery. Behind them sat her sister Caroline alongside the Nicholsons, all looking anxious and out of place. Mr Benson rose to his feet and shuffled past the onlookers to make his way to down to the front of the court, taking his place in the witness box. He swore an oath on the Bible.

'Mr Benson, I am sorry for troubling you,' she began. 'Could you please confirm to the jury what I say is true?'

He took his time, shuffling and clearing his throat before addressing the jury. 'We took in Miss Coppell in the fall of the year seventeen forty-nine. She has laboured in the capacity of house servant and parlour maid for me since then, up until her recent apprehension. I have found her to be reliable and honest in that time. She has learned to read and write and has acted respectably.'

Sylvia felt her shoulders relax a little.

'I was going to the market, wasn't I, Mr Benson?' she prompted.

'The witness cannot testify to the accused's intentions,' the prosecutor cut in.

'But I always went to market at that time, didn't I, Mr Benson?' Sylvia pressed on.

'I believe so, yes.'

'See! Then we just happened on the disturbance, moments before the soldiers arrived. We was caught between the two. When we tried to escape, we got trampled!'

Sylvia looked to the jury, sensing she was winning their favour.

'Very well, Miss Coppell, and what of the gold ring found on your brother's person?' asked the judge. 'Did your brother take the opportunity to pilfer and pickpocket?'

There was a long silence. Sylvia looked at Jacob, tears streaming down his face. He gave the smallest, barely perceptible nod of his head. They'd not been given the chance to straighten their story prior to court, having been held in separate prison wards.

'The ring, Miss Coppell,' the judge repeated.

'The ring belonged to me!'

There was a gasp as everyone turned to see Hugo Somerton raise his hand from the gallery. 'It went missing that morning!'

'Order!' demanded the judge as people began to chatter. Sylvia felt her heart sink. Would her neck stretch because of a single weak moment?

'The ring was nothing to my brother,' cried Sylvia. 'Mr Somerton had lost the ring earlier that day. I found it.'

'Then why was it in your brother's possession? A known thief,' barked the prosecutor.

'I was upset – Mr Somerton accused me of taking it, so—' she sobbed '—so I did! But I was going to return it – I was just upset.'

'Hah!' The prosecutor swung his arm towards the jury in triumph.

'Have you anything to add, Miss Coppell?' asked the judge.

'We never rioted. We were just in the wrong place at the wrong time.'

'Mr Benson, thank you for your testimony. You are dismissed,' said the judge, taking control of proceedings.

Mr Benson remained steadfast, 'Miss Coppell's soul has been cleansed by God's teachings, she's…'

'Thank you, Mr Benson, I will take that into account during sentencing. Members of the jury, how do you find the accused?'

They conferred briefly amongst themselves then, in a show of hands, they unanimously pronounced Jacob guilty. Sylvia clutched the railing around the box as she counted eight of the men raise their hands. For her, it was a partial verdict of guilt.

She reached for Jacob's clammy hand and clenched it in hers. Their eyes met and reflected back the terror they both felt.

'Miss Coppell, you have strayed from the path to redemption. A mistake I hope you will not repeat, when given yet another chance at life. I sentence you to transportation.'

Jacob squeezed her hand. She'd escaped the noose.

'Jacob Coppell, you are of no fixed employment and as we have heard, have practised mischief as a way of life. In light of your past and the unlikelihood of reform, I sentence you to be hanged from the neck.'

A cheer rose from the gallery, delighted to see another ne'er-do-well swing for his crimes. Sylvia pulled Jacob against her. He sobbed as they embraced. The judge banged his gavel and readied himself for the next trial.

Sylvia had been granted her life, at the cost of her brother's. The pain in her heart was unbearable.

27

Dawn light began to seep into Viktor's room and birdsong could be heard through the window he'd left open all night. Fully clothed, Viktor sat on the bed, which he'd pulled in front of the door to prevent it from opening. His cut-throat razor was open, ready, in his right hand, should Charlie make good on his threats. He had lain awake all night, his head twitching at every sound. His few belongings were packed in a hessian sack; it was time to go. As luck would have it, it was the first Wednesday of the month.

He pulled the bed away from the door as quietly as he could, picked up his sack and crept out. Walking behind the tobacco barn, he was shielded from the slave accommodation on the other side, but in full view of the main house in front. The only thing that stood between him and the obscurity of the trees was a brisk walk across the rear lawn. Viktor's heart thumped as he scanned the large windows of the main house. All were empty. He stepped out round the edge of the barn and feigned a casual saunter over the lawn. Other than the birdsong, it was deathly quiet.

He was three-quarters of the way to the trees when he heard a creak from behind him. He stiffened. Peering over his right shoulder, he saw Davey, the oldest of the slaves, hobbled out of his hut, naked, and emptied his bladder onto the grass.

Before Viktor could decide what to do, Old Davey looked up and

238

their eyes met. Eventually, Davey finished his piss. He waved to Viktor and turned back to his hut. Soon, the slaves would all be laughing at him. He reminded himself it didn't matter what negroes thought of him. His father Hans came to mind, arms folded, *I told you so, son.*

Viktor broke into a run. Eager to put as much distance between himself and the plantation as he could, he dashed into the trees and headed for the wharf. On the brow of the slope that looked down to the creek, Viktor hid behind a tree. The water was still, perfectly mirroring the grey of the dawn sky. Frequent glances over his shoulder reassured him he hadn't been followed. His thoughts turned to what Mason would do when he discovered his absence. The air would likely turn blue from his cursing, and he imagined Mason shouting about his spinelessness, how much he'd done for Viktor, and so on.

He reflected on Mason's promise of inheritance – had it just been a lure? Or had Mason been waiting for Viktor to prove himself worthy? Had he been found wanting? The thought saddened him. *Am I destined to only ever be a runaway?* All his grand dreams and imaginations were just that: fantasies, never to be realised.

His sullen mood was interrupted by the gentle splashing of oars pulling through water. Ripples on the water's surface announced Barney's arrival. Wearing a tatty cocked hat, he drifted into view, and pulled his boat up alongside the wharf. He looked about, then gave one sharp whistle, presumably to announce his arrival.

As Viktor hesitated, questions tumbled through his mind. *Where am I going? What if Barney knows Mason? Is anybody else coming to meet Barney?* The last time he'd run with Barney, he'd been led astray.

Everything was quiet.

It was time to go. Now. Yet Viktor hesitated. Where was he headed to? Nowhere. The uncertainty of his future loomed large, walking away from a chance of inheriting a plantation, regular pay, doing what he knew – all because the slaves had threatened him. What did that say about him? He realised there and then, he was a coward. Scared of the slaves, scared of what lay ahead, scared of Barney. He felt disgusted with himself.

Barney looked through the goods under his blanket.

Viktor squirmed as he remembered the scolding from his father after the incident with the bees. *What would Father say? I'm running away – again. Will I run all my life?* An image of Mason came to mind, *'Are you willing to pay the price?'* Viktor bit his thumbnail. What was he willing to do? To tolerate, to endure? Far less than the negroes. If he left, there was no way back.

Barney looked up once more around the wharf and up the track.

Then he cast off the wharf and began to paddle.

Viktor's mouth opened. No words came out as he watched Barney turn his boat around and once more his strokes disturbed the calm of the still waters. He rounded the corner, leaving Viktor dumbstruck, watching his future row away without him.

PART 2

—

1753

28

Mason sat at his desk in the study, seeking refuge from the afternoon heat, the windows open, his shirt unbuttoned to his waist, his feet unstockinged. Grace brought him a cup of tea and smiled briefly as she put the cup and saucer down in front of him. To think it had been over a year since her part in the missing rum. She'd only just got back to managing a forced smile in his presence. He'd been all for stringing her up by her neck, but Mary had insisted she'd deal with it. 'Be practical, Mason!' she'd cried. 'Grace is the best cook we've had. I won't endure months of poor sustenance for the sake of three bottles of your lousy rum.' *It would have been a different matter if she'd stolen your wine,* Mason had thought, but he'd relented. It had been the right decision. He didn't know what Mary had said or done, preferring not to meddle in the business of women, but Grace hadn't put a foot wrong since. She was a good nigger, on the whole, he thought, it was just a shame she'd got herself mixed up in Charlie's schemes. He was another one, too good to be without. Often it was the best negroes who proved the most troublesome.

Mason returned the quill to the ink pot, closed his ledger and sighed as he sipped his tea. He couldn't go without his morning or afternoon tea, reliant on its calming effect to soothe his worries. A moment to stop whatever he was engaged in, to let his mind rest in the balm of the dark liquid. As he drank, he looked out of the tall windows at the far end of his study. The lawn looked resplendent in

243

the afternoon sun. Despite the poor harvest, he was content with the progress he'd made. Viktor had proved a reliable hand in supervising the tobacco; the poor harvest owed to the weather, rather than Viktor's capability. The low yields may at least finally force the obstinate hand of Hans Neumann, who had so far proven more resilient than expected. The old man was fighting tooth and nail to hold on to the little he had. How Hans would meet his obligations this year, Mason didn't know.

He was impatient for progress. He'd written to his lawyer in Fredericksburg, asking for references of any men of means and good character, who would be willing to buy a share in a ship. As yet, he'd received no reply. In the meantime, his thoughts turned to diversifying his crops to end his reliance on tobacco. Pork seemed to offer the most stable source of income, but to keep a few pigs was a mere distraction. If it was to be done, Mason would do it properly. With scale. It was all the more challenging as Mason didn't know the first thing about pigs.

Mary marched into the study. 'What are you doing?'

'I was about to read the newspaper.'

'Why are you in a state of undress?'

Mason frowned. Before he could reply, she went on.

'I saw Grace come out of here a moment ago—'

'Jesus, Mary, you're paranoid.'

'Did you?'

'Did I what?'

'Fuck her?'

'No!'

Mary folded her arms and turned her head away from Mason towards the window.

'She brought me a cup of tea, woman. I was about to read the paper before you barged in here like the Spanish Inquisition with your wild accusations.'

Mary grunted.

'Is that it?' he sighed.

'You haven't paid me any attention.'

Mason groaned. He knew what lay ahead. 'How much have you had to drink?'

Mary's head flicked back to scowl at him. 'Nothing. So what if I've had a bit? I'm a grown woman!'

'Huh, a spoilt child, more like.'

'There you go, bringing children into this.'

'I wasn't,' he said.

'You know I can't have them, so you mention them at every opportunity.'

'Don't be ridiculous, you're making this up—'

'I'd rather be ridiculous than irrelevant.'

'How are you irrelevant? You live on a beautiful plantation. You have slaves to wait on you. I don't force you to mingle with people you don't like – which, by the way, is everyone – what more do you bloody want?'

'Well, you wouldn't know, would you?' she shouted.

'Enough!' barked Mason. 'Out! Now!'

She slammed the door behind her. *What the devil has got into that woman? It's as if she's possessed.* Mason felt his cheeks glowing red. He took a deep breath and rubbed his forehead with the palm of his hand. *Why do I always rise to her bait?* He slumped back into his chair. The effects of his tea – his one bloody pleasure of the day – ruined. As his temper cooled, he wrestled with what had happened to their marriage. Taking his clay pipe out from his drawer, he stuffed it with tobacco and puffed a plume of smoke into the air.

Was it the children, where our problems started? Sometimes, after similar outbursts, he'd wondered if he'd be better off without her. But women were scarce, and it would be embarrassing to be the only divorcé in the colony. He had few friends, and knew that society would take pity on her, assuming – at worst – that his malevolent ways had forced her out, or – at best – that he was unable to control his wife. Both called his honour into question, and that was something he could not allow, particularly at a time when he wanted to venture beyond his plantation.

He took another lungful of smoke and opened the paper, scanning a notice of ships due to arrive in the colony. One caught his eye, the *Relief*: a merchant brig that had left London, bound for Alexandria. Ever more ships had headed for the Potomac in the three years since Alexandria had been founded. It was a good sign; a rising tide lifts all boats. The *Relief,* he read, carried a cargo of indentured servants for sale. It would be the usual dregs of England, bringing with them their diseases and criminal intentions. But still, every so often one uncovered a gem, a competent and reliable man, unencumbered by a trade or ambition. Perhaps this was the omen he'd been looking for. The ship was due to dock next month. He would visit the auction and see who he could buy.

29

A good breeze blew across the stern of the brig *Relief*, filling her sails and pulling her towards the Americas.

Sylvia Coppell savoured the clean air; she should have been below deck with the rest of the convicts. Lucky for her, as she'd waited in prison for the spring crossings, she'd contracted gaol fever. It had started with a headache; her bones began to ache and her worst fears were confirmed once a rash had broken out across her body. It killed half the inmates she'd shared a cell with on the women's ward. For a time, she'd hoped the fever would take her life too, but as she'd huddled in agony amongst the rats, under the ventilation hole, she'd slowly begun to recover. With the cell thinned out, the air improved and with a little extra food, her strength began to return. She awaited her transportation, eager for anywhere outside of Newgate, only to learn from a fellow inmate who had since secretly returned from transportation, that the conditions on board ship would be every bit as bad. The rough seas caused convicts to empty their guts in the hold. It made for a vile and damp confinement, chained together.

They'd been marched in chains, six to a gang, from the prison to the mooring on the Thames where a large ship awaited its human cargo. Shivering, Sylvia had tilted her head to the sky and closed her eyes, savouring the rain that rinsed off her grime-smeared skin. She heard men talking: the ship's captain and the merchant responsible for the sale of the convicts inspected their goods, tallying names against the ship's manifest, £2 a soul. As they'd neared, she recognised a voice. Her eyes sprung open. *It was him.* Tall, his square jaw still set as determined as before when, good to his word, he'd introduced her to Mr Benson.

'Captain Reid?'

He'd squinted at her, uncertain.

Her heart had soared in hope. 'Sylvia Coppell.' She reminded him of their encounter. His face twisted in distaste.

'Load them up,' he'd shouted.

'Please, let me speak with you,' she'd begged, as he'd turned away and walked up the gangplank.

One day later, the river had turned to sea, causing the boat to creak and heave with the waves. Laying on their backs, chained in the hold, the convicts began to retch with seasickness. The air had become noxious, and Sylvia had sobbed herself to sleep that night. The following morning, two seamen had come in search of her. Hearing her name called from the hatch to the hold, she cried out. They'd unlocked her restraints and took her above deck. Squinting against the piercing daylight, she'd felt every sailor's eyes on her as she was paraded across the deck to the Captain's cabin at the stern. A tap on the door and she'd been beckoned in.

Captain Reid hadn't looked up as he'd searched inside a wooden chest.

'Fetch a bucket of soap and water. A comb. Some clean clothes too,' he'd ordered.

'Aye, Captain,' said the sailor, leaving them alone together.

'The years haven't been kind to you, Miss Coppell. I left you in the care of Mr Benson, so why should I find you amongst these dregs bound for Virginia?'

It was the first time she'd had her destination confirmed. The prospect of soap and water brought a tear to her eye. She'd explained the unfortunate events that had led her to his company again, omitting the matter of the stolen ring.

Once the soap and water arrived, Reid had sat down and invited her to wash herself. She'd wet her hair and lathered it with soap, dragging the comb through the knots and tangles. More fresh water had been summoned as she washed her hands and face.

'And the rest of you,' said Reid.

'May I have some privacy?'

He'd shaken his head. 'There's no secrets aboard ship.'

Ordinarily, she might have hesitated, but she longed to be clean again. She'd pulled her shirt over her head, exposing herself to Reid's examination as he'd cradled a brandy in his hand. She washed herself, turning the water brown, her humiliation tempered by his enjoyment. She'd known from the moment she'd met him that she'd be intimate with this man, and perhaps now that moment was close. After everything she'd endured, whatever moral hesitations she might still harbour were of little consequence, if she could finally attain some limited comfort for herself. It was a sacrifice she was willing to make after a long year in prison.

As she'd stood naked, shivering, her pale skin returned to its former beauty, Reid had nodded. 'That's more like I remember.' He'd indicated the fresh clothes on the table. 'You're welcome to stay naked, but if you'd rather dress yourself...'

She did, then accepted a tankard of brandy, savouring every sip. He fed her fruit, bread and cheese. She hadn't eaten so well since prison, such that she began to feel sick at being so full.

'What now?' she'd asked, though she knew full well what the answer would be.

'It's a long voyage. You can stay here if you like, but you don't get to share my bed for free... Or you can go back into the hull with the others.'

She'd kissed him.

All their nightly encounters now ran through her mind as she watched the Captain pace about the quarterdeck. She held on to the mainmast, while Reid passed a lead weight to Seaman Jones.

'The sea's a-changing colour. Grease this and plumb the seabed,' he barked, even less forgiving to his men than he had been with her. The more he'd used her with such casual disdain, the more infatuated she'd become. It was infuriating; whatever temporary comfort she'd drawn from his loins, made her want him even more, and him want her even less.

Being a woman had too many disadvantages to list, but Sylvia had turned nature's cruellest disadvantage to her favour. This was a line she'd never been willing to cross until life had become so intolerable. Thanks to that, she stood on deck, savouring the salt spray and clean air on her cheeks.

She watched Seaman Jimmy Jones at the gunwale; he was a short, blond lad, also in his early twenties, and with whom she had struck a platonic dialogue. He dropped the greased weight into the water and lowered it until the rope slackened. Minutes later, the sunken lead was retrieved and inspected by a relieved Captain Reid. A mixture of sand and mud was stuck to the grease, and the presence of small oyster shells, the most reliable of mariner's signposts, indicated they were at thirty-seven degrees of latitude and headed straight for their destination: the Chesapeake Bay, which divided the colonies of Virginia and Maryland.

'Land in the next two days,' bellowed Captain Reid, and a hearty cheer went up among the sailors on deck. He ordered Jones to fulfil the old sailor's superstition and tie the soiled weight to the foremast.

News that the two-month voyage was nearly over would soon permeate below deck and passengers and convicts alike would begin to eagerly anticipate their safe arrival in Alexandria. For Sylvia though, land threatened to end her period of safety. She waited until the Captain retired to his quarters and joined him there.

'What will become of me when we make land?'

Reid shrugged. She walked over to him and took his hand in hers. 'Will you not want to keep me?'

'Be away with you woman, I'm busy.'

She felt a lead weight in her stomach, knowing she would soon be sold again, to begin her long indenture with all its hardships and dangers – but perhaps also its opportunities. For now, the only certainty was that she would never return to England. Like all her fellow convicts, her passage was one-way. England would greet their return with the hangman's rope.

America was now home.

***

Land was sighted the next afternoon and a bottle of whisky granted to the lucky sailor who first spied the coastline. But the promise of heaven turned to purgatory as an unfavourable wind-change stranded the *Relief* at sea for two more days.

Sylvia lay in the arms of Captain Reid, pleading that he may spare her the uncertainty of being sold into indenture. Or at the very least use his influence to gain her a favourable posting.

He was adamant. 'You're cargo. It's more than my job's worth to meddle with the merchant's goods.'

'You could buy me?'

Whatever suggestions she offered fell on deaf ears, until he became angry with her. Once he fell asleep, she lay with her head leant against his bare chest, tears trickling down her cheeks. Crying for so many reasons. The loss of Jacob, whom she'd not seen or heard of since they'd appeared together at court. The impending loss of Captain Reid, a man whose self-interest had at least shown her more love and kindness than anyone, though he tortured her just as much by denying her the very freedom he took for granted. Perhaps his was the cruellest punishment of all. Yet, she didn't regret lying with him, as well as the privileges that came with the space in his bed. She wept too, for the uncertainty that America would offer. Alone in a foreign land, with no one to protect her and only herself to rely on.

The following morning, they dropped anchor off Cape Henry and signalled for the pilot to come aboard. Two hours passed while he rowed out from the shore. Having fastened his boat to a tow, he came aboard and guided Captain Reid between the middle ground and the horseshoe shoals that lurked in the bay's entrance, the resting place of many an inexperienced captain. Coins were passed and the pilot departed at the mouth of the York river, leaving a tense Captain Reid to navigate further north.

Sylvia and Jimmy Jones stood together on deck, leaning against the gunwales under the mainsail. Their staccato conversation was interspersed with her first views of the wooded coastline of this far-off land which was now her future. It was flat, the only features a succession of inlets and rivers, each one as large as the Thames.

'Look,' said Jimmy pointing down at the water, 'a jellyfish.'

Sylvia peered over the side at the lurking menace, its clear flesh tinged with a pink and blue hue, floating on the murky brown water.

'I've been stung by one of those – Portuguese man o' war,' said

Jimmy. 'Brought tears to my eyes, it did.'

Sylvia shuddered and gripped the wooden rail. As they continued, the waters filled with a great variety of boats: flat-bottoms, ferries and sloops sailed up, down and across the river. Others bobbed peacefully at anchor off the shore.

'There's the navy,' said Jimmy, his voice weary as he pointed at a frigate that lay peacefully at anchor at the mouth of the Potomac. Its sails furled and the Union Jack and ensign fluttered in the gentle breeze.

They sailed slowly past it, close enough for a shout to be heard by the men on deck.

'Don't you think those gold and black stripes along its side make it look like some sort of wasp?' Sylvia remarked.

A frown spread over Jimmy's sun-freckled face. She caught herself looking at the scar on his chin as he shook his head.

'I'd rather be stung by a thousand wasps than be forced to serve on her. If they're short of men, they can board us and seize any sailors to serve. I'd rather be dead.'

'Would it be so different?'

'Yes, it bloody would. You speak to any sailor unlucky enough to suffer the press. It'd make life on this ship look like paradise. I wouldn't treat a stray dog like they treat sailors in the navy. They'd whip you soon as look at you.'

Sylvia's eye was caught overhead by an enormous flock of ducks heading inland.

'What you going to do when we get to shore, Jimmy?'

'I ain't allowed on shore, girl. Captain got a bond on all of us; if he returns home with one less sailor than he left with, he'll lose his money. I'll be on board all winter. Captain will keep us busy though. Hopefully I won't be drawn to clean out the hold. It's awash with your friends' fluids.'

Sylvia shook her head in revulsion, glad to have been spared the indignity.

'We'll be allowed off to load the tobacco, once he's sold the space in the hold...'

Jimmy continued regaling her with trials of the winter ahead, while Sylvia's thoughts turned to her own future and the many unknowns which lay in store. Her fate would be decided by the nature – good or evil – of the man who would eventually buy her, with all the dispassion of a farmer buying livestock.

'You worried?' asked Jimmy, sensing her attention had wandered.

She nodded.

'Don't be. If you ask me, colonies are better than home. It's warm. There's plenty to smoke, plenty to eat – even a man like me can afford sugar here. No shortage of work neither. The air's clear, no slums, people aren't on top of one another like in London. They got it better here than we have. Certainly better than aboard Reid's ship – well, for me at least.' He nudged Sylvia with his elbow, grinning at his own joke.

I'll allow him that, she thought.

'Can you keep a secret, Sylvia?' He lowered his voice, a solemn expression on his face. 'I ain't told no one on here, but you.'

'Of course.'

'I ain't going back home.'

'Me neither.'

He smirked. 'I'm serious, life on this ship ain't life at all. I plan to desert when we make land. I've had enough of ship's biscuit, salted beef and buggery. Living here's like being trapped in a barn with wild animals.'

'What will happen if you're caught?' whispered Sylvia.

'I'd be lashed to ribbons, good and proper. But I don't plan on getting caught. I'll ditch these stripy trousers and hide out in the woods until the ship's gone.'

'What about the Indians?'

Jimmy grinned. 'You read too many fairy tales, girl! They long cleared out the savages from these parts. This is white man's land now. Besides, I won't have to hide for long. There's plenty of work for able sailors in the Americas. Reckon I'll soon find a captain willing to turn a blind eye to my background when he sees me shimmy up a mainsail faster than any man.'

Sylvia laughed. She liked Jimmy. Despite his hardships, he always managed a smile. She had a feeling life would be kind to him.

'You can come too, if you want?'

She smiled. It was sweet of him to ask her. He was a good soul, and he probably would look after her, without imposing his desires on her flesh, but the offer of a fugitive's life with a bounty on their heads was not one she wished to repeat. Mr Benson's words rung in her ears. Her days of crime were behind her. For the sake of one gold ring, she'd learned a very hard lesson. Never again would she risk imprisonment.

'Thanks, Jimmy, but a woman would just slow you down.'

'Right, strumpet,' boomed the large boatswain, resting his oversized hand on Sylvia's shoulder as he came up behind them. 'We're nearly there. It's time for you to rejoin your mates on the chain below deck.'

She looked pleadingly into his large brown eyes.

'Captain's orders, love. Let's not have a fuss.'

'Good luck, sweetheart,' said Jimmy.

'You too, Jimmy.' Her voice cracked.

Jimmy winked at her with a grin across his face. She stifled her tears and was led below deck, into the dark.

Soon, she'd emerge into a new life as a Virginian. Hopefully a better one – no matter how painful the birth.

30

When the knock on his new office door finally came, Governor Dinwiddie was composing a verse of poetry, lost in thought. For his consumption only, he found writing eased his mind. A younger man may have desired to expend his surplus energies in other ways, frustrated by the slow progress of governance, but Dinwiddie was happy to pen shoddy verse and indulge in rose-coloured memories of Britain.

The bulk of Major Washington's frame filled the door, sporting a new red and navy uniform. Since he'd last seen the lad, his shoulders and face had grown squarer as he'd thrown off the last signs of youth. He wore his face without blanc, and what remained of his pox scars was no longer as distracting. 'Major, good to see you're dressed for the part.'

'Good afternoon, Governor. I came as soon as I got your letter.'

The pleasantries exchanged bore no trace of any residual tensions from their last encounter. Since then, Washington had pursued responsibility for the more prestigious northern district of Virginia's militia. The post had become vacant when the former incumbent had left the colony, and Washington had roused his various patrons to make the post his own. Dinwiddie had acquiesced; it was better, he reasoned, to have someone brimming with enthusiasm – if not experience.

'Drink?'

255

The Major declined and took a seat. Dinwiddie poured himself a generous measure of brandy from the decanter he kept on his desk, along with a stack of papers, an ink pot from which a feather quill protruded, and a large map of the Chesapeake region. 'George, are you still eager to serve your country?'

'Of course.'

Dinwiddie slung a letter across the table. 'Your orders.' He sat back and waited for the young man's reaction as he broke the seal and began to read the letter.

'It's signed by the King!' said Washington, his face illuminated.

'Indeed. You won't get a better chance to make a name for yourself, Washington. It is time you came out to play with the real men.'

Washington swallowed the lump that had formed in his throat. Dinwiddie allowed himself a wry smile.

'Rumour has it our French friends are creeping south into the Ohio Valley and hassling our traders.'

'Governor, if you don't think me rude for asking, we've known of their attack on the Twightee for over a year. Why is it we are only acting now?'

'Because,' said Dinwiddie, getting agitated, 'if you go and build a fort and harry them off our land, then we risk starting a bloody war, and I don't want that falling on my shoulders.' Dinwiddie took a sip of his brandy and regarded Washington. What young men so often failed to recognise was that, whilst action might be prudent, if – or when – it failed, there was always an inquiry afterwards and blame to be dispensed. Dinwiddie had worked in politics long enough to know never to issue an order that wasn't countersigned by his superiors. In this instance, the letters had taken four months to cross the ocean and back, but he reasoned that delays weren't normally as bad as people made them out to be, especially when they came with the benefit of absolving himself of any responsibility.

'But the King granted this land to the Ohio Company...' said Washington.

Dear me, this fellow is naïve, thought Dinwiddie. 'Ordained by God, was it? Guess what, the King of France didn't get the message. He must have been busy that day. Really, Major,' snapped Dinwiddie.

He'd suffered enough fools throughout his career that he'd become decidedly impatient.

Washington blushed. 'What do you think they're up to?'

Dinwiddie turned to the map on his desk. 'I assume they want to keep us penned in, east of the mountains.'

'Why take the risk of provoking us?'

'Global politics is not that different to a marriage dispute,' Dinwiddie smirked. 'Both sides are certain of their righteousness. They'll have their reasons for their actions; all that matters is we stop them from going south of this point,' the Governor gestured to the fork in the Ohio River, where it split into the Allegheny and Monongahela rivers. 'This is where the Iroquois want us to fortify,' he said, jabbing his fingers on the map.

'And if the French refuse to leave?'

'The problems you encounter will be yours to resolve, Major.'

'Very well. What provisions are you giving me?'

Dinwiddie leaned back in his chair. 'None.'

Washington looked confused. 'What should I tell my recruits? They'll want paying…'

'Too bad, there is nothing to give – not for you or for them. The House won't vote through any funds. We can thank Fry for that.'

'How am I to recruit people without pay? I can't go alone!'

'Evidently you know lots of people in this colony, Major,' said Dinwiddie referring to the letters he'd received from Lord Fairfax and other members of the Freemasons, all vouching for Washington. 'I'm sure you'll find someone; perhaps take somebody from the Ohio Company.'

Washington cut an indignant figure as he stared at Dinwiddie, imploring him to help.

'You wanted to serve your country, Washington. This is what it looks like: servitude.'

'Literally!'

'I'd get used to it, if I were you. I have found Great Britain to be an ungrateful mistress.'

Washington reread his orders. 'It says here I should drive the French off by force?'

'It does.'

'But surely, if the King commands it, then the Lower House must make provision…'

'You'd think so, but it doesn't work that way. Perhaps in France, but us British like to confuse matters with our pesky notions of individuals' liberties.'

'Then how am I to fulfil my orders?'

'Welcome to politics, George. Stuck between a rock and a hard place.'

Washington's mouth hung open.

Dinwiddie finished his brandy. 'Do your best, lad. Just don't *start* a fight. Not on my watch. Find out what's happening. Do what you can, then come back in one piece.'

31

Mason's chest hurt from coughing. Mary held open the bedroom door, letting the morning light spill into the darkened room. The curtains shifted in the breeze.

'Are you better yet?'

Mason allowed his eyes to fall shut. A gentle shake of his head was all he was prepared to offer. He could count on one hand the number of times he'd been confined to bed in his life. But when his body finally succumbed, he wasn't a good patient.

'You've worn yourself out. I've told you, you need to rest,' she said in exasperation.

She had. Repeatedly. But relaxation didn't come naturally to Mason. And no sooner had he found a moment's peace, she interrupted it with a demand or complaint. It had become a perpetual vocation for Mason to ensure he spent as little time in his wife's company as possible. This only served to stimulate her grievances.

'Well, what about your visit to Alexandria? I want my post,' she said.

Mason grunted.

'Perhaps if you came to bed at night, rather than jotting every measly penny into your ledgers, you wouldn't be ill,' she went on.

'I'll have to send Viktor,' he mumbled.

'But the harvest is in. Is he capable of selling our crop? You trust our fate in *his* hands?'

259

'What choice do I have?' said Mason, summoning a measure of his normal aggression. Viktor had accompanied him to the warehouse on previous visits; he knew the ropes.

Mary mumbled something to herself before leaving the room.

Mason opened his eyes and propped himself up against his headboard. Yesterday morning, he'd woken with a headache. He'd been instructing Billy on an extension to the wharf he wanted built, when he'd felt faint; the fever had begun that afternoon. Reluctant to abandon his trip to Alexandria and the many pressing affairs to attend to – not least the transportation and sale of the crop – he'd retired to bed in the hopes he might sleep it off.

Alas, he'd continued to worsen. He wiped the sweat off his brow, thankful at least that fall afforded the comfort of cooler evenings. He swung his legs over the edge of the bed and felt light-headed as he sat upright. Reaching down, he slid the chamber pot from under the bed. Unable to stand, he knelt on all fours and lowered himself so he straddled the pot, resting his head on his hands. He exhaled and began to top up the pot with a trickle of orange urine.

'Mason?' Viktor entered the room.

'Not now, you bloody fool!'

Viktor apologised and retired from the room.

Mason finished and climbed back into the damp sheets of his bed. He called for Viktor to come back.

'Sorry, sir. Mrs Fitzbarton had sent for me.' Viktor stood at the end of the bed, holding his hat by his waist.

'I need you to take the crop to Alexandria,' murmured Mason.

Viktor's mouth broadened into a smile.

'It'll be sold once it arrives in London, so all you need to do is negotiate a crossing with a ship's captain. But don't use a slaver, his ship will stink worse than my chamber pot. It'll taint the tobacco.'

Viktor nodded confidently.

'There's more: a ship is due to land in Alexandria. Buy me a servant. I want someone who knows about pig farming. No more than fifteen pounds, able-bodied, not too old.' Mason pushed himself up against his pillows and continued to list other errands: collecting his and Mary's post; sending letters of instruction to Mason's agent in London; picking up supplies from the store. 'Here, take this letter of introduction, it will grant you the ability to act on my authority.' He passed Viktor a sealed letter, marked, *'To whom it may concern'*.

Viktor took the letter. Finally, after two and half years, he was being entrusted with the plantation's affairs. He would prove himself worthy. He walked towards the open door with a spring in his step.

'Don't forget the post!' called Mason.

Viktor bounded down the mahogany staircase and was met by Mary at the bottom, her arms folded across her chest, blocking his path.

'What's he told you to do?'

Viktor relayed his instruction of finding a pig man.

'Hmm,' Mary pursed her lips and squinted at Viktor. 'Get a man who can read and write. A man capable of numbers, to keep Mason's ledgers for him.'

'But, Mrs Fitzbarton, Mason said...'

'Listen to me,' she hissed. 'You do as I say, or I'll part you from your balls.'

Viktor stepped back. Before he could protest, she continued:

'Swear it.'

Viktor frowned. *How can I please two masters?*

Mary stood resolute.

'Very well, ma'am, I'll get somebody who can bookkeep.'

Viktor side-stepped her and headed for the front door. In under a minute, he'd been doomed to fail. Whatever he did now, he would inevitably disappoint one of them. *These people are impossible.* He went outside, cursing his misfortune, but very glad to be getting away from the Fitzbartons.

Viktor oversaw the safe loading of the hogsheads of tobacco, the modest fruits of his supervision, as the lack of rain had left the plants stunted. Once the barrels were securely stacked three-high onto the flat-bottomed boat, he dismissed all but three of the slaves: Thursday, Sam and Musa. They each had children on the plantation, so were unlikely to attempt an escape. They cast off and the slaves punted and rowed their giant raft-like boat up the Occoquan River. A gentle starboard breeze greeted them as they entered the larger Potomac River. Viktor sat atop a hogshead, savouring the journey. Outings on the boat were rare and today the water was calm, the riverbank lined with gold and copper-coloured trees of the early fall. They hugged the bank, avoiding the larger vessels in the middle of the river. With the flood tide in their favour, they were carried north with ease.

Viktor had Mason's letters and pocketbook stowed safely in a leather bag, together with the signed letter of introduction. He pondered how to avoid falling foul of both Mason and Mary on his return. *A pig man who could keep books?* Seemed impossible. At least he had the rest of the day before he had to make a decision. He was desperate to make a success of his visit, hoping he might be entrusted with more responsibilities in future. This was what he'd imagined when he'd daydreamed of working for Mason Fitzbarton. He felt *mature:* a man, on man's business. Of course, one thing was still missing before Viktor could really be considered a man… Perhaps this time, Alexandria would supply the cure to his desire: a woman.

Viktor took a big breath, savouring the fresh air on the gentle breeze as they silently glided with the current. They drifted past a slope overlooking the riverbank; upon it was a pleasant clapboard dwelling, its mooring signposted 'Mount Vernon'. It was the sort of simple, well-situated house that Viktor had always wanted for himself. Yet today he noticed that his usual wants felt blunted. Having seen the Fitzbarton plantation up close, he knew now that such homes contained a darker underbelly. He thought of Charlie, hanging from the whipping post, his blood-soaked flesh hanging from his back, all because of a few bottles of rum. For years, he'd idolised the Fitzbarton's grand plantation, willing his father to emulate it. Viktor sighed. Perhaps Hans *had* been right after all. The beauty of wealth and civilisation couldn't mask the seething resentment from its slaves, its massive gains enjoyed by one man at the expense of many. To say nothing of the marital feuding the house contained. Nobody at that plantation was happy, including himself. How many other places in Virginia shared a similar tale? Luxury crafted from suffering.

They rounded Point Lumley and entered the crescent-shaped bay. To the left, the hull of a ship was emerging from a crude dock cut into the bluff. In the centre of the bay arose a fine mansion adorned with scaffolding. Yet to be roofed or glazed, the bricks were only at the level of the first-floor windows. When complete, it would enjoy a commanding view of the bay, no doubt for one of the town's important men. A cluster of other brick buildings was emerging in the neighbouring plots. Soon this would be a bona fide town. At the far end of the bay, on higher ground, stood the tobacco warehouses. Viktor could see that a wharf was yet to be built, though that was no issue for their flat-bottomed boat. No doubt the ferry that operated back and forth to Maryland made a handsome living unloading the boats.

Viktor marvelled at the larger vessels: three sloops, a snow with tatty sails and a schooner without her ensign, all lay at anchor off the far point of the bay. Here, the tidewater ended, marking the farthest point upstream where large boats could still navigate, being the ideal site for a tobacco inspection warehouse. All the growers of the interior transported their hogsheads here for inspection, sale and shipping.

The warehouse was surrounded by large brick buildings catering to the needs of the tradespeople; two large taverns to house the merchants and sailors while they were in port, a chandlery store selling supplies to sea-going vessels, and another store brimming with goods and luxuries imported from Britain: furniture, clothing, haberdashery, tableware and crockery; tea and cotton from the Orient; sugar from the West Indies, and rum from the northern colonies. There were a few simple wooden houses and a brick building, the offices of the town. No church, yet.

'Land us there,' shouted Viktor, pointing to a suitable part of the shoreline.

The negroes paddled and punted as fast as they were able to gain speed to beach the boat. There was a gentle crunch as they ran aground on the pebble shoreline.

Viktor spat out his tobacco and stepped ashore. The air bustled with the fizz of opportunity as people busied themselves, preparing for all the trade that would pass through the town now the growing season was finished.

'Right, let's get these hogsheads on dry land.'

Familiar with the routine, the slaves manhandled the first barrel over the bow, rolled it up the slope and onto the grass, beyond the reach of the river water.

Once the hogsheads were on dry land, the boat was dragged further out of the water. The slaves began the tedious task of rolling the barrels further up towards the inspection warehouse. Viktor introduced himself to the inspector, a small, bookish man with glasses perched on the end of his button nose. One by one, the hogsheads were weighed, opened, checked, declared free of trash, resealed and fire branded 'MF' with the weight, tare and gross, and grade of the crop. Finally, all was stacked in the warehouse, and Viktor passed the afternoon chatting to others who eagerly awaited the arrival of the next English ship. A Scottish factor had pleaded with him to sell him the crop now, with the promise of credit in his uncle's store. Viktor steadfastly refused; Mason only ever sent his crop to London. Free of debt and well insulated against the risks of shipwreck, shrinkage and damage, he could afford to hold out for the higher prices fetched in the capital.

The inspector wrote up the crop note, making a small deduction for his fee, and passed it to Viktor. He always found it a strange notion that a year's work – thousands of pounds in tobacco – resulted in a small scrap of paper. He placed it carefully in his leather bag and left the warehouse.

No sooner had he stepped back out into the afternoon gloom, than a tall man with weathered skin and dark hair approached him.

'James Reid, Captain of the *Relief*. How many heads you got?'

'Where you headed?'

'London. Soon as I'm full. How many you got?'

'How much you charging a head?'

'Let me buy you a drink.' He put his arm on Viktor's shoulder and ushered him towards the tavern door. The tap room was busy. Men occupied all the tables, their drinks, pipes, cards, dice and papers all out on display. A small fire burned in the grate. It was warm with the heady smell of alcohol, smoke, and sweat.

'Captain Reid's buying,' said Viktor, a grin on his face as they approached the bar. 'While you're doing that, let me check the post.'

Viktor walked round the side of the bar into a small wood-panelled room, bare except for a six-foot table, on top of which was a collection of sealed letters. Viktor scanned the names and found two letters for Mason and three for Mary. He put them in his bag and returned to the bar, where Captain Reid had a cider waiting for him. They toasted, swigged and began negotiating.

Viktor was halfway through his drink when Reid placed his empty glass on the bar. 'Your round.'

Viktor hesitated. Having waited so long to earn it, he was saving his money and didn't want to squander it on Reid. 'Sorry, Captain, but I'm a little short.'

'You work for a planter, a good one at that. What do you mean, you're short?'

'Well, I...'

'Spend some of Mason's money,' interrupted Reid. 'You're working, you've got your expenses to cover.'

'I wouldn't want to anger him.'

'Jesus, lad, you're wet behind the ears.'

Viktor frowned.

'Look, you grow his tobacco, yes?' said Reid.

Viktor nodded.

'Who else has he got to do that for him?'

Viktor took a swig of his cider. 'Anyone he finds to do it, I suppose. I'm here to buy some people tomorrow, as it happens.'

'Trust me, Vik, I've just shipped a bunch of vagrants and mongrels out here. How many of those lemons do you think know the first thing about tobacco planting?'

Viktor shrugged.

'They wouldn't know a tobacco plant if they tripped over one,' Reid scoffed. 'Far less, able to tend to it. Without you, your governor would have to poach somebody from a neighbouring plantation – which would piss his neighbours off – hire a runaway who can't be trusted, advertise the job with a pay rate that would turn every planter against him – or worse still – whip his niggers himself. A man like him won't want dirt under his fingernails. There's more work out here than there are men to do it. Why do you think we keep shipping in Africans? It ain't for their sweet aroma. Trust me, your governor *needs* you. Least he can do is buy you a drink. Least *you* can do is buy me one back, if you want me to haul your leaf home.' Reid rapped his knuckles on the bar, 'Two ciders, please!'

Viktor didn't protest. For the first time it occurred to him how lucky Mason had been to chance upon him.

Two pints later, they had settled on £7 a ton, and the crop note, together with Fitzbarton's outgoing post, was entrusted to Captain Reid on the promise he'd personally deliver it to Mason's agent in London. Reid spat on the palm of his hand and held it out.

Viktor did the same, glad that he'd had some drink to settle his queasiness at the custom. He wiped the spittle from his hand on his breeches.

'Now, I must be getting on. Say, Viktor, you wouldn't mind helping us out this evening. would you?'

He'd enjoyed Captain Reid's company and didn't relish the idea of chatting to strangers. 'What is it?'

'Nothing much, just got a bit of cargo to load, nothing too strenuous – ten minutes work.'

'Now?'

Reid shook his head. 'Nah, we'll wait till it gets dark.' He left.

Viktor felt flush with the warmth of the cider and a touch of pride. He'd struck a good deal and completed the first part of his errand. But why was Reid shifting cargo at night? He shrugged and decided to celebrate with another cider.

32

November 1st, 1753
Alexandria

George Washington led his horse between the building plots of Alexandria, the same that he'd surveyed years before. If only Lawrence could see what was becoming of his fledgling town. What had started as a mere idea, was fast becoming the reality Lawrence had envisaged; it was bittersweet. The reminder of the hole that his brother had left in George's heart was fleeting, for he had pressing issues to resolve. Whatever concerns Dinwiddie may have had over his starting a dispute with the French, George was regretting his former enthusiasm. He had to journey to an unfamiliar destination, with only a conspicuously blank map to guide him. Then persuade an obstinate enemy to depart, in a language he couldn't speak, all amidst sparring native peoples who moved like ghosts and whose shifting allegiances were equally opaque. He'd stopped in Fredericksburg, yet without the means to recruit anyone, he was facing the unwelcome prospect of undertaking his mission alone.

He'd stopped at Mount Vernon to pay his respects to Anne, who he was pleased to see was managing well, given the circumstances. When he'd complained about his predicaments, she'd wasted no time in pointing out it was him who'd wanted to be a soldier, before quoting Epictetus, *'Don't seek for everything to happen as you wish it would, but rather wish that everything happens as it actually will.'* It had left George feeling guilty for neglecting his own studies, and for his indulgences. On top of that, he'd forgotten to write to Anne, a widow alone, raising her children in a house that reminded her every day of the man she'd loved and lost. *There's always someone worse off.* She'd ordered her slave to prepare some victuals for George's saddlebag while he changed out of his formal clothes into buckskins for the journey to the frontier. He'd also grabbed a copy of the new novel by Daniel Defoe, *Memoirs of a Cavalier*. He hoped the English civil war might prove an adequate distraction.

As he watched negroes labouring, carrying bricks on their shoulders, lumbar for scaffolding boards, he wondered how he was going to get help. All around him, people were gainfully employed. He had nothing to offer the few white people here. He headed for the tavern up on the hill; most problems could be solved in a public house, he reasoned.

George tied his horse to the rail and entered the tavern just as a tall man with creased skin was leaving, brushing by him. *Where do I start?* thought George as he surveyed the tap room. He moved beside a broad-shouldered man with blond hair, sunk in the last of his drink. The man belched and pounded his glass back on the bar.

'Another?' asked the tavern keeper, a burly man whose shirt sleeves were rolled up to his elbows.

'Why the hell not, Ginny!' replied the young man, a broad smile across his ruddy face.

'A good day?' asked George, leaning his musket against the bar and putting his bag down.

'By my standards, very! Thank you.'

George envied the man, who must be the same age as him.

Ginny returned with a full glass and noticed George. 'Hello George, long time no see. How are you?'

George smiled. 'I have my health, thank you, Ginny.'

'Anne, is she well? I haven't seen her since Lawrence...'

'You don't need to worry about Anne, that woman is made of stern stuff.'

'Send her my best.' Ginny turned her attention back to the blond man, as he put the drink down in front of him. 'Do you want that on Fitzbarton's account?'

'Mason Fitzbarton?' said George, remembering the incident after court when Fitzbarton's wife had collapsed in drunkenness. 'There's a name I haven't heard for a while. You work for him?'

The man nodded but his smile seemed to fade, piquing George's interest.

'Major George Washington, pleased to meet you.' He offered his hand.

'Viktor Neumann.' His grip was firm. Well-cut clothes for a working man. 'Never met a Major before, thought you'd be older.'

George grinned but stopped himself from indulging further; better to be modest in front of strangers. He ordered a warm milk from Ginny, then returned his attention to his new acquaintance. 'How long have you been in Mason's employ?'

'Two and half years already.'

'Must be suiting you if time passes quickly?'

Viktor grunted. 'They've passed pretty slowly, to be honest.'

'You a native Virginian?'

Viktor nodded and elaborated on his upbringing. George thought there was something endearingly plain and honest about the lad. Well-mannered, but without the stifling social habits of the gentry class. Native too – they always did better in the backwoods. An impulse gripped George.

'Mason, we rarely see him out and about,' he said. 'Why does a man with so much to offer this colony keep to himself, do you think?'

Viktor shrugged.

'How's his wife, is she still a bit of a handful?' George probed.

Viktor nodded. 'It isn't the happiest marriage. We all know to keep out of the way.'

'Can't be much fun. Say, would you be interested in a proposal?'

Viktor's eyes widened. 'Sure.'

'Have you heard the rumours of French incursion into Ohio country?'

Viktor shook his head.

'I am departing to reconnoitre the area. I'd be grateful of some company, to help with trapping and the travails of the journey.'

'You're going west on your own?'

'Well – no – I – I am recruiting suitable companions en route.' George was unsteadied by Viktor's sceptical frown. 'It's a once in a lifetime opportunity.'

'Sounds dangerous.'

'Serving one's country isn't supposed to be safe.'

Viktor smirked. 'My family's German. Forgive me if I don't share your enthusiasm for dying for England.'

George explained the political implications, sharing some of Dinwiddie's theories of the global tensions (and claiming them as his own). As Viktor's cider ebbed, George thought he was becoming more interested.

'Then what – *if* – you get back?'

George shrugged and flashed a dashing smile. 'The whole point of adventures is that you don't know how they'll end. But I have every confidence it will be truly remarkable.'

'Does it pay, to be your camp assistant?'

George tried to hide a grimace. 'No. It's a service.'

Viktor gave a laugh that shook the boards on the bar.

'So, if I've understood,' he said, recovering, 'you're inviting me to run away from my employer, join you on a dangerous wilderness adventure – for no pay, and with no prospects on my return?'

George smiled as broadly as he could manage. 'That's exactly right, yes. It will be fun.' He stared intently at Viktor, who, despite his laughter, was giving it serious consideration. *Clearly, he isn't fulfilled at the Fitzbartons,* he sensed. He produced his orders from King George II from his coat pocket. 'Here, read this.'

As Viktor stared at the paper, the long silence between the two men was accompanied by the noises of the tavern replete with newly paid men: laughter, whispered gossip, debate, gamblers celebrations, drinks orders, the bell to sound that supper would soon be served. *I think I've got him,* thought George as he watched Viktor staring intently into the suds of his empty glass.

'Major, thank you for considering me worthy of your mission,' Viktor said eventually. 'I am flattered. It sounds, well, memorable, certainly, and something tells me you are mad enough to pull it off. But it's not for me. I am sorry and I wish you luck.'

Damnation. So close! 'Sure?'

Viktor's face was tormented by the offer. 'I can't. It's too – no. I mustn't. No.'

'Very well. It's been nice to meet you. If you change your mind, find me.' They shook hands and George finished his milk. He had a choice to make: leave this evening or hang about in Alexandria until he found someone else. Talking to Viktor of his mission had renewed his enthusiasm. As implausible as it was, there was something so daring about it. Buoyed despite his failure, he was confident things would go his way. He just needed to be patient.

***

Viktor stepped outside, his legs wobbly from drink, wondering if he had done the right thing. The dusk air was cool and foggy, thick with the scent of wood smoke. He emptied his bladder and took a few moments to sober himself. He'd been tempted. Something about the young Major had drawn him in. But as he looked out at the twinkling lights of the boats moored in the bay, he decided the Major's mission was nothing more than a fool's errand. The sensible course was to try to win Mason's favour and get paid. Mason's illness meant his wages were overdue again, but Viktor was certain he would get paid on his return. He settled himself down to wait for Captain Reid.

A short while later, once the sky had turned black, leaving only the light of the full moon shimmering on the river's surface, a voice called out to him from the dark. It was Captain Reid, lantern in hand.

Viktor hopped to his feet and followed him down the slope towards the river's edge. Viktor had entirely forgotten about the boat and the negroes, and was relieved to see it where he'd left it and the negroes huddled together around a small fire, playing one of their dice games with slaves from other boats. Captain Reid's skiff was beached further down the shoreline.

Reid passed Viktor his lantern. 'Hold this.' He took off his shirt, exposing his bare chest, muscled from years of climbing rigging, hauling rope and shifting cargo. 'Here,' he draped his shirt over Viktor's outstretched arm and began to unbutton the flap at the front of his breeches.

Viktor froze. *Is Reid a molly?* Reid began to fish for his manhood, while Viktor took a step back, realising he'd been lured here in the dark so Reid could sodomise him. He was about to yell for his negroes when Reid began to piss.

271

Viktor breathed a half-sigh of relief.

Reid finished and re-fastened his breeches. He took back his shirt from Viktor's arm and held it up in front of the lantern, hiding its light. He lowered the shirt, illuminating his face in the yellow glow of the flame. He repeated this strange performance ten times, concealing and exposing the lantern's light.

'That should do it. Come, let's have a smoke.'

They sat at the brow of the beach head. Reid stuffed his clay pipe with tobacco from a small leather pouch he wore on a necklace. Once lit from the lantern, the tobacco glowed orange in the dark. He sighed as he puffed smoke up into the night sky. They passed the pipe back and forth, Reid recounting stories from home in England. Viktor found his attention wandering, simply savouring not being on the plantation. Mixing with people other than Granville and Billy. So far, he'd completed his tasks with competence. All that remained was to buy either a bookkeeper or pig man tomorrow, pick up materials from the store and sail home to face the wrath of whichever Fitzbarton he'd disappointed. Even when he was gone, they had a way of imposing themselves to spoil his enjoyment.

As Reid droned on, a thought struck Viktor: Mason was ill. What would happen if he died?

He was toying with what would become of the plantation, when a rowing boat quietly scrunched against the pebbles directly in front of them.

'Ahoy there,' came a gruff voice.

'Barney, that you?' asked Reid.

'Aye, Reidy, 'tis I,' said Barney as he clambered out of his boat, his feet splashing in the shallows. He dragged his boat further onto dry ground. 'And I have a wee stash of bulk for you.'

Captain Reid tapped the tobacco from his pipe and stood up to shake Barney's hand.

'Hi Barney,' said Viktor.

'Is that you, Viktor?' said the Scotsman in surprise. 'Still whipping niggers for Fitzbarton, are ya? Found yourself a woman yet?'

Viktor flushed with embarrassment. Did everyone know what he'd done to Charlie? And had Barney told everyone he was a virgin?

'Here we are then,' said Barney, pulling back the blanket to expose a mound of loose tobacco in his boat. 'Virginia's finest. What you got for me?'

'What about the inspection?' asked Viktor. 'Are you smuggling?'

Both men stopped and stared at him. Reid swung his arm and clipped Viktor's head. 'No need to announce it to everyone, you moron.' He leant over and inspected the leaf, rolling it between his fingers and inhaling its scent.

Viktor stayed quiet. Tobacco was regulated by Britain to ensure its quality. It was supposed to be inspected, graded and, if it was of suitable grade for export, Virginia levied a duty to pay for the colony's administration.

'Come on then, what you offering?' said Barney.

'Coin. Spanish silver dollars. Won them off my new boatswain who'd been on a sloop in the West Indies. Poor lad can't play brag to save his life.'

'You can have the lot for three dollars,' Barney offered.

A deal agreed, a tariff avoided, Viktor offered to have his negroes load the tobacco into Reid's skiff.

'Pleasure doing business with you, Reidy,' beamed Barney. 'You want anything, Viktor, be sure to let me know, eh lad.' The gentle splash of water from his oar strokes was the only indicator of his presence as he slipped out into the dark of night.

'Right, time for me to say good night, Viktor,' Reid sighed. 'Thanking you for your help and your business. Your master's crop's safe with me.'

'What if you got caught with this?' Viktor pointed to the loose tobacco in the boat.

'Pah! Who'd want to catch me? This here's the hobby crop of everyone in the county, what they tend to in their own gardens. Justices of the peace, clergy – you name it! Judge, jury and executioner will all have a hand in this here bulk. Probably Governor Dinwiddie himself!'

Viktor felt foolish and thought of his father: he was either too honest, or too naïve, to make it in this land.

'Come now, give us a push,' said Reid. 'I'll have my boys stash this load tonight, so I won't be back. You can take my room at the tavern as a little gratuity.'

Viktor helped his negroes push the bow of the fully-laden skiff. The water took its weight and it vanished into the dark.

33

November 2nd, 1753
The Relief

Sylvia emerged from the ship's hold to be blinded by the daylight. Sun burned through the scattered clouds, the air was mild, its scent muddy, a contrast to the salty odour of the sea crossing. She filed across the deck behind her fellow convicts. For them, it was the first opportunity to walk unshackled, as Captain Reid hadn't wished to draw unnecessary attention to their status as felons, lest they fetch lower prices. Like a platoon of soldiers, they lined up across the main deck. The First Mate issued an order to undress. Their initial hesitancy was quickly overcome as a whip cracked. Sylvia looked imploring at Captain Reid, who nodded his agreement; she was spared the indignity. She sensed this was more due to the fact she was clean already, rather than any lingering affection Reid had for her – he'd remained immune to her pleas to stay on board as his companion.

As the others stripped, buckets of water were placed in front of every third person. They were instructed to wash and make good their appearance. The ship's crew made no attempt to hide their stares as they took in the display of nudity. Sylvia contemplated the new start that awaited her. Uncertain what life had in store for her, she resolved to bury her terror and do whatever it took to prosper in this distant land.

Jimmy Jones walked along the line, handing out clean clothes, flashing her a wink as he passed. She was grateful for her brief friendship with Jimmy. However unlikely, she hoped one day she might see him again. Of the hundreds of souls aboard the *Relief*, his was perhaps the kindest. Though he had little to offer a woman, he had a good heart and she hoped that would suffice for someone deserving one day.

Once they passed the First Mate's inspection, they were ordered to the starboard gunwale. She took one last look across the ship that had served as her home for the past months. Captain Reid stood on the quarterdeck, clutching his lapels as he supervised the unloading of his freight. Their eyes met. Would he miss her? His face betrayed no such sentiment. From here on, she was on her own.

Her knees began to tremble as she clambered down the rope into the waiting rowing boat, and found a seat, squeezed between two fellow passengers. It was a short row to the shore, before her feet touched American soil for the first time. The crew ushered them up a slope where the grass had worn away. At the top, they were met by four men with bloodhounds on leashes. Legs weak, she was led towards a crowd of well-dressed men assembled outside a clapboard tavern. The dog handlers arranged the immigrants in lines of ten while the crew went back to the ship to fetch more, leaving the men to begin their inspections. Her export was complete.

Of the lot, Sylvia was the most attractive woman and soon found herself the subject of examination from several men. The first was a broad blond man who couldn't have been much more than twenty. There was a simple purity to his appearance that made her feel his honesty. She returned his stare and felt a thrill when he averted his gaze. She smiled and his eyes took in her face.

'What's your name?' she asked.

'Viktor,' he said, his cheeks flushing.

Before their conversation could continue, a short, gruff man invaded the space between them. 'My, what have we here?'

Sylvia said nothing. His face was puce, laced with tiny red veins and beads of sweat. His yellow eyes and fat belly indicated he lived too well, yet he smelled unwashed beneath his fine clothing, the odour taking her back below the *Relief*'s deck.

He stuck his stubby fingers in her mouth and parted her lips. They tasted of beasts, musty and soiled. She could smell the whiskey on his breath as he leant in to inspect her teeth and gums.

'Turn around,' he ordered.

Sylvia complied, her resentment building. She felt like a cow at Smithfield cattle market.

'About face.'

Sylvia turned back round. He stretched one eye wide open with his grubby fingers, then the other. He smiled, exposing his missing front teeth, as he cupped her breast with the palm of his hand. 'Mmm.'

'Don't touch me, you—' She knocked his arm away.

The men around him chuckled, all except for the blond man, Viktor, who looked shocked.

The fat man suddenly pressed his fingers against her vagina. 'You'll make me a fine wife.'

'Fuck off!' she seethed, kicking him in the shin, and thrashing her fists against the dead weight of his chest. 'I won't!' she spat at him. 'Over my dead body – and yours too!'

He cuffed her round the head and wiped her spittle from his cheek.

'No handling the goods, please,' called out one of the men, a bloodhound straining against his leash.

The fat man straightened his scruffy waistcoat, while the onlookers chortled.

'Tell me, what did you do wrong, little lady?' he whispered.

'I killed my husband,' she said, flashing her teeth, determined to deter his interest.

'So you lot *are* convicts then?' a grin on his face. Many people volunteered passage to the New World to escape the bondage of the old world, believing the tales that a better life awaited them in the colonies. Such folk were believed to make for better indentured servants.

The onlookers fell quiet. Sylvia sensed her mistake; she glanced at the blond man whose eyes flared. A tense silence lingered, and Sylvia's heart sank as people drifted away to appraise the others in line – all except the short fat man.

'Don't worry, love,' he winked at her, 'we'll be very happy together, and you just got a lot cheaper.'

She spat in his face again.

He wiped it off and blew her a kiss.

'Viktor?' she called out, but the young man had moved away.

She stood frozen, staring blankly at the American dirt. All around her, people were examined while she remained alone, damaged goods, buyer beware. She reflected on the events that had conspired to bring her here, desperately wishing she could have her time again, to do things differently. But it was no use. British justice had spoken. England had cashed her in.

Growing up poor and attractive had accustomed her to the attention of men, which, when met with refusal, all too often led to violence. She'd had to learn to protect herself. Most men couldn't conceive of a violent woman and were usually ill-equipped to deal with it. Occasionally – like today – her behaviour backfired.

***

George had spent the night at Mount Vernon with Anne, who'd been surprised to see him return so quickly. He hadn't admitted to her that he'd been anxious about setting out on his own, she'd only have offered him cold-comfort by reminding him it had been *his* choice to volunteer for such an undertaking. His efforts to recruit a volunteer had been wasted. After Alexandria, the only settlements this side of the mountains were scattered farms, ferry crossings, roadside taverns and occasional hamlets at road junctions. His odds of finding anyone fell the further he ventured from the coast.

Hearing that there was an auction in Alexandria the next day, he'd opted to wait and see if he found anyone capable of making the journey to the Ohio with him. He'd mooched about the tobacco warehouse, the taverns, the store, but nobody he'd encountered had fancied a wild goose chase in search of national glory. His confidence was ebbing as he walked over to the auction, where he could see people being inspected.

The usual rag-tag array of sun-deprived people stood, trying to appear as if the ocean crossing hadn't taken a toll on them, despite their hacking coughs, pallid skin and withered bodies.

'Viktor?'

'Oh, hi George.'

Viktor was staring intently at a young woman with auburn hair, clearly the most attractive of the bunch.

'Got your eye on something?' George commented.

Viktor grinned, a boyish excitement on his face. 'George, tell me, what should I do?'

'Come to the Ohio with me!'

'No, that's not what I meant. Mason has told me to buy a pig farmer. That man over there claims to have experience,' Viktor pointed at an elderly man with greying hair and a robust physique. 'On the other hand, Mrs Fitzbarton wants someone literate, to do the administration – I think it's so Mason loses his excuse to avoid her in his study. Who should I disappoint?'

George laughed. 'A man can't serve two masters, Viktor.'

'What would you do?'

'Run away to the Ohio.'

Viktor dismissed George's persistence with the wave of an arm. 'I'm serious. Who?'

'Happy wife, easy life, isn't that what they say? Mason will see the sense of it eventually. There will be another boat and another pig farmer.'

'Do you think?'

'Good luck, Viktor.' George patted him on the back. 'I'm sure you'll make the right decision. If you change your mind and want to join me, it looks like I'll be staying at Mount Vernon again tonight. Come by, it's the first house on the far side of the creek. I'd be glad to have you as a companion.'

People were milling about. It was worth one final look in the taverns, thought George as he walked up the slope, all but resigned to going it alone. As he approached the tavern, the door swung open. A tall Dutchman, unkempt and dishevelled, filled the door frame.

'Van Braam!' George called out. 'Just the man!'

'George, long time no see, how are you, boy?' Before George could reply, Van Braam continued, 'I was sorry to hear of Lawrence's passing. Very sad.'

George nodded, but was eager to avoid the subject, lest it provoke emotions he'd prefer not to show. Besides, seeing Jacob Van Braam was a stroke of fate. He'd served in the army with Lawrence and was tailor-made for the expedition. George wasn't going to let this bit of luck slip through his fingers.

'Jacob, I need your help.' He explained his mission and watched as Van Braam considered his reply.

'You speak French!' George implored. 'Please, Jacob, I'm desperate.'

'I'm not letting you go on your own! This is what we trained for,' said Van Braam, referring to his stays at Mount Vernon when he'd taught George the basic drills of soldiering.

Relief surged through George. 'Thank you.'

Then and there, their journey began.

***

An hour passed before the auction got underway. The auctioneer, a tall man with a Scots accent stood on an upturned crate and welcomed the bidders to the sale. By his side stood Captain Reid, whose eye Sylvia couldn't tempt her way.

The men were sold first. Before each lot, the auctioneer invited them to say their name and profession, then the bidding began. The best amongst them fetched up to £30. At home, such a sum would have taken two years of continuous work – which was as unlikely as a sunny English summer. Here, that ensured the successful bidder seven years free labour. Such was the easy lot of the rich man. Sylvia wondered if they appreciated the enormity of their advantage.

As the men were sold off, the crowd began to drift away with their purchased goods. By the time Sylvia stepped forward, three-quarters of the bidders had left. Unfortunately, the short, fat man remained. When invited, she said her name, attempting to sound genteel. Thanks to the charity of Mr Benson, she was able to state her profession as parlour maid.

The fat man scoffed loudly.

His was the first bid received.

Sylvia began to tremble in the long silence that followed. She looked beseechingly at Viktor, who stood at the end of the remaining bidders. He'd bid on one of the men but had lost out once the price got high. The frown on his forehead and heavy weight of his cheeks gave him an anxious appearance. She mouthed at him, *'Please.'*

He glanced left at the other bidders.

'Eight pounds. Going once,' said the auctioneer. 'Too pretty a woman to only fetch one bid!'

Sylvia locked eyes with Viktor, pleading with him to bid.

He looked uncertain.

'Going twice.'

The fat man grinned at Sylvia. He was going to win. It was her fault, she'd scared the other bidders off. She felt sick.

'Nine pounds!' It was Viktor.

Her heart soared. Her whole future rested in the hands of a man she knew nothing of, save that he had to be preferable to the alternative.

'Ten,' countered the fat man.

'That's more like it,' said the auctioneer. 'Do we have eleven?' He looked at Viktor.

Sylvia nodded frantically.

His jaw twisted.

Damn you, bid, you coward! thought Sylvia.

He nodded.

She breathed a sigh of relief.

'Twelve?' The auctioneer passed the bidding back to the rotund monster.

He nodded. 'I can go all day,' he announced for all to hear.

Sylvia's hopes plummeted. She looked at Viktor in desperation. His head twitched as he tried to decide. *Come on.*

'Twelve, going once,' declared the auctioneer.

The fat man leaned forward and glowered at Viktor.

'Come on,' Sylvia gritted.

'Going twice.'

For Christ's sake, bid! Sylvia willed him.

Viktor's mouth twisted with uncertainty.

'Sold!' declared the auctioneer. 'To Mr Bowler, for twelve pounds.'

Sylvia fell to her knees, unable to restrain her tears.

The fat man rubbed his hands together in anticipation. 'We'll be very happy together, once I've broken you in.' A laugh rippled through the crowd of remaining bidders.

Viktor, hands cupped over his mouth, had missed his opportunity.

So had Sylvia.

34

Sylvia had always thought herself a fast learner. It was an ability which had evaded her this morning. She cursed her stupidity as she watched Simon Bowler, the squat, gap-toothed creature – her new owner – load his wagon.

Bowler, a foul specimen, accustomed to handling unreceptive livestock, must have been used to such reactions from women, and wasn't in the least intimidated by her malevolence. She'd realised he liked it: intimidating those he perceived as weaker.

Overawed by her arrival in a distant land, she promised herself she'd act with more cunning from here on.

Bowler dismissed the negro who'd finished loading the goods onto his wagon. Since the auction, he'd kept Sylvia restrained, tying her hands behind her back until she'd calmed down. He'd lifted her onto the flatbed of his wooden wagon, then introduced himself as Mr Simon Bowler, planter and farmer. He owned a homestead a day's ride west of here, a simple log cabin he'd built himself. He proudly announced he owned two negroes, Tweedle-dum and Tweedle-dee, who worked his land. Her role would be to keep his home, cook, clean, and keep him satisfied – the latter was said with a wink.

'It's a pleasant place,' he smirked. 'You'll have seven years to learn to appreciate it.'

Sylvia's face didn't betray the turmoil that occurred in her gut.

'So you don't get any ideas, there'll be no escape. West is full of

Indians; they won't think twice about feeding you to their children. North and south are mountains; you'll freeze – if the wolves don't get you first. I know every man between here and where we're headed, so you're best advised to make your peace with your circumstances.'

He took a sliver of dried meat from his pocket and gnawed at it. A passer-by congratulated Bowler on his purchase.

'You got your hands full there, Simon!' he joked.

With an outstretched arm, he offered Sylvia a bite of the meat. 'Deer?'

She shook her head.

'You can be my wife if you like, but I'll rut with you either way. God willing, you'll sire my children. Under the law, you'll be free to leave after seven years. Any children will be staying with me.'

He walked away and went to give some grass to the mangy horse hitched to the wagon, leaving Sylvia to contemplate her life sentence.

When the judge had declared her guilty, she'd felt so relieved to escape the gallows. Exportation to the colonies had, for a passing moment, seemed like a chance at a new beginning. She knew better than to hope for a bed of roses, for rarely had life given so freely, but she'd never imagined herself trapped in a frontier wilderness, shackled to a man who was barely more refined than the animals he tended. The noose would have been quicker.

Bowler returned. 'Now, if you're calm, I can untie you and you can come for lunch.'

She acquiesced. He bought them a lunch of vegetable soup and turkey cuts at the tavern. He refused her request for a gin, but allowed her a cider while he enjoyed three glasses of wine.

Then they'd gone to the store. He spent more in that half an hour than she'd done in the last year: fifty nails, ten hinges, a saw, a chisel, five sacks of flour, one of sugar, five bottles of rum, three wooden handles, a length of rope, and then – after complaining about the price of gunpowder – added a large pouch of the black powder to his haul. Finally, he picked up a saucepan and an apron.

'You'll need them,' he laughed at his own joke.

Having attended to his practical needs, he invited her to choose some new clothes. The choice was limited, but she took two cotton chemises, a coif and a woollen red dress.

'That'll do, lady,' he'd declared.

'We'll need some soap too,' she said, grabbing a cake of it. If she had to share anything with this stinking man, he'd have to learn to wash regularly.

'No, you'll make your own,' said Bowler, replacing the packet on the shelf.

Sylvia insisted. She placed the soap back on the counter. Under the watchful eye of the storekeeper, Bowler relented. To Sylvia's surprise, they left the store without parting with any money, everything having been put on account. It was unthinkable to her; in London, if you didn't have the money, you didn't get the goods. It seemed temptingly open to abuse.

Bowler made a final inspection to satisfy himself that all his goods were packed securely into the wagon. He tapped the plank that served as a bench, indicating Sylvia to take her place next to him. She felt a tug at her wrist. Bowler had grabbed her arm and quickly tied it to the bracket that held the back of the bench to the seat.

'Is this necessary?' she demanded.

'I expect so.'

Having secured her, he slapped the long reins and the nag reluctantly trudged forward, jolting Sylvia in her seat. She turned to take a last look at the river that had brought her here.

It was mid-afternoon and the western sky had turned a menacing shade of grey that threatened rain. Bowler stuffed some tobacco into his mouth. He didn't offer her any. It was a rough and unforgiving ride. The road passed through the farmland that surrounded Alexandria, though she could barely look as she gritted her teeth to stifle her tears. A gang of negroes, shackled to a long chain attached to their ankles, walked in the opposite direction. In London's taverns, she'd overheard men debate the wisdom of investing in slaves. Anyone could buy a slave, or as many as they could afford, and hope for a return from their share in the sugar or tobacco trades. In London, it had been simple commerce; here it was the reality of people's existence. Whatever colour one's skin, she saw clearly that there were two types of people in Virginia: slaves, and those who owned them. She was the former.

'Will we ride through the night?' she asked.

'Nah. We'll find a quiet spot and camp under the stars. Romantic,' he chortled.

After a few bumpy hours of travel in silence, they pulled off the road and took shelter beneath a tree. Mercifully, the rain had stayed away and the sun cut pink through the grey clouds above the hillside.

'Time to make camp,' said Bowler. He took his knife and held it to Sylvia's throat, 'I'm going to untie you – there's nowhere for you to go, but if you try, I'll cut your throat.'

Sylvia nodded. She knew it was an empty threat. The man wasn't foolish enough to damage goods he'd only just paid money for.

'You get a fire ready.' He slipped the knife back into his coat pocket.

Once the feeling had returned to her freed hands, Sylvia set about collecting firewood. Bowler opened his rum. He took some tinder from his pocket and proceeded to light a fire. The flame slowly took hold of the wood.

'There're some provisions in that chest. Make us some dinner,' he ordered from the height of his wagon seat.

Sylvia did as instructed.

She served him a simple bannock bread and a fried egg. Having washed it down with rum, Bowler cut a satisfied figure, sitting beside his campfire in the last of the daylight.

He took the knife from his pocket once more. 'Now then, better get the inevitable over and done with.' He unbuttoned his breeches and lay down, staring fiercely at her. Sylvia had expected as much.

'Sir, I'll offer you no resistance, I'm yours to do with as you please. All I ask is that you put the knife away. I'm not going anywhere – not in these shoes. If we are to live together as the Lord determines, let it be an arrangement based on mutual trust and free of violence.'

His small, round eyes narrowed as he weighed up her words. After a moment's thought, he shook his head. 'Not yet, little lady.'

'Well, at least let me make one request, for my own comfort?'

He nodded.

'Let me wash you clean first.'

'Very well.'

Sylvia stood up and emptied some water into the saucepan he'd bought. Placing it on the embers of the campfire to warm, she found the soap and gave Bowler a tot of rum, sneaking a swig for herself. Kneeling in front of him, with the water warm and soapy, she gestured for him to stand. She pulled down his breeches to his ankles, taking her first look at his manhood. He hummed with satisfaction.

A man on his own, living in the frontier with only animals for company, this would at least be over with quickly, she consoled herself. Working a lather between her hands, she took his manhood; it swelled immediately. She took a deep breath and pulled his foreskin back. Soaping it thoroughly, she began to rub it back and forth and Bowler purred in delight, a large grin spread across his podgy face.

'Put it in you, woman.'

'Ssssh.' She rinsed her hands in the water and washed the soap suds from his erection. Satisfied it was clean, she leant forward and took it in her mouth.

He groaned as she moved her head back and forth, summoning her resolve. From the corner of her eye, she could see his grip on the knife loosen.

She kept going, his breathing becoming faster which each motion. Sensing the end was nigh, she brought him to the edge of climax – then suddenly clenched her jaw shut, sinking her teeth into the head of his cock as hard as she could.

Roosting birds fled their nests as his howl filled the evening air. He slapped her across the face, knocking her sideways into the embers of the fire, raking her teeth across his member in the process. He bent double, clutching his crotch, shouting obscenities. Sylvia dashed to the wagon. She went straight for the pouch of gunpowder in his bag and threw it on the fire. The explosion was far more violent than she'd imagined, causing her to stumble against the wagon. Bowler was thrown back, hitting the trunk of the tree. The horse started; only the weight of the wagon restrained it from bolting. Sylvia picked herself up, groaning in pain since her back had collided with the side of the wagon. She summoned up spittle in her mouth and spat it out, ridding herself of his taste.

She surveyed the scene. Bowler, the wind knocked from his lungs, lay in a crumpled heap under the tree. He twitched and moaned; blood pooled in his lap.

She knew whatever she did next would determine the course of her fate in the colonies.

She picked up the knife Bowler had dropped on the ground.

35

November 2ⁿᵈ, 1753
Alexandria

Viktor ordered another cider on Mason's account. *What does it matter?*
I'm done for.

He sat at the tavern bar, staring into the golden liquid. His father
had often said that there were never answers to be found in booze,
only comfort. Yet this evening, it provided Viktor with no comfort,
simply an unavoidable truth: he'd choked at the auction. Again, he'd
been found wanting. He'd leave Alexandria empty-handed, with
nothing to show but a bar tab. He would be scolded – and rightly so,
he conceded to himself. *Why can I not make a decision?* Since leaving his
family home in a fit of temper, he'd proved himself incapable of acting
when it mattered.

Viktor took a sip. The tavern was quiet tonight, most folk having
concluded their business and returned home. A trio of men played
dice in the corner. A married couple finished their meal and mopped
their plates clean with hunks of bread. Two middle-aged men
approached the bar and ordered drinks. He eavesdropped on their
conversation while they waited:

'He was about to cross into Maryland, upstream by the falls. I set
the dogs on him. You should have seen the look on that nigger's face,
he turned paler than you!'

The other man laughed. The first man went on to explain how he'd
returned the escaped slave to the plantation and staked him to the

ground, then made all the other slaves shit on him.

The image brought much amusement to the man's companion. It turned Viktor's stomach. He knew he didn't have it in him to enact the punishments and torments that his job required of him. A vision of Charlie's bleeding back lashed to ribbons came to his mind. He took a large gulp of his drink.

He turned his thoughts back to the pretty girl who'd been auctioned away from him. She'd looked terrified at being sold to that man. Viktor cursed himself for not buying her, but the man had been determined to have her. What would he have said to Mason? He hadn't been sent here to buy a fancy for himself. The Fitzbartons would never have forgiven him. What did he have to offer such a woman anyway? *Anything*, he concluded. For a woman like her, he would do anything, forever. To see her laugh, to make her smile, to touch her, taste her, hear her groan – he would submit himself to anything. And yet, his moment had passed. He hadn't done *anything*. He'd been too damned scared of the consequences. *You're a coward, Viktor Neumann. You don't deserve a woman like her.*

He drained the last of his cider, feeling thoroughly despondent. He didn't want to confront the Fitzbartons, having failed both of them. Once the negroes got word, even they would mock him. Billy and Granville wouldn't take pity on him. His cards were marked with Mason. Perhaps it was for the best.

His only other option was George Washington; it wasn't a job, but at least it was a way out. The Major seemed a decent sort, but this was a quest into the wilderness. He'd have to contend with Indians – he didn't much fancy being relieved of his scalp in the dead of night.

Captain Reid? Would he offer him a job? Everyone wanted sailors, but Viktor barely knew one end of a boat from another. And if he didn't take to it, he would be trapped at sea.

His thoughts were interrupted by a burst of laughter by the window.

He ordered another drink and Ginny rang the bell for last orders. Viktor hadn't realised it had got so late. He was accustomed to turning in for the night shortly after dark, but once the candles were lit indoors, it was easy to lose track of time.

He took a large swig of cider and promised himself he would act decisively in future, devil may care the consequences. He wouldn't be going back to Mason's. *First decision made.*

When it came to what he wanted to do instead, he was less clear. He knew he couldn't cope with a life at sea, and that wouldn't get him the one thing he knew he wanted: a woman. That left only George's offer. *Come on Viktor,* he said to himself, *be decisive.*

'Barkeep, toss me a coin, would you?'

Ginny grinned. 'Sure.' He fished a shilling from his pocket. 'Heads?'

'Heads is…sea. Tails, Indian wilderness.'

'They ain't great choices, my friend,' said Ginny as he tossed the coin up with his thumb. The coin seemed to spin for an age before landing back in the palm of Ginny's hand. Viktor was numb with cider; the die of his life had been cast, the coin had fallen. The barkeep slapped the coin over onto the back of his other hand.

'Tails. Indian wilderness for you, lad.'

Viktor was disappointed and relieved in equal measure.

He'd desert Mason's negroes and walk to Mount Vernon instead. He'd seen it from the boat on the way over, so it would be easy to find, even in the dark. It was a few hours on foot; he'd be there for sunrise, ready to meet George.

He left the tavern and found the negroes dutifully waiting for him outside.

'You lot rest up tonight, we'll leave in the morning,' he said as he staggered past them.

The night air was fresh. The moon was full, giving him some light for his journey. It cast a milky shine on the river, illuminating the moored boats, lanterns marking their positions. It was a peaceful scene.

He walked down the slope towards the centre of the bay, where the mansion and foundations of future buildings were rising from the ground like brickwork saplings. His footsteps giddy, the slope helped him bounce along. He decided to give the buildings a wide berth in case they harboured trouble. He veered to the right and reflected on what a fine man George had seemed, when something suddenly caught his left foot. He fell forward, thumping into the hard ground.

Everything went dark.

***

Sylvia's fingers gripped the horse's mane tightly as she cantered through the Virginia countryside. Eager to put as much distance between her and the crime scene as she could, she'd travelled back on the same road – the only road she knew – heading east. With every passing mile, the relief of escaping Bowler faded as she began to contend with her next problem. She was a fugitive. She knew no one and had nowhere to go, so she kept heading east, back towards what passed for civilisation.

In the early hours, she crested the brow of a small hill and saw in the distance the light of the moon shimmering across the expanse of river water. She drew the animal to a halt. Alexandria was barely more than a village. In all likelihood, she'd be recognised from the day, her behaviour at the auction having drawn attention to herself. Panic set into her belly. *A boat. I need to talk my way onto a boat and get out of here,* she decided.

***

It was still dark when Viktor came to. He had a headache and was sore from his fall. Instinctively he checked for his shoulder bag. It was still there, where it should be, unopened, Mason's crop note still inside. He sat up and tried to remember what had happened. He felt the ground, his wrist catching against a piece of string. It was pegged into the ground, forming a large square. He suddenly realised what he'd done. The string denoted the plots of land that had been auctioned to the first investors in Alexandria. They were left out to make sure no property boundary disputes broke out. In his silly state, he'd blundered straight into one. He got to his feet and relieved his bladder before proceeding with care to avoid any further string markers.

He worried about Mason's crop note as he journeyed west on the road. *Is it theft? Maybe I can post it...* His thoughts were interrupted by a woman's voice.

'Excuse me, sir.'

In the dim light of early dawn, Viktor saw the silhouette of a horse behind a tree on the verge. Beside it, a woman, her hand behind her back.

'Yes?' Was this a robbery, he wondered, tensing in readiness.

'Can you help me? I need to find a boat to take me.'

'Where to?' Viktor glanced over his shoulders to make sure they were alone. He stepped towards her to get a better look. 'You alone?'

'Yes. Don't come any closer.'

There was something familiar about her voice. 'Do I know you?' Viktor's tired mind grappled.

'No.'

Viktor squinted at her, the moonlight just enough to make her out. 'It's you. From the auction yesterday. I bid on you. What are you doing here?'

She stepped forward, tentatively. 'Viktor?'

'That's right.'

'Oh, thank God. I need your help!'

36

'Just take me back with you,' Sylvia pleaded with Viktor. 'You were going to buy me anyway, so let's just pretend you did.'

Viktor cursed his fortunes. He'd summoned the courage to finally leave the Fitzbartons. And within a few hours the one thing he'd wanted more than anything – a pretty woman – was begging him to take her back there.

'What about the man who bought you?' he asked as they stood on the road that led to Mount Vernon.

She took his hand in hers. 'Don't worry about him. We'll have no bother from him. Come on, let's go.'

Viktor frowned, his mind too tired for such big decisions. 'But I was supposed to buy a pig farmer.'

'Then why did you bid on me?'

'Well...' He'd felt sorry for her, but didn't like to say so.

'What do your employers need?'

'I'm sorry, I can't.' There was too much to explain. Having finally made up his mind, he didn't want to change it.

She sniffed and wiped tears from her eyes.

Oh God, please, no...

'I'm alone,' she sobbed, 'I've nowhere to go. I never wanted to come here.'

'Look...'

Before Viktor could continue, she pressed herself against him,

weeping into his shoulder. He wrapped his arms around her. *Poor girl.*
'Come now, it will be all right.'

She shook her head. 'I'll be dead within a month.'

'No, that won't happen.'

'It will. No one will help me.'

Viktor pulled her into his embrace, a flicker of shame passing
through him as he found himself enjoying the touch of her body.

'Please, I beg you. I'll do anything.' She looked longingly into his
eyes.

Is this really happening? Viktor wondered as he felt his heart
beginning to melt. She was beautiful. Desperate. All the journeys he'd
made in the colony and, finally, he had found his wish fulfilled. If he
went to meet George Washington, he'd be leaving her behind and
would never see her again. God had tested him, repeatedly, for years.
Is this my reward?

'You'll take me?' she breathed.

He remembered the feeling of regret he'd felt as soon as she'd been
sold to the other man. In her, he had a chance to return to the
plantation, having completed his errand. And best of all, he'd have her
companionship. He couldn't say no.

'Come on then.'

She kissed him. On the lips. His cheeks flushed. In that moment,
he knew he'd made the right decision.

They turned the horse free and returned hand in hand to the boat
to rouse the sleeping negroes. Musa used the pole to ease the flat-
bottomed boat away from the shoreline, bobbing into the river's swell.

Viktor bubbled over with excitement, but doubts were beginning
to surface. 'What about the money – we should have a receipt for you.'

'We'll say they forgot to file the paperwork. No one is going to
complain about not being charged for goods. We'll change my name.
Instead of Sylvia, I'll be… Sarah!'

'Take a seat, *Sarah*,' said Viktor with a grin. She joined him at the
bow, snuggling against him for warmth. As they sailed in silence,
Viktor looked at the dawn sky burning pink above the Maryland
horizon, welcoming him. A smile was plastered to his face, cold,
thirsty, tired – yet with a woman on his arm. He felt something he'd
dreamed of but had never experienced: complete. He couldn't wait to

kiss her once more, but knew an opportunity would arise again – it was enough for now. To be patient, like the rich folks. She was no tavern whore, after all; she would be his lady eventually, and he would treat her as such. Chance had brought her back to him, as if it had been divined.

'Tell me of your master,' said Sylvia, breaking the silence.

Viktor recounted a version of life on the plantation, leaving out the more unsavoury aspects. As he spoke, he was reminded he needed to square his decision to buy her. 'Now, what are you good for?'

'I can do cooking, cleaning – any domestic work.'

'They have negroes for that.' Viktor's stomach churned with worry.

'I can sew, stitch and mend.'

'Can you read and write?'

'A bit, yes.'

'Numbers – can you bookkeep?'

She nodded. 'I can do money.'

Viktor breathed a sigh of relief; at least Mary would be pleased.

***

The opposite was the case: on being introduced to Sarah, Mary had walked back down the hallway and slammed the drawing room door behind her, without a single word.

Mason had taken it better. He'd remained in the doorway, appraising his new servant.

Well, I can see why he bought her, he thought, a brief grin escaping at Viktor's temerity, who stood by Sarah's side looking pleased with himself.

'Your new bookkeeper, Mr Fitzbarton: Sarah Broadwater.'

She did a small curtsy. Her clothes were ill-fitting, but she appeared healthy.

'How much?' Mason demanded.

Viktor looked worried.

'Eight pounds, and worth every penny,' said Sarah, in his place.

Mason turned his attention to Viktor. 'I wanted a farmer.'

'Yes, well, there weren't any. The only man experienced with pigs was old and sold for over thirty pounds,' Viktor rambled on. 'Besides,

Mrs Fitzbarton had recommended I get you a bookkeeper, so you could enjoy your evenings again.'

Mason snorted. *So, it had been Mary's idea! She's not going to like this one bit, but that will teach her to interfere.* He wondered how he would make this right. At least she couldn't accuse him of introducing this new temptation into their home; he'd had nothing to do with it. He appraised Sarah. She was tall and plain, with an unblemished face and good teeth. He decided to keep an open mind about her. He certainly had no objection to having someone around who was so easy on the eye.

'Lovely to meet you, Sarah. Forgive my wife, she's prone to moods.' He held out his hand. 'Let me show you around.'

Sylvia followed him inside. Mason dismissed Viktor, forgetting to ask for his crop note.

***

Sylvia waited in the hallway while the Fitzbartons argued in the next room.

'I won't have that woman sleeping under this roof!' cried Mary.

'It's no use you flying off the handle at me. It was Viktor who bought her.'

'I don't care. I don't want—'

'It's not like she's faulty goods we can just exchange at the store!'

At least Mr Fitzbarton sounded calm, thought Sylvia as she listened from the other side of the door. In time, she would have to win Mrs Fitzbarton round. It wouldn't be easy but it was better than a life with Bowler.

'It was you who tampered with my instructions to Viktor. Serves you right for interfering,' said Mr Fitzbarton, raising his voice. He cut Mary off as she tried to reply. 'Enough! It's not her fault, let's give the girl a chance. If she's no good, we'll sell her. That's settled,' he declared.

Sylvia straightened up and shifted a few feet away from the door. Mr Fitzbarton emerged, his cheeks reddened by temper. Without further ado, he showed her round the ground floor of the impressive house. It was modern, and by some margin the grandest she'd ever stepped foot in. The stuff of her dreams. The master's study, where she was to work, was bedecked in artworks, shelves of books, and long velvet drapes fit for a queen. She had no experience of keeping ledgers, but thought better than to confess. She would try to make sense of it first, and if she couldn't, she would find other ways to endear herself to her employer. Their visit to the dining room, which was equally grand, was cut short at the sight of Mrs Fitzbarton pouring herself a drink from a decanter. Her glare was enough to freeze water, so they withdrew before she could voice her displeasure. In the kitchen, Mr Fitzbarton introduced her to a negro girl called Grace and an older man, Zebedee, who was the footman. Their reception turned frosty when Sylvia volunteered to help with any house duties.

Mr Fitzbarton led her out of a door to the rear of the house. It occurred to Sylvia, who'd had occasion to observe the ways of lords and ladies, that Mason never once held the doors open for her. It was an ungentlemanly way to behave for someone seemingly so well-to-do.

'I'm sorry about my wife,' he commented. 'She doesn't accept change too readily. Stay out of her way and she'll come round, in time.'

Sylvia nodded obediently.

He led her round the back of the house, across a lawn to a long single-storey wooden clapboard building that served as the accommodation for the white workers. Two negro women, one carrying a wicker basket full of linen, walked past them, stealing a glance at Sylvia. She turned to see them whispering to each other.

'You'll be sleeping here,' Mason said as he held open the door to the building.

Sylvia stepped into the dark hallway. The familiar smell transported her back to London: men. The musty, salty fug of working men, confined to small spaces. She would open the windows and give this building the airing it needed.

She followed Mason to the far end of the corridor and he showed her into her room. It was a small square space, wooden floor and bare walls, interrupted only by a small window over the bed frame.

'I'll have Grace fetch you some linens,' said Mason.

There was a chamber pot under the bed, a small desk, covered in dust, with an empty water jug and wash bowl atop it. A chair. No candles. A few cobwebs. The room needed a clean, and despite being a far cry from the main house, it was pleasant, and would more than suffice. Most importantly, it didn't have Simon Bowler in it.

Mr Fitzbarton stood in the doorway, gauging her reaction. He had the clean, unblemished and serious face of a powerful man, one acquainted with money and accustomed to getting his own way.

'Thank you, sir,' she said. 'I hope I will please you and your wife with my labours.'

'Take a few days to familiarise yourself with the plantation. Stay out of the house unless you're invited. If you need anything, Viktor's next door. Billy and Granville too.' He lowered his voice. 'Sarah, if any of them lay so much as a finger on you, I'll have them flogged.'

Reassured, she smiled and nodded again. 'Thank you, sir.'

His eyes narrowed as he took one last look at her, then left.

Sylvia wondered if he would likely proposition her. In her experience, rich men tended to do as they pleased. It would be easy for him to make life impossible for her. She would avoid being flirtatious, especially while Mrs Fitzbarton took such exception to her.

She sat on the bed. *Here I am,* she thought. *In America. Home?* She closed her eyes and let out a deep sigh. It was the first time she'd heard silence in months. The noise of the past weeks was gone: the lapping of waves, the creaking hull of the ship, the chatter of the crew and cargo, the auctioneer's booming voice, the trundling wheels of a wagon, horse hooves thudding against the dirt road, Simon Bowler's screams, all were gone. In their place, the pure simplicity of peace. Her mind turned to her family members. What had become of Jacob? Had his execution taken place? She assumed she would have sensed the moment of his passing, but as yet nothing. Or had being at sea disconnected her? It wasn't unheard of for sentences to be relaxed, especially if somebody stood to profit. What of Caroline, living in their former hovel with the Nicholsons? She was now all alone. How could it be, thought Sylvia, that it was herself who was finally convicted for a crime, only to end up living in more comfortable surroundings than those she'd grown up in.

She recalled Captain Reid's advice when they'd first met in the London tavern: *'Your past doesn't matter in the Americas. Far easier to make an honest living, they're always short of labour. Regardless, though, a pretty woman like you – you'd find a man easy enough...'* She dared to hope life in

Virginia would be better. Her heart felt a pang when she thought of Reid as his imperviousness to her affection still irritated her, so she thought of Caroline again, instead resolving to write to her younger sister when an opportunity presented itself.

Feeling a sudden and overwhelming tiredness, she lay down. There would be many challenges in the days ahead, but for now, her journey had finally ended. She closed her eyes and felt her shoulders untense. She was safe.

***

It was dusk when she woke to her door creaking open. In the fading light, she recognised Viktor's smiling face.

'You all right?' he whispered.

'Mmm, yes,' she groaned as she eased herself up off the bed, her legs still stiff from the night's ride.

'May I come in?'

She nodded. 'What time is it?'

'Six. I brought you some water.' He came in and passed her a clay mug. She swallowed it all. 'And, these, to brighten your room.' From behind his back he produced a handful of pretty flowers, none of which she recognised; small white petals and little yellow blooms.

'Ah, bless you, Viktor.' It had been a long time since anyone had picked her flowers. She took them and was immediately at a loss as to where to put them; without water they'd be dead by morning. Still, it was a lovely gesture.

Grace brought them a dinner of eggs and bread. They ate together and chatted. She told him about parts of her old life. He was either coy about his past or there wasn't much beyond what he'd told her. His life had revolved around growing and harvesting tobacco.

Billy came and introduced himself, a scruffy working type who made no attempt to hide his interest in her. She glanced at the door, and felt a burst of anxiety as she saw there was no lock. Then Granville, too, came to investigate. He stunk.

Viktor looked irritated by their arrival.

Having had enough of the assorted male attention, she got up to open her window.

'I wouldn't if I were you, not at night,' cautioned Viktor. 'The mosquitos will devour you.'

'Lucky blighters,' joked Billy, nudging Granville.

'Come on, gents, let's leave the lady in peace,' said Viktor, sensing she'd had enough. As he ushered them from her room, he reassured her he was next door if she needed anything.

He's got a good heart, that one, she thought as he closed the door, leaving her in peace. He'd be no trouble, beyond over-fussing her. From the other two, she'd need protection. She felt for the knife she'd stolen from Bowler, still tucked securely up her sleeve. She hid it under the mattress.

37

George felt enormous relief as he stared across the fork where the Ohio River divided to become the Allegheny and the Monongahela.

Up to this point, his fortunes had been as changeable as the weather. He and Van Braam had followed the path of the Potomac northwest. After two uneventful weeks, they'd stopped to rest for the night at Wills Creek, a small hamlet on the northern border with Maryland. The tavern at the crossroads had been a simple affair, a one-storey building with a large bar, and guest rooms to its rear. As they'd stepped into the candlelit bar, George had heard his name called. Shocked, he'd turned to see a large man with lank black hair looking at him. George had approached the man, seated amongst his companions by the fireplace, desperately trying to remember where he knew him from. As the man stood to greet him, his oversized hand outstretched, George remembered him from the trial. He'd sold his slaves to Fitzbarton, who'd neglected to pay for them.

'Christopher Gist! What are you doing here?'

'Last time I saw you was at Fairfax's Boxing Day hunt,' said Gist, 'when they made Lawrence president of our Ohio Company.'

'Yes! I remember,' said George, breaking into a broad smile. His lasting memory of that day had been being cross with Lawrence for appointing Gist as surveyor to the Ohio Company, instead of him. It seemed trivial now.

'I've been surveying out this way,' said Gist. 'These men have been helping.'

George nodded his acknowledgement to the motley crew of Gist's companions. An unsavoury looking bunch.

'Better to travel in numbers on the far side of the mountains,' Gist added.

How prophetic, thought George. 'Actually, I'm headed that way on company business.' George explained his assignment.

'Just the two of you?' asked Gist in surprise.

'Yes. Although we could really use your help.'

'You could. You've no chance without me.'

George prickled at the suggestion.

'The company's chances would be greatly improved if you'd join us,' he said smoothly.

'Well, if these Ohio shares are to be worth anything, I think we'd better come too.'

With that, George's party had grown from two to seven. Things were finally looking up.

Lashing rains had turned to early snow during their ascent of the mountains. They endured a week of painfully slow progress, traversing the rocky trails on foot, leading their horses by the reins should their sure-footedness evade them in the snow and ice. At night, they huddled together for warmth, icy winds buffeting the mountain tops. A diet of dried meat, melted snow and tobacco sustained them until they emerged on the western face. Gist led them downhill to a wooden cabin of a trader he knew. There, they could thaw, and enjoy hot food and drink. The torturous week had seemed to last a month. Shivering between his companions, George had thought of Anne reciting Shakespeare: *'There is neither good or bad, but thinking makes it so.'* Well, if there was anything good about this journey, it wasn't evident to George, who, for the first time ever, feared for his life. Contemplating a fate of being preserved in ice on a mountain top, he remembered Dinwiddie's words: *'You wanted to serve your country, Washington. This is what it looks like: servitude.'*

But those thoughts were all cast aside as he considered how best to cross the river. The point of grassland in the middle, which Dinwiddie had pointed out on Fry's map, was where the Iroquois wanted the

British fort.

'Cannon would make mincemeat of anything coming down these rivers,' said Van Braam as they looked across the fast-flowing flood water of the swollen rivers.

'It's ideal,' said Gist. 'We should cross further up where the river's narrower. There's a track on the other side that will take us to Logstown, the Iroquois village.'

George bristled. Between them, the two older men were gradually assuming leadership.

'Boys, drag the canoes over there,' continued Gist. 'We're crossing to the other side.'

They may be older and know this land better than I, but I *am the one with the King's orders in my bag,* thought George. He kicked his horse, urging it forward into the icy water.

'What the hell are you doing?' called Gist.

George ignored him. Water rose up the animal's flanks, soaking his boots. He felt Lisbeth's hooves treading in the river bed, twitching as they found purchase between the rocks. 'A far cry from the racetrack, old girl!' said George, to ease his own nerves as much as the animal's.

'Oi, George, you bloody idiot! Get back here, you'll get yourself killed!' shouted Gist.

'That's up to him,' George heard Van Braam comment. Behind him, the rest of the party moved upstream to find a crossing point of their own. The water kept rising. George was up to his chest. Lisbeth tilted her head back, to keep her mouth clear of the water. He felt the current push into their flanks. One false step would see them both swept downstream. 'Keep going, girl,' he encouraged her. She tossed her head to the side, but George gripped tight with his thighs as his body turned numb from the icy water. Halfway across, he glanced over his shoulder to see the rest of his party readying the canoes. Lisbeth's hoof slipped. His left shoulder plunged under water as he balanced himself. Her hooves scrabbled, then found their grip.

'That was close!' gasped George, grinning as his fear turned to relief. They finished the crossing and emerged on the strip of land between the rivers. George cast his surveyor's eye over the land. Even in winter, it was solid rather than swampy ground. The low rolling hills on the far banks would serve as good vantage points and a fort here would dominate the rivers. It was ideal. Beginning to shiver, George kicked Lisbeth onward and traversed the river on the far side of the point. To his relief, the water was slower and the river shallower. Waiting on the far bank, he did his best to ignore the cold, calling out, 'What kept you so long?' as the rest of the party approached in the canoes, leading their riderless horses.

'Any fool can be cold,' Gist replied to George's taunts. 'Don't be wanting to borrow my clothes when you're freezing tonight, you bloody idiot.'

George rode off; they could catch him up, he decided. Tensions had been festering in the group since the mountain crossing, their personalities clashing as the hardships had set in. Little digs of disapproval had been met with pointed insults as the men began to grate against each other. George was grateful of some time alone as he rode ahead, leaving a trail of river water seeping from his clothes.

They made the Iroquois village by nightfall.

***

Yet, as it turned out, Tanacharison was off hunting. None of the Iroquois chiefs were willing to parley in their leader's absence. While George waited for Tanacharison's return, he quizzed some French deserters. The four men, eager to escape the brutality of their commander, had been travelling south on the river, stopping at Logstown to resupply. With Van Braam translating, they explained to George that the French were moving downriver into the Ohio Valley, erecting a series of forts to establish their claim.

That night, George confided his thoughts in his journal. Having encountered the enemy now for the first time, he felt conscious of the weight of his mission. He wondered if the other men felt the same. They were certain to be outnumbered by the French. He would need the Iroquois to make up the numbers. Otherwise, they would be dead.

During the day, he milled about the village, feeling a sense of bridled excitement. In the dark of night, excitement turned to anxiety; it was as if his confidence went to sleep, even if he couldn't.

It was three days before Tanacharison returned from his hunting trip.

'He pulled that trick when I last came,' whispered Gist in George's ear.

Eager to get on, George asked for an audience right away. Tanacharison declined, needing to rest after his hunt. He would see them again tomorrow. George bristled at the further delay.

The following day, George, Van Braam and Gist passed time by taking a walk along the river's edge. George listened to the two older men debate how to handle the Iroquois.

'It should be me who speaks to them,' said Gist. 'I was here when we negotiated the Logstown treaty. They already recognise my authority. It was I who had Croghan swing it Virginia's way.'

'I'm tasked with leading this mission, Mr Gist,' George reminded him as he glanced away from the icy water towards his companion. 'I will address the Chief.'

'It won't just be Tanacharison we see. Though he may be their natural leader, the Iroquois are an alliance of tribes, each with their own chief, responsible for his people. Each will demand a say in how their council responds to our visit.'

'Surely their leader, Tanacharison, will decide...'

George was interrupted. 'We may have one king, George, but that doesn't stop the people of Virginia, or Maryland, or Pennsylvania having some sway in matters that concern them.'

George began to up his pace. He'd had enough of being lectured by older men, more intent on jostling for leadership. They must have hurried to keep up with him, because he failed to put any distance between them. When they arrived back at the village, George strode towards Tanacharison's tepee, which occupied a prime spot near the longhouse. His path was blocked by an attractive young woman, kneeling on the ground in front of the tepee. She busied herself scraping a knife blade across the inside of an animal pelt, dragging away the sinews. George ignored her greeting.

'Excuse me, Chief. I am ready to talk.'

The leather flap was pulled aside, releasing a whiff of tobacco smoke. The Chief stepped out and stood tall, measuring up to the same height as George.

'Please let us not delay further,' said George, holding his ground.

Van Braam and Gist arrived.

'Very well, English men. I see you all now,' said the Chief, looking at Gist.

George shook his head. 'Chief, I will see you in private.'

George sensed his two compatriots sharing a glance. The Chief shrugged. 'Suit yourself, English.'

George followed him to the stone longhouse, relieved to leave Van Braam and Gist in his wake. Inside, they escaped the winter gust that cut through the settlement. A small fire glowed in the middle of the building. The two men were alone.

From what George knew of the Indians, he assumed he'd meet with their whole council. It must be a good sign they were alone, he thought; they could reach an agreement much quicker. They sat down cross-legged by the fire, and George warmed his hands against the flames before presenting the Chief with gifts of wampum and tobacco, just as Gist had counselled.

'Great Chief,' George began eagerly, 'our enemy, the French, are coming.'

The Chief, a bearskin still draped around his shoulders, nodded.

Encouraged, George continued. 'I have orders to repel them, from the Great British King over the water.' He produced his orders and proudly showed Tanacharison the King's seal. 'I request your safe escort to meet with the French, so I can remove them from our land.'

The Chief's eyes narrowed. 'They will see this as hostility, revenge for their attack on Pickawillany.' A faint smile flashed across his weathered face.

'Without an escort, their allies, the Huron, may cut us down before we even arrive.'

The Chief nodded. 'You must build fort at forks to keep them away.'

'Yes, of course. I've seen it for myself, it's a fine site.'

'Your people too slow to protect us from the French.' Tanacharison's frown appeared hostile, which George thought unnecessarily rude.

'That is what I am here to do,' George stuttered. 'But I need your help.'

'You come to build fort?'

'No, not me!' exclaimed George.

Before he could continue, the Chief threw his arms in the air. 'The French bad people. They come take this land. You don't build fort. Why I believe anything you tell me, when you English don't keep promise?'

'Look here. I haven't come here to argue with you,' said George, trying to remain calm in the face of the Chief's aggressive manner. 'I have been sent by the King of England to remove the French, so you may live in peace.'

'English good people, they don't want our land – do they?'

George felt his stomach twitch. The Ohio Company's founding charter required it to settle the land with one hundred families. Gist had warned him about Iroquois sensitivity to the white man encroaching. The Chief's stare burned into him.

'No,' lied George, 'we desire only to trade with you, our friends.'

The Chief moved his arm behind his back, and appeared to be fishing for something, all the while keeping his face expressionless.

'Smoke with me, my brother.' Tanacharison produce a pipe and stuffed it with a pinch of the tobacco George had given him. He lit the pipe from the hot cinders of the fire, took a puff and then exhaled a long trail of grey smoke, before passing the pipe to George. He inhaled a small puff.

George was surprised how quickly the Chief's mood appeared to have quietened. Seizing the change in atmosphere, he reminded the Chief of his obligations: 'We have a treaty, signed here last year,' said George as he passed the pipe back. 'Our great peoples are bound to assist one another, so we may continue the trade that strengthens our bonds.'

The Chief nodded. 'But you not build fort?'

'We are raising the funds.' Another lie. Fry and his contingent had blocked the funds from being raised in the House of Burgesses.

'Fort build with stone, wood, earth – not money,' said the Chief.

George decided not to get drawn into an unhelpful diversion. 'I need an escort. Twenty men, to show the unity between our peoples.'

'You want my men, yet you not build fort – for one year now.'

George felt himself getting irritated. He took another puff on the pipe and coughed, having taken too much. There was a long silence.

'Chief, you have a treaty with us. You are legally obliged to help us.'

A flash of anger crossed Tanacharison's face. 'English are a good people. I call council meeting for tomorrow.'

***

The following day's council meeting was a near copy of the previous day's between George and Tanacharison. It was longer and more formal, but George, conscious of the crowd, patiently repeated his requests, made the same points and absorbed their criticisms over the fort. Again, he falsely reassured them the British wanted only to trade. He was pleased with his efforts, dignified, yet firm. Lawrence would have been proud.

The Iroquois talked between themselves in their native tongue. After much debate back and forth, the Chief confirmed their decision.

'We are brothers. We support your voyage.'

George couldn't contain the grin that spread over his face. One by one, he had overcome the challenges: no resources, no companions, snow, biting winds, icy tracks, swollen rivers, squabbling rivalries… Now he could add overcoming Iroquois reticence to his achievements.

'We leave now,' he declared.

Chief Tanacharison shook his head. 'No. Very important that first we send wampum.'

What?

'Very important.' All the Iroquois were nodding. 'We show we make peace, not war.'

'Very well,' said George. 'We send wampum now and leave tomorrow?'

The Chief shook his head again. 'Will take a few days.'

George stared hard at the Chief. *This is all for show. They're wasting time.* 'Very well. Then we travel north with twenty men?'

'Yes, of course, we great friends.'

George sighed as he left the longhouse. He didn't make friends easily, but never would he consider that beastly man approaching a friend. All the delays left George with a bad feeling for what lay ahead.

38

November 22nd, 1753
Fitzbarton Plantation

It had been nigh on three weeks since Sylvia had arrived at the Fitzbarton plantation and by now she was beginning to feel distinctly surplus to requirements. Her initial relief at arriving somewhere both safe and opulent was fading with each day she felt further from home, and increasingly disorientated. Life in London had been hurried, people rubbing together cheek by jowl, on the make, surviving, a lucky few thriving. Here, time passed even more slowly than it had with Mr Benson and Mr Somerton. Having endured the stares and the unwanted attentions of Billy and Granville, she relied on Viktor for company and had barely seen the Fitzbartons, who, believing they had paid for her, put her to no use whatsoever. She hoped to be given some meaningful duties to help the time pass, for her idle mind began to churn darker thoughts. Would her escape from Simon Bowler come to light and her real identity be discovered? And what punishment might she suffer if apprehended for this crime? How such things were attended to in the Americas, she had no idea.

In the meantime, the silence that first had comforted her now tormented her. The native bugs and birds made such a racket, they woke her at dawn, which only served to make the already long day even longer. Thank heaven it got dark early so she could go to bed, where, for the first time in many years, she had the most vivid nightmares. She was chased, tortured and under attack. The lack of activity during the day was made up for in her imagination at night, when her mind was free to wreak havoc.

Grace knocked once and came in, carrying a plate. Each night, around six, she brought something over from the house for Mr Fitzbarton's white workers to eat. Tonight, it was boiled eggs and bread. She placed the plate on the table.

'Thank you, Grace,' said Sylvia.

Grace nodded and turned to leave.

'Won't you stay a moment?'

Grace shrugged. Sylvia stood up and closed the door.

'Please take a seat.'

Grace frowned, and shook her head. 'It's not my place to sit here.'

'Come, don't be so silly, it would be nice to talk. Tell me about our master.'

Grace remained standing and glanced nervously towards the door.

'What's the matter, Grace?'

'I'm not meant to be talking to you. Master don't like it.'

'Nonsense,' said Sylvia. 'There's no harm in two women having a natter. We're both workers.'

Grace scoffed. 'I'm no worker. I'm slave!'

'Well,' bristled Sylvia, 'so am I, I suppose, I'm here for seven years. I sure won't be getting paid either.'

Grace shook her head. 'Seven years is nothing. I here for twenty already. I never leave.'

'Surely you—'

Grace interrupted. 'You don't know how it is here. We not the same…'

Sylvia changed the subject. 'Tell me, what is Mrs Fitzbarton like?'

'Things here are bad. She always unhappy, but worse since you come.'

Sylvia felt a knot of fear in her gut. She knew it was the woman of the house who steered the thoughts of the man. If she remained out of favour, her safety was at risk.

'Grace, what makes Mrs Fitzbarton happy?'

'Nothing. Devil in their souls. You'll see.'

The door opened; Viktor appeared bearing his plate of eggs.

'Evening, mind if I join you?' Then he spotted Grace, 'Oh!'

Sylvia noticed Grace turn away from Viktor.

'I must go. Slaves can't mix with white folk,' said Grace. Head down, she pushed past Viktor.

As Viktor came in and took his usual seat at her table, Sylvia wondered what had caused the ill feeling between him and Grace. Surely Viktor was too sweet and naïve to have troubled her? But the atmosphere had definitely changed once he'd appeared. Had he forced himself on her? Beaten her? Sylvia believed herself a canny judge of character. She couldn't believe that of Viktor. His innocence was still childlike. In the time she'd been here, he'd never once done anything that even passed for flirting. From his regular attention and glances at her body it was obvious he was keen on her, but he was too shy. He was sure to still be a virgin, for he possessed no confidence or apparent experience in courtship's simplest rituals.

The rest of the evening passed in a similar matter to all the others. They chatted. He told her about tobacco. She told him about London. His childlike fascination with the world outside of Virginia was endearing. He was a sweet boy and she felt safe in his somewhat unremarkable company, but she didn't have the luxury of an alternative. She wondered what she could tease out of him about the Fitzbartons.

'Viktor, the Fitzbartons don't have any children, does that strike you as odd?'

'Oh. No. Master says the Lord never blessed their marriage with children.'

'I see. That must be very upsetting for them.'

Viktor puffed out his chest a little. 'Tell you the truth, that's what brought me here. Mr Fitzbarton promised me that if I work hard, he would pass the plantation to me once he dies.'

'*You?*'

'Yes.' His face showed a trace of defiance at her tone.

'But you're not...their sort, are you?'

'What do you mean?' Viktor blushed.

'Well, aristocracy...they don't usually bequeath their worldly possessions to people outside of their class.'

'What do you mean?' he repeated, his brow furrowing.

'They're obsessed with siring heirs, hereditary privilege, titles – they don't normally entertain common people. We're different.'

'Maybe in Britain.' Viktor shrugged.

Sylvia was astounded. The idea that someone in Fitzbarton's position could even consider leaving a plantation like this to a pauper like Viktor was beyond credulity. Yet Viktor believed it. No commoner in England would ever fall for such a ruse. As he prattled on, the thought kept whirling around her mind. Being an imbecile in England didn't preclude you from the aristocracy – indeed it was practically a birthright. But not even the most capable person could transcend the boundaries of their class at birth. Was America really so different?

***

The following day, Sylvia had been relieved to finally start work. Mr Fitzbarton had come to fetch her, and she'd followed him to the house and into his fine study. He presented her with his ledgers, pointing to a half-inch pile of neatly stacked receipts, invoices and bills of exchange. She sat, her buttocks cushioned in his soft padded leather chair, while he stood over her explaining how he kept his books. Where the debits and credits went, that he liked everything divided into categories so he could keep a close watch on his expenditures. She nodded while his words went in one ear and out the other. He may as well have been speaking Dutch. She asked an occasional question to keep up her pretence of understanding.

'Now, we'll start by doing a letter. I'll dictate, you write.' His manner stopped short of rude, but she sensed he wasn't one to suffer fools gladly.

She took a leaf of paper, dipped the quill in ink and readied herself, sparing a thought for Mr Benson who had patiently taught her to write. She felt a pang of guilt for stealing his partner's ring. Fitzbarton moved to the window, looking outside as he dictated a letter to his agent in London. She scribbled furiously in an attempt to keep up, asking him to pause occasionally, to which he huffed disapprovingly, but obliged. In the letter she composed, he ordered two silk blouses, in whatever style was considered fashionable, four silver candlesticks, a lady's hand mirror, a lady's wig, a purse, an evening dress, three pairs of ladies' shoes – one for everyday use, one for evenings and a pair for formal engagements, a parasol in either pink or pale green, silk underwear, stockings and perfume – something floral, nothing with sandalwood.

Sylvia scratched away in disbelief. This man was spending more in the course of one letter, than she'd spent in the course of her entire life. This was the price of keeping Mrs Fitzbarton happy, she realised. *This is because of me.*

Finished, he approached from the window and she passed him the quill for his signature.

'Your writing looks like a cat has scratched this together with its claws. In the dark. It's embarrassing.'

'I'm sorry, it has been some time since I used a pen, I had to write quickly to keep up. I – I will do better next time, I promise,' she assured him, flashing a dutiful smile.

'Do it again, then I'll sign it. And I don't want my ledgers defaced with that scrawl. You take as long as you need with them. I want them neat. Understood?'

'Yes, sir. Forgive my asking, but will you send money with this letter?'

Fitzbarton shook his head. 'The cost is deducted from my account; all our colonial funds are held in London.'

Before Sylvia could ask more questions, the door to the study opened. Mrs Fitzbarton entered the room and folded her arms.

'What's taking so long?' she demanded.

'We're done.' Without looking at her, he left the room. Sylvia sat frozen, staring at the floor, while Mrs Fitzbarton glared at her. Without a word, she followed her husband out and shut the door.

Sylvia breathed a sigh of relief to be left alone.

***

For the next two weeks, her days were spent with her head buried in ledgers. Before committing ink to paper, she spent two days studying them, trying to build an understanding of how the numbers added up and tallied. She then practised adding entries on a separate piece of paper, adding and subtracting, checking her counting. She'd handled money in the taverns and shops so she knew the principle, but the numbers were bigger than she'd ever seen. Fortunately, Mason Fitzbarton rarely looked in on her, presumably not wanting to antagonise Mrs Fitzbarton. When satisfied, she gingerly made her first entries.

The work wasn't demanding, so she used the time to peer through the mass of papers in the study. She'd hold a letter under the desk, in case she was interrupted, and glimpse into the Fitzbarton affairs. In her old life, she'd had little use for paper, but she quickly learned that you could tell a lot about people by the paper they accumulated. Her heart would flutter with excitement as she leafed through his accounts and their personal correspondence from the preceding years. Mason was making handsome returns from his tobacco. Evidently, he'd built himself a reputation for settling his accounts. Amongst his letters, his agent in London thanked him for his prompt payment. Other agents sent him letters of solicitation, inviting him to try their services and extending him generous offers of credit. He had several letters unable to oblige his offer to invest in various ships. Most intriguingly, it seemed the Fitzbartons had been refusing social invitations from other notable persons in the colony. There was a letter from a Lawrence Washington, expressing regret that the Fitzbartons had been unable to join them for the weekend, and extending the invitation should Mrs Fitzbarton's health improve. *Was Mary ill?* she wondered as she leafed through the pile. Then another letter from a Colonel Thomas Lee, saying that he regretted Mason's absence at the recent weekend at Stamford Hall, where all involved discussed profitable business opportunities for westward expansion. He hoped Mrs Fitzbarton would recover in time so they could join the party at the horse races in Williamsburg this summer. Sylvia saw a picture emerging: *The Fitzbartons are isolated,* she realised. They seemed to attribute this to Mary's ongoing ill health, but from the little Sylvia saw of her, cholera, the pox and typhus had more to fear of Mrs Fitzbarton than she did of them. If a frosty demeanour were all that was required to keep illness at bay, then Mary Fitzbarton could look forward to a long and healthy life.

Sylvia was staring out the window wondering why Mary, who had so much, had cause to be so bitter with her lot, when the evening bell rang; it was five o'clock. She'd already closed the books and returned today's stash of private correspondence to the drawers, so she quickly left Mason a note accounting for how she'd spent her time. It was a practice she had decided upon herself to do. It seemed to her a ridiculous waste of paper and ink but when her master, despite being under the same roof, seemed unwilling to communicate, she didn't want to take for granted her employment. She was fed and watered. Bored, admittedly, but for a young woman, far from home, and without the protection of a man, boredom was a price worth paying for the safe blanket of the plantation.

Sylvia got back to her room, reflecting on the latest personal insights she'd gleaned into the Fitzbartons. Grace, the negro servant, had left her a pile of clean laundry. Sylvia chuckled to herself. She'd been convicted of a crime, sent to the far side of the earth, sold at auction, supposedly indentured – and yet her washing was done for her. What had been a punishment was in fact an elevation in privilege. The Lord did indeed work in mysterious ways, for he'd given this cloud a very silver lining. Her satisfaction was tempered by the thought of her brother, Jacob, who hadn't been so lucky.

I must write to Caroline, she thought as she sorted through today's pile: a clean cotton bed sheet, underwear, a chemise, and four sanitary rags. Sylvia stiffened at the sight of the small strips of cotton. When did she last have her curse? Her mind skipped back – it had been on the ship, shortly after they'd departed London. She quickly did the maths and her blood ran cold. She'd lost track of her cycles during the voyage, but as she double-checked her timings, she became increasingly certain she'd missed her monthly bleed. She was due around the new moon; if tonight was a half-moon, then she was late.

She crumpled onto the bed, her head buried in her hands as tears welled in her eyes, fearing she carried Captain Reid's baby in her womb. A momentary sacrifice for comfort and protection now risked landing her in very dangerous waters. Nobody took kindly to one of their workers falling pregnant. Without the baby's father to support her, she'd be cast out.

'Shit,' she cursed, then tried to calm herself. *Check the moon. If it's the worst, then you'll have to do whatever's necessary.*

There was a knock at the door. 'Hold on.' She blotted her teary eyes with a sanitary rag. 'Come in.' It would be Viktor; he always called by when he'd finished for the day. His beaming face appeared round the door. His smile faded to confusion.

'You all right?'

Sylvia nodded. He asked if he could come in. She nodded again.

He sat down beside her and started talking about his day. She didn't absorb a word of it, her mind still racing to plan for her potential circumstances.

He placed a hand on her forearm. 'Sarah,' as he always referred to her since rescuing her, 'are you sure everything's all right?'

'You know, Viktor, I am a little tired. Do you mind if I have some time alone this evening?'

His furrowed brow softened in disappointment. He'd visited her every evening since bringing her here. They ate their evening meals together and had taken to playing cards to pass the time. She planned on telling him what she'd learned about the Fitzbartons, but that now seemed little more than idle tittle-tattle.

'What's wrong?'

'Please, Viktor, not now.'

'Sure, should I find you a book?'

She shook her head. His concern, whilst well intended, felt stifling.

He stood and as he was leaving, turned to ask, 'This Sunday, I had planned a surprise for you, if that's all right?' A small, innocent smile crept back across his face.

Sylvia felt a moment's guilt for sending him away. 'That would be lovely, Viktor, thank you.'

He closed the door, leaving Sylvia to await the rise of the moon. She lay on her bed, resting the palms of her hands on her belly, wondering if she was cradling a new life inside her. Should she feel something, she wondered? She prodded her tummy. Nothing.

As the room fell dark, she dreaded looking out the window. Unable to put it off any longer, she heaved herself up and scanned the dusk sky. She couldn't see the moon from her vantage point, so she walked outside. There was a chill in the air, and the trill of the last field crickets of the year. Stars twinkled their diamond sparkle across a black canvas. There, low in the sky, just over the treetops, was the bright mottled white of the moon: a perfect half circle.

39

November 30th, 1753
Logstown

'You promised me twenty men!' George was unable to hide his anger as he stood by the riverbank, ready to depart. 'You delay me for days while you mislead me, and then when it's finally time to leave, I discover there are only four of you coming?'

Tanacharison was unmoved by George's anger. 'It better this way. We don't want to provoke the French.'

'We are supposed to be showing our strength and unity. We couldn't even fill a dinner party! It's hardly going to scare the French off.'

'This is how it is, Major Washington.' Tanacharison headed back into the village, leaving George and his men looking at each other.

'You won't change his mind, George,' said Gist. 'Indians do as they please.'

'They are supposed to be our allies!'

Van Braam chuckled. 'My wife vowed she'd be obedient – don't always make it so.'

George looked around in search of an answer. Thick snowflakes tumbled from the sky, carpeting the muddy ground, hushing the sound of the swollen river and the village.

'A soldier has only one task,' Van Braam cut into his thoughts, 'to fulfil his orders and survive the day. You've a message to deliver and a report to make. Let's go.' He signalled to one of his men to fetch back the Chief.

317

'But the French, we need to—'

Van Braam shook his head. 'Your job is written on that paper.'

'Yes, and it says to drive them off by force of arms, signed by the King himself.'

'Then that's what we do. Come on, let's start moving before I freeze out here.'

With the late winter dawn breaking the sky, George, Tanacharison, and their party of six white men mounted on horseback, and three walking Iroquois, all bedecked in animal skins and fur, began their journey to meet the enemy. With enough provisions to last, should they be delayed.

The sixty-mile trek north took five days, their going made punishingly slow by the short days and the precarious, snow-covered routes that the Indians insisted were the most direct. It was six extremely cold, bedraggled white men who first laid eyes on the French outpost. George crouched behind a tree next to Tanacharison and studied the position. One large log building, smoke drifting from its brick chimney into the late afternoon dusk. Another smaller one set to the side. Its defences were limited to the land between the confluence of two rivers.

'Time to carry out your orders, George,' said Van Braam, standing against the canopy of a rhododendron bush.

Now is the time, thought George. It had been a long and debilitating journey to reach this point. He'd had enough of Van Braam's endless badgering in his ear and was eager to get it over with. What sort of reception he would receive, he wasn't sure. He returned to his horse and unfurled from his saddlebag his other outfit: breeches, stockings, shirt, waistcoat, cravat, and tailcoat. After much hopping from one leg to the other as he struggled to don his breeches on the snowy ground, he almost looked fit to attend a dinner party. He retied his hair into a queue and smoothed the creases in his clothes. Only his muddy boots were at odds, but satisfied he looked like an English gentleman, fit to deliver the King's orders, he commanded the horses to be tethered and the party into the canoes. They slipped across the fast-flowing river and stepped foot on French soil – which George had to remind himself was actually English – just as the day's light was fading. George puffed out his chest and, with his party in tow, walked up to the large cabin door and knocked.

The door was answered by a short man with a lazy eye. '*Bonsoir.*'

'Indeed. I am Major George Washington, seeking an audience with your commanding officer.'

The man looked confused, so Van Braam called out a translation from over George's shoulder.

The man at the door said something in reply and indicated with his head towards the other building. The door closed.

At the next, smaller cabin, George was invited inside, taking Van Braam with him. Candles burned on the table in the middle of the room. The cabin was simply appointed; a raised bench ran around the edge, strewn with bags and clothes, and seemed to serve as the sleeping area for the inhabitants. The Frenchmen all stopped what they were doing to appraise the newcomers. They were invited to warm themselves by the fire, George relishing the tingling in his cold cheeks.

'Major Washington, Captain Joncaire, I am pleased to make your acquaintance,' said the French officer, his English, despite being accented with the unmistakeable French drawl, was fluent. He was shorter than George and wore deer skins. His hair was dark, untied, hanging loosely around his shoulders, and his face was wide with a flat nose and high cheeks. George suspected he must be part Indian.

'I regret to inform you,' said George, trying to sound imperious, 'that this is British land, and I am required to ask you to leave.'

'*Naturellement,*' said Joncaire, chortling to himself.

George was irritated by the Frenchman's irreverence. 'I have here a letter from Dinwiddie, the Governor of Virginia, requiring you to depart the Ohio Valley.' George handed the letter over. The Frenchman took a cursory glance.

'*D'accord.* My orders are to fortify this post,' the Frenchman said.

'Mine are to have you removed,' said George. 'By force, if necessary.'

The Frenchman's face turned serious. 'How many men have you?'

'Nine, sir.'

Joncaire and his fellow officers began to laugh. George's cheeks flushed red and it occurred to him perhaps he should have exaggerated his strength.

'Major Washington, my orders are to remain here. You will need to take the matter up with my commanding officer, Captain Legardeur de St Pierre.'

'Where can I find him?'

'Fort Le Boeuf, forty miles north of here.'

George hesitated.

'Come, Major Washington, join us for dinner. Your men can house themselves with mine, in the other cabin. It would be a dishonour to France to turn you out into the night, so far from your homeland.' He put a hand on George's shoulder and ushered him to sit on the bench. He issued an order in rapid French and a man departed to show the rest of George's companions the accommodation in the other cabin. George felt very alone as the door closed. He didn't relish the idea of further journeying in these wintery conditions, deeper into the bosom of the French. An image of Colonel Lee at his dinner party came to his mind. *'Possession is nine-tenths of the law,'* he'd said. George, now some three hundred miles from his own home, finally understood what Lee had meant. How could Britain claim a territory as her own, when it was the French who were already stationed there?

That night, Joncaire talked as freely as he drank. Over a delicious roasted rib of beef, George listened intently as Joncaire told him of French designs to connect Louisiana to New France, via the Mississippi river. He boasted of the chain of French forts that was being established to contain the British colonies and prevent their expansion beyond the Appalachian Mountains that George had crossed for the first time only a week ago.

Later, as he lay on the timber bed, listening to the drunken snores of the Frenchmen, George's earlier despondency was replaced by a sense of excitement. He now knew intimately what the French had planned and what they'd achieved so far. He might not succeed in removing them on this visit, but all that was needed was to overwhelm them with soldiers and settlers. They may have been here first, but he'd seen for himself the shiploads of vagrant people arriving in Virginia. As long as the boats kept coming, the company could fill the Ohio Valley – and he would be rich. Very rich.

***

The next morning, Tanacharison woke at sunrise. He'd slept in the larger cabin, thick with the smell of white men. Their slumbering chorus of snores, farts, coughs and shuffling was a poor substitute for the dawn songs of the birds. He crept out, donning his bearskin to guard against the winter cold. More snow had fallen overnight, dusting the trees of the surrounding valley white. It was a fine morning: a clear sky, rising blue from a yellow horizon. Today would be crisp, and despite the snowfall, ideal for travelling.

Tanacharison walked the few paces to the end of the spit of land that nestled between the rivers. The water from the smaller river swirled as it met the faster current of the larger, before finally being swept along, its identity melded away into a new river, the water indistinguishable from its origin. It reminded Tanacharison of the fate of his people. Not just the Seneca, or the Iroquois Six Nations, the alliance formed in response to the white man's encroachment into their lands, but all those native to this land. Their once endless herds, now thinned by the arrival of the white men and their diseases, left the Indian peoples so dangerously reduced they were losing the very land from under their feet.

Deer and beaver had both suffered similar fates. The white men's insatiable appetite for their pelts had made the once common sight of these creatures increasingly infrequent. British, French, Dutch, or German – it made no difference. Whatever their words, their intentions were the same: land. The trade had been good, but competing tribes, sensing their chances to settle ancient rivalries, had sought short-term advantage by allying with the white men. Their muskets and powder hadn't been sufficient to wipe out the blood debts between the Indian peoples. Instead, they'd increased them. It had been the white men who'd grown rich; they sat back as the native peoples inflicted damage upon themselves, creating the space the white man desired. Tanacharison watched the water travel into the distance and thought about his life, the mistakes he'd made and how he would account for those in the spirit world. He would atone for his greed by setting his people on a better course. No longer would they be swept along in the water of the white man's game.

He stooped and washed his face in the icy river. He quenched his thirst, while his belly protested its hunger. With the white man's larder, he wouldn't need to hunt this morning. Behind him, the camp began to creep to life. He was joined by his three braves, and together they watched the loathed white men go about their morning tasks. Major Washington was early to rise, still wearing his longcoat and white breeches. He walked with a briskness which suggested he was in a hurry. Tanacharison watched him inspect the French camp. He was more sober and purposeful than the average white man. There was a youthful impatience to his manner, which made him prone to rash actions. *Perhaps he is the perfect choice for my plan,* thought Tanacharison, recalling the stories about the Major's ancestor, 'Conotocarious'. Four generations earlier, George's great-grandfather had murdered five Indian chiefs who had journeyed under a banner of truce to negotiate a peaceful resolution to their disputes. One of countless treacheries committed by the white men. Eighty years may have passed since, but that man's seed now roamed, with dubious designs of his own, inhabited by the evil spirits of his ancestors *Yes, Major Washington must suffer for the deeds of his family, for he too is a devourer of villages. I will name him Conotocarious also.*

'*Bonjour,*' said Joncaire, approaching from behind.

Tanacharison nodded. He knew this man and his Indian line, but Joncaire acted under the banner of the French, using his Indian roots only when it suited him.

'You are to guide Major Washington north today?' asked Joncaire in Seneca.

Tanacharison's eyes narrowed as he nodded.

'Brother, I have a better idea. Keep the English here for a little while.'

Tanacharison squinted at the half-breed. *Could he be trusted?*

'I'll see that you'll be comfortable. If you do as I ask, I'll ensure your safe passage. The Huron could make life difficult for you and your friends.'

Joncaire's threat hung in the air.

***

Having completed his survey of the French camp, George had a clear picture in his mind of the best landing point, the best place to cross the river and a suitable vantage point to observe the post. If an attack were ever required, he was confident he could execute such an order. He found his men standing outside the smaller cabin, in the midst of a lively discussion with Joncaire.

'Ah, there you are,' said Gist. 'There's a problem – it's the Iroquois.'

'They're drunk,' added Van Braam.

'On French brandy,' said Gist, pointing at Joncaire.

The Frenchman raised his palms. 'The supplies were intended for your onward journey.'

'And you thought it was a good idea to entrust them to the Iroquois?'

'I didn't know—'

'Poppycock!' said Van Braam.

'Where are they?' asked George.

He followed Gist round to the back of the cabin where they found Tanacharison nestled between some trees, brandishing a half-eaten loaf of bread. Beside him sat his three braves, passing a bottle between them. George interrupted their laughter. 'What is the meaning of this?'

'We eat,' said Tanacharison.

'You're drinking brandy,' George pointed out.

The Chief shrugged.

'You were supposed to prepare the horses, so we could leave,' George said, raising his voice.

'We not stop you. Tack your own horses,' said the Chief, taking a bite of bread.

The other Iroquois grinned at George. He suppressed the anger that swelled in his belly.

'You ask us take you to see French. We done that. We finished now.'

'We're not finished until I say so,' George gritted. 'You are required, by treaty to help us – we are your ally.'

'You go. We catch up.' Tanacharison took a large swig from the brandy bottle.

'Damn you Indians!'

The grin on Tanacharison's face fell and his forehead furrowed. His stare turned menacing.

George suddenly felt the limit of his bravery, his anger checked by self-preservation. He walked away.

'We could go without them,' said Gist, following him.

George shook his head. 'If we leave, we'll never see them again.'

'So?'

'It's essential that the French see the Iroquois in alliance with us. They won't leave here because of English threats. It's the fear of the Iroquois that will drive them off.'

'Then we don't have much choice, do we?'

George stalked off, finding Joncaire inside his cabin. 'Sir, this is your doing; I regard it as foul play!'

'What is the hurry?' asked Joncaire, not even trying to deny his complicity. 'Please, it is unfortunate. Why don't you stay here, as my guest?'

This is a trap, thought George. At best, they'd sent a warning north of the English arrival. At worst, they'd be imprisoned. It was true what people said of the French: they really were as slippery as a snake in the grass.

40

Sunday took an age to come. Viktor woke earlier than normal, excited at the prospect of a day with Sarah, but nervous too, in case she didn't like what he had planned.

In the few weeks since she'd persuaded him to bring her here, his life had altered immeasurably. The days stood watching the negroes labour now passed slower than ever. With this season's crop shipped, the work had shifted to clearing the remaining woodland and harvesting the trunks for Billy to work in the shop. The scrub would be burned and the bare land brought into tobacco cultivation for next season's crop. With many of the existing fields burned clear after several seasons of tobacco over-production, Mr Fitzbarton had instructed him to sow wheat. Viktor had no experience of growing wheat but, in the words of Fitzbarton, 'being as you failed to buy me a farmer, you can learn. If you get it wrong, you'll discuss the matter with the lash.' Though the threat had hit its mark at first, as the days passed, Viktor had realised that Fitzbarton couldn't very well whip his slave driver – it would demean him in front of the negroes. Besides, Viktor had learned an important lesson on his trip to Alexandria: it paid to be decisive. Whilst events hadn't transpired in the way he'd intended, they had worked out very much for the better. Had he sat there crying into his cider in the tavern, he'd have never met Sylvia, or Sarah as he now always called her. She was heaven sent and had provoked in Viktor a new hunger.

325

He loved her. She made him want to succeed. He'd plant the wheat, tending it night and day if he must. He'd show Mason what he was capable of. Viktor would prove to him and everyone else that he was the natural choice to entrust the plantation to.

Viktor bit off a chaw of tobacco and rubbed his cold hands together. Mason's two Cuban mastiffs, muscular bulldogs with clipped ears, strained at the leash, dragging him round as he patrolled the fallen trees of the woodland they were clearing. He passed Charlie and Musa, their ankles shackled together as they stood on each end of a saw, cutting a tall trunk in half.

'You had the white girl yet, Boss?' called Charlie, a grin on his face.

Viktor frowned, dismissing the comment. He ought not to tolerate the cheek of Charlie when others were about, but he too often found himself lenient since the whipping. Despite Charlie's retaliation, pragmatism had returned on both sides. He needed Charlie's help, and in return, Charlie benefited from Viktor's mercy.

'He's in with her every evening, I hear,' said Musa, grunting, imitating the sounds of lovers.

Viktor stopped and shot both men a glare that would give Satan pause. 'Cut the damn tree,' he snarled. It was another instance of Charlie's over-familiarity spreading to the other slaves.

'The English girl's made the virgin's heart dark,' said Charlie defiantly.

Viktor walked away, cursing under his breath. The truth of Charlie's observation cut deep. Viktor was exasperated that it was so plain that even the slaves could see. How could he be all things to all people, a good protégé to Mason, an accomplished man in the eyes of Sarah, and a solicitous driver of slaves? He chomped hard on his tobacco, wondering why the negroes were abusing his kindness. The dogs jerked at the leashes, sniffing an area of brush on the margin. Viktor was glad to be led away from Charlie and Musa.

The dogs barked, bringing Viktor's attention back to the fore. Shirking behind a tree, the dogs had discovered Benji, the young boy whom Viktor had enjoyed snowball fighting with last winter. The boy's brief, sullen smile, suggested he knew he was caught.

Infuriated, Viktor swung his whip over his head and around before flicking it forward in one smooth motion. There was a loud crack.

Benji fell to the ground, terror in his eyes and began to cry. He was unharmed but the fierce crack had frightened him. Seeing the little boy's fear, Viktor's anger melted into guilt, then regret. He knelt to comfort the crying boy. The dogs approached, sniffing around the boy's head.

'My daddy says we're going to heaven and you're not!' Benji cried. 'None of you are.'

Viktor sighed, he suspected Benji was right. The boy broke free from his arms and scuttled away. He stopped and turned to Viktor, 'My daddy says you people can't hurt us in here,' he pointed to his head, then turned and ran away.

'What happen?' said Charlie, who had approached.

Viktor jolted up. 'Get back to your sawing.'

The men stood gazing at each other. 'Back to your task,' Viktor commanded.

Charlie remained still as he sized up Viktor. 'You hurt the boy?'

Viktor shook his head. He felt pathetic. He was supposed to terrify the slaves. To treat them as farm animals, and yet he was answering to them, afraid to inflict even the mildest of corrective punishments. Viktor knew it was he who was finished. He walked away without saying a word.

He lay in bed that night thinking only of how he could win Sarah's heart. To offer her his love, a home, a family, all the things a woman would want.

***

His heart beating faster than usual, Viktor knocked on Sarah's door and entered when her sweet voice called out. She looked radiant, her long auburn hair thick and lustrous, her eyes sparkling even more than usual. The colonial diet was beginning to put some weight on her slim frame and a hearty colour in her cheeks. She put on her shawl and they walked out side by side, passing a pair of negro slave women pounding maize, who shared knowing looks behind their backs. There was a bitter chill to the morning air, but as yet no snow had fallen. Viktor led her through the woods, down to the wharf overlooking the creek. The water was black and still, the trees bare, but the sun made

327

frequent appearances between the grey streaks of cloud. It looked a lot nicer in the fall, but it was still the most peaceful spot on the plantation.

'I've made us a little meal,' he said as he invited her to sit on the planks of the wharf. He produced a bouquet of red and purple Indian grass, which was all he could find at this time of year. 'For the lady.'

'Ah, bless you, Viktor. You're very sweet. What have I done to deserve all this attention?'

Viktor thought about confessing his feelings. Then, embarrassed, thought better of it. 'Why not!' he quipped instead, producing a folded linen pouch, from which he produced some sausage rolls.

'Oooh, my favourite.' Her slender fingers reached out to grab one. 'Mmm, still warm.' She delicately bit into the roll, wisps of steam eddied in the cold air. 'Viktor, I love you, these are delicious!'

His cheeks coloured. *Did she mean that? Really?*

'Fancy some rum to wash it down?' He produced a small hip flask from his pocket. He'd borrowed it from Billy and curried favour with Grace. She'd made the sausage rolls and decanted a little rum from Mr Fitzbarton's reserve. Mason would likely be livid if he found out, but it was a risk Viktor had to take.

Sarah took a swig from the pewter hip flask and passed it back to him. He upended it and let the dark liquid trickle down his throat, savouring the sugary burn. He eyed the sausage rolls, but despite their fantastic smell, he couldn't eat. Not yet. In fact, he couldn't wait any longer. In the spirit of recent events, he didn't dither, opting instead to come straight out with it:

'Sarah, will you marry me?'

41

Tanacharison and his braves had consumed French supplies until they were too drunk to move. Finally, on the third day, their hangovers sufficiently cleared, and with much provocation from George, they readied themselves to leave. Joncaire winked as he wished them good luck and their journey north began. A driving wind buffeted them all day. The temperature fell below freezing, and their progress was slowed by periodic snowfalls. The Iroquois talked amongst themselves and Tanacharison appeared to tolerate protracted arguments about which route was fastest or – as George was beginning to suspect, slowest – for they were met with as many frozen ponds, steep slopes and dense undergrowth as a man might imagine. His attempts to rebuke Tanacharison were met with indifference, for they both knew the Iroquois could desert at any point, abandoning George and his men to perish in the wilderness.

The next three days saw George's party suffer more setbacks as Van Braam and Gist's men had all fallen prey to frostbite. They'd sheltered overnight in a trapper's hut. With Van Braam and the others too weak to continue, George reluctantly realised if he was to fulfil his orders, he had no choice but to leave without the injured men. By the time George, Gist and the Indians finally laid eyes on the French fort the following evening, they too were in a sorry state. It was too dark and he was too desperately cold to appraise it. If they didn't get in the warm soon, they wouldn't survive the night. This pressing need overshadowed any consideration George might have otherwise given to their appearance; as the British delegation sent to assert their hold over the Ohio territory, it would have been desirable to arrive with some dignity, if not strength.

The Frenchmen took pity on them and left them by the fire with hot soup. George, still cold to his bones, slept the sleep of the dead. He awoke the next morning, exhausted and irritable. After a warming breakfast of porridge, he was shown to the fort's commander, Captain Legardeur de St Pierre. An elderly man of few words, his skin was weathered by the elements, his long hair greyed with age, and his eye patch was a testament to a career of soldiering.

'Thank you for your hospitality, Captain. I am here to ask you to leave,' said George laconically, eager to dispense with surplus formalities. He handed over a copy of his orders for the Captain to read, who fortunately was competent in English.

George looked about the Captain's room, which served as both his quarters and office. The bed, desk and chair were all made of crudely sawn wood, scavenged from the surrounding area.

The Captain passed back George's paper. He said nothing.

'Sir, this land belongs to the King of England. I will be requiring you to leave.' George made no effort to disguise his temper. This mission had damn near killed him and he was in no mood to mince his words.

The Captain smiled. 'You've come a long way, Major. *Très fatigué.* Rest here while I compose my reply. Recover your strengths for your journey home.'

George left the Captain's room. *What was the point in further discussion? Wasted words. They won't leave. How can I even pretend to force them?* Two Englishmen, racked with exhaustion, and four Iroquois were a mere embarrassment to any pretence of a British claim to the territory.

He found Gist in the main barn, sitting by the fire. 'Well?'

'Well. We've been wasting our time,' grimaced George. He pulled up a chair and sat close to Gist, keeping his voice hushed, but unable to conceal his frustration, 'This whole mission's been a waste of time. I ask you, what was the point of it?'

Gist smirked. 'If Van Braam was here, he'd tell you to do your duty and get home safely.'

'For all I know, Van Braam could be dead in that cabin. For what? Were the French ever just going to abandon their fort and go?'

'Of course they weren't. Your trouble, George,' said Gist, his voice calm and low to avoid the prying ears of the French, 'is your expectations. You thought you could march into the Ohio and boot everyone out? Return to Virginia the hero? Pah. Life isn't just going to neatly conform to your desires, just because you want it to.'

'I could throttle Dinwiddie…'

'Why? You accepted the mission. You're here because you wanted to be. Don't blame Dinwiddie, or the King, or anyone else you can think of.'

George grunted.

'Get over yourself, Washington. I've got several years on you and let me tell you, life is a succession of defeats, so you better get used to it. If you're going to sulk each time fate goes against you, you're going to be a miserable and bitter soul.'

George bristled at Gist's unwelcome lecture. 'They're snatching this land from under our noses!'

'Maybe they've got their own Ohio Company.'

'We're going to have to fight them for it, aren't we?'

'Yes, we are. If we still want it.'

George wasn't certain he still did.

***

When they weren't sheltering from the cold, George and Gist spent the next three days covertly surveying the fortification that the French had named Fort Le Boeuf. In its centre was a square surrounded by wooden buildings. Encircled by an outer wall made of wooden stakes driven into the ground and a pointed bastion at each corner, it was undeniably a military outpost. Attacking it would present a much more demanding task than the previous French camp they had stayed at. The two hundred canoes that were moored against the creek's edge suggested that the hundreds of French soldiers didn't intend to stay holed up here indefinitely. George shuddered at the odds now facing the Ohio Company. The French effort appeared organised and determined to push out into this hinterland to claim it for their nation. By contrast, Britain's rival schemes for westward expansion had stalled to a squabbling halt in the Virginia government. Unlike France, Britain had sent no supplies or support, its King hampered by Parliament, leaving it to the endeavours of his subjects – who'd so far only mustered six Englishmen and a Dutchman, four of whom now languished with frostbite deep in no man's land, and four Iroquois allies. Hardly *Great* Britain.

Having recovered sufficiently from the journey, George felt his exhaustion replaced by embarrassment at his blustering attempt to remove an enemy dug in deeper than a tick. The next day, he attended the summons from his host, Captain Legardeur de St Pierre.

Pleasantries dealt with, Legardeur came to the subject at hand. 'Major Washington, I thank you for coming here, bearing your request for France to retire. I do not think myself required to obey it. As you English say, possession is nine-tenths of the law, *c'est vrai?*'

To offer any protest, George decided, would make him look even more naïve.

The Frenchman passed George a note. 'Take this to your Governor. It sets out the French position, so there are no further misunderstandings. The journey home is long, so I have prepared you a canoe with provisions.'

'Thank you, Captain, your hospitality has been very much appreciated.' To wish the Frenchman any luck would have appeared disingenuous. He had at least acted the perfect gentleman, so George opted for a straightforward goodbye as he left the Frenchman's quarters. He found Gist waiting outside.

'We're going,' said George. 'He's given us supplies to get us home. You ready the horses, I'll fetch the Iroquois.'

Tanacharison and his men were in the mess hut, playing dice with some French soldiers. *Fraternising.*

'Chief, we're going now.'

Something in Tanacharison's expression made George's gut twitch. 'Now,' he repeated. 'Finish your game, we need the daylight.'

Tanacharison remained still.

'Come on.'

'We stay here,' said Tanacharison.

Christ, not again. 'No, you don't. Come on, we're leaving. Now.'

Tanacharison rolled his dice and looked at his French opponent.

George took a deep breath and composed himself. He noticed the four muskets leaning against the table. 'Whose are those?' he asked, a sinking feeling in his stomach.

'They're ours,' said Tanacharison.

'Where...did he give them to you?' He pointed towards Legardeur de St Pierre's quarters.

'French captain, he give them to us. You give us no guns. We stay here.'

'No! No you don't, you treacherous shits!' George pushed the table away, knocking over their muskets. 'Your people have a treaty with us,' he bellowed as the startled Iroquois and Frenchman darted out of the way. 'I don't care what he's promised you, I'll make you a promise: you come with me – now – or on my mother's life, I swear not one Englishman will ever buy your goods. I'll see to it that you're abandoned and left to the mercy of the Huron and the French!' George's cheeks glowed red with rage. The futility of his mission, the wrangling with his older companions, the truculent Iroquois, the precariousness of the Ohio Company, the deceit of both the French Captains, even the death of Lawrence that still ran raw – all those feelings coalesced, sharpened, and pointed at Tanacharison for his duplicity. The Indian Chief's wide eyes suggested he didn't think the youthful leader capable of such an outburst.

'I'm leaving now. If you value your people, I suggest you come too.' George turned his back and stomped out of the mess.

Tanacharison's eyes narrowed. *Careful what you wish for, white man.* He nodded to his braves. They picked up their fallen muskets.

***

Watching from the fort wall, Captain Legardeur de St Pierre waited until the two British men and their Iroquois guides were safely across the river. He called for his aide-de-camp, who hurried across the muddy courtyard.

'It would be better if those men never make it home to Virginia. Contact the Huron, have them ambush them and dispose of their bodies.'

'Certainly, sir. What should I offer them for payment?'

'Give the Huron whatever they ask for. If Major Washington makes it home, it will panic the ponderous British into action. The longer we can keep them out of our land, the better.'

42

December 12ᵗʰ , 1753
Fitzbarton Plantation

To have fallen pregnant was a disaster. Sylvia cursed herself for cosying up to Captain Reid, who had proven frustratingly unsusceptible to her charms. She had known the risks she'd taken laying with him, but she had believed she could win his heart, from the very moment she first saw him. If he knew she was pregnant, would he be more attentive? It didn't matter, for he would be an ocean away, wherever his cargo took him. Soon, Sylvia would be fettered with a child, and there was her problem entirely. Out of wedlock, she'd be disgraced. No employer would retain her. For a woman already in hiding from the authorities, in a foreign land, none of her options were good ones. Viktor's proposal of marriage seemed like the most immediate solution. She ruminated on it as she walked over to the house to start her work for the day. He was naïve with women and would most likely think the child his own if she were to lay with him.

The house was quiet, the study cold. She piled up some kindling in the fireplace. The tinderbox was empty. She went to fetch some from the fireplace in the dining room.

'Good morning, Sarah.'

Sylvia jumped out of her skin. She hadn't noticed Mason sitting at the far end of the dining table, taking his breakfast.

'I didn't mean to startle you.'

'No harm, sir.'

'Come here. Take a seat.' He waved his knife towards the chair beside him.

She walked to the far end of the room and sat on the edge of the seat as instructed, wondering what was happening.

'How are you finding it here?'

'Very comfortable, sir, thank you.'

'There's no need to call me sir.'

Sylvia frowned. Mason proceeded to talk about himself and his lineage – which amounted to nothing more than a grandfather who had emigrated to Virginia and started the plantation. All the while, he stuffed his open mouth with food and waved his knife and fork about like a medieval swordsman.

'Tell me,' said Sylvia, 'what did your grandfather do? Before he came here.'

Mason shifted in his seat.

'He was a fishmonger. And yet he had the bravery to travel the ocean, and shape this land into the productive enterprise you see today.'

Fishmonger? Now it made sense. Despite the façade, there was no actual nobility in this household. If Mason could pass for gentry in Virginia, then so could anyone – even Sylvia! *With a following wind.*

'You must be very proud,' she commented.

'Grandfather had a saying: cream rises to the top.'

Sylvia smiled, pretending to be impressed.

Mason finished his meal. He called for Grace and demanded more coffee. He smirked at Sylvia, taking enjoyment from commanding his negro slave in front of her.

'We live very well, as you can see.'

'Indeed,' agreed Sylvia, wondering why she was being kept in his presence.

'Truly, Mary and I want for nothing. All life's luxuries…'

'Come, sir, all men want for something, surely?' said Sylvia, interrupting his self-indulgence.

He leered at her. 'Sarah, if I want something, I can have it.'

She raised her eyebrows. His eyes narrowed. She held his gaze. His insinuation was obvious.

'Are we done?' she asked.

Mason grunted.

'Thank you for the conversation, most enlightening.'

Mason bristled as she rose to her feet without invitation.

She had reached the door when he called after her.

'Sarah, I must check your work. I'll visit you very soon.'

'Naturally. I'll look forward to your visit.'

Sylvia, you'd better tread carefully, she thought as she lit the fire in the study. Defying a powerful man tended to either bring out his vindictiveness, or bring him back looking for more. As the flames took to the kindling, Sylvia wished her grandfather had been possessed of the good sense to come to America. How different her life would have been if he had, then she too could be gentry by now. She sat down at the desk and imagined the life Viktor might offer her; it would be honest and loving, most likely. He was loyal, and would probably make a good father, despite his naivety. It would certainly be frugal. Hand to mouth, one bad harvest away from destitution. Dull, definitely. Was she willing to settle for that?

But time wasn't on her side. She had to decide.

***

The following day at breakfast, Mason's mouth tingled. For some reason, the yolk of boiled eggs had started to mildly irritate his mouth. He didn't find it an agreeable sensation. Finished, he wiped his lips with his napkin.

At the other end of the table sat Mary, looking at peace with herself. Her recent bouts of brooding brought to a mutually dissatisfactory conclusion, Mason's resistance had finally caved under a sustained campaign of irrational anger and vitriol. Until Sarah's arrival, he'd had the convenient necessity to attend to his ledgers in the evenings. Since that fool Viktor had introduced her into the equation, his excuse was void and he'd once again been subjected to spending evenings with his wife – who, following too much Madeira wine during the day, berated him for his lack of attention, his meanness, and a long list of other failings. How this was supposed to endear him to her, he couldn't understand. Placating her with gifts, the promise of a trip to the springs out west next summer, and various attempts at cordial conversation all failed to have the desired effect. She'd suggested granting her access to his account, held in London, so she could order things from his agent, without needing his permission. The idea was intolerable and he'd flatly refused. That night, she'd woken him by scratching his face with her nails. In a fit of anger, he'd had to restrain himself from beating her. This morning, before breakfast, he'd acquiesced to her demand. Just like that, her mood had lifted.

'I think I'll go for a ride,' she announced. 'Care to join me?'

Mason shook his head in disbelief. He wanted to check on that Germanic mongrel Viktor, who should by now have cleared the block of woodland between the north field and hillock.

Mary left and Mason poured himself another cup of tea. Grace shuffled into the dining room and brought him a copy of last week's Virginia Gazette. He left it laying on the table, his mind too preoccupied with the mess of his and Mary's relationship. When they'd met, she'd been a minx. What she'd lacked in looks, she'd more than made up for in bed. There was a time, before they were married, when lovemaking had lasted all afternoon. The thought that she would even attempt to rouse him once, let alone twice, seemed like an alternative reality that had never existed. He'd made mistakes, calling her barren in a drunken argument. She'd accused him of dead seed. Over the years, the goodwill had ebbed to become a distant memory.

Mason looked up from his daydream and took a deep breath, as if to exhale all the difficulties of recent days. His tea finished, he leapt up and banged his fist repeatedly on the mahogany table and snarled, which had the effect of restoring his prestige and purpose. Chest puffed out, he strode from the dining room into the hallway. He fetched his boots and longcoat from the cloakroom and made his way to the front door. As he crossed the hallway, the door opened and in rushed Sarah, cloaked in a shawl and shivering from the cold. He didn't acknowledge her, but the sight of her put an idea in his head. He went upstairs and waited for Mary to leave for her ride. As soon as the front door clicked shut, he slipped downstairs.

He said nothing as he let himself into his study and pushed the door shut behind him. Alone at the desk, Sarah was warming her hands. He stood and stared at her. Her cheeks were flushed. Her hair, lustrous and vibrant, was tied behind her long neck. Her eyes were bright with life. After a pause, she raised her eyebrow to invite him to say something.

'I think it's time we look at what you've been up to. See what my money has bought me.'

'As you wish.'

She's not short of poise, this girl. Her assuredness baited him to bring her back down to her station. He strode over and stood behind her. She slid the ledger to her right and opened it to the most recent page. He was pleased to see her writing was neater than before. He ran his finger down the debit column. She'd listed everything correctly. Pounds, shillings and pence all looked about right. He checked her addition. 'Mmm.' He checked it again. 'Look.' He pointed to the column. 'This doesn't tally.'

She said nothing.

Mason looked back at the previous page. Again, the addition was out. 'Basic errors.' He felt his teeth beginning to grind. 'This is all wrong.' He counted the numbers. 'You've not carried over the fractions.' He slammed the book shut. 'I've kept these ledgers for years. Now it's all wrong!' His voice beginning to rise, he gripped her arm and hoisted her out of his seat. The look of disdain on her face was nothing to that which was swelling inside of him.

'What have you to say for yourself?'

'I am sorry for my error.'

She held his gaze. An empty apology if ever he heard one. He expected her to be scared, yet she stood in front of him, brazen in her defiance. He had half a mind to strike her, but thought better of it. There was the promise of a better punishment.

'You've caused me a lot of bother, Sarah.'

'I never intended to make your life anything but better. Sir.'

'Huh! Well, if I'm to keep you, tell me what are you good for – it certainly isn't bookkeeping!'

He could see the resolve in her eyes ebbing away.

'What is it you want, Mason?'

'Don't address me by my Christian name!' he snarled.

He leaned into her, forcing her to move backwards, trapped by his desk. 'Be very careful, young lady. Those who play with fire get burned.'

339

Her eyes narrowed, her fear turned to determination. It made him want to kiss her, just to spite her. He hesitated. 'I could have you any time I wanted.'

'Now you're the one playing with fire, Mason.'

He raised his hand to slap her but she didn't flinch. He strode out of the room, cursing her temerity. *How dare she!*

***

Sylvia breathed a sigh of relief when Mason left her alone. That could have gone any number of ways. Mason was taken with her, which came as little surprise; he regarded himself as a powerful man, though one who suffered an obvious rift in relations with his wife. He'd been angered when she'd resisted him, which hadn't been her intention, but if she'd have capitulated, he would soon reduce her to his concubine. She took a deep breath to steady her trembling hands. As her compose returned she looked at the closed ledger on the desk and wondered what she could do. Again, her choices seemed to narrow. Mason wouldn't tolerate his records being defaced. Yet he was the only one with the ability to teach her mathematics sufficiently well. He would exploit her in exchange. Powerful men measured themselves by how often they got their way. She briefly considered the consequences of just letting Mason have his way with her. How would he react once her pregnancy was discovered?

She leaned back in the chair and gazed out of the window and to the extensive lawns that unfurled in front of the house. How long could she last here? She'd dreamt of living in such splendour, she'd never been so comfortable; and yet she stood to lose it all. Perhaps it would have been better to never have had it. Her mind jumped back to an image of Simon Bowler. She consoled herself that whatever dilemmas she faced here were preferable to the life she'd escaped. Then she thought of her poor brother. Was Jacob even alive? For all the crimes they'd committed in the past, it had been the most innocuous misdemeanour that had been the one to upend her life, and to end his.

43

The knock on Sylvia's door came at the end of the day as usual. Viktor's smiling face appeared round the door.

'I brought you a biscuit.'

'Bless you, Viktor.' She put it on the windowsill. 'I'll eat it later.' Sylvia sat on the bed, her arms folded. Viktor sat on the chair, pulling it closer to the bed.

'Have you got an answer for me yet?' His hopeful wide eyes betrayed his feeble smile.

'You can't rush a girl on these matters, Viktor,' she said, taking pity on him.

'But I love you, Sarah. I'd do anything for you. What more do you want?' His forehead creased in puzzlement. 'We can live here happily. I'll inherit the plantation, and we'll both be rich.'

She took pity on him, 'Viktor, Mason isn't going to let you inherit all this.'

He looked crestfallen. 'But he has no one else…?'

'That may be so, but men like him just don't behave charitably like that. He's leading you on.'

The look of resignation on his face told her he had begun to suspect as much himself.

Like a child pleading to his mother, he changed tack. 'Even so, you'll be free in seven years; by then we'd have enough to buy some land. I'll build us a house.'

She stopped listening, for he'd say anything to win her. It should have been enough, given her pregnancy. Many women might have taken it, and she still might. Yet Sylvia felt like whatever short-term comfort she might draw from Viktor's companionship, the life he offered felt like purgatory. She had grown up in and around the brick townhouses of London, the biggest, noisiest, most thriving city in the world. Viktor's cabin in the woods... Well, there'd been a time, a month ago, when she might have taken it. But she knew she couldn't exist in isolation. mothering a clutch of screaming brats, scrubbing pots and pans, tending crops before cooking up gruel for an easily pleased husband and their docile children. It wasn't the stuff of her dreams. In want of a better idea, she deferred:

'It's Thursday. You and I will go for another walk on Sunday.' She flashed her eyes in her best coquettish fashion. 'Then I'll give you my answer.'

Viktor looked disappointed. She leant over and planted a long, lingering kiss on his lips.

His disappointment melted away.

***

Early the next morning, Sylvia admired the magnificence of the main house from her bedroom window. Never could she have imagined she would reside within touching distance of something so grand. A far cry from her tenement, or even the mollies' house. Overnight, she'd formed a plan to make herself more useful to the Fitzbartons. When she caught sight of Mason striding across the rear lawn. She dashed outside, catching up with him at the stables.

'Mr Fitzbarton, sir.'

He stopped and his irritation softened as she smiled at him.

'I wanted to apologise. For my errors in your ledgers. It was unforgivable.'

He hesitated. Sylvia relaxed a little as the conversation tilted to her initiative.

Regaining his poise, he said, 'Well, they need to be corrected.'

'I'd like to make it up to you. I know it can't be easy for you with Mrs Fitzbarton being so uncomfortable with my presence. I never wanted for that to happen. So I had an idea, to prove to you both what an asset I could be.'

Mason raised his eyebrows.

'It's Christmas soon. Let me prepare you a celebration to do you both proud. You'll want for nothing. Mary will warm to me then.'

'We no longer celebrate Christmas,' said Mason, looking momentarily forlorn.

Sylvia pressed on, undeterred, 'I could do you proud, it would be the most memorable celebration. Put some fun back in the household.'

Mason squirmed. 'We have Grace and Zebedee for that.'

'Yes, but having negroes serve you is so…colonial. You could invite guests to stay, as many as you like. They'd be impressed by an English lady-in-waiting.'

She sensed he was warming to her suggestion.

'Please,' she took his hand in hers, disarming him. 'Let me entertain you, you won't regret it, sir.' She pursed her lips, flirtatiously.

'I'll consider it.' He shook her off his hand and hurried towards the stables.

44

December 25ᵗʰ, 1753
The Ohio Valley

Tanacharison and his Iroquois feasted on roasted bear, oblivious to the notion that they may be seen to be celebrating the birth of Christ, man's redeemer. By chance, they'd happened across the dead animal. Normally hibernating at this time of year, this one had been caught out in the open, like a gift from heaven. It was a good omen to the starving men. After repeated nights in the cold, George was in need of a saviour, and was happy to delay for the warm meat and an open fire. It was tender, like beef, but flavoured more like horse. Small clouds of warm breath escaped his mouth as he chewed the flesh.

If the journey out had been tough, it had proved only a warm-up for the journey home. The delays at the hands of the Iroquois and the French had proved costly, as the weather had worsened. The rivers had frozen, and the snow had hardened into a solid crust that made the going treacherous underfoot. The horses had been released to take their own chances; too enfeebled to continue, they'd become a hindrance. George had shed a tear when parting with Lisbeth. His faithful steed for years, she'd carried him to third place in the races, then across America. That this futile mission of Dinwiddie's should claim her companionship too, was the final straw. He'd stroked her mane and kissed her cheek, bringing back memories of saying his final goodbye to Lawrence. But when it came down to it, he had to face Hobson's choice in order to survive. As a young boy, his father had used the phrase, declaring that a land as untamed as America demanded the impossible of you, and one had no choice but to accept her terms.

George nestled close to the fire the Iroquois had built, savouring the warmth on his cheeks, his shivers slowing in its amber glow. He and Tanacharison had spoken but ten words to each other in the days since leaving Fort Le Boeuf. In the silence, since Van Braam's withdrawal, George had grown increasingly grateful for Gist, whose laconic manner and efficient habits made him the ideal travelling companion now that he wasn't bickering with the Dutchman. Without the others, George hadn't had to impose his leadership on the party. He and Gist had cooperated fully, finding repeated agreement on all the small decisions: where to sleep, where to build a fire, who would build a shelter, who would collect firewood, which path to take. Small, essential details for survival, all a world away from the global politics that occupied the minds of Dinwiddie and the like. Whose theories and schemes were now slowly playing out in the enormous theatre of the American frontier. The British would have to organise themselves if they were to stand any chance of occupying the Ohio.

George found himself increasingly less interested in the outcome. Faced with the reality, it seemed to him beyond his own reach, as he battled the relentless cold that made each minute of the day and night seem like an hour. He barely cared for anything, bar making it home to the warmth of his empty bed.

At night, he thought of Lawrence. His brother had occasionally, when prompted, regaled curious listeners to light-hearted anecdotes of soldiering, but alone, he'd been unwilling to talk of his war experiences in the Caribbean. In private, he was overcome by a hollowness that George had been unable to understand. To his mind, the glory of distinguishing yourself in battle, behaving honourably in victory, taking pride in the lines of soldiers clothed in brilliant red, assembled under a fluttering flag to the beat of drum and tune of fife. George had imagined an awe-inspiring sight. But, like his own mission to the frontier, Lawrence must have faced similar challenges – not the cold, but disease, and death of friends. For the first time, Lawrence's silence began to make sense.

With a belly full of warm meat and his constitution restored, George got to his feet. 'An excellent lunch. Let's go.' There was an outside chance they could make the forks in the Ohio River by nightfall. He understood very clearly now why Tanacharison had wanted a fort there. It would block the French route south. For British influence in the Ohio to stand any chance, work on the fort would need to begin without further delay.

'We stay until we finish the bear.'

'There's no time.'

'We very lucky to find bear. Gift from spirit gods. We cannot ignore.'

'There's plenty more bears. It's time that's short.'

'No. We eat the bear. Then we go.'

George looked at Gist.

'Come on,' he said, climbing to his feet.

They didn't need to discuss the obvious: they were close to the forks now. If they could make it there, the Iroquois would travel west back to Logstown and they'd be on their own. Gist knew the way back from the forks and George felt he could remember it well enough.

They said their goodbyes to their Iroquois guides and trudged on, George glad to see the back of them. The first three miles were relatively straightforward, picking a path through the trees. They happened on a clearing just as a blizzard came in. The biting wind and poor visibility made it impossible to continue. They huddled together behind the treeline and waited.

It blew all night. Unable to light a fire or set up camp, the two men clung to each other, unable to sleep under their blankets, they shivered together all night.

George was relieved to find both himself and Gist alive in the morning. The storm had passed, the rising sun cast a brilliant pink across the horizon. The woods began to renew themselves. Birds sang and darted between the branches as they emerged into the calm of the new day.

The two men staggered out of the treeline into the clearing. All George could manage to think about was placing one frozen foot in front of the other, every step aggravating the numb flesh. Halfway across, already exhausted, George stopped to take a bite of snow and wet his mouth. *I can't make it.* They must be close to the forks, but for the first time since leaving Virginia, he had nothing left to give and no longer believed he'd make it home.

'Come on,' said Gist, 'stop and you'll die here.'

An hour later, they crossed the clearing, leaving two lines of tracks in their wake. Back in the woods, the snow was lighter. George leant back against a tree, resting his weary legs. *No more.* A whistle pierced the air. His head jolted from side to side, like a rabbit scanning for a predator. Twenty yards ahead was the dark face of a solitary Indian, his bald head interrupted by a tuft of black hair adorned with a long feather. Clad in skins and cloaked in a blanket, he seemed impervious to the cold as he appraised them with a narrow stare.

'Nyah-weh-sgeh-noh,' said Gist, offering the traditional Seneca greeting.

'British?'

Gist nodded. 'Iroquois?'

The Indian said nothing.

George's skin prickled. *What were this fellow's intentions?*

'You help us?' asked Gist. 'We travel to Ohio River?'

The Indian turned and beckoned them to follow. George, unsure, looked at Gist.

'If he wanted us dead, he'd have killed us already,' Gist shrugged.

It was too late now to escape the native's attention. Too tired for much deliberation, George followed. And their walk continued.

As the hours passed, unable to keep pace, George began to fall behind. The Indian waited for him and Gist to catch up. As George slumped against a tree, the Indian took his backpack from him. 'I take.'

George let him. The Indian swung the pack over his shoulders; George, seeing his musket fastened to the top of the pack, thought about keeping his weapon, but dismissed the idea. He was glad to be rid of its weight.

They trudged on for mile after mile, the Indian pulling ahead.

'Surely we must be close?' asked George as he drew level with Gist, who was looking about the woods, shaking his head.

'Something's not right. This doesn't look familiar.'

'It all looks the same to me,' said George. 'Where's our guide?'

'Can't see him. He must be ahead.' Gist ground his teeth. 'Let's keep going, just keep your wits about you.'

George followed Gist's footprints as they made their way between the trees. The wood's silence was interrupted by a crack of gunfire. Gist dropped to the ground. Ten yards in front, the smoking muzzle of George's musket was pointing at them, in the hands of the Indian who'd been guiding them.

'Gist, are you shot?' George panicked.

Gist sprung forward and charged at the Indian. George gave chase. Gist shoulder-barged the startled Indian. Still bearing George's heavy backpack, he tumbled to the ground, and was smothered by Gist's sizeable physique. Gist drew his knife from his belt and pressed it to the savage's throat.

'You missed!' he shouted at his wide-eyed captive. 'You all right, George?'

George checked himself for blood. He was unharmed, his weariness forgotten in the excitement. 'What happened?'

'This treacherous toe-rag ambushed us from behind a tree. He must be Huron. Only he can't shoot straight!'

'What are you going to do with him?'

'Slit his throat.'

'Wait. No,' said George.

'What's got you so squeamish? He's for France.'

'It's not that. But if his people find him dead, they'll use it as an excuse to have a blood feud with any British people. Our mission in the Ohio will be compromised.'

Succumbing to George's logic, Gist asked, 'What else do you want me to do to him? We can't let him go.'

George regarded the Indian pinned under Gist's knees, his face in stern defiance to the fate that awaited him.

'He found us once, he'll do it again,' said Gist. 'We won't be safe unless he's dead.'

'We're never safe out here. If his tribe's close, they'll track us and avenge his death. No, we better our chances by showing mercy.'

'No. I'm killing him.'

'Gist, stop! That's an order. Kill that man and I'll report you.'

Gist glared at George. He lifted his arm and drove his fist into the Indian's nose. The crunch of the bone breaking split the air.

'Enough, Gist. Let's tie him up.'

The remaining delayed hours were taken up with guarding their captive, helping themselves to his supply of dried deer meat and waiting to see if he had companions in wait. The need for silence prevented Gist from giving voice to his frustrations. Once dark, they untied the Indian, and with Gist's knife pressed into his neck, warned him that next time, they wouldn't be so merciful. He scampered off into the dark of the night.

'Come, let's go this way,' said George, pointing in the opposite direction.

'I don't like this, George. We should have killed him while we had the chance.'

***

They walked all night, listening attentively for every foreign noise and looking over their shoulders. At dawn, they happened upon the site of the river with mixed feelings. They were downstream from the fork, so they were at last back in more familiar territory. But with the river in full flood and without their horses or canoes, they would need a way of crossing its icy current.

'We've only one choice,' said Gist, 'We'll have to build a raft.'

The rest of the day was spent fashioning a crude raft from fallen logs and small trees. With only Gist's hatchet, they trimmed the logs to fit snugly, then fastened them together with material torn from their blankets. Satisfied their craft was river-worthy and with the afternoon's light fading, they searched for a suitable place to ford the fast-moving river.

'Look, there's an island in the middle, we should cross there,' said George. They positioned themselves upstream so that the current might carry them ashore. George held the raft while Gist climbed aboard, balancing himself with a long branch to use as a pole. He pressed it into the shallows and held the raft firm. George passed over their pack, which they used as ballast in the middle of the raft. He picked up his own pole and gingerly stepped aboard, taking his position at the bow.

'Ready?'

George eased them away from the bank, keeping his balance as the current swept them along.

'Use your pole to push us across,' said Gist from the stern.

The riverbank began to disappear as they sped past. The island was only fifty yards away, but they would need to make decisive progress lest they drift beyond it. The raft began to tilt sideways as Gist pushed the stern out. George quickly did the same to keep them straight.

'George, ice!'

George looked over his shoulder and saw a slab of ice hurtling towards them. If he could slow the raft down, it would overtake them. He dug his pole into the riverbed to act as an anchor. The pole gripped, spinning the raft on its axis. George's feet were swept from under him. He toppled to the side, soon feeling the water's icy kiss. His breath vanished from his lungs as his head popped back to the surface. He cried out to Gist but no sound came; his legs flailed in search of the riverbed, but it was too deep.

'Grab this,' Gist swung his pole to George.

George managed to grip the pole and was pulled into the swell of the raft. Gist heaved him in. George, his body numb, reached for the outmost log of their raft and gripped with all his strength.

Gist pushed the craft further into the river. 'Kick with your legs, George.'

George began to tremble with cold. *Just keep holding on,* he thought. He could see the island's shore approaching. Gist forced the raft across the middle and began to slow as the water shallowed. Gist pushed and pushed, guiding the craft to the far shore. George felt his knees bump against the bottom, and Gist held out his hand and pulled him up onto the raft. George felt the heavy weight of his body return as he convulsed with cold and Gist threw him to the shore, then stowed the raft on the bank.

'Let's get you warm and dry. Stand up. Walk about. You need to get the soak out of your clothes. Keep moving. I don't care how cold you are. You keep moving, you understand?'

George did as he was told. He stamped around in circles like a man fit for a lunatic asylum.

'We'll spend the night here,' said Gist. 'We'll be safe from the Huron on this islet. I'll light a fire. We'll get you warm.'

George continued his demented pacing, his teeth chattering, his body shivering with a violence he'd not known possible. The rest was a blur until, sometime later, he felt the warm balm of a raging campfire that drew steam from his clothes and returned him to the relative comfort of only being very cold.

45

December 25ᵗʰ, 1753
Fitzbarton Plantation

Mason was plagued by mixed feelings as he dressed himself. When Sarah had first suggested hosting Christmas, Mason had been averse to the idea. Yet entertaining, showing off their wealth, making connections – it was how he and his wife should be behaving. Mary, too, hadn't been in favour, for company unsettled her. Mason had pointed out how frequently she complained of being bored. He'd reassured her they'd have fun. A nice feast. A roaring fire. Some parlour games. It would be like the Christmases from all those years ago. As the wine flowed, she'd warmed to the idea. To Mason's surprise, they'd made love that night. Who would have thought that Sarah would turn out to be the spark to rekindle the embers of their passion? One barn swallow didn't make a summer, but it did remind Mason that he hadn't been handling Mary right, and if he changed his manner, so might she. He clung to the thought as he fastened his cuffs and checked himself in his full-length mirror.

He'd restricted the invite to Mr and Mrs Joshua Fry, the judge who'd found in his favour, before being moved to another district. In a fit of inspiration, Mason had written to them, inviting them for Christmas, fully expecting them not to come. Without children of their own, it transpired that the Frys had no prior engagements. A cold shiver had run down Mason's spine when he'd received their acceptance. At least they weren't tobacco people, so they wouldn't have to suffer the barbed remarks of their rival planters. Nor would

352

Mason need to be guarded with his conversation, and if Mary did act up, as she had at social occasions in the past, at least it wouldn't be the talk of the planting community for months to come.

In the short time since arriving in Virginia, Joshua Fry had become an influential member of the House of Burgesses. He was worth getting to know. Mason was eager to understand more about his land speculation venture to the west, which he'd seen mentioned in the Gazette.

***

Downstairs in the kitchen, Sylvia was having difficulties of her own. The stove was burning, taking off the winter morning chill. The turkey was in and Grace was preparing the vegetables on the rough-sawn table. Zebedee was in the dining room, setting the places. Sylvia picked up a peeler and reached for a potato.

'I do it!' snapped Grace, snatching back the potato.

'I'm only trying to help,' said Sylvia.

'It's not your place to help. This is my job.'

'Grace, I'm not trying to take your work away from you. It's important for me, for everyone, that today goes well. Remember, I see Mason's private matters. Things aren't as good for them as you might think. If they do well, so do we.'

Grace squinted at her.

'Trust me,' said Sylvia.

She shrugged. 'I have the best job of all the slaves. I not want to lose it.'

'You won't. I promise. I'm not here to see you put out in the fields. If you want my opinion, I think it is criminal people can keep slaves. If I steal a loaf of bread to feed myself, I'm a criminal and am sent to the other side of the world. If I steal an African from his home and ship him to the far side of the world, I'm a merchant?'

Grace nodded.

'You should at the very least be paid. As should I.'

Grace chuckled. 'You not been in this house long time. It never work like that.'

Sylvia picked up the potato and began to peel.

Once the food was prepared, Sylvia removed her apron. She took a knife and pricked the point of her finger, squeezing it to produce a drop of blood. Looking in the hallway mirror, she rubbed the blood onto her cheeks: peasants' rouge. Her cheeks reddened, she retied her hair and adjusted her coif. She pursed her lips, plumped her breasts. She looked good, for a servant. Her Christmas plan was shaping up nicely. Mason and Mary both seemed happier to be distracted by the planning of the occasion, something positive into which to pour their energies. Mary was still as frosty as the December weather when dispensing instructions to Sylvia, but the fact they were interacting at all meant Sylvia was becoming ensconced in the house. The relationship between mistress and servant aside, the mood in the house was lighter. Today she would prove herself to Mary.

***

The Frys' carriage drew up at midday, its arrival delayed by a dusting of snowfall. Zebedee helped them out and showed them indoors where Mason and an anxious-looking Mary greeted them in the hall. Sarah swooped in and introduced herself to the guests, then relieved them of their heavy winter coats. Mary's frown softened once Sarah left the room with the coats. Zebedee followed with the luggage. The Frys were shown to their room where they were afforded some time to refresh following their journey. During the afternoon, Mason gave them a tour of the house before they changed for dinner and assembled in the dining room.

The fireplace crackled with burning logs. Candles twinkled on the table and in the chandelier. The last of the day's light reflected off the snow outside. Mary, fortified by wine, clung to another glass. Sarah served wine to the guests as they took their seats.

'Merry Christmas.' Fry raised his glass and the toast was acknowledged by the gentle clinking of glassware. Sarah left the room.

'Tell me, Mason, you have a white servant,' Fry commented. 'Quite old-fashioned for a modern man.'

Mason chortled. 'It's a long story, but let's just say it was more by accident than design.'

Fry nodded. 'I must say I approve. Negroes are fast becoming the bane of this land.'

'By what measure?' quizzed Mason.

Fry set his glass down and pursed his lips as he prepared to share his opinions. 'One hundred years ago, the number of negro slaves in this colony could fit into a single barn. Since I arrived here, I would be forgiven for thinking I was in Africa. A people who soon outnumber their white masters cannot remain enslaved. They will revolt. This place is a tinderbox.'

'Where do you stand on the negro tax, Mr Fry?'

'In favour. Although I can't imagine a planter like you shares my view?'

'*Au contraire,* there is too much tobacco being grown. It's too cheap. Every man in Europe can afford it. It's lost its prestige. Five percent on the sale of each negro is not sufficient to discourage new entrants to the trade.'

'You have sufficient negroes, so others should be denied your advantage?'

'Exactly.' Mason grinned. 'What is politics, if not for the advancement of one's personal agenda?'

'For the greater good?'

'Substantially higher taxes on the sale of negroes would stem the flood of them into this land. The genie isn't yet out of the bottle; if we act now, we can all sleep easier at night.'

'Well, on that we are aligned. But any tax raised shouldn't be squandered on land speculation like the Ohio Company. They antagonise our French enemies and serve only to line the bulging pockets of the already wealthy.'

'You're against westward expansion?'

'On the contrary. Jefferson and I are fully enmeshed in the Loyal Company of Virginia. We aren't bound by the rules of the King; we won't squander public money building fortifications that serve only to provoke.'

'How will you guarantee the safety of the inhabitants?'

'Tell me, Mason, where is the nearest fortification to here?'

Mason shrugged.

'Yet you live peaceably?'

Mason nodded. 'But the Indians?'

'You think a fort would deter Indians? It's no protection whatsoever. The solution to the Indian question is simple. We have to outnumber them. Deluge them in the white man and stop selling them weapons so they can't overwhelm our militias. They are a mobile people. Push them back and they will squabble for land amongst themselves. They can do the job for us.'

'Inspired, Mr Fry.' Mason grew excited by the simplicity of it. 'And how does one invest in such a venture?'

'It's an open book. We don't believe in the entitlement of a controlling elite. Investment is limited to five hundred pounds per person.'

'Done. I'll have my lawyer draw up a draft for you.'

'You're most welcome.'

Mason was delighted. He rapped his knuckles against the table. This was exactly what he'd missed. Making money was easy when you rubbed shoulders with the right people. Something he'd shied away from too readily. Self-confidence coursed through his veins. 'A toast, to the Loyal Company of Virginia.'

They raised their glasses.

'If you two have finished talking about negroes and money, it's hardly in the spirit of the season,' said Mary, scowling at the floor, her wine glass empty.

Sarah appeared at the door carrying all four dinner plates. Mason sighed as he watched her gracefully dispense the plates. So much more elegant than Grace. He savoured her sweet scent as she placed his plate of steaming beef in front of him. Her hand touched his back and her fingers briefly traced across his shoulder blade, unnoticed by anyone else. He glanced at her backside, and pictured the buttocks hidden by her dress.

'Mrs Fitzbarton, let me refill your glass,' said Sylvia.

Mary's scowl was briefly replaced by a smile as the glass was filled higher than custom demanded. Mary took a swig and reduced it to a more socially acceptable level. Mason too, took a refill. The Frys both declined.

Main course finished, a dessert of plum pudding came and went. The food was delicious. The best Mason had tasted at home in years. It must be Sarah's influence. He savoured the fumes from his brandy glass. Life, today, was good. He resolved to make 1754 a better year, to be the Mason of old once again. He would rekindle the ambitions and impulses of his youth before life had jaded him. He was cunning and he'd failed to use it. Virginia wasn't for the indolent, which is what he'd become. No more.

There was a smash at the opposite end of the table. Mary slumped in her chair. Her glass lay shattered on the floor. Her eyelids flickered as she grappled with consciousness. Sarah swooped in and tidied the glass. Mason tensed, *Oh God, it's happening again.*

'I think it's time we retired,' said Fry, looking awkwardly at his wife. 'Thank you for your hospitality, Mason, a most enjoyable evening.' He stood and turned his attention to Sarah. 'Thank you, my lady, a delicious meal, most memorable.'

Sarah smiled and offered a brief curtsy. Small enough to be polite, but not so elaborate to be ostentatious. Mason felt a smattering of pride to have employed someone so adept in circumstances which he needed more of: hosting the good and great of the colony. *How classy to have her, rather than that clumsy nigger Grace.*

Mary tried to stand as the Frys departed. Dizzy from the rush to her head she fell. Sarah caught her and returned her slumped body to the chair.

'Goodnight,' said Mrs Fry as she scuttled round the table, eager to escape the unfolding embarrassment.

Mason nodded politely and was relieved when they closed the door behind them. *Fucking Mary, drunken bitch.*

'I think we'll need to carry her upstairs,' whispered Sarah.

'Here, mind out, I'll remove her.'

He too had had his fair share of fare and drink. He got Mary's limp arm around his neck but struggled to free her from the chair. Sarah stooped beneath Mary's other arm, and with a heave they lifted her free and staggered across the floor, then gingerly up the staircase one step at a time. Mason was livid. Tonight had been a success and Mary had disgraced herself. Again.

Sarah began to giggle.

'What's so funny?' snapped Mason, unable to see her on the far side of his wife's bobbing head.

'I would never have thought someone so small would be so heavy!'

she chuckled through her words.

'She's a greedy bitch!' he replied. Sarah's laugh was infectious and he began to laugh too. Once up the stairs, it was a short walk to the bedroom. Mason shouldered open the door and they dragged Mary into the dark room and dropped her onto the bed.

'Do you need a hand?' said Sarah, indicating her clothes.

'No. I'll sort her out.'

'Very well. I'll go and clear up downstairs. Call if you need me.' Sarah made her departure.

Mason's eyes adjusted to the dark of the room. He picked up Mary's feet and swung them onto the bed. He considered undressing her but then thought against it. It was better she woke fully clothed as a reminder of her behaviour. He knew her well enough to guess she would excuse herself of any suspicion if she woke up normally. Better she suffer, he thought as he looked down at her sullen face. Once so full of fun, it was now as drawn and empty as her womb. *Which came first?* Mason wondered. The barren womb or the barren soul? One begot the other.

He closed the door and made his way across the landing to his room, hearing the clank of crockery being cleared away from the dining room. Sarah was downstairs. He felt an urge to see her again. She'd been excellent tonight. He should thank her. He hesitated as he thought about their encounter in the study. *Nonsense,* he said to himself, this was his house, he'd do as he pleased. As he walked down the stairs, a small part of him knew he was playing with fire, but confident from his success with Fry, along with a bottle of wine and brandy, made him impulsive.

He crept up to the door of the dining room and watched her clear the table. Something told him she knew he was watching, but she carried on with her work.

'Tonight was excellent,' he said.

She feigned surprise. 'Mason, thank you.'

He frowned.

'Sorry, Mr Fitzbarton. Thank you, Sir. Nightcap?' she offered.

He grinned. She was daring him. 'Very well. I'll accept.'

She fetched him a new glass and poured a generous measure of brandy.

'A new glass, for new beginnings,' she said.

Before Mason could fathom what she meant, she continued:

'It went well with Mr Fry?'

'Very.'

'Good. I am pleased for you.'

Mason took a sip and savoured the burn in his throat. 'Yes. He's a rising star in the colony.'

Sarah didn't say anything. She put a log on the embers of the fire and perched her backside on the table. She removed her apron.

The door opened to reveal Zebedee.

'It's all right, Zebedee,' said Sarah, continuing to exhibit an authority which hadn't been bestowed. 'If you're done in the kitchen, I'll finish these last bits in here. You turn in for the night.'

Zebedee glanced at Mason, who nodded his approval.

The door closed.

'You have the measure of them already,' Mason commented.

Sarah shrugged. 'The world's a better place when we get on with those around us.'

She was right; if only Mary would recognise it. He stared at Sarah and realised he knew very little about her. 'Pour yourself a drink. Tell me about yourself.'

She did as invited and pulled up a chair.

She's not in the least intimidated, thought Mason as she squared up to him. She offered her glass. He hesitated, before raising his and they touched with a tiny clink.

'What do you want to know?'

'Why are you here?'

'To make a new start.'

'Go on.'

'I want,' she paused, looking deep in his eyes, 'to rise.'

He frowned. She topped up his glass.

'I'm not content to be a servant. I am not content to merely belong to somebody. America is a virgin land. A man can reinvent himself here.'

'And a woman?'

'That's what I am going to do. To escape the misfortune of my birth. To be the woman I know I am.'

Mason was impressed. Perhaps it was the drink; normally he would dismiss such words from a woman as fantasy, but she meant it. If only Mary had half her determination.

'Tell me, Sarah, what are you prepared to do, to be the woman you are?'

She leant forward, her face close to his. 'Whatever it takes.'

Mason's control seeped away. Sensing his vulnerability, she closed the distance and kissed him. He could give her that life and she was taking it for herself. Her hands gripped his neck, her tongue forced its way into his mouth. Mason knew if he were to resist, now was his last chance. In one movement, she slid onto his lap, straddling him.

Too late.

He caved, his longings flooded to the fore, he kissed her back. He recognised himself in her, and it was too much. Fate had brought her to him. She began to move against him, stirring his loins fit to burst from his breeches. He ripped off her chemise, inhaling her scent, then grasped her backside and stood up, carrying her in his arms. Placing her on the dining table, he pressed her back against the table, sending cutlery crashing to the ground. Mason was too inflamed to care about the noise. His currents were surging like a storm tide. He smeared his lips against hers, bit her neck and her breasts as his hands rummaged her skirts up around her waist. She pulled him towards her as he fumbled at the tie of his breeches and freed himself, while she pulled at his shirt and exposed his chest. He probed her with his fingers, then purred with anticipation as he fed himself into her. He watched her face. Her eyes were open and she was willing him on. He pushed her further onto the table and climbed on top of her, hoisted her legs around his waist and took her with an intensity he'd never experienced. He knew he couldn't resist. He relented and thrust himself forward with all his strength as he spilled himself deep into her. In that lingering moment, Mason was more content than he had been in years. She may be low-born, unsuitable, but he didn't feel a moment of regret. He could never tire of this. She sighed as his body turned limp.

He'd crossed the divide; there was no turning back.

1754

46

January 16ᵗʰ, 1754
The Capitol Building, Williamsburg

The door to Dinwiddie's office opened. 'Major Washington to see you, Sir,' said the orderly.

'Splendid! Show him through.' Dinwiddie cleared some papers from his desk as Washington strode into the room, looking gaunt. 'Good to see you safe and sound, Washington. My, you've shed some weight!'

'I left it somewhere over the Appalachians,' said Washington, his manner curt.

'Take a seat. What's happening out there?'

'It's as bad as we expected. The French are building a line of forts, one at the junction of each river, between the lakes to the Mississippi. They were brazen, Sir. They took no care to hide their designs.'

'They're encircling us?'

'Very much so.'

'Tricky wee bastards. Did you order them to leave?'

'I think it's a bit late for that, Governor,' George grunted. 'I fulfilled my orders, but by that time, I had one companion remaining, and four contemptible Iroquois. The French, on the other hand, had a force of some two hundred men. They did not think themselves obliged to obey my demands, as Captain Legardeur de St Pierre put it. See for yourself, sir.' George passed him a tatty envelope.

Dinwiddie studied the letter within.

'I can't stress the urgency enough, Governor. If the Ohio Company is to have any chance of pegging its claim to the valley, we need a fort at the forks to form a bulwark against further French incursion.'

'It will be a challenge to get money out of the House. Fry has blocked all our efforts—'

'I did not just risk my life in the most inhospitable territory known to man, for you to forfeit your responsibilities, Governor. Find the money,' George gritted. 'Do whatever it takes.'

'Watch your tongue, Washington!'

'I damn near died out there, Governor. If you don't act to stop the French, there will be no Ohio land – not for us, or for Fry. West of our colonies there will be only France, and who knows how far that land stretches west. If the rumours of its vastness are true, we could find ourselves the minority on this continent, so please, do *your* bit.'

'You forget yourself, Major!'

George took a deep breath. 'My apologies, Sir, it has been an exhausting experience. I find myself frustrated at the inaction of men older than I. We need to raise an army and repel them.'

Dinwiddie regarded Washington – the young man had been stripped of all his naivety.

'Yes,' he conceded. 'I'll convene the council.'

'Very well. Now, I have performed a great service to this colony, Governor, may I respectfully ask that you find time, during your meeting, to consider my compensation?'

Dinwiddie frowned. It pained the Scotsman to part with money, even if it wasn't his.

'If it wasn't for me, you would have no intelligence of the French intentions, to say nothing of the Indians…'

'You've made your point, Major. Write up your report and have it to me by ten tomorrow morning.'

The young Major left the room, leaving Dinwiddie to his thoughts. He took a dram of whisky to soothe his fears. He had a bad feeling about this. A boundary dispute was now fast evolving into geo-politics. In the near future, his superiors would question his role in all this. One day, history books would recount his actions. He shuddered at the thought and took a larger measure of whisky. *What to do?* He'd been around long enough to know politicians never emerged as the heroes, even if events went well. His own ambitions had long since been out to pasture. Alas, here he was facing either the fire or the frying pan. There was only one thing for it – he penned a letter to London.

An hour later, he read through his effort. Satisfied he'd distanced himself sufficiently from any responsibility, he signed his name and took another whisky. He'd send it tomorrow with a copy of Washington's report – may as well line the boy up for his share of responsibility, he decided.

He leant back in his chair. *Bloody German fool.* It was after all, the King's land grant that was responsible for once again bringing the British into the orbit of the French.

***

The following afternoon, George waited impatiently in the tavern while the Governor's council debated what to do. It all seemed like a distant memory to him now: the cold, the fatigue, the fear. The apathy he'd endured at the height of his struggles had been replaced by a burning desire to make his journey worthwhile. *What is to come?* he wondered as he waited, supping his warm tea. That morning, he'd met with the Virginia Gazette and regaled them with tales of his exploits. His journey would soon be the talk of the colony. Beyond the headline, George loved the idea that his mission would mean something one day, a small but important initial step in Britain's acquisition of the Ohio Valley for itself. *History in the making,* although he kept that shamefully indulgent thought to himself.

Across the street, the door of the Capitol building opened. Dinwiddie stepped out into the street. George abandoned his tea and dashed over to meet Dinwiddie.

'Governor! What is to happen?'

'Hello Washington. Walk with me back to the mansion.' The Scot's face was expressionless, as hard to read as a card player's. 'We're going to rally the militia, every able-bodied man in the northern counties will be called upon to serve.'

'That's tremendous! I'd like to volunteer my services…'

'Well, it's too late for that, my fellow.'

George frowned.

'You'll be leading the men, Lieutenant Colonel.'

Lieutenant Colonel!

'Congratulations, Washington. I wouldn't want the job for all the tea in China, but fortunately for you, neither did anyone else.'

George could have kissed the Governor, his imagination running wild at the prospect. His mother had denied him the navy, but he'd got himself the most plum job in all the Americas.

'Now, listen to me,' Dinwiddie went on, 'you're to get to the fork in the river and build that fort. Draw whatever expenses you need, within reason, but you're only to defend our position. Under no circumstances should you prod the hornets' nest. I don't want you starting a bloody war! Is that clear?'

'Yes, Sir. Defend the fort.'

Dinwiddie continued pontificating his warnings, worries and stipulations – but Lieutenant Colonel Washington didn't hear a word of it. He'd endured. He'd prevailed. He'd arrived.

47

January 17th, 1754
Fitzbarton Plantation

Viktor was not having a good day. The slaves were working slowly. In frustration, he cracked his whip, but they ignored him. What had once been a lush wood was now a wasteland dotted with tree stumps that would be burned before ploughing. The achievement didn't prove sufficient distraction from his restless mind, that churned over and over with why Sarah was being aloof. She hadn't given him an answer to his proposal, and had been too poorly to walk with him on Sunday as she'd promised. Since then, she'd either been too busy in the main house or too tired in the evenings to see Viktor. He hadn't even seen her on Christmas Day. *She must realise the wait is killing me*, he thought repeatedly. All he needed was a simple 'yes', but the wait made the days pass even slower. He was so eager to make their dreams together come true. He longed to believe Mason would be good to his word and pass over the plantation on his death. It would be perfect for him and Sarah. He could hire somebody more capable to drive the slaves. He would dismiss Billy and Granville, who would never respect him. She could decorate rooms to her choosing, they would entertain… He imagined himself regaling their dinner guests with the story of how he left his father's land and worked his way to prominence here, celebrating his humble roots. They would have children. The boys would be taught to farm. The girls would be groomed for prominent marriages. They would live in blissful comfort and privilege, the stuff of dreams. Warmed by his fantasy, he resolved to find the courage to ask Mason to confirm his inheritance. It should be formally recorded in his last will and testament.

'Hey, Boss,' said Charlie, interrupting Viktor's daydream as he dragged some tree branches to the discard pile. 'You is quiet?'

Viktor shrugged.

'I think you took the news hard,' he remarked, as he passed Viktor.

'What?'

'Your lady Sarah. Very sad.'

'What are you talking about?' Viktor turned to face Charlie.

'Mr Mason is riding her.'

Had he heard right? He asked him again. Once more, Charlie repeated it. *What?* He could barely hear Charlie, who was saying something about Grace finding them together. Viktor's mind was shattering, his thoughts as disconnected and incomplete as broken glass. *No, no, no, this can't be right.*

'Yes, very sad for you, Boss,' said Charlie, looking amused at the impact this revelation was having. 'He powerful man…'

'Get back to work!' yelled Viktor, raising his whip hand. As Charlie sauntered off, Viktor turned his back, his legs felt wobbly, his mind numb. *It must be a lie. She couldn't have.* Tears welled in his eyes. He couldn't stand here, waiting for evening. He had to find out. Now. He ran back to the house. She'd be in Mason's study.

***

Mason lay on the rug. A chair was jammed against the door, his clothes dumped in a heap on the chaise longue next to hers. His hands rested on her thighs as she straddled him, forcing her hips back and forth. Her skin was pale, her breasts modest, pleasingly round, they shook as she rode him. Her hair hung like silk over her face, as if to hide him from the reality of the sin they were engaged in.

She was bewitching. He hadn't been able to think of anything else. Each time he took her, he promised it would be the last, but each time left him needing more. She was an unquenchable thirst. *She's a passing fancy,* he consoled himself. He would soon tire of her, as quickly as day turned to night. Yet at this very moment, as she slid herself back and forth, he knew he could never tire of such pleasure.

Two more pulls and his loins burst; intense pleasure turned quickly to satisfying discomfort as she continued to move. If this woman were the devil, then he wanted nothing more than a long stay in hell.

They lay together on the floor of the study, still joined, neither of them noticing the shadow briefly cast across the carpet from a figure at the window.

48

January 17th, 1754
Fitzbarton Plantation

For want of anywhere better to go, Viktor returned to the site where the slaves were clearing the woods. The afternoon sky had turned grey, and specks of rain were carried on the breeze. He slumped down against a fallen tree trunk and let the rain land on his cheeks. He simply looked at his boots. The cracked brown leather. The laces matted with dust. The toes scuffed. He stared at them all afternoon.

'Boss,' said Charlie. 'The day is over.' Behind him were gathered the rest of the slaves, their emotionless faces studying their driver: worn down, numb.

Viktor nodded. The afternoon's rain had soaked him through. He didn't shiver, despite the cold.

'You coming, Boss?'

He shook his head.

Charlie dismissed the slaves to return to their accommodation. He turned to follow them.

'Charlie, when is Barney next coming to the wharf to trade goods?' asked Viktor.

'Sunrise, this Sunday.'

***

Sunday morning came. Viktor hadn't slept all night, his mind clouded with thoughts that whirled around and around. He dressed, pocketed the savings he'd hidden in his mattress and walked out of his room. He glanced at Sylvia's door. He had nothing to say to her. She'd been his reason for returning here. Now she was his reason for leaving.

She'd come to see him the night before; her words still rung in his ears: 'What's wrong, Vik? You haven't been to see me.' He'd only offered a cold stare in response that said, *I know.* She didn't deny it or apologise. He'd turned away and heard her light footsteps leave the room. Viktor had toyed with the thought of telling Mason she was a runaway. There was nothing to be gained now. It was dawn and the dream was over.

The morning was bright and crisp. He took the trail and waited on the wharf, listening to birdsong, wondering what was to become of his life. He'd left his father because he'd wanted more. *Should I go home?*

The gentle splash of an oar interrupted his thoughts. The water in the creek began to ripple. Barney rounded the corner, glancing over his shoulder as he rowed.

'Ah, you all right, pal?' The boat drew level and bumped gently into the wood of the wharf, the cargo concealed under a large blanket. 'What can I do you for?' said Barney, softening his accent.

'Where are you headed?'

'What's it to you?'

'Because I'm coming with you.'

Barney grunted. 'Do I look like a ferry to you?'

Viktor's gaze hardened.

'Well, you can row,' said Barney finally as he moved to make way for Viktor.

A whistle came from the woods. He swung round to see who it was. Charlie emerged from between the trees and walked over to the wharf.

'I wanted to see you off, Boss.'

Viktor frowned. *Why?*

Charlie held out his hand. Viktor didn't understand, but clapped the man's warm, firm hand in a shake.

'This place bring out the worst in everyone. You have a good heart in there, Boss.' He pointed to Viktor's chest. 'You have always been free to follow your own path, to a better place.'

'Thank you, Charlie. I am sorry for whipping you.'

'Maybe I deserved it?'

Viktor frowned.

'We spoil your father's crop. Mason make me do it. Back then, I just thought you another plantation, so what do I care.'

Viktor's mind raced to understand Charlie's words.

'The flea beetles that ate your father's crop. It was Mason's idea. We had the start of an outbreak here. Master make us dig up all the soil where their eggs lay and for three nights we scatter it around your father's crop.'

'Huh.' Viktor was lost for words. He stepped into the boat, eager to get as far away from this wretched place as he could.

'Good luck, Charlie.' He bore him no ill will. They had both been doing as Mason commanded. In serving the devil, all were to be condemned. Unlike Charlie, Viktor had come here voluntarily. He would leave voluntarily. Charlie could not.

'One day you come back, Boss. You bring guns for us.' He grinned, baring his white teeth.

'Yous two wanna kiss and say your farewells? Your man here's gotta living to make,' grumbled Barney.

Viktor picked up the oars. Barney pushed the boat clear of the wharf and settled back into his makeshift seat amongst his cargo.

Viktor rowed, his back towards the bow of the boat, uncertain what lay ahead. He'd spent over two years at Fitzbarton's, enticed by the promise of wealth. He was leaving with new clothes and a pocketful of money. It wasn't much, but it was a small foundation that he could build upon.

Charlie and the Fitzbarton plantation began to shrink in view as his arms repeatedly dropped the oars into the water to pull himself away from his past. *If I never see this place again, it will be too soon.*

PART 3

—

1754

49

George Croghan hoped that the new year would bring a change in fortune, but the omens weren't good. The mood in Logstown was sour. Indians allied with the French harried their trading. Croghan alone had lost five men, a hundred loads of skins, and trading goods to the equivalent of six hundred bucks, all in the previous year. The remaining Twightee, whose village at Pickawillany he'd narrowly escaped when the French had attacked, had abandoned their alliance with him. Fearing further French reprisals, they'd begged forgiveness and returned to their French masters, costing Croghan his westernmost source of furs. Croghan was now penniless, but worse still, the confederacy of Indian tribes that constituted the Iroquois Six Nations was fragmenting. Fearing retributions from the French for their alliance with Britain, the council argued about the options available to them: swap sides in the hopes all would be forgiven; double down on Pennsylvania, who, despite paying good prices for their goods, showed no sign of defending them; or throw in their lot with Virginia, who many of the elders suspected wanted nothing more than to steal their land anyway. Croghan had every sympathy for them; they had backed the wrong horse. What he had less tolerance for was the sight that greeted him every evening: the Iroquois men splintered into factions, drowning their fears in rum and fighting, only to languish in their tepees the next day, too ill to tend to their families or to hunt. When combined with the encroachment of their enemies, it

375

meant Croghan's supply of furs was becoming ever leaner, and the people at Logstown were going hungry. Worse still, the French had put a bounty on his head, holding him responsible for the murder of their traders in Sandusky all those years ago.

Croghan loaded up the last of his fifteen packhorses with pelts in the early dawn. Whatever relief he might have taken from leaving the proverbial fire was tempered by the reality of the lean comfort of the frying pan to which he was headed. His debts had spiralled. As his various creditors had encountered one another, they had learned the true scale of his outstanding commitments and, in the previous fall, had sent agents out to the Ohio to recover whatever of Croghan's assets they could find. On learning of their approach, he'd taken leave of his farmstead and circulated rumours of illness. But he couldn't hide forever. If he stayed in Logstown, he risked losing the last of his trading stock, so he was making the journey east in the depths of winter. This load – if it arrived safely – was nowhere near enough to clear his accounts, but when combined with his trademark charm, he hoped it would buy him another season's grace. He prayed the French could be kept at arm's length, but judging by the stinking, slumbering state of Logstown, that was a tall order.

Croghan mounted his horse, whose breath blew clouds of steam into the cold morning air. As he readied to leave, he was approached by Tanacharison.

'Safe journey, Buck. I hope we will meet again.' The anxieties of his tribe's predicament were weighing heavily on the Chief's weathered face.

Croghan smiled at him. 'We shall; you've promised me two hundred thousand acres, which I have every intention of claiming.'

'I hope it will still be mine to give. My people grow fearful of the fate that awaits them.'

'All will be well, Chief. Now's not the time for being faint of heart.'

Tanacharison seemed calmed by Croghan's words, but beneath it simmered uncertainty. For trade to continue, all rested on the arrival of the Virginians and the building of the fort at the forks in the river to repel the French from the Ohio. Only if all those things happened, Croghan would get his two hundred thousand acres. Then he could clear his debts and all would be well.

He took the hunting trail east from the camp through the trees. A mile out, he heard a sharp whistle. Fear gripped him; he scanned the woods around him. On his right, the trail was in the shadow of a steep wooded bank. At its top, he saw the head of Thayonih, Tanacharison's eldest son, who had greeted him when he'd very first arrived at Logstown some eight years ago. He spurred his horse up the slope, ducking between the trees. At the top, he found Thayonih hidden in a sunken hollow.

'You've just made a fresh path up to my sentry post!' complained the brave.

Thayonih accepted his apology and said he would cover up his tracks, so as not to be discovered. Security measures were now in place in case the camp were to be raided. A ring of sentries surrounded the village, on both sides of the river.

'Keep an eye out for Huron,' said Thayonih.

'You too. Look after your father. He has the weight of the Six Nations on his shoulders.'

Croghan rode down the slope and re-joined his column of packhorses to begin his journey east.

50

January 21ˢᵗ, 1754
Fitzbarton Plantation

Mason's mind churned, keeping him from sleep. It wasn't affairs of the flesh which niggled Mason tonight, it was business. Something was up. He could feel it in his gut. His tired mind was searching for problems, like weeds between his tobacco plants.

He sighed in frustration. It was the early hours of the morning. His mouth was dry and he had a dull headache from the wine. Mary had been in a cantankerous mood so he'd plied her with drink at dinner. She'd become more objectionable before retiring to bed early, just as he'd hoped. Mason had enjoyed a peaceful cigar, the smoke of which still flavoured his mouth now, and contemplated paying Sarah a conjugal visit in her quarters, but dismissed the notion as too risky.

He gave up trying to sleep and heaved himself from his bed. Tiptoeing from the room, avoiding the squeaky floorboard, he slipped downstairs to the solitude of his study. At night the room took on a quiet readiness, its stillness only a candlelight away from exerting its industrious influence on his thoughts and decisions, like a coiled spring ready to release its potential energy. Mason sat at his desk and felt the cold leather on his naked buttocks. He allowed himself a brief smirk at the recent memories of the last time he'd been naked in this room. He lit a candle and leafed through his books; perhaps a clue would prompt his consciousness. He looked through the ledgers, correcting Sarah's faulty arithmetic. By the time he'd finished, his once beautiful ledger looked like a child's exercise book, replete with crossed-through text and annotations. He'd better do it himself, he thought wearily. She was of no use, bar that of being what she was: a harlot. *What am I to do with her?* There was little sense in letting her struggle on with clerking. *I'll have to find something useful for her to perform and earn her keep, otherwise she's just a waste of money.* Mason sat upright. His mind caught the scent of something: he scanned the debit column, twice. No mention of Sarah. He leafed through the receipts for the plantation. No mention of her. He smirked to himself. Had they neglected to charge him for her? After all, Viktor had conducted the purchase. Perhaps the unfamiliar face had confused the auction clerk. A dilemma formed in Mason's mind: if he ever wanted to sell her, he had no proof of ownership. *Did she know that?* He nibbled at his thumbnail. The thought of selling her made him twitch. The fact it made sense was deeply irritating – Mary would certainly approve. But without title, Sarah's value would be impaired. On the other hand, there was no shortage of flesh-starved bachelors in need of a wife.

Mason certainly hadn't finished with her – yet. The matter of her purchase would need to be resolved regardless. He would ask Viktor in the morning.

Mason didn't return to bed, He waited until dawn, crept back upstairs to get dressed, then went to Viktor's quarters to investigate. He knocked on Viktor's door. No answer. Impatient, Mason let himself in. The bed was empty. He scanned the simple room. No clothes. No boots. He must be up already. A horrible thought occurred to him. He opened Sarah's door. Much to Mason's relief, she was sleeping alone. He savoured a brief look at her smooth pale skin. Could he bring himself to sell her? *I must. Just wait and a moment will present itself.*

His thoughts returned to Viktor. He searched the accommodation block, the slave quarters, the outhouse, the kitchen. No Viktor. Frustrated, Mason paced back to the house to take his breakfast. The bell would ring soon and the working day would commence. At which point he would interrogate the man. He found Grace in the kitchen and chivvied her into making him scrambled eggs. He took his seat in the dining room. No sign of Mary, who would no doubt need to sleep off her wine. He picked up the Gazette while waiting for his breakfast. The front page detailed an attack by Indians on settlers in the

Shenandoah valley. Three families scalped. Mason, who had no interest in such bloodthirst before his stomach had been suitably lined, turned the page.

> *Another appeal by Simon Bowler of Frederick County, who was left for dead when he was attacked by a servant he'd bought the same day at auction.*

Mason chuckled to himself and continued to read.

> *Miss Sylvia Coppell had viciously attacked Bowler without provocation as they journeyed by horse and cart from Alexandria to Bowler's homestead. Miss Coppell struck Bowler's head with a rock. A blow which Bowler insisted was intended to be fatal. Coppell then relieved the victim of his horse and left him for dead at the roadside. Sylvia Coppell had just arrived from London. She is described as twenty years old, auburn hair, tall in figure, measuring approximately 5 feet 10 inches and of pleasant complexion and comely appearance. She has not been seen since and should be treated with caution.*

Mason yawned. They could nearly be describing Sarah, he thought. She might know the girl, they must have travelled here on the same boat. He'd ask her. It was to be expected though; more of England's trash dumped in the New World.

Grace arrived with a plate of steaming eggs. He made light work of them; sated, he wiped his lips on his napkin and stood up to leave just as a tired-looking Mary appeared.

'Good morning,' she said.

Mason grunted as he passed her. 'I'm off to look for Viktor.'

Mary took the seat he'd left warm. She picked up the newspaper.

51

January 23rd, 1754
Alexandria

Viktor was feeling distinctly optimistic as he and Barney drifted onto Alexandria's shore, crunching the gravel under their hull. Wearing the new cocked hat he'd purchased from Barney, he leapt ashore with the enthusiasm of a prisoner set free. He'd spent the past days travelling the riverbanks, helping hawk Barney's stock. They'd slept rough, huddled around campfires, drinking rum together and roasting meat. Despite the cold, Viktor realised he needed very little to be happy. For the first time, he was free of the influence of others. No Mason, or Mary, nor his father – no one at all telling him what to do.

'Thanking thee for your help,' said Barney as he walked up the snow-covered slope towards the tavern by the tobacco warehouse. 'Buy yous a drink?'

Viktor hesitated. 'What if someone recognises me? They might tell Mason.'

'Pah, yous worry too much, lad. You'll be fine.'

Viktor shook his head, a bad feeling holding him back. He'd escaped. He was finally free and he wasn't taking any risks. 'Barney, no, I'm not going in the tavern. Mason's post is kept there. He'll hear.'

'Very well, there's a new tavern just opened, we'll go there instead. Take your mind off that lassie Sarah.'

Hearing her name made Viktor twinge. He'd thought about her constantly. Had he been naïve? Was she just evil? It didn't matter, the future he'd imagined for them was gone. He had a new plan now, inspired by Barney. He'd buy a small piece of land on the frontier, and with his land as collateral, he'd borrow to buy a slave and farm his own tobacco. It was what he knew. He could tend the tobacco, he'd treat the slave well such that he – or she – wouldn't want to run away. He'd build a house, and leaf by leaf, he'd cultivate his future. It wasn't exciting, it would be nothing but hard work, but it was possible. And best of all, it would be his, and his alone. The only thing missing was a wife, but his experiences with Sarah had tempered those desires.

It was only three months since his last visit to Alexandria, and he could not believe how much it had changed in that short time. The houses were roofed, windows glowed from lights burning within, chimneys puffed grey smoke into the late afternoon gloom. At the end of the street, slaves laboured on the unfinished plots. Viktor felt a pang of envy as he saw what real money could do. At least now he had some of his own, safely tucked into his shoe.

He followed Barney into the tavern.

They emerged four hours later, steaming drunk. Stumbling in the snow, emptying their bladders in the street, Barney put his arm around Viktor's shoulder, 'Rite, you wee feckin' eejit, I's got a present for yous.'

Viktor was promptly sick, spattering his boots with the gin, rum and cider they'd consumed. He followed Barney down to the shoreline. At the far end of the bay, marked by flickering lanterns, was a long keel boat, moored against a crude staithe. Fearing he'd fall in, Viktor crawled up the gangplank and tumbled over the gunwale onto the deck with a thud, much to Barney's amusement. Having composed themselves, they stooped as they passed through the door on the bulkhead. Viktor was blanketed by the warmth of a stove burning in the middle of a small lounge area. The men at the card tables fell silent as they watched the two men enter.

'Gentlemen, welcome to the finest boarding house in Virginia,' said an officious-looking woman wearing a stay more suited for someone much younger. Her cheeks were bright with rouge and her long silver hair was tied back. 'Rum?'

'Aye,' replied Barney.

'Please, take a seat.' She indicated a small table by the fireside.

Viktor slumped into the chair and purred in the warmth of the fire.

The chatter at the three other tables resumed.

'What's this place?' he asked.

''Tis ideal for last orders.'

Viktor was past conscious thought. His body acted on instinct as he took in his surroundings with the dumb curiosity of a newborn babe.

Two drinks were placed on the table, startling him. Next, a woman sat down on his lap, the curls of her hair brushing against his cheek. Her perfumed scent danced across his nose.

'Hello. I'm Joy,' she said.

Viktor grinned. He squinted at her. Her hair was black, but not as frizzy as a negro's. Her lips were full and her eyes dark. She was mulatto, and a pretty one; even her worn and blackened teeth didn't detract from her smile.

Opposite him, Barney enjoyed similar company, another mixed-race woman perched on his legs. The old lady stooped by his shoulder as he whispered something to her. She left and Barney raised his glass. 'Cheers, Vik.'

Viktor grinned. Joy picked up his glass and held it to his lips, tipping the sugary liquor into his mouth. She wiped the drips from his lips with her finger.

'You are?' she said.

'Viktor.'

'That's a nice name.'

'Th-thank you.'

He felt her buttocks shift gently back and forth on his lap, stirring his senses.

'You're very handsome, Viktor.' She brushed his blond hair away from his forehead.

'You're pretty.'

'Bless you, Viktor.' She kissed him on the lips.

He had no idea what was happening. Had he died and gone to heaven? He didn't care. He was warm and drunk, and a pretty woman was tending to him. She poured more drink into him, burning his throat.

'What is this place?' he murmured.

'I live here. But I do get very lonely. And it's very cold in the winter. I long to have someone to keep me warm at night.'

'Me too!'

'Do you like me, Viktor?'

'Very much.'

'Would you like to have me, Viktor?' She stroked his cheek.

'Me?'

'Yes, Viktor, I've been waiting for someone like you.' She kissed him, her tongue probing his mouth.

I am in heaven, he decided. He looked over to Barney, he was kissing his woman, his hand cupping her breast, under the watchful eye of the madam who'd welcomed them in.

His attention was recaptured as Joy squeezed his manhood, which responded in kind. 'Come, Viktor.' She stood up and took him by the hand into the shadows behind the stove. Curtains hung from the low ceiling. She crept through, and Viktor felt a touch of excitement as he followed her into this secret world. A narrow corridor with more curtains on his left, they walked to the end and she held back another curtain for him. They entered a small, candlelit space with a straw mattress covered in fabrics and cushions. She turned and removed his coat, tossing it onto a rickety chair.

'Now, Viktor, before we begin, first you need to pay me.' She pressed her finger against his lips to silence any objection. 'Two pounds.'

Viktor grinned, slumping onto the straw mattress and beginning to wrestle with the laces of his boot. Behind the next curtain, he heard a man groaning.

'Let me help you.' Joy knelt and took his boot in her hands. Viktor stared at the deep cleavage that revealed itself from her loose-fitting shirt. She tugged at his boot and tipped it upside down. Paper money and coins tumbled to the floor. She took two pounds, showed Viktor, and put it in her jar on the floor. He watched her put the rest of his money back in his boot.

'Thank you,' said Viktor. His fuddled mind beginning to contemplate what was about to happen to him. 'I'm a virgin.'

'Not for much longer, Viktor.' She lifted her shirt, revealing pert nipples that adorned her large breasts. She unbuttoned his shirt and tugged down his trousers, pushed him onto the mattress, and took his manhood in her hand. 'You lie back, Viktor, I'll take it from here.'

Viktor closed his eyes. *Finally! It's happening.* She eased him inside her. It was better than he could have ever imagined. She rose and fell on him, and everything that had ever happened to Viktor faded into the background, forgotten; he was now a man in *every* sense. He was leaving his past behind. No longer would he be defined by what he didn't have, or hadn't done. She climbed off and squeezed down next to him. 'Lay on me.'

He did as instructed. Instinct took over. He pushed his hips back and forth, grateful for the booze that numbed his senses and prolonged his pleasure. He looked at her face, deep into her dark eyes. He didn't know the first thing about this girl. Whatever happened tomorrow, he would remember her forever. His fists clenched as his excitement climaxed. Viktor heaved a huge sigh; it was the most natural thing in the world.

They lay side by side and Viktor fell into a very deep sleep.

***

The first he knew of the next day was a piercing headache. Then, a mouth so dry it could absorb the waters of the Potomac. *Where am I?* The dim morning light stabbed at his dry eyes. He sat up. *Oh, yes, the boat, the girl!* The memory of her briefly eased the pain. *Where was she?* His clothes were abandoned in a heap on the floor beside the mattress. No sign of her. He reached for his shirt and began to dress himself. The sight of his untied boots sent a shudder through him. He lunged forward and stuffed his hand into the boot. Empty. Then the other. Also empty. *No!* He tipped them both up. Nothing fell out. He'd been robbed. His hands trembled as he rifled through his clothes. He looked under the mattress. Nothing. His money was gone.

'Barney?' he called out, his voice trembling.

It was too much to contemplate. If his money was gone, so was his future. No land. No farm. Tears pooled in his eyes as he dressed himself. He rushed through the curtains and found the older white woman in the room with the tables.

'Where's my money?'

'How should I know?'

'But... You... I've been robbed!'

'If you say so.'

'Where's Joy?'

'She's gone ashore. Your friend is waiting outside, if you'd care to leave?'

'I can't – not without my money. I want it back! I'm not leaving without it.'

'Well, you can't stay here...'

Rage surged through Viktor's fists. Sensing his change in mood, the woman calmly called out, 'Vincent.'

From behind the curtains stepped a large negro, so tall he couldn't stand straight under the low ceiling of the barge.

'We won't have any trouble, young man,' said the woman, 'or Vincent here will throw your corpse in the river.'

Tears spilled down Viktor's cheeks as he walked past her and out into the cold morning air on deck.

'Do come again,' she called after him.

On the shore, Barney was crouched with his trousers round his ankles as he emptied his bowels into the water's edge. 'Ya 'right?'

'No! They've taken my money.'

'Oh, aye.'

'It was a year's wages!' shouted Viktor, his heart still thumping in his chest with the agony of it all.

'I's better buy you a wee breakfast then, aye?'

Damn Barney. It had been his idea to visit this floating brothel. A den of bloody thieves.

'Breakfast?! Then what am I supposed to do?' yelled Viktor.

Barney shrugged. 'Lunch?'

'I'm homeless. Penniless. Jobless. Wanted by my master. My life's in bloody tatters!'

Viktor fell to the ground, his headache eased by the chill of the snow as he sobbed his heart out.

52

Mason dismissed Sarah and refastened his breeches. She left his study and closed the door behind her. He opened the window to freshen the room and waft away the smell of their lovemaking that hung in the air, then poured himself a brandy from the decanter on his desk and sat down. He'd intended to tell Sarah that he was going to sell her. Cut his losses before Mary caught them cavorting under her nose – which she surely would. But the sight of her had lit his flame and he'd taken her. *Next time.*

The knock at the door caused Mason to sit bolt upright. He was relieved to see it was Granville.

'Sorry to disturb you, Master, only I thought you'd want to know. I was talking with the men on the neighbouring plantation – word is Lieutenant Colonel Washington is summoning the militia. To attack the French over the mountains.'

'Yes?'

'Billy and I are both enlisted, we was wondering if you wanted us to go?'

'Certainly not! We have too many negroes, it wouldn't be safe for you to leave, especially since Viktor's disappearance.'

'Fine by us, sir, we've got no desire to go fighting, only, see, we is required by law to go.'

'Don't worry about that. What do you think, that the Colonel is going to come by here and manhandle you away? Nonsense. Ignore it.

387

You're paid by me, and you won't be getting any wages if you leave. We're running an enterprise and my niggers can't very well whip themselves.'

'Very well, sir, grateful, if you'd vouch for us.'

Mason shooed him away. That was all he needed – another war with France to jeopardise the shipping of his tobacco across the ocean. Especially after all the money he'd splurged on Mary to appease her after Sarah's arrival. Damn women were always frivolously expensive.

***

Sylvia was brushing her hair in her nightdress. It was only eight o'clock but with Viktor gone and no one to talk to she was readying herself for another early night. She missed his company but she was at least glad not to have to fend off his advances any longer. She rubbed her stomach; was she starting to show? It was hard to say, but she knew she would have to confess soon. *How would Mason take the news?* The only thing he lacked in life was an heir; in that lay all of Sylvia's hopes. But how might Mary take the news of her pregnancy? All she knew for sure was that the relatively stable boat on which she'd sailed was about to enter very choppy waters. She'd need her wits about her to make sure she wasn't cast out. If that happened, the only person she knew was Viktor. Could she find him and would he take her in? He must have found out about Mason and her. It was the only explanation for his sudden desertion.

The quiet night air was interrupted by a tap at her door.

'Who is it?' Her heart quickened a beat, fearing it might be an unwelcome visit from Billy or Granville.

In fact, it was a bigger surprise; Mary's face, cold as frost, appeared around the door. 'May I?' she said curtly.

Sylvia stood by her bed and held her hairbrush behind her back.

'Forgive me for troubling you, Sarah, I can see you were going to bed.' Mary took a seat by the small wooden table, the only other furniture in the room. A lone candle burned on top, casting its soft light onto Mary's stark face.

Mary indicated for Sylvia to be seated, which she did, perching herself on the edge of her single bed. She folded her arms.

Mary's gaze swept around the room, the corners of her mouth twitching down. 'I haven't been very kind to you, Sarah.' She turned to look her in the eye. 'I apologise.'

Sylvia was taken aback. 'No need, Mrs Fitzbarton...'

'Please, call me Mary. I don't respond to change readily,' she continued, smoothing out the folds of her skirt. 'It must have been very hard for you, coming so far from home, for one so young.' Mary cleared her throat. 'You are a very pretty girl. You cannot blame an older woman for fearing the worst, that you might lead my husband into temptation.'

What does she know?

'You see, Sarah, mine and Mason's marriage is – well, in the season of fall. The bright flowers are gone now and the leaves lie on the ground.' Mary was staring at the wooden floorboards.

Sylvia kept her face emotionless.

'Mason's very upset since learning of Viktor's disappearance. Viktor brought you here, didn't he, Sarah?'

Sylvia nodded.

'Why do you think he left so suddenly?'

Ah, so this is what she came here for. 'I don't think he took to his work very well, Mary. He had a good heart. Too innocent from being brought up in isolation. He's not seen the cruelty of the world. He didn't have it in him to whip the negroes, is my opinion.'

'Oh, I see. Yet he'd been here for more than two years, hadn't he?' Mary's face wore a look of puzzlement. 'I thought...well,' her gazed returned to Sylvia, 'did he harbour a fancy for you, Sarah?'

Sylvia twisted her lips. 'He was lonely and I am sure he would have...well, you know what men are like.'

Mary's face was hard as stone.

'No, please don't think I led him on,' Sylvia said hastily. 'I wouldn't risk losing my livelihood for anyone, not without your permission.'

Mary nodded, her face softening.

She believes me, thought Sylvia.

'I didn't mean to accuse you of anything. It's just that... Mason can't understand it. He'd gone to some trouble to secure Viktor's services.' She chuckled. 'Well, he's like a bear with a sore head when things don't go his way.'

'Maybe Billy and Granville could tell you more?'

'Perhaps. Thank you.' Mary stood up. 'I must leave you to your rest.'

Sylvia breathed a sigh of relief that the sour-faced woman was leaving.

Mary turned at the door. 'I enjoyed our chat, Sylvia... Us girls ought to stick together, don't you think?'

Sylvia nodded, 'Yes, Mary. Good night.'

Mary's eyes narrowed. She turned and left.

Sylvia blew out the candle and lay back on her bed. Her heart thumped as Mary's last words played again in her mind. *How did she know?*

53

George stepped out of the newly completed dwelling that had been loaned to him, nicely situated on the corner of Water and Oronoco streets. The sun threatened to break through the winter clouds, and he was protected from the cool winter breeze by his new uniform, a blue coat with scarlet breeches and waistcoat. George was thrilled with his appearance, but that was about it. He would cut a dashing – but lonely – figure on the frontier. None of the provinces had yet answered his call to send men for his militia. Since the hostile Indians had been pushed beyond the mountains, the Virginia militia hadn't been summoned in decades, bar a few infrequent and rudimentary drills after church. It had withered away as folk tended their own priorities, free from imminent danger. The men he'd spoken to didn't much fancy taking on the French, nor did they see it as their fight, not caring one jot what the French did behind the mountains. If the investors of the Ohio Company stood to lose a few pounds, that was their problem. Obviously, slaves were out of the question; they'd abscond first chance they got.

The town was the usual hustle of slaves lugging materials around, people trading and moving into their new properties. So far, George had recruited one runaway from a merchant ship, Jimmy Jones, who'd been caught stealing eggs. He'd jumped ship and been living rough since. George left Jimmy in the cupboard that passed for a gaol,

391

fearing that if he let him out, he'd simply abscond again. George wasn't yet panicking, for it was too early to cross the mountains, but he had to assemble something resembling a fighting force. The memories of the French forts, their manpower and preparedness, haunted his thoughts.

He stepped into the tavern, always a reliable source of news. It was quiet, only two men hunched over plates of scrambled eggs. George walked up to the bar and as he waited for the tavern keeper, he studied the two diners. He recognised the blond hair and well-proportioned build of one of them. The man looked up as he approached, his eyes red and his pallor that of a man nursing a hangover. The other man, inhaling his breakfast, was a scraggy mess of red curls and beard, interrupted by a scar on his cheek.

'Say, where do I know you from?' called George. 'I remember! We met in the other tavern – you're Fitzbarton's man.'

It took a moment for Viktor's weary mind to recognise George. 'I *was*.'

'Oh. What happened?' George moved to stand by them.

Viktor shook his head, with a look of melancholy. 'Long story.'

'What are you two men involved in today?'

Viktor shot the red-haired man an evil look.

'He's starting afresh today, aren't ya, pal?' said the red-haired man, then tittered at his own comment. He introduced himself as Barney MacGregor. George didn't shake his hand.

'So, you're finished with that rake Fitzbarton. Are you looking for work?' he said.

'Aye, what do yous need?' interjected Barney.

'Gentlemen, consider yourselves recruited into the Virginia militia.' George grinned, convinced of the favour he was doing them. 'We'll be defending British territory. No pay. It's your duty.'

'Oh aye, yous are wanting me to fight for the British army? For nought?' Barney smirked and shook his head. 'I have dodgy knees, pal, I cannae fight…'

'Nonsense,' interrupted George, who'd heard any number of excuses in recent days.

'I'll do it,' said Viktor, putting his knife and fork down. 'So will Barney.'

'Bollocks to you, my man!' retorted Barney, who gave respite to his breakfast for the first time as he glared at his companion.

George pulled up a chair and positioned himself at the head of their table. 'We're assembling an army to cross the frontier. We're to build a fort. Keep the French at bay. I doubt we'll fire a shot in anger.'

'What weapons you bringing?' asked Barney.

'You'll need to bring your own,' George said matter-of-factly.

The Scotsman, who'd finished his eggs by now and was mopping his plate with a crust of bread, chuckled, 'Oh aye, no pay, no weapons – some force you're gonna be. How many men yous got?'

'Four. Us three and one other.' George kept a straight face as Barney laughed again. 'If you men help with recruitment, I'll make you my officers. You can supervise the other men.'

Viktor, who cut a more dejected figure, nodded his approval. George thought the lad was carrying an air of resignation about him.

'Do either of you have military experience?' he asked.

Barney pointed to the wound on his cheek. 'There's mine, right there. Look, pal, I wonnae be fighting in your – well, let's be honest, it ain't no army.'

'Sir, it is your duty!' George countered.

'No. It's *yours*. And I'll be having nothing to do with it. Great Britain's a load o' shite, and you havnae a pot to piss in. But if you're serious, what victuals will you be needing? Here I can help yous.'

'None as yet,' said George, suppressing a touch of embarrassment.

'Yous gonna need victuals. Weapons. Food. Tea. Horses. Wagons. Whatever you need, I can get it for you. Ain't that right, Viktor?'

Viktor wore a frown but nodded.

George felt his head begin to ache as he considered the prospect of dealing with another Scottish hawker. Something told him to be careful about making promises. 'We'll see, but if you want to make money, you'll need to be enlisted.'

'How's about I get you a barrel of flour to get you started? Say one pound and six? Very fair.'

George leaned forward. 'You show me what you can bring to the table, then we'll see.'

'I'll need some credit.'

'Too bad,' said George, satisfied to have the man on the back foot.

'You two fellows finish your breakfast, then you can help me find some vagrants to press into service.'

As George left, Viktor looked at Barney, who seemed to read his mind.

'More fool you if yous wannae be getting shot, but let me tell ya, there's coin to made. War's expensive. No more paddling the rivers trading tobacco and wee bits o' tat – this'll be government money, and I fancy a slice of it. Least they can do for me, seeing as the bastards shipped me over here. After last night, yous could do with a wee earner too, ah?'

Viktor shook his head. He knew Barney well enough by now; whatever was earned would find its way into Barney's pocket, not his.

***

Two days passed. Their numbers hadn't grown, and George's frustrations had got the better of him and he'd taken a boat south, heading for Williamsburg where he intended to hassle Governor Dinwiddie into granting the soldiers pay. Duty to one's militia was a tradition that looked distinctly outdated in the face of a modern and well-resourced opponent. It was a territorial grab, from which the soldiers would see little benefit. Having lands of their own to tend, the promise of more untamed land beyond a mountain range was an altogether different cry from defending one's own from Indian raids.

George departed, leaving Viktor and Barney at the house in Alexandria, with orders to keep the prisoner fed. Viktor had failed in his attempts to have Barney accompany him back to the floating brothel. 'You'll nae be finding me crossing those women, lad. They've spent a lifetime learning to protect themselves against unwanted threats. Your money's gone, for which I am sorry,' had been his reply. Viktor, seeing his future slip from his grasp again, gave up hope. As he sat behind George's desk in the front room, staring out of the window, his growing bitterness left him in the mood to shoot a few Frenchmen.

Barney left the room and returned a few moments later with a tired and cold Jimmy Jones.

'No use this poor fellow freezing himself outside.'

Viktor didn't object – it wouldn't have made a difference anyway. Jimmy was short, and his stooped posture and drawn face suggested he was starving. He'd be easy to overpower if necessary.

Jimmy and Barney pulled up chairs on the opposite side of the desk. Barney lit a pipe and took a lungful of tobacco smoke. He offered the smouldering pipe to Jimmy, who eagerly took some puffs before offering it on to Viktor.

'What happened to you, then?' Barney nudged Jimmy. 'By the look of your stripy trousers, I'd wager you jumped ship?'

'Aye, I came over on the *Relief*...'

Viktor noticed Barney frown.

'The *Relief*, that's Reidy's boat, no?'

'Aye. Captain Reid.'

'Viktor, you remember Reidy – you helped him load up my loose leaf one night after harvest.'

Viktor nodded; he remembered the man, but wasn't really interested. His mind wandered off while Jimmy recounted his voyage over, his abscondment and eventual capture. Listening to another man's story caused him to reflect on his own, the sum of all his actions and decisions had led him to be alone in an empty house with two men for whom he barely cared. He took a swig from the hip flask that Barney passed round. The other two chatted freely as Jimmy began to become more animated. The sailor's revival caused Viktor to withdraw further into his own thoughts, until something caught his ear:

'There was one bird on the boat, Sylvia she was called – absolute cracker. Reddy-brown hair, great body. What an eyeful she were.'

'Sylvia?' said Viktor.

'That's right. Pretty creature.'

'Don't tell me,' said Barney staring intently at Viktor, 'that innae the wee bird you took to Fitzbarton's?'

'Sounds like it.' They conferred dates. It tallied. Jimmy had been on the same boat as Sylvia.

'Wee lassie broke our man here's heart,' joked Barney, enjoying himself too much for Viktor's liking.

'Well, if it's any consolation,' said Jimmy, 'she rode Captain Reid all the way from London to escape the hold. If she int pregnant, Captain's a jaffa.'

Viktor grunted. It was no surprise; he'd misjudged her. Beneath her beauty and charm had lurked a calculating creature. *Surely all women can't be like that,* he wondered, his experience of losing money on the boat still colouring his thoughts.

'See, wee lassie led Viktor here on a merry wee dance, then shacked up with his master. Got a big old plantation, half a day away on the Occoquan River. You should see the place, Jimmy, everything a man could want...' Barney paused. His eyes darted about the room. 'That's it!' he announced as he leapt to his feet. 'Viktor my boy, I've got it. I know what we gonna do – get yous even and me ahead!'

Viktor took a puff on the pipe and leant back in his chair. *Why do I get the feeling this is going to be a bad idea?*

'Rite, I need something to sell to Washington, so he treat me serious. What we'll do is sneak up to Fitzbarton's place in the middle of the night. Chore everything we can from him. Load it up from his wharf and whip it all the way back, then sell it to Washington. He gives me a contract for his army, and I'll be happy as a pig knee-deep in shite.'

'You're mad,' said Viktor.

'Nae, bloody genius, that's me, pal.'

'Forget it.'

'No way. We're going. You're coming. You know the place like the back of your hand.'

Viktor shook his head furiously.

'I need you, pal.' Barney pointed a rough finger at him. 'Look, he stole your woman. We'll steal his stores. George'll be very happy with us. I'll get me a contract, you get yourself a wee promotion, Officer Neumann. Aye, sounds rite, eh?'

'He has dogs.'

'So? They know you. You can settle 'em down – or we'll poison them. Either way, it'll be fine. Jimmy, you can come help. The fresh air'll do you power of good.' Barney rubbed his hands together.

'What if we're caught?' asked Viktor, fearing himself getting sucked into Barney's scheme.

'One, we won't be. Two, if we were – which we won't – but just to humour you, we'll be like Jimmy here: recruited into Washington's army as punishment. Which is right where we all are already! We've literally nothing to lose. Ah, it's so brilliant I can feel me old boy gettin' firm.'

'Barney...'

'Hold your tongue. It's settled.'

54

January 25th, 1754
Fitzbarton Plantation

All good things must come to an end, or so Mason told himself as he made his way to the workers' accommodation block. It was early in the day but he'd fortified himself with a brandy anyway. He'd take no pleasure in telling Sarah he intended to sell her; she'd been the most enjoyable entertainment he'd had in many a year. But she was an immoral pastime, he'd got away with his dalliance, but God was watching and he could not live in perpetual sin. He'd backed out on three other occasions, so this time he'd made sure he had no choice: he'd agreed a sale to another plantation owner, who was recently widowed. He'd told Mary, who'd been delighted, naturally, and had even been civil to Mason since.

Sarah was in her room, sitting on her chair, tying her shoelaces. Mason, his heart pounding, quickly shut the door behind him.

'Good morning, Mason!'

'Yes, morning. Now,' he did his best to sound commanding. 'You're not suitable. You can't bookkeep and I have no need for an extra house servant, so I've advertised you for sale.' The words were out. He felt better.

Her skin turned pale and her eyes went wide.

'Mason…'

'No. I won't be talked round. My decision is final.'

'Mason, I'm pregnant. Your child is in my womb.'

Mason fell backwards against the door. His thoughts raced, which was the only thing that stopped him from being sick.

'Are – are you sure?'

'Yes.' She pulled her dress tight over her small but noticeable bump. 'Mason, we're having a baby.'

FUCK! Despite his entire body rebelling, Mason couldn't help but smile. This good-for-nothing woman had managed the only task that his wife had proved incapable of: bearing him an heir.

'Christ, that's… Sarah, I don't know what to say…'

'Mason,' she took his hand and led him to the bed. 'I'm certain it's a son.'

He didn't hear the rest of what she had to say. It was the best news he'd ever been given and yet also the worst. Mary would…well, it didn't bear thinking about. This was the one aspect of his life that had eluded him, the missing piece of his puzzle, something to make it all worthwhile. He'd been afforded a second chance.

'Now, Mason, if you send me away, I'm taking your son with me…'

Mason fainted.

55

January 25th, 1754
Fitzbarton Plantation

'Well, I'm glad that's out in the open and we'll be rid of that girl,' said Mary.

They were seated on the balcony, overlooking the lawn in the late morning sunshine.

Mason said nothing.

'Mason?'

'Uh, sorry, yes?'

'It's done? You've told her she's leaving?'

'Oh yes, all done. Drink?'

'Let's celebrate!'

Mason shouted for Grace, who soon emerged with a bottle of wine.

'Good riddance to bad rubbish,' said Mary, raising her glass.

'Mary, the poor girl isn't that bad.'

'Don't you be making excuses for her. She's a London tramp. If you ask me, we got off lightly. When is she leaving?'

Mason took a large swig of his wine. Mary was such a poisonous creature. Was he really to spend the rest of his life with her, knowing that his child would be out in the world somewhere? With an heir, all this would have meaning. The plantation. His legacy. A dynasty, rather than the drunken oblivion they were currently heading for. But the child would be a bastard, unless he married Sarah – which he couldn't

because of Mary. He was stuck. Besides, the child might not survive…
But they could have others. A million thoughts rolled through his
head.

Mary topped up her glass, her eyes fixed on him, trying to read his
thoughts.

'I know you, Mason. What's wrong? Tell me.'

Mason waved away her enquiry.

'Well, you don't seem very happy. Are you rutting her?'

'Mary! For heaven's sake, can't you just let things be?'

'Look me in the eye and tell me you're not.'

Mason did as instructed, holding her sharp gaze.

'If you are, Mason, I swear I'll castrate you in your sleep—'

'Enough with you! I've got rid of her, and you're still not satisfied!
Why do we have to go through this ridiculous routine all over again?'

'Because you're weak, Mason, susceptible to a temptress—'

Mason stood up, knocking his chair over. He slapped her hard
across the cheek with the back of his hand. She recoiled and clutched
her reddened cheek, glaring at him with all her venom.

'Pig!'

'There's more where that came from if you don't quiet yourself.'
Mason walked away towards the balcony door.

'That's it? Off to cuddle up to your whore?'

'Her company is a lot nicer than yours.'

'Tell that to Simon Bowler.'

'Who?'

'The man she left for dead on the side of the road.'

Mason turned back to face her.

'Who?'

'That article in the Gazette. It was her. Her name isn't Sarah. She
answers to Sylvia. Sylvia Coppell. A runaway. That idiot Viktor helped
her escape.'

'Nonsense.'

'No, Mason. The truth. Here.' She got up and fetched a copy of the
Gazette, hidden behind a cushion. 'See for yourself.'

Mason took the paper. He remembered the article. 'This is her?'

'The description matches. She came in on that ship. And when I
called her Sylvia, she answered, so yes, it's her.'

Viktor! That explained why he didn't have a receipt for her. *She was a runaway!* And mother to his child…

'You're sure?' he said.

'Yes. We can go and ask her right now if you don't believe me—'

'No! Better we don't alert her.' He sat back down and topped up his wine glass. His hand was shaking. He downed the glass and poured another before topping up Mary's.

'Haven't you got something to say?' asked Mary.

Mason frowned.

She pointed to her red cheek.

'Yes. I – I'm sorry.'

He slipped off into his own thoughts again. He had to find out if it was true. There was no way she could stay now. If she were discovered, it could be argued in front of a judge that he'd harboured a runaway. He'd have to deny it. But she'd attacked a man. Attempted murder. If he turned her out and she was caught, she could well be hanged with his child in her womb.

'Mason, you've sacked people before. Are you getting soft? Next you'll be baking cakes for the niggers,' Mary scoffed.

Mason left without a further word, his hands were trembling, his head light from drink.

He crept out the backdoor, taking care to close it quietly. He found Sarah helping Musa muck out the stables, while the horses grazed in the paddock. He dismissed Musa.

Sarah stood silent, offering a small smile that tempered his anger. He ought to beat her. His fists were clenched but as he looked into the warmth of her brown eyes, he couldn't bring himself to hurt her.

She stepped forward and took his hand to press it to her cheek. Her beauty melted away the last of his anger. She reached up and kissed him on the lips. His body responded. He took her in his arms and kissed her back, forcing his tongue into her mouth. He shoved her to the ground and took her in the straw. He was rough to her, yet she didn't resist. They climaxed together in a chorus of groans, and as his anger ebbed, all his fears, his emotions swept aside in an act of unrestrained desire for the mother of his unborn child.

'Mason, I'm in love with you.'

She kissed him. He should have confronted her. He wasn't even sure of her name. But he couldn't bring himself to shatter the dream.

Mason walked back to the house, unburdened by a sense of resignation for his fate. He would throw the pieces up in the air, and they would land where they fell. Perhaps it was *her* influence; Mason was more accustomed to commanding the events that shaped his destiny, but in the afterglow of Sarah's embrace, he was happy to be a passenger to fate. It was time to throw caution to the wind.

***

Mary was sitting in the lounge, her eyes drooping from the empty bottle of wine on the pedestal beside her. Mason watched her from the doorway. He was calm.

'Mary. I have been with her. She bears my child.'

A wine glass smashed against the wall beside his head, spattering red droplets across his face and clothes. He didn't flinch.

'I knew it. You pig!'

'I haven't sold her. I love her. She will be staying here.'

The vitriol that spewed forth from Mary's mouth was unrepeatable. The wine bottle flew. Mason ducked. It smashed behind him. She bolted for him. He fled into the hallway and closed the door, keeping a grip of the handle to hold it shut. From behind the wood, the tirade of a woman scorned continued.

Zebedee appeared in the corridor.

'Is everything all right, Master?'

'Here, Zebedee. Hold the door shut. Don't let her out under any circumstances.'

***

Sylvia was shaded from the afternoon sun as she walked through the trees at the end of the lawn. She felt at ease. Day by day, she was becoming accustomed to the peace of her new surroundings. London felt like a different life. This was home now. Her secret was out. She'd endured Mason's affections, but she was certain he was hooked. She would only ever be his mistress, but for a poor girl who'd faced the gallows, there was no shame in that. She was certain Mason wanted, needed, a child more than anything. She hoped he may never know that the child wasn't his but Captain Reid's. For the first time in many years, she prayed. *God, please make it a son.* If it was, she'd be safe – at least for a few years.

Her prayers were interrupted by the smash of glass. She ran to the edge of the trees. The sitting room window was broken. Somebody was climbing out of the window. *Is that Mary?* The woman clambered out and fell to the ground. *What on earth is happening?*

Mary picked herself up, dusted herself down, then strode across the lawn, heading in Sylvia's direction. *Stand your ground,* she said to herself.

Mary's nostrils flared and her eyes were wild with fury. 'You harlot! You think you can come in here and take my husband? You bitch, you'll hang for what you've done!'

Sylvia stayed quiet. The woman was three sheets to the wind.

'I know all about you, Sylvia Coppell. I will write to Simon Bowler and tell him you're here. He can come and get you – and that bastard in your belly!'

Sylvia's teeth clenched and her body tensed.

'You'll hang, both of you, for what you did! I'll see to it. You wait, I'll see to it everyone will hear about this. You'll be a laughing stock!'

'You'll disgrace Mason, Mary.'

'No, Mason will have disgraced himself. It's about time the world sees him for what he is.'

She was spoiling for a fight. Sylvia knew better than to give her one; that was where Mason went wrong, by indulging her.

'As you wish, Mary.' Sylvia began to walk away.

'Come back here! Now!'

'No, Mary, the only person I answer to is Mason.'

'You bitch! Come back!'

'Goodbye Mary.' Sylvia took a deep breath to slow her pounding heart. She may have won this battle, but Mary could destroy her if she spilled her secrets.

She spent a fitful night's sleep, wondering how to make the best of her predicament. Amongst the muddle of her thoughts, her one trump card was Mason believing that the child was his.

***

The next morning, she was greeted by Mary, who had been waiting for her at the door to the house. She blocked the doorway, glaring down at Sylvia from the top of the steps. 'Your presence is required in the sitting room.'

A lump formed in Sylvia's throat as she passed Mary and made her way to the sitting room. Mason was standing at the window, his back to the room.

'Sit there, Miss Coppell,' ordered Mary, indicating a simple cane chair that had been deliberately placed in the centre of the room.

Sylvia did as instructed and folded her hands over her lap. Mason turned to sit on the settee and avoided her eyes. Mary took her position next to him but remained standing. To Sylvia, Mary's actions felt rehearsed.

'Since arriving, you have proved largely incapable of maintaining my husband's ledgers,' Mary began. 'You have managed to seduce him and claim to be pregnant with his child.'

Sylvia wanted to protest, but held her tongue.

'Conceiving a child has eluded Mason and I.' Mary forced herself to swallow. 'So, I am telling you now, that you will remain here, deliver your baby, at which point we shall adopt it as our own.'

Sylvia's mouth fell open. Mary paused to let her words sink in.

'Mason is the natural father, so he is entitled to do as he wishes.'

But he isn't! thought Sylvia, unable to speak the truth.

'We will raise the child as our own. It won't want for anything. We will afford it a more comfortable life, and a proper education, that will surpass anything you can offer it.'

It? They may be wealthy but the idea of abandoning her baby to be raised by these people – who drink themselves into oblivion each night, who smash their own windows when they row, who were so beset by evil that they scarcely noticed it amongst the window dressing of Christianity that adorned their existence. It was abhorrent and bought a tear to Sylvia's eye. As she wiped it away, she noticed a glint of satisfaction on Mary's face.

'And what about me?' said Sylvia, trying to keep her voice from wavering.

'You can stay while the infant is young,' said Mason, 'you can feed it, care for it, and then you will be free to leave once the child is weaned.'

'On one condition,' interrupted Mary. 'You stay away from my husband. If you tempt him or have even the briefest moment of unbecoming behaviour, we will report you to the court as a runaway. You will be punished for your crime and returned to the care of Simon Bowler – your rightful owner.'

Sylvia felt herself shrinking into the cane chair. They had her cornered.

'It is necessary that you leave before the child can form lasting memories of you,' Mary continued, rubbing salt into her wounds. 'But you will leave with a satisfactory reference, so you can start a new life elsewhere.'

How could you expunge a mother from her child's life? It was the most unnatural and intolerable punishment imaginable. Tears poured freely down her cheeks.

'Dismissed,' Mary hissed.

Sylvia gritted her teeth and offered Mary the most vengeful look she could summon. She glanced at Mason, hoping to find some pity.

'Stay away from my husband, you whore.'

Sylvia's emotions spilled over the moment she was clear of the house. She returned to her room and sobbed until her tears ran dry. She could muster only one constructive thought: hatred for every misfortune that had ever befallen her, in England and now here, in Virginia. But most of all, hatred for Mary. What sort of child would that woman raise? Certainly not one capable of love or kindness.

When she finally finished crying, she took herself for a walk to clear her head. As she returned, crossing the rear lawn, she happened upon Mary talking to Billy, outside the slave accommodation. Sylvia had never seen Mary conversing with the outdoor workers. Billy was nodding his understanding and when he noticed Sylvia approach, a knowing look appeared on his face. He grinned.

As Sylvia passed, close enough to overhear their conversation, Mary said in a pronounced voice, 'So, to reiterate, you will tell me if you see anything untoward occurring in your accommodation building.' Mary glared at Sylvia as she passed.

This, too, is another bit of Mary's theatre, to let me know who rules the roost, thought Sylvia as she returned to the sanctuary of her room.

She took a seat and thought back over what had occurred that morning. It had been Mason who had voiced that she *could* stay and raise the child. It must have been a concession he'd extracted from Mary. Sylvia was in no doubt that Mary wanted her gone, and was watching, waiting for any mistake. She felt very alone and vulnerable. Without Viktor, she had no allies – and no kindness. Sylvia would have to be very careful.

56

On the western road out of the town of Lancaster stood a solitary clapboard tavern. Smoke billowed from its brick chimney and candlelight shone from the ground-floor windows, the only brightness in a dull winter afternoon. A tall, lonesome figure swept the snow that dusted the pathway leading to his tavern. A whistle caught the man's attention, and he looked up from his sweeping, snowflakes landing on his bald head where they promptly melted.

'Mr Croghan, long time no see,' said the tavern keeper. His voice was quiet with a touch of resignation.

'Good afternoon to you, Paul. If you can stable my horses, I'll be staying the night.'

'You still owe me from your last stay.'

'Ah, put it on my book then.'

'Mr Croghan, sir, your book has been closed.'

Croghan grunted. He'd feared as much. His creditors had most likely complained such that no further bills could be accepted on his account. 'Very well. I'll write you a promissory note.'

Paul stopped sweeping and propped himself up with both hands cupped over the end of his broom handle. 'I'd prefer cash.'

'No cash, but as you can see, I've a caravan full of skins brought straight from the Ohio. You're welcome to some of these. Or I can stay elsewhere, if you'd rather…'

The tavern keeper's head bobbed from side to side as he weighed the matter in his mind. 'Very well. Put your horses in the barn. You can stay for the night.'

'Excellent. I'll be needing a warm meal and a warm woman!'

Croghan led his horses round the back to the wooden barn, where a black stable boy helped unload them and turned out fresh hay. Paul came out to supervise and helped himself to two of Croghan's pelts. Once all was in order, Croghan hurried inside to warm his frozen limbs by the fire. He didn't notice the tavern keeper whispering instructions to the stable boy.

Inside, ensconced at the bar with a beer in hand, Croghan swapped news with the other travellers, most of whom were concerned about the French incursion into the Ohio. It was cause for great excitement, as the patrons feared it might precipitate another war.

Croghan shook his head, the colour having returned to his cheeks. 'No. The French don't want another war any more than we do. Their whole presence in the north depends on the Atlantic being open for shipping. They have no market here for their goods. Everything has to make it back to France, so the last thing they want is to rouse the Royal Navy.'

The men deferred to his knowledge; after all, he was the only man amongst them to have ventured beyond the mountains. He beat them at cards, ate a full meal and then bedded Lilly, the tavern prostitute. The next morning, he slept in, savouring the comfort of a bed after so long on the frontier. After a breakfast of eggs and bacon, he summoned the stable boy and told him to ready his animals.

Sated, rested and warm, Croghan slipped outside when Paul was distracted. The weather was fine, cold but sunny, suitable for his travels. He found the barn locked and no sign of the stable boy.

He reluctantly returned to the tavern, where Paul was seated by the fireplace, reading last week's newspaper.

'Your lad was supposed to ready my animals,' Croghan complained.

The tavern keeper grunted. 'I'm afraid you won't be leaving just yet. Some people want to see you.'

'Now hang on,' snapped Croghan, stepping forward.

From behind his newspaper, Paul produced a pistol, pointed straight at Croghan.

'Stop there, Mr Croghan. If you want to live, you'll go and wait in the tap room.'

'What the feckin' blazes...'

Paul cocked the hammer, ready to fire.

Croghan raised his palms. 'You made your point. Nobody's needing to be hurt today.' Satisfied the situation was calming, he asked, 'Who wants to see me so bad?'

'Edward Shippen.'

Without a further word, Croghan went to the tap room and helped himself to a cider. Shippen was the largest of his creditors, one of the wealthiest merchants in Philadelphia. Paul must have sent the slave boy to fetch him, and would no doubt recover the cost of Croghan's stay as a reward.

It was late afternoon by the time Shippen's tall frame strode purposefully into the tavern, flanked by two bodyguards. Seeing Croghan, he pulled up a chair and sat himself very close. 'Hello George. Glad to see you've recovered from your illness.'

'Fully, Mr Shippen, thank you.'

Shippen had a long nose, flabby cheeks, and a cold stare indicative of a calculating mind. Despite his dapper clothing and air of civilised respectability, Shippen was a man who didn't suffer fools and took no prisoners. Those who crossed him often disappeared or mysteriously suffered life-changing injuries. He lit his pipe and blew a fug of tobacco smoke at Croghan.

Croghan's usual approach was to warm his opponents up a little, but he knew this would only provoke Shippen. Instead, he sat quietly.

'You're a man in demand, Croghan. There's a long list of people who want paying. Seems you've been accepting more contracts than you can fulfil...'

'People want what I can supply—' Croghan interrupted.

'I don't doubt it. Many succumb to your horseshit. Not me, Croghan. Now, what have you got for me?' Shippen demanded.

'I have fifteen loads of buckskin in the barn here.'

Shippen nodded to his companions, who left to take possession of the pelts.

'Is that it?'

Croghan nodded.

Shippen's jaw tensed. 'Take one step in Philadelphia, and you'll be going straight to a debtors' prison.'

Shippen was also a judge, so could make good on the threat. He took out a slip of paper from the inner pocket of his velvet jacket.

'But you're no use to me in prison, Croghan. I want the rest of my money.' He slid the paper across the table. 'This licence permits you to move freely between here and the Ohio – provided you send word to meet me here. If I hear of you paying anyone before me, you'll be in gaol. Do I make myself clear?'

'Clear as water, chief. Only, you should know, the French and their Indians are moving into the Ohio.'

'Then have the Iroquois throw them out,' said Shippen impatiently.

'Our Iroquois aren't much of a threat. They're frightened. They talk of abandoning us.' Before Shippen could interrupt, Croghan continued, 'They lost confidence in Pennsylvania when we refused to build the fort they wanted. Virginia haven't made good on it either. Nobody has ammunition to trade, so as the Iroquois see it, we haven't protected them, so why should they protect us?'

Shippen looked irritated.

'Listen, I'm losing here too,' said Croghan. 'I was lucky as the devil to get this load out. I may not be able to do so again. Throw me in gaol if you want, but if you want your money, we need to get the French out.'

'So, what would you suggest?'

Croghan was thinking on his feet now. 'A gift would…'

'Damn their gifts, they've had enough out of our pockets!' snarled Shippen.

'The Iroquois need food. Their supplies are running thin as the Huron encroach on their hunting grounds. If you were to give me the money, I could trade it for flour and gunpowder…'

'Give you more money?' said Shippen, the incredulity plain on his pale face.

'Fine, then go get the furs yourself.'

'Damn you, Croghan!'

'Damn me, sure, but I'm not the problem, here. It's France. If you want your money, I need to take something back with me – otherwise I can't make good.'

'I've given you enough—'

'But this isn't about me. I'm not asking for *your* money. Just dip your fingers in the Philadelphia treasury; after all, Indian bribes are a legitimate expense. I'll get food and ammunition with it, then bring you all the skins I can carry. You'll sell them, get your money – and then some.'

'How do you expect to get ammunition?'

'I know someone.' Croghan sensed Shippen softening. Using colonial funds meant he had nothing to lose. 'It's a simple solution, Edward, and we're both after the same thing.'

Shippen leaned back in his chair and regarded Croghan through narrowed eyes. After a considered pause, he replied, 'Very well, Croghan. I'll take your pelts now, and I'll be back here tomorrow with a government bill. But I want everything that comes out of the Ohio until your slate is clean. Understood?'

Croghan extended his hand, but rather than shake it, Shippen got up and left, muttering about the interminable Irish.

Croghan breathed a sigh of relief. That had gone well, all things considered. Of course, the ammunition had been a lie. Nor would he buy the Indians food. But with some ready cash, he'd hire the men and materials needed for this damn fort at the forks, and build the wretched thing himself.

Tanacharison would be happy. Croghan would get his land.

He'd pay the colony back in due course. The fort would be his and if Virginia wanted it, they'd have to buy it from him.

As he was staying here another night, he poured himself more cider and went in search of Lilly.

57

February 1st, 1754
The Capitol Building, Williamsburg

'Governor, I have but twenty men, all vagrants and deserters. I scarce consider I'll have any left by the time we cross the mountains,' protested George in the Governor's private chamber.

'What would you have me do, Lieutenant Colonel?' asked Dinwiddie. The Governor's portly frame filled his chair, his hands raised in resignation.

'Let me offer them pay.'

'But that we could. Fry and his faction won't vote the funds through the House. My hands are tied.'

'Governor,' George leant over the desk and faced him at a distance too close to be considered polite. 'The King has an expectation that the Ohio lands will be claimed for his Empire. How do you think he'll feel when he learns his man in Virginia couldn't organise enough men to fill a cricket team in defence of his honour?'

'What are you saying, Washington?'

'That I will write to His Majesty myself, and let it be known that you did precious little when it mattered most! You can look forward to a posting in India, I imagine. I hear the food is terrible.'

'Now steady yourself, Washington, you have a bloody nerve...'

'I *need* a bloody nerve, to fulfil this mission. I've seen the French, remember – we won't last ten minutes unless we prepare ourselves.' George retreated from the Governor's space. Dinwiddie rubbed his forehead.

'I need men, I need money. So do you, Governor.' With that, George left the room.

Washington had timed his approach well: the House of Burgesses was in session. Dinwiddie collared Fry in the corridor after the morning session and ushered him up to the Governor's empty council chamber.

'Mr Fry, I have good news for you,' said Dinwiddie, as he pulled out a chair for Fry. Dinwiddie remained standing.

Fry looked suspicious.

'I'll come to the point; the Council and I have appointed you to lead His Majesty's troops to repel the French from the Ohio.'

Fry's frown deepened during the long silence. Then he erupted:

'Nonsense! You're out of your mind. That's Washington's job.'

'Not any more. It's yours. He'll be your second in command. The mission is too important to be left to a colonial. His Majesty will be comforted to know the charge is being led by a true Englishman.'

'But I'm no royalist. Quite the bloody opposite,' protested Fry, squirming in his seat.

'Be that as it may, your King requires this service of you.'

'Never! The Ohio is your madcap scheme.'

'It's the King's actually, he granted the land after all. And you don't have any choice. Your family has military experience.'

'Yes, fighting for Cromwell – against the King!'

'Well, times are changing, now you're on His Majesty's side.' Dinwiddie sat down beside him. 'Let me make the decision easier for you, Joshua.' He lowered his voice. 'If you don't agree, I'll veto every single bill you introduce to the house. You'll be so ineffective, your electorate will boot you out. I'll have you struck off the judicial circuit, you'll never practise law again, and I'll have you sent back to Britain on the charge of treason.'

'It wouldn't stand!'

'There's only one way to find out, Judge Fry. You know how fickle the law can be. Take the risk and they'll stretch your neck. I could have words with the right people – they'd be delighted to have one less republican in the country.'

'You bastard!'

'Come, Joshua, it's a small service. Take the men over the hills, build a fort – nobody need get hurt. And if you do, I'll see you get a seat on the Governor's council. Can't say fairer than that.'

Fry's demeanour changed. 'A seat in the Upper House?'

'Indeed. Lifetime peerage for you, Colonel Fry. If you can't beat them, join them.'

'Colonel?'

'Yes, it's your militia now.'

Fry looked round the oval office, taking in the chandelier, the mahogany table, the oil paintings, the plush rugs.

Every man has his price, thought Dinwiddie. 'So, you won't oppose the funds for the militia?'

'I accept.'

***

The next morning, Dinwiddie summoned Washington to his office.

'Lieutenant Colonel, good morning. Would you like the good news or the bad?'

George was unsettled by Dinwiddie's easy demeanour, too relaxed and carefree for a man at the centre of an international crisis.

'Good news is always in short supply,' said George.

'Indeed. You'll have your money. A pound a week for each man who completes the service, paid in arrears.'

'Terrific!' said George, shaking his fist, as much in relief as excitement.

'But,' added Dinwiddie, 'you'll be commanded by Colonel Fry, who has agreed to lead the mission on behalf of the colony.'

'What?'

'You heard me. Fry's in charge.'

'You double-dealing bastard—'

'Politics, George.'

'Damn you, Governor!'

'Enough!' shouted Dinwiddie, his cheeks reddening as his temper flared. 'You'll show me respect, you petulant shit.'

Chastened, George took a deep breath and fought to control the anger that bubbled up inside him.

'Look, Washington, I like you, you're a good man. But this has the potential to blow up in our faces. If you'll heed the advice of an older man, it's far better to let Fry take the force of the blast, don't you think?'

'No,' said George. 'The man's a rat. He'll be hopeless. If we're successful, he'll be insufferable. More likely, we'll all be killed.'

'Your time will come, George, trust me. I have a bad feeling about this matter.'

'To hell with your theories! I'm leaving.'

George stormed out of the room and pounded down the staircase two steps at a time. He saddled his horse and rode for Alexandria. He wouldn't be waiting for Fry or anyone else. This was his mission, and he would show those bloated politicians they were lucky to have him. As he cantered out of Williamsburg, there was one thought on his mind: *Joshua Fry, of all people. Lawrence would be turning in his grave.*

58

Sylvia woke with a start as her bedroom door swung open. Someone staggered into the room and slammed the door shut. She scurried backwards in her bed, the headboard blocking her retreat. In the dark, she fumbled down the side of the mattress for the knife she'd stolen from Bowler. She couldn't find it. The figure approached the bed and sat down. She could smell the rum.

'I've missed you so badly.'

It was Mason. It had been almost two weeks since Mary had issued her ultimatum, and Sylvia and Mason had barely spoken since. He reached for her. 'Come here.'

'You scared me, Mason!' she hissed.

'Ahh,' he dismissed her fears. 'I had to see you.'

'Mason, you can't stay. You must leave. Now!'

He grabbed her by the arms, pulling her towards him. She struggled to escape his grip, but he pressed against her. The smell of rum was overpowering.

'I've missed you…'

'Mason, you can't!' She did her best to keep her voice low so as not to wake Billy or Granville. 'If Mary finds out you're visiting me, I'm done for!'

'She won't know,' he slurred, and tried to kiss her. She turned her head away. 'Come here.' He groped her breast.

'Mason, no. Stop. Please.'

His full weight was on her now, flattening her on the bed. He tried to kiss her, but she clamped her mouth shut, so he licked her instead, with all the romance of a heifer cleaning a newborn calf. She pushed him away, but he pinned one arm against the mattress and lay his forearm over her throat. 'Come on, I want to make love to the mother of my child.'

It crossed her mind to tell him the baby wasn't even his, but self-preservation bested her urge for spite. His hips began to gyrate as he prepared himself. She knew there was nothing she could do, gasping for air under the pressure on her throat. Tears welled in her eyes as his fingers reached under her nightdress and prodded between her legs. She winced in pain as he forced them inside her.

She lay there hoping it would be quick. Sensing her resistance had quelled, he untied his breeches, reaching for his manhood. She thought about the knife – could she threaten him? He might beat her. Or – she could kill him.

'You're the most beautiful woman in the New World,' he slurred as he slumped on top of her. He tried to kiss her again, forcing himself into her. She contorted in pain as he found his destination. Tears trickled from her eyes as she lay trapped under his pounding weight, clouded in the miasma of his breath, listening to his grunts. One quick stab and this could all be over, she thought. She reached her spare hand out to the side of the mattress once more and felt for the knife. Her fingertips brushed cold steel. Mason's thrusts quickened, his breathing shallow. She thought better of it; killing Mason would only make her life worse. She closed her eyes and thought of London. The life she'd left behind. The filth and stench of Newgate prison. Her brother Jacob, who'd been sentenced to death for the crime of helping her. Then poor Abe, killed outside the theatre in Covent Garden. All her past sufferings made this one easier to bear while Mason's body writhed as he purged himself of his seed. He reached to kiss her again. She turned her head.

'You're heaven,' he groaned as he withdrew.

She said nothing as he got up and began to make himself decent. Words were wasted on a drunk. He bid her goodnight as he left the room. She poured some water from the jug and cleaned herself, then looked back at her bed in the moonlight. Was this all that life had in store for her?

***

The following night, Sylvia returned to her room, her mind still a jumble of what to do. She'd kept to herself all day, taking care not to cross paths with Mason or Mary. Grace had left two hard-boiled eggs on her table. For all the perilousness of her predicament, she hadn't lost her appetite; perhaps it was the baby that kept her hungry. She nibbled at an egg, lost in her worries, when the door creaked open. It was Billy, his hat removed and held in his hand, exposing his greasy hair.

'Hello darlin'.'

Sylvia was filled with dread.

'Seems you had yourself a visitor in the night?'

'Billy, I was asleep.'

'I wasn't. I heard him come in and I don't need to be a wise man to guess what happened next.' Billy came forward to sit on her bed, leaning back against the wall with his legs spread wide. 'See, Lady Mary wants to know if you're sleeping with her husband. But the way I figure, I can keep a secret.' He winked.

'What are you saying, Billy?'

'Let me ride you, and she won't hear nothing about you and Mason.'

'Get out of my room, you rat!' She flung her plate at him. It smashed on the wall behind him. She dived across the bed and grabbed her knife. Billy leapt to his feet. She brandished the knife at him. 'You come near me, and I swear to God, I'll geld you.'

Billy raised his palms and backed towards the door. 'Careful, lady, I was just offering to help you out, that's all.'

Sylvia spat at his feet. He ran from the room and she exhaled a deep sigh. *When will this ever end?* she asked herself. If Billy told Mary what he'd heard, it was all the justification she would need to see Sylvia out on her ear. She sat back down and finished her eggs, allowing her temper to cool. Her mind was clear: she had to take matters into her own hands, before it was too late.

59

February 9th, 1754
Fitzbarton Plantation

Sylvia was at a crossroads. She knew what she did next would define the rest of her life – and the life inside her. She sat in her room, unaware how fast her foot was tapping. Mary had threatened her, and she was in no doubt the woman would keep her word. How she knew about Simon Bowler, Sylvia wasn't sure. He must have reported her missing. She looked out of the window at the white moon in the night sky and thought of all the twists in the path that had brought her here, an ocean away from her past. She had overcome them all, so far. And yet, misfortune continued to assail her.

She tied her hair back and tiptoed out of the accommodation block, then darted across the rear lawn and around the side of the house. Candles were burning in the dining room. She pressed herself against the brickwork and listened at the window's edge. She could hear Mary shouting at Mason, though her words were muffled.

She waited for what felt like hours while the two of them went in circles, shouting and threatening each other. Mason would leave the room. Mary would follow. Sylvia would scuttle round the outside of the house until she found them again. Doors slammed, objects thrown. She found herself feeling sorry for Mason. Mary was relentless. Finally, he went to bed. Mary followed, her tirade continuing. Sylvia hoisted herself up through the broken window of the lounge, which Mary had climbed out of earlier that day. The room was cool and dark. She moved across the floor, treading lightly lest the floorboards creak, then cracked opened the door to the hallway and peeked through. The hall was empty. Grace and Zebedee were nowhere to be seen, presumably knowing better than to be caught in their master's crossfire.

At the top of the stairs, Mary was banging on Mason's door, screaming at him to come out. Her voice was slurred. She repeated herself endlessly. Sylvia waited, marvelling at the madness of it all. These two had more comfort and possessions than most of London's poor put together, and yet they couldn't see their fortune for what it was, choosing instead to invest all their energies in fighting one another.

As Mary pounded on the door, Sylvia wondered whatever had possessed them to marry. Perhaps it had been arranged. Sylvia's eyes, now well-adjusted to the dark, scanned the shapes of the hallway. The door to the dining room was opposite. It brought back memories of when Mason had fallen for her, taking her on the table. From that spark, a fire had grown, and Sylvia had known just how to fan the flames. In fact, she was poised to pour oil on the inferno.

Finally, Mary fell quiet. Sylvia could hear her footsteps as she staggered to her room. The door opened and closed. The house fell silent, bar the gentle tick-tock of the hallway clock. Sylvia waited an hour. When the clock chimed one, she removed her shoes and went out into the hallway and climbed the staircase, her bare feet taking one step at a time, pausing whenever the wood threatened to creak. Her heart pounded so hard, she could hear it pulsing in her ear. Pressing herself against the wall, she edged past Mason's door. It was silent within. She went past another two doors until she came to Mary's. Her ear against the cold wood: nothing.

She rested her hand on the cold brass door handle and very gently began to turn it. There was a small click as the latch cleared the plate. Sylvia froze.

The clock struck the half hour.

She pushed the door ajar. She could hear Mary's breathing, slow and loud, the sleep of a drunk. Sylvia slipped into the room and pushed the door to, without closing it. Everything was pitch black. Sylvia took one step towards the bed and stopped. Mary continued to snore gently. Then another step. Within a minute, she was standing over the woman who had threatened her only hours earlier. Whose actions could see her hang. Beneath her, Mary was oblivious. Sylvia saw an image in her mind's eye of what Mary would have looked like as a child. Petite, before she'd fattened herself, her innocent face and childlike hopes and dreams, before the drink had taken her into its barbed blanket. That little girl would never have imagined how her life might have ended. Sylvia reached over Mary's body and lifted a pillow from the far side of the bed.

Here at the crossroads, it was time to decide. She pushed the pillow down, smothering Mary's head. Disconcertedly, nothing happened. She kept the pressure on. Seconds passed. Mary remained still. *Am I doing it wrong?*

A muffled cry was accompanied by a jerk of Mary's arms and legs. Sylvia pushed harder, leaning her full weight on the woman. The gasps for air and dampened cries for help were alarmingly loud in the silence. Mary's body writhed as it fought for air. Sylvia gritted her teeth and pushed with all the might of a young woman whose life depended on it. Mary flapped and wriggled like a fish out of water. Her convulsions pushed Sylvia back, loosening the pillow's grip. Forcing the pillow back into place, Sylvia leapt on top of Mary, whose muted cries for help reverberated round the dark room.

Finally, after what felt like a precarious eternity, Mary's wriggling stopped. The groans stopped. Mary's body slackened beneath her. Sylvia held the pillow in place. Aside from Sylvia's pounding heart, everything was deathly still. She waited for five more minutes. Certain Mary was dead, she replaced the pillow and climbed off the bed. Her hands trembling, she did her best to straighten the sheets and hide any signs of struggle and left the room.

There could be only one queen bee in this hive.

60

February 10th, 1754
Fitzbarton Plantation

Mason had risen early and spent the morning outside. He'd ridden his horse around the perimeter of the plantation twice, eager to distance himself from the wrath that he knew waited for him indoors. As the fresh air cleared his aching head, he'd searched his soul for answers to his predicament, which took on a new light in the dawn of a fresh day. The quote from James 4:17 kept appearing in his thoughts: 'So whoever knows the right thing to do and fails to do it, for him it is sin.' *Will I be condemned to hell for abandoning my wife? Or my child?* In the eyes of man's law, he was required to stand by his wife. Bastards were tolerated, but their parents couldn't live in sin before God. Mostly he thought of himself. There was little to be gained by safeguarding the future of the plantation in this world, if he himself were condemned in the next.

The prospect of hell made Mason shudder. He returned the horse to the stable, his mind made up. Doing the right thing meant selling Sarah and honouring his marriage. He would listen to his head, not his heart.

He returned indoors to inform Mary of his decision. In time, she would forgive his transgression. Downstairs, the house was quiet. He found Grace on her hands and knees, scrubbing the kitchen floor. She informed him she had yet to see Mrs Fitzbarton today.

'Go and fetch the idle woman. Once she's decent, I'll speak with her in the dining room. Then you can bring me some lunch.'

He left and, having retrieved the newspaper from the sitting room, took a seat in the dining room. He reread the article about Sarah's escape – or Sylvia's, as she was supposedly called. He would confront her with it after lunch.

His reading was interrupted by a scream. Heavy footsteps pounded down the stairs. Grace appeared at the dining room doorway, her eyes wide with terror.

'What is it?' asked Mason, sensing there was a problem.

'She's dead!'

Mason frowned at her. What did she mean "dead"?

'The lady isn't moving.'

Mason leapt to his feet and barged past Grace to run up the stairs.

There she was: his wife, motionless in bed. He stood in the doorway staring at her ribs, willing them to rise and fall with her breath. Her eyes were open. Her mouth was open. She was gone. He retreated from the room, supporting himself against the wall as he backed away. His mind a scatter of thoughts, he slumped to the floor to sit on the top step. Grace stared up at him from the dining room doorway, shock etched onto her face. Mason nodded at her.

'She's dead.'

***

The coroner arrived the following morning to inspect Mrs Fitzbarton's corpse. Sylvia waited with Grace at the bottom of the stairs while Mason showed the coroner, Mr Johnson, up to the bedroom.

Johnson carried a leather bag in his hand, and his medium build looked comparatively small as he ascended the stairs next to Mason. The coroner's inquisitive eyes suggested a sharp mind behind his kind face. 'Tell me, Mr Fitzbarton, your relationship with your wife, how would you describe it?'

'We'd been married for longer than I care to remember – very happily, for the most part,' added Mason.

They disappeared into Mary's room, where she had remained untouched.

Sylvia strained to hear their conversation, but Johnson spoke in low, measured tones. From what she could gather, there wasn't a hint that anything suspicious had occurred. She felt a moment's respite for her frayed nerves. She hadn't slept a wink since the deed. Reliving the events over and over in her mind, every waking moment was subjected to its own post-mortem, as she sought signs of suspicion towards her from others.

Her fitful thoughts were interrupted by Grace sneezing.

The two women shared a look. Sylvia sensed Grace was fearful. She invited the house slave to share her thoughts, 'You can speak.'

'I not sure how the master react, now his wife dead.'

Sylvia shrugged. Her mind turned back to Christmas, when Grace had feared losing her domestic privileges to her. That same fear was most likely troubling her now.

'It will be all right, Grace,' Sylvia consoled her. 'We'll come through this. Mason needs us now more than ever.'

Grace looked comforted by her reassurance.

Mason came down the stairs, his face ashen.

Sylvia contemplated holding out her hand for him but thought better of it. He couldn't look at her yet.

'Grace, fetch some tea for Mr Johnson,' said Sylvia. Once she'd left, Sylvia touched Mason's elbow, 'How are you?'

He let forth a long sigh. 'I can't believe it. She has been a constant in my life, and now she's gone. She'll…she'll never berate me again!' He snorted in morbid amusement. 'I wonder if I'll miss having things thrown at me and being scratched?'

He finally met her gaze. She saw the thought appear in his mind. He pulled her into the study at the far end of the hall.

'I must ask you, Sarah… For her to die – so suddenly…' Again, he couldn't hold her gaze.

'What are you trying to say, Mason?'

'Nothing. Nothing. It's just – well – since you arrived so recently, it looks…'

'Mason, I fear you're about to accuse me of having some hand in this.'

'No. Well, it's…' He shook his head, 'I'm sorry, my mind is all over the place, I shouldn't have said anything.'

'Come.' She nestled into him to offer comfort.

Their embrace was cut short by the sound of footsteps on the stairs.

Mason went back into the hall and Sylvia stood listening at the door, her heart pounding in her chest.

'She appears to have died of natural causes in her sleep,' came Mr Johnson's voice. 'Her eyes are open, so she must have woken at the final moment, I doubt she suffered much.'

Sylvia felt a sense of comfort hearing that.

'There are no signs of distress, so I'm going to record the death as natural.'

Sylvia thought she might be sick with relief.

'That's a comfort to me, thank you,' said Mason.

'The body will still need to be viewed by a local jury. That may take some days, so I suggest you bury her in a shallow grave and exhume her when they attend. It's just procedure, you understand. But they may want to speak with you and your household.'

Sylvia felt a lump in her throat, and her panic heightened at the sound of more footsteps. She peeked out to see Grace returning with a tea tray.

'Mr Johnson, please, will you take some refreshment with me in the sitting room?' said Mason.

'Splendid, thank you.'

Once they had disappeared, Sylvia slipped out of the study, and went past the sitting room, steadying herself with her hand pressed against the wall. She felt she was walking with someone else's legs. Arriving in the kitchen, she waited for Grace to return. The fact that Mason had felt the need to question her involvement had unsettled her. It was too obvious – after all, she was likely to benefit from Mary's death.

Grace returned.

'Shall we take a tot of rum?' said Sylvia.

The slave looked terrified at the suggestion.

'How about I take one for me and share some with you?'

Grace nodded. Sylvia went into the pantry and drew a draft of rum in a small glass, trying to still her shaking hands. She took a swig, refilled it, then passed it to Grace. The woman shuddered as the liquor made its way down.

'It sad about Mrs Fitzbarton, but if you excuse me, she had a bad spirit, that woman,' Grace said heavily.

Sylvia nodded. 'She must have been difficult to live with.' She took a swig of rum and passed the glass back to Grace. 'You could understand if Mason had had enough.'

'Sarah, you don't think he—?'

'I hope not,' Sylvia shrugged. 'But you know him better than me...'

Grace frowned as she considered the possibility.

'I'm sure he wouldn't have,' said Sylvia, satisfied she had planted a seed of doubt that may take root in the minds of the slaves.

***

The following morning, Sylvia bumped into Billy outside her room. She suspected he'd been waiting there for her.

'Mighty odd, wouldn't you say? Mary dying all sudden like that,' Billy said, his arms crossed.

'What are you implying?'

'Just saying.'

Sylvia didn't have the patience for Billy's games. 'Shall we go and ask Mason if he did it? Makes sense. He can have me whenever he wants now. What do you think he'll do to you, if he's capable of killing his wife?'

Billy's demeanour turned sheepish; she'd called his bluff. 'Worked out well for you, though, didn't it?' he spat.

'We'll see how things work out. No sense making an enemy of me though, is there?'

He squinted at her.

'Mason would be interested to learn that you tried to blackmail me for sex,' she pushed on. 'No master likes having his mistress interfered with. Would be some repercussions for the perpetrator, wouldn't you think?'

'Bitch.'

Sylvia grinned. 'Goodbye Billy.' He was no match for her.

61

February 25th, 1754
Fitzbarton Plantation

The jury members came to exhume Mary. From her bed in the workers' accommodation, Sylvia could hear the repeated crunch of a spade digging into the earth outside. Since her crime, she'd become entangled in her fears and had worried herself sick. Frayed nerves, no sleep, unable to eat, she'd taken ill in the night. Stabbing stomach pains were accompanied by violent diarrhoea and a shivering fever. She lay, motionless, her knees tucked up against her belly, her nightdress cold and damp. Eyes tightly closed, she was too ill to worry further. Every half hour she dashed for her chamber pot and filled it with rotten brown water that spattered the porcelain, filling the room with a hellish stench. She couldn't muster the strength to empty it. Nor could she open her window, for she was so cold, the icy winter air would cut through her. Drifting in and out of consciousness, she wondered if she would survive, and at points felt so ill she no longer cared if she did. Not even the thought of the baby in her belly could rouse any fight in her. Never previously persuaded by religious beliefs, she feared the Lord was punishing her. She would have even contemplated prayer, had she the energy.

The door opened. It was Grace, bearing a cup of rainwater and a biscuit. Sylvia couldn't face a single bite. Grace took the chamber pot away, then returned and dabbed the sweat from Sylvia's forehead with a cloth. Sylvia felt Grace's hand tunnel under the cover and touch her back.

'We need to get you dry.'

Sylvia grunted.

Grace drew back the cover and lifted Sylvia up to peel the sodden nightdress off over her head and shoulders. She gasped.

'You are with child!'

Sylvia's head bobbed up and down, too ill to deny it. While Grace stood staring at her naked body, she curled back up and pulled the cover over her. Grace dragged her back up and wrestled her into a clean nightgown and tucked her back in.

'You must eat.' Grace held the biscuit to Sylvia's mouth. Sylvia took a small bite. 'Is it Mason's child?'

Sylvia nodded. Her eyes still closed.

Grace said a prayer: 'Please God, watch over them, bring mother and baby salvation. God, forgive our master,' she hesitated, 'his sins, let them not cast a shadow on his brood.'

There was a knock at the door. In the doorway stood an elderly man, spectacles and the short white curls of a wig. He sported a portly belly that struggled against his waistcoat.

'Good God, it smells like Satan's closet in here!' he said, covering his nose.

'The lady is sick.'

'I'm with the jury, I need to speak to her,' he said, tilting his head towards the open door.

'She too ill.'

'Who is she?'

'Sarah. She work here.'

'I haven't seen her before. Is she new?'

Grace nodded.

'Another one just off the boat, unused to our climate. I'll fetch the doctor, he's out with the corpse in the garden. He can examine her.'

Grace shook her head. 'No, no, no. No need. She all right. She need rest.'

The man frowned.

Sylvia lay still, her eyes closed, listening to this, her heart quickening at the prospect of being inspected by a doctor. One look at her would reveal her being with child. This would inevitably raise the most awkward questions in light of Mary's sudden death. Fortunately,

Grace had had the good sense to deflect the inquiry.

Grace stroked Sylvia's head. 'I care for her.'

His concerns assuaged, the juryman continued with his inquiry, 'Tell me, what was Mr Fitzbarton's relationship like with his wife?'

'Fine. She drink a lot,' Grace answered. 'I always say she drink herself into her grave.'

'I see. Did Mr Fitzbarton have cause to restrain her?'

Grace shook her head.

'How would you describe his relationship with this woman here?'

'Sarah, not here long. Mrs Fitzbarton in charge of us house servants. Master not have much to do with us.'

'I see. Well, young women have a habit of…'

'Mr Fitzbarton very religious man.'

Grace was doing a great job, but Sylvia's guts began to gurgle. Not daring to leap from the bed for her chamber pot, she tensed her tummy muscles.

The man continued, 'Still her arrival does create complications, I'll need to interview her, can you please prop her up…'

Sylvia's guts evacuated. The gushing sound was muffled by the cover, but the stink filled the room. Grace lifted the cover, exposing a brown mess on the nightgown and the mattress.

'Good God,' the man retched at the sight and dashed out of the room in search of clean air.

Sylvia, too tired to fret over her humiliation, hoped she might have evaded her interrogation.

***

Two days later, she emerged from the putrid air of her room and gingerly walked towards the house. She was short of breath by the time she made it to the back door. Nonetheless, she felt wonderful to be up, moving, breathing fresh air and feeling ready for some sustenance. Grace made her a plate of fried eggs and bread, which she devoured at the kitchen table. With each mouthful, her strength returned.

Mason was out. Grace explained he'd taken the boat to Alexandria the previous morning. Sylvia was relieved not to have to contend with him until she was more recovered. She had been wondering endlessly how he'd be with her. Would he be suspicious of her, or would he welcome her affection?

'How is he?' she asked.

'Master is fine. I hear him crying once. Otherwise, he looks tired. Very quiet.'

Sylvia nodded. 'Do you think he did it?'

Grace shrugged. 'Maybe he want you as his wife. You're having his baby.'

'He forced himself on me.'

Grace nodded knowingly. She didn't appear surprised. *Had Mason bedded his slaves?* Sylvia wondered. There was a mulatto child with the other workers; it stood to reason it was his.

'It is better for a slave not to ask, or to hope, but whatever happen, the lady is dead…'

Sylvia shuddered as her thoughts took her back to Mary's bedroom. She'd felt the resistance in her arms as she had squeezed the last drop of life out of Mary. Her stomach turned at the thought.

'…this can't be changed. I do hope that the master marries you. You would be a much better woman. You are kind to us. Your heart is good. My people are whipped and beaten…'

Sylvia stopped listening as Grace reeled off her list of grievances. She'd heard what she wanted to hear. They trusted her. Grace would, she was certain, speak for all the negroes, they would support her. Whether it would count for much, time would tell.

Loud knocks echoed through the house. They walked together to the front door and Sylvia opened it to the sight of two men in cocked hats and long coats. Behind them was a horse and cart, on which rested a large black trunk.

'Where do you want it?' said the taller of the men.

'What is it?' asked Sylvia.

The man shrugged. 'Came in from London two days ago. Addressed to Mr Mason Fitzbarton.' He looked her up and down. 'You his wife? Lucky devil, eh!'

'You can bring it inside the door, thank you,' she said curtly.

Minutes later, the trunk was lowered onto the floorboards.

'Right then, we need paying.'

'I don't have anything.'

'A note to put it on your master's account will do. Or we can take it back.'

'He's not here.'

'So? You can write it. That'll do for me. Two and six will cover it.'

Sylvia ducked into the study to scribble out a bill, signing it with Mason's name. She stopped to look at it. How it must be, to be Mason. Able to write his own money, and have people accept it without question. To a poor girl from London, it was unfathomable. The man accepted it without hesitation, which put a thought in her mind, but that was for another day.

She and Grace unfastened the buckles on the leather straps that secured the trunk. They lifted the lid to reveal fine paper overlaying neatly folded clothes. Ladies' clothes. Boxes too, arranged in neat rows. The largest contained a lady's hat.

'Mason ordered this for Mary,' said Sylvia. 'I wrote the order. It was the first thing he had me do.'

Grace whistled. Zebedee came up the corridor to see what the noise was.

'We can't leave it here,' said Sylvia. 'You two carry it upstairs to Mary's room.'

'I don't want to go in there...' muttered Grace.

'Oh, come on, you can't avoid it forever. Better for Mr Fitzbarton not to find it abandoned here on his return.'

Without further protest, the two slaves struggled upstairs at either end of the trunk. Rather than watch them, Sylvia went into the study, where she waited until they had returned to their duties.

A few minutes later, she crept up the stairs and into Mary's room. The sight of the bed, stripped of linen, gave her pause. She closed the door behind her. She would have to make her peace with the memories in this room. Mason, if he was of a mind to accept her, might insist that she sleep in here.

She opened the trunk and carefully sorted through all the items. More goods than she'd ever owned. She inhaled the sweet, floral perfume, dabbing some onto her wrists and neck, then picked up a blouse with a décolletage neck, rubbing the silk fabric between her fingers. It was too fine to resist. She slipped off her shift, and buttoned up the blouse, her nipples stiffening from the caress of the material. It was too big around her waist, but that could be adjusted. She pulled it tight and tucked the excess into the back of her dress. Returning to the trunk, she found a box of jewellery and took out a silver necklace. In the mirror on top of the wooden drawers, she watched herself don the necklace, centring the sparkling pendant between the cleavage exposed by the blouse. It was surely the most expensive thing she'd ever handled. Only in her wildest dreams had she imagined herself wearing such a precious article. Mary had no need for it now. As Sylvia fondled it, she thought how different her life might have been, had she been born rich. She turned her shoulders, and held back her hair, posing in the mirror. Her face looked drawn, the illness robbing her of the fuller features she'd developed since her arrival here.

Seeing herself adorned with such beautiful things, she knew for certain: she wanted it. All of it. As she admired her new appearance, she saw an image of Mary's sour face staring at her from the mirror. Sylvia stared back unflinching. *How do I make my peace with this?*

'You're in God's care now, Mary,' she whispered. 'May it prove happier than your life here.' As the image in her mind's eye faded, she saw herself again. Could she live with what she'd done? *People die all the time.* All the dead bodies in London, nobody ever offered a prayer for them. Why should Mary be afforded any better? All her life, Sylvia had been used and abused. Now it was her turn in the light. She pushed her bust forward and ran a hand over her bump. *I will make my peace with what I've done, for your sake.* Mary's miserable life in exchange for her child's happiness. The price was high – but fair – for the life she would offer her child, who would never know the poverty she'd endured. Sylvia gritted her teeth and returned to the trunk.

Once she'd put everything back as she'd found it, she went outside for a walk around the gardens. Grace made her lunch and then she had a nap and woke feeling much stronger. She strolled back to the house and waited for Mason to return.

Just as the skies darkened, the creak of the front door opening rang through the house. Sylvia leapt up from the settee and smoothed the fabric. She found Grace leaving the kitchen, doing just as Sylvia had instructed, carrying a glass of wine on a tray. Sylvia led the way. Mason was in the hall removing his coat.

'Here, let me.' Sylvia took the coat from him and hung it on the peg. 'You must be weary. Would you care for your wine in the sitting room?'

A grateful smile creased Mason's face as he removed his hat. His cheeks were red from the cold air. In the sitting room, a fire crackled in the fireplace. He slumped into the settee with a relieved sigh. Grace placed the wine on the pedestal to his side, then Sylvia thanked her and dismissed her. Mason took a swig and let out a sigh as Sylvia remained quiet. She walked behind the settee and began to rub his shoulders.

'That feels nice,' he said, groaning as her thumbs squeezed the tension out. His head flopped forward. After a while, he murmured, 'I had business to attend to in Alexandria, sorting all of Mary's affairs, her will, letters to her relatives in England. Matters of my own too. But that's all done now.' He gave another long, deep sigh, and went quiet again.

Sylvia removed the ribbon that tied back his hair and let it fall loose to his shoulders. Mason purred as she ran her fingers through it, gently dragging her nails over his scalp.

'Have I died and woken in heaven?' he murmured.

She smiled to herself. He would never have received such a welcome from Mary. When she'd finished, she handed him his wine and he took a large swig.

'Another?'

Sylvia called for Grace, who duly appeared. 'Another wine, please – actually, two. I'll have one as well.' She indicated the space next to Mason on the settee. 'May I?'

'Yes, of course,' he said. She took her place by his side.

'How are you, Mason?'

His eyes began to glisten.

'I'm sorry, I didn't mean to upset you.' She placed her hand on his forearm.

Mason shook his head. 'No, it's just…that's the first time anyone has asked after me in…as long as I can remember.'

Grace came in and set down their wine on a side table.

'Thank you, Grace, that will be all for this evening,' said Sylvia.

Grace nodded. 'There's two meals plated in the kitchen if you get hungry.'

'Bless you. Sleep well.'

The door closed. Sylvia looked at Mason. He was staring into the flames of the fire, lost in thought.

Finally, he spoke. 'I can't believe she's gone. The number of times I wished her dead… And now she is. Do you think God heard me? Did he have a hand in this?' He turned to Sylvia, a helplessness to his expression. 'Will you pray with me?'

Sylvia hoped her face didn't betray her surprise. 'Yes. Of course.'

Mason eased himself down to the floor, his knees pressing into the deep pile of the carpet. Sylvia followed his lead. He pressed the palms of his hands together and bowed his head. His eyes closed:

'Lord, our Father,
We pray that you watch over Mary's soul
As we commit her to your care,
We pray that you forgive her sins
And that our own transgressions can be forgiven
Grant us the wisdom to follow your example…'

Sylvia sneaked a sideways glance as Mason continued to pray. The thought of God watching her every move struck more discomfort in her than usual.

'God bless this house, and all those in it.
Amen.'

'Amen,' added Sylvia, offering Mason a reassuring smile.

They resumed their places on the settee and took a sip of wine. He brushed strands of Sylvia's hair behind her ear.

'This is certainly a nicer homecoming than I would have received from Mary.'

'She's gone now, Mason, you can do as you please. No one will judge you any longer. You don't have to answer to anyone.' She squeezed his hand.

He nodded, his expression distant as he retreated into his thoughts.

'Grace said you've been ill. I'm sorry I didn't come to see you…'

'It's fine, it was nothing. I'm better.'

'And…er,' Mason shifted in his seat as he nodded to her belly, 'he's all right?'

'Yes, our baby's fine.'

A smile broke out across his face.

Sylvia wondered whether to kiss him. She hesitated. *Too early.*

'Life promises to be very different now,' he said.

She nodded.

'But I have to ask you,' he went on, 'your name is Sylvia – you're a runaway and you attacked your owner.'

Sylvia nodded and held his gaze. 'It's true, I did.'

'I need to know what happened.'

'I was sold to him the moment I stepped foot in America.'

'Were you a convict?'

Sylvia winced. She didn't want to talk about *that.*

'In England, you can be sent overseas for stealing a loaf of bread…' Tears welled in her eyes. 'I was…' She began to sob.

Mason put his hand on her thigh.

'I'm sorry, I don't like to talk about it.' She wiped away the tears and sipped her wine. 'I was denied justice, confined in the cramped hull of a ship for three months, subjected to the groping hands and invasive stares of all the unwashed men. It was terrible, Mason. Then, no sooner had we landed that a man called Simon Bowler bought me. He made it clear he wanted me to bear him children. Mason, he was no better than a beast. I couldn't. When he tried to touch me, I hit him over the head with a frying pan and took his horse. I rode all night. That's when I met Viktor. He offered to bring me here.'

'I see. They'll be looking for you.'

She shrugged. 'What could I do? What would you have done?'

He looked away. 'Who else knows about this?' he asked eventually.

'No one. Just you and Viktor.'

'Mary did,' he pointed out. 'It was in the newspaper.'

'Can you make it go away?' she whispered.

Mason nodded. After a long pause, he continued:

'We'll have to say I knew your family in England and agreed to house you. We can forge some letters if required. Someone in Britain must vouch for you – as Sarah, not Sylvia. Do you know anyone?'

Mr Benson would not lie for her. The only person Sylvia could trust was Caroline, but she couldn't read. Her sister would have to pay someone to read the letter and reply for her. She nodded, adding, 'they'll want paying.'

'Money's not a problem, but they'll need to hold their tongue. It would mean writing to them, which creates a trail of evidence if they don't destroy your letter.'

Sylvia's eyes narrowed at the reference to *your* letter. She sensed Mason was canny enough to distance himself from further lies.

'What about the baby? How will we explain it?' she asked.

'Well, there's no denying it. Besides, I'm a grieving widower. I took comfort in the loins of a house guest.' He raised his eyebrows.

She leant over and kissed him. He responded in kind.

'You must be very tired, Mason. Why don't you take me to bed with you?'

Smiling, Mason stood up and led her up the stairs.

62

March 23rd, 1754
Fitzbarton Plantation

I must be mad, thought Viktor as Barney helmed the boat silently up against Fitzbarton's wharf. The new moon offered little light to aid their way. Jimmy stepped ashore and deftly tied the stern to the wooden pilling. An owl hooted as they made their way up the slope and through the trees towards the house. Viktor estimated it to be an hour or two after midnight, his heart quickening as they approached. It was strange to be back; he'd sworn he'd never return, and even under the cover of darkness the place haunted him with memories of flaming banzas, blood-soaked whips, Grace trembling naked, Sylvia's infidelity, and the dispute with his father that had led him here. All of which convinced him that Mason was owed any harm they did tonight.

The first step was to placate the dogs, who would be asleep, chained to the outside of the slave accommodation to guard against runaways. Their plan would live or die on this first encounter. Barney and Jimmy crouched behind the treeline at the edge of the lawn as Viktor casually walked over to the building. He was within twenty paces when he heard one of the dogs growl.

'Sshh.' But the silence of the night was shattered by their hollow barks. As he approached, they strained at their chains, snarling to get at Viktor. His heart in his mouth, he ran the final paces towards them. 'Sshh, boys, it's me, Viktor.' Still, they barked. Once they recognised him, their barks turned to excited yelps. He stroked their heads and settled them down. A door opened and a negro stepped out.

438

'Who goes there?'

'Who's that?' hissed Viktor.

'Viktor? That you?'

'Charlie, yes, it's me.'

'Viktor, what are you doing back here?'

'I forgot something. I came back for it.'

'Master mighty angry with you. Don't let him catch you,' Charlie warned.

'I know. You haven't seen me, you understand?'

'Fine. Be careful, Viktor. Things here are bad. Master kill his wife.'

'What?' Viktor left the dogs and walked to the door where Charlie stood.

'He say she die in her sleep. We not believe him. He with your Sarah now.'

'Are you saying Mason killed Mary?'

'I dunno. All I'm saying is Mary dead. She buried in the woods. Mistress Sarah wouldn't let her be buried near the house.'

'Jesus!' Viktor was lost for words. He'd seen Mason's cruelty – but murder? His own wife? A slave, maybe, but to kill his spouse…

The dogs whimpered as Barney and Jimmy arrived. Viktor went to soothe the hounds.

'Could ye make any more fucking noise, ye careless bastard?' snarled Barney.

'Mr Barney? What are you doing here?'

'Don't worry, Charlie, they're with me. You go back to bed. Best you're not seen talking to me.'

***

Sylvia heard the dogs barking. It was probably just a rabbit straying too close, she decided. She heaved herself up from the bed she shared with Mason and slipped out of the room onto the landing. Her pregnancy, which was approaching six months, was large enough to be unavoidably noticeable and meant she couldn't last the night without needing a pee. As soon as the dogs woke her, she felt the urge to go. Too proud to relieve herself in front of Mason, and lest she wake him, she kept a chamber pot outside the bedroom door. She hoisted up her nightgown and squatted over the pot, sighing with relief as she let go. She returned to the dark of the room and drank down a glass of water. Near constant thirst appeared to be another symptom of her pregnancy. She needed more but had already emptied the water jug. She picked it up and tottered downstairs to refill it from the kitchen. Her body ached from sleeping in one position, so she was glad to move about for a moment. In the kitchen, her eyes not having quite adjusted to the dark, she felt about for another water jug.

Click. The door to the outside opened. A chilly gust of night air blew across her face. She shrieked in terror as she scuttled across the kitchen towards the knives, which Mason insisted on keeping in a locked drawer. Before she could find the key, a shadowy figure crossed the kitchen and muffled her screams with a hand across her mouth, dragging her to the floor. She wriggled but couldn't get free, pinned under the weight of a burly man.

'Stop yourself, wee lassie,' he hissed in her ear. 'Yous be quiet and you wonnay be gettin' hurt.'

Eyes wide, her heart pounding as she struggled for breath against the filthy hand, she lay still, trapped. Her heart sank when she saw the other shadows moving. Her first fear was rape.

The Scottish man whispered to his accomplice in a hushed command:

'Jimmy, by the door. Clobber him if he comes down. Vik, light a candle, so I's can see what I'm doing.'

'But…'

'Don't fucking argue with me, Viktor!' he said, straining to keep his voice quiet.

Did he say Viktor? thought Sylvia wildly.

Viktor, searching for a candle, knocked over the empty water glass she'd left on the sideboard. It fell to the floor and smashed, echoing round the house.

'Viktor, you fucking moron,' barked the Scotsman.

It must be him, Sylvia realised, feeling marginally less threatened. Viktor would never hurt her; she was certain of it.

The kitchen door opened.

'Sarah, is that you?' said Mason.

There was a clang as the man named Jimmy clattered a frying pan against Mason's head. Mason dropped to the ground. Jimmy brought the pan back down for another go. Mason lay still and Jimmy raised the pan again.

'That's enough, Jimmy! You'll kill the poor bugger!' said the Scotsman, no longer making any attempt to keep his voice quiet. 'Viktor. Get some rope. Tie him up.'

'Rope? In a kitchen?'

'String then, I don't know, use your initiative, just tie the bastard up.'

Time passed slowly as she remained pinned beneath the Scotsman. Viktor fumbled around in the dark, before finally lighting a candle and casting a yellow glow across the kitchen. Viktor avoided her eye and he managed to find some butchers twine to tie Mason's hands behind his back. She gasped as she recognised the man helping him. It was Seaman Jimmy Jones. He must have jumped ship like he'd said he would. He winked at her. Viktor finished tying up Mason, then glanced at her, shame clear on his face.

The Scotsman stood and hoisted her up to push her against the sideboard.

'Rite, lassie, we'll have no bother with you. We'll be borrowing a few things from your pantry. Is that going to be a problem?'

She glanced at the other two, both looking sheepish. The Scotsman grinned at her. She spat at his feet.

'While your man's still out cold, tell me, does he think that whelp in your belly belongs to him?'

Sylvia scowled.

'Let me tell you what I know, which old mutton head here,' he pointed at Mason, 'is too dumb to figure out. A wee birdy told me—' he looked at Jimmy '—you spent your sea crossing riding old Reidy dry every night, in exchange for nice quarters. I'd wager that baby's Captain Reid's, aye?'

Panic coursed through Sylvia's veins.

'Ha! I can see the terror in those pretty eyes of yours! Yous onto a good thing here, eh? I know Captain Reid. He'd be delighted to learn he's got a child out here, almost as much as your man here would be heartbroken, eh? But don't you worry, you play nice and your secret's safe with me.'

Sylvia's vitriol cooled as the prospect of a bargain became apparent.

'One day, I'll call for a favour, and you'll be good for it. We clear? Yous be belonging to me, eh? For now, we's just be taking a few things from you. It's for a good cause, I assure you.'

Sylvia's nose twitched as she nodded her agreement. She didn't like being cornered by this poisonous bastard; it left a very sour taste in her mouth. Any man who threatened her made his own wager with the devil, but that would have to wait.

Mason groaned and began to stir.

'Jimmy, you watch these two. Viktor, you show us the pantry and we'll get busy.'

The two men slipped off through the door to the pantry. She could hear the faint chatter of their voices. They returned, arms laden with sacks of food.

Mason pushed himself up off the floor and glanced at her, a mix of confusion and rage in his eyes.

'What are you villains doing?' he sputtered.

'Steady, old fruit,' said Jimmy, nudging Mason back over onto his belly with the frying pan.

Mason protested and hurled abuse. Sylvia kept her thoughts to herself. Unlike Mason, her own shock had subsided; her mind was rational once more. Why were they being robbed? As the Scotsman and Viktor returned to the pantry for another load, she turned to Jimmy.

'What's this for?' she asked.

'There's a war on. Army needs food.'

'What?!' barked Mason. 'This is how our army feeds itself? By robbing innocent patriots?'

'Needs must, great that you could do your bit,' Jimmy quipped.

'Fuck off, you—'

'Mason! Quiet. Don't antagonise them,' she warned.

Fortunately, he followed her advice.

They waited while Viktor and the Scotsman – whom she heard the men call Barney –emptied the pantry of all their supplies. Viktor dashed outside and fetched a cart from the stables. They loaded the stolen goods onto it, the sight of which provoked Mason:

'You've taken all our food, you bastards!'

Barney looked at Sylvia, his eyebrows raised, reminding her what he knew.

'Mason. Be quiet. Just let them go,' she said.

'Let them go? Viktor, you shit! First, you desert me, then you rob me of all I have to eat? You ungrateful bastard. I'll make sure your father hears of what you've become. I'll see you hang for this!'

'Mason, stop!' Sylvia ordered.

Viktor walked over to Mason and crouched down beside him.

'Word is, Mason, you killed your old lady. Mighty coincidence if you ask me. Your mistress falls pregnant, and your wife dies. I'm willing to bet someone would take an interest in that. Imagine then if they found out her real name is Sylvia, and she's a runaway. It would all look very bad. So, you threaten me all you like. But my question to you is, *are you willing to pay the price?*'

Viktor's eyebrows raised as he waited for a reply that didn't come.

Sylvia bristled as another of her secrets found new ears, but despite that she felt a touch of pride on Viktor's behalf. He was finally becoming a man. It was a shame they'd wound up on opposing sides.

'Jimmy,' said Barney, nodding his approval.

The frying pan came crashing down once more, knocking Mason out cold.

She looked at Viktor, the thought of what might have been on his face. He nodded. She assumed this gesture meant good luck, or at least that she needn't fear his betrayal.

They slipped off into the night.

63

March 24th, 1754
Fitzbarton Plantation

Mason was naked as he stomped round the bedroom, slamming drawers and wardrobe doors, while he selected clothes for what remained of the day. Zebedee had found him and Sarah, tied up in the kitchen, where Viktor and his thugs had left them. Once released, they'd returned to bed, having been awake for much of the night, but Mason had been too enraged to sleep. His temper had grown with the passing hours.

'The embarrassment of it. How dare they! After all I did for Viktor. The man's a snake!' He continued his rant as he stepped into his breeches, nearly losing his balance in the dim light of the room. The curtains were closed to keep out the morning sun. Sarah lay in the bed.

'They'll hang for what they did! I'll bloody see to it. I'll write to Joshua Fry. He's a magistrate, it's his duty to bring them to justice, and it's his army they steal for. Serve Fry right for siding with the Ohio Company, after everything he said in our dining room. Why, the man's hardly any better himself!'

Sarah propped herself up, adjusting the pillows against the headboard.

'Mason, that may not be a good idea,' she said calmly.

'I don't care!' He sat on the end of the bed and donned his stockings. He twisted to see Sarah, his forehead creased in a deep frown. 'Why not?'

'Well, I don't think it's wise for us to attract the attention of the authorities so soon after Mary's death.'

Mason leapt up, his arms outstretched. 'But we've done nothing wrong! I expect justice! You can't have people roaming around, robbing—'

'I know,' Sarah's voice remained level. 'But it doesn't look good on us.' She indicated the bulge in her belly that she cradled with folded arms.

'I don't care how it looks! I've nothing to hide. Perhaps you have?'

'I don't appreciate what you're suggesting, Mason. I am thinking of our baby, and the fact I'm a runaway – pregnant by a man who was recently widowed. Think about it.'

'We've a plan for your identity…'

'I know, but why risk attention? What have we to gain? We won't get our food back.'

'We? Huh. Easy to say when you didn't pay for it! That's not the point, I demand justice…'

'Mason! Think.'

It was the first time he'd witnessed her temper and it caught him unawares. He pulled up his breeches.

Regaining her composure, Sarah sat up in the bed. 'Forget justice. Seek revenge. If you must get even, take out your frustrations on Viktor's family.'

His fingers fumbled the buttons on his linen shirt as he considered this. How fitting that Hans, that stubborn fool, should be humiliated by the actions of his wayward son.

Dressed, Mason raced down the stairs two at a time, ignoring Sarah's calls. He paced down the hall into his study. *Hang what she says, my only offence is to harbour a runaway. No one can prove what I did or didn't know, and I wouldn't be the first man in history to sire a bastard with a housemaid.* He took a leaf of paper and dipped his quill in the ink to compose a letter to Fry. He detailed an account of the robbery, naming Viktor Neumann, with descriptions of him and his accomplices: the red-haired, scar-faced Scotsman called Barney, and the shorter man with young features and blond hair.

The letter sealed and ready for posting, he paced up to the window overlooking the front lawn, with one thought in mind: how to avenge himself against Viktor's father. Done well, he could finally get their land for himself.

64

April 1ˢᵗ, All Fools Day, 1754
Alexandria

The new town of Alexandria was abuzz like never before. People moved in all directions, boats came and went, supplies trickled in and out. A visitor from New York or London might have thought it quaint, but for agricultural Virginia, late to the party, it was a meaningful show of intent.

Inside George's borrowed office, the room was silent. George, dressed in his new uniform, sat statue still, his ears pricked and his eyes occasionally glancing at the open window. The artist worked in silence as he put the finishing touches to George's likeness on his canvas. George, forced to sit still for the first time in his life, thought about his task ahead.

His initial disappointment at being placed under Fry's command had quickly turned to defiance. He'd written to Fry, confirming that he was attending to matters in the north of the colony, and that Colonel Fry would be best placed to continue the muster in the south. He hadn't offered congratulations. Fry had replied, agreeing to George's suggestion. He ordered that their forces rendezvous in Alexandria and depart for the Ohio in mid-April.

Reading the reply, George had huffed. The King had entrusted George with the reconnaissance mission, and he'd be damned if he was going to let that dawdling mathematician take all the credit for what was to come. Besides, from what he'd already seen, George knew that the key to the mission's success was securing the fork in the river

447

before the French did. He would need to make haste.

'May I see?'

The artist beckoned him over and George joined him on the far side of the canvas. There he was, staring back at himself, looking contemplative and confident.

'My goodness, it's marvellous. Well done, my man.'

The painter nodded modestly. 'I'll add the background in now.'

George was delighted. The likeness was uncanny. The brushwork was neat and lifelike, it was fit to hang in any building in the colony. He slipped the painter a coin and left him to his labours. What a lovely way to commemorate the encounter that lay ahead. In victory, he pictured himself standing in front of the portrait, regaling guests and grandchildren of his exploits. Or in defeat... *Come now, who'd entertain that,* he thought. But still, people would introduce onlookers to George Washington, who bravely fought the French in the Ohio: *a hero of our age*.

George stepped outside: there was to be a muster at midday, and he was keen to inspect his soldiers. It was important they saw him every day, a simple discipline that Lawrence had used during his time in the Caribbean. 'It reminds them you're there with them,' he used to say. 'If you lead, they'll follow. If you spectate, so will they.' George was grateful for those simple wisdoms, for they were all he had. He may look the part now as he strode down the street, but inside, he knew he was making it up as he went along. So long as nobody else was privy to that little secret, he would be fine.

'Lieutenant Colonel!' a voice called out.

It was that Scottish rogue Barney MacGregor, Viktor in tow.

'A wee minute of your time, sir?'

George waited for the man to arrive.

'How's about givin' us that contract then, to keep your boys fed, eh? I's given you a first load, but you'll be needing more, if the campaign's to be a long one.'

'Barney, tell me: there are reports of robberies circulating, people complaining that their flour and salted meat has been stolen.' George stopped walking and regarded Barney shrewdly. 'That first load, where did you get it from?'

Barney frowned at the offence. 'Colonel, that you should think that, I'm lost for words. I'm an honest factor. The goods were shipped in from Boston…'

'You have proof of their provenance?'

'Oh aye, not with me now, granted, but they are legitimate.'

George's eyes narrowed as he weighed the fellow up. 'Viktor, you're an honest Virginian. Can I trust this man?'

Viktor nodded. 'Certainly.'

'Hmm. Very well. You prove that what you've already delivered isn't contraband, and I'll pay you for it.'

'And…'

'And,' continued George, 'then you can have a contract to supply my forces. I need more food and munitions. I have enough for a month, but we shall need resupplying once we've departed.'

'Fine. Nae problem. We's be having a deal then?' Barney offered his hand.

'Once you satisfy me it isn't you who's been robbing everyone.'

'Sure,' said Barney.

'Good, now if you'll excuse me, I have matters that demand my attention. Viktor, come with me.'

George began to walk, turning down a side street. Barney called out his thanks and made good his disappearance, looking very pleased with himself.

George was glad to be rid of him. Sadly, an army couldn't operate without such scavengers.

'Viktor, you've been with me since the beginning. I need people I can trust,' he began.

A broad smile swept across the man's pale skin.

'I want you to command a section.'

'Thank you, but I wouldn't know how. I've never…'

'Neither does anyone else, Viktor,' whispered George, conspiratorially, 'but it's our duty.'

'Yes, but…'

'Please, Viktor. I wouldn't ask if I didn't think you more than capable. The pay is a pound a month more. Come, let us look at the men.'

Before Viktor could object, George stepped up his pace and strode off towards the grassed area behind town. In his mind's eye, he'd

pictured lines of red-coated soldiers marching in step to drumbeat and
fife, beneath the union flag. The reality was less impressive: a rag-tag
bunch of men milled about chatting, or sitting on the ground playing
cards. With Dinwiddie's government finally agreeing to offer pay in
hard currency, people had started to pitch up in Alexandria. First to
arrive were the dregs of the colony. A stinking, wretched bunch, gap-
toothed, with torn and tatty clothes, some without shoes, all unarmed.
If their desire to traverse the mountains and engage the French had
been one-tenth of their eagerness to get their hands on silver coins,
then George might have been in safe hands. It wasn't, and they
wouldn't get a penny until their service was complete. He would
however have to advance them shoes and guns, later to be deducted.
The militia men were in an altogether better state. All had brought
muskets and adequate clothing. They too, were tempted into service
more by pay than duty, and all sought reassurances they'd be back to
their farmsteads by harvest.

The sight might have filled a lesser man with dread, but George
was determined to fashion these reprobates and farmhands into the
Virginian heroes of Britain's Empire.

'Men,' he shouted, repeatedly, until he'd caught their attention.
'Form up!' From the shifting huddle emerged Jacob Van Braam, his
left hand missing two frostbitten fingers from their last expedition into
the Ohio.

'Afternoon, George.'

'How many do we number now?'

'One hundred and sixty.'

George grimaced. They needed more men, but they also couldn't
wait indefinitely.

'What about the other colonies?' ask Van Braam.

'I very much doubt those Pennsylvanian cowards will be sending
anyone. No word from Maryland. Rumour is the Carolinas may yet
stump up.'

'I received a letter from a friend in the south. Colonel Fry has a
hundred men. Word is they should be here in two weeks.'

George straightened his back. 'We'll be leaving tomorrow.'

'For the Ohio?'

'Of course.'

'But we'd be leaving at half-strength without Colonel Fry and his men,' Van Braam pointed out.

'We're better off without that dithering fool. He never wanted the Ohio Valley for his country. The man's a republican.'

'But, George…'

'Thank you, Captain Van Braam. And it's Lieutenant Colonel Washington. Those are my orders. Have the men ready to leave by morning.' George knew he was taking a risk, but he had no confidence in Fry's leadership. They had to act; he was certain of it.

'But they've hardly practised with their weapons—' said Van Braam.

'Well, best they do so this afternoon.' George turned to Viktor. 'Corporal Neumann, you're in charge of provisions. Have your Scottish friend deliver whatever supplies he can for tomorrow.'

'Corporal?'

'Yes. Congratulations Viktor. You'll be excellent, I'm sure of it. Now, run along.'

George walked down the line of his front rank. They were a pitiful crew, but with proper direction, and their natural English combativeness, they would make mincemeat of the French. One thing was certain: he wouldn't be letting Fry steal his glory.

***

Viktor found Barney on the dockside, watching the boats come and go.

'Barney, we leave in the morning!'

'Oh aye. You can do as ye please, laddie, but I annae going anywhere.'

'You're not coming?'

'Aye. I'm a Highlander. No ways you'll be seeing me fighting under a British flag. I'd soonay shoot the bastards myself. You never heard of the auld alliance? Scotsmen and Frenchies have a lot in common: we both hate the English.'

Viktor frowned. He wondered if he'd ever understand the British. Sometimes it was like those living in America had more loyalty to Britain than those coming over from the homeland, still preoccupied with the ancient squabbles of their forbears.

'If yous any sense, you'll stick with me.'

Viktor thought about it. He'd grown fond of Barney, but at heart Barney was a loner. His instincts told him he'd be better off with George – pay would be a certainty in the army and he was a Corporal now. He decided not to tell Barney, in case it upset him.

'You've a contract to fulfil, Barney. I'll do what I can to help.'

At dusk, they waited outside the customs house, a newly erected brick building overlooking the bay. Barney checked over his shoulder, and seeing no one was about, he slipped through the front door, Viktor following close behind, his cocked hat pulled down over his brow.

Inside, a solitary man was sat behind a wooden desk. He looked up from behind his leather-bound ledgers and ink pot. 'We're finished for the day,' said the tide waiter, a stocky man whose Scots accent was much softer than Barney's. His job was to inspect cargo on board vessels before it was unloaded, making sure it matched the exported cargo lists and to apply the necessary import duty.

'Wonnay take a minute, pal.'

'I'm sorry, you'll have to come back tomorrow,' he said, finishing his notation, blowing on the ink before closing his neatly scribed ledger.

'Thas nay possible. See, I need a cocket, for tomorrow. Wonnay take a wee minute.'

'You need a cocket?'

'Aye, for three hogsheads a' flour. Another a' salt pork.'

'When did these goods arrive? This afternoon?' probed the tide waiter.

'No. They never came.'

'Well, if they didn't arrive, you can't have a note to prove they did, can you?' the tide waiter began to clean the ink from the nib of his quill. 'If you'll excuse me, gentlemen.'

'Thas nay possible either. I need a receipt to show they were shipped in, legal. I's asking kindly. Otherwise,' Barney pulled out a knife, 'I'll cut ya bollocks off and feed em to ya.'

Viktor gulped and glanced out the window, relieved to see no one else was coming.

The tide waiter's eyes narrowed as he assessed Barney.

'Please,' said Barney with a grin.

'That won't be necessary. Put your knife down. I'll write one for you, confirming your goods arrived spoiled and therefore no duty is due. It will cost you two pounds. Cash. Now.'

'Very well. Seems fair.' Barney put the knife back in his coat pocket.

The tide waiter drew up the cocket and stamped it with a customs seal. Barney passed him £2 in coins, which he duly pocketed. Satisfied all was in order, Barney and Viktor stepped back out into the dusk.

They headed for the house Lieutenant Colonel Washington was using as his headquarters. A negro answered the door and showed them to the front room, and they accepted his offer of a drink. Two whiskies arrived, and shortly after George entered in his shirtsleeves and breeches.

'Gentlemen, good evening. I can guess why you're here.'

'Aye. As requested. Proof of authenticity.' Barney held out the cocket note from the customs house.

'The ink is dry then?'

'Aye. Damn cheek of you!'

'Very well, sir. Consider yourself commissioned to supply His Majesty's Virginian regiment.'

Barney stood and they shook hands.

'There is just one thing, Lieutenant Colonel,' said Barney. 'Folk know there's an army being raised and that a war's coming. They get jittery about credit in such time; should, you know, the worst happen, they don't want to be left out of pocket. My suppliers, they'll want half the money upfront.'

George regarded Barney, who held his hands up, suggesting there was nothing he could do.

'Very well. You can have half the money up front. Here.' George fished out £30 in notes from the side pocket of his tunic.

Viktor watched as the two men agreed the quantities of goods. He admired Barney in a way. The man didn't let anything stop him. Whenever he hit an obstacle, he simply skirted round it – or destroyed it. He never hesitated or so much as flinched. The Scotsman would do well in life, he was sure.

Not wishing to dwell on his own future, Viktor put all his fruitless plans out of mind. At least now he was due to embark on a meaningful adventure. Perhaps he'd make a name for himself. Perhaps he'd be killed. Either way, he didn't care. It was a relief not to make any decisions for himself; all he must do was to follow Lieutenant Colonel Washington's orders. That he knew he could do.

'Pleasure doing business with you,' said Barney. 'If you're departing tomorrow, I'll catch you up with the goods.'

'That will do nicely. And should you fail to arrive,' said George, 'or if anything gets lost – you'll hang. Is that clear?'

'Oh. Aye. Rite. Best be getting on. Viktor, you coming?'

Viktor shook his head and offered his services to Washington instead.

***

Barney sported a large grin as he stepped out into the darkness. He squeezed the notes in his hand and headed for the floating bordello. He was due to collect his share of the money the whore had stolen from Viktor. He might even treat himself to a roll under the covers while he was there.

Satisfied he was out of earshot of Washington's property, he couldn't resist voicing his thoughts out loud: 'Last you'll see o' me, you pompous English wanka.'

65

April 17th, 1754
The Fork in the Ohio River

George Croghan bit off a hunk of bread and chewed as he stood back and regarded another long day's work. Finally, after weeks of labouring, his frustrations were beginning to turn towards something resembling satisfaction. The fort was taking shape: a crude palisade of wooden stakes, each sharpened to a point to stop people climbing over, encircled the accommodation and stores built from interlocking logs. It was basic, but all it needed now was for doors to be hung on the buildings, the gates to be hung on the palisade, gun holes to be cut, and a walkway erected to allow the free movement of sentries around the top of the outer wall. Then it would be complete. Just another week's work.

As he looked at his construction, Croghan wondered if it was what King George had envisaged. He chuckled to himself; doubtless any king accustomed to the guilt-edged splendour of Europe's palaces would think it a rather poor effort at a fortification. Well, perhaps they might, thought Croghan, but if it hadn't been for him, there'd be nothing here whatsoever. Despite the King's requirement – and Tanacharison's insistence – the colonists had proved themselves completely ineffective. Pennsylvania had steadfastly refused to commission anything that would offend God's sensibilities. The Virginians still squabbled over its necessity and who should bear the cost. Exasperated by their inactivity, Croghan took the bull by the horns, using the colonial funds from Edward Shippen, and instead of

455

buying food and weapons for the Iroquois, he'd hired a team of labourers, some tools and materials, and returned to the Ohio to build it himself. Pennsylvania had funded it after all, but Croghan was certain God would understand. Better still, when the Virginians finally decided they needed it, they could lease it from him, or he'd sell it to them for a tidy profit. There was still a French bounty on his head, and he wasn't certain he could trust any of the Indians not to cash in his scalp; they didn't take much persuading to change allegiances.

Building the fort was his last gamble to hold on to his claim of two hundred thousand acres in the Ohio. All his hopes rested on the arrival of that upstart Washington, for a fort without soldiers wasn't much use. Fortunately, all had been quiet; occasionally, a friendly hunting party came by, waving from the far riverbank. It was so peaceful, with the gurgle of the river, fish leaping, the songs of birds, an eagle circling overhead, that it was hard to believe that this small spit of land was destined to be the centre of an international dispute.

Croghan took another mouthful of bread and washed it down with water. The light was beginning to fade. The men would need feeding before they lost the light. Croghan called out to signal the end of the day's work. The other four downed tools and stretched their aching bodies. Croghan went down to the water's edge, the sight of the river reminding him of the day he and Tanacharison had ridden here and overlooked the fork in the rivers. He washed his face and hands in the cool water, satisfied that he'd transformed the Chief's vision into a reality. He'd kept him on side, lured the Virginians in, and once they arrived, the two hundred thousand acres Tanacharison had promised him would be his. He was so close, he could feel it.

As soon as the Chief died, Croghan would parcel up the land and sell it off. He'd be the richest man in America. The pauper from Ireland would join the ranks of the elite. He'd host balls, eat his own bodyweight in rich food, drink himself sober on fine wines and brandy. He'd have a collection of courtesans – blonde, brunette, Indian, oriental, African – one for every day of the week.

He submerged his head into the cool running water, savouring the wash of the current as it drew the dust and grit from his scalp. He held his breath until his lungs could no longer stand it, then emerged to gasp for air. As the water ran from his face, he opened his eyes. A shadow cast across the river. He glanced up: the wooden bow of a canoe drifted into view. Croghan jumped to his feet. Three men sat in a canoe right before him, holding the boat in the current with their paddles.

'*Bonsoir, mon ami,*' said the man at the stern, a broad grin on his face.

Croghan stared in disbelief. More canoes drifted into view. He looked upstream. It was swarming with canoes, like a shoal of fish crowding the brown waters of the river. French tricolours hung limp from their sterns. They began to beach and their inhabitants stepped ashore.

Mary, mother of Jesus, no...

He glanced to his left. The river was clear. He could make a dash for it. He hesitated while his mind weighed up his options.

'*Non, monsieur,*' said the Frenchman at the bow of the nearest canoe, an arm's length away. Croghan looked at him. A gap-toothed smile on his face and a flintlock pistol in his hand – pointed at Croghan.

66

April 17ᵗʰ, 1754
The Fork in the Ohio River

'You are the British trader George Croghan, yes?' asked the French commander, a narrow-eyed man with dark hair, in his mid-thirties. He stood tall in his blue longcoat and cocked hat, announcing himself as Joseph Coulon de Villiers. He, and the one thousand Frenchmen in his command, had captured the fort without firing a shot. Resistance would have been futile.

'No. Not at all,' pleaded Croghan on bended knees, his hands raised in denial.

Coulon de Villiers continued, gesticulating with his flintlock pistol. 'You murdered our traders, you turn the Twightee against us…'

'Honestly, that ain't me, sir. I know Croghan. Last I heard he was at Logstown, a day's ride west of here. If you—'

'Nonsense. It is you—'

'On my mother's life, I'm not him! Ask them.' Croghan pointed to his men, also lined up and on their knees, under the watchful eye of French guards. 'Lads, tell the man—'

'Silence from you,' barked the officer, 'What is this man's name?'

'He be Edward Ward,' said one of Croghan's men.

Croghan could have kissed him. That was his brother-in-law's name. It was a feint he could work with. He could sense the officer falling for it, as the rest of his men confirmed it.

'Gentlemen, there is a large reward on the head of George

Croghan. All you have to do is confirm that this man here is him, and you'll be rich.'

Croghan tensed. *Please, God, no. Hold firm, boys.* He glanced right and winked at his men. Before anyone fell to the temptation, he intervened, 'Listen, I know Croghan. If you like, I'll fetch him for you.'

The French officer turned his attention back to him. 'You will say anything to save your neck.'

'No. I could use that reward. I could have Croghan here the day after tomorrow. I'd wager Chief Tanacharison would give him up, for the promise of leaving the Iroquois in peace.'

The officer's gaze narrowed as he considered it.

Go on, you wee bastard...

'*Non.* You are not to be trusted.'

'Look, what have you to lose? You have the fort. You have my men. If I can get you Croghan – well, I'd reckon the form you're on, they'll make you a General.'

The Frenchman smirked. 'I think it is better if we keep you here.'

Croghan's shoulders slumped. 'Suit yourself, but you could be a national hero...'

'We'll see. Monsieur, remind me, what was your name?'

'It's Ward, Edward Ward, of Pennsylvania.'

The Frenchman pursed his lips as Croghan's deception held firm. *You'll need to do better than that, you froggy bastard.*

'I shall consider it,' said the Frenchman, before ordering Croghan and his men to be kept under armed guard.

All night, they lay on the ground, huddled against the palisade, while the French guards paced about, chatting and smoking tobacco.

Having evaded identification and remaining in possession of his scalp – for now – Croghan's thoughts turned to what was at stake. With the capture of the fort, and the forks of the Ohio River under French control, all they needed to do now was travel south and fortify the Monongahela River, then the door to the interior would be closed. The British would be held east of the mountains, permanently encircled by the French. Could the two peoples live cheek by jowl in peace? Nobody knew for sure how much of America there was to the west. If it was as large as rumours suggested, the French could reap its rewards for themselves. That would cost George Croghan his livelihood, to say nothing of the two hundred thousand acres Tanacharison had promised him. *Damned Frenchies.* Someone needed to stop them. With a calm mind, Croghan thought about the problem, breaking it into logical steps: the longer he stayed here, the more he risked being identified. All it would take was one slip of the tongue, or one of his men breaking rank, tempted by the French bounty. He had to leave.

He needed pelts too, though that meant getting rid of the French. But there were simply too many of them. Aided by compulsory national service, all young men in New France were required to serve at their Governor's behest. He resolved to tackle his financial problems once he got out of this first jam. Somehow.

Uncertain, he lay on his back and looked up at the beautiful blanket of twinkling stars. *Ah George Croghan, you're so close. Where there's life, there's hope.* Or so some Roman had said. Hopefully by now the Virginian forces would be riding to the rescue – even if, as word from upriver had said, that fool Joshua Fry had been placed in charge. Hopefully he was a better soldier than he'd been a negotiator, when they'd agreed the treaty at Logstown.

***

The next morning, he persuaded one of the guards to take him to Coulon de Villiers. Everywhere, Frenchmen were rising from their slumber in dawn's early light. The commanding officer was striding across the fort.

'Begging your pardon, Officer, Edward Ward seeking an audience with your highness?'

Before the neatly dressed Frenchman could refuse, Croghan continued, 'I could use that reward, I have debtors to pay. Let me get Croghan for you. Give me an escort of your troops – three should do it – and I give you my word, I'll bring him back to you.'

'If he's in Logstown as you suggest, that would be four of you against a whole Iroquois village. I will send you with one hundred men.'

Croghan's insides somersaulted. 'They might mistake that for a raiding party. They're mighty nervous. Besides, I know Croghan. He rides out each morning. I'll approach him somewhere quiet. He's always keen for news. When he stops to talk, your men can capture him.'

Coulon de Villiers' mouth twisted as he considered it. 'You're his brother-in-law...'

'The man beats my wee sister. I'd gladly do it for free, if I weren't so desperate for the money.'

'Seems you have an answer for everything, Monsieur Ward. Very well, I accept. You will have a guard of three of my best men. You're to leave now and be back here in three days. For every day you're late, I'll execute one of your men.'

'Three days, no problem. Then you'll let me go?'

'Gladly.'

Croghan's face betrayed none of the emotion running amok inside him. That Frenchman had taken his bait, hook, line and sinker. 'We'll need wampum, to show the Iroquois we come in peace.'

Within ten minutes, George Croghan was being escorted out of the fort he'd built, under a small guard of French soldiers, and his pockets lined with wampum. Coulon de Villiers accompanied him to the gate.

'Goodbye, George.'

George didn't respond to his real name and managed a frown. 'Edward,' he corrected, offering his hand to shake the Frenchman's. Without warning, Coulon de Villiers grabbed hold of Croghan's extended arm. Another Frenchman stepped forward from behind and grabbed his other arm. Both his hands were tied together with rope.

'*Mon ami*,' said Coulon de Villiers, 'I do not trust you, but if what you offer is real, it is worth the risk, and you will, I hope, accept my full apology. If, though, you should try to escape, these men will shoot you. I hope you will die a quick death, for alas, if not, it is very bad for you.'

'*Je mange l'Anglais*,' said one of his guards, whose pox-scarred face was missing all his front teeth.

'*Je suis Irlandais*,' replied Croghan.

The man licked his lips.

'I'll see you tomorrow,' said Croghan.

Coulon de Villiers nodded, and they left. The guards canoed him across to the northern riverbank. He took one last look back at the fort he'd built. *So close*. With so many men, the French would have it finished by sunset.

It was twenty miles to Logstown. As they began their hike, Croghan studied his guards. They each shouldered a loaded musket and carried another in their arms. They wore good leather boots and long coats, protected from the elements, unlike himself, who was left in his shirtsleeves. They were well-built men; he had no chance of overpowering them, especially with his hands tied. The river was his best chance of escape, but they steered him up the tree-lined slope, away from the water's edge.

He allowed himself a sigh of relief, for at least he was out of the enemy's bosom and had the rest of the day to plot his escape.

'*Irlandais*, tell me about this man Croghan,' said the gap-toothed Frenchman, who walked in front.

'Ah, the man's a genius,' said Croghan, 'cunning as a fox – but we'll catch him. I know a place we can hide this evening. He's sure to ride past in the morning. How long have you men been in the Americas?' In his experience, everyone enjoyed talking about themselves. No better way to soften up his escort.

By mid-afternoon, a biting wind cut across them. They were a mile from Logstown and the mood amongst the Frenchmen became more serious, scolding Croghan for his continued talking. They followed the hunting trail until they came to the point where Croghan had ridden up the bank to say goodbye to Thayonih at the start of the year. The memory put an idea in Croghan's head. He spoke loudly to make sure he'd be overheard.

'Further up there's a hollow where we can camp for the night. Croghan will pass on this trail in the morning. I'll stop him for a chat, and you can spring down the bank and restrain him.'

Unconvinced, the gap-toothed Frenchman, indicated for Croghan to show him. They made their way up the slope, Croghan discreetly raking his feet as he climbed, to disturb the loamy topsoil. From the top, they could make out the tepees of Logstown in the distance. On seeing it, there was some disquiet amongst the Frenchmen, as they argued in hushed tones in their own tongue.

Croghan sat down in the middle of the hollow and began to relax.

Gap-tooth silenced his men's concerns and ordered them to take sentry positions at the rim of the bowl in which Croghan was sitting. He took his musket over his shoulder and pointed it at Croghan's head. 'No fire. No sound. If you move, I kill you.'

Croghan nodded and stretched out on the floor, wriggling his fingers to get some blood back in them. He hoped it would be a long night.

***

Tanacharison was playing with his grandchildren at the water's edge. He envied their carefree abandon as they chased each other. Rarely could he enjoy them without his mind wandering to the many problems at hand. Being Chief was both the best and the worst thing, for it was down to him to act, and he would be judged for what he did. Word had reached him that the French had arrived at the forks. The time for him to act was nigh. His descendants would tell legends of whatever he chose to do next.

'Chief.'

Tanacharison's thoughts were interrupted as one of his braves came running towards him.

'The French have the Irishman, Buck. I saw them walking this way. He was their prisoner.'

'How many?'

'Only four.'

As they hadn't arrived at the camp, they must be in hiding. Why, the Chief couldn't understand. Was Croghan betraying him? As darkness fell, Tanacharison and fifteen of his best braves spread out and crept up the slope towards where Buck had last been seen.

They smelt the white men, who were fool enough to hide upwind. Tanacharison knew the best spot to hide up on the bluff. They would most likely be there. They crawled one step at a time. It took half the night, but in the pale moonlight, the head and distinctive shape of a white man's hat was just visible above the rim of the dip.

Tanacharison gave the whistle. They rushed the last twenty feet, descending on the white men, knives drawn. Tanacharison leapt through the air, landing his knee on the back of the white man, knocking the wind from his chest. He tilted the man's head up and held the tip of his blade at his throat. Around him, the others did likewise. The small party of French were overwhelmed.

'What kept you boys so long?'

It was Buck. Tanacharison laughed. They put the Frenchmen in the middle of the dip and surrounded them. Buck climbed up and stood next to Tanacharison, who cut the ropes binding his hands.

'What should we do with these?' asked a brave, nodding at the Frenchmen.

'Take them back to the village, unharmed. We must not anger our enemy,' ordered Tanacharison.

'There's plenty more where they came from,' said Buck. 'A thousand.'

That was more than Tanacharison had been expecting.

'Your people are marching north, led by Washington, headed for the forks,' said Tanacharison. 'They are three days away.'

Three lousy days – so close, lamented Croghan. 'How many?'

'We counted one hundred and sixty. Too little, too late.'

'Oh, Jesus. We better warn him.'

'I warn you people. I tell them, you must build a fort, stop French coming. Why only you listen? Now we have war. Because your people hopeless. French are much more organised.'

'Well, look on the bright side, we can only do better,' Buck shrugged.

'I should leave that fool to march his men to their deaths!'

'We can't! Come on, you and I have too much at stake. We must warn Washington. Besides, if you want English support, you better honour your side of the treaty, you can't be denying knowledge of the French. Last thing you need is to make an enemy of the English too.'

'You always very wise, Buck.'

Tanacharison led them all down the hill, back to the village. He ordered his best brave to lock the Frenchmen in the longhouse, tied together. He waited with his brave and, satisfied they would not be overheard, he leant forward and whispered in the brave's ear, 'Release one of the Frenchmen tomorrow night, show him back to his people. They overheard our conversation in the hollow, nobody wants surprises. Showing a little good faith to our enemy may go a long way.'

The brave nodded.

Trading with the English may have been more lucrative, but Tanacharison feared the French were determined to stay. He hoped they would be keen to avoid a costly battle with the Iroquois.

***

Coulon de Villiers took a swim in the slower-moving southern fork of the river, staying near the shore lest the river's current sweep him away. The water was still icy cold, but it revitalised his tired body and mind. The fort was finished. His orders complete. Stealing it had been easy. His Huron scouts had observed the British men building it for some days before they'd arrived. He would name it Fort Du Quesne, in honour of the Governor of New France. Du Quesne had really shaken them into action since his arrival two years ago. He was full of his own self-importance and he would surely be pleased to have such a strategically crucial point named after him. It may help curry a little favour for Coulon de Villiers, perhaps even secure him a cushy administrative post back in Montreal or Quebec.

He'd sent a dispatch rider north with a letter confirming he had secured the gateway to the Ohio River. He now had a few weeks to provision the fort, make peace with the local Indians and wait for his next orders. He was certain they would be to follow the Ohio River, and set up a fort at the next confluence. An assignment, which – should it transpire – would keep him from his sweetheart Marie Anne, who he hadn't seen since departing for the south at the turn of the year.

'Captain!' came a shout from the riverbank.

It was gap-toothed Jean Luc.

'You are returned! *Magnifique!* Did you capture Croghan?' shouted Coulon de Villiers.

'*Non.* We were tricked! That man – it was Croghan all along. He was rescued by the Iroquois.'

Coulon de Villiers slapped the water in rage. *Merde.* He trod back to the riverbank. That reward would have done him nicely and he'd gone and given it away. *Damn that lying swine.*

'You escaped?' he snapped.

'*Non.* They let me go. They kept the others hostage. But I learned that the English are coming. The Indians say one hundred and sixty of them.'

Coulon de Villiers took a sharp breath as he dried himself with a towel. Not enough to dislodge his forces, but enough to hassle their supply lines and create havoc in the surrounding area, especially with Indian help. The last thing he wanted was to start a fight. The Ohio was for France, and he was well-placed to defend it now. But it only took a fool on the British side to try and make a name for himself; before you knew it, the two sides would be warring again. It would be better to warn the British off before hostilities had a chance to burgeon. Coulon de Villiers knew his French force outnumbered the British, who were generally inept on land. But the consequence for him personally would be grave if he provoked them. His orders were clear: don't start a fight. Du Quesne feared their Royal Navy, which could blockade New France, cutting them off from the French homeland, Louisiana and the Caribbean.

As he dressed, Coulon de Villiers became more certain: intercept the British troop early and convince them their mission was futile before they came close enough to engage. He'd need enough soldiers to keep themselves safe from Indian attack, but not so many that the English would mistake their approach as aggressive.

'Did they say who led the British?'

'I think his name was Washington? Something like that,' said Jean Luc.

Coulon de Villiers purred. He remembered the Virginian from his previous expedition to the northern French forts. He'd seemed a sensible officer, cautious and refined.

Coulon de Villiers made up his mind. He had plenty of troops, but he needed to leave Fort Du Quesne well-defended against an Iroquois attack. So, he would take a party of forty uniformed men and personally lead them south to parley with Washington, and save him the embarrassment of seeing how forlorn the English were. To prevent misunderstandings, he penned a letter explaining that he was travelling with the purpose of forewarning the British. He placed it in the pocket of his blue coat.

67

As he crossed the mountain peaks, George was reminded of his last voyage west. This time, the snow was melting, the wind had lost its bite, and the sun was out. It was as if the Ohio Valley was welcoming him, to save it from the clutches of the French. A good omen. Despite being mounted on horseback, progress was at a snail's pace. Behind him, his men snaked along the mountainside. Slowly trudging upwards, their humour fading as the altitude rose.

He took a moment to appreciate the wide expanse of the continent that stretched as far as the eye could see. He recalled the late General Lee pontificating that this vast land was too big for one nation alone to rule. Yet as he gazed out at the vista, it dawned on George that it fell to him alone to ensure this land wouldn't be shared with France. What an immense privilege he was charged with.

There was much to do, but thus far George was satisfied. He'd kept his troops fed, watered and rested at night. Complaints had been minimal but, as he looked west over undulating forests as far as the eye could see, he knew that harder miles were ahead. Supply lines would be stretched; that detestable Scotsman, Barney, had yet to appear and make good on his contract, but George had bought up all the victuals he could as they'd journeyed through Virginia.

On the horizon, amongst the endless trees, the Indian nations would be lurking, like lice on a coat, seeking their advantage. At least, this time, he wasn't dependent on that knave Tanacharison. Once his fort was built, his force could be self-sufficient and free from harassment. Success hinged on establishing a strong defensive position to repel French encroachment.

'Some view,' said Viktor, who had stayed close at hand.

His fellow Virginian had proved eager and reliable, running small errands. Their itinerant existence seemed to suit him, like a child on a big adventure. It was a feeling that George shared. Van Braam joined them at the crest of the bluff.

'Four days from here, even for us. Best we keep moving – if they all stop to admire the view it'll be five!' True to form, Van Braam assumed a commanding manner that exceeded his rank.

George acquiesced, for the Dutchman was right. He kicked his animal's flanks and navigated the mountainside, down into the trees, keeping a north-west bearing. At sunset, they happened upon a clearing, no greater than fifteen acres, that suited as a camp for the night.

The following morning, George was breakfasting on a stale bit of flatbread when a murmur rippled through the camp. All around, his men leapt to their feet and reached for their guns. 'Indians!' George grabbed his musket and ran forward. He saw them standing at the forest edge, watching. No weapons drawn. At their head was Tanacharison.

'Stand down, men!' shouted George, fearing they may panic. He felt the stares of his men amassed behind him as he approached Tanacharison. Standing beside the Chief, George recognised George Croghan, that Irish fur trader he'd met at Governor Dinwiddie's residence.

'Top o' the morning, Washington.' Croghan gave him a broad smile.

George's greeting was courteous but cold. Last thing he wanted was for them to think he was glad to see them.

'You are too late,' said Tanacharison. 'The French have taken the fork in the river.'

George recovered himself, determined not to let his face betray his disappointment. The Indian and Irishmen proceeded to describe the strength of the French force.

'What are their intentions, do you know?' George asked of the French.

Croghan replied, 'They are claiming this land for themselves, unless you stop them—'

'But the King said it was ours!'

'Aye, he can say what he wants in London, but he's not here to argue with them.'

How could a king govern a land so far away, when he'd never even seen it with his own eyes, thought George. And when another king invaded it with troops of his own, how could the land still be determined as rightfully British? It seemed preposterous. And yet, it was George's duty to enforce this British right. His thoughts turned to Dinwiddie. If he'd rallied the House into action sooner, then maybe George could have got out here before the winter, and the French would have been pegged back. Alas, that moment was gone, and so too was George's investment. Unless he could come up with a plan.

Keen to reassert some degree of control over matters, he ordered his troops to disperse and scavenge for food. He invited Croghan and Tanacharison to parley further in his tent, free from prying ears.

Croghan wasted no time in imposing his opinions: 'Look, your choices are limited. You can't beat them in a fight. There's too many of them and they're fortified. But you need to make it clear that the French can't come any further.'

'Thank you, Mr Croghan, I realise that. What are you suggesting?' said George testily.

'Either move north and harry their supply lines so you can force them to retreat. Or get as close as you dare and fortify the river downstream from them.'

George's mind felt blank, there was so much to take in and he was conscious they were looking to him for a decision.

'You should attack!' Tanacharison insisted. 'Too long you have taken.'

'If I were more confident of your support, I might, but from the poor showing of your Iroquois peoples on my last visit to the Ohio, I fear I might find my men abandoned to their fate.'

Tanacharison scowled.

'Hold on, let's not rake over the bones of the past,' said Croghan, keen to appease the Chief.

'Easy for you to say, Croghan,' snapped George. 'But this man here was required by treaty to send warriors to accompany me, and only managed a total of four. Hardly the impressive alliance we needed to deter the French! Now he begs me to attack. You expect me to believe he'll be any less useless this time...'

Tanacharison spat at George's feet.

Silenced, George felt disgust at the savage's behaviour. 'As you sow, so you shall reap, Tanacharison.'

Croghan held out his arm to restrain the Chief from pouncing forward. 'Look, we all want the same thing here, and by Jesus, Washington,' Croghan lowered his voice, 'could you refrain from insulting the man?'

George turned his head away. Croghan tugged his attention back, speaking in a hushed tone, 'Look, don't underestimate the Indians, I've seen what they are capable of...'

'As have I, for the most part: duplicity!' George cleared his throat, 'I've made up my mind. We'll continue until we reach the Monongahela River and we'll build a fort a day south of the French fort, at the fork with the Allegheny. It will give us sufficient time to see a French attack coming. It's not perfect, but it will do under the circumstances. Now, if you'll excuse me, I have duties to attend to.'

George issued them out of his tent and followed them outside. A loud cheer erupted from the troops who'd returned from scavenging. George looked up to see why his appearance should be greeted by jubilation, only to realise their ovations were directed in another direction. Appearing through the trees to the south were troops.

Shouts of 'Reinforcements!' filled the air. George paced forwards through his assembled men, but didn't share in their jubilation. His heart sank when he saw the small, bespectacled figure of Joshua Fry on horseback, clad in a red coat.

'Lieutenant Colonel, I should have you court-marshalled!' Fry boomed. 'You left without me and with half a force. Explain yourself!'

George stiffened. 'I was concerned, Colonel, that so much time had already passed as our hopes would be best served by beating the French to the forks. As it transpires, I was right: we are too late. Too many delays have cost us the initiative in the Ohio. A force of one thousand Frenchmen awaits us.'

Fry frowned.

'The French have the forks, Colonel,' George spelled it out.

Croghan and Tanacharison arrived and exchanged brisk greetings with Fry. They confirmed the news that George had imparted.

'But there is a new plan,' announced George. 'We will travel to the river and build a fort downstream.'

'No, we won't. This is my command now and we'll be staying right where we are.'

'But, Mr Fry—' pleaded Croghan.

'It's Colonel,' snapped Fry.

'We ought to—' continued Croghan.

'We *ought* to wait, until our forces are assembled.' Fry glared at Croghan, then at George. 'More men are coming from the Carolinas. So, before the likes of you and Washington rush off all half-cocked, we'll be doing things properly and with maximum strength. This is a good clearing, we are safe here. Washington, have your men fell some trees and build a palisade wall for us to defend.'

'But—'

'That's an order, Lieutenant,' said Fry, adjusting his spectacles.

George felt his cheeks flush. He could not let this stand. 'Colonel, forgive me, but we need to cover as much ground as possible, to keep the French at bay.'

Fry leant forward. 'We have but two hundred men between us. If there are indeed one thousand French, we are woefully outnumbered. Judging by your stores over there,' Fry indicated the barrels dumped in the middle of the camp, 'you are short of supplies. Probably because you left in a hurry. The further north you go, the more our supply lines will be stretched. Our advantage lies in us being fortified, supplied and amassed. I've no wish to see Englishmen killed on the foolish errand of their King and the ill-discipline of his novice colonial commanders.'

With his fists clenched, George turned and walked off before he did something he might regret.

***

Viktor and Jimmy crept through the forest on the trail of a deer, having spotted the fresh dung and hoof prints. Staying downwind, they tiptoed through the undergrowth, going from tree to tree for a quarter of a mile until they caught sight of the young white-tailed buck. Viktor peered round the tree trunk that sheltered him, raised the musket and took aim. The deer stretched its neck, reaching for the low-hanging berries. Its three-pointed antlers shook as it munched its way through the slim pickings on the bush. Viktor's heart pounded as he aimed for the beast's heart, just behind its shoulders. He pulled the trigger, the crack of gunfire ricocheting around the forest. The buck was knocked off its feet. He ran across to find it thrashing its legs as it struggled to find purchase in the soft, loamy ground. It flicked its antlers in his direction. The shot had gone into the buck's lungs, and blood bubbled from its nostrils. Jimmy arrived beside him, panting.

'You've got a knife. Slit its throat,' said Viktor.

'I ain't doing that, it'll have my eye out.' Jimmy pointed at the antlers as the animal thrashed about, crying out.

Viktor remembered Jimmy was a sailor, born in London. He'd probably never killed his own dinner. He took the knife and, careful to avoid the antlers, sliced the deer's throat. Its movement slowed and it finally lay still as its blood spilled from its neck.

The forest was silent, and Jimmy looked about anxiously. 'This place gives me the creeps. That noise will have travelled for miles. I say we get out of here before Indians do likewise to us.'

Jimmy was just like every other man off the boats, thought Viktor. Full of tales of Indians, fearing their savagery. 'You get the front legs.'

Between them, they carried the fallen deer back to camp.

Jimmy spoke with lowered voice, 'Viktor, you heard the Indian and Irishmen this morning. The French have beat us to the forks, our mission is over. I say we head home. I've got a bad feeling about this now.'

Viktor dismissed the suggestion. He'd been running from things for years: his father, Fitzbarton, Sylvia... He was determined to see this through. He trusted George to know what to do. Besides, Viktor had nothing to return to and the longer this dragged on, the better the pay.

It was late afternoon by the time they found the camp again. The numbers had somehow swollen in their absence, and a few stakes had been cut and driven into the ground to form the beginnings of a crude wall. A nearby man confirmed that reinforcements had arrived, and Colonel Fry was now in charge. The sight of the dead deer caused some excitement as they carried it through the camp and dumped it on the ground by the mess kitchen. Viktor stretched his weary arms now that they were free of the burden, then went in search of George to find out what was going on. Before he got more than five yards from the deer's carcass, he heard his name called.

'Viktor, it's you!'

He thought his eyes were playing tricks on him. A little older than he remembered, but unmistakably, it was his younger brother.

'Daniel! What are you doing here?'

His younger brother embraced him. Viktor was too puzzled to return the sentiment.

'I mean it – what are you doing here?'

'I joined up,' he said simply. 'Viktor, it's so good to see you. I've missed you enormously since you left!'

Viktor couldn't share in the joy of seeing his sibling; not until he understood what had become of Hans. 'What about Father? You should be helping him.'

Daniel looked hurt. 'Why should I be the one left behind to look after him? You didn't.'

'But – I don't understand, why did you leave?'

'It's not been the same since you left, Vik. Father's been even grumpier than usual. Then one day he fell ill – nothing serious, but he rested in bed, so I went to church without him. On the way home, Fitzbarton and his two men…'

'Billy and Granville?'

'I guess so, they accosted me on the track home. They said I needed to sign up for the militia. That I'd be paid, Vik – after all, we could use the money. They said that if I didn't, they'd be entitled to burn the cabin as retribution.'

Viktor clenched his teeth. 'What did you tell Father?'

'Nothing. I waited till he got better, then I left.'

'But you can't just leave him alone! He won't know why you disappeared, he won't manage on his own—'

'You left! Why is it different for me? Why do I have to stay just because you've chosen not to?'

Viktor shook his head. It was a fair point, but Hans couldn't be left by himself, to be harried by more of Mason's tricks. Viktor knew Mason would stop at nothing to get their family's land, especially after he'd robbed him. He rubbed his forehead as a horrible thought occurred to him: *This is Mason's revenge for the robbery. This is my fault.*

'Dan, we have to go back.'

'No. Why?'

'Because Mason will prey on him.'

'What can he do?' Daniel scoffed.

'He'll think of something. Do you remember the flea beetles? That was his scheme, to see us starved out.'

'It's in the past. Besides, if we leave now, we won't get paid. Then this will have been for nothing.'

'Come on. We'll go and explain to Washington.'

They found him supervising the construction work taking place in the middle of the meadow.

'Begging your pardon, Lieutenant Colonel, could I have a word?'

'Certainly, Viktor. What is it?'

Viktor thought it strange that he looked relieved to be interrupted.

'This is my brother, Daniel, he came with the reinforcements today. But he shouldn't be here. He ought to be looking after our sick father. Mason Fitzbarton tricked him so he could take advantage of our father being incapacitated.'

'Tell me, Viktor,' said George after a pause, 'what does this have to do with the Ohio Valley?'

'Well, nothing, sir… Only we need to go home to look after our father…'

'Out of the question.'

'But Daniel was tricked into—'

'It is Daniel's duty to serve his colony, same as it is yours and mine. I won't hear any more of this.'

Viktor felt bitterness surge through him and opened his mouth to respond.

'Think, Viktor, before you speak something you may regret.'

'Permission to leave the camp, sir?'

'Denied. I need you. So does your country.'

'But so does my father—'

'Daniel, please leave us.' Once Daniel had departed, Washington leaned forward, his grim expression only a few inches from Viktor's. 'How dare you question me and then have the temerity to argue my decision, Viktor. I should have you shot!'

Viktor flinched.

'And so you don't you think of absconding,' George continued, 'you'll take sentry duty tonight.'

Viktor nodded and walked away, cursing his foolishness, cursing Fitzbarton's cunning, and cursing Daniel's naivety.

'What should we do, Viktor?' asked Daniel when Viktor caught up with him.

Viktor shrugged.

'I'm sorry if I've made things bad for us, and for Father...'

Viktor put his arm around his younger brother. 'It's not your fault, Dan.' He observed the camp, the men milling about, playing cards, cricket, and chattering. Why must God tolerate the likes of Fitzbarton and reward him with such wealth, when honest folk like his family didn't have a penny to their name?

He bid Daniel good evening, grabbed his musket, and took up a position amongst the trees on the edge of camp.

68

May 24th, 1754
North of British camp, the Ohio Valley

By dawn, Tanacharison and his five best braves were well clear of the English camp. Fleet of foot, they covered ground quickly and silently, heading north towards the French advance party. That night, crouched low behind a tree trunk, he watched as the detachment of Frenchmen made camp for the evening. He signalled his braves to fan out. Then he stepped clear of the tree and whistled, his palms held aloft.

The French were startled, reaching for their guns. Tanacharison stood still. Seeing this, the French commander, a tall man with long dark hair, ordered his men to stand down. Tanacharison held out a string of wampum, to show he meant no harm.

The forest was silent. The French officer beckoned him forward. With his hands raised Tanacharison stepped towards them, stopping within twenty paces.

'I am Tanacharison, leader of the Iroquois people,' he said in English.

The French commander replied in English, 'I am Joseph Coulon de Villiers. I come in peace.'

'As do I. Welcome to these lands. I returned a prisoner to you with valuable information. Did he make it to you?'

'He did. Thank you. I am grateful for your friendship. Can I offer you a drink?'

Moments later, Tanacharison was drinking wine from an animal skin. 'What are your intentions?' he asked.

'I come to parley with the English and deter them from attacking.'

'Their numbers have grown. Three hundred men,' said Tanacharison. 'They have proved good traders, but unreliable allies. To make a peace with the French peoples, I offer to lead one of their commanders to meet you. You can talk with him or capture him – whichever best serves your purpose. In return, I want protection for my people.'

The Frenchman nodded his agreement, stating France wished to trade with all the Indian peoples.

Together, they agreed how they would lure in the English officer and take him hostage. Conversation over, they clasped each other's forearms, eyes locked, plan agreed.

***

The following morning, George was joined in his tent by Tanacharison and Croghan. They huddled conspiratorially, these three distinct men united by their shared opposition to Fry.

Tanacharison spoke in hushed tones. 'My braves have seen forty Frenchmen coming this way. Their leader is among them. If you capture him, then you have the initiative.'

Finally, thought George, *Tanacharison is proving himself a worthy ally.*

'Hold on,' said Croghan. 'You'll need to be careful not to start a fight...'

George dismissed the concerns of the yellow-bellied Irishman; he had no cause to be here anyway, let alone giving voice to his opinions. George left the tent to go in search of Fry. To his disbelief, he found the Colonel peering through the undergrowth, studying plants on the edge of the clearing. *Hardly the time for botany.*

'Colonel, my intelligence sources tell me the French commander is headed for us with a small guard. I request permission to lead a detachment of my men to intercept them and capture the commander. With hostages, we could negotiate—'

'Denied.'

'But, Colonel—'

'But nothing, Washington. Capture one commander and they'll just send another. If what you say is true, then clearly they are coming to negotiate. If their intentions were aggressive, they'd send a larger detachment of troops, wouldn't they? So, we wait.'

More waiting. That was the trouble with old men: rather than shaping the future they were content to simply observe it. Endless waiting and arguing was what had cost Virginia the Ohio in the first place. Infuriated by the inactivity, George returned to his tent and penned a letter to Dinwiddie, complaining about Fry's command. With his frustrations off his chest, he wrote letters to the Governors of Maryland, the Carolinas and Pennsylvania, imploring them to send men, and assist in sparing Britain further embarrassment in the face of the French.

Come the afternoon and his temper restored, George asked himself what would Lawrence do. He'd hated Fry as much as anyone. The more George thought about it, the more he realised there was only one choice: He couldn't, in clear conscience, sit back and let his reputation suffer at the hands of Fry's faint-heartedness. He summoned Croghan and Tanacharison back to his tent to test his plan.

'My spies report the French raiding party is only seven miles away,' said the Chief.

George bristled; they were close enough to reconnoitre the British position.

'Tanacharison, if we left tonight, would you provide an escort?'

The Chief nodded. The thin smile that spread across his face suggested he was happy to help. 'Twenty men.'

'Excellent. Croghan you will come with me and act as an interpreter...'

'I shan't be coming with you.'

'What on earth do you mean?'

'The French, they've a bounty on my head, I've escaped them once...'

'Well, I'll be damned,' said George, making no attempt to hide his contempt. 'This is for your country. It's your duty!'

'Duty? You talk to me of duty? Tell me, whose duty was it to build a fort? The Ohio Company's. And where were you? Nowhere to be seen. I'd half-finished that bloody fort with my own hands and at my own expense, so don't be telling me about duty! You're a year too bloody late and don't be blaming me. If it weren't for me, your company would never have this man here's blessing. You cheeky upstart—'

'Croghan, you are dismissed.' George's cheeks glowed red with fury at the Irishman's rebuke. If he never set eyes on him again, it would be too soon. With Croghan out of the way, he continued planning: 'Right, Tanacharison, I'll assemble forty men and we'll leave at midnight.'

The Chief nodded and slipped out of the tent.

Three hours later, the camp asleep, George had hand-picked forty men and, following Tanacharison's lead, they embarked just as rain began to fall.

George jogged to the front of the line, passing Viktor and Jimmy, both of whom had been sullen all day. Fearing Viktor may be tempted to desert in his absence, he'd ordered them to join him at the front.

***

Viktor pulled his coat tight across his chest to protect himself against the driving rain. It was pitch black under the forest canopy, the new moon providing no illumination to guide their path. He stayed close to George – so close that when he tripped over a tree root, he fell into the back of him, bringing them both down onto the sodden ground. After cursing under their breath, they picked themselves up and resumed their silent march. Viktor had been disappointed to be chosen for this expedition and was certain it was because of his request to take a leave of absence. At least Daniel had been spared selection, on account of being under Fry's command.

They walked for hours, slipping in the mud, tripping in the dark, bumping into one another, sodden wet and tired. Any nerves Viktor might have felt at the prospect of encountering their enemy had never emerged. He was too fed up.

The dark was just beginning to lift when George stopped in his tracks. From the misty gloom, two Indians appeared and whispered to Tanacharison. The Chief turned and spoke to George. Sensing something was afoot, Viktor felt butterflies flutter in his stomach. George motioned for all men to gather round.

While Tanacharison kept a watchful eye on the slope in front, George whispered to his men. 'The French are hiding in a hollow at the top of this slope. We're going to encircle them. The Indians are going round the back of the French to cut off any rearward escape. We'll approach on our bellies and capture them in their slumber.' George raised a warning finger. 'You're only to fire your weapons on my command. We want prisoners, not bodies. Under no circumstance are you to shoot their leader.'

Satisfied they had understood his orders, George turned and crept towards the French. Tanacharison and his Iroquois braves left in crouched runs, leaving the British alone.

Viktor felt the cold wet soil under his fingers as he began to crawl up the slope.

It took half an hour to reach the top. George glanced over first. Viktor poked his head up. A fire smouldered, around which were arranged the peacefully sleeping bodies of the French soldiers, shrouded in their blankets and blue coats. Viktor's heart skipped a beat. It was the first time he'd seen Frenchmen, the eternal enemy of his adopted homeland. In the dim light of dawn, they looked very normal. As he scanned across, his eyes met those of a sentry on the edge of the camp. The Frenchman's eyes opened wide in horror as he realised what was afoot. The sentry raised his pistol and a flash of flame spurted from the muzzle. The bang echoed round the forest and set panic through the French as they leapt up from under their blankets and reached for their weapons.

Someone from the British ranks fired, felling the sentry.

The French returned fire, filling the hollow with flashes, bangs and smoke.

'Halt fire!' yelled George.

Viktor felt a euphoric rush as fear took control of his body. At the word *fire*, he pulled the trigger. The musket thumped into his shoulder as it spat its lead ball towards the French. All along the British line, they fired.

As they reloaded, George leapt to his feet.

'STOP!' he shouted. 'STOP! STOP!'

A shot was returned by the French.

It was greeted by retaliatory British shots from the far end of the line.

'Cease firing!' yelled George, his face puce.

Viktor glanced over the lip of the hollow.

The air was still, thick with the smell of gunpowder, the acrid smoke clinging to the damp ground. The only sounds were the agonised groans from the injured. As the fumes cleared, the toll the ambush had taken on the French became clear. Those that weren't holding their hands in the air, had fallen. The luckier ones clutched at their wounds and writhed in various states of stifled agony.

'We surrender,' called out a heavily accented French voice.

Next to Viktor, George stepped clear of the small tree that had shielded him and descended into the sunken hollow.

I hope this isn't a trap, thought Viktor. The Iroquois were nowhere to be seen.

'Lieutenant Colonel Washington of His Majesty King George's army. Who is your commanding officer?'

'I am,' said a tall Frenchman, with long dark hair. 'Captain Joseph Coulon de Villiers.'

'Viktor, Jimmy, Van Braam, come and join me,' George called.

Viktor, with some degree of trepidation, stood and walked down, his musket pointing at the enemy.

The French captain grimaced, his narrow eyes so sharp they could mine copper.

'You have killed ten of my men and injured just as many. This attack was unprovoked.'

George looked down at his feet. 'You are sneaking about these woods, land claimed by our King, coming to spy on us. Your intention was to attack,' George retorted.

The Frenchman was incredulous. 'I've never laid eyes on the British forces on our side of the mountains. I come bearing a peace treaty to ask you to vacate, so no blood might needlessly be spilled. But because of your rash actions—'

'I must protest – if your intentions were so peaceful, then why do you take a troop of soldiers with you?'

'Lieutenant Colonel Washington, I note that you have the same size force as I, and it is you who sneaks about in the night, murdering us while we sleep!'

Viktor watched as George shifted on his feet, uncomfortable with the Frenchman's accusations.

'Believe me, Lieutenant Colonel,' the French captain continued, 'from what I have heard of your army, I have enough men to wipe the British from the Ohio. That you mistake my force as weak, is a sign of your own weakness.'

'Well, alas, what's done is done,' George said quickly. 'You have surrendered, and this cannot be undone. Please prepare yourself and your men to return with me as prisoners of the British army.'

***

This was the moment Tanacharison had been waiting for. He watched the white men in discussion, events having gone as well as he could have expected. He'd been right to rely on Washington's over-eagerness, and the young Virginian had unknowingly played his part perfectly. It was now time for the Iroquois to play their part. He signalled to his braves and they crept down the far side of the hollow, towards the Europeans. He recognised the French commander from their meeting in the woods the day before. He was pleased to see he was unharmed by the British incompetence. Tanacharison joined Washington and Coulon de Villiers, offering a nod to each of them. Washington looked flustered, his face pale and mannerisms jittery. Coulon de Villiers looked expectantly at the Iroquoian chief. As he returned the man's gaze, Tanacharison thought, *May your spirit wander freely.* He reached inside the fold of his fur coat and gripped his tomahawk. In one swift motion he swung his arm, burying the blade in the Frenchman's forehead with a dull thud. The pained surprise would be etched on the Frenchman's face for eternity. He dropped to the ground.

'What the fucking hell are you doing?' barked Washington.

Tanacharison clicked his fingers. His men stepped forth and with axe blows, and slashes of knives, they murdered the remaining Frenchmen, all bar one. The wounded were relieved of their scalps.

'Stop this!' yelled Washington, waving his arms in protest.

Tanacharison shook his head. This would not be stopped. This was the destiny of not just his people, but all the native peoples, who had been forced to share their lands with the cancerous white men, and their insidious notions of land ownership, private property and law.

The lethal weapons and poisonous drugs they'd inflicted on the continent. The legal sleights of hand and duplicitous treaties.

As the slaughter subsided, he felt calm, despite Washington's protestations.

His descendants would judge what happened today, but in his gut, Tanacharison believed it would be his name that the elders of the future would intone as they sat around campfires and inside their tepees, telling children stories of the great Tanacharison, who restored the dominance of the Native American peoples.

'What the fucking hell are you playing at?' screamed Washington.

Tanacharison raised his tomahawk. It was enough to silence the imbecilic Englishman.

'Goodbye Washington. I have fulfilled my treaty obligations. I wish you a quick death in the forthcoming war.'

He clicked his fingers again and his braves, scalps in hand, followed him out of the hollow. They were going home. They took the one remaining Frenchman with them. He would be returned to his people, so the French might learn of the murderous brutality inflicted on them by the British attack.

***

George steadied himself, fearing his legs might give way. At his feet lay the bodies of thirty-nine Frenchmen. He felt bile at the back of his throat, bent over and vomited, spattering his boots. Never again would he trust an Indian. The consequences of where he stood, of what he'd seen began to dawn on him. What would he say to Fry? This was the Iroquois' fault; yet the jumped-up little maths teacher would be sure to exact full reprisals on George for disobeying him. The repercussions rippled thick and fast through his thoughts.

'What should we do?' It was Viktor's voice.

George turned to see Viktor, Jimmy and Van Braam, all pale, stunned. Not even Van Braam, usually so quick to offer suggestions, had anything to say.

'Lieutenant Colonel? Viktor prompted.

'How the fucking hell should I know?' screamed George.

Disconcerted, Viktor looked at Jimmy, who raised his eyebrows.

George wiped the tears that welled in his eyes. Lawrence's wife, Anne, came to mind. He recalled her quoting the Stoics at him: 'Wish life as you find it, not as you would have it.' What a load of codswallop.

The remainder of the company began to move down the slope into the hollow. Quietly, they began to rifle through the pockets of the slaughtered.

'Sir,' said one of George's men. 'We've a single casualty. Shot in the head he was.'

George needed time to think. 'Dig him a grave. We'll give him a Christian burial.'

'What about the French?'

'What about them?'

Viktor and Jimmy slid into the background as the rest of the men looted the French corpses. Though Viktor wasn't the most worldly-wise of men, he knew enough to realise that what had unfolded this morning was a cause of great shame to Washington and all involved. Jimmy's face mirrored his.

'Shall we?'

Jimmy nodded.

They sneaked up the side of the hollow. Once clear of the lip, they broke into a sprint. Ducking branches and swerving trees, the two ran as far and as fast as they could. When their legs could no longer stand it, they came to an abrupt halt, bent double and wheezing for air, their hearts thumping. Once recovered, they continued east. After a few miles, they came to a track that led them back south. They would need to circumnavigate the British camp and trek back over the mountains.

As they walked, doubts began to form in Viktor's mind. If the French were to retaliate – and there was no doubt in his mind that they would – then Daniel would be amongst the British ranks. The prospect of his brother caught up in a battle against a superior force appalled him. He had to get Daniel out. Would Jimmy even be willing to return? And if they were spotted returning on their own, before or after the rest of the company, they would certainly face tough questions.

Unless… An idea occurred to Viktor. Washington's company had sneaked out of camp under the cover of darkness. They could return and inform Fry of Washington's disgrace, turning desertion into an act of loyalty. He was just about to pitch the idea out loud when Jimmy stopped in his tracks.

'Sshh.'

They stood still.

'Can you hear that too?' Jimmy whispered.

Viktor strained his ears. There was a sound of creaking wood.

Together they ran into the undergrowth and hid behind a thicket. There was a crack of a whip, a horse blowing hard.

'Come on, ye wee bastard!'

Viktor peered through the bush and couldn't believe his eyes. Crossing a stream and struggling up the slope was a horse and cart. Sat atop it was the familiar face of a Scotsman. What on earth was Barney doing out here alone?

69

May 24ᵗʰ, 1754
Somewhere in the Ohio Valley

Viktor and Jimmy leapt out from behind the bush, shouting 'Boo!'

The horse reared, straining against its harness. Barney fell backwards from the bench and rolled over onto his cargo.

Viktor and Jimmy rolled about with laughter.

Dusting himself down, Barney said, 'Argh, ye pair o' bastards, ye frightened the life out o' me!'

It was a welcome release to laugh again after the tragedy they'd just endured. Jimmy settled the horse.

'What are you doing?' asked Viktor.

Resuming his seat, Barney, who hadn't entirely seen the funny side of their prank, said, 'Selling this lot.' He indicated the barrels tied to his cart.

'You've gone too far. We're camped south of here. There's only French that way.'

'Oh aye,' Barney shifted in his seat, looking away.

'Except you weren't looking for us, were you, Barney?' said Jimmy.

'Eh?'

'You'd have known that – the tracks of three hundred men traipsing through the woods – even a drunk could follow. You've swerved past the British on purpose, haven't you?'

'So what if I have?'

'That would make you a traitor!'

'A traitor?' Barney laughed. 'These pricks dumped me over here,

486

and now they expect me to supply the same army that slaughtered my kinsmen? Nae thanks.'

Viktor shook his head in disbelief. *What is it with these people?*

'Anyways, I best be getting on,' said Barney.

'I wouldn't if I were you. Washington just presided over the slaughter of forty Frenchmen. Soon as they learn what happened, they'll be out for vengeance.'

'Wasnae me, pal, auld alliance will hold firm.'

Viktor lifted his musket, pointing the muzzle at Barney. 'No you don't. We incriminated ourselves to get you this contract, and you're going to honour it, Barney. We're taking you back with us, and you're going to split the monies three ways.'

'Oh aye? Says who?'

'I do, Barney. I've just killed French soldiers. Trust me, I won't think twice before shooting you. Don't you be thinking anyone will miss one traitor, out alone in the woods. Then me and Jimmy will split the monies fifty-fifty.'

'Oh aye? Somebody's grown a pair of sweetbreads.'

Viktor nodded. 'You decide, Barney.'

Jimmy lifted his musket too.

'Alrite, but nae word of this, aye?'

Viktor nodded. 'You were lost. That's all.'

With some difficulty on the uneven ground, Barney turned the cart around and Jimmy and Viktor climbed aboard to perch on barrels of salt pork. They made good pace and were back at the camp by late morning, circling round to approach from the south.

'Who do we speak to?' asked Barney, pulling the cart to a halt on the edge of the meadow.

'Colonel Fry's in charge. I'll fetch him,' said Jimmy, climbing down.

He returned shortly, pushing his way through the small party of onlookers the cart's arrival had drawn in, all eager for news and gossip from the far side of the mountains.

'He's exercising his horse, should be back soon. Best we wait here,' said Jimmy.

***

Joshua Fry rode a rising trot: it was safe, measured and gave both him and his animal a bracing workout that demanded discipline and concentration. Discipline was something that was sorely lacking in his force. Yet what could one expect of colonials, so accustomed to doing as they pleased? If Washington, supposedly the best of them, was wanting, then what chance did the rest of them have? Fry had bottled his anger when he'd learned that Washington had disobeyed him and taken a company of men out for reconnaissance. They'd been gone for some time, but if the Lieutenant Colonel thought that meant Fry's anger would be abated, then he would soon discover his notion was erroneous. He would be stripped of his command and sent back to Virginia in disgrace. The British army couldn't function with his sort amongst the ranks.

Earlier that morning, Fry had penned a letter to Governor Dinwiddie, informing him of Washington's disobedience. He carried it now in his breast pocket, and would complete it once he could fully detail the scale of Washington's blunder.

His composure restored from his exercise, he arrived back at camp by lunchtime. All the men were either queueing for food or sitting about eating it. By the entrance to the meadow, he saw a cart laden with supplies; a welcome sight, for they were running low. He rode forth to address the men standing guard of it.

'Colonel Fry, we were contracted by Lieutenant Colonel Washington to supply goods for the army. In his absence, could you please sign a receipt for us so we might draw payment?' said a young blond man.

The man with wild red hair stepped down from the cart. Fry noticed a scar across the fellow's cheek. His instincts warned him there was something unsavoury about this man.

'I see. What are your names?'

'Barney MacGregor,' answered the scar-faced man in a Scots accent.

Fry frowned. 'And you?'

'Viktor Neumann, Colonel.'

He'd heard that name before, but couldn't think where. Fry looked at the other man, short and fair-haired. Recognition dawned.

'Are you men from Fairfax County, by any chance?'

They nodded, looking quizzical.

It must be them. The name Viktor Neumann tallied and the other two matched the description Mason Fitzbarton had given in his letter. Fry took a chance: 'Then you are under arrest, for the assault and theft of goods from Mason Fitzbarton.'

Their mouths fell open. *I bet they hadn't reckoned on their crimes catching up with them out here,* thought Fry with no small degree of satisfaction.

'Thas nae us…' protested the Scotsman.

'I have sufficient suspicion to bring you to trial. The law will do the rest.' Fry straightened his spectacles. 'If these lands are to be considered British, then our laws apply. You'll be tried for your crimes in Williamsburg.'

The Scotsman snarled as he stepped forward and kicked the belly of Fry's horse. It neighed in pain and reared up. Fry fought to retain his balance, gripping the reins. As the horse's front legs returned to the ground, he slid out of the saddle and over the horse's neck. The ground rushed up to greet his fall. He heard a crunch as his head slammed into the ground, a sharp pain in his neck. Then his world went dark.

***

The three of them stood over Colonel Fry, staring at his motionless body. The horse shuffled, settling from its trauma.

Jimmy looked nervously over the cart to see if anyone had noticed. The rest of the camp was preoccupied with lunch.

Fry lay motionless. Viktor bent down and felt his neck for a pulse. Nothing.

'Barney – you've killed him!'

'I never. Was falling off his horse that killed him!'

They all three looked at each other.

'What are we gonna do?'

***

George returned to camp just after lunch, still uncertain of what he was going to tell Fry. Following in his wake, his men were sullen. His numbers had shrunk by six. Five had deserted, with one British casualty, but it was the fate of the French that weighed on their tired minds. George ruminated on how the expedition had descended into a firefight, despite him never once giving the order to fire. Soldiers were supposed to follow orders. If they had, none of this would have happened. As for Tanacharison's treachery, well, that was no less than he expected. He vowed never to trust Indians of any persuasion again.

As he walked through the camp, he felt stares following him. Soldiers stood about in groups, appearing to await a reaction from him. *Did they already know?*

One of Fry's officers approached. He looked as pale as George felt.

'Lieutenant Colonel, there's been an incident. Please, sir, if you'd accompany me?'

George was defiant. 'This incident has nothing to do with you, I shall speak to Colonel Fry, not some—'

'Forgive me, Lieutenant Colonel, the incident to which I refer involves Colonel Fry.'

George was confused. He followed the man into Fry's tent. Laid out on the ground was the motionless body of Joshua Fry. His eyes and mouth were open. George stared at his chest, waiting for the rise and fall of his ribcage. Standing at the back was MacGregor, that Scots hawker, alongside Viktor and Jimmy. He'd last seen them in the hollow, and assumed they'd fled, never to be seen again. He'd deal with their offence later.

'What happened?' he demanded.

'Poor bugger's horse reared up, dumped him on the ground. Landed on his head,' said Barney.

'That's it?' asked George in disbelief.

'Aye. Freak accident. Very sad.' Barney shook his head in condolence.

Viktor and Jimmy both nodded their support.

The officer piped up, 'We found him dead on the ground, next to his horse. There's no marks or wounds on his body. Appears it was just bad luck. What would you like us to do, sir?'

George looked up from Fry's silent corpse. The man had had a lot to say in his short time in Virginia; but no more. *Does this make matters easier?* He wasn't sure yet.

The officer paused, then said, 'You're now the ranking officer, Lieutenant Colonel.'

'Indeed.' George was ashamed to feel a brief sense of relief that he wouldn't have to offer an explanation for his night-time fiasco. 'Have your men dig a grave.'

The officer left the tent.

'Why do I smell foul play?' said George.

Barney shrugged. 'I brought your supplies, as promised.'

George knelt to inspect Fry's body. His head was at an odd angle. Beyond that, he looked in order, with no rips or scuffs to his clothing. He noticed the corner tip of a bit of paper protruding from the man's breast pocket. He took it out and unfolded the letter. After reading a few lines, he re-folded it and put it in his own pocket for safekeeping, lest anyone else read its damning contents.

'MacGregor, find yourself a weapon, you're staying here.'

'But...'

'Or I'll have you arrested for the murder of Joshua Fry.'

'I never!'

'I don't know what happened here, but you two should have been with me. As the three of you were found standing over the dead body of our commanding officer, it'll be your word against mine. So, get out there. You'll be in my regiment, Barney, under Jimmy Jones' command. If you desert, you'll be shot. Dismissed. You too, Jimmy.'

Barney's jaw rippled. He looked like he was about to protest but took himself out of the tent. Jimmy followed.

George stood up and squared up to Viktor. 'You're a good lad, Viktor. I'd rather not have you shot for desertion. Why did you come back?'

'For Daniel.'

George nodded, satisfied it was the truth. 'I need someone to take a letter to Governor Dinwiddie in Williamsburg, explaining what occurred this morning. It's better coming from someone who witnessed what Tanacharison did. If you do that for me, then you're free to attend to your father's situation, so you won't need to desert again. Take Fry's horse.'

'Thank you, Lieutenant Colonel.' Relief spread over Viktor's face, then his eyes widened as a thought occurred to him. 'Can my brother

Daniel come too?'

George shook his head. 'No. He's to stay here. I need every available man.'

Viktor frowned.

'I'll have him transferred, and Jimmy Jones can look after him. Now, wait here while I write a letter.'

***

With Washington's sealed letter in his pocket, Viktor grabbed a loaf of bread and led Fry's horse in search of Daniel. He found Jimmy first.

'Barney's livid.'

'Never mind him,' said Viktor. 'My brother's being transferred to your company. I want you to promise you'll keep him safe.'

Jimmy agreed, then began to quiz Viktor on how he had managed to get out on full pay. They found Daniel sitting with some soldiers who were beating him at cards. He got up, pleased to see Viktor.

'Daniel, I have to run an errand for the Lieutenant Colonel. I will be gone for some time, but I'll check in on Father on the way back. This is Jimmy Jones, he's going to look after you. You'll get to know Barney – but don't listen to him, he's trouble.'

Daniel looked apprehensive. Viktor embraced him then climbed up on Fry's horse. He turned to wave goodbye as he rode away, and took a long look at their faces, hoping dearly it wouldn't be the last time he saw them. He regretted ever leaving Daniel and his father. He hoped he could make amends for that now, but as he left his brother for the second time, he couldn't ignore the unsettled feeling in his gut.

70

Mason paced up and down in his sitting room, listening to the screams emanating from above. Sarah had been up in the bedroom all day, labouring to deliver their baby. In the morning, Mason had gone outside, ostensibly to cast an eye over the slaves, but really just to get away from it. He couldn't think with all the noise. He'd hoped it would all be done by the time he returned for lunch. Out here at least he was afforded some solitude to reflect on how his life had changed since Sarah's arrival – and Mary's death. It was as if God had conspired to answer all of Mason's prayers. He and Sarah had conceived at the first time of asking, a good omen. Though Mary's death had been unforeseen, she'd abused her body, and since her passing, it was as if a cloud had lifted from over the house. It had taken her death for him to realise how tense he'd become around her. Without the constant criticism and provocation, he no longer feared entering the same room as her, and no longer had to organise his day around avoiding his wife. He'd been freed.

Of course, it now afforded him unrestricted access to Sarah until her pregnancy had advanced beyond what he considered tasteful. In addition to the physical pleasures she offered, she acted the part of wife well: supporting Mason, indulging his needs and his moods. Adorned in better clothes, she dazzled. Strangers could scarcely detect she was a low-born creature. Watching Sarah's transformation into lady of the house had provoked great pride in Mason. He had the ability to gentrify anyone he chose; it felt like God's work.

It had finally rained and the slaves had begun transplanting the tobacco plants from the seed beds to the fields, creating hillocks around the base of the plants to support their growth. They noticeably upped their tempo when Mason arrived. Since Viktor's departure, Billy and Granville had taken it in turns to supervise them, yet they weren't as adept at driving them as Mason was. If only he could find people as capable as himself, he lamented as he walked back to the house, hoping Sarah's groans had quietened.

On the contrary – it was worse. He wasn't a patient man, and the waiting was torturous. His child's safety – and hers – was out of his hands. The notion that his child might not survive was causing him great anxiety, especially given that it had arrived a month earlier than he'd expected. Sarah insisted that they continue to share a bed, despite her advancing pregnancy, but he'd drawn the line at having her give birth in his bed, insisting that she use Mary's old room. She'd protested but when the time had come, she'd been too terrified to argue. Grace had prepared towels and warm water to assist with the birth, as she did with all the slaves.

After a particularly long scream, in which some very choice words could be distinguished, he relented and poured himself a rum. Since Mary's death, he'd eased off the drink and felt the better for it. His sleep was deeper, and he found himself more productive, even rekindling his efforts to buy a share in a ship, and to diversify into pork and wheat. He could now also attend to the outstanding matter of the neighbouring Neumann land. Not that he really needed it, but he couldn't be seen to be trumped by a German pauper.

He'd enjoyed his visit to see Hans three days ago, taking Billy and Granville with him. They'd approached at dusk, stopping outside for Billy and Granville to light their torches. Entering without knocking, they'd found Hans asleep in his chair. Presumably tired from working his land without his other toe-rag son, whom Mason had persuaded to leave a few weeks earlier. Mason had nodded to Billy, who'd held his flaming torch under Hans' foot. It had taken a few seconds for the old kraut to leap out of slumber.

'What are you doing?' he'd shouted, struggling for balance as he wobbled on one foot.

'You're going to sell me your farm,' Mason had drawled.

'I am not!' Hans had held the back of his chair to steady himself.

'You are, because if you don't, I'm going to bring a case to court against your son, for robbing me in the dead of night.'

The old man had gone silent. That Mason had already told Fry mattered little, for Hans wouldn't know.

'Nonsense. He never…'

'Oh yes, he did, Hans. A right little criminal you raised there. He'll hang for sure. Unless you save him. We can make the whole thing go away.'

'How can I trust you?'

Mason had grinned. 'Because you must. I'll pay you ten pounds for the land, which is very fair, considering.'

The old man's eyes had narrowed. Billy and Granville had held the flaming torches closer to the wooden walls.

'You can work for me if you like, Hans,' Mason went on. 'You can join those niggers you're so fond of.'

Hans had shaken his head, hatred burning in his eyes.

'I'll be back in a few days with a contract to sign,' Mason had said, clapping his hands together. 'Take the time to decide what you're going to do next. I hear there's cheap land out west.' With that, they left the cabin.

'Boss,' Billy had said, 'you should have pushed it. We could have got him to agree.'

'Actions speak louder than words, Billy. Burn down the barn.'

He slurped his rum now, happy to have his devilry back and relishing the memory of Han's tobacco barn burning bright in the night sky. He had stayed and watched until the roof had caved in, sending a large column of flames into the air. Hans had been helpless, watching, weeping on his doorstep as the flames took hold.

Mason's memories were interrupted by the unmistakeable cry of an infant. He dropped his glass and ran up the stairs two at a time, then barged into the room to see a bloodstained baby howling in Grace's arms.

'It's a boy!' said Grace, holding up the child.

He checked the genitalia and thought his heart might burst with pride. 'Give it here,' he said taking him from Grace. The child wriggled in his arms, squalling, his eyes screwed tightly shut. Mason kissed his head. 'My son. We shall call you Peter, after Christ's disciple.' He looked at Sarah, propped up in bed, exhausted, her hair a mess, hands held out. He passed Peter to her. She took him to her bosom and kissed his head. They exchanged a loving smile.

'You did it! A son!' As he looked at them together, mother and son in embrace, Mason felt a sense of euphoria. He now had the one thing he'd always wanted: a family. Yet it wasn't so in the eyes of God – or the law. He fell to one knee by the bedside and reached for Sarah's hand.

'Sarah, you're the mother of my son, I'd like you to be my wife.'

She smiled.

'Will you marry me, Sarah?'

'I will!'

He stood up and kissed her on the lips. His life complete, his heart full of love.

71

June 1st, 1754
Governor's Mansion, Williamsburg

Not even the splendour of the mansion, radiating back the brilliant pink of the evening's sunset, could rejuvenate Viktor, who was as tired as he was sore. Every step up the gravel path was agony as his backside and legs protested at the four days on horseback he'd endured. Whenever he'd wanted to stop and rest, he'd thought of Mason Fitzbarton standing over his father, threatening him. Having not seen Hans in two years, he now imagined him as old, frail and doddery from labouring without the assistance of his sons.

He removed his hat and knocked on the vast door. After stating that Lieutenant Colonel Washington had sent him, the servant was persuaded to lead him into the study, where the Governor would join him shortly.

***

Dinwiddie was cursing his diet as he struggled to empty his bowels into the chamber pot. He silenced his grunting upon hearing the knock at his chamber door.

'A visitor for you.'

'Who is it?' he barked.

'A runner, sent from Lieutenant Colonel Washington.'

Dinwiddie leapt to his feet and retied his breeches.

A nervous and dust-streaked blond fellow waited for him in his study.

'Drink?'

The man nodded. Dinwiddie had the footman fetch two large whiskies. They sat on either side of his desk while they waited for the drinks. The lad hadn't introduced himself, but Dinwiddie didn't bother to ask his name.

'Well?' he prompted.

The youngster took a creased letter from his pocket and stretched over the desk to pass it to him. Dinwiddie broke the seal and read the contents. *Oh dear.* He folded it and left it on the desk. The drinks arrived. The young lad sunk his in one go.

'Were you there? Tell me about it,' said Dinwiddie.

'We went to meet the French, who we found sleeping in a hollow in the woods. Everyone starting shooting at each other. They surrendered, then the Indians butchered them. There was nothing the Lieutenant Colonel could do.'

Dinwiddie could think of a thousand things he could have done!

'Tell me, where was Colonel Fry?'

'Dead, sir.'

'Dead?'

The lad squirmed in his seat. 'Fell from his horse. Just one of those things…'

Dinwiddie asked rapid-fire questions. Once satisfied he'd learnt all he could, he dismissed the youngster. He leant back in his chair and looked at the portrait of the King that adorned the far wall of the study. *Shit.* This debacle was sure to provoke a French response, which would lead to a British one, and off they'd all go again: to war. He felt a sense of foreboding. The global war he'd so glibly prophesised at dinner parties now felt a step closer. When he'd been sent back to the far side of the known world, he hadn't foreseen being at the epicentre of it all. He took another draft of whisky and consoled himself that powers far beyond his influence were at work. Having gathered his thoughts, he wrote two letters.

The first was to Washington, congratulating him for his bravery and ordering him to hold his position. It was the only option. Ordering a retreat was unconscionable for his own reputation. The best outcome for him would be if their plucky colonial forces were slaughtered by the French. That would put an end to the whole Ohio nonsense. If so, Dinwiddie could offer to resign and – with any luck – return home to Scotland.

The second letter was to the Board of Trade in London, responsible for all Britain's colonies, and as such all communication home passed to and from them. He detailed Washington's foolhardy actions and his failure to secure the strategic entrance to the Ohio Valley, which was now fortified and under French control. He added that Washington had failed to control his Indian allies, who had proceeded to kill a host of French soldiers, including their commanding officer. With the blame laid firmly and neatly at Washington's door, Dinwiddie asked the Board how he should proceed.

He put down his quill and picked up his pipe, satisfied he'd absolved himself of any responsibility. He took a long draw on the tobacco. As the smoke filled his lungs, an idea occurred to him. This wasn't just a Virginian problem. The French could potentially attack any British possession. The more colonies that got dragged into the mess, the more it deflected away from him. It worked for Britain. Her colonies each acted completely independently, but in the presence of a common enemy perhaps they could finally learn to cooperate. The King's grant of the Ohio lands to Virginians would surely provide a sore subject for colonial disagreement. If the colonies could join and repel the French, then they might all profit. The only snag was they were trapped by the King's grant.

Dinwiddie took another lungful of smoke and proceeded to write many more letters, to the governors of the other British colonies on mainland America. *Join or die,* he thought, chuckling to himself. All this might conspire to allow him to exit the stage and return home for a quiet life.

Having finished, he retired upstairs, ready to once again do battle with his chamber pot.

72

June 5th, 1754
The Neumann Plantation

The first sight of his family home brought a lump to Viktor's throat. The cabin's roughly sawn logs had turned green with moss and needed a scrub. The tobacco barn was gone, save for the four charred stumps poking out of the ground, remnants of the corner posts. Ash still stained the ground. A heap of scorched metal, once their tools, now lay mangled. Viktor was certain this was Mason's doing.

Viktor counted quickly on his fingers. It was now twenty-two years since his father had arrived in the New World. This wasn't much to show for the risks he had taken. Viktor had heard new arrivals to the colony naively boasting of making their fortune in America, as if their arrival alone guaranteed riches. They only needed to hear Hans' story, he thought.

Opening the door and entering the musty house, he was shocked to find his father in bed, in the middle of the day. It was an old man who looked up at Viktor from his repose. His face was thin and drawn, the creases on his forehead deeper than Viktor remembered.

'The prodigal son returns?' Hans croaked.

Viktor let the comment slide. Time was when he would have mounted a defence. He fetched a cup of water and offered it to his father's lips. Hans took it and drank for himself.

Viktor noticed a neatly folded pile of clothes, razor and comb on the small table at the end of his father's cramped room.

'Are you going somewhere, Father?'

500

Hans' face assumed a weary look. 'I was getting ready to leave. Then I didn't feel quite myself, so I came to bed. That was two days ago.'

'Have you eaten?'

Hans shook his head.

'I'll fix you something.'

Viktor lit the fire, boiled some water, and cooked up a bowl of oats, stirring in a bit of honey he'd found. He took it back into his father's room and propped him up so he could eat. Viktor sat on the edge of the bed.

'It was Mason's doing. He burned the barn,' Hans said as he took a spoonful.

Viktor nodded. 'Father,' the lump returned to his throat. 'I'm sorry.' He wiped his eyes as they began to water.

'I told you…'

'You did. I should have listened. I'm so sorry.' Viktor wept.

Hans looked better for his porridge. He held out a gnarled hand to take Viktor's and squeeze it.

'I was young once too.'

Viktor sniffed and wiped his tears on his sleeve. It was the closest his father would ever come to an apology. 'What are you going to do?'

Hans shrugged. 'I've no idea. This place is all I have, but Mason won't stop until he takes it. He can't live with the thought of me getting it from under his nose. Little sense in continuing to fight someone bigger and stronger… Perhaps if I were younger…'

'You can't just quit, not after everything—'

'You did. Daniel did.'

'Daniel didn't want to leave you, Father. Mason got to him, too.'

Hans looked up, his blue eyes red-rimmed.

'He joined the army, same as me,' Viktor explained. 'He thought the pay would help.'

'Where is he now?'

'Over the mountains, in the Ohio.'

Hans shook his head, staring into the middle distance. 'Bloody fool's errand.'

Viktor nodded. It was. A shambles that had only succeeded in provoking a stronger opponent. Was this, the family farm, doomed to the same fate, he wondered?

'He's coming back with a contract for me to sign. If I don't, he'll burn this whole place to the ground with me in it.'

Viktor gritted his teeth. The sight of his father reduced to his sick bed by that devil stirred a deep anger within him. If he'd learned one thing during his time away, it was that running from things got you nowhere. You had to face matters and do what was right.

'That's not going to happen, Father.'

'You the man of the house now then?'

'What does it say in the Bible? Put on the full armour of God, so that you will be able to stand firm against the schemes of the devil.'

A proud smile crept across Hans' face. 'I did teach you something then?'

'More than you know, Father. Come on, let's get you better. We'll fix this place up. Rebuild the barn…'

'What about Mason?'

'You let me worry about him.'

***

It was two days later that Viktor embarked on the few miles' walk to the Fitzbarton plantation, turning over the problem of Mason in his mind. Though it was still mid-morning, there wasn't a cloud in the sky and the day promised to be hot. Viktor wiped the first beads of sweat from his forehead. The woods were still, the only movement being the flies circling in tight patterns in and out of the sunlight. Viktor stopped for another piss; he was nervous.

Hans had recovered quickly, but it was a temporary reprieve, for the spectre of Mason loomed large and needed to be permanently banished. Viktor didn't relish the challenge, but he owed his father that much.

Viktor ran through Mason's transgressions in his mind: infecting their crop with flea beetles, burning down their tobacco barn, both of which could be denied. Knowingly harbouring a runaway was a small crime, but Viktor hoped that, when paired with the sudden death of his wife, it might be enough for Mason to fear for his reputation. Viktor's mind was teeming with what-ifs: What would Mason say?

What if he shouted? What if he turned violent? As he neared the estate, Viktor settled on a plan. Mason would surely be angry about the robbery, so Viktor would refuse to get caught up in any tit-for-tat argument. The goal was to achieve a truce for his father.

As he passed the turning for the track that led to the small community church, Viktor wondered why God granted such wealth and power to the likes of Mason. His faith undermined, nonetheless he spoke a prayer as he walked, asking God to grant him strength.

The Fitzbarton plantation revealed itself as Viktor passed through the land that he himself had once cleared, the day the negroes had rounded on him. The house's red brick and white portico columns looked resplendent in the morning sun. His stomach twisted as he walked across the lawn towards the main entrance. Palms sweaty, he knocked sharply on the front door and took a step back.

It was Grace who answered, unable to disguise her shock.

'Viktor?'

'I've come to visit Mr Fitzbarton.'

'He's out. Gone to Alexandria to buy a ship.'

'Oh.' He felt a curious mix of relief and disappointment, for he knew he would have to go through today's anxieties all over again. 'When will he be back?'

Grace shrugged.

'Who's that at the door?' came a voice from deep inside the house. It was Sylvia.

Moments later, she appeared at the door, cradling a baby in her arms.

'Viktor! What are you doing here?'

The look of surprise on her face only served to make her even more beautiful than he remembered. Her auburn curls framed her face, which looked pale save for two blushes of rouge on her cheeks. Her lashes were startlingly dark against her skin, her lips a luscious red.

'Not here to rob us again, I hope?'

He shook his head shamefully. 'No. I'm sorry about that. I'm here to see Mason.' He looked at her longingly, imploring her forgiveness.

'Come in, Viktor,' she said after a pause.

He felt guilty as he entered, thinking of his trespassing not too long ago. It occurred to him that Mason would be even more irate to find him in the company of his mistress. Yet Viktor felt drawn to her. As he followed Sylvia through the hallway into the sitting room, it seemed inconceivable that he had once asked her to marry him. Now here she was, living in the big house. It soothed the still-open wound of her rejection of him; he'd never stood a chance. It was almost as ludicrous as his belief that Mason would have let him inherit all this.

Viktor stole a glance at the baby as Sylvia passed it to Grace. Dark-haired and ruddy-faced, it squawked as Grace carried it down the corridor. Viktor took a seat as instructed, perching on the very edge, not wanting to mark the furniture with his clothes.

'America has been kind to you, Sylvia.'

Her expression hardened. 'I'm Sarah. That's the name everyone knows me by.' She forced a smile. 'Mason and I are engaged to be married.'

How thin the veneer of the life she has made for herself that one mention of her real name should unsettle her. 'Congratulations.'

'Look, I am sorry about what happened,' he said, unsure how to excuse his actions. He saw no forgiveness on her face. Viktor hesitated. 'I loved you, you know? I really did.'

She sighed. 'I guess we've all done wrong, Viktor.'

He smiled awkwardly. She did likewise. His transgression out of the way, he found himself enjoying simply being near her. Since he'd shed his virginity, he'd hoped he would feel less in awe of her, more on an equal footing. But the silk floral dress, dainty leather shoes and the silver pendant necklace that adorned her neck were a stark reminder of how far she'd climbed. In that same time, Viktor had only succeeded in falling further than before. *God's work!* He decided to change the subject:

'Will you be happy here, do you think?'

She smirked. 'It's not a woman's place to be happy, Viktor. But I am comfortable, yes. I have more security here than I've had in my life.'

'Mason burned my father's tobacco barn down,' he stated bluntly.

Sylvia folded her arms. 'How do you know it was him?'

Viktor laughed. 'Really, are you going to deny it?'

She turned her head away.

'Sarah, I've no wish to battle you or Mason. But he wants my father's farm. God knows why, he doesn't need it. I reckon a man like him wants all that he cannot have.' Viktor raised his eyebrows.

The twist in her red lips meant she'd understood his insinuation.

No longer nervous, Viktor knew there was no confrontation to be had between them. The facts were sufficient. He felt very glad to be having this conversation with Sylvia, and not Mason.

'Sarah, I can't stop Mason,' he reasoned. 'He can burn down my family's home, beat us, chase us off our land. But,' he held her gaze, 'we can tell the colony that your real name is Sylvia Coppell, a runaway. We can tell everyone that Mason killed his wife so he could marry you, who he'd impregnated. When your banns are read in church, we can volunteer all these lawful reasons why you may not marry.'

Her face grew thunderous.

Viktor's voice remained calm. 'Or we can tell Mason that the little boy he so loves, actually belongs to an English sailor named Reid.'

The words hung in the air as Zebedee entered carrying a tea tray.

'Not now,' barked Sylvia.

Zebedee retreated hurriedly, the cups and saucers rattling on the tray.

'But we needn't,' said Viktor. 'We could just agree to leave each other alone.'

Her jawline softened.

'It's up to you,' he finished.

She smoothed her skirts, and finally said, 'I think we have an understanding, Viktor.'

Viktor nodded and rubbed the stubble on his face. 'I don't doubt that *we* do; it's Mason I'm worried about. He can be...impulsive.'

'Leave him to me. He'll never bother you or your family again. You have my word.'

'Thank you.' He sat back in the chair, his body trembling with relief.

'You'd better leave,' she said curtly. 'It won't help your cause if he comes back to find you here.'

Viktor got to his feet. 'I'll show myself out.' He was tempted to kiss her – it was his last chance to, but the moment passed. 'Thank you, Sarah. I hope you find the happiness that has eluded everyone else who lives here.'

He left her sitting stony-faced in the grand room.

***

Viktor and Hans walked through the woods, in search of a tree, tall and straight, that would be suitable for the new tobacco barn. They stood at the base of an oak, looking up towards its canopy. Hans placed his gnarled hand on the trunk and nodded. 'This'll do. You'll have to fell it. My back isn't up to it.'

Viktor swung the axe, hitting the trunk with a small thud. A piece of bark chipped off. They would be here for the rest of the day, he thought. As his body settled into the rhythm of chopping, his mind began to wander. Though Hans had been gratified to hear of Viktor's success at the Fitzbarton plantation, a cloud of doubt had grown over the next two days. Viktor had spared him the details and had simply explained that it wasn't in Mason's interest to provoke them, but Hans could never trust the man.

After an hour, Viktor stopped to let his back and arms recover. The oak was a stubborn opponent, conceding only a few inches. Hans took the axe and sharpened the blade with a stone. Sitting on the cool forest floor, they shared a draft of ale.

'Viktor, when you farm, you have to farm as if you're going to live forever. But as I lay ill in bed, approaching my fiftieth year, I began to consider what should happen if I were no longer here...'

To hear his father talk openly of his mortality was rare. Viktor put his hand on his father's shoulder and their eyes met.

'I need to decide what to do with the plantation after I am gone,' Hans continued. 'It has provided enough for you, Daniel and I – but if you boys were both to raise families of your own, then it wouldn't suffice.'

Viktor chuckled inwardly; after all, it was the meagre state of the farm that was in part at fault for the absence of wives for himself and Daniel. The colony's few available women were lured to richer men.

'Let me make it easy for you, Father,' Viktor cut in. 'Leave it all to Daniel. He's better suited to this life.'

'But you're the eldest. You wouldn't mind?'

'Not in the least.' Scratching a living was one thing, but doing it under the nose of Mason and Sylvia would be a wretched reminder of his mistake: his betrayal of his family. There had been a time when he would have relished taking over his father's land, buying slaves and making a life here. But now that he'd witnessed the reality of it at Fitzbarton's, there was a cost that he was unwilling to pay: his soul.

'I can't offer you anything else, Viktor.'

'Don't worry, Father. You've already given me more than you know.'

'You're a good lad, Viktor. It's nice to be free of that worry.'

Viktor took the axe and got to his feet. 'Well, come on, this tree won't chop itself.'

73

The French were coming. George's scouts at the French fort had passed on reports of a large detachment of French soldiers making their way south, guided by the Huron. Unwilling to retreat, George and his troops waited nervously at the camp he'd renamed Fort Necessity. He tried to keep the men busy, building fortifications and cutting a road through the forest so they might resupply faster in future. Perhaps this would convince the men that Britain was thinking long-term about the territory. Alas, the rumours of the oncoming French army had caused nerves to break and men to desert; their numbers had thinned to just two hundred men.

George walked the fort, inspecting the trench that had been dug to encircle the wooden palisade. He was pursued by Croghan and Van Braam, both of whom irritated him with increasing regularity, offering unwanted opinions and neglecting their unkempt appearance.

'Washington,' implored Croghan, 'we're outnumbered. You need the Iroquois, they can harry the French before they get here. If we're defeated by the French, that's the end of the Ohio—'

'It's Lieutenant Colonel Washington,' George reminded him again. 'Don't be so defeatist, the men can hear you!' He peered down at the three-foot-deep trench and nodded his approval to Jimmy Jones and Viktor's brother, Daniel, who'd been digging. They took this as a cue to sit on the spoil heap that formed the trench's outer rampart and reach for their tobacco pouches.

George walked further along the trench and continued addressing Croghan. 'I will not be relying on those treacherous natives. We're left with the bravest Englishmen, who will be more than a match for the French. Unlike you yellow-bellied Irish.'

'You're a stubborn feckin' idiot, Washington.'

'Silence!' George ordered. 'If I want advice on being a merchant, I'll be sure to ask you. Otherwise, leave the soldiering to those of us that know the profession.'

'I was of the understanding that this will be your first engagement.'

George walked away, leaving Croghan to call after him, 'If they have Indians on their side, don't be thinking they'll present themselves in neat lines to be shot at!'

Infuriated, George turned and pointed at Croghan. 'Well, if the Huron are half as contemptible as the Iroquois, then we have nothing to fear, do we?'

Croghan closed the distance between them and spoke in a hushed tone. 'The difference is that the Iroquois know a lost cause when they see one.'

'Well, no wonder you're on such good terms with them, they're as yellow as you are!'

'There's nothing brave in being slaughtered, Washington!'

'We have a fortified position. We have provisions. We'll be the ones doing the slaughtering, Mister Croghan.'

'Aye, you'll most likely be outnumbered. You've no roof on your fort and you're flanked by higher ground.'

George grimaced. Before he could muster a retort, a noise came from the far side of the fort. Cheers ran round the camp as he saw men clad in civilian clothing appear at the mouth of the roadway that had been cut through the trees. At their head was a man on horseback in a green soldier's coat.

George clapped his hands together at their arrival. 'You see, Croghan? There's fight in us yet.' He left the Irishman and strode over to greet the new arrivals.

He introduced himself to the officer on horseback, a stocky man with ruddy cheeks and thick black hair to his shoulders. George placed him in his early thirties. The man introduced himself as Captain James Mackay in a subtle Scots accent.

'Your Governor Dinwiddie managed to persuade the Carolinas to dig you out of your Virginian mess,' the Captain said. 'I bring one hundred men from South Carolina. We're expecting another hundred on the way from North Carolina.'

George resented the rebuke but was glad of the reinforcements. He wondered what spoils Dinwiddie had bargained away to secure the cooperation of the Carolinians. Instead, he remarked it was nice to finally see the colonies cooperating in British interests. With a curt nod, Mackay began to issue orders to his second in command, and George realised he'd better establish his own authority.

'Captain Mackay, your cannon are a welcome sight,' he said. 'We'll position them in the fort and you can station your men on the western side of the camp.'

Mackay scowled. 'I wonnae be taking orders from you, lad.'

'I'm Lieutenant Colonel—'

'You could be a General, for all I care, but you're only a colonial outfit. We are a royal regiment; I paid the King fifteen hundred pounds for my commission, so I won't be taking orders from a colonist who hasn't yet invested himself in the business of war. Can't have any Tom, Dick or Harry turning up and leading armed men, can we?'

'But your men are from the Carolinas…'

'Aye.'

'So, are they not colonial too?'

Mackay nodded. 'They are. But I'm not, and I paid good money for my rank. You didn't.'

'This is absurd!'

The Scotsman shrugged. 'I don't make the rules. But neither do you. My cannon and I will take up a position on the eastern side. The west is flanked by high ground; we'd be too vulnerable.'

George stomped back to his tent and furiously drafted a letter of complaint to Dinwiddie, demanding to know if Mackay was obliged to obey his orders.

With his frustrations moderated, George took a walk around the camp, eager to find fault with Captain Mackay's preparations. He noticed the Carolinians had brought ample supplies: beef and dairy cows, and hogsheads full of flour and salt pork. He found Van Braam holding an empty pail, in heated discussion with Captain Mackay.

'Let me draw some milk from your cows,' said Van Braam.

'No. They're for Carolinians,' the Scotsman responded. 'You want milk, you should have brought your own cows.'

'Captain,' George cut in, 'I've sent my factor, Barney MacGregor, a fellow Scotsman, back to Virginia to fetch more supplies. It would make sense to share and share alike in the meantime.'

'If you're running low, that's your fault, and it's your problem,' Mackay shrugged. 'And if you're relying on a MacGregor, then I fear for you. They're loyal to the young pretender, Bonnie Prince Charlie.'

'What is it with you people and your clannish squabbles?' George demanded. 'MacGregor has proved himself reliable; he's supplied us with all we have to date.'

'Good for you, Washington. But you ain't having any of my food.'

***

Over the next three weeks, George and Captain Mackay's relationship continued to deteriorate. The most galling discovery was that Mackay and his Carolinians were paid more than George and his Virginians. The whole thing left a sour taste in George's mouth. He struggled to believe that the world could be ordered in such an unfair and haphazard manner.

When Barney never returned and the Virginians faced starvation, Mackay begrudgingly shared his remaining rations. There was scarcely an element to this whole endeavour that couldn't have been performed better – a sentiment which he shared in his latest letter to Dinwiddie. Dinwiddie replied that George would soon be reinforced by more Carolinians, this time under the command of a Colonel James Innes. Innes, as the ranking officer, would assume responsibility for the whole force, including George and his Virginian regiment. So, George had been demoted once more. At least this time, Innes was an experienced soldier; he recalled Lawrence mentioning the man, as they'd fought together in the Caribbean.

After reading the letter, George had lain in his tent, contemplating why Dinwiddie had passed him over again. Was it because he felt he couldn't rely on George, or some other reason? It seemed at odds to appoint a Carolinian... Perhaps this was Dinwiddie's method of distancing himself, should it all go wrong. In the end, it mattered not, as every report suggested the French would arrive before the reinforcements. George confided his fears to his diary, recalling a quote from Epictetus: '*He is a wise man who does not grieve for the things which he has not, but rejoices for those which he has.*' Reassured, he reminded himself that with Mackay's forces they now numbered three hundred and, crucially, they were fortified. They were better off without the contemptible and unmanageable Iroquois. Though their food supplies were exhausted, at least the end of the wait was nigh. Hunger would drive the men to fight all the fiercer, so they could plunder French supplies. Above all, they not only had the strength of cannon but the fortitude of being British; their freedom inspired men to fight, unlike the dictatorial French whose tyranny conscripted men into sacrifice for their King and nation. The French leader's judgement would be tainted by his desire for revenge, while George's own was second to none.

***

Early next morning, the tent flap was pulled open. Croghan knelt at the door.

'You got your wish,' he said. 'A scout just returned – they're a mile away. Eight hundred Frenchmen, accompanied by four hundred Huron.'

George cleared his throat and straightened his jacket. The time had come.

He strode out and shouted for his men to take up positions. Under heavy grey skies, the men formed two neat lines, shoulder to shoulder, and loaded their muskets.

Captain Mackay arrived at George's side.

'They won't give us a pitched battle,' the Scotsman said. 'We should take cover in the trenches.'

'You hide if you want to,' replied George, nerves fluttering in his stomach.

'I'm serious, your men will be—'

'You made it clear you're not obliged to follow my orders, Captain,

512

so don't think me obliged to follow yours.'

The two men shared a long stare, which George broke off first. 'If you'll excuse me, I have an enemy to defeat.' His nerves were making him tetchy, but he wasn't in the mood for squabbling with Mackay. The time for talking was over. It was time to fight.

George ignored Mackay's protestations and positioned himself on the left, at the furthest eastern end of his line of soldiers. Lawrence always said an officer should put himself in harm's way. No sheltering behind the lines.

The hours passed. George's stomach groaned and head ached with the pressure of anticipation. He scanned the treeline, searching for any sign of movement. Between his men and the woods was thirty yards of open ground, the grass trodden flat from weeks of people milling about. The twenty yards behind them, to the fort's wooden palisade, was interrupted only by the trench and earth bulwark they'd dug.

As nerves turned to tired irritation, George prayed the French would soon arrive. The men were shuffling on their feet and gossiping. Then – a shot came from his right. Mackay's men had fired.

'There they are!' came a voice from the ranks. On the far right, beyond Mackay's men, George could see the blue coats of the French appearing at the wood's edge.

Damn them. They're in the wrong place!

'Steady men,' commanded George, forcing calm into his voice.

The French retreated to the woods. Flecks of blue appeared amongst the trees as they moved round to George's ranks. George stiffened his back. *Step out and show yourselves.* His men fidgeted, looking to him for orders. He repeated his call to remain steadfast. Within seconds, the treeline before them bore a thin blue line at its edge.

Puffs of smoke were soon followed by loud bangs as the French discharged their muskets. Shrieks sounded across the ranks as George's men fell. Some lay dead, others writhed in pain.

*No…*thought George. *Surely they're not going to skulk in the woods taking pot-shots at us?* The second volley of fire suggested they were happy to do just that. *So French.* The remaining men looked desperately in his direction, wanting orders.

'Charge!' shouted George and broke into a run. His men followed, offering a mild roar. George's body jolted as his feet pounded across the uneven ground. Clouds of smoke concealed the wood's edge. The gunfire was interrupted by the spine-chilling, shrill war cry of the Huron. To his right, a hundred braves leapt clear of the treeline, tomahawks raised, charging at the centre of his line.

'Halt,' he cried. 'Fire!'

His men drew to an irregular standstill and fired their muskets, felling a portion of the Huron. The remainder descended in a wild flurry of swinging tomahawks, hacking into the ranks before they could reload. The Virginians turned and fled.

Seeing his centre melt away, George issued the order to turn and fight. The left and right of the line held and managed to reload in time to fire at the screaming Huron. Yet another volley from the woods felled more of the remaining Virginia regiment, giving the Huron a moment to regroup.

Sensing disaster as he watched his men running back to the trench, George gave the order to retreat. Virginians slumped to the ground, tomahawks protruding from the backs, agonising cries filled the air as the French musket fire spattered out. George chased after his own men, a musket ball whistling past his head as he leapt the earthen bulwark into the trench. It had been so close, whistling past his ear. He felt more alive than ever and a peculiar smile spread across his face.

His excitement faded the moment he glanced above the earthwork. The field was littered with the bodies of his regiment. More gunfire to his right – Mackay's men were still in the field! They unloaded a volley of cannon fire into the Huron. On bended knee, they alternated their musket fire, keeping the enemy at bay. Goaded into action by the prospect of Mackay's gloating, George clambered out the back of the trench and ran towards the Carolinians. More smoke lay thick around him, and he stooped instinctively as musket balls whizzed overhead. Time seemed to slow as more ammunition flew past him. He jumped back into the trench, his feet squelching in the soggy earth and gasped for breath.

Before him stood a milk-pale boy, whom he recognised as Daniel Neumann. George grinned at him, and the boy seemed to settle. Overhead, constant gun fire crackled from the woods. George glanced above the trench to see Mackay's men forced to pull back as they absorbed French fire. George shouldn't have been relieved to see his own side retreating, but he felt his humiliation being spared. His thoughts quickly turned to what to do next. He could see the Huron scalping his men. His eye was drawn to one Huron brave who held up an injured man's head by his hair. George recognised him as Jimmy Jones. He raised his musket and took aim. Pulling the trigger, he kept his aim down the barrel of the gun as the musket thudded into his shoulder with a fierce kick. Acrid white smoked belched from the pan, and he saw the ball shoot forward, curve to the right and thud harmlessly into the grass. The Indian sliced his knife across Jimmy's head, his body dropping to the ground. As the Indian moved to the next man, Dan raised his musket and fired. The shot found its target, felling the Huron brave to the ground.

'Good shot, lad,' said George. 'You're a soldier now.'

Daniel smiled nervously back at George.

George shouted the order to fire. There was an erratic ripple of gunfire from the men around him, but what good it did, George couldn't say, as the French were still cowering amongst the trees. What it did do was provoke return fire. Along the full length of the front, more scattered shots were exchanged. Mackay unleashed his cannon, firing into the trees and raising cheers across the British lines.

While the two sides continued to harmlessly swap lead, George wondered how to take the initiative. If they moved forward, his men would be slaughtered. But the same difficulty applied to the French – there were just so many more of them to absorb the losses. George guessed he had lost as much as a third of his force, shuddering at the thought. But now was not the time for grief.

He looked over the top of the trench once more, scanning the woods for French activity. A musket ball hit the earth bulwark, casting soil in his face. He ducked and wiped the grit from his stinging eye. *We're pinned down.* The words of Mackay and Croghan rang in his ears. He was loath to admit they'd been right, for the French *were* indeed behaving like Indians, skulking in the woods.

'What are we to do, sir?' asked Daniel Neumann.

George adjusted his seat in the trench and gazed up at the sky. The midday sun was hidden behind thick grey clouds, and a bald eagle circled high overhead, soaring effortlessly above George's predicament. He was reminded of Lawrence. *What are you trying to tell me, bird?* With one flap of its wings, it changed direction and flew westwards, out of sight.

George felt a speck of rain hit the back of his hand. Another dropped onto his hat. The earth began to darken as more raindrops fell. What had begun as a light shower became torrential. The clouds turned a menacing dark grey, and within seconds the water was pouring off the edge of his hat. The French became obscured by the rain. George's woollen uniform became cold and heavy with water. Van Braam jumped into the trench, splashing through water that was pooling at its bottom.

'George, we can't load our weapons in this rain,' he said. 'If they attack, we're done for.'

'But neither can they,' George pointed out.

'They have some cover under the trees at least. Our boys don't even have leather cartridge cases – the paper cartridges are wet, the powder will cake. It'll be useless.'

George gnashed his teeth together in defiance. He couldn't let on how hopeless the situation was to his men. They had to believe in the fight. He cursed the miserly old men in power who had put their lives at risk. How much would cartridge cases have cost? The whole campaign would grind to a halt because they couldn't fire their weapons.

'We need to surrender,' said Van Braam.

'Over my dead body!'

'Careful, George, you might tempt someone to shoot you.'

'We've more cartridges in the fort,' George remembered. 'There's a hogshead full of them. We'll retreat there. You tell the western flank.'

'What about Mackay?' asked Van Braam.

'What about him? He didn't want to use our fort. He can fend for himself.'

'You can't leave him out here, George!'

George dismissed Van Braam before he could protest further, ordering him to notify the western flank, but relented on the matter of leaving Mackay. It wouldn't look good.

'Neumann, run over to Mackay – tell him we're retreating to the fort.'

The lad looked worried but scrambled out of the trench and began to run. Shots rang out from the woods. *The French are still able to fire!* George watched Neumann sprint through the shots raining out of the woods. *Go on lad.* Then came a shriek. Neumann went down. Sprays of mud formed around him as the French continued shooting.

He's finished, thought George. *No use following him.*

'RETREAT!' he shouted. The Virginian ranks were quick to dash back to the fort. George made it to safety and turned to see his men in. A few were felled by French fire crossing the open ground. Musket balls thudded against the wooden palisade. The sodden men poured round the back of the fort and took shelter behind the wall. George looked out to where Neumann had been shot. He saw two men, one carrying the other. It was Croghan, helping Neumann, who was hopping on one leg. More smoke emanated from the woods as musket balls landed either side of Croghan and Neumann.

'Come on,' shouted George. Shots cracked from the trees. Croghan slipped in the mud. They fell; Neumann yelped in pain as Croghan struggled to his feet. Seeing their predicament, George ran out to save them. Grabbing Neumann's other arm, he knocked his own hat off in the process. Together, he and Croghan dragged the boy across the field, narrowly avoiding the lead all around them. Neumann became heavier with every step. Finally, they rounded the fort and hobbled through the gate, which was promptly barred behind them.

They dropped Neumann on the floor. He was alive; a musket ball had clipped his ankle. He wriggled in pain and cried out for Viktor.

'Quiet, man,' said George. 'You'll be fine.'

'This is what happens when you don't listen, you pompous arse!' wheezed Croghan, recovering from the run and squaring up to George. 'All those men died because you thought you knew best.' He jabbed at George's chest with an outstretched index finger. 'I told you: Don't expect them to fight in neat lines. But you're more bloody interested in playing the hero, so you can impress your aristocrat mates at your fancy dinner parties! You think this is all some bloody game. Men died today because of you!'

George swung his fist at the Irishman's cheek. Croghan swerved the punch and lunged forward, grabbing George's lapels. He staggered as Croghan tried to throw him to the dirt. George gripped Croghan's shoulders and tried to throw him down, resulting in an awkward dance in front of the onlooking soldiers, crowded into the palisade.

'Enough!' shouted Van Braam, emerging from the crowd. 'The enemy's out there. Save it for them!'

George and Croghan broke free of one another, their clothing dishevelled, hair wet and bedraggled. Croghan spat at George's feet.

'Any time, Washington.'

George would have like nothing more than to order him shot. Unfortunately, Croghan wasn't recruited as a soldier, so George's rank didn't apply. Instead, he straightened his jacket and turned to face his soldiers. 'Stop gawping, all of you.'

There was nowhere else for them to look. They were crammed into the small fort like salt fish in a barrel. Stood shoulder to shoulder, under the pouring rain, they looked a frightened and dishevelled group. One man dropped his britches and spilled the contents of his bowels into the mud.

'Right, place the injured men in the store,' said George, regaining his composure, referring to the small hut where the camp's provisions were stashed. 'Anyone with dry powder, take a position at a loophole and fire at the French.'

The fort emitted a few cracks of gunfire that did nothing more than ricochet off the trees, but it was enough to give Mackay's men the cover to retreat and crowd into the fort. Mackay gave George a knowing look as he entered, covered in mud. Fortunately, he had the good sense not to comment.

The afternoon passed and the men became more disgruntled as they struggled to stay warm, huddled together, hungry, under the relentless rain.

With the British men hiding behind their palisade, the French turned their attention to the British livestock, corralled in a crude pen at the rear of the camp. Their snipers summarily executed all the helpless horses and cows.

By mid-afternoon, George heard laughter from the supply hut. He forced his way through the crowd and looked inside. The injured had discovered the rum and were roaring drunk. George's rebuke elicited nothing more than defiant laughter. From every angle, George felt the glares of unhappy men. Croghan was huddled with some of them, their faces grim, no doubt sharing criticisms.

Mackay approached George and whispered in his ear, 'Game's up. We should surrender.'

'Nonsense. The French must be suffering too. They'll crack first.'

'Washington, look at us.'

'He's right,' added Van Braam.

'You surrender if you want to, Mackay,' said George, loud enough for all to hear. Mackay shook his head as if trying to shake off his disappointment.

At six o'clock that evening, the rain stopped. A shout came from one of the fort's loopholes, followed by muted cheers. George barged forwards to see what the commotion was.

A white flag waved its way across the open ground and stopped in the middle.

George adjusted his jacket and called Van Braam to his side. Mackay joined them, which gave George the opportunity to say, 'I told you they'd blink first, Mackay.'

Together, they made their way to the centre of the open ground to meet the Frenchman holding the flag. He was short and stocky, with narrow eyes and a pointed nose.

In French he said, 'I represent our commander, Louis Coulon de Villiers, whose brother your men murdered. He offers you the chance to surrender. If you leave the Ohio, you can retreat with full honours.'

'What's he saying?' George asked Van Braam, who understood some basic French.

'Surrender and we can return home, with honours.'

'Out of the question,' said George. 'Tell him this land is ours and we shall not retreat.'

Van Braam's eyebrows raised in disbelief. George nudged him to continue.

He translated and the Frenchman laughed.

'It will be dark soon,' he said. 'You won't see us as we overrun your fort. Our cannon will tear open your palisade.'

In the gloom, George saw cannon being dragged from the trees and put in position.

'Then,' continued the Frenchman, 'the Huron will attack you from behind. They will butcher your men, and our soldiers will fire

TIM HOLDEN

relentlessly into your open fort. Not a man will be left standing.'

George looked to Van Braam for a translation.

'They're going to kill us,' was all he said.

George grimaced. Mackay spoke up, 'Van Braam, tell him we accept.'

'Pah!' dismissed George. 'Tell them this is our land.'

'Come on, George, really?' said Van Braam.

'The King gave this land to Virginia's Ohio Company—'

'Washington, a soldier needs to know when he's beat. To carry on is suicide.'

Observing their disagreement, the Frenchman asked Van Braam, 'How many men have you lost already? One hundred? We have three French dead. That's it.' He held out three fingers to George. '*Trois Français mort. C'est tout.*'

George understood, but still couldn't concede.

'Leave with full honours or be slaughtered,' the man said. 'The choice is yours, but either way, this land is now France.'

Van Braam repeated the threat to George. 'You won't get a better offer, Colonel,' he added.

'We accept.' Mackay stepped forward and shook the Frenchman's hand.

As he felt the floor dropping beneath his feet, George was eager to maintain some authority. 'Very well. We shall retreat with full honours, but I won't be conceding the title to this land.'

Van Braam translated. The Frenchman simply shrugged and spoke rapidly.

'He says, don't the English have the expression *possession is nine-tenths of the law*?' said Van Braam.

The Frenchman held out his hand. George reluctantly shook it.

'France accepts. Now we must complete the surrender papers.'

Once Van Braam explained, George replied, 'They want to draw up a contract?' Only the French could be so bureaucratic.

'I'll leave you to it,' said Mackay, 'being as you're the senior officer here.' He chuckled as he strolled back towards the fort. The Frenchman continued conversing with Van Braam, who explained the process to George.

'They want you to talk with the French commander and sign a

document of surrender.' Van Braam lowered his voice. 'You'd best be careful. It was his brother Tanacharison murdered.'

George's skin prickled in warning. This could be a ruse to exact revenge. 'You go, Van Braam; you speak the language. Bring it back to the fort for me to sign.'

It took an hour for Van Braam to return, during which time George reassured his men that a solution was imminent, though he doubted he had hidden his disappointment at the surrender. Fortunately, the rain returned and discouraged further debate. Croghan remained silent, but the smug look on his face was insufferable. George went outside of the palisade to confer with Van Braam, who clutched a scrap of paper in his hand.

'The articles of capitulation.'

The word turned George's stomach. Van Braam passed him the paper, on which was scrawled their impromptu peace treaty in French. George, like all true Englishmen, prided himself on never learning French, so he asked Van Braam to summarise their terms: 'They want to avoid a war, so they're saying this attack was merely a reprisal for the unprovoked death of Coulon de Villiers.'

'But that was Tanacharison.'

Van Braam shrugged. 'They're happy for us to return to Virginia unmolested, if you agree to this.'

'But, for them to call this revenge, is nonsense, they've come south building forts as they travel.' George stopped talking as it dawned on him how his actions, together with Tanacharison's complicity had handed the French the ideal excuse to evict Britain. He felt deeply shamed at playing into their hands. In his imagination, an image of Fry crowing was followed by another of Lawrence berating him.

'Lieutenant Colonel, you don't have a choice. They're ready to attack now. If I'm not back within half an hour, they'll start,' Van Braam cut into his thoughts.

George took the paper, the ink spreading in the rain. 'Have you got a quill?'

Van Braam shook his head. George cursed; he couldn't even surrender in an orderly fashion. He had a quill in his luggage, which had been packed away with his tent, in the fort, amongst his dejected troops. Twenty minutes passed while he rooted through his trunk, suffering the groans and drunken gibes of his injured men crammed into the stores. Finally, he scratched his name on the rain-sodden document.

It was over.

***

George announced to the men that they would be returning home tomorrow, but it was received with muted celebrations.

'We did our best,' Mackay said, in a gesture of appeasement. 'This time, it wasn't enough.'

It was scant consolation. The whole debacle was a disaster and George made no effort to hide his disappointment. In his head, he railed at the King for granting them the land but not the means to secure it. The scheme had got bogged down in petty colonial politics. Had he ever stood a chance? He would refuse to accept the blame that would surely be pinned to him.

George was tired, hungry, cold, defeated and very fed up. Musters accounted for one hundred men dead, in exchange for three French souls, and those who Tanacharison had murdered. They would crawl out of the Ohio with their tail between their legs, and George could wave goodbye to his £200 investment in the Ohio Company. It was the first time in his life that George was glad Lawrence wasn't alive, sparing him the sight of the fist his younger brother had made of his scheme.

As the fort was awash with mud and piss, George took himself off to a quiet spot to lament his errors. His tears were of frustration rather than sorrow, and he would willingly have thrashed any man at the slightest provocation. *At least I'm going home alive,* he consoled himself. Then his mind turned to the reality awaiting him there and the people he must face: The Fairfaxes, Lawrence's in-laws, Ann, his widow, George's mother, his other brothers. His neighbours, every tavern in the region. The newspapers. This would be the talk of the colonies and he would be cast as the architect of the defeat. He'd wanted so badly to be the hero, but fate had conspired to make him the inevitable scapegoat.

He didn't sleep that night. In the early dawn, with a mist blanketing the bodies of the fallen, George ordered a breakfast to be prepared from the dead livestock. As soon as it was eaten, he had the men form up, ready to march home. They would salvage whatever dignity they could on the return. A guard of French soldiers came to see them off. They drummed a beat, and their commander saluted George.

He tasted bile in his mouth as he returned the salute, and made himself a promise: *Never again will I surrender. Next time, I will be the one saluting the gallant defeated enemy.*

George and Captain Mackay led the line on foot, for their horses had been slaughtered along with the other animals. Behind them, Van Braam carried a union flag, after which trailed two columns of men. At the rear came wagons loaded with the wounded, the camp luggage and the remains of their supplies. The mood was of sombre relief to be returning home alive, with at least the prospect of compensation. As the bedraggled British troops left the field, their heads bowed, French soldiers set fire to Fort Necessity. They cheered. They had taken the Ohio.

As they marched, George began to fret. How would his surrender be received at home? Being shot for cowardice was the worst of the fears that ran amok in his mind.

'Washington,' said Mackay, as they left the meadows for the cover of the trees, 'it will be better for us if we agree the facts we wish to report.'

George frowned. 'The facts speak for themselves.'

'Jesus, you're naïve, man. Your and my accounts will be the only two official records of these events. To have lost over a hundred men in exchange for three French lives will hardly benefit our reputation.'

'Are you suggesting we alter the truth?'

'That's exactly what I'm saying. Three hundred French dead is a more respectable outcome, don't you think?'

'But that would be a lie...'

'It would. But rarely does the truth serve one well.'

George ruminated on the idea as they travelled further into the woods, failing to notice the eerie silence.

The air was pierced by the shrill cry of Indians. From all sides, the Huron appeared and ran down the banks towards the rear of the column where the luggage was being transported.

'We've already surrendered!' shouted George in defiance.

'They're not bound by any agreement between us and France,' said Mackay. They watched in dismay as the warriors piled onto the luggage wagons.

George gave the order to fire but no one's muskets were loaded. Instead, his men broke into a run. The Huron didn't give chase, content to loot the wagons, carrying off the barrels and trunks. George yelled at two braves, who were heaving his own trunk up the slope.

'We have a treaty!' he yelled to no avail.

Those Huron who didn't get their hands on the spoils of war set about slaughtering the men too injured to flee. Each British scalp commanded a bounty back in Montreal or Detroit. They yelped in joy as they fled back up the hill. George walked alone to see if any injured had survived the assault. Bodies lay prone atop each other, on the wagons or on the ground. It was the sight of Daniel Neumann that made George freeze. Blood was seeping from the hole where the young man's scalp should have been. He lay face up on the forest floor, an arm outstretched, eyes vacant. Dead.

74

June 15th, 1754
Fitzbarton Plantation

The time had come. Today, Sylvia and baby Peter would become Mason's property. She would cease to be his mistress and become *the* mistress of the Fitzbarton plantation. It was wealth and security beyond her wildest childhood dreams.

But Viktor's visit had unsettled her. For the first time in her life, she had a lot to lose, more than just her freedom – which had been taken and won back many a time – but a son, who had bred feelings of love in her so strong, she hadn't known them possible; to say nothing of all the worldly possessions and deference that came from her attachment to Mason. What little remained of her former family, Caroline and Jacob, God rest his soul, seemed like a different lifetime. Her old life was an ocean away and all but forgotten. Now she had a family of her own, she had been *truly* reborn, as her former Methodist teacher, Mr Benson, would have said.

But in the back of her mind lurked inescapable truths that threatened the delicate life she had constructed for herself. She'd never mentioned Viktor's visit or his threats to Mason, but as her fears began to consume her, she sought reassurances from him. One night, lying in bed together while the baby slept in the new nursery next door, she'd asked Mason about the reading of the banns in church and what might happen. He'd dismissed her worries:

'We'll just buy the marriage licence. Saves having to read the banns altogether.'

'But what about in church, if someone objects during our ceremony?'

Mason stroked her hair, 'It's common here for people to get married at home. Many people live too far away from a church. I'll pay the pastor to visit and marry us here. Nobody need attend.'

Sylvia's relief was tinged with sadness. As a little girl, she'd imagined herself as a beautiful bride, adored by an envious congregation, given away by her father, her mother in tears. But such childish sentimentality caved under the demands of practicalities.

'Won't people think it odd, you marrying your servant?'

'It's always been that way in the colony. There's never been enough women to go round,' he pointed out. 'Men have simply married whoever was available. My grandmother was an indentured servant. My grandfather bought her at auction and two months later she was pregnant.'

Sounds familiar. How different it was to England, she thought. Here, class and custom were sacrificed to the realities of the possible. At home, she could only have risen as far as concubine; society would never accept a servant girl in the circles of the well-to-do.

'Better still,' said Mason, 'I can divorce you too, for any number of offences you commit.'

She pinched his nipple and he yelped, laughing away her protests. 'Don't worry, it cuts both ways. You can divorce me too, provided you have sufficient justification.'

'*Really?*'

'Oh yes. No Act of Parliament is necessary, you simply petition the court. But you needn't worry about that.' He kissed her, running his hand over her hip.

Sylvia broke away from the kiss. 'Wouldn't I be disgraced?'

'No. With women so scarce, you could remarry straight away.'

That explained why Mason had no compunction about remarrying so soon after Mary's death. Sylvia shook the memory of that night from her mind. She was still haunted by Mary's face, and no doubt would remain so forever. She'd wake in the night to see Mary's miserable scowl, judging her for her crime. She would have to learn to live with it.

Another thought occurred to her, which she was happier to

indulge: 'Mason, why didn't you ever just divorce Mary?'

His raised eyebrows suggested the thought had occurred to him many a time.

'Perhaps I should have. But there aren't many unaccompanied women here, and it would have reflected badly on me to divorce. Mary would have caused trouble, smearing my reputation.'

'But her drinking damaged your reputation, anyway, didn't it?'

He nodded, looking rueful. 'Maybe you're right, but it's all in the past now.'

Sylvia didn't say any more, for fear of embarrassing Mason, but it surprised her that Mason, like so many men, had been willing to tolerate an unhappy marriage for so long. Whether it was the fear of being alone or a matter of pride, she didn't know, but in a land of such freedoms it seemed an unnecessary endurance.

That night she dreamt of Mary again, but with a new day dawning, she washed away her thoughts in the bowl of water. Today was about Sarah, she decided as she sat at the dressing table, looking into the mirror to adjust Mary's earrings on her lobes. *I am Sarah Fitzbarton now,* she mouthed to her reflection. *Today Sylvia dies too.*

Sarah puffed her chest out and turned to check how her petite cleavage protruded from the elegant blue dress. Marrying Mason in his late wife's clothes was not what she would have chosen, but immediately after their engagement, she had written to his agent in London to order a vast quantity of new clothes, cosmetics, jewellery, and bed linen. It would cost a fortune, but Mason had plenty of money, and she'd signed the order using Mary's name. The London agent wouldn't know of her passing and if Mason protested, Sarah could simply blame him for letting Mary have access to his account. It seemed most people in Virginia waited until the winter to get married so the wedding didn't interfere with the labour, but Mason was eager to defy convention. He worried that the sin of a child born out of wedlock would offend God. Eager to see that the Lord had no justification to take his son from him, the sooner he made it legitimate in the eyes of God, the better. *If only he knew the half of it,* thought Sarah, who was happy to settle for the security of a quick marriage, for reasons entirely her own.

Mason entered their bedroom only partially dressed. Tight, white breeches hugged his muscular legs, and a cotton shirt with lace cuffs and collar hung still undone. He strode across to her in his stocking feet.

'The pastor is here. Grace is fixing him a drink while he waits for us.' Mason had a childlike grin on his face.

She smiled back, feeling a flush of nerves. He squeezed her hand and moved to kiss her, but she pulled away.

'Problem?'

'You must promise me something, Mason,' she said. 'I am very pleased to be marrying you—'

'I should think so!'

'—But we have much to lose. I want you to promise me you will leave the Neumanns alone.'

His demeanour grew stern. 'What are you worried about them for?'

'They're not worth it.'

'That little shit robbed us at knifepoint!'

'Mason,' she calmed him with a touch of her hand, 'I don't want anything to come between us, especially if it is for the sake of people who mean nothing to us. We have everything we need.'

'That's not the point,' said Mason dismissively.

'No, that's exactly the point. I am a runaway. Viktor knows that. I am not going to be returned to Simon Bowler.'

'You'll be my wife. I'll compensate him...'

Her voice was steel now. 'No, you won't, Mason. You will promise not to make trouble for me, for us.'

'Fine.' He walked over to his wardrobe.

Sarah got up and took the Bible from the bedside table. She held it out to him. 'Swear it.'

'You can't be serious?'

'I am.'

He glared at her, but she held his gaze as she waited for him to place his hand on the Bible.

He rolled his tongue round his cheek.

'Mason,' she prompted, 'I won't marry you if you won't grant me this one request.'

'Very well.' He put his hand on the book. 'I swear I will leave the Neumanns alone.'

'Forever?'

'Yes, forever.'

'Thank you.' She stood on tiptoes and kissed him full on the lips, rekindling his smile. She knew he feared God; it was a promise he would surely keep. Her secrets were safe.

'That reminds me,' he said, 'now that you will be mistress of the house, I need to talk to you about your relationship with the slaves.'

With that conversation also concluded, they readied themselves for their wedding.

***

The ceremony was a simple event, conducted in the sitting room, which had been cleared of its furniture. The pastor was a young man, no more than twenty years of age, with neatly cropped brown hair and a round face. Sarah and Mason stood opposite one another and recited their vows. Billy and Granville witnessed the marriage, while Grace held baby Peter and watched beside Zebedee. Charlie came to represent the outdoor slaves. Mason's voice and hands wavered as he produced a diamond ring from his waistcoat pocket.

Sarah's heart soared. She gazed, spellbound by the stone's sparkle. She offered him her hand and he struggled to force the ring past her finger joint, but finally it fitted. The pain she had briefly suffered was as nothing, for never in her life had she expected to have a diamond of her own. She thought back to everything she'd had to overcome, to finally find herself standing here, in front of her prince. This ring would have cost more than all the money that had ever passed through her hands, and here it would stay, forever on her finger.

'Mason, it's beautiful.' Tears welled in her eyes.

'Like you,' he replied.

She clenched her fingers together, clasping the ring tight in her grip as she leant forward and kissed Mason firmly on the lips.

When they finally parted, the red-faced pastor said, 'I now pronounce you man and wife.' A small ripple of polite applause rang round the room.

'I love you, Sarah.'

The Pastor congratulated Mason. Billy and Granville admired

Sarah's wedding ring. Charlie came forward, his head stooped to present Sarah with a small figurine, carved from dark wood. She looked confused.

'It's a small gift from the workers,' he explained, 'to celebrate your wedding. This is Babalú-Ayé, our God of good health and healing.'

She smiled and nodded her head in thanks.

Charlie continued, 'We are very pleased to have you as our master's wife. You have been kind to us, and we hope Babalú-Ayé will bring you good health and in turn, you may help heal our people's suffering, now we work for you too.'

She nodded.

Encouraged, Charlie continued. 'We are hungry, perhaps you allow us some off-cuts of meat from the kitchen, to celebrate the wedding?'

Sarah didn't smile. This is what Mason had warned her of, the slaves seeking to take advantage of her good nature. She narrowed her eyes and did as she'd been instructed, 'Charlie, let me make one thing clear: you're my niggers now.'

Very slowly he nodded his head as if he'd seen in her something familiar. A look of resignation fell across his face. He took a step back, never losing her stare. As her words hung in the air between them, she knew she had crossed a line, from which there was no return. She felt the briefest pang of shame, but that was the price she must pay for becoming the princess in the palace of her childhood imagination.

She dismissed the onlookers. Sarah, Mason and the Pastor feasted on the meal that had been prepared for them.

75

July 1st, 1754
Alexandria

The Virginia regiment's departure from the Ohio battlefield may have enjoyed a modicum of ceremony, but their return into Alexandria was a pathetic spectacle. As they'd travelled east towards the mountains, repeated Indian raids on their column had decimated their cargo, drums, flags, and a great many of their men. Any attempt to restore some pride on those men remaining was futile, they wanted their pay and nothing more.

For Croghan, the return to Alexandria wasn't a homecoming any more than it was a celebration for the safe return of the soldiers. He looked across the anxious faces of the crowds who had gathered to witness their deflated return. There were no flags being waved, no fifes or drumbeats; only subdued faces bearing witness to the colony's humiliation. The older folk seemed relieved to have been spared the ordeal, while women anxiously scanned the rabble to see if their men had returned unharmed. Negro slaves looked on with indifference. The younger men, who'd had more sense than to enlist, had their avoidance of duty vindicated. Many failed to locate their loved ones, breaking down in tears, scowling at Washington, hurling curses. The mood was sour, and the young commander bore the brunt of it all. Ashen faced, he walked by in stunned silence, numbed by their outpouring. For the first time, Croghan felt sorry for Washington, who'd fallen victim to his own courage. A novice saddled with the expansion of the British Empire. His hubris on the battlefield had

531

been quickly disabused by the French. Now, though, despite his uniform and large physique, he seemed to have shrunk in stature, and made no effort to conceal his shame. Perhaps this experience would serve him well. *We were all young and foolish once,* thought Croghan, *but I'm content to just be foolish these days.*

Croghan took in the sight of the gleaming new town of Alexandria. Like so many in the New World, perfectly straight streets were lined with regularly spaced buildings of sharp-edged bricks and brightly coloured mortar or freshly sawn wood. It was like a fairy-tale dream; everywhere lacked the scars of time. For him, this visit would be a mere interlude, for he had nowhere to go. His foray into the Ohio was over for now. The French bounty remained on his head. His trading partnership with the Iroquois was over, they'd abandoned the alliance he'd brokered at Logstown. With it, Tanacharison's promise of vast lands had blown away on the breeze as quickly as it had come. His mother would say, in her broad Dublin brogue, *'If it seems too good to be true, it usually is.'* The boy who'd arrived penniless and hungry from Ireland, wouldn't be joining the ranks of the newly well-to-do in the New World just yet.

Indeed, Croghan's financial predicament was uppermost in his thoughts. All his hopes had rested on the Ohio. He'd robbed Peter to pay Paul so many times, even he had lost count of his creditors. What was certain: he couldn't return to Philadelphia. The eternal spring of his promises, of money just around the corner, of just one more month, one more deal, had all run dry. With no furs, no Indians, no Ohio lands, he was broke and destined for debtors' prison the moment he stepped foot in Pennsylvania. He was left with nothing but the smile on his face.

Mackay had already left the column to return to South Carolina. He was approached by a distraught looking Washington, who looked like a man who needed to do something with himself. They'd barely spoken a word since their bout of fisticuffs in the fort.

'What do you think will happen to the Ohio now?' he asked.

'Maybe it'll stay French,' Croghan shrugged, 'or maybe it won't. It's for cleverer men than us to decide.'

'What will you do now?'

'What will I do now? You mean now that you've fucked up the entire Ohio Valley for me and left me penniless?'

Washington's face grew red at the accusation, which Croghan easily diffused with a wink and a grin. 'I'll think o' something. What about you, George – still keen to play soldiers?'

'Depends on what he says,' said Washington, indicating a bloated-looking Governor Dinwiddie, who was standing with his thumbs tucked under his lapels, waiting outside his newly completed mansion in the centre of town. His wide eyes betrayed concern at the sight of the remnants of his forces. As they approached, neither the Governor, Washington nor Croghan said a word. The silence was sufficient to suggest that nobody wanted to dwell on the causes of their shared disaster. Bad news travelled fast and had evidently reached the coast before the returning men.

'Tell me, Governor,' said Croghan, 'what now? Is the Ohio project done for?'

Dinwiddie's lips puckered and his eyebrows raised. He didn't know, and he certainly wasn't going to put his name to anything now. It was London's problem.

Croghan continued looking at him expectantly.

'It is over, as far as this colony is concerned,' the Governor said. 'There won't be any support in the House after…' He looked at the dejected figure Washington cut and thought it best to leave it there. Dinwiddie had warned the lad, but he had been too petulant to listen. 'How many dead?' he asked instead.

'Ours or theirs?' said Washington.

'Ours. From what I hear, none of theirs were hurt.'

'One hundred killed. Then the Huron finished off our wounded.'

Dinwiddie's head spun as he took in the facts, which were as bad as the rumours suggested. He put his hand on Washington's shoulder. 'We can't deny our dead, but it would be helpful if your report suggested we'd done rather better at killing the French.'

Washington didn't look surprised by the suggestion; his sullen look indicated he was finally taking all the advice he could get.

'What about the Iroquois?' asked Dinwiddie.

'They weren't persuaded to stay,' Croghan said enigmatically. 'They forsook our treaty.'

'Good,' said Dinwiddie, 'see that your report majors on their treachery.'

'Gladly,' said Washington.

Croghan shook his head. 'I'll leave you scoundrels to your politics.'

'What will you do now?' Dinwiddie called as Croghan began to walk away.

'I think I'll find a tavern, beat someone at cards, get drunk and try to bed a woman of ill repute.'

'The Red Lion on Water Street should fulfil your needs adequately.'

Croghan thanked him and wandered off. Dinwiddie turned back to Washington and commented on Croghan, 'He'll either be penniless or a very wealthy man by the time he dies. His sort never settle for middle ground.'

'He certainly didn't carry the influence with the Iroquois that he led us to believe,' Washington grunted.

Dinwiddie appraised Washington's expression. It seemed to him that it was Washington's influence that was wanting.

'So, what happens now?' asked Washington.

Dinwiddie decided to be direct. 'Failure demands its scapegoats, George. The Virginia regiment is to be broken into ten individual companies with a captain commanding each one. It is my hope that you would command one of them.'

'You're demoting me again?' Washington's eyes began to glaze.

Dinwiddie nodded. He would spare the man the full recount of his errors, lest it cast his own judgement in a poorer light.

'But we didn't have proper equipment, no uniforms, our powder was soaked...'

'George, a lot of the colony's money was squandered on this mission.'

'If we'd had proper funding from the start, instead of entertaining rival schemes, a hundred poor souls would still be alive,' George insisted.

'Certainly, George. This isn't France. Our politics rests on the art of the possible.'

Washington ground his teeth in frustration and looked away.

Dinwiddie put a hand on his shoulder. 'We did the best that Virginia could muster. After all, we're only a colony, George, our resources are limited, as are the mechanisms available to us. This is a matter for Britain now; the men in London will have to decide if they want to keep America for themselves or share it with France.'

'But we can't just give in,' Washington protested. 'We can't let our home become a crowded outpost, denied of opportunity, simply because we lacked the courage to stop France!'

'George, you are young and therefore blessed with simple logic. If you ever go into politics, you'll learn things are rarely simple.'

Washington's cheeks turned red.

'Go home, George, you've earned a rest. You did your best, which is all we could ask of you.'

'Very well. But before I go, I would like to state my disappointment for the record. My mission wasn't funded properly, I wasn't adequately recompensed for my troubles. Mackay was paid more than me, I dare say Fry was too.'

Dinwiddie groaned before adopting the stern manner he adopted when discussing money. 'You just started a fucking war – and now you're asking for money?'

'No!' protested George. 'The French themselves said it was just a reprisal. They don't want war.'

'Of course they don't. They got what they wanted. But you watch what happens next. Our King just had his eye wiped and when he finds out, he won't like it one little bit. What's more, a lot of people just lost a lot of money. They'll want a bloody war, you mark my words.'

Despite the admonishment, Washington stood still, his expression indifferent to his shortcomings.

Disbelieving, Dinwiddie added, 'You confessed to murdering a French officer.'

Defiant, George retorted, 'Yes, it appears I was a poor choice, which will lead people to think you found me an affordable solution, Governor, rather than an adequate one. People will question the judgement of Dinwiddie, a tight-fisted Scotsman.'

The cheek of him! Dinwiddie thought. *Bargaining his reputation in exchange for my own. Lest everyone forget, I wasn't spoilt for choice.*

'I'm not a wealthy man, Governor,' Washington went on. 'I fear this episode will do little for my reputation. All I'm asking is that my service to my country be properly acknowledged. If it were, then my report would highlight the excellent support I received from my Governor, rather than drawing attention to, for example, the lack of cartridge cases to keep our powder dry.'

'You've made your point, Washington,' snapped Dinwiddie. 'But may I remind you that it's in neither of our interests to draw attention to the expedition's shortcomings.'

Washington stood unfazed, and Dinwiddie felt himself being drawn into the one thing he'd hoped to avoid: recriminations.

'It's the House who controls the purse strings, not I,' he continued. 'Nevertheless, I shall recommend they recognise your bravery in the face of overwhelming odds.'

'And hundreds of French soldiers killed. I am most obliged, Lieutenant Governor.'

'Indeed. Now, go home, George.' The Governor turned his back on the conversation and headed to the sanctuary of his mansion.

At the gate, he called out behind him: 'Washington, you should go into politics. Unlike soldiering, you have a flair for it!'

With Dinwiddie's back-handed compliment ringing in his ears, George attended to his men. He thanked them for their bravery and directed them to the quartermaster, so they could draw their pay before being discharged.

***

Word of the troops' return had spread across the colony like wildfire. Viktor was eager to meet them, not least to draw his pay, but also to see his brother. With the future of the family plantation settled, he was excited to tell Daniel of the treaty he'd brokered with the Fitzbartons. Their lives were set, and they could celebrate tonight before going their separate ways.

Before he left, he embraced his father, something he hadn't done in years. Though he said he hoped to be back for Christmas, Viktor had other ideas. If he were to come back, he would be sure to come bearing expensive gifts – or better still, to have married so he could invite his father and brother to see his new house, wherever that might be. With his newfound confidence, he was less concerned about the future; he knew it would work itself out somehow.

He walked to the Potomac and caught the ferry to Alexandria. Judging from the hustle of activity at the waterfront, he was too late to see the army return, for young men with grim faces and dirty clothes abounded. Two of them stepped into the floating brothel where he'd been deprived of his savings. *Good luck to them,* he thought. Walking up the slope, he kept his eyes peeled for Daniel. There was a long queue outside the house that Washington had used as headquarters. He saw a few vaguely familiar faces, but none he knew sufficiently well to talk to. He joined the queue, and his name was ticked off the muster roll. One shilling a day, less the cost of rations, came to a paltry £6. Viktor pocketed the coins and asked the clerk if Daniel Neumann had drawn his pay yet. From behind his desk, the clerk looked down the muster roll and shook his head.

Viktor emerged from the house with an ominous sensation in his gut. The men ahead of him in the queue made their way straight to the tavern. He was about to follow when he caught a glimpse of a blue coat on the other side of the street. 'Lieutenant Colonel!' he called out and broke into a run.

Washington looked drawn and sheepish.

'I'm looking for Daniel. Have you seen him?'

Washington's eyes were dark and his face still. A rushing sound rose in Viktor's ears as he watched the officer's lips curl and his head shake.

'Daniel won't be coming home.' Washington walked off.

Viktor was left numb in body and mind. '*You cunt,*' was all he could think to say.

Fleeting thoughts blew through Viktor's mind, but none of them took root. He steadied himself against the wall of a nearby house. Should he be crying? No tears were forthcoming. *What did that mean?* He loved Daniel. Surely, he should be mortified and yet, he just stood in a daze, waiting for emotion to strike. The idea his brother was gone from the Earth forever was more than he could contemplate.

The world around him, the streets, the people passing by, the horses and carts – all seemed separate from him. He was a ghost, watching at a great distance. Uncertain what to do, he saw some men leave the tavern where he'd first been recruited by Washington after having lost all his money. Something urged him to go inside – he needed a drink.

A cheerful hubbub spilled out through the open windows as he approached. Within, the smell of unwashed men and stale beer filled the warm, moist air. Viktor ordered a beer, wincing at the high price. Evidently, the tavern keeper was keen to take advantage of the surplus of recently paid soldiers in town. Viktor looked around the tap room. At a table on the far side, he spotted Barney playing cards with the Irish fur trader, Croghan.

'Mind if I join you?' he said.

'Aye, Viktor, you old turd,' said Barney, affectionately. 'Where've you been? I'm just relieving this Paddy here of his money.'

'Do you know what became of my brother, Daniel?' asked Viktor as he pulled up a chair.

'Aye, he was injured in the battle,' said Croghan. 'I carried him back to the fort, which was the last I saw of him. But on the march back, the Huron plundered our column, killing many of the wounded. I imagine he was among them.'

Viktor stared into the middle distance and sipped his beer, considering his younger brother's fate. *Poor bastard never did anything wrong, he deserved better than that.* As he began to settle, he just felt confusion, quietly numb, while the two men beside him continued their game of three card brag. He knew he ought to go home, but he couldn't face his father with this news. *I'm still a coward after all,* he thought. Viktor sank the rest of his drink and ordered another.

An hour later, the door to the tavern flew open and Captain Reid strode in, ruddy cheeks and a large smile on his face. 'Barney!'

As he joined their group, he saw Viktor, taking a moment for recognition to dawn. 'Viktor, isn't it? Good news, your tobacco fetched a good price. You owe me one, eh?'

Viktor forced a smile, feeling the drink beginning to take effect. More money in Fitzbarton's pocket, he lamented. While Croghan introduced himself to Reid, Viktor contemplated telling the Captain he'd met his son by Sylvia, born into wealth, comfort and iniquity. Then he thought better of it.

Reid returned with a drink and sat down at the table. 'Deal me in.'

Barney looked at Viktor who shook his head. He preferred to spectate, so he could drink himself into oblivion.

'Right, lads,' Reid announced, 'after this debacle in the Ohio, everyone is expecting a war. The French navy is up north, at the entrance to the Lawrence River. It can't leave Montreal and Quebec unguarded. All their merchant shipping in the Caribbean is unprotected.'

'So?' asked Barney.

'War, you cloth-eared fool. Means we're free to go privateering. Plunder some French bounty for ourselves, eh? We can take their ships, their cargo, whatever we can get our hands on, all with His Majesty's blessing. Sooner we strike, we might catch them napping.'

A grin spread across Barney's scarred face. 'With the rate I'm losing to Paddy here, I could use some extra cash, I'm in. So's Viktor.'

'I'm not a pirate,' said Viktor, his words beginning to slur.

'You'd look nice – Viktor the cabin boy, wee parrot on your shoulder, pieces o' eight, eh?'

Viktor dismissed the image.

'That's your trouble, Viktor, nae imagination!' said Barney. 'We can pilfer a ship, run goods up and down the coast, from the Caribbean to as far as New England. With our own vessel, we'd make a fortune! It's the chance of a lifetime. Fifty-fifty, unless Croghan wants in? Can you sail?'

'Nah,' said the Irishmen, 'I don't care for boats.'

'Is it safe?' asked Viktor.

'Not at all,' said Reid, a mischievous glint in his eye. 'Once we're out at sea, we'll change the ensign and paint over the name of the *Relief*, call her something French, I don't know, *Le Grand Bateau*, something like that.'

Croghan laughed, spraying beer from the rim of his glass.

'Enough,' declared Reid, 'let's go, time waits for no man.'

Barney slapped Viktor's shoulder, his ginger beard wet from the last of his drink and a grin so wild even Viktor found himself smiling. They piled out of the tavern into the evening air, merry with hope and anticipation. Croghan pocketed the money he'd won from Barney and bid them farewell.

'Yous not coming, ya daft bastard?' asked Barney, no doubt eager to win his money back.

'No, lads. There's two hundred thousand acres of the Ohio Valley with my name on it. I leave you to your plan while I come up with one o' me own.' Croghan waved goodbye and made good his departure.

Viktor felt a touch of remorse that Croghan wasn't joining them. He was charming company, but the Irishman seemed pulled by his destiny, which he believed was entwined in the Ohio Valley. Viktor wished him well as he watched him disappear into the town.

As they walked to the waterfront, Viktor quizzed Reid on how long a return voyage would take. Thoughts of his father on his mind. He would cope, he supposed; in some ways, it was better if he didn't know of Daniel's fate. This voyage and its spoils would be the new start he needed. And after everything he'd been through, it was time to put his own needs first. If Daniel's death proved anything, it was how fragile and brief life was. Viktor resolved he'd visit his father as soon as they returned, with plenty of money in hand, then he'd give his father whatever he needed.

At the water's edge, they climbed aboard Reid's skiff.

As they pushed off, Viktor heard shouting along the quayside. He craned his neck and saw the tall figure of Fitzbarton, dressed in white. He shuddered at the spectacle of his former master berating one of his slaves. It was Charlie. Mason slapped him round the face, barking abuse towards him. Charlie held up his hands in deference, nodding his understanding. Mason punched him in the face. Charlie fell to the ground. Passers-by paid little attention. Mason kicked Charlie, who lay prone. Again, and again. It was needless cruelty for the sake of cruelty. Viktor was certain that whatever Charlie had or hadn't done, it was a misdemeanour that in no way warranted this punishment.

Finally, Mason unbuttoned his breeches and urinated on Charlie's prone body.

It reminded Viktor how, for all his apparent civility, Fitzbarton's heart was dark beyond reason or rationality. It occurred to Viktor that no matter the threat he held over Mason and Sylvia, Mason would never be cowed. Not even Sylvia might hope to have sway over him; no one could stop his viciousness. Living in his shadow, Hans would never stand a chance.

'Gentlemen, I'm sorry, but I'm going to have to sit this one out,' said Viktor, rising unsteadily to his feet.

'What? Why?' asked Barney, but Viktor didn't respond as he leapt out of the boat into the shallow water and waded back to the mooring. Barney called out to him, but he never looked back. This was about his family, what little remained of it.

Parents gladly sacrificed their lives for their children's benefit, never expecting the same in return. Viktor would do the right thing. He had bad news to bear, and his father would need him now more than ever. Mason wouldn't waste the opportunity that Daniel's death presented.

Careful to avoid being seen, Viktor ran up into the town and hired a bed for the night. The next morning he took the ferry upstream, headed home, against the relentless current of the river.

***

His administrative duties completed, an exhausted George returned to Mount Vernon, unwilling to spend another night alone. As he approached the house, memories of Lawrence came flooding back. Since Lawrence's death, his widow Anne had wasted no time, remarrying before the year was out. When George arrived, she was upstairs putting her young daughter to bed. Clarence, the house slave, prepared him a drink while he waited, explaining that Anne's husband was away, supervising the construction of their new house.

Eventually, Anne came down the stairs, her beauty strained by the demands of time: births, life and deaths. Yet to George she looked more desirable than ever as she smiled at the sight of him. She bounded down the final few steps and they embraced. George's eyes began to water.

'My Goodness, George, you smell ripe! We'll need to get you washed.'

George savoured her floral aroma as their bodies pressed together. He could have held her all night, reminded of his other needs he'd neglected. The absence of a woman's love had been a constant in his life. Returning from battle, his mood as low as it had ever been, he realised he needed a shoulder to cry on, a sympathetic ear, and a bosom to cling to – the duties women so routinely performed without complaint and without acknowledgement. Anne was at once family, and yet, since Lawrence's death, no longer so. George wished she could be his. For a fleeting moment, he imagined this house to be his home, and her to be his wife. He could be a father to her child, his niece, and together they could raise more. A simple life.

Ever intuitive, she sensed his sadness and gripped his fingers. 'George, what's wrong?'

'Anne, I fucked it up.' Saying the words sent tears streaming down his cheeks and he began to sob openly. Emotions that had been bottled up, the fear, the shame, the horror, all released. His body began to shake. She led him to a chair and the slave passed him another tot of rum, which he drank in one go, hoping it might fortify him.

'They'll blame it all on me,' he said, 'I've brought disrepute to the Washington name, I've been such a fool. Men have died because of me. I'll never forget the looks on their faces.' He stared blankly as he pictured the anger and sadness of his soldiers and the loved ones of those who remained graveless, abandoned on the far side of a mountain range in enemy territory. In his late brother's house, he realised now, finally, why Lawrence preferred not to discuss his experiences. It was too fucking painful to bear.

Anne kissed his forehead. 'Come, George, stop punishing yourself, be kind to yourself.'

He sighed and wiped away his tears.

'Remember, George, 'tis neither good nor bad, but only thinking makes it so.'

'Anne, I wish I knew what that means.'

'What it means is,' she removed his empty glass and placed it out of reach, 'what's done is done. All that matters now is what you do next. A gift is hidden in your misfortune, but you won't find it by swilling rum.'

'Well, it's certainly well hidden!'

'Perhaps so, and it may take you years to find it, but you now know more about fighting in the backwoods than any man in America. Think how useful these lessons could prove to be in future.'

'But they demoted me...'

'Well then, you'll just have to get yourself promoted again.'

He tutted. No. He was certain he'd be forever tarnished by the events in the Ohio. He would resign. What he might do then, he wasn't sure. A family might be nice. He looked deep into her eyes. There was no pity to be found, only steely resolve.

'I'm lucky to have you in my life, Anne.' He thought about telling her he wished he could have more of her in his life. But, despite their similar age, he somehow remained her junior. The die was cast, and her role in his life was only to be maternal.

'That's sweet of you. Now, you make sure somebody else is glad to have you, in *their* life, George Washington.'

An involuntary smile escaped. 'Do you know anyone who'd want a stubborn, pox-scarred, ex-Lieutenant Colonel, with a proven ability to make a mess of things?'

She smiled, bringing a drop of joy to his heart. 'You'll find someone, George, and I have every confidence they'll worship you for your great many strengths, even if you overuse them on occasion!' She sat on the arm of the chair and pulled his head to her bosom, smoothing his chestnut hair. 'It's a nice evening. Everything feels better after a walk. Come on.'

Arm in arm, they went outside and enjoyed the warm evening air, taking in the sounds of and the unending beauty of their homeland's countryside as nature readied itself for the night, and the new day to follow. In her infinite wisdom, Mother Nature never judged, only restored life's perspective. In time, George would learn that life's tragedies – and its triumphs – are as temporary and as fleeting as life itself.

76

The First Lord of the Treasury, mockingly referred to as the Prime Minister, Thomas Pelham-Holles, 1st Duke of Newcastle, was seated at his desk. At a glance, the office appeared stately, with all the trappings of Georgian elegance: marble fireplace, oil paintings, chandeliers, plaster-decorated ceilings and cornices. Yet in the three months since he'd succeeded his late brother Henry to the top of British politics, it was evident that the building, like the job itself, was a bodge. Draughty, rickety, and prone to subsidence.

Prior to taking on the top job, he'd won his spurs purging Britain of its Jacobite tendencies. Now it was the Duke's turn to run matters, and he was determined to rein in the treasury's spending by curtailing the expensive folly of foreign wars. Europe's monarchies wasted fortunes robbing territory from one another. Whig dominance rested on their enormous individual wealth, and thus, his government would create wealth: by trade, not war. Pelham-Holles, like many of the Whigs, understood the nature of the modern world: the accumulation of capital-derived power. Increasingly, British policy wouldn't hinge on a king's whim. In this modern age of enlightened thinking, Britain and its growing Empire were now firmly a Whig endeavour, dominated by London's wealth from its burgeoning trade. There was much to do and much to look forward to for the Duke.

His reflections were interrupted by a knock at the door, and the podgy face of a worried Charles Townsend peered round. 'Sorry to disturb you, Thomas – only, there's some worrying news from the colonies. I thought you should know, before rumours spread.'

'Come in, Charlie.' The Duke indicated he take a seat. Townsend was a member of the Board of Trade.

'I've just received word from Dinwiddie, our man in Virginia.' Townsend paused and took a deep breath. 'There's been an incident. In the Ohio.'

'Ohio – where's that?'

'The American interior. On the far side of our mountains.'

'Is it ours?'

Townsend pulled a face that suggested the answer wasn't clear. 'The short answer is no, it isn't. But it transpires, a few years ago, Kingy issued one of his land grants, for half a million acres of the Ohio Valley.'

Pelham-Holles groaned, knowing where this was headed. 'Don't tell me – France?'

Townsend nodded.

'What's happened?'

'It seems a young colonel, leading a Virginia regiment…'

'Wait, we have a Virginia regiment?'

'They formed their own, sir.'

Pelham-Holles shook his head in despair.

'Well, while this Virginia regiment was staking a claim to the Ohio lands, to secure King George's grant, the colonel in charge attacked a small party of French soldiers reconnoitring the area.'

Pelham-Holles waved his hand. 'Send the French an apology.'

'Ah, well, there's more. The Virginian killed the French captain,' Townsend paused, '*after* he'd surrendered.'

Pelham-Holles frowned in confusion.

Townsend continued, 'The French then mounted a successful counterattack. Each side is alleged to have killed a number of their respective subjects, with the Virginians, led by the same colonel, fairing worse. He surrendered, which is bad enough, but in the articles of surrender, our colonel confessed to assassinating the French officer.'

'What? Why in God's name would he do that?'

Townsend shrugged.

The Duke held his head in his hands. Finally, he slumped back into his chair and let out a long sigh. 'This is going to be a diplomatic nightmare.'

It all had a familiar feeling to the Prime Minister. Britain and France had been to war so often he'd lost count. King George would fret over his damaged prestige and demand restitution. Then the French King would do the same, and off they all would go again.

The Duke poured himself a large wine from the decanter on his desk. Townsend declined.

'What's this damned colonel's name?'

'Washington, sir, George Washington.'

'See to it I never hear this man's name again. Cut short his army career.'

'Certainly, consider his cannon spiked.'

This was exactly the sort of self-inflicted mistake Pelham-Holles was determined to extricate Britain from.

'There is a potential upside to the situation,' said Townsend. 'Our tax take in the American colonies is negligible. The colonists are adept at evading our duties, smuggling is rife, and they are the only British subjects who don't contribute to the exchequer. It never used to matter, but there's a lot of them now. If this colonel's indiscretions *were* to lead to another war, this time on American soil, now might be a good time to enforce our taxes and even levy some new ones, to fund our defence of the colonists.'

'Are we defending our colonies, or enlarging them?'

'Fair point, Thomas. This pretext will create pressure from the patriot Whigs here to send in troops. They already chatter about the opportunity of profiting from the American interior.'

Pelham-Holles sipped his wine and thought about it for a moment. Finally, he shook his head. 'The taxes will have to wait for another day, I've only just got into office. Let's not pick a fight with our own side, as well as the French. Better we avoid one war than start two.'

'It might lead to problems later, Thomas. Our people here are already the most heavily taxed in Europe. It hardly seems fair that they alone should be burdened with the cost of defending the colonies?'

The Prime Minister shrugged. That was a problem for a different minister, on another day.

'Charles, what will be, will be.'

To be continued...

*"It was the volley fired by a young Virginian
in the backwoods of America,
that set the world on fire."*

Horace Walpole

Historical Note

This book melds together the real and the fictitious. Some of the characters need no introduction, others are my own creations, a list of which are below.

George Washington is a titanic figure in American history, but his pre-revolutionary days are much less known on this side of the Atlantic. I was interested in exploring his conversion from eager participant in the British Empire, to latter-day nemesis. Even now, as I write him, I am yet to be fully comfortable walking in his rather large shoes. He's a man about which much is *known*, but how can we ever *really* know what someone is thinking and feeling, and what insecurities drive him. This is where I believe historical fiction can make a valid, if speculative, contribution to historical opinion, adding a degree of context absent in recorded events. Whether you approve of, or disagree with, *my* George Washington, is entirely your own judgement to form.

His early chapters are my invention. His timeline becomes accurate from the occasion of his accompanying Lawrence to Barbados. Thereafter a version of everything contained in this story occurred. There are some minor inaccuracies such as the timing of his portrait painting, but none which materially affect the passage of the story. My account of his relationship to Anne, his sister-in-law, is notional. What Washington's relationship with Joshua Fry was I can't say. Not much about Fry is recorded. He was a magistrate in Albemarle County, VA. Fry's political views are my imagination. Together with Thomas Jefferson's father, Fry formed the Loyal Company of Virginia to rival Washington's Ohio venture. But it was Fry's untimely death that played the biggest part in Washington's life. He was indeed killed by falling from his horse, but this happened en route to the Ohio Valley, prior to him joining up with Washington. It is not an event that is recorded as suspicious. The consequence being that Fry had no hand in the goings on at Fort Necessity; they are all laid at Washington's feet.

I found varying accounts of the battle at Fort Necessity, so I have opted for the version that felt most plausible. More contested are the events of Jumonville Glen, where French officer Joseph Coulon de Villiers was murdered. Given the incendiary impact of this event, it is perhaps not surprising that British and French accounts should differ. The French claim that Coulon de Villiers was shot by British soldiers whilst surrendering, and that they were spared further slaughter only because the Native Americans intervened to stop the British. This strikes me as a politically convenient version from a French perspective, who would have hoped to form cordial relations with the Iroquois, once the British were defeated. I have opted for the more conceivable account as offered by Washington himself. However, Tanacharison didn't abandon Washington's forces until a little later when the main French force arrived, not as in my account, after the murder of the French officer.

Little is known of Tanacharison's views, but he certainly found himself in an increasingly impossible position caught between the French and the competing British colonies. I must ask for forgiveness for having hugely simplified the structure, and nature, of the Native American people. I am not qualified to do it justice and any attempt to more fully convey the complex alliances and rivalries that underpinned their society, would, I fear have made the story unwieldy and potentially inaccessible to a reader of casual interest.

All the slaves in this book are fictional. My account doesn't come close to showing the horrors and suffering they endured. Nor have I so far written any chapters from their point of view. The conditions of their bondage afforded them so little, if any, agency, that I felt very limited to what I could achieve with their characters. Something I may attempt to rectify in the next book.

George Croghan's timeline sticks very closely to recorded events. He witnessed both the murder of the French trader at Logstown and the Sandusky massacre. The French raid on his trading post at Pickawillany occurred, but not when Croghan was present. Likewise, he was also absent when the French captured the fort at the fork in the Ohio River. His brother-in-law, Edward Ward was supervising construction at the time. In my version, I have had Croghan impersonate Ward to aid his escape. He, together with Gist and Fry, brokered the deal with Tanacharison at Logstown, and was promised his acreage. In his pursuit of wealth, Croghan ran up large debts, Edward Shippen amongst them. He spent his life trying unsuccessfully to secure his land grant and then to establish a new colony of Vandalia. The exact nature of his relationship with George Washington is unknown to me. They did though, end up on opposing sides of the American War of Independence.

The Ohio Company was founded by Colonel Thomas Lee, and included Lawrence Washington among its founder members. Christopher Gist was contracted as a surveyor, and he did later accompany George Washington on their ill-fated wilderness mission. Robert Dinwiddie became involved in the company once he returned to Virginia, and his timeline is accurate as described in the book, although the scenes themselves are imagined. His relationship with Washington did appear to ebb and flow.

There were frequent riots in London during the eighteenth century. Those I describe at the Strand did in fact occur, although three years earlier than happens in this story.

The fort at the fork in the Ohio River is today the site of the city of Pittsburg. Logstown was located near the site of modern-day Baden, Pennsylvania. Bar London, I am yet to visit any of the places featured in this book. I very much hope to do so one day.

Fictitious Characters:
Viktor, Daniel & Hans Neumann
Barney MacGregor
Mason & Mary Fitzbarton
Sylvia (Sarah) Coppell and her London associates
Jeremiah Benson & Hugo Somerton
Captain Reid
Charlie, Grace, Zebedee, Benji, Billy, Granville and all those at the
    Fitzbarton plantation
Jimmy Jones

This year, in the US and UK alone, over 460,000 new books have been published. For any to stand out among that crowd is a near-impossible task.

If you have enjoyed this story – tell your friends! There is one thing above all others, that you can do to help this book fulfil its potential:

Please leave it a positive review wherever you bought it from.

If this story wasn't for you, then I thank you for persevering with it until the end. Feel free to keep your thoughts to yourself!

To stay up to date with future releases, follow Tim Holden
www.timholden.com
Facebook: Tim Holden – Author

Also by Tim Holden:

SPIRALS OF FATE

Acknowledgements

There are two people above all others for whom I reserve the greatest thanks for their unending support in helping bring this novel to life: Katherine Skala and Ella Micheler. Both of whom frequently demanded more from me, the story, and the characters. Whilst internally, this would sometimes fill me with despair at having to do yet more writing, I fully concede the novel is a fuller, richer and better book for it.

Writing a book about poIlical turmoil, unprovoked invasions, colonialism, financial misconduct, misogyny, human trafficking, migration, slavery and racial segregation has felt unhappily prescient, given the news agenda during the course of the book's creation. Ella's efforts in helping guide me carefully across the tightrope, as I attempt to balance the need to reflect the appalling attitudes prevalent at the time, whilst attempting to be conscious of the array of cultural sensitivities of our own time. I am certain I won't have struck this impossible balance right for all readers, but I hope to have conveyed the suffering of the eighteenth century sufficiently, without causing undue offence to the majority of readers.

Katri and Ella, it has been a pleasure to work with you both and I hope to do so again.

I must also thank Anne Gillion for her painstaking removal of my errors and my excellent beta readers: Jon Witte, Amy Beck, Cheryl Cooper, Emily Richards, Chris Albert, and Mike Villalard. My wife Heather and her colleague Claire Blackledge for another wonderful cover design.

My gratitude also to Sean Johnson and Cheryl Cooper, who were not only subjected to my latest manuscript, but continue to tolerate my leadership and, despite this, demonstrate unending commitment to my business. Without you both, such fictitious diversions would not be possible. Also, Mark Fisher, for his wisdom and support. You always point me in the right direction and remind me what I shouldn't have forgotten. Thank you.

And saving the best to last: My family, Heather, George and James. I love you all beyond words.